1001 Dark Nights
Bundle Six

1001 Dark Nights Bundle 6
ISBN: 978-1-682305-75-1

Published by Evil Eye Concepts, Incorporated

1001 Dark Nights
Bundle Six

Seven Novellas
By

Jennifer L. Armentrout
Lorelei James
Alexandra Ivy
Laura Wright
Donna Grant
and introducing
Rebecca Yarros
and Kennedy Layne

1001 Dark Nights

EVIL EYE
CONCEPTS

Table of Contents

One Thousand and One Dark Nights

Once upon a time, in the future…

*I was a student fascinated with stories and learning.
I studied philosophy, poetry, history, the occult, and
the art and science of love and magic. I had a vast
library at my father's home and collected thousands
of volumes of fantastic tales.*

*I learned all about ancient races and bygone
times. About myths and legends and dreams of all
people through the millennium. And the more I read
the stronger my imagination grew until I discovered
that I was able to travel into the stories… to actually
become part of them.*

*I wish I could say that I listened to my teacher
and respected my gift, as I ought to have. If I had, I
would not be telling you this tale now.
But I was foolhardy and confused, showing off
with bravery.*

*One afternoon, curious about the myth of the
Arabian Nights, I traveled back to ancient Persia to
see for myself if it was true that every day Shahryar
(Persian: شهریار, "king") married a new virgin, and then
sent yesterday's wife to be beheaded. It was written
and I had read, that by the time he met Scheherazade,
the vizier's daughter, he'd killed one thousand
women.*

*Something went wrong with my efforts. I arrived
in the midst of the story and somehow exchanged
places with Scheherazade — a phenomena that had
never occurred before and that still to this day, I
cannot explain.*

*Now I am trapped in that ancient past. I have
taken on Scheherazade's life and the only way I can
protect myself and stay alive is to do what she did to
protect herself and stay alive.*

*Every night the King calls for me and listens as I spin tales.
And when the evening ends and dawn breaks, I stop at a
point that leaves him breathless and yearning for more.
And so the King spares my life for one more day, so that
he might hear the rest of my dark tale.*

*As soon as I finish a story... I begin a new
one... like the one that you, dear reader, have before
you now.*

Dream of You
A Wait For You Novella
By Jennifer L. Armentrout

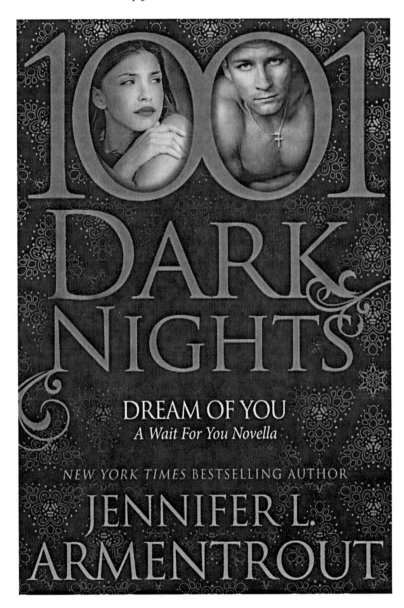

Acknowledgments from Jennifer L. Armentrout

I can't start off these acknowledgements without thanking my agent Kevan Lyon, who has always tirelessly worked on my behalf. A huge thank you to Liz Berry, the 1001 Dark Nights team, and everyone who worked on Dream of You. Thank you to my other publicist with the most-est K.P. Simmons for helping do everything to get the word out about the book.

I would go crazy if it weren't for these following people: Laura Kaye, Chelsea M Cameron, Jay Crownover, Sophie Jordan, Sarah Maas, Cora Carmack, Tiffany King, and too many more amazing authors who are an inspiration to list. Vilma Gonzalez, you're an amazing, special person, and I love you. Valerie Fink, you've always been with me from the beginning, along with Vi Nguyen, (Look, I spelled your name right), and Jessica Baker, among many, many other awesome bloggers who often support all books without the recognition deserved. THANK YOU. Jen Fisher, I heart you and not just for your cupcakes. Stacey Morgan—you're more than an assistant, you're like a sister. I'm probably forgetting people. I'm always forgetting people.

A special thank you to all the readers and reviewers. None of this would be possible without you and there isn't a thank you big enough in the world.

Chapter One

You'd be really hot if you'd just lose some weight.

My fingers curled around my car keys as I stormed out of the bar and into the thick, muggy air of July. The jagged edges dug into my palm as I resisted the urge to walk back and shove the keys into one of the jackass's over-inflated muscles.

From the moment Rick asked me out, I knew the date was going to be a bad idea.

The second I'd stepped foot on the elliptical at the gym that was a part of the Lima Academy, I'd seen Rick buzzing from one chick to the next, wearing his nylon sweats and babyGap shirt, so tight I always expected it to burst at any given moment. I hadn't even realized he worked for Lima Academy until tonight, employed in their sales and marketing department, and I felt like I knew *everything* about him because that was all Rick did.

He talked about himself.

God, why did I even agree to go out with him? Was I that lonely and sad? The clicking of my heels across the sidewalk was my only answer. Parking in the city on a Friday night was ridiculous. It was going to take a year to get to my car.

You'd be really hot if you'd just lose some weight.

My lips thinned. I couldn't believe he actually said that to me, like it was a compliment. What in the actual hell? It wasn't like I didn't know I could stand to lose a few pounds or thirty, but in my twenty-eight years of life, I had long accepted that I would never, in the history of ever, have a thigh gap, my butt would always have strange dimples in it, and no amount of sit-ups were going to counterbalance my love of cupcakes.

Deep down, I knew why I agreed to go out with him. I hadn't been on a successful date in two years, and my last serious relationship had evoked the "to death do us part" clause.

I was twenty-eight.

A widow.

A twenty-eight-year-old widow who needed to lose weight.

Sighing, I turned the corner as I reached up, tucking my hair back from my face. A fine sheen of sweat dotted my brow. I stuck close to the edge of the sidewalk, walking under the street lamps and staying away from the dark shadows that bled out from the numerous alleys. I could see my car up ahead, at the end of the silent block. It was early for a Friday night, but I was going to go home, crack open that can of BBQ Pringles that had been calling my name all evening, and forget about Rick while diving into the latest Lara Adrian romance.

Why couldn't alpha vampires with a heart of gold be real?

A sudden pained grunt snagged my attention as I was halfway to my car. Instinct flared alive, a burning fire in my gut urging me to keep walking, but I looked to my right. I couldn't help it. My head turned on its own accord, a reflex, and I stumbled.

Horror seized me, freezing my muscles and shooting darts of ice through my blood. Terror slowed time, throwing the scene into stark detail.

Dull yellow light formed a halo over the three men in the alley. One stood further back from the other two. His hair bleached blond and greasy, sticking up all over his head. He had a scar. A thin slice across his cheek, paler than his skin. Another man was leaning against the brick wall of the building, crowding the alley. I couldn't make out his features, because his head was hanging from his shoulders, and he appeared barely able to stand, obviously injured. The other man, his head completely shaven, stood directly in front of the injured man, and even though I only saw his profile, it was a face I'd never forget.

Hatred bled into every line of the man's face, from the dark slash of brows and squinty eyes, to the hooked nose and distorted, curled upper lip. He was a big guy. Tall. Broad in the shoulders. He wore a white tank top, and as my gaze tracked down his arm, I could tell his skin was shadowed with markings. A tattoo. But I wasn't thinking about the tattoo when I saw what he held in his hand.

The bald man was pointing a gun at the injured man!

Instinct was screaming like a five-alarm fire. *Run. Get away. There's a gun! Go.* But I couldn't move, torn between shocked disbelief and some inherent, possibly suicidal urge to do the right thing, to intervene and to—

A small light burst and thunder cracked overhead. The injured man crumbled as if some grand puppeteer had cut his strings. He hit the ground with a fleshy smack, and for a moment, all I could hear was my heart beating fiercely, pushing blood through my veins.

That popping snap wasn't thunder. The burst of light was a spark.

Reality slammed into me as I stared at the fallen man in the alley. A dark puddle formed, spreading from where he lay face first on the dirty pavement. My heart seized in my chest as I opened my mouth, dragging in air.

No. No way.

The man with the scar was talking to the one with the gun, his voice an excited, high-pitched squeal, but I was beyond hearing the exact words. My hand spasmed, and the keys slipped from my grasp. They clattered off the sidewalk, as loud as me trying to run on a treadmill.

Bald man's head swung sharply in my direction, and if I had felt like time had slowed before, it stopped right then. Our gazes locked, and in an instant, a horrifying connection was formed. He saw me. I saw him.

I saw him shoot someone in *the face*.

And this man, this killer, knew that.

His arm started to lift. All my muscles reacted and unlocked at the same moment. Pulse pounding, I spun around and started running back toward the bar, my lungs burning as a scream tore out from me, a sound I was sure even in my darkest moments, I'd never made before.

Brick exploded to my left, showering wickedly sharp chunks into the air. Flashes of pain erupted along my cheek, and I stumbled. The heel on my shoe snapped and slipped off, but I kept running, leaving the shoe behind.

I needed to find someone. I needed to call for help. I needed—

Rounding the block, I slammed into someone. A startled scream was cut off as I bounced back. There was a grunt, and I felt a hand grasping for my arm, but it was too late. I went down, landing hard on my side. A flash of pain jarred my bones, knocking the air out of my lungs.

"Holy shit," a male voice boomed above me. "Are you okay?"

I gulped and wheezed air as I flopped onto my front as I heard a woman say, "Of course she's not okay, Jon. She kamikazed into you!"

Lifting my head, I peered through the hair that had fallen into my face. I saw them—the one with the scar and the bald man, the cold-blooded murderer, running away, down the sidewalk, beyond where my car was parked. I watched them until they disappeared.

"Miss?" the man asked. "Miss, are you okay?"

Hands shaking, I pushed up onto my knees. The whole world took on a startling clarity. Cars driving by sounded like airplanes. Nearby doors closing sounded as if they were being repeatedly slammed, and my own heart was beating like a steel drum.

"Yes. No." I rasped out. Pressing my fingers to my burning cheek, I jerked my hand back when I felt the wet warmth. Darkness smeared the tips of my fingers. My gaze shot back to where I'd run from. "We need to call the police. Someone has been shot."

Chapter Two

I'd never been inside a police station before. One might think I lived a boring life. No parking tickets to appear for. I'd never been fined for speeding. Even as a teenager, I obeyed the law.

Well, I did do a little underage drinking here and there, and I most definitely smoked a bit of weed in my day, but I'd never gone overboard.

And I'd been clever enough to not get caught.

But now I was sitting in one of those rooms that I'd only seen on reality TV. I was sure the camera in the corner wasn't for show. Although I'd done absolutely nothing wrong, I half expected a barrel-chested detective to burst through the door and start throwing accusations at me.

My fingers curled around the crumbled tissue I'd been holding for what felt like hours. The man I'd *kamikazed* into had called the police since I hadn't been able to figure out how to get my phone out of my purse and use it.

Shock.

That's what the EMTs who'd arrived right behind the flashing red and blue lights of the police cars had told me. They had wanted me to go to the hospital to get checked out, but the responding officers were understandably impatient. They needed answers. I was a witness to a—to a murder.

Because that man in the alley was dead.

And there was nothing seriously wrong with me. My palms were a bit raw and my body ached from my tumble. The cuts on my cheeks were nothing compared to what had happened to the man lying facedown in the alley.

I would be fine.

My breath caught, and I refused to close my eyes for anything longer than a second because when I had as the police officer drove me to the station, I saw the bald man firing the gun. I heard it crack. I saw the man fold like a paper sack.

I saw the bald man pointing the gun at me.

Terror resurfaced, and I shut it down before it took hold, but it was a struggle to not think about the fact that the murderer had seen my face. He knew that I was a witness. That was terrifying because there was no doubt in my mind that he would have no problem putting a bullet in me.

He had no problem doing it to that man.

Folding my arms across my chest, I stared at the near-empty paper cup in front of me. I'd all but gulped it down when the officer had brought it to me. A shiver rolled across my shoulders. It was so chilly in here. Even the tip of my nose was icy.

Instead of keeping my thoughts blank, I focused on what had happened. How much time I thought had passed between when I left the bar and had walked in front of the alley. What I saw was important. Someone was murdered, and I'd seen the persons responsible. Whatever information I had would help bring them to justice.

So I replayed the events over and over, up to the horrifying moment the gun had gone off, despite how badly it made me shudder and how I wished I had kept walking. That may be wrong, but I knew that until my dying day, I would never forget tonight.

That man died with his face pressed into an alley that smelled of urine.

I shuddered again. Never in a million years had I thought accepting a date with Rick the Dick would end with me sitting in a police station after witnessing…a murder.

I had no idea how long I'd been sitting in this room, but at some point an officer had shown up with my car keys. After confirming the make and model, the officer had left again to retrieve my car from the scene. I wasn't sure if that was protocol or not, but I appreciated the gesture.

The last thing I wanted to do was return to the scene.

A shaky breath puffed out as the door opened, causing my chin to jerk up. Two men entered. The first thing I noticed was that both were dressed like I expected detectives to be. The first man wore tan trousers and the other one had on black. The first man's dress shirt was slightly wrinkled, as if he had gotten the call in the middle of the night and had picked the first thing up from the floor. He was older, possibly in his fifties, and his dark gaze was sympathetic as he moved closer to the table. The scent of fresh coffee wafted from the cup he held. He placed a closed file on the table.

"Ms. Ramsey? I'm sorry to keep you waiting. I know you've had a long night. I'm Detective Hart." He stopped, turning halfway. "And this is Detective…"

I was already looking up at the other guy, taking in how the pressed, white polo was loose at his trim waist and a bit tighter along a clearly defined chest and shoulders. Right now really wasn't the best moment to be checking out a guy, so I forced myself to look up. My gaze had just moved to his face when Detective Hart introduced the second detective.

My heart stopped for the second time that evening.

Oh my God.

I could feel my eyes widen as I gawked at the second man, who was openly staring back at me with the same look of disbelief on his unbelievably handsome face. I didn't even need to hear his name spoken. I knew who it was.

Colton Anders.

Oh my God, there was no mistaking him. Those high, angular cheekbones, the cut line of an often stubborn jaw, his full lips and those bright and piercing blues eyes had spawned an embarrassing amount of fantasies in high school and beyond.

God, it probably made me a terrible person. I had a boyfriend all through high school—a boy who ultimately became my husband—but there had always been Colton. He was the untouchable god in high school, the boy you went to school for and lusted for from afar, even though an icicle had a better chance of surviving in hell than you did when it came to gaining his attention.

Colton was classically handsome, just like his younger brother, Reece, and he looked more ready to arrive at a fashion shoot for a men's health magazine than he appeared ready to investigate a homicide.

So shocked at the sight of him, the question blurted out of me. "I thought you worked for the county?"

"I did, but I transferred to the city." Colton lifted his arm, running his hand over his dark brown hair. Did he still live in Plymouth Meeting? Had he moved to Philadelphia? Those questions were so inappropriate, and I was amazed I kept my mouth shut as he stared at me. "Damn, Abby. I had no idea it was you in this room."

He knew my name? Let alone, remembered it? The Kool-Aid dude could burst through the one-way mirror and I wouldn't be any more surprised. Colton and I hadn't run in the same circles, and I was sure, a hundred percent positive, I hadn't been on his radar in high school.

"You two know each other?" Hart asked with a frown as he glanced between us.

Colton gave a tight shake of his head. "We went to high school together, but I haven't seen her…" He lowered his arm. "I haven't seen you in years."

Oh, but I had seen him around town. Not often. At the grocery store once in a while. Once at the movies. I'd been with my friend and he had been with this statuesque blonde.

"I…" Swallowing hard, I glanced at Detective Hart. Off kilter from what had happened, I already felt like I was stuck in a dream. Or a nightmare. "I left for college and then moved to New York after I graduated. I've been back for about four years."

Colton stepped around Hart and those blue eyes, framed by a heavy fringe of lashes, narrowed. "Are you okay?" His head jerked back toward the other detective. "Has she seen an EMT?"

"From what Officer Hun said, she was treated and refused to go to the hospital."

That narrowed gaze landed on me sharply. "You need to get—"

"I'm fine." How bad did my face look? I resisted the urge to glance at the one-way glass window. "Really, I am."

"You were shot at," Colton stated.

I flinched, unable to stop myself. Either the responding officer had filled him in or that info was in the file. "The bullet must've hit a nearby wall. It was chunks of brick." Pausing, I wetted my lips. "It's not…"

Colton's gaze dipped to my mouth for a second too long for me to have completely imagined it. His eyes met mine quick enough as he slid into the seat closest to me on my left. "Have you called your husband?"

What the…? I blinked once and then twice. He knew I'd married? Granted, it wasn't like it had been a secret or anything. Kevin and I…we'd gotten married right after graduation, during the summer, and by winter we had moved. Yes, we all went to school together, but I had been completely invisible to him.

Drawing in a shallow breath, I loosened my grip on the tissue as I refocused my thoughts. "Kevin passed away four years ago. It was a car accident."

"Shit." Colton straightened as the look in his steeling blue gaze softened. "I didn't know." He reached over, placing his large hand on my shoulder. The weight was shockingly comforting. "I'm sorry, Abby."

"It's…" It wasn't exactly okay even though I'd long come to terms with the loss of Kevin. Some days it was still hard. Something small, like a certain scent or a song on the radio would remind me of him and how uncertain life could be. "Thank you."

He squeezed gently and then lowered his hand, the tips of his fingers brushing the bare skin of my arm. "Okay. Let's get this over so you can go home."

Hart arched a brow as he eyed Colton. He took the seat across from me. "I know you've already given your statement to Officer Hun, but we're going to want you to start from the beginning, okay?"

I nodded slowly. "I was leaving the bar Pixie's and walking to my car. It was parked a couple of blocks away. Maybe three or four blocks. It was early. Maybe around eight-thirty. I was on a…a date, but the guy was a total douchebag." My cheeks heated as my gaze darted to Colton. "I'm sorry. That's not really important."

Colton's lips twitched. "Everything is important."

I forced myself to take another slow, steady breath. "All right. I was walking to my car and I really wasn't paying attention. That area of the city isn't bad and so I wasn't expecting anything to happen, you know? I was just walking and I saw my car up ahead. I was thinking about going home and reading this book," I continued, knowing I was rambling again. "I heard someone groaning and it was like I had no control over my feet. I stopped and I looked to my right. There was an alley and that's when I saw them."

Extending an arm, Colton snatched up the file on the table and flipped it open. His brows burrowed together as he quickly scanned it. "You said you saw three people."

"Yes. There was a man just standing there. He had...he had a scar on his face and bleached blond hair. The other man, the one with the gun, his head was shaven and he had a huge tattoo on his arm. I couldn't make out what it looked like. It was too dark. I'm sorry."

He glanced up at me, his gaze roaming over my face. "That's okay. You told the officer you could recognize them, right?" When I nodded again, he smiled tightly. Not the big, warm smile I'd seen him throw around when we were teenagers. Not even a hint of it. "They're compiling some mug shots of those who've met your description right now. So we'll go over that in a few." There was a pause as he sat back in the chair. "How many times did you hear the gun fire?"

"Once. No. Twice," I said. Detective Hart was scribbling something down on a small notebook he must've had hidden somewhere. "He shot...he shot that man in the alley, and I dropped my keys like a dumbass. Oh!" I smacked my hand over my mouth. "I'm sorry."

The blue hue of Colton's eyes had lightened. "Honey, saying dumbass around here isn't going to offend anyone."

"No truer words ever spoken," Hart added dryly.

The smile that curved up the corners of my lips felt weak and brittle. I'd also never in a million years thought I'd hear Colton call me honey. Hell, never in a million years did I think I'd be sitting in front of him.

I really needed to focus, but now it was a struggle. Adrenaline had long since faded and it was way past my normal bedtime of eleven-thirty. "Um, after I dropped the keys, the man with the gun, he turned to me. I saw him. He…he saw me." My fingers tightened around the poor tissue as a slice of panic cut across my chest. "I turned and ran. He must've fired at me, but missed. The bullet hit a nearby building." I raised my hand toward my cheek and then immediately dropped it back to my lap. "I kept running and that's when I ran into the man."

Detective Hart asked a few more questions. Did I notice if they had gotten in a car? No. Was a name even spoken? Not that I recalled. Did they say anything to the man they shot? I wasn't sure. Eventually, he got up and left the room to retrieve some photos they wanted me to look at.

I was alone with Colton.

Any other time I probably would've been beside myself with nervousness, but at this point, I barely registered his presence. All I wanted to do was go home and forget this night.

"Abby?"

My gaze slowly lifted at the sound of my name. His voice was deep and gruff—a morning voice.

He leaned toward me, placing his arms on the table. Short dark hairs dusted powerful forearms. The few times I'd seen him over the years, I hadn't been in close proximity to him, but now I could see the tiny differences between the Colton I'd admired from afar in high school and the one sitting in front of me, some ten years later. Fine lines had formed around the corners of his eyes. His jaw seemed harder, and the five-o'clock shadow was something new.

Something sexy.

I really needed to stop thinking in general.

"Are you sure you're okay, Abby?" he asked, and real concern filled his voice.

I shook my head slowly as a shiver raced down my spine. "Yes. No? I'm sorry. I'm so tired."

"I can imagine." He glanced at the door as he moved his shoulders, as if working out a kink. "We'll get you home soon."

Slouching in the metal chair, I sighed. "Is this…the start of your shift or…?"

Colton's cobalt gaze tracked back to me. "I usually get off

around eight, but we work in cycles for homicide calls. It was our weekend."

"Sorry," I whispered, and then frowned. "I don't even know why I apologized. It's got to be hard working those kinds of hours, having to be on call."

"I imagine it is for some, especially those with a family." One side of his lips quirked up, and despite the dire situation, my stomach dipped a bit. He lifted his left hand. "Obviously, I'm not married. I wouldn't know."

I thought about the beautiful blonde I'd seen him with at the movies. "No girlfriend?" My eyes widened. Did I seriously just ask that?

That half grin spread, revealing the one dimple he had in his left cheek. "No. Not really."

Not really? What in the heck was that supposed to mean? Did it matter? No. Not at all. I dropped my gaze to the table. A moment passed and I didn't think about what I was saying. It just…came out. "I'd never seen anyone die before. Never saw the exact moment life was snuffed out. I'd lived through death. With my parents and then with Kevin, but…" I'd seen my husband after he'd passed away. He'd been a pale, waxy shadow of himself and as traumatizing as that was, it was nothing compared to witnessing a life end. "I won't ever forget tonight."

"You won't," he said, and I lifted my gaze to his. "I'm not going to lie to you. It's going to hang with you. Seeing death like that isn't easy. It's a darkness you just can't explain and can't understand."

That was so true. "You see it a lot?"

His head tilted to the side. "I've seen enough, Abby. Enough."

The need to apologize again rose, but I squelched it now. It was a terrible habit of mine. Apologizing for things I had no control over. Without apologizing, I had no idea what to say to him.

"I need to ask you one more time," he said, all softness gone from his eyes. They were like chips of blue ice. "Are you positive you didn't hear any of their names?"

"The one guy was talking—the one with the scar, but I didn't hear what he was saying. I was too…shocked by what I was seeing. I wish I did, but I couldn't make any of it out, but I got this impression that he…I don't know."

"What impression?" He leaned forward, gaze sharpening.

Unsure if what I was saying was correct or more of just a feeling, I squirmed a little in my chair. "I got this feeling that he wasn't okay with what was happening. He appeared upset. Like he had his hands in his hair. Like this." I raised my hands to my shoulder-length hair and scrubbed my fingers through it. "He seemed upset. I know that's not much—"

"No, that's definitely something. That's good."

"How?"

Colton smiled tightly. No dimple. "Because if this guy didn't like what was going down, then he could turn against the one who pulled the trigger."

"Oh." I thought that made sense.

He was quiet for a moment. "What a horrible way for you and I to run into each other again, huh?"

My answering smile didn't feel as forced as the one before. "Yeah. Not the greatest circumstances." I reached up, tucking my hair behind my ear. I started to yawn, weary with exhaustion, but the stretching of my face caused me to wince. "Ow."

Colton had somehow moved closer and before I knew it, I could catch the scent of his cologne. It was crisp, reminding me of mountain air. A single finger curved under my chin, startling me. The touch was simply electrifying, like a jolt of pure caffeine to the nervous system. The grasp was surprisingly tender. That softness was back in his gaze.

And it had been so long since I'd been touched in what felt like such an intimate way.

For some god-awful reason, tears started climbing the back of my throat. Granted, there were currently a lot of reasons to begin sobbing hysterically, but the last thing I needed to do was cry over Colton.

I knew I should pull away from him because the comfort his slight touch offered was too much. The wall I had built around the nearly consuming terror started to crumble. "That man…that murderer? He saw me," I repeated in a hushed voice. "If I can describe him, he can describe me." My voice caught, cracked a little. "That's terrifying."

"I know how scary that is, but trust me, Abby." The hard glint was back in his icy eyes as his hand shifted slightly and his thumb smoothed under the tiny cut along my cheek. "I'm going to make sure you're safe."

Chapter Three

None of the pictures that had been splayed out in front of me or had been included in the most disturbing photo album ever were of the men I'd seen in the alley.

Strangely, I felt like I had failed.

I wanted to be able to point at someone and say that was them. The bad guys would be found, and all of this would be over. I wanted that so badly.

But that was not what happened.

Colton had been called out toward the end and even though he'd said he'd be back, I hadn't seen him while I was ushered out of the police station and guided to my car by Detective Hart.

They'd be in touch.

I had no idea what that meant and I was too exhausted to figure it out. The drive from the city to the townhouse I'd purchased when I moved back wasn't particularly quick, even at damn near close to three in the morning. By some kind of miracle, I made it home, parked my car, and hobbled up the steps and let myself in. It was only then that I remembered that my one heel was broken. I didn't recall how I got the shoe back. Maybe Officer Hun?

Or was it Colton?

God.

Please not Colton.

I really didn't need him knowing that I was near caveman size when it came to my feet.

Flipping the light on inside, I quickly closed the door behind me and kicked off my ruined shoes. My pinched toes sighed in relief as I stared up at the narrow staircase directly in front of the door. More than anything I wanted to climb those steps and throw myself into my bed, but I felt disgustingly dirty and my throat felt like the Mojave Desert.

The section of townhouses had been built in the early nineties so the entire first floor rocked the whole open concept. The living room area was cozy with a couch and chair, situated around a TV and coffee table. The space opened right into a dining room that I honestly never used. Most of my dinners were on the couch. All the appliances had been new in the kitchen, and I'd fallen in love with the gray granite countertops the moment I walked into it.

I turned on the light in the kitchen and went straight to the fridge. Diets be damned. I picked up a can of Coke, popped the lid, and nearly drank all of it while the fridge door was still open, throwing out cold air.

"God," I whispered, lowering the can slowly as I closed the fridge door. "Tonight..."

There were no words.

I turned around and walked out of the kitchen, carrying my can of soda and purse with me. As I walked back through the dining area, my gaze fell over the framed photos nailed to the wall. When I moved in, it had taken me nearly two years to hang those portraits.

Some were easier than others. Like the picture of me and the girls from college, standing in Times Square, or the really terrible college graduation photo. For some reason, I ended up looking cross-eyed in it. Most people would want to hide the photo, but it made me laugh.

It had made Kevin laugh.

My gaze tracked over to the photo of my parents. It had been taken in their home, in the kitchen I'd grown up in. It had been Thanksgiving morning and Dad had snuck up on Mom, wrapping his arms around her waist from behind. Both were smiling happily.

They passed away in a car accident my second year of college. It had been a huge blow, shattering. Dealing with the loss of both parents at once had been nearly impossible, but naïvely, I had believed that would be the only real loss I'd suffer. I mean, come on, what was the statistical probability of losing another loved one to something as unfair and unpredictable as another car accident?

The only photo I had hanging of Kevin was the one of him standing alone at our wedding, dressed in the tux he'd rented from a cheap wedding shop in town. It was outside, in the bright July sun, and he was more golden than blond. I loved this photo so much because it captured the warmth in his brown eyes.

That was Kevin. Always warm. Always welcoming. He was the kind of person who never met a stranger. I pressed my lips together as I stared at his boyishly handsome face. As the months had turned into years, it became harder and harder to pull his features from memory alone. The same with my parents. There were days when all of them would appear in my mind as clear as day, while other days they were nothing more than a ghost.

I'd loved Kevin. I still did. And I missed him. We had been high school sweethearts, and he'd been the only man I'd been with. Looking back, I knew we didn't have the kind of passion that curled the toes or woke you up in the middle of the night, wet and ready, and we were simply…familiar with one another, but we loved each other.

And I didn't regret a second I spent with him.

I just regretted the moments afterward because I knew that Kevin would've wanted me to move on, to find someone else to love. He wouldn't want me to be alone.

My throat clogged and I briefly squeezed my eyes shut against the rush of tears. Holding it together, I trudged on, heading upstairs. There were three bedrooms, but one of them was barely large enough to hold a bed, so it had become my office. Which was perfect because the room faced the backyard and the garden down below, enabling me to procrastinate for hours when I should be working.

I passed the tiny hallway bedroom and entered the master at the front of the townhouse. The room was spacious, complete with its walk-in closet and attached master bath. The Jacuzzi tub had become my best friend forever since I moved in.

Flipping on the nightstand light, I walked my purse over to the dove-gray sitting chair near the door. I dug my phone out and then plugged it into the charger on the nightstand. All I wanted to do was plop face first onto the bed, but I went into the bathroom and peeled off my clothes. I started to dump them in the laundry basket, but instead, I rolled them up in a ball, panties and bra included, to take down to the trash in the morning. I didn't want to wear the clothing again, let alone see it.

Tired, I cranked the water up and waited with my back to the mirror above the sink for the water to heat up to near scalding temps, the way I liked it.

I tried not to look at myself in the mirror when I was completely nude.

I didn't like to see my reflection.

I wasn't...comfortable with it.

It wasn't the tiny dimples or the roundness of certain parts of my body that made me uncomfortable. It wasn't physical. Or maybe it was, because I hadn't felt...attached to my own skin in a while. I knew that sounded crazy, but it was almost like I no longer even knew my own body. It was something that I wore. I wasn't intimate with it beyond using my trusty vibrator every so often. Maybe I'd just gone too long without intimacy.

And tonight, for the first time in years, I actually felt *something* when Colton had touched my chin. And how sad was that? The guy had touched my chin and that was the closest to physical interaction I'd gotten since Kevin.

This was the last thing I wanted to think about tonight. My body ached as if I had overexerted myself as I stepped under the steady spray. The shower felt like the longest of my life and slipping on the worn Penn State shirt and thin, cotton shorts was literally a chore.

Finally, after what felt like forever, I was in bed, but I couldn't sleep. I stared at the silently spinning ceiling fan and I couldn't stop thinking about the man who died tonight. Did he have a family? A wife who was going to be getting that horrific knock on the door? Did he have kids? Were his parents still alive and would soon be burying their son? Would they ever catch the man responsible?

Did I have something to fear?

Reaching over, I picked up the remote and turned the TV on, keeping the volume low, but it did nothing to stop the steady stream of thoughts.

I'd seen someone die.

Squeezing my eyes shut, I rolled over onto my side and for the first time in years, I cried myself to sleep.

* * * *

The following morning, I stood directly in front of my coffee maker, bleary-eyed and impatient as I waited for pure happiness to stop percolating. All I'd managed to do so far was scoop up my hair and toss it up in a messy twist, but already, shorter strands were either slipping free or sticking out in every direction.

In other words, I looked like a hot mess, but I really didn't care as I poured the steaming coffee into a cup halfway full of sugar, and I still stood there, taking my first drink, my second, and my third as the cool tile seeped through my bare feet.

I'd overslept.

Well, sleeping past eight a.m. nowadays was sleeping in. It was close to nine before I dragged myself out of bed. It wasn't that big of a deal. The only thing I had planned later in the day was to meet up with Jillian Lima for dinner.

Jillian and I met each other at a book signing in the city. She was almost ten years younger than me, but the age difference had quickly evaporated. Jillian was a hard cookie to crack. She was almost debilitating shy, but love of books crosses all barriers. We bonded over our favorite authors and themes, and once she discovered what I did for a living, she started to open up.

For the last year, we met every Saturday night to discuss books over dinner. Sometimes we'd grab a movie or head to the bookstore, and I was going to miss her. In the spring, she would be transferring to a college in West Virginia. I still didn't know why she was doing that. That was a little nugget of info I couldn't wiggle out of her.

I'd just topped off my cup of coffee when the doorbell rang, surprising me. I wasn't expecting anyone. Leaving the cup on the counter, I padded across the floor and peered out the front window, but since there were always cars I didn't recognize parked out front, that made no difference. Rolling my eyes, I reached for the door handle, cursing the fact that there wasn't a peephole in the door.

My jaw unhinged on a sharp inhale, and the ability to form comprehensive thoughts fled.

Colton Anders, in all his blue-eyed babe glory, stood on my stoop. "Good morning, Abby."

Chapter Four

I was beyond responding.

He stood there with a medium-size pink box in one hand and the other shoved in the pocket of his trousers. The five-o'clock shadow was heavier, giving him a rough edge that my sleep-fogged mind found incredibly sexy.

Okay. I would find that sexy anytime.

Any. Time.

He was dressed as he was the night before, and I had the distinct impression he hadn't been to bed yet, which really wasn't fair, because how could he look *this* good without sleeping?

One side of his lips curled up, revealing the left-sided dimple. "Can I...come in? I brought crepes with me."

I blinked.

"You like crepes, right? You have to like them," he added, grinning. "Everyone loves crepes and these are the shit. They are rolled in cinnamon and brown sugar."

"I...I thoroughly enjoy them." My ass also thoroughly enjoyed them. Moving back, I stepped aside. "How do you know where I live?"

Colton stepped in, his chin dipped down. I wasn't a small lady, coming in at five foot eight, but standing next to him, I felt small, delicate even, and that was an odd feeling. "It was on your statement. I probably should've called first, but I was on my way home from the station and your house was on the way. So was the bakery."

I didn't know what to say as I closed the door behind him, but my heart was pounding in my chest and my stomach was wiggling in a weird way, sort of like the way I'd seen described a thousand times. Butterflies. But more powerful. Like large birds of prey or pterodactyls. "You live nearby?"

His grin spread. "I live over on Plymouth Road."

That was nowhere near my house. The butterflies increased. "Oh. In the apartments over there?"

He nodded. "Did I wake you?"

"No. I..." That was about when I realized that I was wearing nothing but a pair of sleep shorts and an old shirt that pretty much hid nothing. I didn't even need to look down to know that my nipples were most likely noticeable. And my thighs? Oh, dear God.

My hair.

"I smell coffee though," he said, glancing toward the kitchen. "So I'm guessing not?"

He spoke as if he hadn't noticed I had some major headlights and chub rub going on, but then again, why would someone like Colton even notice that in the first place? My attention flipped to the stairway. A huge part of me wanted to rush upstairs and throw a Snuggie on. Or at least a bra.

I really needed to put a bra on.

"No. You didn't wake me up," I said, glancing back at him. The air suddenly punched out of my lungs.

Colton was so not looking at my face.

He was looking below the shoulders, his gaze lingering in some areas longer than others. Like at the edge of my shorts and then across the chest, as if he were committing the words Penn State to memory. A tingle buzzed to the tips of my breasts. His gaze gradually drifted up to my face and those blue eyes...they reminded me of the core of a flame. Heat blossomed deep inside me, infiltrating my veins. The intensity of it was shocking.

So much so I stepped back. "I'm going to...I'll be right back."

That half grin remained in place. "Mind if I help myself to the coffee?"

"No. Not at all." I edged toward the stairwell. "Help away."

Spinning around, I dashed up the stairs and into my bedroom. Once inside, I pressed my palms to my warm cheeks. "Oh my God."

I headed into the bathroom and saw, thank God, that my face wasn't blood red, but my cheeks were flushed and my hazel eyes, more brown than green, seemed bright. Feverish. Turning on the cold water, I bent over and quickly splashed it over my face. Oh goodness, I had only ever read about men staring at women in a way that it felt like a physical touch before. I hadn't really believed it possible.

It was.

Straightening, I grabbed my toothbrush and quickly got down to business, all the while trying to get a grip on reality. It didn't take a genius to figure out that Colton was here because of what happened last night. There could be no other reason, so I needed to keep my overactive imagination where it belonged, at work. Yes, it was odd that he'd just pop over, but maybe he felt like he needed to tell me in person. And the checking me out? Maybe he was just reading my shirt.

Okay. That was stupid. He had definitely been looking at my breasts, but he was a dude and I was a chick, so these things happened.

Especially when you were nipply and you weren't wearing a bra.

I grabbed a bra and a pair of yoga pants I'd never in my entire life ever worn while doing yoga. I quickly re-twisted my hair and then resisted the urge to put makeup on. At this point, if I went back downstairs with a peachy glow and to die for lashes, it would be way too obvious.

I couldn't believe Colton Anders had seen me braless before I had my first full cup of coffee. What is my life?

Ugh.

Ignoring the near constant flutter in the pit of my stomach, I headed back downstairs. What I saw had the weirdest, bittersweet feel to it.

Colton had placed the box of crepes on the dining table and moved my cup of coffee to the seat catty-corner to where he was sitting, at the head of the table. A fresh cup of coffee was placed in front of him. There were even plates and he'd found my napkins. And utensils.

It was so...familiar, and again, intimate.

"How are you hanging in there after last night?" he asked without looking up.

"Okay, I guess. I mean, I'm trying not to think about it." Except that was a terrible lie. It was almost all I thought about last night.

He glanced up and the side of his lips quirked up. "I must say, I sort of liked what you were wearing before more."

My cheeks flushed red as I made my way to the table. "You must be exhausted then."

One eyebrow arched. "Oh, sweetheart, I'm never too tired to appreciate the beauty of a woman who just woke up and is still walking around in the clothes she slept in."

I sat down, eyeing him like he was a foreign species. "I didn't know you were a charmer."

"More like an outrageous flirt," he corrected, opening the box of crepes. "Obviously I'm not very good at it."

Clasping my hands in my lap, all I could do was watch him pluck up a crepe and plop it down on my plate. Was he saying he was trying to flirt with me? That was definitely not typical detective protocol.

Well, not outside romance novels.

"I'm still shocked that it was you when I walked into the office last night. God. How many years has it been? Too many." He moved on, picking up another crepe and placing it on his plate. "I really am sorry to hear about Kevin. The one thing I've learned over and over is that life is not guaranteed. Ever."

"That's true." I glanced at the crepe. It looked delish, but nerves were conquering my appetite. "It's hard to deal with and move on, but you do, even when there are a lot of moments when you don't think that'll happen."

"And you have?" He picked up a knife and fork, cutting into the crepe. "You've moved on?"

"I..." The question caught me off guard, and I glanced at the photo of Kevin. "It was four years ago and I...I will always love him, but I have…I have closed that chapter of my life."

His gaze flicked to mine and he didn't look away as he lifted a piece of crepe to his mouth. He ate it with pure enjoyment, as if it was the first and last piece of food he'd ever devoured, and I couldn't help but think if he ate food with such gusto, what he was like eating—

I cut that thought off and quickly turned my attention to my plate. Oh my God, what was wrong with me? Why I was thinking about Colton eating…well, definitely not food. Then again, who wouldn't think about that when they saw him and those lush lips?

"So what have you been up to, Abby?"

My chin jerked up as my heart turned over heavily. "I graduated from Penn State. Um, I worked in New York at a publishing house."

His brows flew up. "Really? That's impressive."

I shrugged a shoulder. "Well, it was not an easy job to get. I had to put my time in. Luckily, I was able to spend a summer interning while in college. It helped open connections, but I was still an assistant editor by the time I left. Kevin worked at a different publishing house. He made senior editor in record time. Of course."

"Why?" He was almost done with his crepe.

I smiled faintly. "The publishing industry sure loves their boys."

"Interesting. I didn't know that." He paused. "And you left after Kevin passed away?"

I nodded. "I just…well, I wasn't a fan of the city. Even Philadelphia has nothing on New York. It was so damn expensive and I didn't see a point in staying there afterward."

He picked up a second crepe. "And do you still work as an editor?"

"Freelance." I reached up, tugging a strand of hair that came loose back and behind my ear. "I still freelance for publishers and for indies."

"Indies?" Genuine curiosity colored his tone.

"Independent authors—those who don't work with a publisher. Right now I'm working on Jamie McGuire's new novel. It's called *Other Lives*, and it's freaking fantastic. Sometimes my job is hard, though."

"Why? Dealing with authors?"

I laughed. "All the authors I've worked with have been great. Like Jamie? She's one hell of a firecracker, but she's a sweetheart. But sometimes I just suck at remembering this is a job. Like I need to be paying close attention, but I get caught up in the story and the next thing I know I have to go back and reread an entire chapter. I'm hoping she hires me for her next Maddox Brother's book. I'm a huge…" I laughed, a bit self-consciously. "Sorry. I can be a bit of a fan girl."

"It's okay."

I bit down on my lip. "There's nothing more amazing than seeing a book you've worked on get talked about and loved or when it hits a list. You feel like you're a part of something bigger."

Colton was grinning as he watched me closely. "You really love your job."

"I love books," I said simply. "There's nothing more powerful than the written word. It can transfer you to a place that exists right now that you'll never get to visit or it can take you to a world that doesn't. It can show you things you'll never experience otherwise in life, and books…most importantly, they can take you out of your own world, and sometimes you need that."

"I feel you." He was still watching me with those intent blue eyes.

A moment of silence passed between us. "I'm sure you didn't come here to hear about all of that."

He put his fork down. "Actually, yeah, I did."

I blinked. "What?"

Colton leaned toward me with his gaze locked onto mine. "I didn't know you in high school, but I knew of you."

"You did? I can't imagine it was anything interesting. I was boring as—"

"I never got the impression you were boring," he interrupted, and goodness, I could fall into those eyes and never come back out. So cheesy sounding, and if I saw it in one of my author's books, I'd redline the hell out of that, but now I got it. It was possible. "I just thought you were this pretty girl who sat two seats behind me in history class and was shy."

Several things occurred to me at once. He remembered that we shared history class together? Holy crap on a cracker. And he thought I'd been pretty? I was sure I probably weighed twenty pounds more back then and I wore these god-awful glasses that were so trendy nowadays.

Colton *was* a flirt.

"Looking back, I wish I had the balls to talk to you then." He returned his attention to his crepe while my jaw hit the table. "But you were with Kevin and…yeah, that's not my style, you know?" He glanced in my direction. "You're going to eat the crepes, right?"

"Yeah," I murmured, cutting into one side. I forced myself to eat a bite, and it was like heaven just orgasmed in my mouth. Wow. That was inappropriate. I resisted a giggle. "What about you? You've been a cop this whole time?"

"Yep. It's what I always wanted to do. Started off as a deputy, then became a detective for the county before transferring to the city. I love working as a detective, but with my hours all over the place, Reece, my brother, has pretty much straight up adopted my dog. She doesn't even stay at my house anymore." He finished off the second crepe with an impressive quickness and then settled back against the chair, stretching out his long legs. "Almost got married."

Thank God I had just swallowed a piece of crepe because there was a good chance I would've choked. "Almost?"

"Was engaged." He grinned, and I felt my tummy dip in response. "Nicole and I were together for…hell." He glanced up at the ceiling, pursing his lips. "For about six years."

Holy crap, six years? That was a long time. I wondered if she was the woman I'd seen him with at the movies that one time, but that was like, maybe a year ago.

"Got all the way down to planning the wedding date when we came to the realization that we wanted different things in life."

I picked up my coffee, more intrigued than I should be, but I couldn't imagine what more this mystery woman could've wanted beyond having Colton putting a ring on it. Granted, there was more to life, to a relationship, than having a hot guy to wake up to, but Colton and his younger brother, Reece, had always given the good-guy vibes. Colton could've changed since high school, but I didn't think so. "How so?"

"At first I think Nicole liked the idea of dating a cop." He laughed as he ran his finger along the rim of his cup, and damn, he had long fingers. "But it's not an easy life. Odd hours. Then there's the danger factor. I make decent money, but I'm never going to be rolling around in it. I think she hoped that I'd grow tired of being a cop."

I didn't understand. "But you guys were together a long time. Why would she think it was something you'd grow tired with?"

He raised a shoulder. "I think some people pretend at being okay with something because they think there's some kind of payoff in the end. That they'll eventually get what they want, and when they realize that's never going to happen, they just can't pretend anymore."

I shook my head. "I still don't get it. Why would someone waste their time pretending—waste the other person's time? There's no point in pretending in a relationship. It'll never work."

His dark lashes lowered, shielding his eyes as a small smile played across his lips. "Agreed."

Sipping my coffee, I tried to ignore the wild fluttering and the thousand questions whirling around in my head. I peeked over at him as I lowered my cup, and our gazes locked. Air leaked out of my parted lips. Colton didn't look away, and neither could I. Absolutely struck helpless by the intensity in his stare, the wisps of excitement building in my belly gave way to a slow burn that got my pulse pounding. How could a single look from him draw such a response? That gaze of his dipped, and I drew in a shallow breath and felt the warmth travel through my veins. Was he looking at my mouth again? Oh Lord, it was getting hot in here.

Goodness, this man...even his stare was pure...pure sin.

I cleared my throat. "So...um, when did you and Nicole part ways?"

"About six months or so ago."

Ice chased away the warmth as I schooled my expression blank. Six months? That wasn't a long time ago, especially considering they were engaged to be married and were together for six years. Six months was...was nothing. After I lost Kevin, six months had changed nothing for me. How could he be over the failure of a relationship in six months?

And why did it matter? No, it didn't, but there was no mistaking the rise of disappointment. I wanted to smack myself.

Colton leaned forward. "I did have another reason for stopping by. It's about what happened last night."

"Of course," I murmured, slapping a smile across my face as another surge of dismay made itself known.

He looked at me strangely. "I don't want to go into the gory details—"

"I can handle them." Or at least I thought I could. I was pretty sure I could.

That half smile was back. "When I got called out when I was talking with you, it was because the coroner had picked up the...body and had some evidence. Obviously, we know what the cause of death is, but I wanted to stop by and let you know that we are probably going to have an ID sometime today."

"Oh." I took a drink of my now lukewarm coffee.

"I also want you to contact me immediately if you see anything weird, okay?" Reaching into his pocket, he pulled out a business card and placed it on the table.

My gaze fell to the card. So formal. "What could be weird?"

"Just if you notice anyone hanging around here that you're not familiar with. Anything that gives you a bad vibe. That sort of thing."

I glanced up at him, the unease from earlier returning. "Should I be worried?"

"No." The smile he gave me this time didn't reach his eyes. "Just careful."

That really didn't make me feel warm and fuzzy, but couldn't he have just called me? If he had my address, then he had my cell.

The smile transformed and his face softened. "Yeah, I could've called you and told you that."

My chin jerked up as I almost dropped my cup. "Can you read minds? Oh man, I hope not."

His gaze did that slow slide again. "Now I'm curious to what I'd discover if I could read your mind."

I widened my eyes and said nothing because seriously, my mind was one step from face planting in the gutter when he was around.

Reaching over, he tapped his fingers on my arm. "I didn't want to just call you."

"Oh," I repeated. Goodness, I had this conversation thing down pat. It wasn't my fault. The tapping of his fingers had sent a fine shiver up my arm.

"And I was in the mood for crepes," he continued. "And when you're in the mood for crepes, you want to share them with a pretty lady."

My mouth opened but there were no words.

He chuckled as he rose. "I have to get going."

"Okay," I murmured, putting my cup on the table. I stood, following him to the door, and when he stopped suddenly, I nearly bounced off his back. His playful grin once again made an appearance. "Sorry."

Colton tilted his head to the side. "I'll be in touch, Abby."

As he left and I closed the door behind him, I leaned forward, gently knocking my forehead against it as I tried to stop my wayward thoughts from making a bigger deal out of his visit than I should.

But it was hard.

"Ugh." I pressed my forehead against the door and groaned.

Colton was an admitted flirt—an outrageous one. That was what he had to be doing because there was no way that it could be anything else. After all, how could it? Not when he was engaged six months ago, and he hadn't said who ended the relationship.

Besides, I wasn't his type. I wasn't cutting myself short by acknowledging that. Colton was...he was gorgeous. The kind of masculine beauty that could grace the covers of the books I edited, and he was also sweet—charming, and from what I remembered, intelligent to boot. And me?

I was the kind of woman who got the guy in the books.

But not in real life.

Never in real life.

Chapter Five

"Oh my gosh, that is so scary." Jillian brushed the heavy fringe of dark brown bangs out of her wide brown eyes. "Are you okay?"

"I'm fine." A little concealer had covered the tiny cuts on my face, and the palms of my hands only stung every so often. "It was scary and so unexpected."

"Who would expect that? Ugh." Jillian glanced down at her empty plates. We'd demolished our dinner and then our cheesecakes. "I can't even imagine. I probably would've run screaming and flailing in the other direction."

"That's pretty much what I did." I eyed the tiny crumb of cake on my plate and wondered how gluttonous I'd be if I ate that last piece.

"And that's probably why you're alive," she replied. "Even my father would have a hard time justifying a fight strategy rather than a flight one."

Jillian's father owned Lima Academy, and the sprawling building in downtown Philadelphia was more than just a gym. It was one of the premier mixed martial arts training facilities in the world. Jillian's father, skilled in his native Brazilian jiu jitsu, could've probably used his ninja stealth and taken the guys out with his karate skills.

"Speaking of your father, how is he handling the idea of you leaving in the spring?" I asked, changing the subject.

She cringed as she leaned back against the booth, folding her arms across her chest. Tension seeped into her pretty features. "He's still not exactly thrilled about it. He doesn't like the idea of me not being within his eyesight. Like something's going to..." She trailed off, shaking her head. "Anyway, do you still want to go to that signing Tuesday night?"

"Tiffany King's signing? Hell yeah." I relaxed when a genuine smile crossed her face. Conversations about her dad were usually a dead end. "She's going to be signing *A Shattered Moment*."

Jillian knocked her bangs out of her face. "I loved that book. Isn't there going to be another author with her, though?"

"Yeah, I think Sophie Jordan and Jay Crownover are going to be there." I glanced over at the couple walking past our table. "You want to meet at the bookstore?"

She nodded as she picked up her glass. "So," she drew the word out. "This Colton guy you mentioned? You went to high school with him?"

I bit back a sigh. I didn't know why I even brought him up, but I had, and I was woman enough to admit that I wanted to obsess over every little thing he'd said to me, but all I managed was a tight nod.

Jillian turned her head to the side and shot me a sidelong glance. "You know, when you brought him up earlier, you blushed."

"I did not."

"Yes, you did."

My eyes narrowed, but I laughed because yeah, I probably did. "I had the biggest crush on him in high school, and I know that's terrible because I was with Kevin and that probably makes me a terrible person."

"No, it doesn't." She rolled her eyes. "Just because you were with someone doesn't mean you're blind to everyone around you."

"True." I paused. "And Colton was hot."

Jillian giggled. "Was?"

"And now he like puts an extra 'o' and 't' in hot. He...he actually remembered me. Like he knew what class we shared."

Her brows rose, disappearing under her bangs. "Really?"

I nodded as I scrunched my nose. "And I think he was flirting with me. Okay. He was definitely flirting with me, but I think he's just a flirt. And guys who are flirts will flirt with anyone." I paused. "I wonder how many times I can say 'flirt' in a sentence?"

Jillian gave a close-lipped smile. "Oh, I know all about guys who will flirt with anything that's breathing." She glanced over at the empty table. "Anyway, maybe he's interested."

"Ah, I don't know about that." Caving in, I scooped up the last little crumb of cake.

She frowned. "Why? You're smart and funny. You're pretty, and you love books. Why wouldn't he be interested?"

"Thanks," I laughed. "But he was engaged up until six months ago."

"Oh." Her lips pursed.

"And I'm not judging the fact he was in a previous serious relationship because so was I, but…" I stopped myself, laughing again. "Why am I even thinking about it in that kind of manner? I saw him last night because he's the detective investigating a homicide I witnessed and he stopped by this morning." I shook my head, clearing those thoughts away. "I don't even need to think about this in that way."

"I don't know," she replied after a moment. "But this whole thing sort of reminds me of a romance trope."

Another laugh burst out of me. "It sure does, except in real life, it never works out that way."

The truth was, even though that kind of thing only ever happened in books, I secretly dreamed of it happening to me. Sort of like a grown version of a girlie fantasy.

She shrugged as a far-off look appeared in her gaze and her response was soft. "I don't know about that. I like to believe—I need to believe—that happily ever afters exist in real life too." In that moment, she suddenly looked far older than nineteen. "For all of us."

* * * *

After dinner, I stopped at the grocery store in town, picking up a couple of necessary work items.

Coffee.

5-hour Energy drinks.

Skittles.

Chocolate.

Coke Zero.

Without these things, I was pretty much useless when it came to editing. When I worked in New York, I had a drawer in my desk full of three of those five things.

Checking out was a breeze and as I headed back into the waning daylight, I stowed the shopping cart and held on to my bag and case of soda with a death grip. Even though it was Saturday night, I would be working once I got my butt home and into comfy sweats. Working from home meant I kept weird hours.

Or in other words, I simply worked nearly every day.

I most definitely worked more now than when I traveled into an office every day. Then it had been easier to separate home from work. Not so much now.

As I neared my car, my steps slowed. When I'd gone into the store, the parking space beside my car had been empty, and I'd walked past plenty of vacant spaces on my way in and out, but now there was a van parked on my driver's side.

Not just any van. The creepy, white with no windows, kidnapper-type van.

My stomach dipped as I stopped a few feet from the van. Maybe I was just being paranoid after last night. Or maybe it had to do with Colton's warning about paying attention to anything weird, but either way, a tiny ball of dread had formed in the pit of my stomach.

The bag was starting to cut into my fingers and the case of cola was getting heavy. What could I do? Drop my groceries and run? Call Colton because there was a creeper van parked next to mine?

God, I watched way too much Investigation Discovery channel.

Then, before I could make up my mind to do anything, the passenger door creaked open and a male stepped out. My heart plummeted. He didn't look like he belonged stepping out of a work van. No way, no how. I wasn't trying to be judgie-mc-judgers, but his dark trousers, tucked in dark blue shirt, and polished dress shoes did not fit the rusted, broken-down creeper van.

Dark sunglasses obscured his eyes, but I had the distinct impression he was staring at me. Probably because I was standing there like an idiot, but then again, at this time of day, I couldn't figure out why he needed sunglasses. Ignoring the shiver slithering down my spine and the numbness in my fingers, I started walking again, fully prepared to turn the bag of groceries into a deadly weapon.

"It's a nice night, isn't it?" the man called out.

My aching fingers tightened around the strap of the plastic bag. I didn't smile. I didn't reply. The creep factor was off the charts, and as I neared the back of the van, I gave it a wide berth, ready for a posse of insane clowns to jump out and try to kidnap me.

Of course, the doors didn't open. I was going to walk to the passenger side and try to see if there was anyone else in the van before I went to the driver's door. Sounded legit.

"Your name is Abby, right?" the man said.

The air froze in my lungs, like I'd walked into subzero temperatures. Tiny hairs all along my body rose as if an army of cockroaches was running loose on my skin. I looked over my shoulder at him.

He stood by the back of his van with a close-lipped smile. A cold one. Predatory. "The Abby Ramsey, born and raised in Plymouth Meeting? Married her high school sweetheart who tragically passed away in a car accident about four years ago? The same Abby Ramsey who works from home as a freelance editor?"

Holy shit.

Holy shit balls on Sunday.

"Yeah, that's you," he continued. "You saw something last night that we need to chat about."

Talking was the last thing we needed to do. My heart pounded in my chest as I faced him. Why did the parking lot seem so empty now? It wasn't. People were milling around, but no one was paying attention to us. My gaze darted to the entry of the grocery store, trying to determine the distance if I had to make a run for it.

I wasn't much of a runner.

He took a step forward, and I blanched, lifting the heavy bag, prepared to swing if he got any closer. He raised his hands. "I'm not going to hurt you."

Famous last words. "Don't come any closer to me."

"I'm not. We can have our little conversation from a distance if that makes you happy." He smiled again, but it was chilling. "All I need you to understand, and I need you to really get this, is that you're not going to be able to identify anyone from last night."

An icy knot balled in my stomach.

"That's all, and that's not a big deal, is it? Just keep your mouth shut from here on out and nothing bad will happen. And you don't want anything bad to happen, do you?"

I was beyond responding, my heart thumping heavily in my chest. That was a threat, a very thinly veiled threat. Part of me couldn't believe this was happening.

"We want to make sure you keep your mouth shut," he said in the same friendly, conversational tone. "And I think you'll understand fairly quickly how serious we are."

Just then, the passenger window rolled down and all I saw was an arm extend out. A hand popped the side of the van, causing my heart to jump. The man backed up then, clapping his hands together as he said, "Now you have a nice evening."

I didn't move as he walked back to the van and climbed in. I didn't move when the old thing hunkered to life or when it pulled straight through the empty spot in front of it, turning left to head out of the parking lot.

"Oh my God," I whispered.

In a daze, I shoved my groceries into the trunk of my car with jerky, quick motions, and then I climbed in behind the wheel. I didn't even think for one second about what to do next. There was no way I was not going to call the police. Forget that. Before I left for dinner, I had shoved Colton's card in my purse. My mind raced. It made sense to call him because he knew what was going on. Calling 911 meant I'd have to tell them everything all over again.

As I pulled my cellphone out of my purse with a shaky hand, its unexpected shrill ring startled a tiny shriek out of me. Jesus. I looked down at the screen. It was a local number I didn't recognize. Normally I wouldn't answer, but for some unknown reason, this time I did.

I placed it to my ear and croaked out, "Hello?"

"Abby?"

My free hand landed on the steering wheel. I recognized the voice immediately. "Colton? I—"

"Thank fucking God you answered," he said, cutting me off. "Where are you?"

I blinked slowly, completely thrown off. "I'm...I'm sitting in the parking lot of the grocery store near...near Mona's."

"I want you to listen to me, okay?" There was the sound of a car door slamming and an engine keying on. "I want you to go inside and stay there, okay. Do not go home."

Chapter Six

I had kind of done what Colton had demanded. I'd gone into the grocery store and waited near their pharmacy, and when I spotted Reece, his younger brother, prowling through the sliding doors, I knew something really bad had happened.

Reece, a deputy with the county sheriff's office, had been in his uniform. I saw Reece around town a lot and knew he was seriously dating one of the bartenders over at Mona's, a girl we'd gone to school with, but for him to be the one to show up sent a chill over me.

"Something has happened at your house," he'd said, and that was all he would tell me.

He was supposed to wait with me until Colton could get from the city, but I wasn't having that. How could he just say something had happened at my house and then just expect me to stand around and wait? That was my *home*. After much arguing and more than a handful of concerned looks shot in our direction, Reece agreed—or relented—to escort me home.

Stars had started to dot the sky as we walked outside, all the while Reece muttering, "Colton's going to kick my ass."

One look at Reece told me that would be easier said than done.

Yeah, Colton had an inch or two on him when it came to height, but Reece could hold his own.

In his county cruiser, he'd led me the short distance to my house. My hands had ached the entire drive and the moment I pulled into my parking space, I'd wanted to cry.

I hadn't.

Not when I'd climbed out of the car and saw the two officers standing by my open front door. I hadn't cried when I saw the shattered front window. And right now, as I stepped around Reece and went inside, I couldn't let the weight of everything that had happened in the last twenty-four hours get to me.

The TV, which sat near the window, was knocked over, shattered on the floor. Lying next to it was a huge cement block. I had no idea how someone could throw that thing through a window.

"Nothing else appears damaged," Reece said when I looked over at him. His hands rested against his duty belt. "But we're going to need you to look around to make sure nothing has been stolen."

Drawing in a shaky breath, I nodded as I tried to process what I was seeing. There was no way this wasn't related to what happened last night or the swarmy guy outside of the grocery store, but I still had a hard time believing it. Not because I was ignoring the evidence right in front of my face.

"Both the neighbors on either side of your townhouse weren't home," Reece explained. "No one else heard anything. When your neighbor on the right came home and saw it, she immediately called the police."

I needed to thank Betty, the elderly woman he must've been referencing. Coming home to this, on top of everything else, would've been horrifying.

"Are you okay, Abby?" Reece asked, stepping closer. "I know it can be hard to deal with the fact someone has done something like this to your house."

"I imagine you see this a lot, huh?" I worked my fingers together, hoping to ease the blood flow back in them as another officer scooped up the heavy cement brick with gloved hands. Something occurred to me right then. "How did Colton know about this?" This was so not his jurisdiction.

Reece watched the other officer carry the block out of the house. "He mentioned what happened last night when I saw him this afternoon—he mentioned you." A half grin appeared, nearly identical to Colton's. "Which is odd because he normally doesn't talk about witnesses or the fact that he shared crepes with one this morning."

My hands stilled and my eyes widened.

"I was the second officer to respond," Reece continued, the smile slipping away. "Once the neighbor next door said your name, I called Colton."

Was that allowed? I didn't know. Suddenly bone weary, I walked over to the chair and sat down, exhaling heavily. Over the years, since Kevin's death, I had learned how to deal with things. Last night, I had let myself have that little breakdown. It was understandable. I'd been a witness to a murder. If you were going to flip out about something, that was high up on the list of things to freak out over. But I needed to get it together now. I wasn't a shrinking violet, nor was I someone prone to hysterics.

The responding officer came in and I answered all his questions. When had I left the house? Where had I been? When I told them about stopping at the grocery store and the subsequent creeper dude in the creeper van, Reece snapped to attention.

"Why didn't you say something at the store?" he demanded, his eyes sharpening as he reached for his phone in his pocket.

"Um, I was kind of distracted by the dire message of not going home," I said. "But I'm telling you now."

Reece opened his mouth but seemed to rethink what he was saying. "I'll be right back." Stepping outside, I saw him lift his phone.

I wasn't sure how much time passed before I got up and accomplished what Reece had suggested. I checked everywhere, concentrating on my office and my bedroom. Nothing of any value was missing, which is what I told Reece when he appeared in my room.

I knew what the brick through the window was.

A message.

As I stood in front of my untouched jewelry box, I shuddered. Message was received, but that didn't mean I was going to listen. I'd already told the one officer and Reece, and I would tell Colton.

"Abby?" a deep voice boomed from downstairs. "Reece?"

I turned at the sound of Colton's voice and Reece's answering, "We're up here."

A handful of seconds later, Colton appeared in the doorway. He had changed since this morning, wearing a different police-issued polo. His blue eyes were fastened on me as he stepped into the bedroom.

"Are you okay?" he asked.

"She's okay," Reece answered, and then rolled his eyes when Colton shot him a look.

"I'm fine," I insisted, smoothing my hands along my skirt. "I'm just shook up."

Colton crossed the room and within a heartbeat, he was standing right in front of me. One hand curled around the back of my neck in a familiar, comforting gesture. The other landed on my shoulder. Our eyes locked, and my lips parted.

"The man at the store, he didn't harm you or anything?" he demanded, his gaze intently searching mine.

"No," I whispered, swallowing hard. "He just told me that I...I needed to keep my mouth shut. That I better not identify anyone from last night. And then he said that I'd understand quickly how serious the message is."

A muscle flexed along Colton's jaw as his gaze swept over my face. "Why didn't you call me?"

"I was going to. I was picking up my phone to call you, but you called me first. I was so caught off guard by what was happening here that I focused on that," I explained.

His hand tightened along the nape of my neck. It wasn't a constrictive or threatening move. It was one that was oddly tender. Intimate. Way beyond what he had to do, as a member of law enforcement, to comfort me.

The moment, whatever was going on between us, stretched out. There was something there, a jolt. Like touching a live wire. He sucked in an audible breath. His fingers spread along my shoulder, and the sudden urge to obliterate the tiny distance between us, to press my body against his, rode me hard. Without thinking, I stepped forward.

Reece cleared his throat.

Flushing, I looked away from the unnerving intensity in Colton's gaze. A shiver chased after his hand as it slipped off the back of my neck and dropped to his side.

"I need you to tell me exactly what happened at the store," Colton said after a moment, his voice rougher than normal.

I did exactly that.

It was odd to have both Colton and Reece in my bedroom. Their presence made it feel much smaller than it was. Any other time I would've been amused by having two extraordinarily attractive brothers who were also cops standing in front of me, but I was too thrown by everything.

The murder last night.

Colton showing up this morning with crepes.

Creepy van dude.

Vandalized property.

And now the way Colton behaved when he showed up and that...that spark? My skin was still tingling.

All within twenty-four hours. It was insane. My life was normally boring.

By the time I answered all of Colton's questions, it was just us in the house. Reece had left not too long after the other officer to answer another call, and it was close to ten.

Colton had gone downstairs to make a few calls and I was slow to follow him. A warm breeze stirred the curtains in front of the broken window and may gaze drifted to the floor. The glass was gone. The TV was also righted, its broken face a sad sight.

Stepping off the stairs, I looked into the kitchen just in time to see Colton dumping the glass in the trash can. He was still on the phone.

"That's what I thought," I heard him say as he placed the dustpan on the counter. "You know how he operates. We all know how he works." There was a pause as he turned around. His eyes met mine. "Yeah," he spoke into the phone. "I'll be in touch."

Suddenly self-conscious, I glanced at the window and then back at him as I stood near the stairwell. "Thank you for cleaning up. You didn't have to do that."

He placed his phone on the counter and started toward me.

Goose bumps raced across my flesh. "Do you have something to cover the window with tonight? Tomorrow I can head down to the hardware store and get some boards to cover it until someone can get out here and replace it."

Did I fall and hit my head? "You don't have to do that. Thank you, but—"

"I know I don't have to do it. I want to do it." With his long-legged pace, it took him no time to end up standing in front of me. "I'm off tomorrow, and I have time now unless I get a call."

I tilted my head back to meet his stare as I weighed whether I should accept his help. It seemed stupid not to, but it was a lot for him to do for...for me. "I don't want you to go out of your way, Colton."

One side of his lips kicked up. "I don't mind going out of my way for you." He put his hand on the stairway railing above me. "Not at all."

The crazed, possibly carnivorous, butterfly flutter from this morning was back, wiggling around in my stomach.

"Let me help you with this," he urged softly.

I drew in a shallow breath. "Okay."

The smile grew as he lifted his hand from the railing and caught a piece of my hair, brushing it back from my cheek. "Now that wasn't so hard, was it?"

It was and I didn't even understand why.

"Do you have a tarp that I could use to cover the window?" he asked.

"There is one in the shed out back. It was there when I moved in and I don't know if it's any good or not."

"I'll check it out." He started to turn and then stopped. Placing the tips of his fingers under my chin, he tilted my head back. There was a good chance my heart stopped. "Can I ask you something?"

At that moment, he could probably do anything he wanted. "Sure."

The dimple appeared on his left cheek and then he bit down on his lower lip. Something about that tugged at the very core of me. I wanted to be his teeth. Or his lip. Hell, I'd be down for any part of that.

"Do you believe in second chances?" he asked.

That was not the question I was expecting him to ask, but my answer was immediate and it was the truth, something I felt deeply. "Yes."

"Good." His finger slipped up my chin and his thumb smoothed along the skin under my lip. "So do I."

Chapter Seven

Luck was finally shining down on me. The tarp Colton gathered from the shed was useable. I put on a pot of coffee while he broke out the duct tape, and then I pretended not to be watching him cover my window.

I was totally watching him. I mean, who wouldn't? When he'd spread out the tarp, he'd bent over and good Lord in sweet, sweet heaven, that man had a *great* rear end. And then when he started hanging it up, I was witness to the amazing display of muscles rippling and straining under his shirt.

What I would give to see that man in the buff.

During this, I did make a mental note to contact my insurance company on Monday morning, so I wasn't a complete fail at prioritizing.

I walked his cup over to him, placing it on the coffee table. Working on one corner, he glanced over his shoulder. "Thanks."

Since I had tried to help already and was virtually shooed away, I sat on the couch. "I really do appreciate this."

"It's no problem." He ripped off the section of the tape. "There're a couple of things I need to talk to you about. I was planning on filling you in tomorrow. Maybe over some pancakes this time."

I squeezed my eyes shut briefly and wished his words meant

more than just charming flirtatiousness. "Okay."

"We've identified the victim." He stretched the tarp down the right side as he filled me in. "Not the most upstanding citizen, but his record was mostly petty crimes, a few drug infractions. Looks like what went down Friday night might have been more of a turf thing, but obviously it's bigger than that."

My spine stiffened. "I figured as much. Creepy van dude gave me that impression."

"The man murdered worked for Isaiah Vakhrov. Have you ever heard of him?"

"No. Should I have?"

He shook his head as he tore off another piece of tape. "Not if you want to live a long, healthy and safe life, no. Isaiah Vakhrov pretty much runs the city, but not from the right side of the fence, if you get what I'm saying. His fingers are in everything. Some of his business is legit and some of it's not. Lot of drugs come in and out of this city because of him."

I frowned. "So, he's some kind of crime lord? And everyone knows this? How is he still doing what he does?"

"Cause like I said, he's got his hands in a lot of things, and that means he's got a lot of people in his pocket. He's Teflon. Nothing sticks."

"Wow," I murmured.

"Anyway, the man murdered worked for Isaiah, and one thing every shitbag in this state and the ones touching ours knows is you don't mess with Isaiah's people unless you want a target on the back of your head. Whoever the shooters are, either aren't the brightest or they have more balls than brains. And whoever they work for doesn't want that connection made," he told me. "Which explains what happened at the store and this. Someone ID'd you. Could've been anyone hanging around the crime scene Friday night or…"

Or it could've been someone in the police department. Good God, this was unreal.

"The thing is, knowing Isaiah, he's going to find out who pulled that trigger before us." His laugh was without humor. "He almost always does. And he's going to take care of it. But what I don't like is whoever the punks work for coming after you." He yanked on the tape. "They're not going to get close to you again."

The way he said it almost had me convinced he could single-handedly ensure that. I wanted to believe that, but he couldn't be around me twenty-four hours a day. The fear I'd been holding back pressed on me. "Should I...should I be worried about this Isaiah?"

"Honestly?" The muscles moved along his spine. "No. But he's not a good guy. Don't ever mistake him for that, but he has his own sense of moral code and conduct. Violence against women or children is a surefire way to get on his bad side. He will leave you alone."

"That's sort of comforting," I mumbled, taking a sip of my coffee. "Kind of."

"Gotta say, though, you're handling all of this like a champ."

I got a wee bit distracted by the way his bicep bunched and blurted out, "I cried myself to sleep last night."

Colton stilled.

My eyes widened. "Oh my God." I placed my hand over my forehead. "I cannot believe I just said that out loud."

Lowering his hands, he let the tarp flap to the side as he faced me. The roll of duct tape dangled from his fingers.

Warmth invaded my cheeks. "I mean, I didn't like sob or anything, and I don't cry a lot. It's just that—"

"Honey, you don't have to explain anything. You saw some shit last night." Dropping the roll of tape on the arm of the chair, he walked around the coffee table and got right in between it and me. Plucking the cup out of my hand, he placed it beside his and sat on the corner of the table in front of me. He was so close our knees pressed together when he leaned in, resting his arms on his thighs. "Having an emotional reaction is expected. If you hadn't, I would be concerned. To be honest, I didn't like the idea of you being alone after seeing something like that."

"Why?" I asked before I could stop myself. "Why do you care?"

He tilted his head to the side. "I'm not sure what to think about that kind of question."

I exhaled slowly. "I mean, do you treat all your witnesses this way? Bring them crepes in the morning and fix vandalized windows?"

Colton raised a brow. "No."

Well, that was a blunt answer. "Then why are you doing it now?"

"When I asked you if you believed in second chances, I was hoping you'd say yes." Those thick lashes lifted. "I don't like the way our paths crossed again, but I'm glad they did."

There were no words.

A playful grin appeared. "I noticed you in high school, Abby. I thought you were pretty and smart. I liked how you were always the first one in the class and the last one out."

Oh my God, I was always the first one in and the last one out.

"I liked how you were nice to everyone, even the assholes who didn't deserve it," he continued, those azure eyes glimmering. "So, yeah, I noticed you, but you had a boyfriend. You always had a boyfriend. I respected that, but I know you noticed me."

The warmth increasing in my cheeks had nothing to do with embarrassment.

"You know, every couple of years, you've crossed my mind. That's the damn truth." His eyes met mine and held. "It was always unexpected. Never unwelcomed. Did you think of me?"

"Yes. I've thought of you," I whispered.

His grin turned smug. "Hell yeah."

Stunned by what he was admitting, it still didn't make sense. "I've seen you around town, Colton, since I moved back. At the store or the movies." I left out the part that he was with someone else because that was irrelevant. "You never noticed me then."

"Then I'm a fucking idiot if that's true."

I blinked and my gaze centered on his well-formed mouth. What did his mouth feel like? Was it hard? Soft? A mixture of both? And what did he taste like? I bet a marvelous mix of coffee and man. "Colton—"

"I should've noticed you. Damn, I hate the idea that I hadn't." Sincerity filled his tone. "I notice you now, Abby."

My heart started tripping all over itself. "This doesn't seem real."

A chuckle rumbled out of him. "Why not?"

"Because these things don't happen in real life," I told him, leaning back and needing the space before I decided to find out exactly how his mouth felt and what he tasted like. "They don't."

His brows knitted together. "This is happening. It's real life."

"You are not getting what I'm saying." I drew in a deep breath. "Extremely gorgeous men like you—"

"You think I'm extremely gorgeous?" His grin reappeared and so did the left dimple.

I shot him a bland look. "Like you don't know that. And see, that's the thing. You're the gorgeous, confident cop and I'm not the worst thing walking on two legs, but I'm not the type of woman who snags the interest of a guy like you. That only happens in books."

He stared at me for a moment and then he shook his head. "First off, what the hell do you mean by woman like you?"

"Do I really need to spell it out for you?"

His eyes narrowed. "Yeah, yeah you do."

Frustration rose, racing across my skin like an army of fire ants. He couldn't be serious. "I don't look like the woman I saw you at the movies with. She was a tall, thin *beautiful* blonde. No one in this world would describe me as *that* beautiful woman with the hot guy. They would be like, wow, he's really with someone quite average. And I'm totally okay with being that average chick. I know what I am, so this doesn't make sense. I mean, unless you're just horny and want to get laid and you have no other prospects at the moment, then that makes more sense, I guess."

He opened his mouth, closed it, and then tried again. "If I'm horny and want to get laid?"

Yeah, I sort of couldn't believe I said that myself.

"Honey, how old do you think I am that all I'm about is getting laid?" he asked.

"Well, I mean, I get horny and want to get laid too, and we're roughly the same age." I really needed to shut up. "All I'm trying to say is that it's human nature."

"Human nature?" His blue eyes brightened as he laughed under his breath. "Can I just tell you that I'm thrilled to hear you get horny, and honey, you want to get laid, I'm your man, but you don't really know me, Abby."

I was still stuck on him being my man if I wanted to get laid, and boy, did I ever want to get laid. Hadn't even really considered it seriously in the last four years. No guy had sparked my attention, but right now? An ache had already blossomed and my breath came in and out in little shallow bursts, a reaction just to the mere idea of sleeping with him.

"And we're going to change that," Colton said. "You and I are going to get to know each other in a way that's long overdue."

My breath caught as a tight shiver coiled. "We are?"

That half grin did crazy-insane things to me. "Oh, we are. You know why? Because we got a second chance to do so and we aren't going to miss that, are we?"

I couldn't look away. "No?"

"That's right." Lifting his arm, he cupped my cheek with his hand. "Here's an important piece of information about me. If I'm looking for just a lay, I'm not going to bring that woman crepes in the morning or fix her window. And I'm sure as hell not going to risk my career to just screw around with a witness. If I'm going to take that risk, it's going to be worth it." His thumb dragged under my lip, causing me to suck in a shallow breath. "And honey, I have a good feeling, you're worth it."

Before I could respond, before I could say anything that would probably ruin everything he'd just said, he slipped that hand along my cheek, his fingers tangling in my hair as he leaned in, forcing his knee between mine. I took a breath. My heart beat. All I saw was the blue of his eyes.

And then Colton kissed me.

Chapter Eight

Every enjoyable, exaggerated thing my authors have ever written about being kissed was totally true, and it had been so long since I'd been kissed that I'd forgotten that.

The moment his lips touched mine, my body flushed hot, and it was a gentle kiss, nothing more than a light sweeping of his lips across mine—once and then twice. As if he were slowly mapping out the feel of my lips, he took his time familiarizing himself.

And then he caught my lower lip between his, creating a mad flutter in my stomach. The hand on my cheek shifted and his long fingers cradled the back of my head as he lifted his mouth from mine. His eyes burned a blue fire. There was a questioning in his gaze, and when I didn't pull away, his hand tightened.

Colton kissed me again, full on, and his lips *were* an amazing combination of soft and hard, satin stretched over steel.

My hand fell to his chest and the other to his knee as I felt the tip of his tongue tracing the seam of my mouth. My lips parted, and that kiss deepened. I tasted the coffee on his tongue and I knew he tasted me.

At first, I didn't really move. I let him lead the way, take that kiss in a direction that caused my blood to simmer, but when his tongue touched mine, it was like I woke up. My senses came alive. Every nerve ending in my body fired all at once.

This…*this* was what I had been missing.

Tilting my head to the side, I slipped my hand around his neck, anchoring his mouth to mine. I kissed him back, devouring *him*.

"Fuck," he groaned, and then he was moving.

Not away, but standing, and then he was hovering over me, his other hand curving around my hip. He lifted me, and I wasn't a small girl. I marveled in the act as he laid me on my back, his mouth never leaving mine. One elbow planted into the cushion of the couch beside my head, and he kept his body off mine even as the demand of his lips increased and the pleasure of his mouth moving over mine heightened.

I didn't know a kiss could feel like this.

Like he was touching every part of me.

I clung to him, willing him to lower his body to mine so that I could feel his weight. A shiver worked its way across my skin as my fingers sifted through the soft brush of hair along the nape of his neck. He tasted decadent, a deep, rich maleness.

And when he lifted his mouth again, I whimpered from the loss. Actually, *whimpered*. "I like that sound," he said in a rich, sensual voice. "Really fucking like it."

Colton kissed me once more. "There're a few things I want to get straight."

"Does that require talking?"

His answering chuckle brushed my lips. "It does." There was a pause as his mouth brushed the corner of my lips. "But I can multitask."

"Thank God," I whispered.

His body shook with another laugh and then his mouth was moving along the curve of my jaw. "You're not pretty."

My eyes flew open and widened. "Excuse me?"

"I don't think you're pretty." His mouth found my pulse. "I think you're fucking beautiful."

"Oh." I gasped as my hand curled around the straining bicep. A warmth grew in my chest.

"I thought you were beautiful damn near a decade ago." The hot, wet lick against my pulse caused my back to arch. "With your dark hair and fair skin, you were like a living Snow White." That mouth of his was on the move, coasting down my throat, scattering my thoughts. "I don't have a type, Abby. I don't go for just blondes or whatever." With his other hand, he worked my shirt to the side, baring my shoulder. "Checkered?"

At first, I didn't get what he was referencing, but then I felt his finger trailing the lacy strap of my bra. "I think checkered print is underrated."

He laughed and then he pressed a kiss to the hollow of my throat. "And something else I want you to understand, Abby. You're not average. You could never be average."

My breath caught. "You barely know me."

Blazing a trail of fiery little kisses across my collarbone, he dragged his hand down my side, over my waist, to the flare of my hip once more. "Nothing about you screams average. Never did. I know damn well that hasn't changed."

This had to be a dream.

His hand squeezed my hip as he coasted those lips all the way back to mine, kissing me slowly, deeply. Blue fire still burned in his eyes when his gaze met mine.

Then he slowly pressed down, the hardest part of him against the softest part of me. I gasped at the feel of the heavy bulge. Liquid heat pooled. A tempting warmth built inside of me, a raw fire. God, I hadn't felt this way in…

"That's what you do to me," he said, nipping at my lip as he rocked his hips against mine. Desire darted through my veins. Goodness, he was—there were no words. "You get what I'm showing you?" he asked, lust hardening his words.

Part of me did. There was the other part that couldn't comprehend his interest, and finally, another part that wanted to stop talking and start kissing again.

But that second part of me won out. "Where do you see this going?"

He didn't answer immediately, and in that short space, reality kicked in. Maybe this wasn't the best time to ask that question, but what were we doing? Last night had been the first time we'd talked in years and now we were kissing? Hell, we were doing more than kissing. I was flat on my back and he knew I was wearing a checkered print bra.

And I also now knew that all areas of his body were

exceptionally well-proportioned; something in my wildest dreams I never thought I'd ever have personal knowledge of.

I thoroughly believed in insta-lust. Criminy, I'd experienced it several times at the gym, but I was never one to act on it. Or was I? I never really had the chance to do so. I'd never given myself the chance.

But this seemed so fast, because it was fast. Possibly record-breaking fast, but he, the guy I'd admired from afar for quite some time, thought I was beautiful. And he thought there wasn't a single thing about me that screamed *average*.

My wry gaze flicked over his handsome face as the seconds ticked by. Uncertainty slammed into me. "Colton, I—"

His mouth silenced my words, but the softness of his kiss, the tenderness behind it, quelled the brimming disquiet. When he spoke, his nose grazed mine. "That's a hard question to answer, but you know what I do know, Abby? Despite how you came back into my life last night, I was thrilled to see you. I came over this morning because I wanted to see you again and I didn't want to wait for a better excuse. I'm impatient like that," he added, and I felt his lips form a grin against mine. "And I kissed you and I am right where I am because I want you. I think you can feel that."

"I can feel that," I said, my voice throaty. There was no way I couldn't feel that.

"And I think the way you kissed me back tells me you are right where you are because you want to be here." He kissed me softly, stirring up the flutter into a crazy spiral. He lifted his head slightly and stared down at me. "I don't know where this is going or what to expect, but I know what I want and I'm the type of guy that goes for it. Why would I wait getting that message across? It doesn't feel like something that's going to change in a week or a month."

The type of guy who goes for it.

Was it really that simple? He wanted me, so he was going to go for it. Why waste the time? Could it really be that simple for me? Because I did want him. I wanted him so badly it was a physical ache. And why did I really need to even think about the future, where this could lead? We were both consenting adults, and there was no mistaking the fact that he was attracted to me. Could I pass this up?

Pass up the chance to feel again? To be alive?

Because that would be what I was doing if I listened to the tiny, annoying voices in the back of my head. In the hours spent here and there with Colton, I'd felt more than I had in the four years since Kevin passed on. The most I felt was through the words and stories I edited. Was there something wrong with wanting to feel alive again, for wanting more?

I hoped not.

"Okay," I whispered, placing my shaking hand on his cheek, drawing his mouth back toward mine.

Colton came willingly, and his breath hitched before he closed his mouth over mine. There was nothing sweet about this kiss. Our lips parted, and his tongue was a hot, moist demand inside my mouth. He took complete control, as if he was staking his claim, and there was a possessiveness in the way he kissed that shattered memories of any other kiss.

He splayed his palm flat against my cheek, still for a moment, and then he glided it down my neck. His hand stayed there, the touch gentle and so at odds with the fierceness of the kiss. I moaned, my body arching toward his, wanting to melt into him. Between my thighs, I pulsed and I ached. I was so into the taste and feel of him, but that voice was in the back of my head, this time preaching a different story.

Could I actually get naked in front of him?

Speaking of getting naked, I was pretty sure the Hanes boy shorts I was wearing were the least possible sexy thing I could have on, along with the checkered bra.

Would he still be so aroused once he realized there was more cushion for the pushin'?

His pelvis thrust against mine, scattering those fears like ashes in the wind. He nipped at my lower lip, the tiny bite sending a wave of pleasure through my veins.

Making a deep sound in the back of his throat, he lifted his mouth from mine. "I really need to fix that window."

"What window?" I murmured, dazed.

Colton laughed as he dipped his head into the space between my neck and shoulder. "Cute."

"What?"

"You're cute." He kissed my neck. "You can be cute."

I opened my eyes. "I thought I was beautiful?"

"You're both." Pushing himself up, he paused just long enough to kiss me again and then he popped up onto his feet with grace I was envious of. "It's good to be both."

"Uh-huh." I was still lying there, half sprawled on the couch, trying to get control of my thoughts and breathing. I wetted my lips that felt swollen.

Colton extended a hand. "If you stay like that, I'm going to be way too tempted."

I glanced up at him. "What's wrong with being tempted?"

His lips parted. "Damn if I remember right now."

That brought a smile to my face. Placing my hand in his, I let him pull me up into a sitting position. "The window," I reminded him.

"Oh yeah, that. Guess we need to get that fixed so we aren't giving your neighbors a show."

My eyes widened. Holy crapola, I hadn't even thought of that.

Colton started to turn away, but stopped. A soft smile played across his lips. "You know something? It's been a long time since I started a day and ended it with a woman. Glad it's you."

Chapter Nine

Sunday morning, I did something I hadn't done in a very long time. When I stripped off my pajamas and shoved the shower door open, I didn't allow myself to gloss over my reflection or to pretend that I wasn't purposely avoiding catching a glimpse of myself. Because that was what I'd been doing for a long time. Almost like if I didn't see myself, I didn't have to acknowledge how I felt.

But this morning, I looked.

The hollows of my cheeks were a bright pink and my gaze wary as I took in my disheveled hair. It was probably my imagination, but my lips looked swollen. There was no way that was the case, but I didn't have to try hard to remember Colton's kisses. My lips tingled. Those kisses were something I wouldn't forget.

My gaze drifted down, over the slope of my shoulders and then across my chest. I pressed my lips together as I lifted my hands, placing them over my breasts. The skin was smooth, nipples puckered. Steam began to fill the bathroom, dampening my skin. I lowered my hands. My breasts were round and full. Definitely nowhere in the general vicinity of perkiness, but they…they matched the rest of me. My waist curved in slightly and then flared out, forming round hips. The shadowy area between my plump thighs drew my attention. Brazilian wax? Uh, no. I almost laughed out loud at that thought.

God, it had been so long since I had sex.

Could I do it? An image of Colton formed in my thoughts, and the flush raced down my throat. Biting down on my lip, I was pretty sure that I could do it. The man neared perfection when it came to his body.

That would be a lot to overcome.

As I twisted to the side, peeking at my behind, I tried to come to terms with how I felt about myself. It wasn't easy and the steam covered the mirror before I had any answer. I stepped into the shower, letting the hot water beat down on me. I wasn't sure if it was a lack of self-esteem or a lack of action that had my confidence bouncing all over the place. Or maybe it was the fact that I spent every day caught up in the fictional worlds of the authors I edited, experienced their love, their heartbreak and everything in between that I hadn't, in the last four years, experienced anything in the real world or taken any time for myself.

When Kevin passed away, I had thrown myself into work. If I was honest, that was when I started to lose sight of myself, of who I was. I didn't want that any longer. Last night I had decided that I couldn't pass up the chance to feel again. And what I saw in the mirror wasn't horrifying. It was the same body Kevin used to refer to as Botticelli beautiful. Curves weren't a bad thing.

I just needed to get my mind on board with all of that.

Since I had gotten up early, I hit the computer after I'd showered and changed into a pair of jeans and a loose, cap sleeve blouse. I was able to work on a couple of pages before my phone dinged. It was a text from Colton. He was outside.

Heart jumping all around like a bouncing bean, I saved my work and closed the laptop. My bare feet were silent as I came down the stairs. The fresh pot of coffee I'd put on scented the air. Reaching the door, I opened it with a deep breath.

And the same breath punched out of my lungs.

The jeans he wore were faded along the knee and the old screen T-shirt stretched across his broad shoulders. He lived in these kinds of clothes. Not dress shirts and pants, and while he looked good in his detective getup, he looked *damn* good in jeans.

"Mornin'," Colton drawled, stepping inside. He held a white cardboard box that smelled like heaven, and as I moved to close the door, he swooped down, pressing his lips against my cheek. The innocent brush of his lips across my skin sent an acute shiver down my spine. "I swung by the hardware store and picked up the stuff."

Closing the door, I ordered myself to pull it together. "And the bakery?"

"Always the bakery." He tossed a grin over his shoulder as he headed toward the kitchen, where he placed the box on the counter. "I got some muffins and éclairs. You haven't eaten yet, right?"

My tummy grumbled happily. "No. Thank you for doing that—for doing all of this."

"Like I said before, my pleasure. Do you prefer chocolate or fruit?"

I watched him from under my lashes. "Chocolate. Always chocolate."

He chuckled as he plucked the chocolate éclair out, placing it on a napkin. "I'll have to remember that." Picking up a fruity éclair, he faced me and leaned back against the counter. "Did you sleep well last night?"

At first, I had tossed and turned, thinking about his kiss and what he'd said. I'd been turned on and I had to take care of that. Not that I was going to share that piece of info. Obviously. "I slept okay. You?"

His lashes lowered as a small grin tugged at his lips. "It took me a while to fall asleep."

Could he have had the same problem as I? An image of him took hold in my thoughts, vibrant and seductive. I saw him in bed, his hand beneath the sheet, gripping his cock. My stomach hollowed at the thought, my mouth dried. His back would definitely be bowing and his head would be kicked back against the pillows as he worked himself...

He tilted his head to the side. "What are you thinking about, Abby?"

"Nothing." Turning away hastily, I all but shoved the éclair in my mouth. "So...um, how much do I owe you for the stuff to fix the window?"

"Dinner."

I dabbed at my lips when I turned back around. My brows rose. "Dinner?"

A half grin appeared. "Yes. Dinner. You know, where two people, sometimes more, go out to eat?" He took a bite of his éclair while my eyes narrowed. "Tonight."

I started to ask why but managed to stop myself before I looked like a complete idiot. Well, I wasn't sure I would look like a moron, but it would be so evident that my confidence in what was going on between us was somewhere between crappy and craptastic.

So I smiled as excitement and hope bubbled, and prayed there wasn't chocolate on my teeth. "Dinner would be nice."

* * * *

Colton was as handy as he was good looking, and I really could get used to him doing work around the house. Actually, I could get used to him just being in my house in general.

As he boarded up the window, making it more secure until the window guys could come out, an easy conversation flowed back and forth between us, and it was the same when he reappeared later that evening to take me to dinner.

After he'd left in the late afternoon, the struggle had been real when it came to concentrating, but I managed to get some work done on McGuire's novel. I was lucky; her manuscripts were typically clean.

Nervous giddiness had my heart and pulse jumping all around as I picked out a dress that I hadn't worn in what felt like forever. Actually, there was a good chance I'd never worn the sleeveless pink and blue floral dress. I sort of felt like I was wearing my grandmother's couch when I slipped it on over my head, but the high waist and heart-shaped neckline were super flattering. I felt pretty in the dress.

Maybe even a little sexy.

I carried a pair of pink heels downstairs and then slipped them on mere moments before there was a knock on my door. Colton had texted, letting me know he was there. With my heart lodged somewhere in my throat, I opened the door and my tongue nearly lolled out of my mouth and rolled across the floor.

Once again dressed in jeans, he'd paired the dark denim with a plain, white button-down shirt with the sleeves rolled up to his elbows, showcasing powerful forearms. I didn't know what it was about sleeves rolled up, but it had always been a huge turn-on for me.

I was so weird.

Colton's gaze glided over me as a small grin appeared. "You look lovely."

Like I was love-struck or something equally silly, I felt my cheeks flush. "Thank you. So do you. I mean, you don't look lovely. You look hot. Sexy. Very nice."

His brows rose.

I wanted to smack myself. "I think I'll stop talking now."

He chuckled as he lowered his head, kissing me softly. "Actually, keep talking. It's doing wonders for my ego."

"I don't think you need any help in that department."

"True," he admitted, straightening. "My head is probably already too big."

The thing was, Colton was confident and self-assured, maybe even a little cocky, but he wasn't arrogant. He was like a unicorn.

"You ready?"

"Just one second." I grabbed my purse and keys off the coffee table and then joined him outside, pulling the door closed behind me. The heat was near stifling, coating my skin as I glanced at the boarded window. I cringed. "That looks terrible."

"Not the greatest curb appeal," he agreed, placing his hand on my lower back. We started down the short set of steps. "Did you get in touch with anyone today after I left?"

"I called my insurance company—the one-eight-hundred number. It doesn't make sense to file a claim, not with the deductible, but they did give me a list of companies to call tomorrow." Despite the heat, I couldn't suppress a shiver when he slid his hand to the center of my back.

He cast me a knowing side-look as we stepped onto the sidewalk. "I want someone to get out here quick. I don't like the idea of the window being like that for long."

"Me neither. I feel like—"

A loud pop caused me to jump and lose my grip on my purse. It slipped from my fingers, falling to the pavement as I whipped around. Heart racing, my frantic gaze searched for the source of the sound, terrified I was about to come face-to-face with the bald man.

He wasn't there.

"Are you okay?" Colton placed his hand on my shoulder, turning me toward him. Concern was etched into his handsome face. "Abby?"

"Was that a...a gun?" The moment I spoke the question, I already knew the answer. If it had been a gun, I doubted Colton would just be standing there. "I'm sorry." My cheeks burned as I looked away. "I know that wasn't what that was."

"It was a car backfiring. Probably down the street." His hand curved around the nape of my neck and he guided my gaze back to his. "I get it."

That was all he needed to say and I believed him. Nodding slowly, I forced an even breath in and then out. "I guess...I'm just a little jumpy after Friday. When I heard that, I thought..."

"I'm not surprised." His hand shifted and he curled his arm around my shoulders, drawing me to his chest. "You freaking amaze me, Abby, with how you're holding it together after Friday, but I know it has effected you and that's okay. That's normal."

The citrusy scent of his cologne surrounded me and my heart rate slowed. The embarrassment from overreacting eased off. "Thank you."

"There is no reason you need to thank me." Leaning back, he brushed his lips over my forehead and then lowered his arm. He swooped down, picking up my purse. "But I want you to feel safe. Nothing is going to happen to you."

I didn't respond as he took my hand in his other one. Still holding my purse, he led me to where his truck was parked under a large oak tree. The leaves stirred in the warm breeze. "Reece has been keeping an eye on your place during the night and throughout the day, doing drive-bys."

I stared at him, floored.

"It's not perfect, but I doubt you're ready for me camping out in your place like I want to until we get those shitheads and put them behind bars." Stopping in front of the passenger door, he let go of my hand and opened it. "Up?"

I didn't move, not even when he placed the purse in my hands.

"You have Reece watching my place?"

"Yeah. And the other deputies know to keep an eye out." He cocked his head to the side, studying me. "You look like I just dropped my pants."

I liked to think I'd be rocking a totally different look on my face if he'd done that. "I'm just surprised. That's a lot of trouble for them."

"It's nothing." His gaze met mine. "And they're glad to do it. You're important to me. They know that."

For the umpteenth time since he appeared Friday night, I was absolutely flummoxed by Colton. I was important to him? Since when? That question sounded like such a douche-tastic thing to think, but could he really be telling the truth? Did I have any reason to doubt that he was?

"You have that look on your face," he said.

I snapped out of it. "What look?"

"Like you don't believe a word I'm saying."

My eyes widened. Was I that obvious? Holy crap. But he didn't get it. He didn't understand that there was a part of me, no matter how much attention or attraction he tossed in my direction or what he said, that couldn't truly believe he really wanted all of this with me.

"That's okay." He tapped my hip with his hand, motioning me to get into the truck. I did just that, staring at him as he closed the door and jogged around the front. When he climbed in, he started the truck, cranking up the air conditioner. Snagging aviator-style sunglasses off the visor, he slipped them on and looked over at me. "Do you know why it's okay?"

I shook my head. "I'm guessing you're going to tell me?"

His lips kicked up on one corner. "Nah, sweetheart, I'm going to show you."

* * * *

I'm going to show you.

Those words lingered in the back of my head throughout dinner, a tantalizing distraction that resurfaced whenever our gazes collided. Conversation wasn't lacking though.

While we waited for the food to arrive, along with the wine, we chatted about high school and he asked about college. I talked about what it was like to live in a city like New York, and he'd admitted that he could never handle day in and day out in the city, not even Philadelphia. During the dinner, he led me into a conversation about editing, something that many people outside of the publishing industry would have absolutely no interest in, but he seemed genuinely curious about it.

And when I started to go fan-girl over the authors I worked with and hoped to work with in the future, he said I was cute. Again.

We didn't talk about the investigation. I hadn't brought it up, figuring it would kind of ruin the lovely dinner.

Sometimes I found myself missing what he was saying, just tiny bits, because as terrible as it sounded, I ended up just staring at him. It wasn't just because he was that attractive. It was more than a physical thing. A mixture of his charm and kindness, the fact that he was actually here, after all this time, having dinner with me, had a lot to do with it. And yeah, some of it had to do with him simply being so freaking hot.

And I was woman enough to admit that.

I had to wonder what people thought when they saw us together. Like when the waitress's gaze lingered on Colton, what crossed her mind? Did she wonder how the hell I ended up on a date with someone like Colton, who was universally attractive? No one wanted to admit it, but I knew people thought things like that. Hell, I had. After all, if they didn't, there wouldn't be a thousand articles online showcasing couples that didn't match on the attractive scale.

Maybe I wasn't giving myself enough credit. I didn't want to think about things like that right now, because the dinner was sort of perfect, and the steady internal stream of nonsense was ruining it.

Night had fallen when we left the restaurant and bright stars blanketed the onyx sky. He kept his hand on my lower back until we reached his truck. It was such a simple gesture, but I felt like there was so much meaning to it.

The ride back to my place was quiet as I was lost in my own

thoughts, replaying the dinner over and over. I wasn't even aware of the fact that we were at my house until he parked the truck.

I glanced at him in the dark interior of the truck, half hopeful that he would come in and partly terrified that he would.

One hand rested on the steering wheel as his gaze met mine and held. His features were shadowed, so I had no idea what he was thinking. "Walk you to the door?"

"Sure." Disappointment snapped at my heels. So he didn't want to come in? Did I want him to come in? Colton dropped his hand from the steering wheel and reached over, and as he unbuckled my seatbelt, his hand brushed along my stomach. A series of shivers danced over my skin.

Oh yeah, I wanted him to come in. Like that door was wide open.

We walked to the front door, silent with the exception of the humming of crickets. I didn't know what to say when we reached my door and I dug my keys out, unlocking it. I wished I could be brave and confident, invite him in with a sexy little grin, but it had been so long since I'd done this.

Actually, I'd never really done this before. Kevin and I had done the dating thing while in high school. Parents were involved then. Dates ended at the door and picked up again with late-night phone calls. This was a whole different ballpark I had no experience in. I looked up at him, drawing in a shallow breath.

He was staring down at me, and even though I couldn't see his eyes, I could *feel* his gaze, it was that intense. "I had a really good time tonight."

"So did I." I was breathless as I opened the door and stepped inside. When I turned to him and looked up once more, whatever I was about to say faded, lost in the space between us.

There was a certain intent to the line of his mouth, and I knew before he even lowered his head, that he was going to kiss me. The breath I took got stuck in my throat as he cupped my cheek with one hand, tilting my head back. He brushed his lips over mine like he had done the night before, tentative and questioning. There was something so sweet about the kiss as we stood with me just inside the door and him leaning in.

Last night had been the first time I'd been kissed in four years.

This being the second time, instinct quickly took over. Or maybe it was simply just arousal. Pleasure darted as I tilted my head to the side, and when the tip of his tongue touched the seam of my mouth, sweetness was the furthest thing from my mind.

The kiss deepened as our tongues tangled. My hands ended up on his chest and his delved into my hair as his arm circled my waist, drawing me tight to his front. I felt him then, hard against my belly, and feeling just how effected he was had my blood simmering.

The fear of things escalating took a backseat, still there but not consuming my attention. I couldn't think around his kisses, could barely breathe, and somehow, we were moving. I heard the door slam shut behind us and then my back was pressed against the wall and there was no space between us.

"I've been wanting to do that since I saw you in this dress," he admitted, and then kissed me before I could respond.

I clung to his shoulders as his hand slipped down my side, curling around my thigh, just below my hip, leaving behind a wake of shivers.

Lifting his mouth from mine, he breathed heavily. "I told myself I was going to behave tonight."

My hands clenched over his shoulders, wrinkling the material of his shirt. "You're not?"

He kissed my jaw. "Well, I was planning on being a gentleman."

"Why?" I asked, surprising myself.

"Hell. Good question." His lips moved over my neck as I tipped my head back against the wall. "I'm not even sure."

I gasped when I felt his tongue circle where my pulse pounded.

"I just can't keep my hands off you." He lifted my leg just enough that he was able to settle his hips against my core, and oh God, the ache that blossomed almost made me weep. "Damn," he groaned, burying his face in my neck. "That didn't help."

My chest rose and fell sharply. "No. No, it didn't."

A deep groan rumbled out of him, and I felt his hand on my thigh move, slipping under the hem of my skirt. The glide of his palm against my bare skin shook me, pushing a soft moan out from between my parted lips, and that was nothing compared to what came next. He dragged his hand up and over, cupping my rear as he pushed his hips in. Muscles coiled in response.

He dragged his lips up my throat, finding my mouth as his hand kneaded my bottom. The kiss rocked me, and there was little doubt in my mind that I'd stop him if he pulled my panties down and took me right against the wall. The mere thought of him doing so burned my skin, twisted up my insides in a crazy way.

The attraction I felt toward him was startling.

His kiss slowed as he dragged his hand out from under my dress. "Okay," he murmured. "I told myself I wasn't going to do this tonight."

I opened my eyes, barely making out his features in the soft glow radiating from the stairwell light. My heart thundered. I wanted to tell him to ignore what he'd told himself. I was damp between the thighs, ready and wanting. I *wanted* him.

Colton lowered my leg as he rested his forehead against mine. His chest rose just as rapidly. I didn't say anything as we both struggled to gain control over what our bodies demanded, but him putting the brakes on where this was heading was obviously the smart thing to do.

All of this felt so fast and I knew it could quickly get out of hand, but I…I wanted it to do that. I liked Colton. I'd liked him in high school. I'd liked him from afar when I'd moved back home. I really, *really* liked him now.

And that was terrifying.

Chapter Ten

Hitting *send* on the e-mail, I smiled at the computer screen. I'd busted ass since I'd woken up, foregoing showering and even changing out of pajamas until I reached the last page.

The glamorous life of an editor.

Finished with the edits, I pushed out of my chair and picked up a dry erase pen. Carrying it to the whiteboard hung near the desk, I scratched a line over *Other Lives*. Nothing made me more giddy than marking something off from my to-do list.

Actually, that wasn't entirely true.

Colton took the top spot of things that made me giddy right about now.

This last week had been…absolutely amazing, almost like I was a teen again or in my early twenties, buzzing around happily. I'd forgotten how it feels, to be…to be caught up in the excitement and anticipation of seeing someone, to actually be feeling something strongly again, because if this week had taught me anything, it was that the last four years had been only about my career and nothing else.

But this week had also taught me a lot more.

Since Colton worked ten-hour shifts, he had three days off—Sunday, Monday, and oddly, Wednesday. Of course, he was on call those days and it didn't seem like he really had them off. Due to the shooting last week, he was in the office both Monday and Wednesday, following up on leads, but both evenings I spent time with him. Monday was the movies, something I hadn't really enjoyed since Kevin. Wednesday we grabbed dinner at this restaurant in town, one I'd never been to before because it seemed like a couples kind of place.

Both nights had ended like Sunday night, in a way. He would kiss me at the door, but somehow we ended up on my couch, his body covering mine, his mouth claiming mine, and his hands doing crazy-insane things to my body. Just thinking about it now, as I rolled the pen between my hands, created a heady rush of sensations. I flushed and my body responded as I remembered how his hand felt between my thighs and how easily his skilled caresses worked my body into a frenzy.

And he always stopped before either of us found any release. He was an expert tease. Or maybe he just didn't want to go that far and—I cut that thought off, slapping it away like it was nothing more than a worrisome fly. That thought didn't even make sense. It was stupid.

I was done with being stupid.

Besides, things were already progressing crazy fast between us. It made sense that some area of our relationship would be slowed down, which is basically what he'd said. I could and did respect that, and part of me was glad that there was something holding us back. Deep down, I knew I wasn't ready for that. Well, my body was. I had a feeling that what beat strongly in my chest was also on board, but my head…my head had a hard time letting go of the noxious, poisonous whispers.

I'd never thought of myself as someone who had self-esteem issues. I had my body hang-ups, like any normal woman, but the lack of intimacy and the reintroduction of it shined a really harsh light on the way I viewed myself, on how unconnected I was with my own body.

The way Colton looked at me, how he touched me, drew my focus back to myself. He probably would have no idea what that meant for me…or probably what that was *doing* to me.

I placed the pen back in the coffee cup an author had sent me, pulse pounding in all the interesting, distracting places. It was

Sunday and we'd made plans to see each other this evening, nothing further or more concrete than that, and I was still edgy with anticipation.

To be honest, I wasn't sure I ever felt any of this with Kevin. Not because my feelings for him were weaker, because they weren't, but we'd gotten together so young. What I felt then was nothing like what I felt now, and maybe if Kevin and I had met when we were older, I would be experiencing this with him.

All the maddening rush of emotions was a bit too much to handle. It was like seeing only in black and white, and suddenly everything was in vibrant colors. My stomach dipped as a thread of realization weaved its way through my thoughts.

Was what I was feeling something more powerful than lust and the excitement that came with new relationships? Was it love?

I swallowed hard as I turned from the dry erase board, my gaze crawling over the spines of the books I'd edited while in New York and from freelancing, but I really didn't see any of the titles.

Had I already fallen in love with Colton?

That sounded so, so ridiculous. We'd only come back into each other's lives a week ago, and we really hadn't been in each other's lives before. Not really. But what I was feeling was powerful, reminiscent of what I felt for Kevin.

It was strange to think about him while thinking about the four-letter word and Colton, all in the same sentence. It wasn't a bad feeling, like it was wrong or anything, but just odd.

Tucking my hair back behind my ears, I pressed my lips together. It wasn't like I never wanted to fall in love again. I had hoped that I would, but it wasn't something I had imagined happening in a long time. For one thing, I really didn't put myself out there to even meet anyone. To do that, I'd actually have to go out more often.

Feeling what I was caught me off guard for multiple reasons. I wasn't expecting anyone to waltz into my life, especially not Colton Anders. I wasn't expecting to feel this strongly, and although many of the books I'd edited featured characters falling in love hard and fast, I hadn't believed it was possible. Insta-love didn't exist in the real world.

Or maybe it did exist and I was actually experiencing it.

The flutter in my stomach increased. A twisty mixture of thoughts and emotions invaded me. Falling in love was exhilarating. It was arousing, possibly the most powerful aphrodisiac.

It was also scary as hell.

Because I'd already loved and lost once.

And knowing what I knew now, that I would lose Kevin, I still wouldn't go back and change a damn thing. Love, no matter the amount of pain it could rain down on your head, was worth it.

Then that meant if what I was feeling now was real, no matter how crazy it sounded and felt, it was also worth the possibility it wasn't returned, that it would never grow into something mutual, that it would cut deep in the end.

No matter what, I wasn't going to hide from what I was feeling. What happened to Kevin and what I'd seen Friday night proved that life was truly too short to not live it.

To be a coward.

Walking into my bedroom, I kicked off my flip-flops as I glanced at the dress I planned to wear tonight. It wasn't fancy, just a cotton eyelet pattern dress, but I was trying to get more comfortable in my own skin. Reaching down, pulling my shirt off, cool air washed over my breasts and the already hardened nipples tingled sharply. As I pulled off my bottoms, I couldn't help but imagine Colton doing it. I could easily see him on his knees, staring up at me with those ocean-blue eyes.

My stomach hallowed as I sat on the edge of my bed. I needed to shower and get ready, but my hand floated to the base of my throat. There was a moment of hesitation as I bit down on my lower lip. I knew what my body wanted—what I wanted. The tension had been building all week and I felt like I was going to crawl out of my skin.

Getting off had been kind of clinical in the past, almost as if I was detached from what I was doing and feeling. It was just about feeling a few moments of pleasure, but this, right now, was so much more potent. My hand trembled as I realized what I wanted to do and this time, it was so different.

The sharp swirl of pleasure built as I drew my hand down. My arm brushed over the tip of my breast, causing me to suck in a shallow breath. I wasn't thinking as I dragged my fingers down, my nails scrapping lightly over the puckered nipple. Colton consumed my thoughts as my hand drifted down my stomach, beyond my navel. The moment my fingers brushed through the gathering wetness, a breathy moan escaped me. I slipped a finger in as I pressed the palm of my hand against the nub of nerves.

Pleasure pounded, heavy and intense. I let myself fall back against the bed as I widened my legs. My eyes were opened into thin slits. I could see the tips of my breasts, the curve of my stomach, and my hand moving between my thighs.

I'd never watched myself before, but I couldn't look away this time, and my heart thumped fast as I lifted my hips, meeting the thrust of my finger. There was something wholly erotic about this—about watching what I was doing.

My breathing turned shallow, and in an instant, I saw Colton's head bowed between my thighs instead of my hand, and it was his fingers instead of mine, his mouth. The tension coiled and then unraveled without warning, whipping throughout me. I kicked my head back, crying out in the silence of my bedroom. The release was more intense than anytime I'd ever done this, shocking me.

Closing my eyes, I let out a long sigh as I slowly pulled my hand away, letting it rest on my belly. God, my hormones were out of control.

Actually, my emotions were out of control, but in a very good way. My lips curved up at the corners, forming a small, sated smile. I blinked open my eyes, my gaze focusing on the ceiling. My muscles were nothing and moving from this bed was the last thing I wanted, but I...

I felt...alive.

* * * *

Colton really did know the way to my heart.

Crab rangoons.

When he showed up Sunday evening, he'd brought a delicious array of takeout, including my weakness, which existed in the form of crab and cream cheese. He'd also brought a movie with him since I'd replaced the TV a few days ago. It wasn't nearly as nice or as big as the first one, but it would have to do until I could justify spending hundreds of dollars on a larger TV. He'd brought with him a remake of an old-school horror film that had traumatized me as a small child, and when we finished dinner, he popped the movie in.

We started off sitting side by side, but before we were even fifteen minutes into the movie, Colton stretched out his long body across the couch. He managed to coax me down so I was lying beside him, my head tucked against his arm and his hand resting lightly on my hip.

At that point, I pretty much stopped watching the movie.

Kevin and I had done this so many times, favoring bumming around the house many Saturday nights instead of going out. I expected there to be a pang of sorrow, but what I felt was a shadow of the hurt I had lived with in the months and even years after his death. I knew beyond a doubt that if Kevin was aware of what I was doing right now with Colton, he would be happy. Knowing that made it easy to relax against Colton.

But that relaxation quickly turned to keen awareness. With every breath Colton took, I was conscious of just how close we were. The scene of a screaming girl on the TV became nothing more than background noise as I focused on every part of our bodies that touched. The front of his thighs pressed against the back of mine. My bottom was almost cradled in his lap and his hard chest was against my back. I bit down on my lip as I wiggled a little, stopping the moment his fingers of the hand resting on my hip curled, bunching the thin material of the dress.

I thought about what I had done this afternoon, touching myself while thinking of him, and my body flushed hot. Not from embarrassment, but from sharp arousal.

"Are you watching the movie?" Colton asked, his voice deeper, rougher.

I had a choice. I could pretend that I was or I could fess up to the fact I had absolutely no interest in the movie at the moment and that it was him who had my attention. It wasn't...easy to initiate this. My seduction skills were below amateur level, but what had I decided earlier? Not to be a coward. To live life despite the risk of getting hurt. To...to just let go.

Before I could give myself time to overthink, I shifted onto my back and lifted my gaze to his. Our eyes held for a moment and then his gaze dropped to my mouth. I knew that whatever I would say would probably be completely idiotic. I decided action was probably better than words.

Because words could be really hard.

I lifted my hand, pressing my palm against his clean-shaven cheek. My heart stuttered as he turned his head slightly, dropping a kiss against the center of my hand. Oh God, that was too sweet, almost too much. I started to pull my hand away, but I stopped myself as his gaze returned to mine. Drawing in a shallow breath, I guided his mouth to mine.

I kissed him, and I don't know if he could read minds or if he really was a damn unicorn, but he let me set the pace, allowed me to play. I mapped out his mouth, covering every delectable centimeter, and when I wanted more, he opened his mouth to my searching kiss. I leisurely explored him, breathing in the taste of him.

Far too immersed in the sensations kissing him created, I wholeheartedly welcomed the moment he took over. His lips were demanding, and I yielded to him, letting out a breathless moan against his hot mouth as his hand *finally* moved from my hip, smoothing up over my breast. I sucked in a sharp breath. The dress had a built-in bra, and the thin cotton was no barrier against the heat of his hand.

I moaned into his mouth as his hand closed over my breast and kneaded gently. His chest rumbled against my side. "God, we're not even twenty minutes into the movie."

A tiny laugh escaped me. "Is that a bad thing?"

"Hell, do you even have to ask that?" His deft fingers found my pebbled nipple through the dress. Liquid fire poured through me. "I like to think it's a damn good thing."

I gasped for air. "I...I like the sound of that."

"You do?" He shifted so his weight rested on his left arm as his right hand slipped under the neckline of my dress. My back arched. "Yeah, you do."

"I do," I admitted.

He lowered his mouth to mine once more, kissing me. "I don't think I can do the gentleman thing any longer. I want to touch you." His fingers plucked at my nipple, wringing a cry out of me.

"But I really want to touch you elsewhere."

My body shuddered. I had a good idea that I knew where "elsewhere" was. I closed my eyes and whispered, "I want that too."

"Thank God." His hand left my breast, and I nearly ached from the loss, but his hand was on the move again, smoothing down my stomach.

I blinked open my eyes, watching as he glided down my stomach, over my thigh. My breath lodged in my throat as he worked his hand under the skirt of my dress. I bit down on my lip as I gripped his arm. His gaze flicked to mine. "Don't stop," I said.

"No?" He kissed me, nipping at my lip as he lifted his head. When I shook my head, he fused our mouths together. His hand skated up my bare thigh, and then over the lacy edge of my panties.

I held my breath, partly due to the swirling pleasure building inside of me and I knew he could feel just how soft I was. There wasn't an ounce of hardness to my thighs or my hips. He didn't seem to notice or care, because his hand had made its way underneath my panties.

My hand tightened around his arm as his fingers reached the apex of my thighs. He brushed his lips over mine. "Open for me?"

Never in my life had there been three words that were hotter than that. My thighs parted, and his finger skimmed over my damp skin. The touch was barely there, but I jerked nonetheless.

"So sensitive," he murmured. "I like that."

My heart was pounding as he ran a lazy finger over my wet center and then he eased one finger in. A low sound worked its way out of me, and when his thumb pressed down on the buddle of nerves, I gasped out, "Colton."

His mouth covered mine as fierce heat surfaced, building and building until I was sure I would combust. My hips bucked against his hand and blood pounded, creating a ringing in my ears.

No. Wait. That wasn't in my ears. It was a phone—Colton's phone. He ignored it—thank God—as he worked his finger in and out, devouring me with kisses. The tension coiled and I suddenly wanted, needed, to feel his skin against mine. I grabbed a fistful of his shirt, yanking it up. His body jerked and he made a harsh sound the second my hand touched the hard planes of his stomach.

Good God, there wasn't an ounce of *him* that was soft. My eager fingers traced each tightly packed ab. My hand dipped, brushing the button on his jeans.

The phone started ringing again, a few seconds after it had ended, and this time, Colton's hand stilled between my thighs. I almost prayed he didn't stop, but he did.

Groaning, he lifted his head and glanced over at where his phone rested on the coffee table. His hand slipped away from me. "It's work. I'm sorry."

"It's okay," I murmured, dazed by the rioting sensations in my body.

Rolling over me in one fluid move, he snatched up his phone and stood. "It's Anders." There was a pause. "Yeah, I couldn't get to my phone. What's up?"

I looked over at him, clearly seeing the hard ridge of his erection straining against his jeans.

Damn, what a waste.

I suddenly wanted to giggle, except I saw Colton stiffen and caught a brief glimpse of a frown as he turned away from me. He picked up the remote, pausing the movie. "Yeah, you know where I'm at."

My brows knitted.

Colton glanced back at me, his expression inscrutable. "Are you serious? Hell." He shook his head, glancing at the now repaired window. "I'm not surprised, but didn't think it would happen this quickly.

Glancing down, I saw that the skirt of my dress was hiked up to my hips, revealing the black undies. Face flushing red, I hastily reached down and fixed it. Then I figured I should sit up.

"You need me in tonight?" he asked, and I worried my lower lip, hoping nothing serious had happened, which was a stupid thought. Colton was a detective. Serious stuff happened all the time. "Shit. Yeah, that's good and that's bad."

My gaze shot to him as icy motion stabbed my stomach.

"Okay. I'll see you tomorrow." Colton disconnected the call and placed it back on the table. Sitting down beside me, he exhaled slowly. "Sorry about that. It was my partner—Hart."

The cold feeling was still there. "That's okay. Your job is

important. When you get a call, you have to answer."

"I do." He rested his hands on his knees. "I have kind of good news."

"Kind of?"

Colton nodded. "We've identified one of the two men you saw last Friday." He paused, his jaw hardening. "There's no easy way to say this. Apparently he was pulled from Schuylkill River."

I stiffened, eyes widening. "What?"

"One of the men you saw that night is dead, Abby."

Chapter Eleven

All the heat vanished and a different kind of tension built in the pit of my stomach. At first, I didn't think I heard him right. The bomb he dropped came out of nowhere.

I said the first thing that came to mind. "Are you sure?"

And that was a dumb question.

He nodded. "It's not the man who did the shooting. It appears to be the other suspect."

Leaning back against the cushion, I tucked my legs under me as I tried to process what had just happened. My thoughts were running in so many different directions. Not the man who pulled the trigger—the one with the cold, dead eyes? "How did he die?"

Colton twisted his body toward me. "Sweetheart, that's not something you need to know."

Part of me wanted to know, as morbid as that sounded. "But how?"

He glanced at the paused movie. "Remember when I told you about Isaiah Vakhrov?"

The mob guy. How could I forget him? I nodded.

"As far as I know right now, there's no evidence pointing to him having a hand in this, but I'd be willing to bet my retirement it was him." Colton lifted his hand, sighing as he scrubbed his fingers through his hair. "It's messed up, you know? These guys have their set of moral codes, twisted moral codes, and while those guys killed someone, murdering them isn't the answer."

"Agreed," I whispered, shivering. "I...I don't even know what to say."

"There's really nothing to say, but with the one dead, the shooter is probably going to be on the run. If he's smart that is."

My gaze flipped to his as pressure squeezed my chest. "What about the guys who warned me in the parking lot? They won't think I ratted their guys out?"

His jaw hardened as his gaze turned icy. "They'd have to be fucking idiots to think you had anything to do with this."

But they had been idiotic enough to approach me in the first place. Another shiver tiptoed its way over my shoulders. I hadn't forgotten about them or the fear they'd induced this past week. It was just something I tried not to think about. I didn't like the idea of living with that kind of fear.

Maybe that wasn't wise.

"There's one more thing. Hart was able to pull some more photos of those who match your description of the shooter," he explained. "We'd like you to look at them as soon as possible."

I nodded again.

Colton reached over, placing the tips of his fingers under my chin. He lifted my gaze to his. "I'm going to make sure you're safe, Abby."

"Is that why you've been spending so much time with me?" The moment that question left my mouth, I wanted to dropkick myself in the face. I couldn't even believe those words came out of me. It was like they existed in a dark, stupid as hell place that I had no control over.

His brows lifted as he stared at me. "Come again?"

Oh God. My cheeks heated. "I mean, I know I'm a witness and keeping me safe is a part of your job, but I..." I mentally strung together an epic amount of curse words. "I don't even know what I'm saying."

Colton dropped his hand. "I think you kind of do, Abby."

Uncurling my legs, I nervously smoothed my hands over the skirt of my dress. Was my question a Freudian slip in a way? Of course it was. Because that stupid as hell, ugly part of me still couldn't fathom Colton being here because he was sincerely attracted to me, even after what had just gone down between us.

I was an idiot.

His eyes narrowed. "Do you really think that me being here has to do with what happened last Friday?"

"Well, that's how we crossed paths—"

"You know that's not what I'm getting at," he interrupted. "And I know that's not what you were trying to say. You think I'm here, with you, with some kind of ulterior motive?"

A sick feeling expanded in my chest. "I don't think..." I trailed off because if I was being honest with myself, I was lying.

"I'll do anything to keep a witness safe and to get the job done," he said, shaking his head. "But I wouldn't go that damn far, Abby. I'm here and have been here with you simply because I want to be. I'd think the fact that I had my hand between your thighs ten minutes ago would be proof enough of that."

Warmth infused my cheeks as I bit down on the inside of my cheek. A moment passed. "I'm sorry. I didn't mean to insinuate anything."

"You don't need to apologize."

It was my turn to shake my head because I did need to apologize. "But I do, because...because saying something like that isn't saying great things about you as a person." I let out a long breath. What could I say? That I was trying to improve my confidence? That I just... "I'm stupid."

One eyebrow rose. "You're not stupid. That's not the problem."

A slice of unease lit up my chest as I glanced at him. He was staring straight ahead, his gaze fixed on the wall. A numbness settled in the pit of my stomach.

His shoulders tensed. "You're a beautiful woman, Abby. And you're smart and kind. You're funny." He turned to me, a distant gleam in his eyes. "And it's a damn shame you don't see that."

The numbness spread like icy drizzle, coating my skin. Underneath it, embarrassment burned. Were my hang-ups that obvious? I squeezed my eyes shut. *God, this was humiliating.*

"I'm going to...I'm going to go ahead and head out," he said, and my eyes snapped open. He was staring at the wall again as disappointment, remorse, and a hundred other messy emotions churned inside me. "Keep the movie. We'll watch it later."

A knot formed in the base of my throat. For some reason, I didn't think "later" was going to come soon.

"Okay?" he asked.

Pressing my lips together, I nodded as he rose and then I forced a smile when he bent over, pressing his lips against my forehead. My chest squeezed at the sweet gesture, and somehow I managed to walk him to the door and to say good-bye. And when I closed the door, I leaned against it, pressing my balled hands against my eyes.

The sick feeling expanded, circling my heart. There was a good chance that in such a short period of time, I'd fallen for Colton and I...I might have already lost him.

Chapter Twelve

Colton had texted Monday morning asking if I could stop by the office today to look at the photos again, but when I got there, he wasn't there. I tried not to take it personally as I was handed off to Detective Hart and taken into a private room, but it was hard. My stomach churned as Detective Hart spread glossy photographs across the scratched surface of the table.

I wanted to ask where Colton was. Hell, I wanted to whip out my phone and text him. Call him.

"Just take your time," he said, sitting back in the metal chair. "There's no rush."

My gaze flickered over the photographs as my heart started pounding in my chest. I needed to focus. Priorities. Right now, what had happened with Colton wasn't the most important thing going on.

The shooter was still out there.

Taking my time, I looked at each of the photos spread out in front of me. At first, they all looked alike—men in their upper twenties, bald with tats on the neck or just on their arms. I'd looked at twenty or so before Detective Hart added five more photos to the mix. I glanced over at them.

My heart stopped as I sucked in an unsteady breath. I reached over, picking up the third photograph, and held it close. There were three shots: full frontal and two profiles.

"Ms. Ramsey?"

For a moment I couldn't get my tongue to work. Like it was glued to the roof of my mouth. My hand trembled as I stared at the face of the man I'd seen shoot someone—kill someone. My throat was dry. "It's him."

Detective Hart leaned forward, placing his forearm on the table. "Are you sure?"

"Positive." I cleared my throat. "That's him." Unable to look at the photo any longer, I handed it over to the detective. Satisfaction gleamed in his eyes. "What's his name?" I asked and then frowned. "You probably can't tell me that, can you?"

He slipped the photo in a file. "You'd be correct. At least not right now." Standing, he reached into his pocket and pulled out his phone. "There's just a couple of forms we need you to sign and then you'll be on your way."

Taking several shallow breaths, I ignored the unease twisting up my insides. Detective Hart paused at the door. "You're going to put this man behind bars, where he belongs." His smile was tight. "And you've probably saved his life."

* * * *

Monday was weird.

I couldn't focus on the new manuscript, not that anyone would blame me. I'd identified a murderer this morning and according to Detective Hart, I'd probably saved his life by doing so. Unless the mob guy Colton had mentioned got to him first.

Colton.

Throughout the day, I engaged in some major wishful phone checking. As if somehow I had missed his text or call. Of course, there were no missed messages. My stomach dropped. After identifying the shooter, I figured Colton would be in contact, even if it was in a purely professional sense.

Monday slowly churned into Tuesday. No calls. No texts. I could've messaged him, I realized that, but I was the one who messed up and I honestly had no experience in these things. Dating was so far out of my realm of understanding. Was I supposed to give him space? Give him time? Or was he waiting for me to reach out? Or was he just really busy? The latter made sense. He was probably trying to search down the shooter.

Sitting at my desk, I groaned as I leaned over, resting my forehead against the cool wood. I was such an idiot. I'd let that stupid, ugly voice in my head get the better of me. I was still letting it get the better of me, wasn't I? Because why hadn't I messaged Colton?

Messaging Colton would be the normal thing to do.

I lifted my head and gently lowered it back to the desk. Rinse and repeat. What was I doing, other than banging my head on a desk? Because that wasn't weird or anything. Okay. I needed a plan. My heart skipped a beat when I lifted my head and saw my cell. I could text him, something small. I could totally do it.

Snatching up my phone, I tapped the screen and then the little green message icon. My pulse was kicking around as I hit Colton's name and started typing out the first thing that came to mind. I didn't let myself stop and think about it or let myself feel stupid for typing it out. The message was just four words.

I miss your crepes.

Okay. That was kind of a cute message and sort of stupid. A lot stupid. Before I hit send, I deleted the message.

I was such an idiot, geez.

I didn't text Colton and I didn't hear from him.

My life had been so crazy the last two weeks it was almost hard to believe that only that short amount of time had passed. I didn't know how to feel about witnessing a murder, knowing one was dead, and the other one, the shooter, would soon be—hopefully—apprehended.

I didn't know how to feel about a lot of things.

Actually, that wasn't entirely true. When it came to Colton, I knew exactly how I felt. Crappy. I didn't think his text Monday was an excuse to not see me. After all, after what happened, he would be busy, and since he normally worked on Tuesday, I wasn't expecting a visit.

I didn't get one either.

And he hadn't texted or called. There was a part of me that wanted to listen to the small and probably more reasonable voice that claimed his lack of contact didn't mean anything. He had to be busy, and I also hadn't reached out to him. Mainly because I didn't know what to say.

I still couldn't believe I had asked him that question. If he was angry, which I knew he had been even though he'd said I hadn't needed to apologize, it was within his right. Insinuating that he had some kind of ulterior motive to spending time with me and doing the things we had been doing was downright insulting.

I'd fucked up.

And as Jillian sat on the edge of my couch early Wednesday evening, watching me pace back and forth in my living room, I told her just how badly I'd fucked up while she sipped the latte she'd brought with her.

"So, that's about it." I dropped down on the couch, eyeing the cappuccino she'd brought me. It was all gone. "Not only does he probably think I'm a jackass, he also knows I have the confidence of a sewer rat."

Jillian frowned from behind the rim of her cup. "I don't think he believes you're an asshole. He told you not to apologize."

"That's because he's a good guy and he's not mean to anyone. Even in high school he was that way. Standing up for the kids that got picked on and friendly to everyone, and this last week has taught me he hasn't changed in that department." I grabbed the empty cup and stood, unable to stay seated. I walked into the kitchen, tossing it in the trash. "If he thought I was a jackass, he's not going to say anything."

"That may be true, but I just don't think that's the case." She placed her cup on the coffee table and waited until I returned to the living room. "And about the confidence thing? You shouldn't be embarrassed by it."

Stopping near the TV, I arched a brow as I folded my arms across my chest. "Lack of confidence is seriously one of the most unattractive things out there."

Jillian rolled her eyes. "And it's also seriously one of the most normal, common things out there."

"True," I murmured.

"I always thought being told you should be more confident, because confidence is sexy, was like getting a bitch slap in the face,"

Jillian said. "Like 'thanks for pointing that out.'"

I laughed dryly. "It's weird, you know? I hadn't even noticed this about myself in the last couple of years. I just sort of stopped thinking about myself as a woman. I know that sounds stupid, but that's the best way I can explain it. I think..." I sat back down, resting my hands in my lap as I gave a lopsided shrug. "And I was always so comfortable with Kevin. It wasn't something I ever had to think about, and I think the newness of all of this rattled me."

"That's understandable."

A weak smile crossed my lips as I glanced at my phone. Colton should be off tonight, unless he was still handling the investigation. My stomach dropped a little. "I guess in a way it's a blessing in disguise. At least now I know how I feel. I can do something about it."

She twisted toward me. Thick brown hair slid off her shoulder as she tilted her head to the side. "Like what?"

I really wasn't going to admit to the whole staring at myself naked thing. "Mostly I think I just need to be more aware of myself. Take some time for myself, you know?"

"You do work all the time," she agreed after a moment. "I thought my dad worked a lot, but I think the only time you take off is when we get together."

That would be an affirmative.

She peeked at me through the thick fringe of bangs. "Do you...want to change yourself?"

"Who doesn't want to change themselves, just a little bit?" I laughed as I brushed my hair back behind my ear. "I mean, I could probably be a wee bit healthier. Stop drinking cappuccinos every day. But I'd rather be happy with myself than to really try to change everything about myself."

"That's good." Her gaze lowered. "I wish I thought that. About myself, I mean."

I frowned. "Do you want to change yourself?" When she didn't answer, understanding set in. "Is that why you're transferring colleges? To start over?"

Her shoulder rose in a halfhearted shrug. "I just want to...yeah, I want to start over, and I can. I will."

Concern flickered through me. I reached over, placing my hand on her arm. "Is everything okay?"

Jillian nodded in response to the loaded question. The girl had never been very forthcoming with information, only dropping bits and pieces here and there. I knew she wasn't close to many people, except…except a guy named Brock. He was some kind of fighter with her father's organization. From what I had gathered, he'd been around her family for a long time.

And whenever she did talk about him, which wasn't often, her face would always get this look of absolute adoration on it.

"Jillian—"

"I just don't want to end up doing what my entire family does. Everything is about the Academy, and that's not what I want to do. The only way I'm going to escape that is by leaving now. Anyway," she said, pursing her lips as a thoughtful look crossed her face. "One of the things you never really see in a romance book is a woman who has self-esteem issues. I mean, I'm sure they're out there, but they're few and far between. Like they can have eating disorders, post-traumatic stress from sexual assault or mental abuse. They can be sold into sex trafficking and they can carry epic amounts of grief. We have female characters who have suffered every loss imaginable and ones who are scarred physically and mentality, but where in the hell are the average women? Ones who look in the mirror and cringe a little? Like, why are all those others acceptable to women, but reading or knowing another woman who has a low self-esteem is, like, worse than all that drama llama? Dude, I get reading for wish fulfillment, but you've got to have a little reality in the story."

Brushing her bangs out of her eyes, Jillian exhaled loudly and then continued. "Whatever. It doesn't matter. You're normal. I'm normal. We're not perfect and not having the greatest confidence doesn't make you any less of a person."

What Jillian said was so true.

Holy crap, the raw truth of it all floored me.

Women wanted other women to have high self-esteem and confidence. No one wanted to ever admit that their confidence was lacking, that they had a hard time looking at themselves in the mirror.

It was wrong that we weren't able to have our weak moments.

That we had to hide the fact that we were uncomfortable with our imperfections. That the journey to loving yourself doesn't exclude recognizing there were days when you just didn't want to see yourself naked.

And that there were worse things than having some confidence issues.

I glanced over at Jillian. This was one of those moments when I forgot that she was so young, because damn, she really could be a hell of a lot wiser than me. "You're right."

Her face transformed prettily when she smiled. "I know."

I laughed. "And modest."

"Whatever." Leaning forward, she smacked her hands off her knees. "Do you want to go out?"

"Go where?"

"I don't know. You live pretty close to the bar near Outback."

"Mona's?" I started to grin. "Jillian, I don't think you're allowed to go there."

"I've been there before. As long as they don't serve me, Jax is cool with it."

My brows rose. "Jax?"

"He's the owner. He's good friends with Brock." She stood.

I eyed her. "So…is Brock going to be there?"

"I doubt it," she said. "He's usually training now."

For some reason I didn't quite believe her.

"Come on. It'll be good to get out." She paused. "Plus, you know who's the bartender there, right?"

It took a second to click. "Wait. That's where Roxy works and she's dating…"

"Colton's brother," she finished.

The tumbling in my stomach this time was something altogether different. "How do you know that?"

She rolled her eyes again. "Brock is really good friends with all of them and I'm a really…listener. So, you want to go? I'll be good and order a Coke."

I shot her a look. "Wild child."

Jillian giggled, and I had to grin because I wasn't sure I'd ever heard her giggle. "So?"

Glancing at the clock, I saw it was still early. I'd planned on cracking open the new manuscript I'd received, but wasn't I supposed to start taking more time to myself? And besides, if I stayed home, all I would do is end up staring at my phone, engaging in wishful thinking.

"Okay," I said, standing up. "Let's do it."

* * * *

It had been about a year since I'd been in Mona's, and while the bar had a dive feel to it, it wasn't a creepy place. Jillian and I took our own cars since she lived in the opposite direction, closer to the city.

The moment I saw Jax, I remembered who he was. How could I have forgotten? Even though he was a few years younger than me, he was the kind of man who gave off the vibe that said he knew how to take care of things.

He was behind the bar when I led the way to a table. Since Jillian was underage, she couldn't sit at the bar. Jax had the greatest smile and laugh, which he handed out freely. Right now, he was laughing at something someone was saying at the bar. Tipping his head back and letting loose a deep, infectious laugh.

"You just want a Coke? Anything to eat?" I asked.

Jillian was scanning the heads bowed over one of the pool tables. "Nah. Coke is fine."

There weren't a lot of people at the bar when I walked over to it, so the girl behind it quickly came to where I stood. I knew who she was. This was Roxy—Reece's girlfriend. As she drew nearer, I saw that she had a streak of color in her brown hair that matched her purple glasses. Envy filled me. I always wanted to have a wild color in my hair, but I didn't have the face or the personality to pull that off.

Her shirt read *I'm like a self-cleaning oven*, and under it was a happy little oven, and then below that were the words *I'm self-sufficient, bitches*.

I wanted that shirt.

"What can I get...?" Roxy's hazel eyes widened behind the glasses. "Hey, how are you?"

Shocked that she recognized me, I floundered for a moment. "Good. I'm good. You?"

"Great. I haven't seen you in a while. Wow. It's been forever." She leaned against the bar, grinning. "I wasn't even sure you still lived around here." The door opened and a group rolled in, heading toward the bar. "What can I get you?"

"Just two Cokes." I paused. "And a menu."

Roxy nodded. "Coming right up."

I glanced over at the table. Jillian was staring down at her phone, her fingers flying a mile a minute.

"I'm giving them another minute, and if he's not out, I'm going in," I heard Jax say as he reached around Roxy, grabbing a bottle of liquor.

"For rescue?" she replied, her brows raising as she scooped ice into two glasses.

"Hmm," he grunted, screwing off the lid.

"I have no idea what's going on there. I thought they weren't together," she said, placing the two glasses in front of me. She grabbed a menu as she looked over her shoulder at Jax. "He needs to hurry up anyways. Reece has already texted asking where his brother is."

My heart stopped. They were talking about Colton. Holy crap. Okay, there was a tiny part of me that hoped he'd be here but also was terrified of the fact if he was, because then that meant he wasn't at work. And he hadn't gotten in contact with me.

And I hadn't gotten in contact with him either.

And it didn't sound like he was alone.

"Here you go." Roxy smiled as she placed the menu down.

I numbly handed over the cash, and had just picked up the glasses, along with the menu, when I saw him.

He appeared on the other side of the bar, and even from where I stood, I could see that his jaw was a hard line. My heart started racing. I tightened my hands on the glasses. Roxy said something, but I really didn't hear her.

Then I saw *her*.

The tall blonde I'd seen him with before. She was as gorgeous as I remembered. Hair shiny and straight, well past her shoulders, and she was thin. Like I would probably hurt her if I sat on her level of thin. Blood drained from my face as I realized who this woman was. In my heart of hearts I knew it was her, his ex-fiancée.

Oh my God.

"I was getting worried about you," Jax said, placing the bottle back.

Colton glanced over at him, and his gaze was icy as it moved past Jax and Roxy and then over me. He stopped. Literally stopped walking, jerking to a halt.

Our eyes met, and I couldn't even think. There were no thoughts as we stared at each other. My heart...it felt like it stopped, just like him.

"Um," Roxy murmured.

The woman with Colton said something. Her bow-shaped lips moved, but he didn't react. Not at first, and then he did.

"Shit," he said, and he turned to the stunning blonde, who had placed her hand on his arm. The touch was familiar, as if she had done it a thousand times before.

I whipped around, my skin tingling as I walked the drinks and menu to the table. I put them down before I dropped them.

"Are you ok...oh my God." Jillian's eyes doubled in size.

The twisting in my stomach made me nauseous as I flushed hot and then cold. "I think—" I shook my head, my cheeks burning. "God, I'm so sorry, but I really need to go."

Jillian rose, sympathy crossing her face. "Oh my gosh, I'm sorry. I didn't think something like this would—"

"I know." A knot formed in my throat, and the ache pouring into my chest told me that what I felt for Colton was not simply like or attraction. "I hate to do this." Pressing my lips together, I breathed out of my nose. "This is so embarrassing."

"It's okay." She squeezed my arm. "Go. Just call me when you get there, okay?"

Nodding, I bent down and kissed her cheek, then I grabbed my purse. I didn't dare look back as I headed for the door, and I knew even as I yanked it open, I was being such a coward.

My confidence sucked and I was a coward. Great. Winning combination. I didn't remember much of the drive home and as I walked inside, I kicked off the heels and left them just inside the door.

After I texted Jillian, I felt horrible. I shouldn't have bolted. I should've sat there and pretended like what the fuck ever. Tossing my phone on the couch, I pressed my palm against my forehead. The whole being an idiot thing was a running theme.

But Colton had been there with the same beautiful blonde. The fiancée—ex-fiancée, and Sunday, he had been kissing me, touching me, and telling me that I was beautiful and smart, and tonight he was with her?

What in the hell?

Anger surfaced, and I dug my phone out from between the cushions of my couch. I didn't even know what I was going to do. Text him? Call? Throw my phone? All seemed like a viable option.

A knock at the door stopped me.

I turned around and for a moment I didn't move. Despite the fact I'd just seen Colton with her, hope sparked deep in my chest, and how incredibly stupid was that? I doubted they just happened to run into each other. Then again, it had been purely coincidental that I'd even been there.

I shouldn't have left.

The knock came again, and my feet came unglued from the floor. With my phone in one hand, I opened the door.

It happened so fast.

A shadow—*a person*—shoved inside, slamming the door against the wall. There was a glimpse of a band of dark ink around thick biceps. A scream built in my throat and ripped loose a second before pain exploded along the side of my head, stunning me.

I stumbled to the side, my phone slipping from my fingers and hitting the floor. A door slammed shut and a second later, the wind was knocked out of me as my back hit the floor. My lungs seized as I stared up.

It was *him*—the shooter.

Holy shit.

Had he pistol-whipped me? Wet warmth trickled down the side of my neck. The whole left side of my head throbbed.

A fine sheen of sweat dotted his forehead as he towered over me, a gun in his hand. "You couldn't keep your fucking mouth shut, could you?"

My heart lodged in my throat as I scrambled backward, my hands slipping over the wood floors. A flip-flop came off as I reached the edge of the throw carpet.

He followed me. "All you had to do was keep your fucking mouth shut. That was all. Now Mickey is dead and the son-of-a-bitch Vakhrov is gunning for me, all because you couldn't keep your cunt mouth shut."

My vision blurred a little as I tried to remember who Mickey was. It took a moment for my brain to process the fact that Mickey must be the other man I'd seen him with. "I...I didn't identify hi—"

"Shut up! Shut the fuck up!" He shouted, his finger twitching over the trigger of the gun he held. "You're going to tell me you didn't say shit? Because Mickey is dead and the Goddamn police raided my momma's house yesterday."

I scooted back against the wall, my heart pounding so fast I thought I'd be sick. This was so bad, so freaking bad I could barely process what was happening. The only thing I knew was that I was staring death in the eyes.

His lip curled, just like it had right before he'd shot that man. "Stupid bitch. Lift your hands."

Swallowing hard, I raised my shaking hands as my thoughts raced. I had no idea how to get out of this. Could I reason with him?

His dark eyes held a certain glassy sheen to them and his pupils were way too dilated as he jerked the gun at me. "Stand up." When I didn't move, he screamed, "Stand the fuck up!"

Okay. I was standing.

Slowly, I pushed to my feet, losing the other flip-flop in the process. "We can work this—"

"Shut. Up." He stepped forward. "What part of that do you not understand? There's nothing—"

The muted sound of sirens silenced him. Hope exploded in my stomach. Had someone—one of my neighbors—heard my scream and his yelling?

I really needed to thank my neighbors. Bake them a cake or something. If I actually lived through this.

He heard the sirens, and in seconds, the whirling noise grew closer and louder. "Shit. Fuck. Damn."

My wide gaze darted across the room, searching for some kind of weapon. Unless I could grab a lamp before he shot me, I was screwed, but I had to try something. Through the front window, I could see flashing red and blue lights beyond the curtains. The cops were here and I seriously doubted this guy planned on walking out of here alive or letting me go.

Sudden shouts from the front of the house erupted, and horror settled in as I recognized one of the voices. No. No. No.

A loud knock on the door caused me to jump, sending a wave of dizziness through me. "Abby? You in there?" a voice boomed through the closed door. "It's Colton. Open the door."

Before I could open my mouth, the guy lurched forward, slamming into me. The back of my head knocked off the wall. His hand clamped down on my mouth as he got right up in my face.

"Abby!" Colton shouted, and the front door rattled as he or something slammed into it.

The man's breath stunk of stale cigarettes and booze as he pressed against me. "Fucking cops, motherfucking cops," he grunted, pressing the muzzle of the gun against the side of my head. "You say one word, I will blow your fucking brains out right now."

Right now, I thought dumbly. Versus later? A hysterical giggle climbed up my throat. The banging at the front door didn't stop, but I no longer heard Colton. How was he here? If the police were called there was no way he would've found out that quickly. It didn't make sense, but at this moment, it didn't matter.

If Colton somehow got through that door, I knew this man would shoot him. My stomach hollowed in fear.

"We're going to go out your back door, okay?" he said. "And you're going to make sure I get the hell out of here. You get me?"

Squeezing my eyes shut, I nodded. He was going to use me as some kind of shield, and I knew the moment he got outside, he was going to shoot me. It was either in here or out there, where he'd have a chance to shoot someone else—a neighbor, one of the cops, or Colton.

I couldn't let that happen.

No way.

I might have the self-esteem of a sloth, but I wasn't a coward. No. I survived my parents' death. I survived New York City. I survived my husband's death. I *survived*.

I was *not* a coward.

He grabbed ahold of my shoulder and pulled me away from

the wall. With one well-place shove in the center of my back, he guided me through the living room. Someone was yelling at the front door again, but it wasn't Colton.

"Keep quiet," he urged, and when I didn't move quickly, he shoved me again.

I stumbled into the small dining room table. The impact knocked over the heavy ceramic vase, spilling plastic flowers across the surface. The vase rolled toward me.

"Get moving," he ordered.

My gaze zeroed in on the vase. It was within grasp. Right there. My heart rate seemed to slow. Everything slowed down actually.

"Goddammit." He balled his fist in my hair and yanked my head back sharply. Pain tore down my neck, shooting into my back. "Get your fat ass fu—"

My brain clicked off as I grabbed the vase and spun around. The man cursed and he leveled the gun again, but I was fast when it counted. The gun went off just as I slammed the bottom of the vase into the side of his head. There was a sickening crunch and something warm and wet sprayed into the air and across my face. The gun went off again, just as wood splintered on the back door. It flew open just as the shooter crumbled to the floor.

Colton barreled in, dressed as he was at the bar, in jeans and a worn shirt. He had a gun aimed and his bright blue gaze took in the situation. Behind him, uniformed cops streamed in.

He took a step forward, keeping his gun on the shooter. "Abby?"

I was still holding the bloodied vase as I croaked out, "I'm not a coward."

Chapter Thirteen

"You're becoming a repeat customer," Lenny, the repairman who'd previously replaced my broken window, said with a wry grin. He'd just finished fixing the broken back door, which ended up being an entirely new back door. Placing the bill on the TV, he started past me with his toolbox in hand. "I'm glad to see you're okay, though. I heard about it on the late evening news last night. This town is getting crazy. All the violence coming in from the city."

I smiled faintly as I followed him to the front door. "Thank you for coming out on such short notice. I really appreciate it."

"No problem," he replied, stepping outside. "If you need anything else, you know to call me."

"Thanks." I closed the door, sighing.

Turning around, I eyed the freshly plastered wall behind the dining room table. Lenny had also covered the two bullet holes. All I needed to do was match up the paint and then it would be like nothing had ever happened.

Last night felt like forever ago.

I'd spent the bulk of the night sitting in the ER, getting checked out and then answering a thousand and one police questions. Come to find out, the shooter had a name—Charles Bakerton. Didn't sound like a homicidal maniac's name, but Charles was still alive. I hadn't killed him with the well-placed vase of death swing. I was relieved to hear that. I didn't want to know what it felt like to kill someone.

Through the endless hours that had crept into early morning, Colton had remained beside me, mostly silent and very pissed-off looking. Those blue eyes were practically on fire. We didn't get a chance to talk, nothing other than the basics before he was called out. Surprisingly, Roxy and Reece had showed up at the hospital and had driven me home. That was…weird.

I was so lucky. Everyone kept telling me that. I had looked a lot worse than I was. Not even a concussion, and the crack upside the head hadn't even required stitches. A fistful of ibuprofen had taken care of that ache and the rest of the minor pains.

I could've died last night, so yeah, I was really lucky.

Moving to the couch, I started to pick up the remote when there was a knock on my front door. My stomach dropped. Placing the remote down, I went to the front window first. Totally learned my lesson last night. I peered out the front window.

It was Colton.

"Oh my, wow," I murmured, settling back on my bare feet. I didn't let me head race into fantasy land. Him showing up after what went down last night wasn't a surprise. In a daze, I slowly walked to the door and opened it.

His hands were planted on each side of the doorframe and he was leaning in. Blue eyes met mine. "Abby."

Somehow I plastered a smile on my face, and I had a feeling it was a crazy looking smile. "Hi, Colton!" The enthusiasm was a bit much, but I couldn't tone it down. "How are you—?"

"Don't do that," he cut in, and I felt my creeper smile wobble and then fade. "After what happened yesterday, don't pretend with me."

Well then.

He lowered his hands. "We need to talk."

We did. I stepped aside, pressing my lips together. "Come in."

Colton closed the door behind him, but instead of walking to the couch, he stopped in front of me. My breath caught as he clasped the sides of my face in a gentle grasp. His intense gaze swept over me. "How are you feeling?"

"I'm okay. Really." I forced a less weird smile. "Thanks for asking."

The skin around his eyes tensed. "I wanted to get over here earlier."

It was then when I realized he was wearing the same clothes from last night. Needless to say, he probably had a lot of…cop things going on. "It's okay. I—"

"It's not okay. It fucking killed me not to be over here. Fuck." He dropped his hands and ran one through his hair as he stepped back. "Seeing you last night, with blood on your face—fuck," he cursed again, looking away. "Damn, I said I would protect you. I didn't."

"What?" I blinked. "You couldn't have known that was going to happen. Even Detective Hart had said he figured the shooter would've run after his friend or whatever was found dead. That's not your fault."

The look on his face said he wasn't so sure of that. "He followed you to your house and he hit you with a gun. You could've died, Abby. I—"

"Colton," I tried again. "I'm serious. It wasn't your fault. Okay? And you didn't have to come over here to check on me. I'm okay. You've…you've done enough. You got your brother and Roxy to take me home and—"

"I've done enough? Obviously, I haven't done enough." His gaze found its way back to mine. "I need to make a couple of things clear. When you left Mona's last night, you were upset. I get that. You just saw me walk out with Nicole and you left before I could say a single thing to you. Don't pretend like you didn't see that."

"Okay. You, um, seemed busy." I swallowed, taking a step back. "So that…that's your ex-fiancée? She's gorgeous."

"Yeah, she is." His brows knitted as he stared down at me. "You know, I was hoping I would hear from you. I figured after Sunday, I was going to leave the ball in your court."

He had? Had he given that message through man code? I wasn't good at reading man code.

"Obviously, you need to work through some issues and I was hoping that you would let me help you with that," he continued. "I'm impatient though. I was planning on calling you last night, but my brother does this thing every week at his place—game night. It's stupid, but fun. I thought I'd swing by his place for about an hour and then call you."

I didn't know what to say about any of that, but I wasn't going to stand here like I was mute. I had a voice and I was going to use it. "But you were at Mona's, with Nicole."

"I was," he said, a muscle flexing along his jaw. "I met her there on the way to Reece's. When we broke up, there was a watch that my grandfather had given me before he passed away. One night at her place, I had taken it off and I never found it after that. Nicole finally found it." Lowering his one hand to the pocket of his denim jeans, he fished out a gold watch that looked like it cost a pretty penny. "She wanted to talk. That's why we were in Jax's office."

I stared at the watch and then watched him place it back in his pocket. Part of me felt like an idiot, but how would anyone really react in this situation? "What did she want?"

Colton didn't lie. "She misses me. That's what she wanted to talk about."

Sucking in a sharp breath, I schooled my expression blank. "Okay."

His eyes narrowed. "Is that all you have to say about that?"

The frustration rose again, rushing over my skin like an army of fiery ants. If last night had taught me anything, it was that I wasn't a coward. I was a survivor. I *really* found my voice then. "What do you want me to say, Colton? How do I respond to that? I'm not mad that she misses you. You probably miss her too. You were together for a long time, but…" My words started to fade, and while there was a part of me that just wanted to show him the door and retreat, I refused to do it. "But we just reconnected and I don't know where our relationship is going. And you know what? Yes. I don't have the greatest confidence in myself right now. I haven't seriously dated anyone besides Kevin, and the last four years have been a really long dry spell. And I know that's not the greatest issue to have, but whatever. I like you."

I'd blurted those last three words out and then I couldn't take them back. "I *really* like you, Colton. I've always liked you, but I'm going to be honest. I'm going to suck at this whole dating thing and I'm going to have moments when I doubt why you're here. And it doesn't help when your ex-fiancée looks like a *Sports Illustrated* model. I shouldn't have run from the bar. That was stupid, but guess what, I'm probably going to do a lot of stupid things. That's just the beginning."

His lips started to twitch.

My eyes narrowed. "You think this is funny?"

"No." His eyes said he was lying. "Not at all."

"Uh-huh." I folded my arms across my chest and parroted back what he'd said earlier. "Is that all you have to say about that?"

"No. That's not all." His lips did curve up at the corners then. "I don't think less of you because you don't see what I see, what I know, when I look at you. That's the issue I'm more than willing to work with. You get that?"

I nodded as I pressed my lips together.

"I like you, really like you," he repeated, and that hope in my chest sparked into a wildfire. "I've *always* liked you, too. And yeah, Nicole is great looking, but she's not the person I'm standing in front of and she's not the person who gets me hard when I think of her. And she isn't the person I almost lost last night. That's you, sweetheart, all you."

Warmth invaded my cheeks. Oh…oh wow.

"I can tell you where this relationship is going. Or at least where I hope it is. We're going to spend more time together. We're going to really get to know each other, and I'm going to chip away at that low confidence shit until you see what I see," he said, and a shiver curled along the base of my spine in response to his steely determination.

My breath caught as he took a step forward and lifted his hands, gently holding my cheeks once more. "I want this to work," he said, his voice low. "Because like I said before, I believe in second chances and I don't believe in coincidences. There was a reason why you and I reconnected, and I don't want to pass that up. And we almost lost that last night, so really, we're working on a third chance. I want this to work."

"I…I want this to work too." My heart was thumping like a steel drum.

"Then we are on the same page."

"We are," I whispered.

"Good."

Then he kissed me, and in the back of my head, I realized we were still standing just inside the foyer, but I didn't care. His kiss started off sweet and tender, but I wanted more. So did he. My hands found their way to his chest, and I could feel his heart beating just as fast as mine.

I broke the kiss, breathing heavily. "Do you want to stay?"

"Hell yeah, but if I…if I do, I'm not leaving tonight." His thumbs dragged over my cheeks. "And if I don't leave tonight, I'm going to be upstairs and I'm going to want to be in that bed and in between those pretty thighs of yours. If you don't want that or you're not up to it because of last night, let me know now. I can wait, but either way, I'm not letting go of you tonight."

"I'm *fine*." There wasn't a moment of hesitation. "I want that."

Chapter Fourteen

Colton didn't waste a single moment.

He tilted my head back, lowering his mouth to mine in a deep, demanding kiss that brokered no room for denial. Not that I wanted to. That was the furthest thing from my mind as his tongue tangled with mine.

Backing me up, he kept going until we reached the bottom of the stairs; only then did he lift his mouth from mine. Blue eyes met mine, and my throat dried at the intensity of the passion in them. I turned and made it up three steps before his arm came around me from behind, curling around my waist. A second later, his front pressed against my back and I could feel him long and hard against my rear.

"I'm so damn impatient," he said, placing a kiss against my neck. "That bedroom seems awful far right now."

My laugh was breathy. "It's not that far."

"Fuck it ain't." The arm around my waist tightened, sealing our bodies together as he blazed a hot path of tiny kisses down my throat.

Carefully tipping my head back and to the side, I let out a soft moan as his hand drifted up my stomach and cupped my breast through the dress. With unerring expertise, his fingers found the aching tip of my breast. Then I felt his hand between my legs, and the thin, delicate material was no barrier to his seeking hand on my heat.

Without even thinking, my legs spread, giving him more access, and he took it, pushing the dress in as he cupped me. He pressed his palm in against the bundle of nerves. My hips jerked, and the sound he made in response sent a wave of little bumps over my skin. There was no control. I gripped his wrist with one hand and my other flew out, blindly seeking for the railing. I held on to both as I moved against his hand, grinding, seeking, right there, in the stairway. Pleasure built and swelled, pounding through me.

"Damn," he groaned, dropping his hand from my breast. "We aren't going to make it to the bed if we keep this up."

"You started this," I reminded him.

"True."

Pressing one last kiss to my neck, he backed off. My knees were a little wobbly as I started back up the stairs. I was already dazed and breathless and we hadn't even reached the bedroom.

The hallway upstairs was lit from the nightstand lamp I'd left on in the bedroom, and when I turned to glance back at Colton, I found myself suddenly pressed against the wall just outside my bedroom, his long and lean body against mine.

"I'm really fucking impatient," he admitted.

I looped my arms around his neck, giving in to the crazy sensations building in me. "Me too."

Colton kissed me and then pulled back. My arms fell to my sides as I dragged in air. Grabbing the collar of his shirt, he quickly pulled it up and over his head, letting it fall to the floor.

I'd seen him shirtless before, but memory didn't serve any justice. From his well-defined pecs to the way his stomach coiled tightly, he was an artwork of tone and lean muscles I wanted to touch and taste.

I reached for him, my fingers finding the button on his jeans, easily flicking them open. I caught the zipper next, and as the material folded to the sides, my fingers brushed over the long, thick length straining against his boxers.

"Fuck." His hands clasped the sides of my face again and the kiss was so much fiercer. Our teeth knocked together. My lips felt bruised, but I reveled in the raw passion.

Pressing me back against the wall, his hips pushed into mine in a slow, tantalizing roll that caused me to cry out. His hands slipped down my throat, over my arms. Pulling me away from the wall, he led me into the bedroom. Only then did he let go of my hands.

"You sure about this?" he asked.

I moved so I stood in front of my bed. "I'm sure. Are you?"

"Never been more sure about anything in my life." Toeing off his shoes, he whipped off the socks in record time. "I want you."

My stomach constricted. "I want you."

Reaching around, he pulled out his wallet. A silver foil packet appeared between his fingers. I arched a brow as he tossed it on the bed behind me. "What?" His grin turned sheepish, almost boyish. "I always like to be prepared."

"I guess it's a good thing that you are because I don't have any."

Something about what I said had an effect on him. He groaned. "Then we need to make this one count, huh?"

I watched as he walked toward me, his jeans inching down his hips. God, he was beautiful in a purely male way. I almost couldn't believe that he was real, standing before me. That we were about to do this.

"I want to see you." He slipped his fingers under the cap sleeve of my dress, drawing it down my shoulder.

As ready as I was, it occurred to me in that moment that I was going to have to get completely buck-ass naked to do this. I knew he wasn't going to want to do this with clothes on. Oh no, he was a skin man. All the confidence pranced right out of the room on two twig legs. Twig legs with perky breasts, which were two things I didn't have.

I stepped back, drawing in a deep breath as I looked up at him. I hated the sudden insecurity, absolutely loathed it. It was my skin, my body, and it was a part of me, but in this moment, it felt like an itchy, uncomfortable sweater.

Colton stepped closer, his hand lingering on my shoulder. "Are you okay?"

Biting down on my lip, I nodded as I glanced at our bare feet. Next to his, mine actually appeared somewhat small. Still not feminine. Not these cave feet. Okay. My feet didn't look like cave feet. I was being too hard on myself.

"Then what's going on? You've left this room. Probably even this house." He paused. "Is this about Nic—"

"No." My gaze flew to his, and that wasn't entirely a lie. I couldn't help compare myself to her, because hell, I was human, but it was more than that. "I…It's been so long since I've done this, Colton."

His fingers skirted down my arm. "I know."

Did he really know? "Four years."

He threaded his fingers through mine. "I figured that."

Closing my eyes, I exhaled softly. "You want to see me, but I'm not sure you really want to. I don't look like—"

"I know what you look like," he said, his voice low as his gaze met and held mine. "I have two eyes and I've been checking you out often. Enough that it would probably make you uncomfortable if you knew. I fucking adore what I see." He drew my hand to his groin, folding my palm over the rigid length. "I want what I see."

My breath caught on a soft inhale as I held him lightly in my grip. I thought I could feel him pulse. My gaze dropped to where his much larger hand folded over mine. Colton was right. He had two, completely functioning eyes. Wasn't like the clothing I wore hid what was really there, and the heat burning my palm told me that he did want this, just as badly as I did.

I could do this.

Slipping my hand away from him, I reached down, catching the skirt of my dress. I couldn't hesitate at this point. Now or never. Before I could change my mind, I pulled the dress up over my head and then I let it drop to the floor.

I lifted my gaze as I held my breath.

His eyes were glued to mine and a slight, soft smile tugged at one corner of his lips. Then his gaze dropped, gliding slowly over me, and I knew those brilliant blue eyes didn't miss a thing. Not the dainty, blue lace edging along the straps of my bra or the cups. Not the way my waist curved in and then flared out. The undies weren't sexy. They were just cotton boy shorts, and they didn't even match the bra, but as his gaze traveled down to my painted toes, I had a feeling he really didn't care about that.

"You know what, Abby?" His voice was gruff, like he'd just woken up. "You're unbelievably sexy. Every last fucking inch of you." He brushed the back of his hand over my shoulder. "This is." That hand then dropped to graze the swell of my breasts. "So are these, and so is this." He trailed a finger down my belly and around my navel. "And I want to lick these hips." His hand smoothed over one and then around, cupping my rear. "Actually, I want to taste every part of you."

My heart pounded. "I'm...I'm totally down for that."

He chuckled as he stepped closer. With one hand on my shoulder, he guided me down until I was sitting on the bed. Keeping my attention fastened on him, I scooted back and refused to allow myself to get caught up in my head again.

Not that I could when he was taking off his jeans. The way the muscles of his stomach bunched and flexed was fascinating to me. It also made me think of what he'd said he wanted to do to me, about tasting me all over. I actually wanted to do it to him.

He left the tight, black boxer briefs on as he walked around the bed, placing one knee on it as he came down beside me. There was little space between us. Neither of us spoke as our breaths danced over each other's lips.

Slowly, tentatively, Colton touched my cheek with the tips of his fingers. He seemed to map out the curve of my cheek and then my jaw, before skating those rough fingers over my parted lips. The light touch was powerfully seductive, and my response was consuming. The fire surged back to life, keeping me from getting stuck in my head.

His fingers trailed down my throat and then over each cup. My toes curled as I felt my nipples harden. He reached around, deftly unhooking my bra. The straps slipped off my arms, dropping to the bed. "These..." His voice was still hoarse. "These are perfect."

The way he touched me then made me believe that he truly meant that. He cradled the heavy globe as if it were the most treasured thing. He dragged his thumb over the rosy peak, smiling at the immediate response. He did the same to my other breast.

There wasn't a time when I knew of Colton that I hadn't fantasized about him. Only when I was married had I filed those thoughts away, but it had been so long that I dreamed of this, that I wanted this.

My mind finally joined where my heart and body already were, and when he stretched out, I did something that shocked me. Sitting up, I moved onto my knees, placing them on either side of his hips. His hands immediately settled on my hips and I lowered myself down, swallowing a moan when I felt his erection straining against his boxer briefs, hot and hard against the thin material of my panties.

"I really like where this is heading," Colton said, his hands gently squeezing my hips.

I didn't let myself think too much as I leaned down and admitted what I'd been thinking about a few seconds ago. "I've fantasized about this for so long."

Thick lashes lifted as he stilled. His stare was piercing, intent. "Are you serious?"

"So serious."

His fingers curled around the edges of my panties and then one hand trailed up the line of my back and curved around the nape of my neck. "You really shouldn't have told me that."

"Why?" I whispered, my heart thumping.

"Because I have no idea how I'm going to be able to slow this down now."

Colton dragged my mouth to his with a curl of his arm. There was nothing soft or gentle about the way he kissed me. It was fierce and passionate, a kiss of pent-up desire exploding the moment our mouths fused together, a kiss of need. He drew in my breathy moans as he circled his arm around my lower back, sealing our bodies together, chest to chest.

Everything about him swamped my senses and I whispered, "Make love to me."

Colton let out a near feral sound and then he rolled me onto my back, moving so quickly my heart nearly came out of my chest. As he stared down at me, concentration marked his features.

Then he brought his mouth to the tip of my breast. I let out a strangled cry as my back arched off the mattress. He reached between us, working the last of his clothing off as he moved to my other breast. Sensation raced up and down my body, and that was what I got lost in, the way his tongue laved at my nipple, how he nipped at my skin and soothed the sting with a kiss, a caress of his fingers.

Barely aware of him easing my panties down and then off, I was shocked and thrilled to suddenly feel the entire length of our bodies flesh to flesh. His hand slid up, his fingers splaying around my cheek, holding me there as he brought his mouth back to mine. He kissed me until there were no more thoughts, no holding back or getting lost in fear. I could feel him burning against my thigh, and my body moved on its own accord. I writhed and my hips moved, seeking him.

"You sure you're up for this?" he asked.

"Yes."

"I can't wait any longer."

I gripped his arms. "Neither can I."

He rolled, reaching for the condom. My stomach tumbled as I watched him rip open the foil and roll the condom onto his thick erection.

This was seriously going to happen.

Part of me still couldn't believe it as I dragged my gaze up to his and found him watching me. Unable to stop myself, I reached out, smoothing my hands over his hard chest and packed, tight abs. His skin was like silk stretched over marble. I dipped my hand, my fingers brushing over the sparse, short hairs. His chest rose with a deep breath and he seemed to hold it as the back of my hand brushed his cock. He made a deep sound that warmed my skin, and I reached around, folding my hand around his heavy sac.

"Fuck," he grunted. "Abby…"

Slowly, I pulled my hand back. For a moment, neither of us moved, and then he prowled over me, his strong body caging me in. Colton laid claim to my mouth, but those kisses slowed and became something…infinitely more as I felt his tip press against me. Moaning, I rolled my hips, bringing him closer, but not enough, nowhere near enough.

Colton rested his weight on one elbow as he lifted his body slightly and reached between us, wrapping his hand around his dick.

His eyes, a heated and vibrant cobalt, met mine. "I want this to be good for you."

My lips parted on a soft exhale.

"No," he corrected softly. "I want this to be perfect for you. It's gonna kill me trying to take this slow."

I dragged my hand down his back as my heart pounded. "Don't take this slow. I'm ready." The peaks of my ears burned. "I'm wet...for you."

He said something I couldn't quite understand under his breath and then his hips thrust, plunging into me with one deep stroke I felt to the tips of my toes. I cried out, tossing my head back as he stretched and filled me. Nothing ever in my life had felt like this.

"Are you okay?" he asked, his voice harsh as he stilled, seated deep.

"Yes." I grabbed onto his arms as I swallowed. "Yes. Don't stop."

"Stopping right now is the last thing on my mind, sweetheart." He rolled his hips back, pulling out halfway, and then he thrust forward again. "Stopping would kill me."

It would kill both of us.

But he didn't stop. Oh no, he moved and contrary to what he said, he used slow, languid strokes as his hand brushed the damp hair off my forehead. He built a fire deep within me as his breath danced over my lips, our gazes locked together. There was a connection there, flowing back and forth between us, something intense and consuming.

It was love.

I knew that, felt it in every cell of my being, and I closed my eyes, unwilling to show him the deepest part of me because it all felt too soon, and love had never been spoken between us.

Curling my arm around the one he rested his weight on, I wrapped my legs around his hips, drawing him in even further and eliciting a ragged groan from him. I rocked my hips and he tossed his head back, his arm trembling.

"Don't hold back," I ordered in the space between us. "Please."

And he didn't.

Restraint broke. Those tentative strokes turned deep and

powerful. He grabbed my hand, stretching it above my head, and clamped his hand down on my wrist as he moved over me and in me, his hips plunging wildly.

Pressure built, zipping through my veins and crackling over my skin. I cried out his name over and over as the tension coiled deep in my core. It was too intense, too much and still not enough.

Shifting his weight, he caught my other hand and joined it with the one he held. In one fluid move he had me immobile under him, completely under his control, helpless to him and yet entirely safe in his arms. Something about that combination undid me.

I came apart, shattering as the sound of his name and my cries mixed with his groans. He thrust once and then twisted, hard and deep, and then his huge body spasmed over mine as he buried his face in my shoulder.

When he lifted his head and pressed a tender kiss to my lips, I wasn't sure I was still existing on Earth. I felt like I was floating to the clouds, maybe even all the way up to heaven.

"You okay?" He eased his hand away from my wrists, drawing my arms back down.

I drew in a shallow breath. "I think I might have died in a totally…good way."

Colton chuckled and then brushed his lips over my forehead. "Be right back."

An aftershock stole my breath as he eased out of me. I was nothing more than a puddle as he rolled onto his feet and disposed of the condom in the bathroom. When he returned, I hadn't moved. Every part of me was sated, but I told myself I needed to move. Put some clothes on. He'd be leaving soon, and I didn't need to be lying here with everything on display. I started to rise onto my elbows.

"Where are you going?" He climbed onto the bed, half on his side.

"I…I thought I should grab my dress."

"Why?" Shaking his head, he snaked his arm around my waist. "No. Don't answer that question."

"But—"

He tugged me down so my back was curled against his front and his arm was a heavy, pleasant weight across my waist. "I'm not going anywhere, Abby."

I squeezed my eyes shut tightly. Could he read minds?

"Do you understand?" His voice was quiet, and when I didn't answer, his arm tightened around my waist. "I'm not."

But he would, because—

I stopped myself. I shoved that ugly part of me away. In my head, I bitch slapped it. I told it to shut the fuck up, because that nasty part sure as hell hadn't been entirely helpful in the past.

"Okay," I said, placing my hand on his arm. "I…that was wonderful, you know, what we did—you did."

"Of course I was."

I laughed lightly. "Wow."

There was a pause. "It was, Abby. It was perfect." He pressed a kiss against my shoulder. "And it wasn't me. It was you. You made this perfect."

Chapter Fifteen

Perfect was a theme I was getting used to, or at least trying to. It wasn't entirely hard. Not when Colton excelled at making me feel like I was perfect.

A month had passed since the night Charles came through that front door. He was still in the county jail and from what I'd learned, I doubted there would be a trial where I would have to testify. Charles would plead guilty to murder and attempted murder. He would go away for a long time.

Unless Isaiah got ahold of him.

But that wasn't something I was going to focus on. Every once in a while, I had…nightmares. Sometimes Colton was there to ease those troubling memories. Other nights, it was up to me to get through them, and I did.

I couldn't believe how much could change in a short time.

While Colton had a role to play when it came to the changes I was making, the feeling of self-worth and confidence had to come from within. Yeah, the external stuff helped, but using a guy's attention to build your confidence wasn't something that would last long. It would be dependent upon him, a strength that could be flimsy.

The strength needed to come from me.

And the best way I could gain back the stronger part of me was through actually experiencing life.

I wasn't working myself to the bone any longer. Meaning after I put in a normal eight-hour shift, I forced myself to stop. Who knew how much extra time existed when you weren't avoiding...well, avoiding actually *living*?

I visited the museums in the city with Jillian, something I hadn't actually done in years, and I even started going out with Roxy, Colton's younger brother's girlfriend. Through her, she introduced me to Calla, who was dating Jax, and to Katie, a very...odd stripper who apparently had gone to the same high school as Roxy and I.

For the first time in years, I had a circle of girlfriends, and I had forgotten how incredibly important that was. When Kevin had died and I'd left New York City, it was like I'd closed a door on the life that had existed with him, including all our mutual friends. It seemed a little late now, four years later, to try to rebuild those bridges, but it was something I'd thought about a lot and wanted to try.

And like Katie had said last Sunday, while the four of us had breakfast at IHOP, "What's the worst thing that could happen? They ignore you or think you're some crazy cat lady reaching out to them?"

I was also thinking about taking cooking lessons. That was something else I'd forgotten that I'd loved—baking and all things food related. Colton was a hundred percent behind the idea, mainly because I think he just wanted to eat the food.

Speaking of the devil...

Colton reached around me, his finger aiming for the homemade peanut butter icing. I smacked his hand away. "Don't even think about it."

"I just want a little taste." He looped his arms around my waist.

I grinned as I placed the plastic lid over the chocolate cake. "You're going to have to wait."

"I can wait for the cake, but..." He lowered his mouth to my neck, placing a kiss against my pulse. "But there's another taste of something I'm not sure I'm going to be able to wait for."

My stomach hollowed in response. All he had to do was make an innuendo and my blood heated. Colton was *that* good. "We're going to be late."

"It's Jax's BBQ, not a wedding reception." His hands slid across my belly and then down my hips. He kissed the space just behind my ear.

I bit down on my lip as I leaned back into him, feeling his arousal pressing against my lower back. He was insatiable.

I loved it.

"We really should try to be on time," I said as I tilted my head to the side, giving him more access.

With his hands on my hips, he turned me around in his embrace. "We can be late."

Colton kissed me as he slid his hands down, gathering up the skirt of my dress and skating his fingers on the bare skin of my thighs. When he reached my panties and effectively slid them down my legs, every nerve ending took notice. He helped me step out of them.

We were so going to be late.

Our kisses quickly turned frantic, his tongue plunging in and out of my mouth, and our hands were greedy. One of his on my breast, teasing the aching tip through the thin material, his other firmly planted on my ass. I squeezed him through his jeans, loving the way his hips moved against my palm and the deep groan he made against my lips.

He broke the kiss and turned me back around. A fine shiver curled its way down my spine as he brushed my hair aside, then he placed his hand on the center of my back, bending me over slightly.

"Hold on to the counter," he all but growled. I heard the tinny sound of his zipper.

Oh my goodness.

I did just exactly what he said and when he lifted my skirt again, I felt him against my behind, so hot and hard.

His hand slipped around and delved deep between my thighs, and his fingers immediately went to work, testing my readiness. And he didn't have to test that out. I was already ready.

With one hand on my hip, holding me in place, he entered me from behind in a long, deep thrust. I cried out, gripping the edge of the counter. "Oh God, Colton…"

"I love hearing you say my name like that." He started moving, his strokes slow and steady. My inner muscles began to clench around him. "Fuck, you feel so good."

"So do you," I breathed.

His thrusts became harder and faster, and I came within moments, screaming his name as it powered through me. He gripped my hips now with both hands and I was drawn up onto the tips of my toes. When he came, he shouted my name as his arm circled around me, sealing my body tight to his, and damn if that didn't almost make me come again.

I could barely move when Colton turned me around, holding me on weak legs. I draped my arm over his shoulder. His warm breath danced over my lips. "Now I really want some of that cake."

I laughed as I let my head drop to his shoulder. "I'm never going to look at cake the same again."

* * * *

Roxy clasped her hands together under her chin. "Oh my God, I just want to shove my face in it."

"Please don't do that," Calla said as she passed us by, her long blonde hair swinging from a ponytail.

"I have something you can shove your face in." Reece walked up behind Roxy, tugging on her purple streak.

"Please don't do that in my house," Jax replied, appearing in the backyard, a fresh case of beer in his hands.

"We're not in your house." Reece sat in the lawn chair, dragging Roxy down in his lap.

Jax flipped him off.

"Just pointing it out, buddy." Reece grinned.

My chocolate cake with peanut butter icing had gone over well, but the scent of hamburgers being grilled had my tummy all kinds of happy.

Colton draped his arm over my shoulders as he lifted the mouth of his bottle to his lips. When he lowered the bottle, he dipped his head and pressed his lips to my temple.

"You guys are so freaking adorable," Roxy said, splayed over Reece like he was her own personal chair.

"I know." Colton grinned.

I laughed as I rolled my eyes. "He's incredibly modest."

Reece snorted. "Don't I know."

Calla headed past us. "I'm going to grab the plates and stuff. Anyone need anything?"

"I'll help," I volunteered, breaking away from Colton. Or at least trying to. He was like an octopus. I only got so far before his arm dragged me back.

He smiled down at me, revealing that one dimple. "You're forgetting something."

There was no stopping the smile when I stretched up and kissed him. Someone, probably Reece, catcalled. When I settled back on my feet and turned around, Colton smacked my ass.

"So freaking adorable!" Roxy yelled this time.

Face turning about five shades of red, I hurried in to catch up with Calla. She held the door open as we headed in. "You guys are adorable," she said as she headed for where all the condiments and plates were placed on the counter.

"Thanks." My smile was probably going to split my face in two.

She grabbed a large tray. Sunlight from the window above the sink reflected off her scarred cheek. The first time I'd seen her, I couldn't help but notice the thin slice that traveled the length of her face, but now it was something I barely registered. Calla was stunning nonetheless, and it was so obvious that she and Jax were deeply in love.

My stomach tumbled in a pleasant way. Love? God, it was something I'd been thinking about a lot lately. There wasn't a part of me that doubted how much I cared about Colton. I was fully embracing my insta-love and hugging it close.

"Are you going to be here next weekend?" I asked as I gathered up the napkins and plastic spoons.

Calla was splitting her time between Shepherdstown and Plymouth Meeting until January, when she would move up here full time. "No, but Jax is coming down next weekend."

"That's good. I love how you guys do the long distance thing."

"Me too. It's working, but I can't wait until I don't have to dread him going home or me leaving." She grabbed the now loaded up tray as I reached for the million and one bottles. Who seriously needed so many versions of mustard? The doorbell rang, and Calla sighed as she started to put the tray down. "It's probably Katie."

"I'll get it," I offered since I didn't have my hands full.

"Thanks." She smiled, turning to the backdoor. "Hurry back out. Those three guys can eat about a dozen hamburgers between them."

"Wow."

Calla laughed. "Yep."

My sandals smacked off the hardwood floors as I made my way to the front of the house. Wondering what kind of outfit Katie would be wearing, I opened the door, prepared for something pink and sparkling.

The black, silk sleeved tank dress so did not belong to Katie.

Standing on the front porch was the last person I was expecting to see. It was Nicole, Colton's ex-fiancée.

Chapter Sixteen

A feather could've knocked my ass over. I was in such shock, all I could do was stand there and stare.

Over the past month, I thought about her every so often, just like I thought about the man I'd seen murdered, the man who ended up in the river, and the one who nearly killed me. How could I not?

And now she was here.

Since I'd only seen Nicole from distances, I wasn't prepared for just how stunning she was up close. Her blonde hair was ridiculously straight and shiny, her complexion absolutely flawless and without a wrinkle in sight. Lips plump and full and nose pert, paired with high cheekbones, she was the poster child for perfection.

There was no recognition in her blue eyes. "Hi," she said, her voice soft. "Is Colton here?"

My heart pounded in my chest and I said the first, most obvious thing that popped into my head. "This isn't his house."

And I thought that was a super-valid statement.

She glanced over my shoulder. Her hands were clasped together in front of her. "I know that. I saw his truck outside."

Then she knew damn well he was here.

"Can you get him please?" she prompted, giving me a tight-lipped smile. "I really need to talk to him."

Why would she show up unannounced at a friend of Colton's house? Who does that? I didn't think most people did. A hundred thoughts formed at once. Maybe it wasn't entirely unannounced. Maybe she and Colton had been in contact with one another and I simply didn't know. Maybe he wanted—

I pulled the brakes on that train wreck of a thought process. Colton was an honest man, and the stupid as fuck, evil voice in the back of my head wasn't going to win.

But I realized then that I had started to turn around to go retrieve Colton, and that was like a smack in the face. What in the hell was I doing? His *ex*-fiancée had come to Jax's house looking for him—for *my* boyfriend, and I was just going to walk off and get him?

Oh hell to the no.

I faced her. "Why do you want to see him?"

Nicole blinked, obviously surprised by my question. "I don't mean to be rude, but that's really none of your business."

"Actually, it is, Nicole."

Her eyes widened this time. "How do you...?"

"I know who you are." My pulse was pounding so fast I thought I might be sick. "You're Colton's ex-fiancée."

Her slim brows furrowed. "I'm sorry, but I don't know you. You're not seeing Jax or Colton's brother."

"I'm not." I paused and then I smiled. "That's because I'm seeing Colton."

Any other time I might've laughed at her reaction. Her jaw seemed to come unhinged. She gaped like a fish out of water. My lips pursed as her eyes doubled in size. Was it really that hard to believe? Geez.

"I d-didn't know," she said after she recovered. "He hasn't said anything."

My stomach joined her jaw, falling somewhere on the floor.

"I mean, I haven't really talked to him," she quickly added, lowering her gaze as she shook her head. "I've messaged him a couple of times—called him, but he hasn't answered."

Relief poured through me, and I didn't even feel terrible for that.

Nicole cleared her throat. "I...God, this is so embarrassing." She laughed, but it was hoarse and thick sounding. "I honestly wasn't planning to come here, and I know I probably look like a stalker, but my friend lives nearby, and when I drove past and saw his truck I thought I..."

I had no idea what to say. "I'm sorry?"

God, that was pretty lame.

She laughed again and the sound was worse this time. Her gaze lifted to mine. "Do you really care about him? Because I know if he's with you, he really cares about you. He doesn't date idly."

"I know," I whispered, and in that moment, I really did know. With my hand still on the door, I exhaled softly. "I've dreamed of him—of someone like him—for a long time. I'm in love with him. I don't know if he feels the same way, but I know...I know how I feel."

Nicole's eyes closed briefly. "Make sure you tell him that," she said, her eyes filling with tears. "Make sure you show him. I...I never really did, you know? I was stupid. Don't be stupid like me." She stepped back, her throat working. "Can you do me a favor?"

"Yes," I heard myself whisper. For some reason I wanted to cry.

She smiled weakly. "Please don't tell him I was here. I'm not going to try to get in touch with him again. Not when he's with someone. Okay?"

Pressing my lips together, I nodded.

"Thank you," she said, and then she turned around. I watched her leave and then closed the door.

In a daze, I gathered up the bottles and walked outside. Everyone was huddled around the table, scooping up heaps of potato salad and putting together their buns.

Colton looked up, the look in his eyes soft, and my heart squeezed. "I was starting to get worried about you."

"Yeah, who was at the door?" Jax asked.

"No one," I answered, putting the bottles on the table as I took a deep breath. "I mean, it was someone trying to sell candles. It took me a while to close the door."

Roxy snatched up the ketchup bottle. "If it had been Girl Scout cookies, I hope you would've let them in."

I smiled as I moved over to where Colton stood, Nicole's words echoing in my head as I wrapped my arms around his waist. "If it was them, I would've rolled out the damn red carpet."

* * * *

Later that night, I laid in Colton's bed, the fine sheen of sweat cooling on our bodies as our hearts slowed. It had taken some major effort on Colton's part to pull the sheet up to our waists.

He lay on his back and I was on my side beside him. His hand trailed up and down my spine, an idle and tender caress I wasn't even sure he was aware of.

In the silence of his dark bedroom, the conversation I had with Nicole replayed in my head. It had several times while at the cookout. I hated not telling Colton about her, but I also couldn't find it in myself to break the promise I made to her.

I didn't think Nicole was going to be a problem. If anything, her unexpected visit had been eye opening. I needed to tell Colton how I felt. It could be risky. Hell, it could scare him off, but the words were burning the tip of my tongue and twisting up my heart.

And I wasn't a coward.

Worst-case scenario, it was too soon and Colton ran for the hills, but if he didn't feel the same way now, would it really change later? It wasn't like people couldn't grow to love one another, but I was a firm believer that you knew pretty quickly if love was in the cards.

I drew in a deep breath. "Colton?"

"Hmm?" he murmured.

"You're still awake, right?"

His chuckle rumbled through me. "Yes."

"Good. I need to tell you something."

Colton's hand stilled along the center of my back. "You have my attention."

I closed the hand that rested on his chest because it was starting to shake. "I...I really loved Kevin. He was more than my husband. He was my closest friend too, and when he died, I wasn't sure if I'd ever feel that way about someone else. I wanted to, but I...I just wasn't sure."

He didn't move. There was a good chance he wasn't breathing.

"Even though I was with Kevin in high school, I still noticed you and I still…God forgive me, had a crush on you." I squeezed my eyes shut. "And well, what I'm trying to tell you is that I…I love you."

He still didn't move. Or breathe.

My eyes opened and I added in a rush, "And I know it's soon and it's probably too soon for me to be saying that to you, but I wanted you to know that I do. I do love you, and I know you probably are seconds from freaking and—"

"I am freaking out."

Oh dear.

Colton rolled onto his side and suddenly we were eye to eye. "I'm freaking out in a good way."

"Oh," I whispered.

His hand curled around my cheek. "It's not too soon. Or if it is, we're both feeling it too soon."

My breath caught. "You…you love me?"

"Yeah. Yeah, I do." His lips brushed over mine. "I think I fell in love with you the moment you said you thoroughly enjoyed crepes."

I laughed as tears, the good kind, filled my eyes. "Really? It was the crepes that made you fall in love with me?"

"They had something to do with it." He kissed me softly. "And so did your sweet ass," he added, and then I laughed again. "Your smile had a lot to do with it. So did your strength. And your kindness. Everything about you actually."

"Wow," I whispered, resting my forehead against his. "That's all very sweet."

"It's the truth." His hand slid into my hair, holding it back from my face. "I love you, Abby."

With my heart full of love and my mind empty of all fears and concerns, I threw the sheet back, pushed him over, and climbed onto him, straddling his hips.

Colton grinned widely. "I like where this is heading."

Laughing, I placed my hands on his chest. "You know what?"

"What?" His fingers skimmed my sides.

I leaned down and kissed him. There was barely a space

between our lips when I spoke. "I've dreamed of you for so long."

Colton picked up my hand and brought it to his mouth, kissing my palm. "You don't have to dream anymore."

My lips curved into a smile.

He was right. I didn't have to dream anymore.

About Jennifer L. Armentrout

#1 New York Times and International Bestselling author Jennifer lives in Martinsburg, West Virginia. All the rumors you've heard about her state aren't true. When she's not hard at work writing. she spends her time reading, watching really bad zombie movies, pretending to write, and hanging out with her husband and her Jack Russell Loki.

Her dreams of becoming an author started in algebra class, where she spent most of her time writing short stories....which explains her dismal grades in math. Jennifer writes young adult paranormal, science fiction, fantasy, and contemporary romance. She is published with Spencer Hill Press, Entangled Teen and Brazen, Disney/Hyperion and Harlequin Teen. Her book Obsidian has been optioned for a major motion picture and her Covenant Series has been optioned for TV. Her young adult romantic suspense novel DON'T LOOK BACK was a 2014 nominated Best in Young Adult Fiction by YALSA.

She also writes Adult and New Adult contemporary and paranormal romance under the name J. Lynn. She is published by Entangled Brazen and HarperCollins.

Also From Jennifer L. Armentrout

FOREVER WITH YOU
FALL WITH ME

By J. Lynn
STAY WITH ME
BE WITH ME
WAIT FOR YOU

The Covenant Series
DAIMON
HALF-BLOOD
PURE
DEITY
ELIXER
APOLLYON

The Lux Series
SHADOWS
OBSIDIAN
ONYX
OPAL
ORIGIN
OPPOSITION

The Dark Elements
BITTER SWEET LOVE
WHITE HOT KISS
STONE COLD TOUCH
EVERY LAST BREATH

A Titan Novel
THE RETURN

Standalone Novels
OBSESSION

FRIGID
SCORCHED
CURSED
DON'T LOOK BACK

Gamble Brothers Series
TEMPTING THE BEST MAN
TEMPTING THE PLAYER
TEMPTING THE BODYGUARD

Forever With You

By Jennifer L. Armentrout
Now Available

In the irresistibly sexy series from #1 *New York Times* bestselling author Jennifer L. Armentrout, two free spirits find their lives changed by a one-night stand...

Some things you just believe in, even if you've never experienced them. For Stephanie, that list includes love. It's out there. Somewhere. Eventually. Meanwhile she's got her job at the mixed martial arts training center and hot flings with gorgeous, temporary guys like Nick. Then a secret brings them closer, opening Steph's eyes to a future she never knew she wanted—until tragedy rips it away.

Nick's self-assured surface shields a past no one needs to know about. His mind-blowing connection with Steph changes all that. As fast as he's knocking down the walls that have kept him commitment-free, she's building them up again, determined to keep the hurt—and Nick—out. But he can't walk away. Not when she's the only one who's ever made him wish for forever...

* * * *

"Nope." His hands settled on my hips and my eyes flew to his. He held my stare. "And neither are you. You're done with these questions, too."

"I am?" My breath caught as his grip on my hips tightened.

"Yeah, you are." He lowered his head so that his mouth was near my ear "Want to know how I know that? You started to get hot from the moment I said fucking was my hobby." He lifted one hand and without breaking eye contact, he brushed his thumb over the tip of my breast, unerringly finding and grazing my nipple. "And these have been getting harder by the second."

Oh, sweet Jesus. The bolt of pleasure shot out from my breast and scattered, lighting up every nerve. I was struck speechless, which was a new thing for me.

"And I just want to thank you for wearing this top." Both hands were at my hips again. "I like it almost as much as I liked those shorts."

I placed my hands on his chest and slid them down the length of his stomach, the tips of my fingers following the hard planes of his abs. "Then I think you might like what I have on under these jeans."

A deep sound rumbled out from him as his hands slipped around to my lower back and then down, cupping my ass. "I cannot wait to find out."

"Then don't." I tugged on his shirt, and his answering chuckle was rough. Glancing up, I let go of his shirt. "This is only about tonight."

"Then we're on the same page, aren't we?" He stepped back and reached around to his back pocket. He pulled out his wallet, flipping it open. Out came a silver foil, and I had to laugh.

"A condom in a wallet?" I said. "So damn cliché."

"And so damn prepared," he replied with a wink. He tossed his wallet and the condom on the counter. Grabbing the hem of his shirt, he tugged it up and off. Muscles along his shoulders and upper arms flexed and rolled as he threw the shirt to where he laid his jacket.

Good God, all I could do was stare. Boy took care of himself. His chest was well defined and his waist was trim. His stomach was a work of art. His abs were tightly rolled but not overdone. He reminded me of a runner or swimmer, and I wanted to touch him.

"Your turn."

My breath shuttled out of me. I wasn't necessarily a self-conscious person, but my fingers trembled nonetheless as I wrapped them around the hem of the cami I wore. In a weird way I didn't understand, the fact we really didn't know each other made it easy to take the top off. Maybe it was because there were absolutely no expectations between us or because this was only about tonight.

Nick's gaze slowly left mine, and I stopped thinking in general. The taut set to his lips and jaw was like stepping too close to an open flame, but the heat and intensity in his gaze was what started the fire. The look was hungry, and it was a punch to the chest, stealing the air right out of my lungs.

Silently, he lifted one hand and cupped my breast. The gasp that came out of me sounded strangled. He ran his thumb over the hardened tip and then he caught it between his fingers. My back arched and a smug half smile graced his lips.

"You're beautiful," he said, voice gruff. "I bet the rest is just as fucking stunning."

Stripped Down
A Blacktop Cowboys® Novella
By Lorelei James

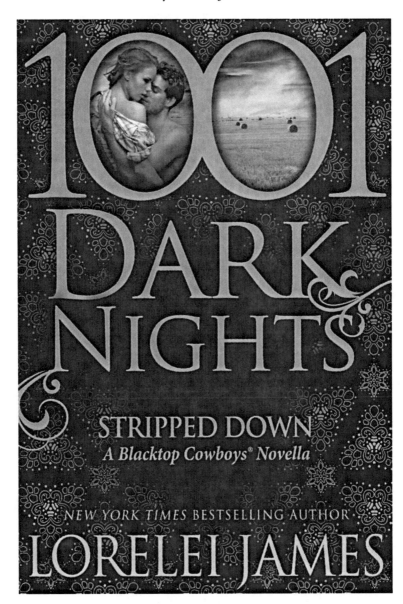

Acknowledgments from the Author

A 1001 thanks to the fabulous Liz Berry for all her love and patience with me—and for asking me to be a part of this amazing project.

And thanks to my readers who wanted to know more about Sutton Grant's brother Wynton, and London's pal, Mel. This love story is for you...

Chapter One

"Weddings make me horny."

Best man Wynton "Wyn" Grant turned to look at Melissa Lockhart, the curvy redheaded maid of honor. Today was the first time they'd met, so the comment threw him off—as had the other sexual remarks she'd made over the past two hours. Wyn wasn't sure if she was playing him...or if she wanted to play. He offered her a nonchalant, "Really?"

She smirked at him. "A strapping, handsome rancher such as yourself doesn't have anything to say to that besides...*Really?*"

Enough. He angled his head and put his mouth on the shell of her ear. "Gonna get yourself in trouble, you keep teasing me."

"You think I'm teasing?"

"Only one way to find out, ain't there?" He traced the rim of her ear with the tip of his tongue. "Words don't mean nothin' if you can't back it up with actions. And darlin' I *am* a man of action."

That caused a quick hitch in her breath.

He smiled and backed off.

After the last guests passed through the receiving line, Wyn's younger brother Sutton, aka the groom, snagged his attention. "The photographer wants a few shots of us alone, so can you—"

"Make sure the wedding party gets to the head table?" Wyn supplied. "No problem."

"Thanks."

Wyn's new sister-in-law, London, whispered something to Melissa.

Melissa leaned over, giving Wyn a peek of her magnificent tits. She attached the train to the back of London's wedding dress so it didn't drag on the ground. Then she straightened up and looked at Wyn.

He offered his arm. "The party waits."

She slipped her arm through his. "Such a gentleman."

Cres, Wyn's youngest brother, snorted. "Gentleman, my ass. He's been pullin' one over on you, Mel. My big brother is the biggest manwhore in three counties."

Little did his baby brother know that Wyn had been damn near a monk the past eight months, but he didn't bother to try and mask his playboy reputation. "Actually, I prefer the term man-slut," Wyn replied. "Manwhore implies that I take money for something I do very well. For free."

Melissa laughed. "You and I must be slutting around in different counties, Wynton Grant, because I don't have your name in my little black book of bad boys." She paused. "Yet."

They stared at one another with identical "bring it" challenges in their eyes.

And that's when he knew, without a doubt, his sexual dry spell was about to end.

"Oh for the love of God. You two have been eye-fucking each other all day. Just sneak into a horse stall and get it over with already," Stirling, London's sister, and the other bridesmaid, complained.

Cres's annoyed gaze flicked between the best man and the maid of honor. "Take Stirling's advice. And don't even think about givin' one another head beneath the head table. Tonight ain't about your uncontrollable urges." He paused. "Got it, Super Man-Slut and his new sidekick, Slut-Girl?"

Wyn struck a superhero pose and Melissa snickered.

After heaving a disgusted snort, Cres muttered to Stirling and they started the trek to the reception hall.

"I do believe I'm offended," Melissa drawled. "My sidekick name should've been *Amazing* Slut-Girl at the very least."

He laughed. "Come on, Melissa. Let's see what kinda dirty, dastardly deeds we can get away with."

"Deal. But call me Mel."

"Mel? Nope. Sorry. No can do."

"Why not?"

"Mel is the name of a line cook. Saying, 'Suck harder, Mel,' or 'Bend over, Mel,' brings totally different images to my mind than 'I'm gonna fuck you through the wall, Melissa.'"

"I see where you're coming from, cowboy." She paused outside the sliding wooden doors that led to the lodge. "But that just means I'll be calling you Wynton—even when you're not making me come so hard that I scream your name."

"Darlin', you can call me anything you like as long as I get to bang the hell outta you tonight."

"Oh, there will be banging. But I'm gonna make you work for it to see how bad you really want it." Her eyes danced with a devilish glint that tightened his balls.

"That ain't gonna scare me off." Wyn let his gaze move over her, taking in every feature. From her cinnamon-colored ringlet curls to the broad angles of her forehead and cheekbones. From her bee-stung lips to the pointed tip of her chin. Then down her neck, noting the smattering of freckles across her chest and the plump breasts. Moving down her torso, imagining softness and curves beneath the long, emerald green dress. He took his time on his visual return, mentally shoving her dress up to her hips, pinning her against the wall, feasting on her skin from neck to nipples as he drove into her over and over. Finally his eyes met hers. "I love a challenge."

Inside the lodge, it was obvious London's parents had gone all out for their oldest daughter's wedding. The ceremony itself had taken place in a meadow on the Gradsky's land. One of the few places—according to London—that wasn't a horse pasture. Even the weather, always iffy in October, had cooperated, filtering autumn sunshine across the meadow grasses, creating a dozen shades of gold against the backdrop of a clear, vivid blue sky. After the simple ceremony, the newlyweds had hopped into a horse-drawn carriage. The wedding guests were loaded onto flatbed trucks—a fancier, classier version of a hayride—and returned to the lodge for the receiving line and reception.

"Isn't this magical?" Melissa said with a sigh. "It fits London and Sutton so perfectly."

"That it does," he murmured. Strands of lights were hanging from the rough-hewn log rafters and twisted around the support poles. Centered on each table was a lantern bookended by mason jars filled with flowers in earth tones ranging from gold to russet. Shimmery white tablecloths were tied at the edges with coarse twine—a mix of elegant and rustic.

He glanced at the far corner of the enormous room and saw a band setting up behind a large dance floor. A makeshift bar had been erected in the opposite corner, coolers stacked on top of hay bales and bottles spread across a wooden plank. Long buffet tables stretched along the wall. Beneath those serving dishes was beef raised on the Grant family ranch. Wyn had checked out the slow-cooked prime rib prior to leaving for the ceremony. Between family, friends, and Sutton's rodeo buddies, as well as the Gradsky's big guest list, he suspected there wouldn't be many leftovers.

"Whatcha thinking about so hard?" Melissa asked.

"Food. I'm starved."

"Me too. I hope the photographer doesn't keep the newlyweds forever. At least being in the bridal party, we get to eat first."

Cres and Stirling were standing in front of the head table with guests crowding around them.

"Looks like our receiving line duties ain't quite over yet."

Wyn steered Melissa to the other side of Cres so any well-wishers would have to talk to them first—even after the bride and groom slipped in.

It turned out that these few stragglers had skipped the receiving line and were looking for a private word with the newlyweds. Wyn kept his smile in place as he repeatedly told the guests that the bride and groom were finishing up with pictures. He had no patience with people who didn't listen to the announcements or thought they were above the rules.

"I hear you growling between guests," Melissa whispered.

"I don't like the unspoken sense of entitlement. Every one of these people should've just waited in the damn receiving line like everyone else."

"Agreed. I'm glad Sutton and London aren't being bombarded with this. They deserve a little time alone, away from the maddening crowd."

Melissa's smile tightened when the last couple approached them.

Breck Christianson whistled. "Mel, you're lookin' fine. Damn girl. I thought maybe you'd turned into one of those binge and purge kinda chicks at the beginning of the rodeo season. Skinny as a wild dog. Then here you are. Back to all those plump curves."

Wyn didn't bother to bank his annoyance with this blowhard. He'd never liked Sutton's rodeo buddy and he liked him even less after that bout of verbal diarrhea. "I don't know if you're already drunk or what, but sayin' that bullshit to her ain't gonna fly with me."

Breck's eyes narrowed. "Who the hell are you to tell me what I can and can't say to an old friend?"

"I'm a man who won't put up with your disrespect because from what I hear, you do this all the time. So it ain't happening at my brother's wedding."

"Jesus, Mel, are you dating this guy?" Breck asked.

"Doesn't matter," Wyn said coolly. "What does matter is telling Melissa you're sorry for bein' a loudmouth."

"Or what?" Breck challenged. "You gonna pound on me, tractor jockey? I throw down steers bigger than you every damn day."

"Breck," Cres said sharply. "You're bein' a jackass. Knock it off and move on."

Breck leveled Cres with a dark look, but Cres didn't back down. Then Breck dropped his arm over his date's shoulder. The miniature-sized bleached blonde barely reached the center of Breck's chest.

Her sneering gaze rolled over Melissa and Wyn from head to toe. "They're not worth your time, Brecky."

Melissa held in her reply until the obnoxious couple drifted away. "How the mighty have fallen. It looks like *Brecky* had to buy a bargain basement escort to the wedding. The idiot has lost a lot of friends in the past year." She stood on tiptoe. "Thank you for calling him out on his lack of tact." She brushed her mouth over his ear, sending a shiver down the left side of his body. "But you didn't have to do that to impress me, because Wynton, I am a sure thing tonight."

Wyn nudged her chin with his shoulder, forcing her to look at him. "I did it because he was outta line. Had nothin' to do with how crazy I am to taste the freckles on the back of your neck as I'm driving into you from behind."

Desire turned her light-brown eyes almost black. "Gonna be hot as a brushfire between us, Super Man-Slut."

"For right now we'll have to settle for a slow burn, Amazing Slut-Girl. Shall we take our seats?"

* * * *

The bride and groom finally made an appearance half an hour later.

Evidently Sutton was starving because he pushed back speeches, reception games, and dancing until after everyone had eaten.

Then Wyn was so busy shoving food in his mouth and seeing to his best man duties that he didn't have a chance to talk to Melissa privately until over an hour later.

He grabbed a beer and sat beside her. "Hey. Did you get enough to eat?"

"Too much. The food was great." She propped her elbow on the table and rested her chin on her hand. "When you disappeared for so long I thought maybe there was an emergency that only Super Man-Slut could handle."

"And not invite my trusty new sidekick, the Amazing Slut-Girl? Not likely." He sipped his beer. "Why? Did you miss me?"

"Yes. We had a very...promising conversation going and then the Injustice League split us up."

He laughed. "I don't know what the hell Cres's problem was." Wyn and Melissa had taken the two chairs on the other side of the groom's seat at the head table. But Cres and Stirling insisted the setup was groomsmen next to the groom and bridesmaids sat on the bride's side. So it *had* seemed like they were purposely being separated. "Anyway, great toast."

"Yours was good too."

"Glad it's over. I ain't much on public speaking." He set his forearms on the table. "And while you were talkin', I noticed you have a hint of a drawl. Where are you from? Texas?"

"As if. I'm from the great state of Kentucky."

"That didn't sound real sincere."

"I used to be all *Rah! Rah! Go Wildcats!* But I grew up, moved away, and haven't been back to the Bluegrass State for more than the occasional weekend since I graduated from college."

"A Kentucky college girl. So what's your degree in?"

"American literature with an emphasis on twentieth century authors."

"Huh." Had she noticed his eyes glaze over? "So uh, what do you do with that degree?"

"Exactly."

Wyn blinked.

"I would've liked to teach—I still would—but earning a degree was secondary to why I attended UK."

"And why's that?"

"I went to school there to be part of their equestrian team. Train with the best, win a team collegiate championship, compete individually, and qualify for world finals with the end goal of competing in the Olympics." She sipped her drink. "Bored yet?"

"Are you kiddin'? Lord, woman, you're a Kentucky blueblood from a horse training dynasty or something, aren't you?"

"I was, now I'm not. Now I..." She shook her head as if to clear it. "This year, I've been teaching at Grade A Farms. Chuck and Berlin Gradsky have...shall we say, affluent clientele who prefer their children train in the English style rather than western."

"Well, Kentucky, I'll bet your horse cost more than my house."

"But you own your house. I never owned my horse. My parents' corporation did. And when I was competing I leased my horse from Gradskys."

"You're not competing anymore?" He didn't remember what her rodeo specialty was. Since she'd gotten the horse from Gradskys, he'd put money on her being a barrel racer.

"How did I end up blathering on? It's your turn." Melissa stared at him expectantly.

Wyn shifted in his seat, feeling uncomfortable with her for the first time since they'd met.

"Don't." She squeezed his knee beneath the table. "This is why I don't tell people about where I came from. I'd rather they see me as a rodeo road dog who gives it the almighty try year after year but never *quite* makes it to that top tier."

"That's intentional, isn't it? Not competing on the highest level?"

"I had enough of that. Now I drift from town to town and occasionally toss out a Sylvia Plath quote or a passage from William Faulkner to keep people guessing about me." She squeezed his knee again. "You were about to spill all of your secrets to me, Mr. Grant."

"That's one thing I don't have are secrets. I grew up a rancher's kid and never wanted to do anything else. When it became obvious that Sutton was better than average with his rodeo skills, I knew he wouldn't want to ranch full time, so I stepped up and learned everything I could. Figured it'd be up to me'n Cres to keep the ranch goin'. My folks did insist on shipping me off to vocational school for three years."

"What's your degree in?"

"Associate degrees in engine repair and veterinary science." He sipped his beer and smirked at her. "Granted, it's no Elizabethan poetry degree, but it's helpful around the ranch knowin' how to doctor up machines and animals."

"Elizabethan poetry? Nice shot, grease monkey."

He laughed. Damn he loved her sense of humor. "You had that comin', Kentucky."

Her eyes turned serious. "Why is this so easy with you?"

"Because we're both easy?" he offered. "It's easier knowin' how things are gonna end between us tonight."

"You two look awful cozy over here," a cooing female voice broke the moment.

Wyn looked up at Violet McGinnis. Then he leaned back and draped his arm across the back of Melissa's chair. "Hey, Violet." After spending one night in Violet's bed, she decided they were destined for each other. Not because the sex was off the charts explosive. Not because she was crazy about him and wanted to spend the rest of her days with him. Her sudden interest happened after she'd turned thirty and decided to settle down. He'd never been interested in that with her, or any other woman, and hadn't hidden that fact from anyone. But she hadn't taken the hint. Evidently it was time to broaden that hint.

"We are very cozy," Melissa said, pouring on a thick drawl. "In fact, we may not move from this spot all night, it's Super"—she caught herself and amended—"that me and my best man are hanging."

Violet crossed her arms over her chest. "I hope that's not true because Wyn promised me a dance."

"When did I promise you a dance?"

"It's a figure of speech, Wyn, meaning I want to dance with you."

"Ah. Well, I wouldn't want you turnin' down all the other fellas who're eager to squire you around the dance floor on the off chance I'll tear myself away from this lovely lady's side tonight. Because I doubt that's gonna happen."

Violet didn't know how to respond. She spun on her boot heel and stormed off.

"Recent conquest?" Melissa asked.

"Eight months ago or so."

"She lousy in bed?"

"Not that I recall."

"So why no repeat?"

Wyn watched Violet move to the back of the room. "That'd give her the false expectation there might be a three-peat. I'm not interested in settling down with her. Or anyone else."

"That's another thing we have in common. But there seems to be...a few haters, here, Super Man-Slut. So how many women in this place have you nailed and bailed?"

He scanned the tables. "Six?"

"You're not *sure* how many women have slicked up your pole, grease monkey?"

"Funny, Kentucky. You say that like you didn't admit, two short hours ago that you're equally as slutty as me."

"Fair point."

"Lots of people from the world of rodeo here. How many guys have you mounted and discounted, Amazing Slut-Girl?"

"Mounted and discounted." She snickered. "That's a new one. I might have to steal that." Melissa tried to discreetly crane her neck to scan the area. After several moments, she said, "Four. Five if I'm counting the same guy but two different times."

"Nope. Still only counts as four. But I *am* interested on what he did that earned him a second go."

"He was breathing."

Wyn choked on his beer. "What the hell?"

Melissa shrugged. "All right, it was more boinking from boredom. We ended up at the same after party. Other people started hooking up so we were like...you'll do. How close is your horse trailer?"

"Has he been eye-ballin' you?"

"Some. But I'm not interested in ballin' him, because that'd be a three-peat rule violation and like you, I don't raise false hopes." She cocked her head. "But I'd make an exception to that rule for you."

"You know what I like about you so far, Kentucky? You don't make excuses for bein' a highly sexual woman."

"And?"

"And you said you were gonna make me work for it. Since we're bein' open about everything else, explain how. Because I want a piece of you like you wouldn't believe." Wyn pushed to his feet. "I'll be right back."

Chapter Two

Mel, you are in deep with this man and you've known him less than half a day.

She watched Wynton Grant amble off. And she couldn't help but notice other women sizing up the rancher hottie too.

From the moment she'd set eyes on him she had that overwhelming punch of want—a feeling that happened to her so rarely lately. So seeing the identical look of lust sizzling in his eyes? The balls to the wall woman of action who'd been in hiding for the past six months had awakened with one thing on her mind.

Sex.

Lots of it.

Hot and dirty sex.

Fast sex.

Slow sex.

And it turned out the very sexy best man was more than happy to oblige.

This was turning out to be the best wedding ever.

The object of her lust stopped to speak to an older woman, giving Mel ample opportunity to study him. The man had it going on. His shoulders were so broad that he blocked the view of the woman entirely. Pity he hadn't taken off his western cut suit coat so she could check out his ass; she'd bet his buns were grade A prime beef too. Not only did he have a big physical presence, he carried himself with confidence. He had an easy smile—which was a sexy-as-his wicked grin. From the back she noticed his dark hair brushed his collar and held more than a little curl. The groom and groomsmen had removed their cowboy hats as soon as the wedding pictures were done. As much as she appreciated a man in a hat, Wynton looked better without it.

Hands landed on the back of Mel's chair and a soft rustle of fabric tickled her neck.

"Staring at him that intently won't make his clothes disappear," London murmured in her ear.

"That obvious?"

"Yes. But if it helps, my brother-in-law is staring back at you the same way."

"Then maybe I'll get lucky on your wedding night too, Mrs. Grant."

London plopped down in Wynton's chair. Her wedding dress was a stunning mix of ivory satin and chiffon. Intricate beadwork of rhinestones and pearls stretched across the bodice of the off-the-shoulder dress. Folds of satin were ruched below her breasts and then floaty, filmy panels of chiffon fell in a column to the floor. It was simple and elegant—exactly like London herself.

"So you'll get a kick out of this, but you cannot tell anyone." London leaned in close enough that a long tendril of her hair touched Mel's cheek. "Earlier, when Sutton said the photographer wanted pictures of just us? Total lie. My husband insisted we have some alone time. And by alone time I mean us in the ready room, with my wedding dress pushed up to my hips, Sutton's tux pants around his ankles as he proved how much he loved me by immediately consummating our marriage."

Mel grinned. "Sounds like him."

"He said he didn't want to wait hours to finally claim what was legally his forever."

"If I didn't love you so much I'd hate you. That's so freakin' romantic."

"I know. I'm so lucky. I am such a sucker for that man. He keeps trying to get me…" She sighed. "Look, I need you to do me a favor."

"Anything."

London tucked a key into Mel's cleavage. "Keep this away from me. And definitely keep it away from Sutton."

"What is it?"

"The key to the ready room where we already rocked the countertop. I have to tell him that I lost it because if he had his way we'd be in there right now. I understand this is a celebration for everyone else, so I can share him for a few more hours. But I promise we ain't gonna be here all night."

"Everyone will expect you to take off."

"Speaking of expectations…You've been such a huge help to me throughout the wedding planning. Mom and I couldn't have done it without you."

Mel teared up. "My pleasure. But if you would've turned into Bridezilla at any point, I would've bitch-slapped you."

"And that's why I love you." London hugged her. "But don't think for one second that I'm not aware there's been some serious shit going on with you the last six months. You can talk to me about anything. So I'm telling you that you *will* be spilling your guts to me as soon as I return from my honeymoon, got it?"

"Yes, bossy-pants."

"That's *Mrs.* Bossy-pants to you." London whispered, "Thank you for being my maid of honor, Mel. Thank you especially for being the sister of my heart."

The tears she tried to hold back fell freely. "Same goes."

"You have your own special chair, my darlin' sister-in-law, so get outta mine," Wynton said behind them, "and quit hoggin' my wedding partner."

"I'm goin', I'm goin'."

After he sat, he noticed Mel's damp cheeks and he looked at London sharply. "You made her cry?"

"They're happy tears, I promise," Mel said with a sniffle.

"So you weren't here warning her off me?" Wynton asked London.

"I should, because you're a serious pain in my ass. But I kinda like you, Wyn, so I'll take the high road and not fill her in on your many conquests." London winked. "His little black book rivals yours, Mel. So I'm thinking you two might be a match made in heaven."

He laughed after London flounced off. "Love that girl."

"Me too."

A voice boomed over the loudspeaker. "Let's kick off the festivities with the bride and groom's first dance as a married couple. Sutton and London, take the floor please."

Wynton scooted his chair closer. "Will you cry when you hear the song he chose?"

"Maybe. This part and the father/daughter dance always make me cry." Her eyes narrowed. "Wait. What do you mean the song *he* chose?"

"Sutton asked London if she trusted him to pick a first dance song and surprise her."

"So you know what it is?"

He nodded. "And trust me, Kentucky. You're gonna need more tissues."

Turned out, he was right.

* * * *

Ten minutes later, when she and Wynton were on the dance floor with Cres and Stirling, the newlyweds, and both sets of parents, Mel still had a lump in her throat thinking about the song Sutton had picked. Billy Joel's "She's Got A Way."

"You all right?" Wynton murmured.

"No. I'm just so happy that London found the perfect man for her. Sutton...gets her. I never would've pegged him as the romantic type."

"Yeah. Me neither. He told me she makes him a better man. I guess that's something to aim for in a relationship." Wynton smiled against her cheek. "I'm happy for him too." He paused. "Maybe a little jealous."

"Jealous? You? Mr. I'm-not-settling-down?"

"From a strictly competitive point of view," he explained. "I'm the oldest. I should've gotten married first."

Mel tilted her head back and stared into his eyes. "I call bullshit on that. Nut up and admit you want that." She pointed at the happy couple.

"Fine. I want that. Someday. How about you?"

"Of course I want it. When I'm lucky enough to find the one."

The DJ called for all the guests to join the wedding party on the dance floor. And although people crowded around them, it seemed as if they were the only ones in the room.

"What makes a man 'the one' Melissa?"

The husky way he rasped her name sent a slow curl of heat through her. "Not wanting anyone else. Everything you do, everything you are with that one person is enough."

"I never thought of it that way."

"It's logical. The literature degree allows me to break anything down to its most basic component. Even love."

"No, baby, that romantic notion of 'one true love' is all you, and logic won't play into it at all when you find him."

And...she melted. "I really want you to kiss me right now."

"I really want to take that pretty mouth you're offering, but not here." He brushed his lips across her ear. "Dance with me. Let's both of us take the time to enjoy the journey for a change. Since it sounds like we both jump to the good part first."

Mel was beginning to believe being in Wynton's arms *was* the good part.

The tempo changed to a fast tune and he eased them into a two-step. They danced four songs together. When it came time for the father/daughter dance, he draped his arm over her shoulder and wordlessly pulled a tissue out of his pocket when she started to sniffle.

He excused himself to dance with his mother, and Cres whisked her back onto the dance floor when he saw Breck approaching her. After that, Mel danced with London's dad, London's brother, Macon, the wild bulldogger Saxton Green, and Sutton's boss.

By the time she returned to the head table for a drink, she realized the dizzy feeling wasn't just from dancing and she needed a quick snack to keep her blood sugar in check. She cut to the bar and downed a glass of orange juice. She turned around and Wynton was right there.

"I saw you slam that."

"I was thirsty."

"So it appears." He drained the contents of his lowball glass and set it on the tray. "I like dancing with you, Kentucky. Come on." He clasped her hand in his and led her to the dance floor.

She nestled her face against his chest and murmured, "I like dancing with you too, cowboy."

At the start of the second slow song, Wynton said, "Most dangerous place you've had sex, Amazing Slut-Girl."

If it was anyone else, she'd be surprised by the question. "Against the pen that housed the bulls after a rodeo. I kept waiting to get rammed in the back by a horn. It didn't last long, if I recall. How about you, Super Man-Slut?"

"In my high school girlfriend's parent's bed. We'd just finished when we heard the front door open. We had no choice but to dive into the closet. But her parents were in the mood and they ended up goin' at it on the floor—on the other side of the bed so we didn't get a floor show, thank God. But my girlfriend was horrified. She was even more horrified when her dad said if he caught us doin' it, he'd cut off my cock and send her to a convent. We broke up the next day."

Mel laughed. "The one time I remember getting caught I almost bit off the guy's dick. He assured me that he and his girlfriend had called it quits. I'm in his camper, giving him a blowjob, and the 'ex' girlfriend walks through the door—turned out they weren't broken up. She's pissed, I'm pissed, the dude is about to piss himself, so of course he suggests he's willing to share himself and maybe we both oughta blow him at the same time and then do each other."

"While he watched."

"Of course."

"Jesus. Some men are idiots. What happened?"

"I apologized to her and she broke up with him on the spot. We went to the bar, ended up doing blowjob shots all night and became fast friends."

"I call bullshit on that." Wynton tipped her head back and gazed into her eyes. "Aw, hell. That's how you met London, isn't it?"

She smirked. "I'll never tell."

"So have you been in a threesome?"

"Yes. More than one. You?"

Wynton smirked back. "Yes. More than one."

"Well, shoot. We *are* evenly matched in slutting around." Mel decided it was time to kick up the competition. "Ever fucked a famous person?"

"Define famous."

"If you said the name I'd know it."

He shook his head. "How about you?"

"Yes, I have. But I will qualify that by saying he wasn't famous when we fucked, and it lasted like thirty seconds."

"Who was it?"

"Sorry, cowboy, I don't kiss and tell details. But I have no problem giving a general overview of my sexual exploits."

"Same. But to be honest, I don't have anyone in my life who wants to hear about the kinky things I did. So I've stored up all my happy endings—"

"In an impressive spank bank?"

A beat passed, then Wynton threw back his head and laughed.

That single, spontaneous expression of joy moved her. Given their raunchy subject matter, she expected he'd toss out a few lewd vibrator references, but his laugh seemed a more genuine response than trying to one-up her.

"What's so damn funny over here?" Sutton asked.

Mel and Wynton had been so deep in conversation they hadn't noticed the bride and groom dancing right next to them. With very curious expressions on their faces.

"We're just swapping bad sex stories," Wynton said without hesitation. "Why? Did you need us to do something official?"

"Shots of tequila!" London said, pumping her arm in the air.

Sutton grabbed her arm and returned it to his neck. "Behave, wifey-mine, or I'll have to take you over my knee."

"Were you two talking about bondage games?" London asked. "Because while I appreciate my husband's rope expertise, I think turnabout is fair play, don't you? Shouldn't I get to tie him up sometimes?"

The groom blushed and whispered in London's ear. Whatever he said made her eyes glaze over and put a cat-like curl on her lips.

Mel glanced up at Wynton, expecting to see amusement in his eyes, but the longing she saw made her ache. He wanted that same connection his brother had more than he wanted to admit.

Don't you too?

"We came over to remind you that the bouquet toss and garter removal is happening soon," Sutton said. "We'll stick around for maybe an hour and then we're takin' off."

"We're at your command," Wynton deadpanned. "But there's something I've got to do first." He kept ahold of Mel's hand as they exited the dance floor.

She had no idea what was going on. When it appeared they were headed to the bar, she started crafting excuses on why she couldn't do shots with him. But Wynton strolled right past the bar and out a rear exit.

It had gotten chilly since the sun had set. Mel shivered, wishing she'd grabbed her wrap.

Then she found herself absolutely burning up, pressed against the side of the building by two-hundred pounds of hot cowboy. Good Lord. The heat in Wynton's eyes nearly set her skin on fire.

There was no speech about how much he wanted to kiss her. He just did it. Lowered his head and planted his mouth on hers.

He didn't have to prove he was a passionate man by thrusting his tongue past her lips and into her throat. He proved it with tender nibbles and teasing licks. A gentle pass of his mouth. Again and again. As if he had all the time in the world.

Each time Mel parted her lips ever so slightly, breathing him in, she felt his tongue softly licking into her mouth. So when he finally kicked up the heat into a full-blown soul kiss, it seemed as if they'd been kissing for hours.

Wynton wrapped one hand around the back of her neck; his thumb stroked the bone at the base of her skull, sending tingles down her spine. He'd stretched his other arm across her back and clamped onto her right butt cheek. The hard wall of his chest pressed against hers, leaving no place to put her hands except to grip his biceps.

She was just glad she had something solid to hold on to because the way he kissed her left her breathless, boneless, and mindless.

And wet.

His mouth left hers to drag kisses down the column of her

throat. "If we weren't needed inside in like a minute, I'd already be inside you." He stopped and breathed heavily against her skin. "Goddammit, Melissa. What you do to me. Kissing you is ten times better than fucking most women. I don't think my brain can process how fantastic the real deal will be."

"Listen to you sweet talk me."

Wynton lifted his head. "Meet me back here in ten minutes."

Mel forced her arms to work and slid her hands across his shoulders. "I have a better idea. There's a private room for the bride to get ready around the back of the lodge." She brought his mouth down to hers for a teasing kiss. "I just happen to have a key. And a condom."

His smile lit up his whole face. "Is it too soon to say I think I love you?"

She laughed. "Save that for after I blow your...mind, cowboy."

The DJ invited all the single ladies to the dance floor for the bouquet toss.

"That's our cue."

Right before they walked into the lodge, Wynton murmured, "These next ten minutes might actually kill me, Kentucky."

"Don't worry. I know CPR. I'd revive you."

Chapter Three

Wyn watched London toss the bouquet. He thought it was telling—and maybe a little sad—that Melissa didn't even try to catch it.

Then he stood in a circle with the other guests as Sutton removed London's garter. He thought it was telling—and an indication of how smitten his younger brother was—that he refused to toss the garter and kept it for himself.

The events dragged out much longer than he'd expected and his gaze was continually drawn to Melissa. He couldn't wait to have his mouth on her skin. He couldn't wait to have those wild curls crushed in his hands. He couldn't wait to hear the noises she made as he touched her. When Cres elbowed him and muttered, "Dude. Quit eye-fucking her," Wyn actually blushed.

So what if he felt like a teenage boy locking eyes with his crush; his heart raced, sweat prickled on the back of his neck, and his dick started to harden. Melissa appeared to be in the same lustful state. Her cheeks were flushed and she alternately bit and licked her lips. The best part was when her eyes kept darting to the door.

He couldn't remember the last time he felt this level of anticipation. Maybe...never. It wasn't bragging that he didn't have to work too hard to find a hookup. Not because he was a smooth-talking Casanova. He just liked women, he liked sex, and he didn't pretend he wanted anything more than a good time.

So why haven't you gotten laid in months?

If his smartass brothers knew how long this dry spell had lasted, they'd claim it was because he'd bedded every available single woman in the area. The truth was, he'd gotten more selective after he'd watched his brother fall in love.

Finally, the newlyweds were ready to leave the reception. Cres pulled Sutton's truck up to the entrance. Earlier, they'd decorated it with dozens of tin cans and beer cans tied to the tailgate and dragging on the ground. They'd written "Just Married" along both sides in huge white letters. They'd filled the inside with rolls of toilet paper and paper streamers. Cres had even tracked down an old pamphlet "What To Expect On Your Wedding Night" and taped it to the steering wheel. But Wyn's favorite part was the two-dozen rainbow-colored condom packages he'd affixed to the hood in the shape of a bow.

As soon as the happy couple pulled away, Melissa was beside him. "Did you save any of those fun-colored condoms?"

He faced her and smiled. "Nope. I had to special order them. Hard to find a place that carries extra small rubbers."

She laughed. "You didn't."

"I did. He'd do the same damn thing to me."

They stared at each other. Moved toward each other.

He dropped his gaze to her lips. "You have the sexiest mouth I've ever seen."

"It's yours. However you want it." Her soft fingers circled his wrist. "We're doing this now?"

"Unless you've changed your mind?"

Melissa brought his hand to her mouth and sucked on his pinkie. "Does that *seem* like I've changed my mind?"

"Christ. Give me the key to the room."

She took two steps backward and an evil smile curled her lips. "Now…Where *did* I put that key? It's on me someplace. Guess you'll have to pat me down or feel me up to find it." She disappeared around the corner.

Wyn followed half a step behind her and he was on her, pushing her up against the door as his mouth crashed down on hers, kissing her with hunger and desperation that seemed totally foreign to him. His hands landed on her hips and he flattened his palms over her abdomen, traveling up her ribcage. Then he cupped her tits, sliding his fingers across the top of the dress and pulling the material away from her skin so he could reach into her cleavage.

Score. The pad of his finger brushed a metal ring.

Rather than scooping it out that way, he broke the kiss to bury his face between her breasts. Licking those full swells of flesh, inhaling the scent of her skin, snagging the key ring with his teeth and pulling it out.

"My, what a talented tongue you have, Super Man-Slut," she said breathlessly.

He grinned and the key dropped into his hand. Snaking his left arm around her waist, he yanked her against his body and jammed the key in the lock. The door popped open.

Once they were inside, he gave the place a cursory look. A single lamp lit the entire room. Three folding chairs were spread out in a semicircle, a low countertop and mirror took up one wall, and a loveseat had been shoved in the corner. Good enough.

He slammed the door and pressed her against it, fusing his mouth to hers again.

She tasted sweet. Like juice and wedding cake. He kissed her until he felt drunk just from the pleasure of it. His hands roved over as much of her as possible, but he needed more.

Wyn ran his hand up her spine until he found the zipper tab at the top of her dress and eased it down to the small of her back.

Melissa broke the kiss on a gasp. "Thank heaven. Now I can breathe."

"Pull the fabric down to your waist," he murmured against her throat.

Hooking her fingers into the side panels, she shimmied it down, baring her tits completely. "The bra is built in—"

Whatever she'd been about to say was lost in a soft moan as he dragged his fingertips over the upper curve of her breast. He locked his gaze to hers. "You want pretty words? Or you want my mouth sucking you here"—he swept his thumb across her nipple—"until I get your pussy wet enough to fuck?"

"That. Yes. Please."

Wyn palmed and caressed her while he feasted on her nipples.

When her squirming forced him to release that rigid tip before he was ready, he said, "Hands above your head, gripping the top of the door frame."

She complied with barely a whimper of protest.

His dick was so damn hard it hurt. He didn't have to drag this out, but that's partially why he wanted to; she wouldn't expect it.

So he sucked and bit and licked her tits, even gifting her with a suck mark on the fleshy outer edge that nearly sent her through the roof.

His mouth drifted back up to her ear. "Do I fuck you sitting down or standing up? Choose."

"Standing up."

Wyn pulled a condom out of his pocket, holding it to her mouth with a husky, "Hang on to this for a sec."

How fucking sexy was it to see her teeth sinking into the plastic. He undid his suit pants, shoving them and his boxer briefs to his knees. He took the condom from her mouth with his own. Then he ripped the package with his teeth and reached down to roll it on.

That's when he noticed Melissa's hands were still above the door. Her chest was heaving. Her eyes...Christ her eyes were heavy-lidded and expectant.

The satiny fabric of her dress brushed against his bare thighs as he lifted the material up and tucked it behind her. He inched his fingers down until the tips connected with the waistband of her panties. "Hold still." As he pulled the panties down her trembling thighs, he crouched slightly, needing to know her scent before he fucked her. Wyn ducked his head and placed an openmouthed kiss on the curve of her mound. "A natural redhead," he murmured against that fragrant flesh.

Once her panties were off, he pressed his body to hers again. He grabbed behind her left thigh and lifted it up to wrap around his hip. Wyn planted his mouth on hers as he aligned his cock to her wet center. He pushed in slowly the first couple of inches and then snapped his hips, filling her in one fast thrust.

Melissa's moan vibrated in his mouth. She rolled her hips forward in a signal for him to move.

Keeping one hand around her thigh, he slid his other hand up her arm, pulling it away from the wall and setting it on his shoulder. He flattened his palm above her head on the door to brace himself as he started to fuck her.

The slow, steady pace didn't last long, even when he wanted to savor every glide of his cock into her tight, wet heat. But as the sensations built, he sped up.

The kiss had become frantic—thrusting tongues and hot, fast breath exchanged in openmouthed kisses.

When he kicked up the pace again, Melissa let her head fall back, leaving her neck wide open.

He nipped and nuzzled. Used his teeth. Lost his mind whenever she released a throaty sigh when his tongue connected with a hot spot. His cock rammed into her faster and harder, but he kept his mouth gentle. If he didn't consciously think about it, he feared he'd turn into an animal, leaving bite marks and broken flesh in his wake.

"Wynton."

"So fucking perfect, how you feel around me."

"I'm close," she panted.

"Tell me what'll get you there."

"Move side to side. Yes. Like that." She groaned. "Don't stop."

His grip tightened on her thigh. "Your pussy's squeezing me like a fucking vise. Take it baby, it's right. There."

That did it. She began to come immediately, her body bucking and grinding against his. The sexiest noises he'd ever heard echoed around him, taunting him to join her. But he gritted his teeth and waited until the last pulse pulled at his cock and she slumped against the wall.

Wyn couldn't hold off. Six hard strokes later, he buried his face in the curve of her neck, his hips pumping as his cock erupted.

Her lips in his hair roused him. He raised his head and feathered his mouth over hers. "That was... Hell, I'm pretty sure we *are* super fucking heroes."

She smiled.

"I don't want that to be it for tonight, Melissa."

Her eyes clouded.

"What?"

"Let's see how the rest of the night plays out."

"Got someone else lined up?" *I'll beat the fuck out of them if you do. Because no one is getting a taste of you. No way. No how.*

"No, and way to ask me that when your cock is still buried inside me. I promised London I'd keep an eye on the reception. Make sure people were still having fun. As soon as this ends, I'm all yours."

Wyn relaxed and slipped out of her. He lowered her leg to the floor and took his time kissing her before he forced himself to take a step back—mentally and literally—to get dressed and remind himself he had best man duties to fulfill too.

After they exited the room, Wyn slung his arm over her shoulder. "I could use a drink. How about you?"

"I have to drop off the key so we're not tempted to misuse the ready room again." She gave him a smug smile. "And then I'll meet you inside on the dance floor."

* * * *

Wyn had knocked back a couple of celebratory shots with Cres and Sutton's coworkers, when Melissa appeared a half hour after they'd parted ways.

"Is everything all right?"

"I had a few things to do that I'd forgotten about. Why?"

"I would've tracked you down if you'd tried to turn this into a fuck and run encounter."

She hip-checked him. "You rocked my world, Wynton Grant. I'm ready for more."

A Pitbull song started and she grabbed his hand. "You didn't think they'd play only country music tonight?"

"I could hope."

* * * *

Two songs later, Wyn and Melissa were leaving the dance floor when he saw his dad stumble back. Then he clutched the left side of his body and hit the floor. Wyn's mother, always the picture of calm, screamed and froze in place.

Wyn raced across the dance floor. That last shot of tequila

threatened to come back up when he noticed the ashen tone his father's face had taken. And the fear in his dad's eyes sent Wyn's alarm bells ringing louder.

"Dad? Can you hear me?"

He nodded.

"Stay still. We'll get you some help."

By that time Cres was next to him, as well as Mick, one of the guys Sutton worked with at the gun range.

Mick said, "I have medical training. Let's focus on slow and steady breathing until the ambulance arrives."

Jim Grant nodded.

Then Mick glanced at Cres. "Can you deal with your mother please?"

"Of course."

"Stay with me, Jim," Mick said soothingly.

Wyn listened while Mick asked basic questions that didn't require more than a nod or a head shake. He vaguely heard Melissa advising guests to return to their tables because everything was under control.

It seemed like an hour passed before the EMTs arrived. Wyn pushed to his feet and looked around while medical personnel assessed his father. He sidestepped them and moved to stand beside his mother and Cres.

"What's going on?" his mother demanded. "Is it a stroke? A heart attack?"

"I don't know. They'll get him stabilized enough to hand him off to the docs in the emergency room."

"How far is the hospital from here?"

London's mother, Berlin, stepped into the circle. "About twenty minutes. The staff is top notch. But if the issue is out of their level of expertise, they'll Life Flight him to Denver." She slipped her arm around his mom's shoulder. "Take a deep breath, Sue. We don't need you passing out too."

The EMT interrupted. "Is anyone riding in the ambulance with him?"

"I am," Wyn said and took his mother's hand. "Cres and I have both been drinking so we can't drive to the hospital. You haven't. So I'll need you to drive Cres so we have a vehicle there, okay?"

She blew out a breath. "Okay." Then she turned to Berlin. "Could you—"

"Chuck and I will handle everything here as far as explaining to the guests. No worries."

"Thank you."

Wyn walked alongside the rolling stretcher, his entire focus on his father. Although he had been drinking, the instant they closed the ambulance doors, he was stone-cold sober.

* * * *

As soon as they were through the emergency room doors, the medical team whisked his father off, leaving Wyn to wait for the rest of his family to arrive. He couldn't fill out anything regarding his dad's medical history. That helpless feeling he'd experienced riding in the ambulance expanded. He'd watched in near shock as his dad had become completely unresponsive. His skin had turned the same gray color as his hair. And beneath the oxygen mask he wore, Wyn thought his lips looked blue.

He paced in the waiting room for a good thirty minutes before other family members arrived.

His mother seemed calmer. The staff immediately took her back beyond the swinging doors, leaving him and Cres alone.

"How is he?" Cres asked.

"He was unconscious the entire way here."

"They give you any indication of what might've happened?"

"I overheard heart attack when the EMT was on the police scanner."

Cres removed his suit jacket, then his bolo tie. He unbuttoned the top two buttons on his white dress shirt and rolled up the sleeves.

"How was Mom?" Wyn asked.

"Doin' that freaky-quiet Mom thing. I suspect Dad's siblings will show up within the next hour. They caught me on the way out and asked which hospital. I explained we were lucky there was even one this far out. They just don't get it."

Wyn sighed. His dad's family hadn't understood why he'd left California and used his inheritance to buy a cattle ranch in rural

Colorado. And the times the Grant family had visited their relatives in Santa Ana, they didn't understand why anyone would choose to live among so many people. But despite their differences, they remained close.

Several long minutes of silence passed between Wyn and his brother, which wasn't unusual since they worked together and didn't yammer on from sunup to sundown. When Wyn glanced at the clock he was surprised to see thirty minutes had gone by.

The emergency doors opened and a whole mass of people walked in. His uncle Bill and his wife Barbie, his aunt Marie and her husband Roger. Cousin April and her husband Craig. Plus Ramsey, Sutton's boss from the gun range, Mick, and Melissa.

Uncle Bill approached first. "Any word?"

"No. They let Mom go back there as soon as she got here."

"That's good," Uncle Bill said, absentmindedly patting Wyn's shoulder.

"It was great of all of you to come, but you don't have to stick around. Cres and I can call you with updates."

"Nonsense. You boys don't need to deal with all of this yourselves. We're here. Besides, the forty years I spent as a nurse will come in handy," Aunt Marie said.

"She has a point, Wyn," Cres said.

"It'll likely be another hour at least before you know anything, so maybe we could all do with a cup of coffee to keep us alert." She signaled to her husband, daughter, and son-in-law to accompany her to the beverage station.

Ramsey moved in. "I'm assuming you haven't called the groom on his wedding night and let him know what's up?"

Wyn shook his head. "No sense in disturbing him when we don't know a damn thing about what's goin' on."

"We're heading back to the hotel. So if anything changes and you need someone to wake up the bride and groom, just call me and I'll knock on their door."

They exchanged numbers.

As Ramsey and his head instructor walked away, Wyn caught Cres looking at Mick with regret. He leaned over and murmured, "So much for your post-wedding hookup tonight, huh?"

"Fuck off."

"Is that the kind of guy you go for?" Wyn asked. Since Cres had come out to his family, they'd avoided talking about their sexual conquests. But when Wyn thought back, any talk of hookups had always come from him, not his brother.

So it shocked the hell out of him when Cres said, "The dude's a cowboy. A hot cowboy. A hot military cowboy. He knows his way around guns and he knows how to ride."

"Point taken. I'd probably wanna tap that if I swung that way."

"Christ. I cannot *believe* we're havin' this conversation." Cres snorted. "Speaking of hookups..."

Melissa wandered over. And Wyn didn't pretend he wasn't checking her out. Her dress wasn't excessively wrinkled from their smokin' hot encounter. He smirked, knowing she had a suck mark on the inside of her right breast. His gaze moved up to her lips. Oh, hell yeah. Her mouth was smooth and plump from the insane amount of time they'd spent kissing. When his eyes connected with hers, that spark of desire remained.

"How are you doing?"

"As well as can be expected without knowing anything," Wyn said. "I'm surprised to see you here." Shit. That'd come out wrong. "I mean—"

"I know what you meant, Wynton. I had your family members follow me here since I've been to this hospital a number of times."

"You were okay to drive?" Cres asked. "I swear I saw you knocking them back too."

Melissa shook her head. "Sleight of hand. I avoid things that put my judgment into question. Alcohol certainly does that."

"Amen, sister." Cres stood and stepped right in front of him. "I need caffeine. You want a cup of coffee, *Wynton?*"

Since Melissa couldn't see him, Wyn mouthed "fuck off" at the snarky way Cres enunciated his full name. "I'm fine."

"Suit yourself." Cres lumbered off.

Melissa plopped down beside him. "Did I interrupt something?"

"Nah. We're both a little punchy."

"I imagine."

He braced his forearms on his thighs. "So you weren't drinking tonight? Or you don't drink ever?"

"I did the champagne toast, but that's it. I drank sparkling water with lime or juice the rest of the night. I've learned if you don't want people to catch on to the fact you're not drinking, then don't talk about it and no one notices."

"But London said you guys were gonna do tequila shots."

"*London* did a tequila shot. I reminded her that me and tequila were on a permanent break."

Wyn smiled. "Gotcha." His smile dried. "I want you to know I was sober when we locked ourselves in that ready room."

"I know or I wouldn't have gone with you."

He reached out and brushed a few stray hairs from her cheek. "You are so freakin' sexy. I'd planned on takin' you back to my hotel room tonight—"

The doors to the back of the hospital opened.

His grim-faced mother was followed out by a man wearing a white coat and a stethoscope.

Wyn's stomach churned. He rose to his feet and Cres was instantly beside him. "Mom? What's goin' on?"

"Dr. Poole will explain."

"Bluntly put," Dr. Poole started, "Mr. Grant suffered a heart attack. To what extent the damage is, we're not sure yet. I've ordered blood tests that measure levels of cardiac enzymes, which indicate heart muscle damage."

"Whoa. You can tell that with a blood test?" Cres asked skeptically.

"Yes. The enzymes normally found inside the cells of the heart are needed for that specific organ. When the heart muscle cells are injured, their contents—including those enzymes—are released into the bloodstream, making it a testable entity."

"Thanks for the explanation," Wyn said. "What else?"

"After discussing the symptoms with Mrs. Grant, I suspect Mr. Grant's heart attack started before he hit the dance floor. We know the heart attack was still ongoing when they brought him in here. We immediately medicated him."

"But?"

"But the medicines aren't working so he's been sent to the cardiac cath lab."

All this medical terminology was making his head hurt. "What's that?"

"A cardiac catheter can be used to directly visualize the blocked artery and help us determine which procedure is needed to treat the blockage."

"You're telling us this because you've made the determination there is a significant blockage?" Wyn asked.

Dr. Poole nodded. "Once Mr. Grant has been stabilized, we'll send him to Denver, via ambulance."

"Not medevac'ing him now?

"No."

"That means...it's not that serious?" Cres asked.

"Oh, it's serious. But given that he was brought here immediately, if we observe him overnight, we'll have a full assessment to give the cardiac team in Denver tomorrow, which will save time."

"But by keeping him here and not sending him to a cardiac hospital, you're not takin' unnecessary chances with his life? 'Cause I ain't down with that at all, doc."

"Wynton," his mother softly chastised.

"I'm with Wyn on this, Mom," Cres inserted. "If Dad needs to be in Denver, fire up the helicopter and get him there. Pronto."

"I understand your concerns," Dr. Poole said. "And you have every right to question my recommendation. But I spent a decade in the cardiac unit in Salt Lake City, so I am more qualified than your average country doc."

That gave Wyn a tiny measure of relief. "Okay."

"Any other questions?"

"Can we see him?" Cres asked.

"Not right now. We'll see how the night progresses. It's up to your mother whether she stays back there with him or out here with you all."

Sue Grant lifted her chin. "My husband has suffered a major health trauma. Of course I'm staying with him." She stepped forward and offered Wyn and Cres each a hug. "As soon as I have any news, I promise I'll be out here to tell you."

Then she and Dr. Poole walked back through the swinging doors.

Wyn turned around and searched for Aunt Marie. "Did you

catch all of that?"

"Yes. From the sounds of it, Jim will be out for the rest of the night. And since there's no reason for us all to be exhausted tomorrow, we'll head back to the hotel. But I promise we'll be back first thing in the morning." Her gaze winged between Wyn and Cres. "I don't suppose I can convince either of you to return to the hotel and get some rest?"

They both said "no" at the same time.

"That's what I thought." She, too, gave them both a hug. "Any change, you call me." She pulled a deck of cards out of her purse. "To pass the time."

Wyn kissed her cheek. "Thank you. You sure you're okay to drive?"

"Sober as a judge, my boy." Her brown eyes narrowed. "Last question. What about Sutton?"

"What about him?"

"He deserves to know his father is in the hospital."

"He deserves a wedding night with his wife," Wyn retorted.

"So you're suggesting we don't tell him that Dad is in the ER and headed for Denver tomorrow, possibly for surgery?" Cres demanded.

"That's exactly what I'm sayin'."

"But—"

"End of discussion, Cres."

Arguments started—and all seemed to be directed at him. So Wyn tuned them out and wandered over to the window.

He'd glared at the juniper bushes lining the sidewalk for several minutes when he felt a soft touch on his arm. He saw Melissa's reflection in the window. "What?"

"You have to tell Sutton about your dad being in the hospital, Wynton. It's his decision whether he leaves on his honeymoon tomorrow or stays here, not yours. By not telling him, you're making it *your* decision. That's not fair to him, to you, or to your father. If something unforeseen happens, and Sutton returns home to the worst news imaginable...he'll blame you for a multitude of things—starting with him not getting to say good-bye. That's too deep a burden for you to undertake."

"Do you have any idea how much this honeymoon means to

my brother?" For months, Sutton had planned the four-week getaway in the tropics. Wasn't out of sight, out of mind better in this instance? Would Sutton even be able to relax and enjoy this special time with London if he was constantly calling home to check on Dad?

"I'd venture a guess...it doesn't mean as much to him as your father does."

"Jesus, Melissa."

"You need someone to be the bad guy and you don't want it to be you. But by letting Sutton know what happened and giving him the choice of what to do next, you are doing the right thing."

"It doesn't feel that way."

"I know." She swept her hand across his shoulders. "But trust me because I speak from personal experience, not telling Sutton is worse."

Wyn turned and looked at her. "This happened to you?"

"My sister had an accident while I was at camp. And instead of bringing me home, my parents let me finish out the full two weeks. We weren't allowed to have cell phones, so I didn't have a clue she almost died until after my dad picked me up. And naturally, my sister thought I wasn't there because my training camp was more important than her. It was ugly."

Before he could ask what kind of accident, Cres strolled up.

"You done bein' unreasonable?"

"Yeah."

"So you're in agreement that Sutton needs to be told?"

"Can we do it early in the morning? And at least give him the rest of this night with London? The doc pretty much told us nothin' will change tonight anyway."

"Makes sense. You cool with Aunt Marie bein' the one who knocks on the honeymoon suite door at six a.m. and tells him what's up?"

"That'd be best. He won't punch her. And she does have that calming nurse demeanor."

Right then, Aunt Marie yelled at the receptionist.

"On second thought..."

Cres chuckled. "She seems feistier than usual. I'll walk them out." Cres headed to the desk.

Melissa squeezed Wyn's arm. "She followed me here, do you want me to lead them back to the hotel?"

"If you wanna go, that's fine."

"That's not what I asked."

Wyn studied her. "Why would you want to stay? We just met today. For all you know I could be a total dick."

"A total dick usually doesn't know he's a total dick, so that argument doesn't apply. Try again."

"Do you *want* to stay?"

"Yes."

He exhaled. "Good. Because to be honest, I didn't know how to ask you to stay. This is"—he gestured to the hospital and to her—"screwing with my head."

She stood on tiptoe to whisper, "I'd rather be screwing with your body, but since that's not in the cards..." Then she stepped back and pointed to his hand. "Speaking of cards...playing strip poker would be a great way to kill time."

"Strip poker, huh?"

"Virtual strip poker, beings we're in public."

"How's that work?"

"We keep score. The next time we're alone together, we'll have a specific order in how we remove our clothes."

For the first time in two hours he had a sense of hope about something—it sounded like Melissa didn't want this thing with them to be a one and done either. "You keep score, baby, and I'll deal the first hand."

Chapter Four

Mel laid down her cards. "Full house, jacks over sevens."

"Damn. I thought I had you this time." Wynton spread out three twos, a six, and a ten.

"Three of a kind with deuces?" she tsk-tsked. "With two players that's never a good gamble." She eyed his shirt collar and imagined peeling that pristine white shirt off his broad shoulders and down his muscular arms. Her gaze caught on the thick column of his neck. She wanted to sink her teeth into that hard flesh. Taste the salt and musk on his skin. Fill her senses with the overpowering maleness of him.

"Melissa, darlin'? You okay?"

Her focus snapped back to him. "I'm fine. Why?"

"You moaned like you were in pain."

She leaned forward. "That moan was your fault. See, I imagined stripping you out of that pesky shirt and my mind wandered south from there."

"You're already kicking my ass at poker and now you gotta give me a hard-on in the waiting room?"

"Just keeping you updated on how eager I am to get my greedy hands all over your naked body. You had way too many clothes on before."

"The feeling is mutual."

But he was distracted when he said that so Melissa turned toward the front entrance when he muttered, "I'll be damned."

The good-looking military guy who'd first offered Jim medical assistance at the wedding paused inside the doors and scanned the waiting area. At the end of the row, Cres straightened up and ran his hand over his hair before he stood.

The guy saw him and smiled. Cres met him halfway and they shook hands, but not in the usual way guys shook hands. Their connection lingered.

Holy crap. Cres Grant was gay.

She sent a sidelong glance at Wynton. Did he know?

He watched the two men, not exactly circumspectly, as he shuffled the deck.

"Is that a friend of your brother's? I saw them talking at the wedding. And he left with Sutton's boss when I got here. Think he came back to see how your dad's doing?"

Wynton said nothing but then she felt him staring at her.

When their eyes met, she got her answer—wariness. Like he was afraid she'd pass judgment on his brother.

As if.

Other people's sexual preferences weren't her concern—she had enough issues with her own sexual needs to worry about someone else's. "How long have you known that Cres is...?"

"Gay?" he said softly. "He came out to us last year. Right after Sutton and London got engaged." His eyes narrowed. "But it's not common knowledge."

"Those two keep looking at each other like that in public and it will be," Mel said dryly. She picked up her cards without really looking at them. "I'd never take it upon myself to point out the obvious to others who can't see it."

"Thank God for that."

"Were you surprised when he came out?"

"Honestly? Yeah. I guess the signs were there if I cared to look. He hadn't had a serious girlfriend...ever really. Hadn't dated any girl since high school. He didn't like trolling the bars with me. Even before I hit pause on my libido last year, he preferred that we hang out and play video games on the weekends."

What did he mean...*hit pause on his libido?*

"And he always did love men's wrestling a little too much."

Mel's gaze snapped to his. "Seriously?"

He smirked. "Nah. Just seein' if you're paying attention."

"Jerk." She tossed her cards down. "This hand is crap. Re-deal."

Wynton shuffled again. Surprisingly, he kept talking. "As an adult, Cres has always seemed preoccupied. When I think back...I just wish he would've told us sooner. Because right after he told us, it was as if a giant weight had been lifted from him. I hated that he carried that weight at all."

You sweet, thoughtful man. He was a good brother—did *his* brothers appreciate that? "So your family is fine with everything?"

"Cres has always been tight-lipped. But like I said, it filled in some of the pieces about Cres that hadn't fit before. So he's got our acceptance, and I think that's all that really worried him. Who else he chooses to tell ain't my concern. It sure as hell ain't my business who he dates. I'm just happy he can be himself and date who he wants."

Mel held her fist out for a bump. "Amen. I'll just throw it out there that we wouldn't be having this conversation if Cres was on the rodeo circuit. If there's even a whisper of that kind of relationship, they're unofficially blackballed."

"That's what Sutton said too." Wynton dealt them each a new hand. "So tell me about your sister. You said she had an accident. What happened?"

How did she explain this? The few times she'd bothered, she worried she'd come off sounding like a poor little rich girl or resentful, which wasn't the case. So she usually avoided the topic entirely with men by just dropping to her knees.

A rough-skinned hand skated up her arm. "With all that we've been through today, I hope you won't start holdin' back on me now."

She inhaled a deep breath and let it all spill out. "My parents are loaded, okay? One of those requirements of being a Lockhart was making sure I excelled at riding, horsemanship, dressage, the whole package. The camp I attended when my sister Alyssa was injured was an exclusive, by-invitation-only camp at a training facility for Olympic athletes. The best trainers in the world were there. So in my parent's eyes, pulling me from camp would've been viewed in the same horrifying light as dropping out of the program because I couldn't cut it. And the Lockharts couldn't have anyone believing that of them or their human progeny." She closed her eyes. The ache of that time had lessened but hadn't disappeared completely.

Wynton cupped her jaw in his hand and lifted her face to his. "Hey. If it bothers you too much to tell me—"

"It doesn't. I just haven't talked about it in a while."

"Then I'm flattered you're sharing all this with me."

"Anyway, throughout my entire life I'd been groomed to win the gold medal in the Olympics while riding a Lockhart horse, thereby increasing its worth and mine."

"Harsh assessment, baby."

"But it's true."

"How old is your sister?"

"Alyssa is six years younger than me."

"What happened?"

"She was at a birthday party. There were go-cart races and she crashed through a fence. The fence crushed her legs and she ended up paralyzed from the waist down."

His jaw dropped to the floor. After he picked it up, he said, "Keep goin'."

"My parents focused completely on my sister—as they should have. Alyssa was really awful after the accident. She especially hated the sight of me. She resented me. Not solely because I wasn't by her side immediately after the accident, but because I was...whole, if that makes sense. As accomplished a horsewoman that I was, Alyssa was better. I'd always known if I'd failed to meet my parent's expectations, the Lockharts had another shot of having an Olympian in the family with Alyssa. I stopped riding and training after her accident because I wanted to be there for her. But she didn't want me anywhere near her. After enduring two solid months of her screaming at me to get the hell away from her, the doctors and my parents asked me to stop coming to visit her, at least until she wasn't so angry. And because it was in Alyssa's best interest, I left."

Wynton picked up her hand and kissed the inside of her wrist.

"So while my sister recovered from a near-fatal accident, I reset my priorities."

"Ran away with the rodeo, did you?"

She smiled. "Something like that. I continued to check on her, but since I was out of sight, I wasn't on my parents' minds. And don't think I was resentful because I wasn't. I was an adult. Alyssa needed them so much more than I did."

"Did your sister come around? Stop resenting you?"

"Yes. I never held the way she acted against her because she suffered a horrible life-altering ordeal at such a young age. Eventually we mended all fences. But I had no interest in going back to that world and competing on the level I'd been at before her accident. After two years, Alyssa set her mind to competing again. She trained for the Paralympics and won several national equestrian championships. She's competed in the international Paralympics, winning a silver and a bronze medal. She's so determined to succeed for herself—not just for our parents—that she won't quit until she's won a gold medal. I'm so proud of her. She's turned out to be an inspiration to so many people."

"I wish I had your attitude. I'm ashamed to say I didn't. Not either time Sutton was injured. The second time I was so mad at him when he opted to go back into rodeo. It seemed selfish of him to continue. And when he was in the hospital, I stayed away. I claimed I had extra ranch work to do because Dad was at Sutton's side, but that wasn't the reason. I just couldn't handle seein' my brother like that. I don't do well when it comes to illnesses and hospitals."

She experienced that familiar punch of sadness. She'd heard that so many times—not only over the last six months, but whenever she talked about her sister's struggles. She'd walked away for her sister's benefit—not because she couldn't deal with it. Now their relationship was solid, but she hadn't even considered calling Alyssa when she'd gotten her diagnosis—especially not after how their mother had reacted when she'd finally told her.

"Hey, Kentucky, where'd you go?" he said softly.

Mel returned her focus to him. The man had the most expressive face. More rugged than handsome, if she had to put a name to it. His features weren't as sharply defined as either of his brother's—Sutton Grant defined gorgeous and Cres Grant was almost pretty—but Wynton's raw-boned features gave him an equally striking look. His hair, in the vivid brightness of the fluorescent lights, held a dark red hue, which made the pieces curling around his ears more boyish looking.

"Darlin', you keep lookin' at me like that and I'm gonna start searching for a supply closet."

"Don't toss out suggestions you won't follow through with," she said.

He cocked a dark eyebrow. "Why don't you think I'll follow through?"

She threaded her fingers through his. "Because even with all this flirty and sexy banter, and me trying to convey my complicated past to try and take your mind off the present, I see the strain in your eyes. You're worried about your dad. But you're also worried about your mom. You feel guilty that you have someone out here with you—even if I wasn't here you'd still have Cres to kill time with—whereas your mother is back there alone."

"You caught all that?" He paused, brooding look in place. "What else?"

"I figured you'd play another two hands of poker with me, letting me believe I was successful at distracting you, before you wandered to the front desk to see if you could go back there and check on your mother, or try to get some kind of message to her to see how she's doing."

"How do you do that?"

"What?"

"Read my mind. It's a little spooky."

"Why?"

He frowned. "Because we've only known each other for a few hours."

But I've known about you for almost a year. The man London claimed had sadness behind his perpetual smile. The man who used sex to combat loneliness, just like I do. The man I refused to let my best friend set me up with—and yet somehow, she did it anyway, without even knowing it.

"Melissa?"

She glanced up from staring at his hard-skinned knuckles. "But in those few hours we've fucked, swapped life stories, and shared some brutal truths, so we're beyond the 'what's your favorite movie?' first date type of bullshit." She brought his hand to her mouth. "So go do what you have to. I'll hang around in the off chance I can continue to be a distraction."

He kissed her. "Thank you. I'll be back."

* * * *

While Wynton was in the back with his mother, Mel did a little exploring. The hospital wasn't very big and most of the private areas were in the back beyond the swinging doors, so that put a wrinkle in her plan.

When Wynton appeared about fifteen minutes later, Mel couldn't help but watch him saunter toward her—his tall, muscular body a visual feast even covered in clothes. He exuded confidence, despite the worry wrinkling his brow, and it made her realize all the guys she'd been playing around with were just boys compared to this man.

Cres intercepted him before he reached the sitting area, and she tried to decipher their grim conversation. Cres nodded, clapped Wynton on the shoulder and stepped aside.

Then Wynton's eyes met hers and she was on her feet by the time he stood in front of her. "No change."

"Sorry." She touched his cheek. "You look like you could use some fresh air."

"That I could." He squinted at the thin wrap covering her shoulders and shrugged out of his suit jacket. "Needing to clear my head don't mean I want you to freeze, darlin'." He draped the coat around her.

His scent enveloped her and his gesture warmed her more than the actual coat. "Thanks."

"Let's take a walk." They exited through the emergency room doors and paused outside the building. The October air had a sharp bite. When Wynton exhaled, she saw some of the tension leave his shoulders. The rancher definitely didn't like to be cooped up.

He dropped his arm across her shoulders and pulled her close so he could kiss her temple. "If I haven't said it enough, I appreciate you bein' here, Melissa."

The security lights lit the sidewalk as they walked around the building. They didn't speak, but the silence didn't seem forced or awkward.

When they reached the edge of the parking lot, Mel said, "My coat is in the car and I'd really love to change out of these shoes."

"Of course."

She hit the unlock button on the Jeep Cherokee and skirted the front end to slide into the driver's side. Wynton slipped into the passenger's seat. She started the engine. "No need for us to sit in the cold." She felt his questioning gaze when she turned the dashboard lights off.

"This is a nice SUV," he said. "It's got enough horsepower to pull your horse trailer?"

"This isn't mine. It belongs to the Gradsky's. I borrow it when I'm not on the road." Mel twisted around to dig on the floor behind Wynton for her athletic shoes. "It gets considerably better gas mileage than my Chevy Tahoe." She kicked off her high-heeled boots and slipped her feet into athletic shoes.

"I never asked how much you're on the road?"

She skirted his question with, "Give me the play-by-play of your multiple ménages, Wynton. Girl/girl/guy?"

"Yep."

"Girl/guy/girl?"

"That too."

"What about guy/girl/guy?"

"Yep, and before you go on, never been in a guy/guy/girl threesome."

She grinned. "That's funny because that's the only type I've ever been in. And talk about scorching hot, watching the two guys together, their hands, mouths, and bodies all over each other. It was fucking powerful."

Wynton reached over and tucked a flyaway curl behind her ear. "Same thing with the girl on girl action. Those soft hands and mouths exploring all that smooth and supple skin. I still remember the sucking sounds. The feminine squeaks and sighs. Then how hot it was to have them turn all that focus on me. Only time I wish I'd had a cock and a strap-on so I could fuck them both at once."

"Put that in your spank bank, did you?"

"Hell, yeah." Even in the dark she could see his eyes glittering when he ran the back of his knuckles down her jawline. "That encounter in the ready room is gonna go in there too."

"I'm flattered." Mel turned her head and rubbed her lips across the base of his hand. "Unzip your pants and pull your cock out. I'll give you something else to file away for a future round of self-love."

Those amazing eyes of his burned black with desire. He kept his gaze locked to hers when he unbuckled his belt. When he lowered the zipper. When he lifted his hips off the seat. When he tugged his pants and his boxer briefs to his knees. Then he eased the seat back and folded his arms behind his head.

Mel dropped her gaze to his groin, not surprised to see he already sported a full-blown erection. She shifted in her seat, angling forward across the console. Bracing one hand on his muscular thigh and the other on his chest, she parted her lips—after kissing the head—and let that hard satin heat pass over her teeth and tongue. She held her breath through the gag reflex when the tip connected with her soft palate and bumped the back of her throat.

Wynton made an inarticulate moan.

Encouraged, she started the long glide up and down his thick shaft, the wetness in her mouth easing her way, each pass progressively lower until she was deep-throating him every time. She didn't use her hands. Just the wet heat of her mouth, the sassy flick of her tongue, and the suctioning power of her cheeks.

She shouldn't have been surprised when his hand landed on the top of her head and held her in place the moment his cock was buried deep. Her eyes watered and her pulse whooshed in her ears, but she still heard him say, "That's it, baby. Take it all. Now swallow. Fuck, yeah. Do that again."

She did what he asked because she had no problem taking direction—except when she didn't. But this wasn't one of those times. And she didn't intend to tease and drag this out. She knew they didn't have much time, so she'd make this fast.

"You could own me with this mouth," he said gruffly when she began bobbing her head, using shallower strokes and stopping to suckle on the tip.

The heater finally kicked out some warmth, turning the inside of the car sultry.

Mel felt that rush of primal satisfaction when he started to pump his hips up to meet the downward motion of her mouth. His grip tightened in her hair. He muttered something about her never fucking stopping when she earned her reward.

His cock got harder yet. In the next instant, it jerked against the roof of her mouth in hot bursts, sending his seed flowing down the back of her throat. She swallowed repeatedly, the mantra in her head *gimme, gimme, gimme* as he shot his load until he had nothing left.

Even when Wynton attempted to pull her head away, she sank her teeth into the base of his cock, keeping him in place so she could suck and lick as his dick softened.

Before she released him completely, she nuzzled his pubic hair. She loved giving head. Every man reacted differently—well, they all acted grateful—but besides that, she reveled in their reaction in the aftermath. Some men wanted to kiss her and taste their come on her tongue. Some men avoided kissing her mouth entirely. Some men wanted to return the favor and practically dove between her thighs. Some men actually stared at her in awe and spent several long moments just tracing her swollen lips. Some men wanted to cuddle. The men with phenomenal recovery time were ready to fuck. So her heart raced when she glanced up to see how Wynton would act.

As soon as he had her eyes, he fisted one big hand in the front of her dress and curled his other hand around the back of her neck as his mouth crashed down on hers in a blistering kiss. He sucked her tongue hard, as if trying to take his essence back from her.

Oh. That was hot as hell.

The kiss made her dizzy and who knows how long it would've gone on if the seatbelt latch hadn't jabbed her in the side, causing her to break away.

"What? You okay?" he asked.

"It's ironic that I'm at the wrong angle now."

"There sure as hell wasn't anything wrong with the angle you were at before." He followed the upper bow of her lip with the pad of his thumb. "That was awesome. Thank you."

"Spank bank worthy?"

"Definitely."

Mel gave him one last lingering kiss before she returned to her seat so he could adjust his clothing. When she reached back for her coat, he grabbed her hand and brought it to his mouth.

"Are you wet?"

"Very."

"I could slip my hand up your dress and get you off." He kissed her palm again. "Or I could stay like this and watch you get yourself off. That'd be hot."

"It would be. But I didn't blow you because I expected something in return."

His eyes searched hers. "Why *did* you blow me? To take my mind off the family medical stuff?"

"No. I blew you because I wanted to get up close and personal with your cock."

"That's it?"

"You were expecting a more dramatic reason?"

"Maybe a more believable one."

Do not get angry. "Explain."

"In my experience, most women don't mind givin' blowjobs, but when they do it's definitely in expectation of me spending time between their thighs."

"So is eating pussy just a reciprocal thing for you?"

"Meaning I only do it when it's expected of me?" He paused and shook his head. "If I'da had my way at the reception? Before we fucked I would've been on my knees with your thigh wrapped around the back of my neck until I ate my fill of you and made you come at least twice."

Her pulse leapt at the image of Wynton's head beneath her dress and his hungry mouth showing her what he'd learned during his years as Super Man-Slut.

"I ain't proud to admit this, but I've had women blow me in hopes of getting an introduction to my world champion bulldogger brother, Sutton. I've had women blow me after an expensive dinner because they felt they owed me." He scowled. "How I kept my dick hard after hearing that is a mystery. I've had women blow me because I've asked them to put their mouths on my dick. Have I ever had a woman blow me because she just likes sucking cock and she's good at it?" Another pause, another soft kiss to the center of her palm. "No, ma'am."

Mel laughed. "Glad I'm unique and brought something new to the table."

"That you did. And while I love spending time with my cock in your mouth, I'm happier that you showed up at the hospital and have given me a chance to get to know you beyond that."

Not for the first time, Mel thought it was a shame they didn't live closer to each other because she'd like to explore this connection for longer than one night.

"We'd better go inside. I doubt anything has changed, but I need to be there in case something does."

She kissed him. "Let's go."

Chapter Five

Wyn awoke with a start when someone jostled him. Melissa immediately sat upright.

Sutton loomed over him. He didn't look pleased. London hung back behind him, covering her mouth with a yawn.

"Mornin' newlyweds."

"While I appreciate that *someone* told me the news about Dad this morning, I ain't too happy that I wasn't told last night."

"Well, excuse the fuck outta me for not wanting to interrupt your wedding night," Wyn snapped.

Cres ambled over and squared off against Sutton. "Both of you need to chill out. Nothin' has changed in the six hours that we've been here so there was no need for you to be here, okay? Mom's the only one allowed back there. We've seen her one time. We'll know more when the doctor makes rounds this morning."

"Any idea when that'll be?"

Wyn shook his head. "But even last night the doctor indicated they'd be sending Dad to Denver via ambulance. Whether they're doin' surgery or what is up in the air." He watched his brother try and get control.

Guilt and sadness crossed Sutton's face when he looked at his wife. "I hate to say this, sweetheart, but you'll have to go on the honeymoon by yourself so we don't lose the deposits. I'll catch up if—and when I can."

Beside him, Melissa sucked in a soft breath and muttered, "Wrong answer, bud."

"Go on our honeymoon by myself," London repeated. "Because that's what I care about, more than making sure your father is okay, more than making sure I'm there for you so *you're* okay, that we don't lose the fucking deposits?" London got in Sutton's face. "Let me tell you something, asshat. I am your *wife*. I am part of this family. Do you think I could just kick back on the beach with a fruity drink in my hand when your dad is fighting for his life? Do you think I'm so—"

Sutton covered her mouth in a silencing kiss. Then he said, "Point taken."

"Good. If we have to cancel the honeymoon—"

"You don't need to cancel the honeymoon," their mom said from behind them. "You might have to delay it a few days, that's all."

Wyn stood. "Mom. Sit. You look exhausted."

"I am exhausted but I've been sitting all night." She looked at each one of her sons and her daughter-in-law, giving Melissa and Mick both a quick, questioning glance before she spoke. "Dr. Poole has already been here this morning. The damage from the heart attack wasn't as bad as they'd originally believed. All that means is your dad most likely won't need surgery, but the cardiac unit in Denver will make the final determination. They'll be transporting him soon. What hasn't changed is the fact that he had a heart attack, and even if they just check him out in Denver for a day or two and then send him home, he is out of commission for at least eight weeks. Eight weeks in which he is to do nothing but recover. Not a half-assed 'I'm fine, the doctors don't know shit' kind of recovery that he *thinks* he might get away with."

Cres laughed.

"So what I need from you boys is your promise that you won't let him do diddly squat for the next two months. You won't let him get in his feed truck. You won't even let him ride along and open fences."

"Harsh, Mom."

"I have to be harsh, Wyn. I'm not going to lose that man

because of his stupid pride." Her chin wobbled and Wyn wrapped an arm around her.

"We've got your back. We promise not to let him pull any crap," Cres said.

"Easier said than done because you're shipping cattle in the next two weeks," his mother said. "Yesterday, before any of this happened, your dad mentioned being shorthanded with Sutton off on his honeymoon. So you know his first response will be to climb on his horse and round up the herd to help you boys sort cattle."

"That ain't happening," Sutton said. "If you can put off shipping even for a week, we can cut the honeymoon short so I can come back and help."

Wyn shook his head. "Because of the wedding, we're starting this a week late as it is. The last thing we need is to lose all our calves to an early blizzard or freezing rain like happened in South Dakota and Wyoming last year."

"If you've got no one that can fill in for Dad, then we'll postpone the honeymoon." Sutton sent London a pleading look. "Sorry, sweetheart."

But London was studying Melissa. "Mel, what do you have going on the next couple of weeks?"

"Not much. I have a break in teaching."

"Good. Then you can help out at the Grant Ranch."

Wyn, Cres, and Sutton all said, "What?" simultaneously.

"Oh, for God's sake. Mel is a cutting horse champion. You guys all know what the main skill is for a cutting horse, right? Sorting livestock. Her horse is at my folk's farm. She can load Plato up and spend the next couple weeks in the field doing what she's trained to do."

Wyn looked at Melissa, who seemed equally shocked by the suggestion.

"London, doll, as much as I love you, you can't go offering Mel's help without askin' her first," Sutton drawled.

"You heard her. It's not like she's got other plans. And Wyn has an extra room where she can stay. So does Cres. That way your mom"—she flashed Sue a smile—"can be with your dad all the time so there's no chance he'll go against doctor's orders and jeopardize his recovery."

"That would be a huge relief to me," his mom admitted.

"Plus, not only is Mel a cutting horse champ, the past five years she's been working as part of a penning team. Shoot, I'll bet she can cut your sorting time down to nothin'. Am I right, Mel?"

All eyes zoomed to Melissa.

"About the sorting time? No. The Grant boys are ranch born. They'll ride circles around me. But if you need an extra horse and rider, I'd be happy to help out in any way that I can."

"Then it's settled," London declared. "You all can figure out where Mel is staying later."

Wyn knew exactly where she'd be staying for the next few weeks.

Everyone started talking and Wyn leaned down to speak to Melissa privately. "You really okay with this?"

"I was thinking to myself earlier that I wished you and I had more time together, and now I've got my wish." She smirked.

"What?"

"This wasn't as altruistic of London as you might believe."

He chuckled. "Yes, it *is* fortunate that they won't have to miss more than a day or two of their honeymoon, isn't it? Because the ranch matters are handled."

"That and you know she's been trying to fix us up since she and Sutton got engaged."

That took Wyn by surprise. "Then why is their wedding the first time I met you?"

Melissa looked away. "I have no idea."

Like hell. He'd find out more about that later. "The circumstances suck, but I'm glad you're staying with me."

"Me too. I'll be happy to bunk in your guest room."

"I'd rather have you in my bed, but I'll leave that up to you."

∗ ∗ ∗ ∗

Wyn gave Melissa his address and the key to his front door. She had a few loose ends to tie up before she made the two-and-a-half-hour trek to the Grant Ranch, and she wouldn't arrive until late tomorrow afternoon. Normally, he didn't like people in his house when he wasn't there, but she didn't feel like a stranger. He might've obsessed on that if he hadn't been obsessing on coordinating family and vehicles as they caravanned to Denver.

Before the orderlies loaded "Big" Jim Grant in the ambulance, the doctor allowed Wyn and his brothers to see their dad for a short visit. The old man looked better than he had the previous night. Sometimes Wyn forgot that his dad was in his late sixties. He didn't look his age, nor did he act it—having a heart attack while dancing to "La Bamba" pretty much summed that sentiment up perfectly.

Now they watched the ambulance pull away and Wyn felt a pang of worry again.

"Mom seemed more relaxed about all of this," Cres commented.

"She puts on a good front in front of Dad."

Wyn looked at Sutton. "I suspect you're right."

"I ain't a doctor, but if Dad's condition was a life or death matter, they would've airlifted him last night. Hospitals don't fuck around with that stuff," Sutton said.

"You would know."

London nestled her head on Sutton's chest. "We are all staying in the same place tonight?"

"Sounds like. It's within walking distance to the hospital."

Cres looked up at the grayish cast to the sky. "I'd better get. Sure hope it doesn't snow."

"I hate that you're goin' home to check cattle by yourself." This time of year and this close to shipping, the cattle couldn't be unattended for even a day. Wyn had stayed behind yesterday morning when everyone else had gone to Gradsky's to get ready for the wedding. Today, one of them had to go home and take care of the herd, and Cres had volunteered. So it'd be at least eight hours before he got to Denver.

"Mick has offered to help me, if that's all right."

Wyn looked at the deep red flush on his brother's face. This was the first time since Cres had come out that he'd shown an interest in a guy around his family. Normally, Wyn would give him a rash of shit, but this was new territory for all of them.

"That's great," Sutton answered. "Mick mentioned when we were workin' at the range that he grew up on a ranch in Montana before he joined the service."

"Yeah, so he ain't just a pretty gate opener."

Both Wyn and Sutton's jaws dropped. They said nothing. What the hell could they say?

London laughed. She dug out ten bucks, crumpled it into a ball, and tossed it at Cres. "Remind me never to bet against you." She nudged Sutton. "Cres bet me he could say something that'd leave both of you tongue-tied."

"Bettin' against me on the second day we're married, Mrs. Grant, is gonna get you in a whole passel of trouble," Sutton warned.

She murmured something to him that made him grin.

"Jesus. Can we just go already?" Wyn complained.

"Yep. See you guys later. Without bein' a dick, I hope I don't hear from you at all until I walk into the hospital in Denver," Cres said.

"Amen, brother. Drive safe."

* * * *

Late the next afternoon, Berlin Gradsky asked Mel, "Are you sure you'll be all right?"

Berlin mothered Mel way more than her own mother did. "I'll be fine. I'm actually really excited to put Plato through his paces."

"London was right about one thing. This is what Plato was trained for."

After Mel climbed in her truck, Berlin rested her forearms on the window jamb. "Nosy question."

"Hit me."

"Is there a reason why you're staying at Wyn Grant's house and not house sitting for London and Sutton while they're on their honeymoon?"

Yes, because I plan on riding Wynton Grant as hard as Plato for the next three weeks. "Sutton said something about liability issues because of his indoor gun range. I didn't question it. And given my...condition, it's probably smart."

Berlin squeezed Mel's shoulder. "No one knows, do they? Not even my daughter?"

She shook her head. "London didn't need that extra stress

during her wedding planning. We both know she would've stressed about that too." But her friend wasn't dumb. She'd asked Mel several times if she was avoiding her. She'd asked if something had happened on the circuit to make Mel drop out. Mel would tell her the reason she'd been distant the last six months as soon as her bossy-pants BFF returned from her honeymoon.

"You're right. I'm happy for my daughter and son-in-law, but I'm glad the wedding is over." She smiled. "Now I just have to worry about you."

"I promise not to take any chances with Plato if I'm not feeling up to it. You know I'd never risk his safety. I'll be fine as long as I follow the rules."

"I've watched you get a handle on this, sweetie, so I trust you with him."

"Thanks for everything."

"You're welcome. Drive safe. Text me when you get there."

"I will."

Berlin stepped back and Mel slowly pulled the horse trailer down the long road leading away from Grade A Farms.

The drive to the Grant Ranch was a little over two hours, and Mel didn't have any reason to hurry. Chances were good she'd beat Wynton there. The family had been in Denver since yesterday, and today they were getting the final diagnosis on the Grant patriarch. She'd stalled as long as she could at Gradsky's. She'd even driven into town and loaded up on groceries because she wasn't sure what type of food a bachelor rancher would stock.

In the last six months, after being diagnosed with type 1 diabetes, Mel had no choice but to monitor every morsel of food that went into her mouth. She also had to reduce her physical activity because she was still learning her limits—which weren't even close to the same as they'd been before her diagnosis.

She hadn't been lucky enough to "get" type 2 diabetes, which allowed her to control her blood sugar levels with modifications to her diet. Her regulation came in the form of daily shots of insulin. Keeping snacks within reach for those times when she felt her glycemic index was low. Carrying glucose tablets with her. Making sure she always had her blood glucose meter, glucose strips, lancets, her needle disposal container, and insulin with her. Thankfully, she could inject herself with an insulin pen, and the type of insulin it used didn't have to be refrigerated.

Even after six months, she wasn't sure she'd ever get used to any of this. It still seemed surreal.

After fighting fatigue, excessive thirst, and weight loss for two months, when she was in LA she finally went to the ER because she thought she might have mono. She'd had it once before and the symptoms seemed similar. The doctor hadn't been convinced her body would react that way to the stress of being on the road, so she'd ordered a battery of tests. When the blood and urine tests had come back positive for diabetes, and further testing indicated type 1 diabetes—a rare diagnosis in a thirty-two-year-old—Mel had literally passed out.

After she'd come to in the hospital, she'd learned the meaning of diabetic shock. She learned her life would never be the same. Ironically, she'd chosen a hospital that had an entire department devoted to dealing with diabetic patients. She learned how to inject herself with insulin. She'd taken a two-day course on proper nutrition, the dangers of excessive physical activity, and how to monitor her blood sugar. She'd soaked it all in. The only time she'd outwardly balked was during her appointment with a counselor who blathered on about emotional changes affecting the body.

Mel had been numb to that. The physical changes concerned her because she realized she'd have to quit competing. It wasn't just her and her horse in the arena, like a barrel racer, or a bulldogger, or a tie down roper. No, in the cutting horse division, it was her, her horse, and ten or more cows. During team penning competition, there were two other riders on horses and up to thirty calves. In other words—mass chaos. She couldn't take the chance that she'd have a low glycemic moment and pass out on top of her horse.

Again.

It had happened to her during a competition, prior to her diagnosis. At the time she'd blamed it on excessive heat in the arena, or being overly tired. She was lucky she hadn't injured herself or someone else.

Especially since she hadn't remembered anything that had happened.

Mel had withdrawn from all competitions. She'd been in limbo, trying to figure out what to do with her life now that her life had changed. Being a trust fund baby did have some perks—she didn't have to decide immediately.

The scenery kept her interest for the remainder of the drive. When she turned down the dirt road that the GPS indicated led to Wynton's house, she envied him and this view every day. Hills and flat land and those gorgeous snow-topped Rocky Mountains in the distance.

His house wasn't what she expected. It was an older ranch house with one old barn, one enormous new barn, and loading pens off to the side of the corral. She pulled the horse trailer up to the pasture Wynton had recommended. She'd keep Plato segregated for a few days until he became acclimated to the area and the other horses.

Since she'd exercised Plato first thing this morning, she checked him for any new marks after being cooped up in the horse trailer. Sometimes the temperamental horse would kick the walls and she'd open up the back end to see him bleeding. But he didn't look worse for the wear, so she fed him and turned him loose.

The next thing Mel did was open the house and cart all of her stuff inside, dumping it in the guest bedroom. She wanted to set the parameters from day one. She couldn't wait to fuck Wynton in every way she'd fantasized about—okay, maybe she had actually written down a list of all the positions and scenarios she wanted to try with Super Man-Slut—but she would be sleeping and waking up alone every night.

You are such a chicken-shit. Why don't you just tell him the truth?

Because she didn't want to blow a good thing. Sexually, they seemed to be on the same page, and that was all that mattered.

She stowed her insulin in the back of the closet. She hid her blood sugar meter in the same drawer as the Glucagon emergency kit. She filled the nightstand drawer with her new best friend—a constant supply of snacks. Then she unpacked her clothes and put them away. She set up her laptop, her cell phone charger, and her e-reader. She spread her toiletries out on the counter in the bathroom across the hallway, including the brand new, unopened jumbo-sized box of condoms.

Then she allowed herself to explore.

Wynton's house was a four-bedroom ranch with a decent-sized living room, and a kitchen that opened into the dining room. Off the dining room was a patio that was completely enclosed by an eight-foot tall fence. The space was homey, although a few things didn't fit. Like the rooster-imaged ruffled curtains in the kitchen and the peach-colored walls in the living room. But the gigantic TV and gaming system, and the oversized recliners and couch did scream bachelor.

One place she didn't even peek into was the closed door at the opposite end of the hallway from her room. It seemed…intrusive to check out Wynton's bedroom when he wasn't here.

And since she had no idea what time he'd arrive, she carried in the groceries she'd packed in the cooler and took stock of his pantry. Good thing she stopped at the store.

Mel had just finished the chicken stir-fry when she heard the front door open.

* * * *

The wait for the doctor's diagnosis today had been nerve-racking. But the good news had been such a relief. His dad had a new diet and exercise regimen. He had eight weeks off to recover because he would make a full recovery.

Before they'd had a chance to celebrate, Jim Grant had announced to his family that he intended to retire from ranching entirely. Starting immediately. Then he'd given Wyn and Cres the option of dividing the land in half. They could each run their own operation, or they could continue to ranch together. He'd take his cut of the cattle sale from this year and then after that, he was out. He planned to fulfill his promise to his wife to see the world. And as soon as he was healthy enough, they'd be off to have the adventures they'd waited a lifetime to experience.

Talk about floored.

Wyn was glad to have several hours to try to sort through everything. But by the time he pulled into his driveway just after dark, he was more than ready to put it all aside and focus on the sweet, hot and sexy redhead he hadn't been able to get out of his mind the past thirty-six hours. The sweet, hot and sexy redhead who was in his house right now. The sweet, hot and sexy redhead who had left the porch light on for him.

Warmth spread through him. It made him a fucking sap, but he hadn't had anyone leave the light on for him since he lived at home. And if the woman had cooked supper? He might just propose to her.

He was so eager to see her he didn't haul in his suitcase. He took the steps two at a time and burst through the door. From the foyer, while he took off his boots, he yelled, "Honey, I'm home." When he rounded the corner, Melissa stood in his living room, her wild curls pulled back into a ponytail. She wore a workout top that showcased her tits, yoga pants—thank you baby Jesus for the genius who invented *those* motherfuckers—and her feet were bare. She looked completely at home in his home.

"Hey. How was the drive?"

"Long."

"How's your dad?"

"Better than we thought, on the road to a full recovery and makin' big plans." He started to stalk her. "Tell me, little redheaded riding girl, what's that delicious smell?"

"I cooked stir-fry but the rice isn't done yet."

"Good. We have time."

Melissa took a step back. "For?"

"For you to tell me why you were trespassing in my kitchen."

"Are you the big bad wolf, Wynton?"

"Yes." He continued slowly moving forward. "Here's where you say, 'Oh my, what big teeth you have.'"

Her gaze zeroed in on his mouth. "Why are you licking your lips?"

"Because you look mighty tasty."

"But I cooked!"

"Don't want food, Red. I want you." Then he was looming over her. The sexy glint in her eyes widened his predatory grin. "Strip off them britches."

Her half-hearted "No" had him wrestling her to the floor. He hovered on all fours above her. "Don't be scared, Red. My big teeth and long wicked tongue are all the better to eat you with. Now take off those pants or I'll tear them off."

Ten seconds later, her bottom half was completely bared to him.

"Drop your knees open. Show me all of you."

Her hesitation vanished.

"My, what a pretty pussy you have." Wyn lowered his head and lapped at the sticky, sweet goodness at the entrance to her body. "I want to fuck you with my mouth, Melissa."

"Yes."

He saw no need to hurry. He explored, mapping her folds with his tongue. He licked fast, then slow. He suckled her pussy lips together, then separately. He grazed her clit with his teeth. By the time he knew the taste of her and the shape of her beneath his mouth, he also knew what maneuver his tongue could do to get her to buck her hips up. Now it was time to know what she sounded like when she came against his face, just how hard she could pull his hair, and how many times he could make her come before she begged him to stop.

Ten minutes later, he had the answers to those questions, and more.

Melissa made a timeout sign.

Wyn chuckled against the top of her thigh.

"You are a menace with that mouth," she panted.

"Come on, Amazing Slut-Girl, you can take some more."

She shook her head. "Not with that lizard-like tongue, Super Man-Slut. But that cock of yours?" She smirked, fished a condom out of her cleavage and flicked it at him. "Bring it on home, baby."

He'd never gotten undressed that fast. He was suited up, on her, and in her. She was hot, slick, tight, and perfect. As he rocked into her, she licked and nipped at his lips, searching his mouth for a taste of herself, which was so fucking sexy, he couldn't stand it.

Then her hands were in his hair, clutching his ass, reaching between them to cup his balls—Christ that felt good.

Melissa arched her back and moaned, "Harder. As hard as you can. I'm close again."

A dozen more deep strokes that sent her sliding across the carpet and she came undone.

Her moment of bliss was a beautiful thing to watch.

When that moment came for him, the last thing he saw before

he closed his eyes was the same greedy look on her face that he knew had been on his when she'd unraveled.

After he was spent, he buried his face in her neck. And blew a raspberry until she shrieked and pushed him away.

She'd left the light on for him, jumped onboard for hot, welcome home sex right on the damn carpet, and she'd cooked for him.

This cohabitating thing might be better than he thought.

Chapter Six

After they finished eating, Wyn said, "Level with me. You haven't been competing this year."

Melissa wiped her mouth and set her napkin on the table. "Not since March. Partially because I burned out on it. Partially because London wasn't on the circuit anymore. Partially because I realized my life hadn't changed in the past seven years. I decided to take a break."

"That's understandable. But why did you hedge when I asked you about it?"

She shrugged. "It's gotten to be a habit. I'm really glad for the chance to try something different."

"And I can't wait to show my appreciation for all your hard work." He waggled his eyebrows.

"So can you give me an idea on what to expect, rancher man?"

"We've left the cattle in the summer grazing areas as long as possible. Starting the day after tomorrow, we'll move them into pastures closer to home. That's always traumatic for the cattle, so they'll need five days to get back up to a saleable weight. Then we'll start separating and loading them. We have different places that take them, and they have set times when they'll accept shipments, so the shipping process seems endless."

"So we'll all be on horseback?"

"For the cattle drive, we'll take the horse trailer and horses to the edge of the summer grazing area. We'll unload the horses and start driving cattle out of there. One thing that sucks is we'll have to cross two roads, but they're not paved roads and we've never had a run-in with a car. Then after the cattle are settled, we'll come back, ditch the horses, and two of us will drive out to retrieve the horse trailer. Usually Dad is the one who does that. He also drives ahead and opens the gate so we don't have to stop the cattle and make them wait. But we'll have to figure something else out since we're shorthanded—even with our hot, new cutting horse expert helping out."

Melissa smiled at him. "Flattery will not get me up at the butt crack of dawn to open gates for you, cowboy."

"Maybe I'll make so much noise in the bedroom that you'll have no choice but to get up."

"I have zero problem locking my door at night to ensure that doesn't happen."

Wyn frowned. "You locking me out of my own bedroom?"

"No, because I won't be sleeping in your room, Wynton."

"Explain that."

"I'm set up in the guest bedroom. I have no problem fucking when and where the mood strikes us, but when it's time to sleep...to be blunt, I want my own space. You've lived alone long enough that you'll probably need your own space too—you just don't know it yet. I'll be here three weeks. I don't want to wear out my welcome on the third day because I've strewn my girl stuff all over your bedroom and bathroom. And some nights I can't sleep, so I'm up late reading."

She had an excuse to cover all the bases. He couldn't argue with them, but that didn't mean he wouldn't try like hell to change her mind. He pushed his empty plate back. "So what are we doin' the rest of the night?"

"Dishes first." She kissed his nose. "Ain't domestic life bliss?"

* * * *

The next morning, Wyn hauled his ass out of bed at first light. He and Cres did chores without saying much besides mumbling every once in a while. They stopped by their folks' place to see how Dad was faring. He was tired—and annoyed by the "no ranch work" edict—so for the first time in years, they talked about other things over lunch. Wyn didn't leave in a rush because he was dodging his mom's questions about his relationship with Melissa, he was just anxious to hang out with her the rest of the day.

Once he got back to his house, he felt stupid, coming home early, expecting she'd drop everything and want to spend time with him. She was here as a favor to them to do ranch work. Since her help wasn't needed yet, he had no right to assume she'd want to spend her free time with him.

She sat cross-legged on his couch with her laptop and looked up, beaming a smile at him. "Hey. You done already?"

"For now. Why?"

"Because I want you to take me for a joy ride across the ranch in your truck, cowboy."

His heart simultaneously stopped and exploded with hope. "For real?"

"Unless you want to ride horses to show me the sights?"

"Nope. Let's go." Wyn would drag this afternoon out. Show her every nook and cranny, every field and stream, every rocky ridge and meadow of this place he loved.

Melissa proved to be an excellent gate opener, and she was properly awed by the ranch. That earned her brownie points when he parked in his favorite secluded spot and undressed her.

The times they'd been intimate had been fast and intense. For this go around, Wyn wanted slow. Maybe a little sweet.

His new roomie proved herself to be excellent at slow and sweet, with lazy kisses and lingering caresses.

Afterward, when they were both sweaty and spent on the seat of his truck, he kissed her chest as they spiraled down from the orgasmic high together.

"We're going to wear each other out," she murmured in his hair.

Wyn didn't see a problem with that. "Is that a challenge?"

She groaned. "Not today. I wouldn't mind going back. I need

to make a phone call and then I want to exercise Plato."

"Okay. But, baby you gotta move off my lap and let go of my hair so I can drive."

"Oh. Right."

He loved that dazed look in her eyes, knowing he'd put it there.

* * * *

Two nights later, after another nutritious—and surprisingly delicious meal—Wyn broke out the PlayStation 4 and they played Borderlands.

"I'm surprised you're a gamer," he said.

"There's not a lot of other things to do on the road once I get the rig parked for the night."

Wyn smirked at her. "You ain't out rounding up a one-night rodeo for yourself every night? For shame, Amazing Slut-Girl. I'm disappointed."

"My cooter is way more selective these days." She shifted on the couch. "And dude, I've never had this much sex, consistently with the same guy. My cooter is clapping with joy, at the same time she's like...you expect me to take the ground and pound twice daily *and* get chafed in the saddle all day? Pass the ice pack, please."

He laughed. Christ. She made him laugh like no other woman he'd ever met. And laughing with her so much felt damn good. "You sayin' you want me to dial it back?"

"No fucking way, Super Man-Slut. My cooter does not speak for me."

Really, really crazy about this woman already.

"So what else did you do to kill time?" Onscreen he dodged a flurry of arrows and slid beneath a boulder.

"I listen to audiobooks when I'm driving. When I'm at an event, I'm out among the contestants and rodeo people because I spend enough time by myself getting to the destination."

"Do you have an apartment that's a home base?"

Onscreen, Melissa chopped a monster's head off with a broadsword, then snagged the jeweled necklace off the corpse with a, "I'll take that, sucker," before she answered. "I had a place in Kentucky. Once I stopped going there...I put my money into the nicest horse trailer I could buy. I have everything I need. I've upgraded it twice. But since I've been working at Grade A, I rented a place in town to see if I liked living in one place again."

"What's the verdict?"

She shrugged. "Still out. At least for there. Why?"

Wyn maneuvered around a patch of quicksand onscreen. "Sutton made great money when he was winning. Bulldogging paid for his house, and he's never been short on cash for anything else. But I heard other guys talkin' like they don't make a living at it."

"You asking how I support myself because you're looking for me to pay you rent while I'm here?"

"No, smartass." He bristled. "Forget it."

Melissa hit pause on the game and faced him. "Let's get this out in the open. I have Kentucky blueblood parents, remember? I have a trust fund. I use it when I need to. I'm not one of those 'Oh, I have to make it on my own even if I have to live in a hovel to prove I'm independent' kind of women. My grandparents set the trust fund up for me at birth. I was a one hundred percent scholarship recipient for college, so I didn't touch my college fund. I made enough money competing to support myself, but I'm lucky enough to have a financial cushion that allows me to not worry that I'll have to eat Ramen noodles for a month so I can afford to fill my truck up with gas to get to the next event."

"You don't have to get defensive."

"I'm not. This is just another example of why I don't tell anyone my background."

He twined a long, red curl around his index finger. "Doesn't that get lonely? Not letting anyone see the real you?"

She laughed harshly. "Being on the road and competing is the *real* me. The girl I was before? She's long gone." She tried to get away from him and succeeded, despite that he'd nearly pulled her hair out in the process.

"Come back here."

"Why?"

"So you can look into my eyes when I tell you this." He stroked her jawline with his thumb. "I like the real you. A lot. And not just because you're the sexiest woman I've ever been with, or that you have a lewd sense of humor, or that you like to fuck as much as I do."

She raised a dark red eyebrow. "You *are* going somewhere with this, right cowboy?"

"Yep. You're the first woman I've invited to stay at my place for longer than a few hours. You're the first woman who's played video games with me. You're not the first woman to cook for me, but you didn't create that meal like it was a wife audition."

"Dude, if I was auditioning to be your wife, I'd cook naked."

Wyn smiled. "See? You're so goddamned funny. I just wanna sit here and talk to you for hours. And this is all new to me, okay? And yet, it's so damn easy. You just slipped in here like you belong. But without permanent ties to anything, I worry that you'll slip back out just as easily." Jesus. Did that make him sound whiny?

Melissa stared at him. "I don't know where this will go, Wynton. I feel like I've known you for years when it's just been days. But I can't promise you anything when I'm taking things—my life—day by day."

Not what he wanted to hear, but it'd have to do for now. "Fair enough." He kissed her forehead. "Let's get back to the game. I believe you were about to pillage the village."

* * * *

For the next week, much to Wyn's annoyance, Melissa had stuck to her guns and locked the door to the guest bedroom after she went to bed. Alone. Every night. It was still locked in the morning—and his need to check that every morning just pissed him off. So prior to them saying good night, he felt entitled to poke her—promising he'd never lock her out of his room and he'd welcome any late visits from her.

He banked his disappointment that she hadn't taken him up on his offer even one time in the last seven nights.

So when a warm body crawled in bed beside him, he figured he was dreaming.

Soft hands floated over his arms and across his shoulders. Cool lips landed on the back of his neck, sending a shudder through him.

"Wynton? Are you awake?"

He groaned. "I am now. What time is it?"

"Three."

Christ. "You know what time we have to get up to start loading cattle?"

"Yes."

"Then what are you doin' in my bed, Miss I-Lock-My-Doors? Did you have a bad dream or something?"

"No. I had a good dream." She licked the vertebra at the base of his skull. "A sexy dream." She blew a stream of air across the damp spot she'd created. "A dirty dream. Starring dirty-minded, hot-bodied you." She sank her teeth into the nape of his neck.

It was as if that particular spot had a direct line to his cock, and it immediately went rock-fucking-hard.

She whispered, "I came in here to see if you wanted me to act out the good parts of my dream."

"Fuck, yeah."

Melissa rolled him to his back. "It's handy that you sleep naked, cowboy."

He kept his room so dark he could only make out her shape in the greenish glow from the digital clock on the side of the bed. "So you're waking me up to reward me with sex?"

"Are you sure you're awake? Or is this a dream starring the sleep sex fairy?" She slid down his body and beneath the covers.

Then her warm, wet mouth engulfed his cock. He clenched his hands and his ass cheeks to keep from bowing up.

By the time she quit teasing—deep-throating him, licking just the head of his cock with the tip of her tongue while she jacked him—his entire body vibrated.

She rolled a condom down his shaft and straddled him, burying his length inside her hot and slick cunt an inch at a time.

"Melissa."

She stretched her body across his and put her mouth on his ear. "I want to fuck you slowly and send you soaring without all the thrusting and straining, so when you do tip over the edge into the abyss, you'll wonder if it all had been a dream."

Wyn sank into the pillows and let her have her way with him, as she sucked and nibbled on his neck, his ears, and his chest. She rocked his cock in and out in the dreamy rhythm she'd mentioned. He trailed his fingertips up and down her spine, pleased to feel gooseflesh erupting in their wake.

When his balls drew up and he felt that tingle at the base of his spine, he grabbed onto her ass and let her body pull the orgasm from his.

She feathered kisses over his lips and disconnected their bodies. She even removed the condom. After one last kiss she said, "Reality is always much sweeter than dreams," and slipped from his room.

The next morning he might've believed it *had* all been a dream...but the hickey above his left nipple was proof she'd been there.

Maybe she was coming around. Maybe next time she'd be in his bed all night.

Chapter Seven

Over the past two weeks, Mel had become a decent ranch hand. After spending long days in the saddle and long nights christening every surface in Wynton's house, she was dragging serious ass today. Ranch work wasn't for wimps.

Luckily, her years of cutting competition had proved useful when keeping stray heifers in line. Seemed those stubborn cows always made a beeline for the creek. She could understand it if it was hot, but the weather had cooled off considerably, and it was always colder down by the water.

She shivered in her borrowed Carhartt coat. She couldn't believe how fast the time had gone. It seemed like yesterday that she'd unpacked her things, half-worried/half-excited to share living space with Wynton. She'd learned so much about him—not just his sexual preferences.

Now she knew little…domestic things. He brewed his first two cups of coffee in the morning as thick as tar. He ate lunch with his parents and brother most days. He read the newspaper from front to back before supper. He liked the scent of laundry detergent in the air so he did one load of clothes every day. He preferred sitcoms to dramas on TV. He shaved every day—not just because she was there.

Now that she also knew the core of him—his fierce love of his life as a rancher and being around his family, his connection to his animals and the land—she realized she'd never find another man like him. She hated that their time together was coming to a close. Wynton had been vague when she'd asked about his plans after the shipping was done, so she hadn't brought it up again.

Plato did a little crow-hop and she absentmindedly reached down and patted his neck. "Easy. I know you wanna work, but we gotta let the boys do their stuff."

Boys. That was almost a derogatory term for the masculine perfection of Wynton and Creston Grant. Seeing them work together was like watching a ballet. Each move and counter move perfectly choreographed. Ropes thrown in unison or in opposition. Both of them taking off on their horses at the same speed. Wynton cut left, while Cres cut right, and the herd was immediately back on track, going where the Grant boys wanted them to go.

She looked around at the pine trees lining this valley that dipped below the rock outcroppings. Some of the grass still had the barest hint of green, but even the brown stalks added to the visual appeal of vastness and serenity. She truly loved it here. It was so peaceful.

When her fingertips tingled and she knew it wasn't from cold, she dug into her pocket and took out a box of raisins. The first few days she hadn't done much strenuous activity—unless lots of hot sex, a couple times a day counted—and she had good blood sugar numbers. She felt great. Better than she had since before the diagnosis. She felt…normal. When her daily activity kicked up the past two weeks, she'd adjusted quickly and had no adverse effects. So she was beginning to think that finally after six and a half months, she had a handle on living with diabetes.

And since things were going better between her and Wynton than she ever imagined, she hadn't seen a need to test their relationship to see if telling him about her condition changed things. A smarmy voice in her head said, *Great plan, Mel. Tell him about it the first time he acts like a total jackass.*

Wynton whistled, drawing her attention to the loading chutes.

Damn, damn, damn but that man was fine. Hard-working, determined, thoughtful, funny, interesting. What you saw with him was exactly what you got. And in her eyes that made him damn near perfect.

You have fallen for him.

Who wouldn't?

She let her gaze scan the panoramic view. She could get used to this life. Working side by side—or at least in close proximity to her man. Raising cattle and maybe a few kids.

Whoa.

Whoa, whoa, whoa.

Putting the cart before the horse, much? Get through the next week with him before you start picking out baby names and knitting fucking booties.

"Melissa!"

Her head snapped up.

All Wynton had to do was point and she knew where she was supposed to be. Her gaze zeroed in on the problem cow. She clicked at Plato.

But before they reached the edge of the herd, the cow headed for the stock tank. On the other side of the pasture.

Then they were off on a wild cow chase.

Plato's withers quivered with excitement. He was in his glory as a cow horse. By the third day, he was penned with Charlie, Wyn's horse, Petey, Cres's horse, and Ringo, Jim's horse. By the fourth day in the field with the Grant horses, Plato had taken over as the leader.

The cow was fast. But Plato was faster.

Mel cut around and Plato's back end slid out so they were almost parallel to the ground. But Plato righted himself and they were in front of the cow, Plato moving back and forth as he tried to gauge which way the cow intended to bolt.

The cow heard the herd mooing behind her. Seeing no escape, she slowly turned around and lumbered back to the corral.

Plato kept on her until she was back where she belonged.

Something was spooking the herd today. Mel had to chase over a dozen runaways. So it took twice as long to sort and load. She'd depleted her secret store of snacks in her pockets and her water bottle was empty.

Wynton wasn't on horseback today. He slammed the back end of the livestock hauler and then jogged up to the driver's side to talk to Cres, who was delivering the cattle.

Mel dismounted. The cold seemed to have settled in her bones, so she led Plato into the barn to warm up as she removed the tack and brushed him down. She had to give him his special blend of oats out of the view of the other horses so they wouldn't fight for their share.

She'd just sent him out into the corral and locked the gate, when a wave of dizziness overtook her. She patted her hand along the fence, trying to squint through the white spots dancing in front of her eyes for the outside pump. There. Red handle. Once she reached it, she pulled up the handle. She had to hold on to the metal pipe as she held one shaking hand out to the stream of water. Very little liquid was flowing into the plastic; it was just getting her hand wet.

Fuck it.

Mel bent down and gulped water directly from the gushing stream. Water had pooled in the rocks, but she didn't care. She was so damn thirsty.

When she'd had enough, she yanked the handle down and cut off the flow. She pushed herself upright and wiped her face on the sleeve of her coat.

Of course that's when she noticed Wyn standing in the doorway of the barn.

He raised both eyebrows. "Thirsty?"

"Very."

"You hydrated now?"

Mel watched him stalk closer with that look in his eyes. A look that said he was about to strip her down and rock her body to the core. "Yes I am."

"Good."

"So, what's going on?"

"You."

"What about me?"

"You are driving me absolutely fucking crazy."

She waited.

"Do you have any idea how sexy you are on a horse? So regal? So intuitive? Fuck, I love to watch you make lightning quick adjustments when you're on the outside of the herd." He moved closer. "I'm surprised I can get any work done at all because I can't take my eyes off of you. For the past two weeks I've watched you. Watched that crazy red hair tossed by the wind as you're chasin' down strays. Watched your cheeks turn pink with color. Watched your eyes dancing with excitement and concentration. You're beautiful, Melissa. But when you're so focused on your task, doin' what you're so goddamned good at, you take my fucking breath away."

Her heart raced. Even when she'd just gulped water, her mouth had gone dry. While he was getting closer, she'd started backing up in a circle, retreating into the barn.

"And every day, when my cock is so fucking hard I could pound horseshoes with it, I tell myself to wait until I can take you in my bed, or on my couch, or on the damn washing machine. But today, Cres is gone, and it's just you and me. Today, I ain't gonna wait."

His eyes were hot and dark and focused one hundred percent on her.

"No foreplay. No sweet kisses or tender touches. I want you, hard and fast and rough. I wanna bend you over and fuck you until the ache of wantin' you doesn't consume me like this."

Two more steps back. "Wynton."

"You want this. I can see it in your eyes. I bet your nipples are hard. I bet your pussy is already wet."

"So?"

"So, stop movin' so we can get on with it."

"Or what?"

"There is no *or*. Don't make me chase you down."

"Think you can catch me, cowboy?" God. Why was she taunting him?

His deep, rasping, sarcastic laugh might've been the sexiest thing she'd ever heard. "Oh, yeah? How about I'll even give you a head start. I'll count to five."

Mel turned and ran.

From behind she heard, "Onetwothreefourfive."

She managed to get out, "That's cheating!" before an arm banded around her waist and she was airborne. She shrieked.

"That's it, baby," he growled in her ear. "Get those vocal cords warmed up because before I'm done with you, you're gonna be screaming my name."

Wynton carried her—one-armed no less!—into the tack room. He pulled a saddle blanket out of the stack and draped it over a workbench. Then he set her on her feet and stripped off her coat. His voice was back in her ear. "Chest on the bench, ass in the air is how I want you. Hold on to the bench with your left hand and drop your right hand beside your leg."

Her need for him overtook any thoughts of arguing. Wynton had been the most spectacular lover she'd ever had, but he'd never been like…this. Desperate to have her and sort of pissed off about it.

At first he didn't touch her besides undoing her jeans, shoving them and her underwear to the tops of her boots, then kicking her feet out to widen her stance.

She heard his labored breaths as he shed his clothing. She heard the crinkle of a condom wrapper. She felt his satisfied grunt on the back of her neck when he pressed his chest to her back and reached between her legs to find her dripping wet.

One finger entered her. Then two. God. He had such long, thick fingers. She made a soft gasp when the callused pad of his thumb connected with her clit.

Wynton kept her immobilized on the bench, his breath hot in her ear as he finger fucked her. And he knew just where to stroke inside her pussy walls and for how long. He knew how much direct contact her clit could take. He knew how to light the fuse and how long before she detonated.

"It's mine, Melissa. Give it to me."

She did cry out when the orgasm blasted through her.

He kept pumping and doing that flicking thing on her clit, dragging out her pleasure. When the last pulse ended, he stilled and pulled his fingers out of her. Then he whispered, "Don't. Move."

No problem. She was pretty sure her spine was somewhere on the hay-strewn floor below her.

He slapped his hands on her ass cheeks hard enough to make that one swat sting. His two fingers, wet with her juices, trailed down her butt crack to her anus. He swept his fingers across her hole until the nerve endings flared to life and the rim was sticky.

She stilled. They'd talked about anal sex, even done a little anal play back and forth, and she knew he wanted to shove his cock in her ass. She wanted that too, but she needed to be more prepared than just a couple of swipes of her come to ease the way.

Wynton's tight grip on her ass relaxed. She felt the damp heat of his breath on her lower back right before he kissed the spot and started to drag his tongue down the split in her ass, making a soft growling noise as he followed the trail he'd made with her juices. And when he reached her anus, he licked and lapped and sucked that tight ring before he plunged his tongue inside.

"Oh, God." He did it a few more times, driving her crazy with the raunchy sensation that she loved.

Then he tilted her hips and inserted just the tip of his cock into her pussy. He dangled something rough against her right leg that caused her to twitch before he slid it into her hand. She squeezed her fingers around it. It felt like...rope.

Holy fuck.

Still breathing heavily, still just resting his cock an inch inside her, Wynton guided her hand between her thighs.

Keeping his hand circling her wrist, he dragged the rope across her clit.

Mel arched up. She tried to pull her hand away, but Wynton wouldn't allow it.

"Ride that line between pleasure and pain."

"I-I...what if it's too much?"

Once again he layered his chest to her back. "There's no such thing." He sucked on her earlobe, impaled her fully, and pulled the rope across her clit all at the same time.

She screamed.

Wynton fucked her as rough and fast and hard as he'd warned he would. His harsh grunts, the sucking sounds of her pussy with his every stroke, the *thump thump thump* of the bench legs echoed around her.

Even before she started to come, Mel drifted to that place where anticipation met intent. She furiously rubbed her clit, her stomach tight every time the twine scraped over that swollen nub. But she couldn't stop. It was so close... It was right...there.

The orgasm ripped through her. Her clit throbbed like she'd

never felt it. Her pussy clamped down so hard on Wynton's cock that she swore she could feel his heart pounding as he plowed into her. Every part of her body tingled. Her ears rang, her head went muzzy. She sucked in a deep breath and the last thing she heard before she passed out was Wynton roaring like a beast.

* * * *

She'd blacked out.

Now Wynton had to know something was wrong with her. Women didn't just pass the fuck out during sex—even as mind-blowing as that sex had been. At least she hadn't checked out before the orgasm that would forevermore be "the orgasm" that all others would be judged by.

She wiggled her naked body. She turned her head. The pillow smelled like him. The scent immediately soothed her. As did the rough-skinned palm that skated down her arm.

"Hey, sleepyhead."

"Uh, how'd I get here?"

"You were seriously out of it after we...you know."

The man was embarrassed? Get out.

"So I carried you into the house, undressed you, and tucked you in my bed."

"How long have I been here?"

"Half an hour." A soft kiss landed on her shoulder. "I fucked you so hard that you passed out, baby." Another kiss. "I've never had that happen before."

Now he sounded so smug. "It's never happened to me before either."

"One for the record books, Amazing Slut-Girl."

Mel smiled in the dark. "True dat, Super Man-Slut." The more conscious she became, the less it felt like she'd had an...episode. Maybe she was just thirsty, hungry, and tired because she'd worked all day, followed by getting spun inside out and upside down by one of the most intense sexual encounters of her life. What woman wouldn't pass out from being exposed to Wynton Grant's pheromones and sating his beastly sexual appetite after he'd made her come so hard she'd screamed? Twice?

"You all right?" he murmured.

"Mmm-hmm. I need to eat something and I'm really thirsty. But besides that…" She stretched. "I feel thoroughly fucked."

He chuckled. "Me too. You sore?"

"A little."

"My fault. Lemme fix that." He slipped beneath the covers and positioned himself between her legs. He planted the softest kisses on her abraded clit.

"Wynton—"

"I just fucked you hard, fast, and rough, Melissa. Now let me make love to you slow and sweet."

Like she could say no to that.

Chapter Eight

In the last three weeks, Wyn's life had changed completely.

He'd fallen in love.

With a hookup.

A *wedding* hookup, no less.

It's been more than a hookup since the first time you kissed her, dumbass.

True.

Wyn was done denying this was a *one and done* or *hit it and quit it* scenario. Melissa was meant to be his. Not for just a few lousy weeks, either. Now he just hoped that Melissa could see he was "the one" she'd been looking for.

How had he gotten so lucky? She was everything he'd wanted and feared he'd never find. She was perfect.

Perfect.

She'd proven it so many times, in so many ways.

She could ride a horse like no woman he'd ever seen.

She liked to just sit around and bullshit.

She liked to play video games.

She liked to play darts and pool.

She liked to curl up on the couch and watch TV.

She liked to cook.

She had a great sense of humor.

She loved sex—anytime, anyplace. She was as inventive in her suggestions as she was adventurous with his.

With each new thing he discovered about her, he fell harder for her.

Why was he reminding himself of all these awesome things about her?

Because Melissa had been a little...grouchy since yesterday. It wasn't his fault that she'd fallen asleep in his bed after he'd made love to her. When she woke up—cranky as hell—she stormed off to her bed, insisting she slept better alone.

How would she know that if she hadn't actually tried sleeping in his bed an entire night?

Maybe he'd man up and ask her that when he got home. He grinned. That'd get her riled up—and that was how he loved her best.

He slowed down and pulled into Cres's driveway.

Cres was out of his house as soon as Wyn killed the ignition. As Wyn wandered up the driveway with a six-pack of Fat Tire beer, Cres said, "That's your *we've gotta talk* look. So it's finally time to deal with Dad's bombshell?"

"I didn't want this to be a pressure thing, Cres. I guess we could've discussed this while we were movin' cattle."

Cres dropped the tailgate on his truck. "Mel's been around and it didn't seem right to talk in circles or exclude her from our conversation. And every other time we've been together it's been with Dad and Mom."

Wyn hopped onto the tailgate beside his brother and handed him a beer.

"Thanks." Cres said, "Does it surprise you that Dad hasn't been bugging us to make a decision?"

"Dad's got other things on his mind for a change. I'm happy to see that. Mom is too. So to be honest, I don't think they care one way or another what our decision is because they've already made theirs. Make sense?"

"Yeah. And Mom's too busy harassing you about what's going on with you and Mel." Cres sipped his beer. "Speaking of Mel...you two seem very happy to be playing house."

Wyn scowled. "I *hate* that fucking term."

"What else can you call it if it's not a trial run for the real deal?"

"Piss off. And her name is Melissa, not Mel. Mel...well, that's more in line with your tastes."

Cres laughed. "True. I like her. She's good for you."

"So if I wanted to play house with her for real?"

"I'd probably come over more often since she's a better cook than you."

"Again, Cres, piss off." Wyn cracked his beer. "I want her there for the long haul. Not just because she's a good cook but because she's...everything. I just feel in my gut she's it for me."

"Does she feel that way too?"

"I hope so."

"Man, Sutton is *so* gonna rub it in your face that you're pussy-whipped."

"I deserve it." He grinned. "I *welcome* it. Anyway, you've had a couple of weeks to think about Dad's offer. Made any decisions yet?"

Cres looked at him oddly. "It never really was a decision for me, bro. I like ranching with you. It'd suck to do it by myself. I say let's keep it together. Same as it's always been."

Wyn held his bottle to his brother's for a toast. "Amen."

A few moments of silence passed.

"Since it seemed like *you* were dragging this decision out, I thought maybe you were gonna suggest we divvy it up."

Wyn pinned him with a sharp look. "Why in the hell would you say that?"

Cres shrugged. "I came out last year. Everyone in the family has been supportive—even more than I expected. But supporting me in my personal life and bein' offered a chance to cut ties with me professionally because of *how* I live my life... We both know it might affect who wants to do business with both of us, Wyn. I could see that dividing it would be an easy out for everyone. I think that's why Dad offered it as a suggestion."

"Bullshit. I thought *you* might be lookin' for an out from ranching completely," Wyn said. "Trying to figure out a way to sell your portion to me."

"And what would I do if I wasn't ranching? I've got no interest in doin' anything else, so selling never even crossed my mind," Cres said. "Besides, knowing us, even if we divided it up, we'd still work together most days anyway."

"True." Wyn swallowed a mouthful of beer. "So we good?"

"I reckon. Be weird not havin' Dad around day-to-day. I'm gonna miss him and those fucked up curse word combinations he uses when he's frustrated."

Wyn smiled. "I'm gonna miss him too. He and Mom deserve a chance to spend the money he's been saving all these years. As for us...dividing the profits by two instead of by three will take some getting used to."

Cres grinned. "That extra cash will come in handy for you since you're playin' house."

"Asshole. What about you and Mick? Any thoughts of playin' house with him?"

"It's casual," was all Cres said. "He's comin' to help load for the Denver trip tomorrow."

"That's an overnight trip."

"Yep. If you gotta problem with that, let me know."

Wyn shot him a *don't be an idiot* look. "I don't."

"Good." Cres exhaled. "Thanks. Christ. I don't know fuck-all about havin' a boyfriend, bro."

"Mick keeps comin' back around, so you must know how to do something right." As soon as that left Wyn's mouth, he groaned. "Shit. I didn't mean it that way."

Cres laughed. "How 'bout we don't go there. *Ever.*"

"Deal." He smirked. "Although...Melissa said you and Mick together...that'd be live porn she'd watch."

"Jesus. No wonder you love her. She's as perverted as you."

* * * *

After almost three weeks of ranch life, Mel hadn't gotten used to waking up at the butt crack of dawn and hauling her carcass out of a toasty bed.

So Wynton's way-too-early, and way-too-chipper summons, "Up and at 'em, Kentucky," as he beat on her door annoyed the crap out of her.

Mel forced herself to respond, "I'll be there in five," somewhat politely, instead of yelling at him to get the fucking battering ram away from her door.

Yeah. She was punchy and cranky.

After taking her shot of insulin, she shoved a glucose pill in her jeans, packed her coat pockets with snacks and filled her water bottle. The last day of shipping cattle meant everyone was in a hurry, so she didn't have time for coffee or breakfast.

Mistake number one.

Once she'd saddled up and the sun had come out, she'd immediately overheated. She took her jacket off and tossed it over a fencepost.

Mistake number two.

Since this was the largest group of cattle going to market, of course everything went wrong. Which meant she spent four hours chasing down runaways and culling cows from the milling herd.

Four hours without a break, without water, and without her trusty snacks.

Mistake number three.

But rather than tell Wynton she hit the hypoglycemic stage and was about to crash, she decided it'd be better to just go off and crash alone.

Mistake number four.

The edges of her conscious began to shrink in on her like a camera viewfinder that starts out close, but objects get smaller and farther away until everything is fuzzy and ringed with black.

She rode to the barn and dismounted. If she could just have a few minutes of clarity to unsaddle her horse while those guys— loaded or unloaded the cattle?—she couldn't remember, she could probably make it to the house before she collapsed.

Wait. The house was collapsing? Why?

She was so confused.

Where was she? What happened to her horse?

Mel spun around and that action caused a quick spike of pain. She tried to pat the top of her head to see if some asshole had buried an ax in her skull, but she ended up smacking herself in the face.

Fuck that hurt.

Take a pill for it.

Good plan. She dug in her pocket—why weren't her fingers working?—and found a round, white thing. She squinted at it. After enclosing it in her fist, she went to find water. She took two steps forward and swayed.

Whoa. When had she gotten on the carousel? Why was everything spinning so fast it was blurred? What was that loud, whooshing noise?

She made it to a bale of straw before the darkness overcame her.

Chapter Nine

After the cattle truck rumbled down the driveway, Wyn did loading chute maintenance—his least favorite part of shipping cattle. But if he didn't fix the problems now, they'd have issues the next time they used the chutes because he wouldn't remember what needed done.

He'd welcomed Mick's help today. Wyn was especially grateful that Mick was riding with Cres to the sale barn, so Wyn could catch up on the piles of paperwork that always accompanied selling cattle. Cres and Mick planned to stay overnight in Denver before heading home. He wouldn't begrudge his brother a little personal time since he'd come to realize how much he needed that in his own life.

Speaking of...he wondered where his hot, redheaded cattle cutting expert had gone. She'd been acting a little weird toward the end.

He saw Plato in the corral, but it looked like he still wore a bridle and bit. Melissa would never turn him out like that.

"Melissa?"

No response.

An eerie feeling rippled down his spine. "Melissa?" he called into the barn.

No answer.

If his head had been turned the other direction, he might've missed her. But the red in her corduroy shirt snagged his attention. He sauntered up to the hay bale she sat on and noticed her eyes were closed. "Napping on the job, Kentucky? For shame."

Melissa didn't acknowledge him at all.

Man, she was really asleep. But as soon as he stood in front of her, he knew she wasn't napping. Something was wrong with her.

He crouched down and took her hand. Holy shit, it was like ice. But he saw her forehead was damp with perspiration and her face was flushed. He tried to shake her. "Melissa?"

She mumbled something.

"Baby, you're scarin' me." Wyn noticed her other hand was closed in a tight fist. He pried her fingers open and saw she'd clutched a white pill. He remembered her complaining of a bad headache last night before she'd gone to bed in her own room. How many of these had she taken?

When her body started to shake uncontrollably and even that didn't wake her up, he dug his cell phone out of his pocket and dialed 911.

After he'd given them the information, hearing the word overdose—which he vehemently argued against, he decided to buck the operator's judgment and move Melissa to the ground.

He'd just propped her head on his jacket when he heard the unmistakable sound of a cattle truck rumbling up the driveway.

His annoyance that Cres had forgotten something *again*, was immediately replaced with a sense of urgency. Mick had medical training.

Wyn carefully lifted Melissa into his arms and carried her out of the barn. He'd made it halfway to the house when both men jumped out of the cab of the truck and ran toward him.

"What happened?" Cres demanded.

"I don't know. I found her like this. Mick, help her," he pleaded.

"Completely unresponsive?"

"Yes. Then she started to shake, almost like she was having a seizure."

"Take her in the house. You called 911?"

"Just got off the phone with them, but they said it'll be at least fifteen minutes."

Once they were inside, Wyn laid Melissa on the couch. He hovered over her as Mick poked and prodded her.

"Is she on any medication?"

"I don't know." He paused. "Wait, she had this in her hand." He passed over the pill.

Mick held it up to the light and frowned.

"What?"

"It's a glucose pill."

"What's that?"

"Diabetics take them when their blood sugar levels are low." Mick looked up at him. "Wyn, is Melissa diabetic?"

"I have no idea. She's never mentioned it to me."

"You haven't seen her testing her blood sugar levels first thing in the morning? Or the last thing before she crawls in bed at night?"

Suddenly, her secretiveness, her insistence on sleeping in her own bed at night and even locking her damn door in the morning made sense. Wyn said, "Fuck. We don't sleep in the same bed. She claimed she's a restless sleeper and needs her own space, so she's been sleeping in the guest bedroom. But obviously it was so she could keep this from me. Why would she do that?"

"Worry about that later. Right now, go into her room and see if you can find a blood glucose meter, some kind of insulin injection instruments. Hopefully she's got a Glucagon rescue kit."

Wyn looked at Cres with utter confusion. "What did he say?"

"Mick, under the circumstances it'd be better for you to do it since you know what to look for," Cres said.

"Where's her room?"

"Last one at the end of the hallway."

Mick took off.

Wyn dropped to his knees beside Melissa. He picked up her hand and kissed her knuckles. "You and me are gonna have a serious talk when you're not goddamned unconscious."

"Promise me you won't yell at her for this when she comes around."

He turned and glared at Cres. "Why the fuck would you even say that to me?"

"For that reason right there. You get angry first and maybe you'll try reasonable later. I'm askin' you not to do that this time.

There's a reason she kept this from you. If you want to understand why, don't scare her off with your blustering and accusations." He softened his tone. "I know you care about her. And I know she's crazy about you. So don't wreck this. Just...tread lightly okay?"

Mick jogged back into the room. He held up a kit. "She's got one."

"You know what to do?"

"Yeah. You gotta move, man," Mick said to him. "Oh, and I found her medic alert bracelet. She is diabetic. Type 1. She's insulin dependent."

Wyn was absolutely poleaxed. This woman that he'd bared his soul to, opened his home to, made love to and had fallen for...hadn't trusted him enough to share this with him.

"This will help her out a lot," Mick said.

"Should I call and cancel the ambulance?" Wyn asked.

"No. The paramedics will need to assess her. They might even take her to the hospital since it sounds like she might've had a seizure."

Seizure. That word twisted his guts into a knot. He couldn't watch as Mick...did whatever he did, because Wyn would be tempted to ask a million questions. The time for questions would come later.

Time passed in an endless void as he paced.

Finally, he heard Mick say, "No, Mel, don't try and sit up."

Melissa said something too low for Wyn to hear. But Mick's response was loud and clear. "Yes, he's here."

She was asking for him?

Wyn crossed the room and stood behind Mick. A sick feeling twisted his stomach again. Until he heard her whisper...

"Tell him I love him."

Say what?

"I'm sure he'll appreciate hearing that." Mick sent Wyn an apologetic look. "She's babbling."

But I want her to mean it.

Mick kept up a running dialogue, if only to keep Melissa from talking. "It's only been twenty minutes since we left. We had to turn around because Cres left the paperwork and his wallet in the tack room."

"Wyn?"

What the hell? She never called him Wyn. She always called him by his full name. It appeared she didn't know what she was saying. "Yeah, baby, I'm here."

Melissa's skin was blotchy, red in spots, pasty white in others. Her eyes were vacant. But when she saw him? Her eyes held fear. And then a film of tears. Her lips started to wobble after she mouthed "sorry" and then she turned her head into the couch cushion, away from him.

The fuck that was happening. She was goddamn *done* hiding anything from him. Wyn stepped in front of Mick and braced his hand on the wall above the back of the couch, so he loomed above her. He reached down and gently turned her face toward him. "Kentucky, look at me."

"Wyn," Cres warned.

"Butt out, bro. This is between me and my woman."

That got Melissa's eyes to open again.

He stroked his thumb over her cheek. "There she is, my beautiful, stubborn filly. Fair warning, darlin'. After the EMTs get here and tell me what steps I need to take to get you back to normal, you and me are gonna have a serious talk."

"You're mad at me," she choked out.

"No, I'm scared for you. Big difference. Now I'm gonna let Mick do his thing. I just wanted you to know I'm here and I ain't goin' anywhere."

Her eyes teared up again and she nodded before she closed her eyes.

The paramedics arrived.

Wyn hung on the periphery and tried to decipher what they were saying as they spoke to her and Mick. Even when he knew it was ridiculous, he had a flash of annoyance that the EMTs were talking to Mick about Melissa's condition when they should've been talking to him. He should know this stuff. Every single bit of it. He vowed he'd never be kept out of the loop again when it came to Melissa's health issues. He'd read everything he could get his hands on so he knew exactly how to help her. And figure out how to prevent this from ever happening again.

The female EMT finally took Wyn aside. "We're not admitting

her to the hospital as long as you're comfortable keeping a very close eye on her the next twenty-four hours."

"Absolutely."

"Mick indicated that you weren't aware she was diabetic."

"No, but I can promise you I'll be up to speed on everything about this in the next few hours."

"There's tons of information online—most of it is excellent. Thankfully she had an emergency kit. You'd be surprised how many diabetics aren't so well-prepared. Anyway, she said she took her dose of insulin this morning, so this…episode isn't due to negligence—aka 'forgetting' to inject herself. It sounds like she overexerted herself the past few days."

Wyn experienced a punch of guilt over that. He *had* been working her hard. "The tablet she had in her hand. Is that part of her daily medication?"

"No, it's supposed to be a quick fix when she feels the effects of low blood sugar. That's just one of many choices to get her glycemic index back in balance. She can fill you in on what foods/drinks/snacks usually work best for her when her body tells her she's hypoglycemic."

He should be recording this conversation—all the words were jumbling together.

"As soon as she's feeling up to it, she needs to eat. She'll need to check her blood sugar levels more often. And if rest, liquids, and food don't get her levels back down into the normal range? Bring her to the ER."

"I will."

She patted his shoulder. "I know you will."

Wyn shot a quick glance over his shoulder. "Can I ask…have you seen this before?"

"What? A diabetic starting to go into diabetic shock?"

"No, people close to the patient bein' in the dark about their condition."

She looked thoughtful. "For some people, talking about having diabetes is an embarrassment because of all the misinformation and misperceptions about it, so it's easier to keep it under wraps. I had a friend in high school that went to great lengths to hide it because she didn't want our classmates or teachers to treat her differently or feel sorry for her. Even at age seventeen, she worried that she'd never find love because it would be daunting for a guy to take on a woman with a chronic illness. Maybe that sounds stupid to us, but the truth is, we don't have to be vigilant about food intake, watch physical activity, take insulin shots, do blood sugar monitoring that the people who have this disease have to deal with every day. And like it or not, type 1 diabetes is an incurable disease. That's not to say it's not manageable, but it is a lifelong condition." She paused. "Did that answer your question?"

"Yes. More than you know. Thank you."

By the time the EMTs left, Melissa was sitting up.

Cres and Mick waited in the kitchen. That's where he went first.

"I know you've gotta take off, and this is one time, baby bro, that I won't chew your ass for forgetting paperwork. I'm thankful that you were here, Mick."

"Glad to help. But you need to get to the bottom of why she kept this from you. Show her you're a standup guy, Wyn. Maybe she's never had anyone show her how to stand your ground when the going gets tough."

"I hear ya."

Cres clapped him on the shoulder. "See you tomorrow. You need anything, call or text."

Wyn followed them out and watched the cattle truck drive away for the second time. Then he went back inside to deal with his woman.

Melissa looked so…frail sitting on his couch with an afghan draped over her.

He crouched in front of her. "You feel like eating anything yet?"

"No. The beef jerky and orange juice will hold me over for a bit."

"Good. You ready to get some rest?"

"I thought I'd stretch out on the couch."

He stood. "You thought wrong." He scooped her into his arms. "Hang on."

She didn't speak until she noticed they weren't going in the direction of her room. "Wynton?"

"From here on out, you're sleepin' with me."

"But all my stuff—"

"Will be moved into my room." He set her on the bed and pulled the afghan away. "In my bed is where you should've been all along and you damn well know it."

Melissa didn't argue.

"Now, do you need me to help you take your clothes off? Or do you wanna do it?"

"Stop it," she snapped. "I don't want you to baby me."

Wyn got right in her face. "Tough shit. I want to take care of you and you'll let me, understand? " He exhaled a slow breath. "I need to do this as much as you need to let me do it."

She reached up and touched his face. "Okay. But no funny business when you help me take my clothes off. I don't have the energy for it."

Do not snap at her for believing you're such a sex fiend that you'd take advantage of her after she had a diabetic episode.

"God, I'm sorry for saying that. I was trying to make light of the situation and it didn't come out that way."

Wyn kissed the inside of her wrist. "You and me are gonna have to come up with a whole new way to communicate, Kentucky."

"Agreed."

He popped the buttons on her pearl snap shirt and tugged it off. He pulled her T-shirt over her head, glad to see she'd taken his advice to dress in layers. He unhooked her bra. He forced himself not to focus on how quickly her nipples puckered into tight points.

"Are you stripping me down completely?"

"Yeah."

"What if I get cold?"

"I'll keep you warm. Stand." He dropped to his knees and undid her belt, then her jeans. He peeled the denim down her thighs and held onto her arm as she kicked them aside. He pressed a soft kiss to her belly as he pulled off her panties. Then he wrapped his arms around her, breathed her in and released all the tension he'd carried in the past hour and a half. She was all right. Soft and warm and in his room, with him, where she belonged.

"Wynton."

"Give me a sec."

Melissa sifted her fingers through his hair. "I'm okay."

"You scared me."

"I scared myself." She clamped her hands around his jaw and tilted his head back. "I'm sorry I scared you. And we'll talk about everything after I've had some time to recover. But for right now, can I please get under the covers? I'm freezing my ass off."

He smiled against her stomach.

When he reached down to remove her socks and she said, "Huh-uh, cowboy. I'll let you strip me naked, but one of the fun side effects of diabetes is my feet are always cold, so the socks stay on."

"Yes, ma'am." Wyn rolled back the bedding. Then he stood and shed his clothes.

From beneath the covers, Melissa stared at his crotch and said, "You're hard."

"Seein' you naked does that to me. It'll behave, I promise."

"You sound like *it* has a mind of its own."

Wyn slipped in next to her. "Sometimes, I swear it does." He tucked her head under his chin and wrapped her in his arms. A sense of peace settled over him as he drifted off.

"Wynton?" she murmured.

"Yeah, baby?"

"I never want to sleep away from you again."

He kissed the top of her head. "Same here."

Chapter Ten

When Mel woke up, she had that same panicked sense of disorientation as she did when she came to on the couch in the living room.

"It's okay. You're still in my bed."

She shifted toward his voice and noticed he was propped up against the headboard, a laptop open on top of a pillow. "Surfing porn sites while I sleep, Super Man-Slut?"

He grinned. "Dammit. Why didn't I think of usin' the Internet to find porn sites? I'm usin' it for pesky research."

Her chest tightened. "What kind of research?"

"Small engine repair for this motor I plan to rebuild."

"Really?"

Wynton rolled his eyes. "No, not really. I'm finding out everything I need to know about type 1 diabetes. You got a problem with that?"

"No." She flopped back into the pillows. "I'd tell you that you could ask me anything you wanted to know, but that's sort of the whole point, isn't it? I *didn't* do that."

"Yeah." He set her blood glucose meter on her chest. "And so the fun begins. It's been two hours, so time to check those levels again."

Her eyes narrowed. "You want to watch?"

"I need to watch so I know how to do it if I ever have to. I also want to watch so I know what you deal with every day. How it's part of your routine."

Stupid, sweet man. Now he was gonna make her cry. "I need the box of glucose test strips, the box of lancets, and the alcohol swabs." She went through the process, poking herself, putting the drop of blood on the glucose test strip, putting the strip in the meter and showing him where the results appeared and explaining what the number meant.

"Wait, I know what that number means. You're still on the low end, so you need to eat or drink something to boost your count and then retest in fifteen minutes."

"Wow. You are a quick study."

Wynton stroked her cheek. "I am when it matters to me."

He definitely was testing her tear threshold.

"Do you want juice? Or raisins? Or honey? Or regular soda? Or a glucose tablet?"

"Juice would be great."

He leaned over and kissed her forehead before he popped out of bed. "Don't move. I'll be right back." The man hustled out and he didn't bother to put on pants.

She loved that about him.

She loved *everything* about him.

An odd sense of...déjà vu niggled in the back of her mind.

Tell him I love him.

The few times she'd gotten to the point she had today, she'd heard from others she'd been spectacularly nasty. She'd also heard of instances where a person blurted out secrets with no recollection of it. So had she confessed her feelings for him? To him?

Given how unbelievably close they'd gotten in the last three weeks, it wasn't a surprise that she'd fallen head over heels in love with Wynton Grant. The man was beyond amazing. But she hadn't wanted him to find out that way, when she wasn't even aware of what she was saying.

But on the other hand, it would be weird if she asked him if she'd confessed her love for him. *Hey, sexy rancher man, I'm not sure if you caught it before because I'm not even sure that I said it, but I love the fuck out of you.*

Ugh. No. That would *not* be cool.

Wynton returned with a tray. He set it on the dresser and handed her a glass of juice.

"Thank you."

"You're welcome. I'll just…" He blew out a breath. "I don't know what the fuck to do. I have so damned many questions but I don't want to bombard you."

Mel sipped the cranberry juice. "Bombard away."

"How long have you had diabetes?"

"Six and a half months."

That surprised him.

"Yeah, it's a new thing to me too. Several months before I was diagnosed I had all the classic symptoms—excessive thirst, weight loss, irritability, no appetite. I chalked it up to the end of the season stress. Then I blacked out, much like I did here today. It scared me and I went to the ER. They ran tests. The results surprised the medical staff as much as it did me because at my age it's almost always a diagnosis of type 2 diabetes, not type 1. So I spent two weeks learning that burying my head in the sand and pretending it would go away isn't the best way to deal with it."

"What happened before?"

She took another swig of juice. "I was lethargic but I competed anyway. I did great in the first go. I did fine in the team penning round. But I was the next to last competitor of the day in the cutting competition and I almost passed out. Hearing people describe the run, they said I sat atop Plato as if I'd been hypnotized."

Wynton brushed her hair out of her face. "Is that how you remembered it?"

"That's the thing. I *don't* remember anything at all. Not dealing with my horse or even getting back to my horse trailer. I woke up the next morning and it was a worse feeling than a blackout drunk."

He kissed her forehead. "Keep goin'."

"That's when I went to the ER. After my diabetes crash course, I took Plato back to Gradsky's because I knew I had to give up competing. I blurted out everything to Berlin. She swore she'd keep it between us. But she insisted I stick around there until I got a better handle on how to live with diabetes and what was next in my

life. I avoided everyone in the world of rodeo. I even avoided
London when she came home."

"So that's what Breck meant when he said you were—"

"All plumped up again? Yes. I'd lost thirty pounds over the
course of three months, so I probably did look anorexic."

"Still makes him a fuckin' ass for sayin' that shit to you." He
absentmindedly stroked her arm. "So you've been hiding?"

"Pretty much."

"You don't gotta hide from me."

*Please don't ask me right now why I didn't tell you. Because you're not
running scared after finding out makes me hope this isn't the end.* She pointed
to the tray. "Could I get some beef jerky and one of those hard
candies?"

"You bet."

"You really did do your homework."

"Like I said, I pay attention when it matters." Wynton pinned
her with a look. "And in case that ain't plain enough for you, I'll
repeat it. You matter to me, Melissa Lockhart. A whole heckuva
lot."

She burst into tears.

Wynton thought he'd said the wrong thing, and Mel tried to get
him to quit backtracking, at least until she got control of her
emotions.

But the man didn't let her sob into her pillow. He simply
picked her up and hauled her onto his lap, forcing her tears to fall
on his chest. He murmured unintelligible things, but they soothed
her with their intent.

After she settled, Wynton kissed the tears from her face. "It
wrecks me to see you cryin'. Guts me like nothin' else. Except seein'
you unresponsive in the barn." He rested his forehead to hers. "I
still have a ton of questions, but I'll let it be for now. You test your
level and then rest a little longer."

"Will you stay in here with me?"

"If you want."

"I do."

He grinned. "See? That wasn't so hard, was it?"

Chapter Eleven

Wyn had thrown a roast, potatoes, and veggies in the slow cooker before they'd loaded cattle earlier this morning, so at least he could feed her properly.

While she'd slept he'd texted Cres, letting him know she was doing better.

He'd done a little more research online.

But the answer he needed the most he could only get from her.

Melissa wandered into the kitchen. "Hey. You let me sleep a long time."

"You needed it." He kicked out a stool. "Have a seat. We can eat whenever you're ready."

"Smells good. What is it?"

"Roast. My mom's recipe. I followed it to the letter so I didn't screw it up. I'm not so good at improvising."

She gave him a smug look. "Maybe not when it comes to cooking."

"True. Is there anything you need to do before we eat?"

"No. I'll shower after dinner. Is there anything I can help you with?"

Wyn shook his head. "It's a one pot deal so I'll just plop it on the counter and dish it up."

Although they sat side by side, they didn't talk during the meal.

He kept sneaking looks at her to see if she was really enjoying the food or if she was just pushing it around on her plate. But her plate was nearly empty.

"Stop looking at me out of the corner of your eye. I'm fine."

He faced her. "It's not that."

"Then what?"

"I'm embarrassed that this is the first time I've cooked for you in my home. I never thought I'd be the type of guy who'd take for granted that you'd cook for me when you stayed here because you're a woman."

She set her hand on his arm. "I cooked for us because I like to cook. And since you've been stewing about this you probably know that the other reason I did it was because I have dietary restrictions."

"So you wouldn't set off my warning bells if I made something that you couldn't eat. And then I wouldn't ask questions if you were doin' all the cooking."

Melissa shoved her plate across the counter. She wiped her mouth and turned her barstool toward him. "We're having this out now? Fine. Ask me."

"Why didn't you tell me?"

"Because you were supposed to be a one-night wedding hookup, Wynton."

He counted to ten. "But it didn't turn out that way. You've been livin' in my house, we've been workin' together, sorting cattle almost every day for three weeks, we've been fucking like bunnies…and not once when you were scurrying off to your room to test your blood sugar and inject yourself with insulin did it ever occur to you to tell me that you're diabetic? And that you could have some sort of serious episode that might send you into a coma? I keep thinking how goddamned glad I am that Mick came back here and had the experience to know all wasn't right with you. Do you have any idea how it made me feel that I didn't know my lover has a life-threatening disease? That I wouldn't know what the fuck to do if something like that happened when we were alone? That you could've died because I wouldn't have known how to help you? That flat out sucks, Melissa. And I know this ain't about me, but goddammit, you *know* it was wrong to keep this from me for even a day, let alone fuckin' weeks!"

Wyn's voice had escalated and he shrank back away from her. Shit. He hadn't meant to yell at her. He scrubbed his hands over his face. "Fuck. Sorry. I just…" He pushed back from the counter.

"Wynton—"

He held up his hand. "Just give me a minute." He walked to the back door. The day had stayed warm and although the sun had set, he welcomed the breeze blowing through the screen, needing something to cool him off because he hadn't gotten a handle on his temper like he thought he had.

Soft arms circled his waist. Melissa rested her cheek on his shoulder blade. "I'm sorry. I can't say that enough and mean it enough. I never wanted you to see me like that."

"Which is why you didn't tell me?"

Her sigh warmed his shirt where her mouth rested. "No. I didn't tell you because I worried that it'd spook you."

"Why in the hell would you think that?"

"Um, I was at the hospital with you during your dad's ordeal, remember? And we had a few conversations about how you didn't know how to deal with health crises situations. You said you either shut down or used avoidance. You admitted you were freaked out by Sutton's injuries—both times—and how relieved you were that he made a full recovery because you weren't sure you could handle him being permanently damaged. So tell me, I was just supposed to blurt out that I have a condition that might end up blinding me? Making me lose a limb? That I had to deal with medication and monitoring every day for the rest of my life? You would've said, 'Thanks for telling me, Melissa. I know we haven't even been on one date yet, but I want to learn everything about your condition on the off chance that I'm not freaked out by helping you deal with this every day forever.' That's bullshit and you know it."

She was right. Fuck he *hated* that she was right. She hadn't even mentioned how horrified he'd been that she had dealt with a permanently injured sibling. And she hadn't called him out on his less than grateful attitude that he'd been spared that.

"Do you want to know how my mother reacted when I told her? She tried to convince me that I was mistaken. I couldn't possibly have 'contracted' type 1 diabetes as a thirty-two-year-old woman. She got all haughty and informed me that what I meant was I had type 2 diabetes. And well, she had little sympathy for me because everyone knows that type 2 diabetes is a disease fat, lazy people and alcoholics bring on themselves by not taking care of themselves."

Wyn didn't know if he could stomach any more of this.

You will listen, asshole. You're the one who demanded to know why she hadn't told you. Now that she has the guts to do so, you ain't gonna puss out.

"Then she said she couldn't believe I was making such a big deal about it. That there were people like Alyssa with real physical problems that couldn't be fixed by a change in diet and exercise. And it was sad that I needed attention for a situation of my own making, and I should be ashamed. That I shouldn't contact them again until I got my life in order."

He spun around and gathered her into his arms when the sobs broke free. "Baby, I'm so sorry."

"So you can see why I'd be less than eager to relive *that* experience."

"No offense, but your family is a bunch of fucking idiots."

"It still hurts."

"I can't imagine." He kissed the top of her head. "Did your sister react the same way?"

"I haven't told her."

"I'm sensing a pattern here, Kentucky."

Melissa head-butted his chest. "I'm sorry I didn't tell you. I haven't told Alyssa because she's been in Europe for fucking ever and I haven't talked to her." She looked at him. "Are you ever going to forgive me for not telling you?"

"Yes. If you'll let us start over."

"Meaning what?"

He took the biggest chance of his life. "As much as I'd like to pretend this has only been about sex between us, that's a lie. It's been about more than that since the second you walked into the hospital and stayed with me all night. I like being around you. I like having you in my house and part of my life."

"I-I don't know what to say."

"Say you'll give me a chance—us a chance."

"I'm supposed to leave tomorrow."

Wyn kissed her. "I know. I'm askin' you to rethink that."

Those soulful brown eyes searched his. "What happened today hasn't scared you off?"

"Exactly the opposite." *It makes me want to hold on to you tighter. It makes me want to prove to you that I can love you like no one else can. It makes me think I've been single all these years because I was waiting for you.*

She sighed and snuggled into him. "You make my head spin, Wynton Grant."

"Is that a good thing?"

"A very good thing. Now, can we curl up on the couch and watch *South Park?*"

"Yeah. Hearing you laugh will do me a world of good, Kentucky."

"I was thinking the same thing about you, cowboy."

* * * *

When Mel felt so restless she thought she might crawl out of her skin, she told him she needed an orgasm to relax.

He told her to take a shower. And he insisted she clean up in his master bathroom since his huge shower had a bench seat in case she got tired.

The man was still babying her.

She sort of loved it.

As hard as she tried to convince him he didn't have to sit on the vanity and watch her, the stubborn man didn't listen.

After she'd washed and conditioned her hair, shaved and loofah-ed her skin with her favorite lavender vanilla body wash, she rinsed off and decided to put her plan to get a little action into action. But the man usurped her intent to give him a show—rubbing one out while sitting on the bench, her legs spread wide—when he entered the shower completely naked with that wicked gleam in his eyes.

"I could tell by the way your ass twitched that you were up to no good, Amazing Slut-Girl. So if you're feelin' up to teasing me then I figure you're up for this." He dropped to his knees and pulled her to the edge of the bench. "Brace yourself, arms behind you." Then he nuzzled her patch of pubic hair and slid his tongue up and down her slit.

"You are so very, very good at that, Super Man-Slut." Melissa felt dizzy for an entirely different reason, but she wouldn't tell him because he might stop doing that swirling thing with his tongue.

Wynton wasn't in a teasing mood. He ate at her as if he was starved for her. The water from the shower flowed over her skin like a dozen softly caressing fingers. Tiny sparkling droplets beaded on his face, the ends of his hair, and those amazingly long eyelashes. His fingers tightened on her ass and he stopped sucking to growl, "Fuck. I know where all the sugar in your body has gone to. Right here. Christ. You're as sweet and addictive as candy."

She trembled at the power behind his meaning. "Wynton. Please."

"Give it to me."

"I am."

"You're holding back. I wanna feel you explode on my tongue."

"Then stop talking and put your mouth back on my clit," she retorted.

His laughter vibrating on her swollen tissues had her gasping.

And the man knew just how to use that skilled tongue.

She shattered—the pulsing, pounding, dizzying orgasm sent her soaring to that other white void.

When she floated back down and opened her eyes, she saw something she'd never wanted to see on her lover's face. Concern.

He opened his mouth—probably to ask if she was okay—and she placed her fingers over his lips.

"Don't. I feel great. I want to feel even better. So get up here and fuck me. I want to lose myself in you for a little while." She scraped her fingers across the dark stubble on his cheeks, loving how the water had softened those bristly hairs. "There's something else I didn't tell you."

"What?"

"You're the first man I've been with since I was diagnosed."

"Why me?"

"Because you're like me—or the me I used to be before. Unapologetically sexual. I liked the way you just took over. I've never had that. Never needed it. Never wanted it. So once we got past the first couple of times we were naked together, I thought if you noticed the insulin injection sites while we were rolling around in the sheets then it wouldn't be as big a deal. That I could tell you the truth and maybe you wouldn't kick me out of bed. When you didn't notice them, for the first time in six months I felt like myself again. You have no idea what that meant to me."

"Yeah, baby, I think I do." Wynton kissed his way up her body, stopping to lick the water off her nipples. When he reached her neck, he sucked and nuzzled the spot that made her wet, made her wiggle, made her moan. "When I was in your room earlier I noticed a package of birth control pills on the dresser. You've been taking the pill?"

"Yes. Why?"

"Because I want you bare. No barriers between us. I'm clean. I haven't been with anyone in eight months." He brushed his lips over her ear. "I've never had sex without a condom."

She pushed him back to stare into his eyes. "Never?"

"Never. I've haven't been interested in a long-term relationship. Until now. Until you, Melissa."

It took every bit of control for her not to burst into tears. She managed to keep her tone light. "Lucky for you I'm so wet we won't even need lube since we won't be using a lubed up condom."

He kissed her then. Kissed her and pulled her into his arms. He maneuvered them so he was sitting on the bench and they were face to face. "You're beautiful."

"You don't have to flatter me. I'm a sure thing, Wynton."

"You're still beautiful." When he kissed her like she was precious to him, and not as if he was being careful because she was fragile, she understood his tenderness came from his strength. And she loved him all the more for it.

Locking her ankles around his lower back, she draped her forearms on his shoulders. When she felt him position the head of his cock at her entrance, she whispered, "Go slowly so I can watch your face."

Wynton kept one hand on her ass and the other cupped her neck as he eased into her fully. "Oh yeah. That feels fucking fantastic."

"Make this last. I want to feel you fill me every single time."

He groaned. "Babe. Cut me a break. The first time with no condom. I don't know how long I can last."

They moved together slowly, taking time to kiss and taste and caress. And when he couldn't hold back any longer, she slipped her hand between their bodies and got herself off the same time he bathed her pussy in his liquid heat.

Only after he kissed her did she notice he'd turned the water off.

"Did you mean it?" he whispered.

"Mean what?"

"Mean it when you said, *tell him I love him*."

Her heart raced. "I didn't think you heard that."

"I did. And I want to know if you meant it."

"Yes, I meant it."

He smiled against her neck.

"Wynton. This is where you tell me this isn't logical. That it's crazy I fell in love with you in three weeks."

"I can't do that. I'm suffering from the same lack of logic, Kentucky, because I fell in love with you too."

Mel eased back and looked into his eyes.

"Don't go tomorrow. Stay with me."

"For how long?"

"Just until the end of time."

She laughed. But her smile faded when she realized he wasn't joking. "Are you sure? Everything is up in the air with me."

"Those things would still be up in the air regardless if you were here or in Timbuktu."

"You do have a point."

He rested his forehead to hers. "Let's figure some of this out together."

"No rush?"

"None."

"Okay."

Chapter Twelve

One week later...

Mel's phone rang and her pulse jumped, as it always did when she saw her sister's name on the caller ID. "Hello?"

"What the hell, sis? I just found out that you have type 2 diabetes?"

"Hi Alyssa, long time no talk. How are you?"

"Pissed. God. I've been gone to Europe for eight months and I don't hear from you at all—we'll get into that bullshit in a minute. So when I ask Mom how you're doing, she just casually fucking mentions that you have 'contracted' diabetes, like it's some kind of venereal disease?"

Mel laughed. She loved her sister. Over the years, Alyssa had taken total control of her life. She didn't take shit from anyone, including their parents, and she'd plow over anyone who got in her way of achieving her many goals. The woman was a muscular beast—on her upper half anyway—and she could inflict some serious damage on anyone dumb enough to assume that being paralyzed from the waist down meant that her brain was somehow impaired. "I can say this to you because you understand, but Mom was a stone-cold bitch when I told her about my diagnosis. And I don't have type 2 diabetes, I have type 1. Which means I'll be insulin dependent for the rest of my life. Of course, Mom being the medical expert on all things insisted I didn't know my own diagnosis."

"Are you kidding me?"

"Nope." And because it felt good to get all of this off her chest with Wynton, she did it again, detailing the entire conversation between her and their mother.

Alyssa was so quiet for so long afterward that Mel thought they'd gotten disconnected.

"Hello?"

"I'm still here. Checking my blood pressure because I'm fuming so hard. First of all, it sucks that not only did you discover you have a serious health issue, you didn't have family support after you found out." She paused. "You didn't keep me out of the loop about your diagnosis to pay me back for bein' such a sorry-assed cunt to you after my accident?"

Mel snorted. How had she forgotten that bloody cunt and sorry-assed cunt were her sister's favorite words? "God, no. I knew you were rolling across the globe, being the world spokeswoman for impaired athletes and inspiring millions. I didn't want to burden you."

"Burden me," Alyssa repeated. "That's horseshit. You've supported me through more than I care to think about. You should've let me rot in my own misery, but you didn't. And it sucks that you wouldn't allow me to be there for you. You didn't have the right to take that away from me. Yeah, I probably wouldn't have flown home, but goddammit, Mel, I have a fucking phone. We could've talked about it."

"I never knew what time zone you were in and international calls are expensive."

Alyssa snarled, "Expensive? What the ever-loving fuck? Jesus, Mel, we both have a damn trust fund! Money hasn't ever been an issue, nor will it ever be. Try again."

Wynton strolled into the kitchen and smiled at her. But his smile dried when he saw she was on the phone. He mouthed, "You okay?"

She nodded.

"Still waiting *Mel-is-sa*." Alyssa singsonged her full name like their mother used to.

"After I told you how Mom reacted, you're honestly surprised that I didn't break my finger trying to dial you up to sob on your shoulder?"

"Fine. You've got me there. But the fact is, I'm back in the States now. I missed you. I want to catch up on your wild, on-the-road rodeo tales. Isn't it about time for national championships to start?"

"Yeah, but I sorta…gave up competing after my diagnosis."

Silence. "Gave up. Please don't tell me it's some kind of stupid safety rule the organization enforces and you're being discriminated against due to your health impairment. Because you know I have a team of lawyers who love to go after those kinds of cases."

"Simmer down, crusader. I had a couple of episodes where I put myself, my horse, and the others in the corral with me in danger. It spooked me. So I've been taking stock."

"That better not be Mel-speak for quitting."

"And if it is?"

"I'll harass you endlessly. And you have to listen to me because I'm *paralyzed* and I still compete."

"Omigod, Alyssa. You do *not* get to play the paralyzed card with me!" She shot Wynton a look and he seemed…shocked by the conversation. Most people would be, but this is how it was between her and her sister, and she wouldn't have it any other way.

Alyssa laughed. "Wrong. I *always* get to play the paralyzed card." She paused. "The question is…do you miss competing?"

Mel locked gazes with Wynton. "Actually, no. I don't miss it as much as I thought I would. I'm thinking about getting my teaching certificate so I can torture teens with words instead of a riding crop."

"You'd kill at that, sis. Good for you."

"Oh, and I *am* utilizing all the equestrian skills I've learned over the years. I've been helping out at this beautiful ranch in Colorado. I've even got this smokin' hot cowboy rancher who wants me to stick around and be his personal ranch hand. He's the lucky one I've been showing all my best riding tricks."

Wynton grinned.

"You have a boyfriend! Is it serious?"

"Yes, it's serious."

"I want to meet this guy," Alyssa demanded.

To Wynton, Mel said, "Alyssa is demanding to meet you."

"She's welcome here any time. I'll even install a wheelchair ramp for her."

She melted. She mouthed, "I love you," at him before she said, "Did you hear that?" to her sister.

"Yes, I heard that and I think I'm a little bit in love with him. Does he have a brother?"

"He has two brothers, but one is married and the other one is gay."

"Story of my life. I'm happy for you sis. Truly."

"Thanks."

"Take care of yourself. You've been feeling okay?"

How weird to have her sister asking about *her* health. "I still miscalculate sometimes, but I'm in the beginning stage of learning to live with it."

"Call me whenever you need someone to listen."

"I will."

"Okay. Love you, and be expecting a phone call from Mom at some point this week because I am going to ream her—and Dad—a new one. It's going to be fucking epic."

Mel was still smiling when she hung up.

Then Wynton was right there, curling his hands around her face. "Sounded like that went...well."

"Alyssa is pissed on my behalf. She can lay on the guilt trip to our folks way better than I can, so I'll let her."

"I can't wait to meet her." He paused. "You're serious about looking in to getting a teaching certificate?"

"It's something I always wanted to do, but I've been too unsettled to follow through with it. Being with you...I feel settled for the first time ever, and not because I settled. But because I'm finally where I'm meant to be."

"I couldn't agree more." He kissed her and chuckled against her mouth.

"What's so funny?"

"Remember one of the first nights you stayed here and we were talking about the difference between love and lust? I told you I warned Sutton that no one falls in love in a month? And you admitted you told London the same thing?"

"Yes. Why?"

"Because we beat them by falling in love in three weeks."

Mel sighed. "Is everything always going to be a competition between you and your brothers?"

"Probably."

"You know, London and Sutton are going to take full credit for us getting together."

"Let 'em. You and I will always know the truth."

"Which is?"

"Super Man-Slut and the Amazing Slut-Girl were destined to hook up and then hang up their unopened packets of condoms for good so they could become the one and only for each other, forever."

"I love a happy ending."

"Me too." He scooped her into his arms. "Speaking of happy endings...you owe me one, woman."

"Hey, I thought you owed *me* one."

Wynton gave her a depraved look that sent her pulse tripping. "You thinking what I'm thinking?"

"Uh-huh."

Then they said *sixty-nine* simultaneously.

And they both got their happy ending...

About Lorelei James

Lorelei James is the *New York Times* and *USA Today* bestselling author of contemporary erotic romances in the Rough Riders, Blacktop Cowboys, and Mastered series. She also writes dark, gritty mysteries under the name Lori Armstrong and her books have won the Shamus Award and the Willa Cather Literary Award. She lives in western South Dakota.

Connect with Lorelei in the following places:

Website: http://www.loreleijames.com/

Facebook: https://www.facebook.com/LoreleiJamesAuthor

Twitter: http://twitter.com/loreleijames

Instagram: https://instagram.com/loreleijamesauthor/

Facebook Reader Discussion Group:
https://www.facebook.com/groups/loreleijamesstreetteam/

Newsletter: http://loreleijames.com/newsletter.php

Also from Lorelei James

Rough Riders Series (in reading order)
LONG HARD RIDE
RODE HARD
COWGIRL UP AND RIDE
ROUGH, RAW AND READY
BRANDED AS TROUBLE
STRONG SILENT TYPE (novella)
SHOULDA BEEN A COWBOY
ALL JACKED UP
RAISING KANE
SLOW RIDE (free short story)
COWGIRLS DON'T CRY
CHASIN' EIGHT
COWBOY CASANOVA
KISSIN' TELL
GONE COUNTRY
SHORT RIDES (anthology)
REDNECK ROMEO
COWBOY TAKE ME AWAY
LONG TIME GONE (novella)

Blacktop Cowboys® Series (in reading order)
CORRALLED
SADDLED AND SPURRED
WRANGLED AND TANGLED
ONE NIGHT RODEO
TURN AND BURN
HILLBILLY ROCKSTAR
ROPED IN (novella)
WRAPPED AND STRAPPED (Nov 2015)

Mastered Series (in reading order)
BOUND
UNWOUND

SCHOOLED (digital only novella)
UNRAVELED
CAGED

Single Title Novels
RUNNING WITH THE DEVIL
DIRTY DEEDS

Single Title Novellas
LOST IN YOU (short novella)
WICKED GARDEN
MISTRESS CHRISTMAS (Wild West Boys)
MISS FIRECRACKER (Wild West Boys)
BALLROOM BLITZ (Two To Tango anthology)

Need You Series (debuts Jan 2016)
WHAT YOU NEED (Jan 5 2016)

Lorelei James also writes as mystery author Lori Armstrong

Roped In
A Blacktop Cowboys® Novella
By Lorelei James
Now Available!

Ambition has always been his biggest downfall...until he meets her.

World champion bulldogger Sutton Grant works hard on the road, but his quiet charm has earned the nickname "The Saint" because he's never been the love 'em and leave 'em type with the ladies. When he's sidelined by an injury, he needs help keeping his horse in competition shape, but he fears trying to sweet-talk premier horse trainer London Gradsky is a losing proposition-- because the woman sorta despises him.

London is humiliated when her boyfriend dumps her for a rodeo queen. What makes the situation worse? She's forced to see the lovebirds on the rodeo circuit every weekend. In an attempt to save face, London agrees to assist the notoriously mild, but ruggedly handsome Sutton Grant with his horse training problem on one condition: Sutton has to pretend to be her new boyfriend.

But make believe doesn't last long between the sassy cowgirl and the laid-back bulldogger. When the attraction between them ignites, London learns that sexy Sutton is no Saint when that bedroom door closes; he's the red-hot lover she's always dreamed of.

The more time they spend together, the more Sutton realizes he wouldn't mind being roped and tied to the rough and tumble cowgirl for real...

* * * *

"Why me?"

"Because we both know the only people who've been able to work with him have been you and me."

She sucked in a few breaths and forced herself to loosen her fists. "This wouldn't be an issue if you hadn't browbeaten my folks into selling Dial to you outright. When the breeder owns the horse and a rider goes down, other people are in place to keep the horse conditioned. That responsibility isn't pushed aside."

"You think I don't know that? You think I'm feelin' good about any of this? Fuck. I hired people to work with him and the stubborn bastard chased them all off. A couple of them literally."

London smirked. "That's my boy."

"Your boy is getting fatter and meaner by the day," Sutton retorted. "I'm afraid if I let him go too much longer it'll be too late and he'll be as worthless as me."

Worthless? Dude. Look in the mirror much? How could Sutton be out of commission and still look like he'd stepped off the pages of *Buff and Beautiful Bulldogger* magazine?

"I hope the reason you're so quiet is because you're considering my offer."

London's gaze zoomed to his. "How do you know you can afford me?"

"I don't. I get that you're an expert on this particular horse and I'm willing to pay you for that expertise." Sutton sidestepped her and rested his big body next to hers—close to hers—against the fence. "I know it'll sound stupid, but every time I grab the tack and head out to catch Dial to try and work him, even when I'm not supposed to, I feel his frustration that I'm not doin' more. I ain't the kind of man that sees a horse—my horse—as just a tool. Your folks knew that about me or they wouldn't have sold him to me for any amount of money."

"Yeah. I do know that," she grudgingly admitted, "but you should also know that I wouldn't be doin' this for you or the money, I'd be doin' it for Dial."

"That works for me. There's another reason that I want you. Only you."

"Which is?"

His unwavering stare unnerved her, as if he was gauging whether he could trust her. Finally he said, "Strictly between us?"

She nodded.

"If it's decided I'll never compete again, you're in the horse world more than I am and you'll ensure Dial gets where he needs to be."

London hadn't been expecting that. Sutton had paid a shit ton for Dial, and he hadn't suggested she'd help him sell the horse to a proper owner, just that she'd help him find one. In her mind that meant he really had Dial's best interest at heart. Not that she believed for an instant Sutton Grant intended to retire from steer wrestling. First off, he was barely thirty. Second, rumor had it his drive to win was as wide and deep as the Colorado River.

As she contemplated how to respond, she saw her ex, Stitch, with Princess Paige plastered to his side, meandering their direction.

Dammit. Not now.

After the incident this morning, she'd steered clear of the exhibitor's hall where the pair had handed out autographs and barf bags. She felt the overwhelming need to escape, but if she booked it across the corral, it'd look like she was running from them.

Screw that. Screw them. She was not in the wrong.

"London? You look ready to commit murder. What'd I say?"

She gazed up at him. The man was too damn good-looking, so normally she wouldn't have a shot at a man like him. But he did say he'd do *anything*...

"Okay, here's the deal. I'll work with Dial, but you've gotta do something for me. Uh, two things actually."

"Name them."

How much to tell him? She didn't want to come off desperate. Still, she opted for the truth. "Backstory: my boyfriend dumped me via text last month because he'd hooked up with a rodeo queen. Because he and I were together when I made my summer schedule, that means I will see them every fucking weekend. All summer."

"And?"

"And I don't wanna be known as that poor pathetic London Gradsky pining over her lost love."

Sutton's eyes turned shrewd. "*Are* you pining for him?"

"Mostly I'm just pissed. It needs to look like I've moved on. So I realize your nickname is 'The Saint' and you don't—"

"Don't call me that," he said crossly. "Tell me what you need."

"The first thing I'd need is you to play the part of my new boyfriend."

That shocked him, but he rallied with, "I can do that. When

does this start?"

"Right now, 'cause here they come." London plastered her front to his broad chest and wreathed her arms around his neck. "And make this look like the real deal, bulldogger."

"Any part of you that's hands off for me?"

She fought the urge to roll her eyes. Of course "The Saint" would ask first. "Nope."

Sutton bestowed that fuck-me-now grin. "I can work with that." He curled one hand around the back of her neck and the other around her hip.

When it appeared he intended to take his own sweet time kissing her, she took charge, teetering on tiptoe since the man was like seven feet tall. After the first touch of their lips, he didn't dive into her mouth in a fake show of passion. He rubbed his half-parted lips across hers, each pass silently coaxing her to open up a little more. Each tease of his breath on her damp lips made them tingle.

She muttered, "Kiss me like you mean business."

Those deceptively gentle kisses vanished and Sutton unleashed himself on her. Lust, passion, need. The kiss was way more powerful and take charge than she'd expected from a man nicknamed "The Saint."

Her mind shut down to everything but the sensuous feel of his tongue twining around hers as he explored her mouth, the soft stroking of his thumb on her cheek, and the possessive way his hand stroked her, as if it knew her intimately.

Then Sutton eased back, treating her lips to nibbles, licks, and lingering smooches. "Think they're gone?" he murmured.

"Who?"

He chuckled. "Your ex."

"Oh. Right. Them." She untwined her fingers from his soft hair and let her arms drop—slowly letting her hands flow over his neck and linebacker shoulders and that oh-so-amazing chest.

Their gazes collided the second she realized Sutton's heart beat just as crazily as hers did.

"So did that pass as the real deal kiss you wanted? Or do I need to do it again?"

Yes, please.

Don't be a pushover. Let him know who's in charge.

London smoothed her hand down her blouse. "For future reference, that type of kiss will work fine."

Sutton smirked. "It worked *fine* for me too, darlin'."

Rage/Killian

Bayou Heat Novellas

By Alexandra Ivy & Laura Wright

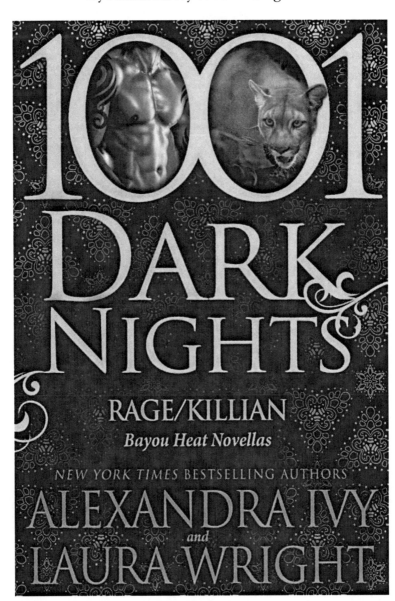

1001 DARK NIGHTS

RAGE/KILLIAN

Bayou Heat Novellas

NEW YORK TIMES BESTSELLING AUTHORS

ALEXANDRA IVY

and

LAURA WRIGHT

Acknowledgments From the Authors

To Our Readers, Current and New: We love you! Enjoy your Pantera. Grrrrowl.

Legend of the Pantera

To most people the Pantera, a mystical race of puma-shifters who live in the depths of the Louisiana swamps, have become little more than a legend.

It was rumored that in the ancient past, twin sisters, born of magic, had created a sacred land and claimed it as their own. From that land was born creatures who were neither human or animal, but a mixture of the two.

They became faster and stronger than normal humans. Their senses were hyper acute. And when surrounded by the magic of the Wildlands in the bayous of Southern Louisiana, they were capable of shifting into pumas.

As the years passed, however, the sightings of the Pantera became so rare that the rumors faded to myths.

Most believed the entire species had become extinct.

Then months ago, they'd been forced to come out of the shadows when it was uncovered that a secret sect of humans have been experimenting with Pantera blood and DNA.

It's a battle for the future of the puma-shifters.

One they dare not lose.

No matter what the cost.

Rage

Chapter One

The Wildlands were exactly what most people would expect for a pack of puma-shifters. Thick foliage, towering cypress trees, narrow water channels clogged with water lilies and banks of sweet-smelling azaleas.

A glorious, untamed bayou that stretched for miles.

But it was much more than a vast swamp. Behind the magical barriers were hundreds of comfortable homes, a state-of-the-art medical clinic, a village green where the Pantera shared meals, and a large, Colonial-style structure with black shutters that looked like it'd been plucked out of *Gone With the Wind*.

The building was currently being shared by the heads of the various factions. Suits, who were the diplomats of the Pantera. The Geeks, who took care of everything high-tech. The Healers, who could usually be found at the clinic. And the Hunters, who were the protectors.

Inside, the HQ was buzzing with activity. No big surprise. Over the past few months they'd endured a crazy-ass goddess, a traitor, and now a human corporation, Benson Enterprises, who'd been secretly kidnapping Pantera and using them as lab rats.

Which was why Rage should have suspected that something was up when Parish led him to a back room that offered them a temporary privacy.

The two male Hunters looked similar at a glance. Both had deeply bronzed skin and dark hair, although Rage kept his cut short. And both had broad shoulders and sculpted muscles that were covered by worn jeans and T-shirts, despite the chill in the air.

But while the older Parish looked like a lethal killer with scars that bisected the side of his angular face, Rage was blessed with the features of an angel. Even more fascinating, his eyes were a stunning violet that was flecked with gold.

Women had been sighing in pleasure since Rage hit puberty.

It took a closer look to see the predatory cat that lurked just below the surface.

At the moment, he looked every inch the deadly Hunter. His eyes glowed with power and if he'd been in his cat form, his tail would have been twitching as he paced from one end of the room to the other.

"No," he growled. "No, no, no."

"I'm sorry." Parish folded his arms over his chest, the air prickling with the force of his authority. The older male wasn't the leader of the Hunters because of his sparkling personality. "Did you think that was a request? Because it wasn't."

Rage grimaced, deliberately leashing his instinctive aggression. He'd discovered at an early age he could use his natural charm to…encourage people to see things his way. It was only when his cat was provoked to violence that it was obvious why his faction was Hunter instead of Diplomat.

"Please, Parish," he soothed. "Send someone else."

"There is no one else." Parish narrowed his golden eyes. "In case you missed the memo we've been having a few disasters lately."

"Exactly. I should be out searching for the mysterious Christopher," Rage said, referring to the head of Benson Enterprises, the shadowy corporation that was responsible for stealing Pantera, as well as vulnerable humans. "Or at least hunting down the Frankenstein labs. We still can't be sure we've burned them all." He pointed toward the window that overlooked the manicured grass of the communal area. Below them a few Pantera mothers were sharing a late lunch while their cubs tumbled across the spongy ground. It was winter in the Wildlands, but the Pantera embraced the brisk air. "Hell, I'll even spy on the military. Someone needs to discover who can and can't be trusted in the human government."

Parish looked far from impressed by his logic. "Are you trying to tell me how to do my job?"

"Christ, no. It's just..."

Parish frowned. "What?"

Rage hesitated. This was the first time he'd ever questioned a direct order, but there was no way in hell he wanted to deal with Lucie Gaudet.

The female Geek had been a few years younger than Rage, and growing up he'd initially felt sorry for the half-feral creature who'd lived in the outer parts of the swamp. She'd slunk around the edges of town with her hair matted and tangled, and her face covered in dirt. Almost like a fabled wood sprite who flitted among the trees, spreading mist and magic

But as they'd matured, his pity had changed to annoyance.

Instead of growing out of her odd preference for the shadows, she'd continued to lurk at a distance, and worse, she'd used her cunning intelligence to torment others. Including himself.

A born troublemaker.

"I'm a Hunter, not a Geek," he finally muttered. "Why doesn't Xavier send one of his own people to track down the female?"

Parish's lips twisted. "Because, like you, they're terrified of Lucie."

Rage scowled. "I'm not scared of her."

"No?"

The two predators glared at one another before Rage, at last, heaved a resigned sigh.

"Okay, I'm scared of her," he admitted. "She's a psycho bitch."

"She's not psycho. She's just..." Parish struggled for the word. "Misunderstood."

"Being misunderstood is shaving your head and drinking so much elderberry wine you puke purple for three days," he muttered,

274/Alexandra Ivy & Laura Wright

274/Alexandra Ivy & Laura Wright

274/Alexandra Ivy & Laura Wright

ignoring Parish's snort of amusement. Okay, it was possible that Rage had done both of those things. "Lucie burned down her grandfather's cottage."

Parish shrugged. "No one was inside it."

"She stole my diary so she could decrypt my private thoughts and posted them in the community center." Something that still aggravated the hell out of Rage. He'd written highly sensitive information about the various females he'd been dating at the time. All of them had refused to talk to him for weeks.

"You shouldn't have been such a hound dog," Parish said with blatant lack of sympathy.

"I wasn't a hound dog," Rage protested. "I just adore women."

Parish rolled his eyes. "A lot of women."

"Not as many as most people think," Rage retorted. It was true he spent a large majority of his time with females, but it wasn't about sex. Or at least, not everything was about sex. More than a few of his dates had been nothing more than two friends enjoying an evening together. "But I'm not ashamed of my appreciation for the opposite sex," he continued. "I love their scent. Their feel. Just having them near."

"Then why were you so upset?"

Because she made him look like an idiot.

He didn't share the sense of mortification he'd never forgotten. Instead, he folded his arms over his chest.

"What about the fact that she hacked into the Pentagon?"

Parish met him glare for glare. Predictably, he refused to back down.

"Xavier took care of her lack of judgment."

"By denying her access to computers?" Rage shook his head. It was a wonder she hadn't gotten every Pantera tossed in the brig. "All that did was give her a reason to leave the Wildlands so she didn't have to follow the rules."

Parish leaned against the edge of the heavy walnut desk, the wood creaking beneath his considerable weight. Pantera had denser bones and muscle than humans.

"None of us liked following the rules. I remember you breaking them more than once."

Rage couldn't argue. He was a hell-raiser when he was young.

But he was an amateur when compared to Lucie.

"I wasn't on the FBI most wanted list," he muttered.

Parish studied him for a long, nerve-wracking moment, then he grimaced, as if coming to an unwelcomed decision.

"You're not being entirely fair, *mon ami*," he abruptly said. "Life wasn't easy for Lucie."

Rage frowned. Parish was the master of the understatement. If he said life wasn't easy, then it must have been hell.

"I know her parents were Suits and spent most of their time away from the Wildlands," Rage said, struggling to recall what little he knew about the secretive female.

"Too much time away." Parish shook his head, his jaw tight. "Lucie should have been raised in the community nursery, but her grandfather insisted that she live with him."

Most cubs spent at least some time in the nursery. It helped to solidify their sense of pack. And children of Diplomats spent more time than others. The Wildlands were far safer for the cubs.

"He was a recluse, wasn't he?" Rage demanded. He barely remembered the cantankerous old man. The only time they'd crossed paths, the bastard had threatened to have Rage and his friends tossed in the bog if they ever stepped on his property.

"Unfortunately. None of us realized that he'd been affected by the rot that had already seeped into the Wildlands." Parish glanced toward the window where the lush beauty of the bayou hid the fact that only a few weeks before there'd been a creeping evil that had threatened to destroy the Pantera. "Not until too late."

Rage took a step toward his friend. "What do you mean, too late?"

"When Lucie was born, she was undersized and dangerously frail. If the Healers had been allowed to treat her, she would easily have outgrown her weakness, but Theo was determined to use what he called old magic to cure her."

Rage arched a brow. "What the hell is old magic?"

The air heated with the force of Parish's sudden burst of anger. "We assumed he meant the traditional herbs and potions from the elders. None of us knew he was tying her to trees during the middle of the night like she was a fucking rabid animal, or forcing her to hunt for her own food when she was barely old enough to shift.

Lucie's early life was a brutal lesson in survival."

A savage sense of guilt twisted Rage's gut.

"Shit," he rasped, hating himself for not taking the time to find out why Lucie had always remained an outsider. And why she'd felt such an intense need to rebel.

Maybe if he'd thought about something beyond his own wounded pride he could have...

Rage abruptly leashed his cat as a growl rumbled in his chest.

He might want to taste blood, but Theo was dead and Lucie missing. He couldn't change the past. All he could do was make sure that he didn't leap to conclusions again.

"Cut her a break when you find her," Parish broke into his dark thoughts.

"*If* I find her," Rage muttered, accepting he'd been efficiently manipulated into going after the missing female.

As if there'd ever been any doubt.

Shoving away from the desk, Parish reached to lay a hand on Rage's shoulder. "I have every faith in you, *mon ami*."

"Fan-fucking-tastic," Rage muttered. "Do you have any clue where I should start?"

"New Orleans."

* * * *

The office overlooking the Mississippi River had the hushed elegance that came from money.

A lot of money.

Not that Lucie was impressed with the contemporary style. The sleek glass and steel desk was a ridiculous statement of fashion, not function. And the low leather seats couldn't possibly be comfortable. Not unless you were a contortionist. Not to mention the fact that the original oil paintings that lined the white walls looked like someone had tossed a can of paint at that canvas and called it art.

Whatever.

She wasn't here to be the interior decorator. Nope. She was here to give her report and get her money.

End of story.

Pacing from one end of the room to the other, Lucie waited for the man seated behind the desk to lift his head and study her with a disgruntled expression.

"How long?" he demanded.

Lucie shrugged. He was asking her how much time it'd taken her to hack into his top-of-the-line computer security system.

"Less than an hour."

"God. Damn." Vern Spencer shook his head.

The middle-aged human was no doubt attractive to most women. He had a well-maintained body, dark hair that was threaded with silver and brushed from his lean face. Currently he was wearing a designer suit that cost more than many people made in a month. His main attraction, however, was the fact he was the CEO of a billion dollar energy company. Human women seemed to be fascinated by a large bank account.

To Lucie, he was another job.

"I spent a fortune on our latest upgrades," the man groused.

"It's good, but not good enough." She nodded toward her report that he'd spread across his desk. "I've made suggestions of where you need to shore up your security." She allowed a rare smile to touch her lips. "And my bill."

"Another damn fortune," Vern grumbled, his gaze lingering on her delicate features before they moved down to her slender body that was hidden beneath a pair of jeans and faded Pat O'Brien's tee.

"Do you want the best or not?" she demanded.

"Yeah, yeah." A cunning expression touched the man's thin face. "I'll have the money transferred into your account."

Lucie rolled her eyes. She was always very clear about her demands before taking on a new job.

"You know I run a cash only business."

Vern shook his head, leaning to the side to open his briefcase. Then, grabbing a thick envelope, he tossed it onto the desk.

"You're a pain in the ass, you know that Lucie?" he asked her, watching as she snatched up the envelope and promptly counted the crisp bills inside.

She didn't trust anyone. Period.

"I try." She strolled toward the nearby door. "Let me know next time you upgrade."

There was the sound of Vern hastily rising to his feet. "What's your hurry?"

Lucie's steps never slowed. "It's late."

"Not that late. We could have a drink or—"

"No."

"What about a quick trip to Paris? I have my jet on standby—"

"No."

There was a strangled sound of disbelief. No doubt Vern was accustomed to women who would do backflips at the chance to go out with him. Like another male that she'd once known.

Bleck.

"Well, you're nothing if not blunt," he said with a small laugh.

"It saves any misunderstandings." She glanced over her shoulder, her ponytail swinging. "Call me if you have a job."

Without giving him time to press his invitation to linger, Lucie headed out of the office and toward the nearest stairs. It didn't matter she was on the tenth floor. There was no way she was going to get into an elevator.

There mere thought of being trapped in a small box made her breath lock in her lungs.

After her grandfather...

No. Lucie gave a shake of her head and jogged easily down the stairs. There was no past.

Only the future.

Within minutes, she was out of the building and moving down the dark street. Her thoughts were still with the easy money she was shoving into her back pocket. It was crazy, really. She'd started hacking in defiance of Xavier and his stupid rules. She hated people telling her what to do. Besides, being able to break into systems that were supposedly impenetrable made her feel like a badass.

And after leaving the Wildlands, she'd needed to hack to support herself.

But in the end, she'd discovered she could earn a shitload more cash by becoming legitimate. Now companies paid her to hack into their high-security systems.

How ironic was that?

The smug thought had barely drifted through her mind when an intoxicating scent of musk had her coming to a sharp halt.

Pantera.

Shit.

Although the puma-shifters preferred to stay in the Wildlands, there were always a few roaming the city. Either to spy on the humans or to keep up on their ever-changing technology. But over the years, fewer and fewer were willing to risk leaving their homelands, and she'd become overly complacent.

Knowing it was too late, she still turned, trying to dart into the nearby alley.

She'd barely manage to take a step when arms were wrapping around her waist and she was being pulled against a hard, male chest.

"You're a hard girl to track down," a low, disturbingly familiar voice whispered in her ear, sending Lucie into an instant panic. Kicking backward, she managed to connect with his shin while at the same time she turned her head, snapping her teeth at his face. "Shit, Lucie." His arms tightened until she could barely breathe, let alone move. "Easy, for god's sake, it's me."

Yeah, like she didn't know that it was Rage who held her?

This male had once figured into her every girlish fantasy. She'd spent hours watching him from a distance, fascinated by his male beauty and the easy charm that made him a favorite among the females.

And much to her embarrassment, she still found herself searching for him during the rare occurrences she returned to the Wildlands.

Now she was desperate to get away from him.

"Let me go, Rage," she growled.

He chuckled. "Long time no see."

Lucie didn't know what bad juju had crossed her path with this male, but she needed to get away. Not out of fear. Xavier had removed the bounty on her head some time ago. But this male...

He disturbed her in a way she didn't fully understand.

With practiced ease she went boneless in his arms, her head sagging against his chest.

"You're hurting me," she whimpered.

"Shit. I'm sorry, Lucie."

On cue, the strong arms loosened their grip and Lucie was

280/Alexandra Ivy & Laura Wright

shoving out of his grasp and scrambling down the alley.

If she could reach the…

With a speed that shocked her, Rage had already caught up to her and was tossing her over his shoulders as he continued down the alley and onto a backstreet.

"Parish is going to pay for this," he muttered.

Lucie scowled as she pounded Rage's back. This wasn't a chance meeting?

"Parish sent you?" she demanded.

"Yes."

She heaved a resigned sigh. "Put me down."

Ignoring her command, he picked up speed, heading away from the commercial district to a quiet residential neighborhood lined with weeping willows.

"Not until we have a chance to speak," he warned.

She slammed her fist against the hard muscles of his back, nearly breaking her fingers.

"Dammit, Rage."

"Temper, temper," he teased, moving in silence despite the fact he was carrying a squirming, furious female.

Lucie made a sound of frustration. If Parish wanted something from her, why the hell had he sent this male? The leader of the Hunters had been one of the few Pantera she'd ever let get close to her. And that was only because the stubborn bastard wouldn't take "no" for an answer. He had to have suspected that she watched Rage more than any of the other males.

Or was that the point?

Did Parish assume that she would be so dazzled by the gorgeous Rage that she would fall into line like a good little Pantera?

She wanted to laugh at the mere thought. She didn't let anything or anyone control her. Not since she escaped her grandfather. But there was nothing amusing in the jolts of excitement that were streaking through her as the heat of Rage's body seeped through her clothing and his musky scent teased at her senses.

Shit. He was hauling her around like a sack of potatoes, but she was getting turned on.

She'd dreamed a thousand nights that Rage would catch sight of her lurking in the trees and rush over to grab her in his arms. And yes, there'd been more than once she'd fantasized he would throw her over his shoulder and haul her into the shadows so he could strip off her clothes and kiss her quivering body from head to toe…

Lucie heaved a groan of relief as they reached the white, plantation-style home set well away from the street that served as a local safe house for the Pantera. Circling to the backyard, Rage was forced to lower her to her feet as he placed his hand against the scanner hidden behind a potted plant. Slowly the door slid open and Rage led her into a large kitchen that was filled with a delicious smell that made her stomach rumble with hunger.

Stepping away from the male, she glanced around the room that was lined with wooden cabinets painted a pretty white. The floor was made of flagstone, and overhead, the open-beamed ceiling had dried herbs hanging alongside a set of copper pots.

A part of her itched to get out of the house that was filled with smells of home. The potpourri that was made from the Dyesse lily that only grew in the Wildlands. Rich moss that had been carried into the kitchen on someone's shoes. And that enticing scent of food that was bubbling in a pot on the stove.

Even worse was the flame of anticipation that licked through her at the realization they were alone in the house.

Dammit.

"Are you going to tell me why you kidnapped me?" she forced herself to mutter.

Rage cocked a dark brow, his gaze taking a slow, leisurely survey of her tense form.

"Kidnapped?" he drawled. "Isn't that a little overdramatic?"

She shrugged. "I was minding my own business when I was snatched off the street and forcibly brought to this house. What would you call it?"

He flashed his wicked smile. "Your lucky night."

"Ugh." She glared at him, pretending her heart wasn't racing and her palms sweating. Christ, what was it with this male? Did he have some sort of direct connection to her deepest urges? "You haven't changed."

"You have." Without warning he prowled forward, the glow of the overhead light adding a gloss to the ebony satin of his hair and shimmering in the amazing violet eyes. Slowly his hand lifted to brush over her cheek before he was reaching to tug at the scrunchie that contained her long hair in a ponytail, allowing the reddish-gold curls to cascade down her back. A low growl rumbled in his chest. "If it wasn't for your scent, I would never have recognized you."

Lucie took a shocked step backward, slamming into the cabinets behind her as she struggled to breathe.

"What are you doing?"

The scent of his musk deepened, saturating the air with his male arousal.

"There's no need to panic." He combed his fingers through her hair, as if he was savoring the feel of the strands sliding against his skin. "Unlike you, I don't bite." He leaned down to whisper directly in her ear. "Not unless you ask really…really nice."

Chapter Two

Rage was lost in sensations.

It was crazy.

He'd spent over six hours searching from one end of New Orleans to another trying to locate Lucie Gaudet. He was tired, hungry, and pissed that Parish was wasting his skills. He should be hunting down the bastards who were responsible for capturing Pantera and treating them as their personal test animals.

But then he'd caught Lucie's scent.

He'd recognized it immediately. A fragrant, enticing musk. Like primroses. Sweet, with the danger of prickles beneath the velvet blooms. He had no idea why it seemed so familiar. As if the smell had been a part of his unconsciousness for years. Perhaps decades.

Then he'd caught sight of his prey and it felt as if his entire world had been turned upside down.

It wasn't just her unexpected beauty, although he'd been stunned at his first glimpse. Who knew that once the tangles were combed out of her hair, it would prove to be a glorious gold that was threaded with hints of fire? Even pulled into a tight ponytail, he'd known it would look perfect spread across his pillowcase. Or that her too-thin face would mature into elegant lines that emphasized the bright gold eyes rimmed with jade?

It was the lingering resemblance to a tiny wood sprite he used to glimpse in the trees. She was elusive and untamable. Like quicksilver.

And it wasn't until he caught sight of her again that he realized just how much he'd missed her presence in the Wildlands. Oh, he'd been aggravated by her outrageous behavior. And his human side had considered her a childish pest. But deep inside it was as if his cat had been waiting, always knowing that he would once again cross paths with Lucie.

The knowledge was terrifying.

Unfortunately, it didn't keep him from being obsessed with the need to touch the wary young female. Not even when she was glaring at him as if she wanted to punch him in the junk.

Stroking his fingers through the warm silk of her hair, he watched in fasciation as it brushed against the milky softness of her cheek. At the base of her throat he could see her pulse fluttering, the evocative scent of primroses clouding his mind.

He had to have a taste.

Now.

Bending down, he skimmed his lips over her forehead. The caress was light, giving her the opportunity to turn away. Just because his cat was furiously trying to get close to her didn't mean she was equally eager.

She stiffened. Was she going to shove him away?

The question was answered when she tilted her head back to give him better access. Rage didn't hesitate. With a low growl, he covered her lips in a kiss that had nothing to do with his usual skilled seduction.

This was raw and needy and way too demanding for a first kiss.

Framing her face in his hands, Rage continued to plunder her mouth, slipping his tongue past parted lips. Oh, hell. He swallowed a moan. She tasted of spring. Sweet. Wild. Thunderously unpredictable.

She shivered against him, her arms wrapping around his neck as she tangled her tongue with his.

Joy blasted through him, his cat roaring with a fierce satisfaction.

At last...

It was the intense approval from his inner beast that had him jerking his head up in shock. He'd enjoyed a variety of lovers. All of them had offered a sensual pleasure that he'd treasured and most had remained dear friends long after their intimate relationship had come to an end.

But none of them had aroused his cat.

"Shit," he breathed, nipping at her lush lower lip. "I didn't bring you here for this."

Her nails suddenly bit into the back of his neck, the tiny pain only intensifying his desire.

"You could have fooled me," she muttered.

Rage chuckled. She might spit and hiss just like she did when she was a cub, but there was no mistaking the intoxicating scent of her arousal. Or the seductive little squirm as she tried to press closer.

The movement against his engorged cock sent tormenting shocks of bliss through him.

"If you don't like it, then why are you rubbing against me?"

She tilted her head back to glare at him, the gold eyes glowing with the power of her cat.

"I don't know."

He kissed the tip of her nose, feeling an odd sense of disorientation. There was something achingly familiar about the female, even as she seemed utterly new and different.

Was it possible his cat had truly been waiting for her to grow up?

"I warned Parish you were dangerous," he breathed, intending to pull back only to find his lips stroking over the softness of her cheek and down the line of her jaw.

"Me?" She shivered. "You're the one who's lethal to females."

He buried his face in the curve of her neck, breathing deeply of her scent. "Madness."

Her nails scraped down his back. "We have to stop."

"Yes." His tongue licked a rough path along the neckline of her tee.

She hissed out a low curse. "Rage."

He squeezed his eyes shut, battling against his cat, who was ready and eager to take this female against the wall. Or on the kitchen table. Or floor...

It didn't matter that they were virtual strangers, despite having been raised in the Wildlands. Or that Lucie had obviously harbored a deep dislike for him when she was young.

Or even that he was here on a mission of utmost importance to the Pantera.

His cat wanted this female.

Period.

With a heroic effort, Rage at last lifted his head, studying her flushed face with a brooding gaze.

"Okay, I'm stopping," he muttered.

He didn't know what he expected, but it wasn't that she was going to suddenly dart beneath his arm and head toward the door.

"I have to go."

"Wait." With a swift lunge, he was standing directly in her path, shaking his head in exasperation. How many times was she going to try and run from him? "I need to speak with you."

She glared at him, tossing back the long strands of her hair as if they annoyed her. Or maybe he was the one annoying her.

"Tough, I have things to do."

"What things?"

"None-of-your-business things."

Rage heaved a sigh. Dammit. He should have kept his hands to himself. If she ran off before he could ask for her assistance, then Parish was going to kick his ass.

Not that it had been a choice, he ruefully acknowledged. Even now his fingers were twitching with the urge to reach out and touch those glorious golden-red curls.

"I told you Parish sent me, but it's Xavier who needs your help," he said, hoping to stir her curiosity.

They were all cats at heart, after all.

"He has an entire posse of Geeks," she grudgingly pointed out, unable to resist temptation. "Why does he need me?"

"They don't have your particular talents."

Her gaze slowly narrowed, the golden eyes smoldering with a dangerous heat. "You mean he needs a hacker?"

"Exactly," he agreed, grimacing as she gave a sharp burst of laughter. That couldn't be good. "What's so funny?"

She stepped forward and poked her finger in the center of his chest. "The self-righteous pricks gave me the option of throwing away my computer or leaving the Wildlands. They claimed I was an undisciplined criminal." More poking. "And now that they need my services, they suddenly aren't so worried about ethics?"

She had a point. Rage grimaced, the guilt that he'd felt since Parish had revealed details about her childhood feeling like a lead ball in the pit of his stomach. No one would blame her for telling them all to go to hell.

Unfortunately, they needed her. And it was his responsibility to convince her to forget the past.

"Things change during times of war," he informed her, not surprised when she rolled her eyes.

"Now who's being overdramatic?"

"Make no mistake, Lucie, the Pantera are under attack," he insisted. "You haven't been around much, but—"

"I know what's been happening."

Rage's brows snapped together. "How?"

She shrugged. "Not everyone considers me a leper."

"Parish?" he guessed.

Her hands landed on her hips, her expression warning that she was tired of his questions.

"Once again. None of your business," she growled.

It wasn't. So why were his hands clenching and his cat pressing against his skin with the need to get out and track down the leader of the Hunters?

Because he was jealous.

The simple answer sent a jolt of shock through Rage. He'd never been jealous in his entire life.

Shaking off the strange desire to punch Parish in the face, he forced himself to concentrate on the reason he'd come to New Orleans.

"Are you refusing Xavier's request?" he demanded.

She folded her arms over her chest, her expression defensive. "What if I do?"

"Then I return home and we figure out a new plan."

She hesitated, licking her lips. "I can just walk away?"

It took a second for the insult to sink in. Then fury pulsed through him.

"Christ, Lucie, what did you expect?" he snarled. "Waterboarding? A couple broken kneecaps? Thumbscrews?"

She at least had the decency to look embarrassed as she hunched her shoulders. "I don't even know what thumbscrews are."

Rage stepped back, waving a hand toward the door. Beneath his anger was a sharp-edged hurt that she would ever believe he would threaten her with violence.

"Fine. Go," he rasped, spinning away with a low curse.

He'd managed to fuck up this meeting on an epic scale. Clearly, Parish should have sent a Suit.

Expecting to hear the slamming of the door, Rage was caught off guard when he heard Lucie heave a sigh.

"Tell me what Xavier needs," she muttered.

Slowly he turned, studying her with a suspicious frown. "Why?"

* * * *

Why.

A hell of a question. A shame Lucie didn't have the answer.

She knew beyond a doubt that it didn't have a damned thing to do with the male who was staring at her as if she'd just crawled beneath a rock. Hell, if it was up to her, she would walk out the door and never set eyes on him again.

He was flat-out, do-me-now trouble.

She'd always sensed it, even when she'd been too young to know why she watched him. Now that she'd actually tasted his lips and felt his touch…she ached for him with a desperation that was downright dangerous.

If she had one ounce of self-preservation, she'd be running as fast as her feet could carry her.

And it didn't have anything to do with loyalty to her people. She'd put aside her life as a Pantera, hadn't she? Okay, her cat demanded the occasional trips to the Wildlands so she could shift and absorb the magic. But she was no longer a part of the pack.

They'd never given a shit about her. Why should she care if they were in danger?

She heaved a deep sigh. The only explanation was that there was a small—very small—part of her that whispered she would regret turning her back if something truly terrible happened.

"Lucie, are you just screwing with me?" Rage abruptly growled, jerking her out of her dark thoughts.

She forced herself to meet his accusing gaze, shuddering as her cat purred in anticipation.

"Tell me what Xavier needs."

"And you'll help?"

She held up a hand. Only a fool would commit to some vague request for "help." She wanted details.

"It depends on what it is."

The violent eyes smoldered with annoyance, his lips parting only to snap together as Rage made a visible effort to accept her hesitation.

"Fine." He pointed at the wooden kitchen table. "Grab a seat."

Lucie frowned, watching as he crossed toward the stove. "What are you doing?"

"I'm starving," he said, reaching into the cabinet to pull out two bowls. "I didn't have time to eat before I left so my mother sent some of her famous gumbo with me." He scooped up two heaping bowls of the spicy stew and placed them on the table. "Don't tell me your mouth isn't watering."

It was. Rage's mom was a Nurturer who'd offered comfort to the sick Pantera with her delicious cooking. Not that Lucie had ever been allowed to be consoled by the warm-hearted woman.

Unable to resist temptation, she slid into a seat and grabbed for a spoon. "Spoiled," she muttered, more than a little jealous.

Rage had been petted and adored by his mother and four older sisters.

"Probably," he admitted, cutting thick slices of bread and grabbing a bottle of wine before he returned to the table and took his own seat. "Eat."

She sent him a glare, but she readily dug into the gumbo. Her loathing for being told what to do was no match for the enticement of Andouille sausage and plump shrimp and chopped okra, all poured over garlic rice.

A groan was wrenched from her throat as the rich flavors

exploded on her tongue. "It's delicious," she muttered, keeping her head down as she cleaned the bowl and soaked up the juices with a slice of bread. "I can see why everyone was so eager to taste your mother's cooking."

She was oblivious to Rage's unwavering gaze until he leaned across the table to fill her wineglass.

"Lucie, it's no excuse, but I didn't know." He abruptly broke the silence.

She glanced up in confusion. "Know what?"

His expression was somber. "About your grandfather."

With a jerky motion she was on her feet, knocking the chair over in her haste to step away from the table. Dammit. Had Parish shared the humiliating details of her childhood?

The thought was...

Horrifying.

The very last thing she wanted was this male's pity.

"I don't discuss the past," she rasped. "Not ever."

He slowly rose to his feet, regret shimmering in his eyes. "You should have been protected. We all failed you."

Lucie wrapped her arms around her waist, her mind locked against the grim memories. It was the only way to survive.

"Are you deaf?"

"I had to say it." Rage rounded the table, prowling forward even as she instinctively backed away. "I'll never forgive myself for not doing something to help."

Lucie stiffened. There was no denying the sincerity in his voice. What he felt wasn't pity for her, but guilt that he hadn't prevented her grandfather's brutality.

Oh hell. Her heart melted. She'd always been fascinated by his concern for others. Well, that and the fact he was gorgeous, charming, and sexy as hell. His ability to display such tenderness was a stark contrast to his cat, who was vicious when provoked.

But she'd never directly experienced his fierce need to protect.

It was...intoxicating.

And oh, so dangerous.

"It wasn't your responsibility," she muttered.

"It was," he countered, moving to stand so close she could feel the heat of his body wrap around her. "I'm a Hunter."

Desperately, she tried to ignore the urge to reach out and run her fingers over his beautiful face. Just to prove to herself he was real.

She needed to put some distance between them.

"And here I thought you were just another pretty face," she mocked.

His mouth twitched. "Actually, I'm pretty all over. Just in case you were interested."

"I'm not."

"The lips say no, but those eyes…" He gave a low chuckle as she lifted her hands to shove him away.

"Are you ever going to get to the point of why you brought me here?" she growled.

His teasing expression slowly faded. "If you've been in contact with the Wildlands, then you know we recently prevented a military contractor from using Pantera blood as a serum to create super-soldiers in the military."

She nodded. It'd been several weeks since she'd been to the bayous, but Parish had called only a few days ago to update her. As always, she refused to tell her friend where she was living, but she couldn't break all ties with him.

"I thought Stanton was dead?"

"He is, but Xavier intercepted an e-mail from one of the researchers who was working with Locke," he said, referring to the human who had been Christopher's right-hand man and responsible for building the laboratories that experimented on Pantera as well as humans. "The mystery man claims he downloaded the data before we torched the place."

"Do you believe him?" Lucie asked. It would be an easy claim to make.

Rage shrugged. "Impossible to say, but we can't take the risk he isn't bluffing."

"Why not contact the human authorities?"

His beautiful features tightened. "We don't know who we can trust."

Lucie snorted. She knew exactly who she could trust.

No one.

"What do you want me to hack?" She went straight to the

point.

"Whoever sent the e-mail was setting up an online auction," Rage explained. "In twenty-four hours, the top bidder will receive the supposed intel."

Lucie hesitated. She had never been able to resist a challenge. Something that'd gotten her into trouble more times than she wanted to remember.

If she intended to walk away, she had to do it now.

Rage wisely remained silent, waiting for her to sort through her inner conflict until she at last accepted the inevitable. She might want to deny the Pantera as her pack, but in her blood, they were still family.

"Show me," she muttered in resignation.

Not giving her the opportunity to change her mind, Rage turned to head out of the kitchen. They walked through a large front room with molded ceilings and a sweeping staircase before they crossed the hall into the library.

Lucie glanced around the large space. It was more or less what she expected. Traditional mahogany furnishings that were arranged around the wooden floor. On the far side of the room was a deep alcove with a brocaded chaise lounge, and at the back was a marble fireplace. Her lips twitched as she caught sight of the velvet Elvis painting that was hanging above the mantle.

Someone clearly had a sense of humor.

Rage headed directly to the large desk that was loaded with high-tech electronic surveillance equipment and a computer system that would have been a wet dream for most nerds.

Lucie, however, had a setup that was illegal in most countries.

"Xavier said he'd send the info to this computer," Rage said. "It's encrypted, but he said you should be able to—" He bit off his words as Lucie slid into the chair and swiftly lost herself in the world of electronic data.

This was the one place she felt safe.

The one place where no one and nothing could hurt her.

Chapter Three

For the next hour, Rage paced the library. From the bay window to the fireplace. From the alcove to the towering bookcases. All the time keeping a covert watch on Lucie as her fingers flew across the keyboard.

She was completely engrossed in her work, unaware that the glow of the monitor was emphasizing the delicate beauty of her face and shimmering in the fiery highlights in her golden hair.

Rage, however, was painfully conscious of her exquisite temptation.

Something that should have bothered him, not filled him with a joyous sense of anticipation.

Of course, now that Lucie had agreed to assist Xavier, his duty was more or less complete. Why shouldn't he savor the attraction that sizzled between them? His cat had already decided she was going to be his lover. Maybe even more.

He might as well enjoy the ride.

Right?

Accepting his fate, Rage made another circle of the room, only halting when Lucie at last rose to her feet and lifted her arms over her head to stretch out her tight muscles.

Rage's cat purred, wanting to lick the pale strip of belly revealed as her tee rode up.

"Whoever set this up was clever," she said.

Rage reluctantly leashed his animal. Later he could lick. And taste. And maybe bite.

"Can you trace them?" he asked.

"Yes. The auction is set up through a remote computer." She lowered her arms and leaned against the edge of the desk. "The program is designed to pick the highest bidder, and once the money is transferred to an overseas account, the payload is released."

Rage frowned. He was a Hunter, not a Geek.

"Payload?"

"The computer files he claims to have taken before the lab was destroyed."

"Ah."

"We need to go to my place."

He studied her in surprise. The last thing he expected was an invitation to her private lair.

"Why?"

She nodded toward the computer on the desk. "Right now I'm being blocked. I can access the auction, but I can't break through the firewall to get a lock on who is responsible. I need to run a trace."

"And you have the equipment to do that?"

She rolled her eyes. "Yeah, I have the equipment."

Okay, it was a stupid question.

"Do you want to take a vehicle?"

"No." She gave a decisive shake of her head. "It's not far from here. I'll call you when I've found something."

"No."

She frowned. "No?"

He moved to stand directly in front of her. "I'm going with you."

"Why?" She squared her shoulders, instantly defensive. "Do you think I'm going to try and escape?"

Rage muttered a curse, reaching out to grasp her shoulders as he glared down at her wary expression.

"I told you that you're free to go wherever you want," he snapped. Christ. He was tired of being treated as if he was a monster. "I'm asking for your help, not holding you captive."

She scowled, refusing to apologize. "Then why do you want to go with me?"

"Because I'm curious," he said. "I want to see where you live."

"And?" she prompted, easily sensing he wasn't giving her the whole truth.

He reached out to cup her cheek in his palm, his thumb brushing her lower lip. "And my cat wants to be near you."

She trembled, her eyes darkening with excitement as her own cat responded to his touch.

"Rage," she choked out, shocked by his blunt honesty.

His lips twisted. She wasn't any more shocked than he was.

"You asked," he said.

With a sharp motion, she was jerking away from his hand, her arms folding over her waist.

"Do you have to flirt with every female?"

"I would usually say yes, but this isn't flirting."

Her scowl deepened. "Then what is it?"

Hmm. Now that was the question, wasn't it?

"Hell if I know," he growled, his animal restlessly prowling beneath the surface. The beast was growing agitated by the space Lucie insisted on putting between them. "I'm hoping you can figure it out."

She sucked in a deep breath, the musky scent that filled the air revealing she was as eager as he was to get up close and personal.

Unlike him, however, she wasn't about to give in to temptation.

At least not yet.

"Let's go," she grumbled, pausing long enough to shut down the computer before she was leaving the library and heading out of the house.

Rage was swiftly at her side, his gaze scanning the darkness for any hint of trouble.

As far as he knew, there was no one who could suspect why he was in New Orleans. Or want to target him. But it was his nature to be on guard.

Especially when he was protecting this particular female.

If someone actually tried to harm her…his jaw clenched. The unfortunate bastards would discover exactly why his mother had named him Rage.

They traveled in silence, surprisingly headed toward the French Quarter. Somehow he'd expected her to have an isolated house on the fringes of town. Instead, she led him directly to Royal Street, pointing toward the house shrouded in shadows.

"That's it."

Rage nearly fell over his feet as he caught sight of the grand mansion.

Built on a corner lot, the graceful three-storied house was framed with towering oak trees. The old bricks had been painted a warm cream and there were covered galleries on both the front and the side of the house that ran the length of the porch, with lacy iron railings.

It was graceful and posh, and whispered of days gone past.

Just how much did hacking pay?

"Yep, this is it," she muttered, pulling a key out of her pocket to lead him inside the black and white tiled foyer.

He had a brief glimpse of an overhead chandelier and a hallway that led toward an inner courtyard before she was jogging up the polished wooden staircase. They bypassed the formal living room and entered what he supposed had once been called the "parlor."

She flipped on the lights, giving him the full impact of the wide room with Corinthian columns that towered toward the fifteen-foot ceilings that still possessed the original medallions. There was a priceless Parisian rug spread across the worn floorboards and furniture that looked as if it'd come out of a European palace.

Once again, he was struck by the elegant sense of history that she'd so carefully mixed with the comforts of home.

"Wow," he breathed, strolling to the center of the room.

"What?" she demanded.

"It's beautiful."

She blushed, as if embarrassed by his genuine admiration. Then pulling an envelope out of her back pocket, she moved to pull aside an antique table to reveal a safe hidden in the wall. Quickly she had it opened and the envelope stored inside.

"The wine cooler is fully stocked," she told him as she straightened, nodding toward the heavily scrolled bar that was built in beneath the mirror that ran the entire length of one wall. "Help yourself."

Rage swiftly moved to block her path as she headed back to the door. "Where are you going?"

She blinked in surprise. "My office is over the garage."

"I want to go with you."

"I…" She swallowed her protest as she met his steady gaze, no doubt seeing his cat's fierce refusal to be left behind. "Fine. Follow me."

To the ends of the world, a voice whispered in the back of his mind.

They left the parlor and headed deeper into the house, at last coming to the end of a hallway where they were blocked by a heavy steel door.

Rage arched a startled brow as she placed her hand on an electronic scanner and then leaned forward to type in a complex code. Only then did she pull out an old-fashion key to open the final lock and push the door open.

"You expecting a zombie invasion?" he teased as they stepped into the narrow room that was nearly overwhelmed by the stacks of high-tech equipment and monitors that looked far too sophisticated and expensive to be sold at Best Buy.

She shrugged, snapping on the overhead lights before moving to settle in front of the nearest computer.

"Not everyone is happy with the work I do." She glanced over her shoulder to toss him a startling smile. "And there is always the off chance the zombies might show up."

Rage felt as if he'd just been punched in the gut.

Christ. She had a dimple.

Reeling from the impact of her smile, Rage was barely aware of her rapidly tapping on the keyboard. Not that he would have known what the hell she was doing even if he'd been paying attention. Still, it came as a shock when she was rising to her feet and studying him with a quizzical expression.

"That should do it," she told him.

He nodded, his gaze lowering to her lips as he remembered her sweet taste of primrose.

"Now what?"

"I'm running the trace. It's going to take a while," she said with a shrug. "If you want to go back to the safe house, I'll call you when I find something."

He stepped forward, his hand lifting to lightly circle her neck with his fingers. "Are you kicking me out?" he murmured, his thumb resting against her fluttering pulse.

She instinctively tilted back her head, offering him greater access to her throat. "This could take hours," she cautioned.

His cat rumbled in anticipation. "Good."

She shivered, her eyes molten gold in the bright overhead lights. "Good?"

"We have some time to get better acquainted," he informed her.

Before she could react, he bent down to scoop her off her feet, heading back to the main house.

He didn't know exactly where he was going, but he was sure there had to be a bedroom somewhere. He wasn't going to stop until he found it.

* * * *

Lucie told herself she should protest. She hated when men thought they could grab her as if they owned her. And she certainly never allowed them to haul her around like she was some helpless doll.

But gazing up at Rage's achingly familiar face, she knew she didn't want to protest. Not when her entire body was shuddering with an eager need she couldn't disguise.

The fantasy of this male had tantalized, teased, and tormented her for years.

Could she truly live with herself if she didn't discover if he could actually fulfill her dreams?

Shutting out the tiny voice that warned she wasn't thinking clearly, she made no move to escape when he entered her private rooms and headed directly for the bed that was arranged next to the bank of windows that overlooked the inner courtyard.

She loved New Orleans, but there were times when she felt trapped by the press of buildings and narrow streets. She liked to be able to open her windows and allow the sunshine to spread over her naked body.

Bending down, Rage gently settled her in the middle of the mattress, staring down at her with eyes that glowed with the heat of his cat.

"I thought you said you wanted to become better acquainted?" she teased.

He stilled, his jaw clenching as he visibly struggled to contain his primitive instincts. His beast was clearly anxious to do more than exchange chitchat.

The knowledge sent a shiver down her spine. Her own cat was equally eager.

Unlike humans, Pantera didn't always equate sex with some rigid morality. Sometimes it was about warmth, and companionship, and pleasure.

And sometimes it was about being with the one male who stirred her on a soul-deep level.

"Do you want to go back to the parlor?" he asked. "Or if you want, we can go out for a drink."

She lifted herself on her elbows. "What do you want?"

"You." His voice was low and rough, his heat brushing over her like a physical caress. "I want you."

It was the perfect thing to say.

Holding his gaze, she gave a slow nod. "Then we stay here."

Easily reading the invitation in her voice, Rage kicked off his boots and yanked his Tulane sweatshirt over his head. Then, unzipping his jeans, he shoved them down to reveal his hard, bronzed body in its full glory.

And it was glorious.

Her mouth went dry as she studied the hard, sculpted muscles that flowed with a fascinating ease. His chest was broad and tapered to a slender waist, with a puma tattoo just below his collarbone. His arms were ripped without unnecessary bulk, and his legs were long and lightly dusted with dark hair.

A perfect male specimen.

Yum.

"A good choice." A slow, wicked smile curved his lips as he moved to crawl onto the mattress.

"You approve?"

"Oh, I approve." He lowered his head to press his mouth to a spot just behind her ear. Lucie's cat purred in pleasure. Who knew a mere kiss could be so erotic? "In fact, I'd be happy to demonstrate just how much I approve."

"It's fairly obvious," she said, pointedly glancing toward his cock that was fully erect. Her mouth watered at the thought of wrapping her lips around that broad head and sucking him deep.

She rarely performed oral sex on men. It seemed too...intimate.

But she desperately wanted a taste of this male.

"I suppose it is," he agreed in a husky voice, nipping her earlobe. "Christ, I feel like I've waited for this moment for my entire life."

Her breath tangled in her throat at his words, a bittersweet ache clenching her heart. She wanted to believe him. But while she'd dreamed of this male night after night, she wasn't stupid enough to think that he'd ever given her a second thought.

"You don't have to say that," she muttered.

"Say what?"

"That I'm special," she said. "I know there's been a lot of females."

He heaved a sigh as he reached down to slip off her shoes, then with obvious expertise he easily rid her of her jeans and tee.

"Why does everyone assume I'm some sort of player?" he groused, kneeling beside her to run a scorching gaze over her body, now covered in nothing more than a pair of lace panties.

Lucie quivered beneath the hungry gaze. "Because you are?"

"I've had a few relationships that I'll always cherish, but none of them made me feel as if I was going to lose my mind if I couldn't kiss them."

Leaning forward, he planted his hands on the mattress as he moved to settle on top of her. She sighed at the sensation of his weight deliciously sinking her into the mattress. Instinctively, she allowed her legs to widen so he could settle between them.

Lowering his head, the raven hair brushed against the puckered tips of her nipples.

"Rage," she choked out.

His tongue flicked over her nipple, the rough stroke wrenching a moan from her throat.

"It's your turn, Lucie."

She scored her nails down the smooth skin of his back. How was she supposed to think when his touch was sending streaks of white-hot pleasure through her?

"My turn for what?" she at last ground out.

He continued to tease her nipple, his cock pressing with flawless precision against her pussy. Oh...yes. It felt good. But she wanted that thick length sinking into her aching body.

"To tell me that I'm not just another male," he said, stroking a line of kisses between her breasts. "That this is different for you."

How could he doubt it? She'd never melted from a mere kiss. Or groaned with impatience during foreplay.

And certainly she'd never considered the possibility of handcuffing a male to her bed so he couldn't escape.

Of course, it seemed better not to share that particular sentiment.

"Your ego is big enough," she informed him.

Rage abruptly lifted his head, gazing down at her with a smoldering intensity. "You think this is about my ego?"

Her lips parted to give a flippant retort, only to have the words falter beneath the hint of vulnerability in his violet eyes.

Her answer mattered. She wasn't sure why, but she wasn't going to deliberately ruin this fragile moment.

"I don't know," she confessed with blunt honesty. "If you know my past then you have to realize that I don't have much experience with relationships. I don't understand the rules to the game."

With a low groan, Rage surged upward to claim her lips in an openmouthed kiss that was hard with unrestrained hunger. She could taste the musk of his cat. Feel the heat of his need blazing through her like wildfire.

Any lingering hesitation was seared away.

"This is no game to me," he whispered against her lips. "Not this time."

Her hips arched upward in blatant invitation. "Why is it different?"

"Because my cat has never been so hungry for a female."

She retained enough self-preservation to flinch at his

possessive tone. The only thing in her life she was certain of was the fact that she couldn't depend on anyone but herself.

Something she was in danger of forgetting.

"Just for tonight," she warned, scraping her nails up his back. She exulted in his violent shudder of pleasure. "As soon as I'm done with the hack, you'll return to the Wildlands and I'll stay here."

"Lucie," he breathed. "Can we enjoy a few hours together before you start talking about getting rid of me?"

"I just don't want you thinking..."

She forgot how to speak as his mouth skimmed restless kisses along the length of her neck, over her breasts, and down the clenched muscles of her belly.

"Let's make a mutual promise to stop thinking," he rasped. "It's a highly overrated habit."

It was, Lucie discovered when his tongue dipped into her belly button. Why think when it was much better just to feel the shocking throb of longing between her legs, the clever fingers that knew exactly where to touch, the warm brush of his lips, the hard promise of his cock...

It was like standing in the middle of a violent inferno with no desire to avoid being burned.

"I promise not to think, if you promise not to stop," she managed to breathe.

Chapter Four

Rage gave a low chuckle.

Stop? He was fairly certain that nothing on the face of this earth could make him stop. Not when his body was primed and ready to please this female.

Of course, he would prefer if there wasn't still a hint of wariness deep in her eyes. And that he sensed she would flee in terror if he confessed that his cat was more than just hungry for her.

That it had decided to claim her for his own.

Right now, beggars couldn't be choosers. He would take what he could get until he could convince her to accept him as her mate.

Allowing his hands to glide up her bare thighs, he grasped her panties and with one jerk, he had them ripped off her body. Only then did he move so he could spread her legs, his gaze drinking in the sight of her wet pussy.

Exquisite.

A roar of approval echoed in his head as his cat took full appreciation of her naked beauty, startling Rage. He'd never had his animal so close to the surface during sex.

It was intense and intoxicating, and viciously erotic.

With a low growl, he leaned forward to stroke his tongue through her luscious cream. The taste of primroses exploded in his mouth, clouding his mind with pure lust.

He heard Lucie suck in a sharp breath as he licked her with a growing urgency, the sound filled with the same raw need that clawed at him.

"I could become addicted to your taste," he said thickly, his hands exploring up her body to cup her breasts, his thumbs teasing her hardened nipples.

She gave a strangled groan, her hips lifting off the bed as her fingers clenched the quilt spread over the mattress.

"Rage," she moaned.

"Yes, my sweet Lucie?"

"I want you inside me."

Rage chuckled, giving her pussy a last, lingering taste before he was kissing his way back up her body. His cock was aching, desperate to give in to her command.

Not just to feel her slick heat wrap around him, but he wanted her skin to be marked with his scent, imprinting himself on her as he emptied his essence deep inside her.

Easily sensing his possessive animal instinct, Lucie abruptly sat up. Rage tensed, afraid he might have spooked her with his hunger. But even as he prepared himself for her rejection, she was leaning forward to trail a path of wet, mind-destroying kisses over his chest, her hands grasping his hips as he jerked in shocked pleasure.

His cat understood it was her power play. She needed to feel as if she was in control of the encounter.

He hid a smile, willing to let her play as he planted his knees on each side of her hips. At least for now.

His brief spurt of amusement was lost as she spread the tormenting kisses, heading ever lower.

Rage clenched his teeth. Oh, hell. He was already close to the edge. He moaned, his desperation to toss her back on the mattress and enter her with one thrust tempered by the fierce pleasure of her maddening kisses.

Clearly enjoying her power over his body, Lucie used the tip of her tongue to trace a path from his bellybutton down to his balls. A groan was wrenched from his throat as she sucked them into her mouth, driving him to the edge of madness before she turned her attention to his aching cock.

"No more," he rasped as she slipped the tip between her lips. He reached down to grab her shoulders and pulled her up.

She flashed a smug smile before he was abruptly turning her around and leaning her forward, so she was on her hands and knees. Then he grasped her hips, pulling her into the perfect position.

"Rage?" Her eyes widened with shocked pleasure as he thrust forward, and with one smooth motion, impaled himself in her damp heat. "Oh, hell."

Smoothing his lips up her back, Rage sank his teeth into her shoulder, savoring her low moan of pleasure. Her pussy clenched around him, making him shudder with sheer bliss.

"Shit, Lucie," he rasped. "I'm not sure how long I can last."

Tightening his hold on her hips, Rage withdrew to the very tip before slowly sinking back into her welcoming heat. She rolled her hips at the same time and Rage muttered a curse, waging war against his looming orgasm.

Dammit. There was no way he was going to embarrass himself by coming before his female.

Quickening his pace, he reached around her body to stroke his fingers over her tender clit. The air was perfumed with her arousal, her slender body bowing beneath him as she tipped back her head and moaned in pleasure.

"Faster," she choked out, her voice harsh as her climax neared.

Rage used his free hand to grasp her hair, turning her face so he could kiss her with savage pleasure at the same time he pumped into her with an insistent rhythm.

"Whatever you desire, Lucie," he swore against her lips.

He plunged his tongue into her mouth, their bodies moving together with a perfect tempo. Then, with a burst of relief, he felt Lucie stiffen, her sharp cry of release echoing through the room.

Rage hissed as her climax gripped his cock, his hips pistoning as he at last gave into the wild hunger of his cat. He gave a shout of satisfaction as his orgasm exploded through him, a tidal wave of rapture rippling through his body.

* * * *

Lucie collapsed on the bed, too sated to protest when Rage stretched out beside her and possessively tugged her into his arms.

Okay. That'd been…

Stunning. Beautiful. Life altering.

And overall, terrifying.

She liked her sex straightforward and uncomplicated. No weird emotional attachments or expectations. But even as a voice in the back of her mind was urging her to panic, her body was happily snuggling against his hard body, her cat purring in utter contentment.

She would panic later, she promised herself.

After Rage had left her to return to his home.

Lost in her thoughts, Lucie didn't realize that Rage had lifted his head to study her with a brooding gaze. Not until he broke the thick silence.

"Why did you steal my diary?"

Lucie blinked. Wow. That was not at all what she'd been expecting.

She didn't want to talk about the childish stunt. Not because it'd been embarrassing for him. He'd only become more popular with the females after they'd decided his private musings about his lovers somehow enhanced their reputations as desirable mates. Idiots. But because it revealed how desperately obsessed she'd been.

And still was, for that matter.

Acutely aware of his deepening curiosity, she forced herself to shrug. "I was a brat," she said in light tones.

"No." His fingers brushed through her hair, his touch achingly tender. "You were hurt and striking out. I'm just not sure why I was singled out for public humiliation."

"Because…" The words stuck in her throat.

"Lucie?"

She heaved a resigned sigh. He wasn't going to let it go. Not until he coerced her into revealing the painful truth.

"Because I had a crush on you," she grudgingly muttered.

The violet eyes shimmered with flecks of gold as the dawning sun splashed through the windows.

"A crush?"

She grimaced. She might as well confess the rest. If she were being honest, she probably owed him.

"Don't act surprised. You had to sense that I watched you from the trees."

"I thought you were plotting my death."

"I was young and impressionable, and I was fascinated." Her gaze ran over his lean, perfect features. "You were so gorgeous."

"True." He grunted as she elbowed him in the gut. "Ow."

"But it was more than that," she finished her confession. "You had a...kindness that I desperately wanted for myself."

His teasing expression melted to one of regret, his fingers sliding over the curve of her shoulder.

"I would happily have been kind to you if you hadn't bolted whenever I got near you," he murmured.

She believed him. Rage might have been spoiled, but he'd never been deliberately cruel. His nature was to protect the weak and vulnerable.

"I didn't know how to tell you," she admitted with a wry smile. "So instead I struck out."

His fingers drifted down her collarbone, his enticing musk scenting the air. "From now on, I have a better way for you to express your feelings for me."

She instantly stiffened. It was one thing to confess her feelings when she'd been an idiotic youth. There was no way she was going to share the fact he'd never left her dreams.

"Who said I still have feelings for you?" she belligerently demanded, ignoring the fact that she was lying naked in his arms. "That was a long time ago."

He chuckled, not fooled for a second. Damn him.

"Fine, then I'll show you how I feel," he murmured, lowering his head to brand a path of tiny kisses over her brow and down the length of her nose. Then, at last reaching her mouth, he nibbled at her bottom lip. "In fact, I intend to show you how I feel several times a night for a very, very long time to come."

His words were no doubt the empty promises he made to every woman. We'll be together forever, blah, blah, blah.

But they didn't feel empty.

They felt like a pledge that resonated deep in her heart.

Instinctively, she lifted her hands to press them against his chest. "Rage."

He raised his head, staring down at her with a fierce determination. "Do I frighten you?"

"Yes," she admitted without hesitation. "This is all happening too fast."

She caught a glimpse of his cat lurking in his eyes...hungry, possessive. Then, with a visible effort, he gained command of his animal.

A rueful smile touched his lips. "I know."

"I need to check the trace." Lucie muttered a curse, slipping out of bed and heading into the shower.

A charming Rage was as lethal as a possessive Rage.

Twenty minutes later she was scrubbed clean, with her hair braided and wearing her usual uniform of jeans and a long-sleeved T-shirt. Adding a pair of jogging shoes, she returned to the bedroom to discover that Rage had used the guest shower and was already dressed and waiting for her.

His beautiful face was carefully bland as he folded his arms over his chest. Smart male. The intimacy of the night had left her feeling raw and unnervingly vulnerable. One smartass comment and she would have him tossed out of her house.

Without a word, she left the bedroom and headed back to her hidden computer office. Acutely aware of the male prowling a few inches behind her, she slid into her chair and forced herself to concentrate on the computer screen that was blinking with success.

"I have a hit," she murmured, resisting the urge to give her trusty computer a pat.

Not everyone understood her habit of treating her equipment like they were old friends.

Leaning over her shoulder, Rage surrounded her in his warm, male musk. "You found the bastard?"

"I located the computer that is running the auction," she cautioned. "Whether or not the person who's ultimately responsible for setting it up is physically there..." She shrugged. "That's impossible to say."

He nodded. "Where is the computer?"

"Bossier City."

"Damn." Rage abruptly straightened, pacing from one end to

the other of the long, narrow room. "That's where Locke was setting up the military lab."

Lucie grimaced, easily understanding his frustration. Stanton Locke had been the human who'd been experimenting with Pantera blood and intending to share it with a military contractor. If the computer was in the same spot, it couldn't be a coincidence.

"So the mystery man might actually have the research notes." She spoke his fears out loud.

"Yep," he growled.

Lucie hit a button on the keypad, then reached to the side as the printer spit out a paper with the information she'd located. Rising to her feet, she handed the printout to Rage.

"Here's the address."

Folding the paper, he shoved it in the back pocket of his jeans, moving to stand directly in front of her.

"The Pantera is in your debt," he assured her, his fingers lightly tracing her jaw.

A tiny shiver raced through her. God. She loved the heat of his touch. It felt as if she'd been branded. Claimed.

So dangerous...

"I'll come up with a payment plan," she muttered.

Without warning, he leaned to press a light kiss to her lips. "I have to deal with this, but I swear I'll be back."

Lucie stepped back, her brows lifting in surprise at his words.

Did he think that she was just going to sit home like a good little girl while he had all the fun?

"I'm coming with you."

Rage stiffened, his eyes narrowing. "No way."

She folded her arms over her chest, not for the first time wishing she wasn't so tiny. It was hard to be intimidating when she was a foot shorter than everyone.

"I wasn't asking permission," she informed him.

"You're a Geek, not a Hunter," he growled.

She rolled her eyes. "I'm aware of that."

He leaned down until they were nose to nose, the power of his cat pulsing through the air.

"You've done your job. Now it's my turn."

Her animal prowled beneath her skin, instinctively wanting to back down beneath the stronger male, but Lucie refused to be intimidated. Not just because she was stubborn and overly independent, but because there was no way in hell she was going to let this male walk into danger alone.

That was unacceptable.

"You need me," she told him, meeting him glare for glare.

Taking advantage of their proximity, he swiped his rough tongue over her bottom lip. Such a cat.

"That's true," he agreed in husky tones. "But first I have to put an end to this threat."

She pulled back, resisting the urge to do a little licking of her own.

Later...

"I mean, you need to me to stop the auction," she insisted. "Unless you've become a computer expert?"

His brooding gaze lingered on her lips. "With enough encouragement, I can force the bastard to end it."

She didn't doubt that. For all of Rage's easy charm, he was a ruthless predator who would do whatever was necessary to get the information the Pantera needed.

A knowledge that she intended to use to force him to take her along.

"And if he won't? Or if he manages to escape?" she demanded. "Or you accidentally kill him?" She held up her hand as his lips parted to assure her that he could take care of the enemy. "The auction is set on a timer. It's going to happen unless I can gain physical access to his computer and stop it."

His lips snapped together at her indisputable logic.

They both knew that right now, nothing mattered but halting the sell of the technology that would use Pantera blood as some sort of weapon.

"Dammit." Reaching into his pocket, he yanked out his cellphone. "I need to call Parish."

Knowing she'd won, Lucie turned and headed forward to the door. "I'll wait for you in the garage."

Chapter Five

Rage completed his call to Parish and then took a few minutes to regain control of his temper.

Damn, Lucie. She was supposed to be in her beautiful home, doing whatever it was she did on her fancy computer system. She wasn't supposed to be directly confronting their enemy and putting herself in danger.

Unfortunately, he couldn't deny her logic.

They knew nothing about the person responsible for setting up the auction. Or even if they were still in Bossier City It was only reasonable to have a backup plan to make sure they could prevent the information from being spread to some unknown buyer.

Once he'd managed to gain command of his anger, he followed the scent of primroses to the narrow flight of stairs that led to the garage. Entering the small space, his brows lifted at the sight of the Harley-Davidson Sportster motorcycle.

It was a sleek, fast work of art.

Just like his Lucie.

"Why am I not surprised?" he murmured.

Tossing him a helmet, she tugged on her own before she straddled the bike and started the engine with a throaty roar.

"Get on," she commanded.

Rage put on his helmet. It wasn't that he was afraid of an

accident. Pantera could take one hell of a beating. But they didn't have time to be stopped by the local police.

Crossing the floor, he studied the female who was impatiently waiting to leave. "Why can't I drive?"

She sent him a wry glance. "You got to drive in bed."

Heat streaked through him at the vivid memory of her bent in front of him as he took her from behind. Instantly, he was hard.

"True," he murmured.

She flipped down her visor, revving the engine. "Are you coming or not?"

Swinging his leg over the bike, he settled in close behind her, wrapping his arms tightly around her waist.

"This gives me ideas," he said, rubbing his erection against her lower back.

"Stop that," she chided, trying to pretend her arousal wasn't scenting the air. They just had to be in the same room for desire to combust between them.

She pressed a small device that was mounted on the front of the bike, opening the narrow door of the garage, then gunning the engine, they shot onto the narrow side street that was thankfully empty at the early hour.

Rage gave a low chuckle. If he couldn't keep Lucie tucked safely at home, then he was going to enjoy their time together.

Keeping his chin planted against her shoulder, he held on tight as they headed out of New Orleans. The morning air was edged with a sharp chill as they hit the highway and headed north, but neither noticed. Instead, they silently appreciated the close press of their bodies.

Finally, it was Lucie who broke the silence, speaking through the Bluetooth that was built into their helmets.

"What did Parish say?"

Rage grimaced. The leader of the Hunters hadn't been any happier than he was at the thought of Lucie being exposed to their enemy.

"That he would slice off my balls if you got hurt," he admitted, his ears still ringing from the older male's angry warnings. Then, unable to resist his primitive instincts, he asked the question that was gnawing at him. "Are you going to tell me what's up between the two of you?"

"Nothing's up." She easily weaved through the thickening traffic, clearly as at ease on the bike as she was behind her computer. Her skill was oddly erotic. "Parish is my friend."

He believed her. Parish was not only happily mated, but if he'd wanted this female, then nothing on this earth would have kept him from her side.

"Why him?" he demanded.

She snorted. "Because he's a pushy pain in the ass who refuses to take no for an answer."

"That sounds like Parish," he swiftly agreed. "What did he do?"

"He came to me after my grandfather died."

Rage clenched his teeth. Christ, he wished he'd known what her grandfather had been doing. He'd have given the bastard a taste of his own medicine.

"Is that when you burned down the cabin?" he asked.

"Yes." He felt her shiver and he tightened his arms, trying to offer her comfort. It was too late to do any good, but it was all he had. "I had to destroy the memories of that place."

"I don't blame you."

She shrugged. "Maybe someday I'll be able to accept that it was the sickness that made him so cruel, but not yet."

He hoped she did find some peace in the memory of her grandfather. Bitterness would only eat away at her soul.

"Did Parish help you leave the Wildlands?" he inquired.

She nodded. "Once Xavier told me that I was no longer allowed to work on the computers, he offered me an apartment and gave me some money. I think he was afraid I might do something crazy."

Rage gave a short laugh. Like she hadn't been doing crazy shit before then?

Of course, he wasn't stupid enough to point out her habit of striking out without warning.

"I'm glad that Parish was there for you," he said instead, ignoring his cat's growl in protest.

His animal might be convinced that he was the one who was supposed to protect her, but at the time he hadn't given her what she needed. Thank the goddess, Parish had.

He shook off his cat's urge to pout. He hadn't taken care of Lucie in the past, but he fully intended to be the only one to see to her needs in the future.

"You know that Xavier's going to do everything in his power to get you back after this?" he warned.

She buzzed around a truck pulling a wagon of hay. "There's nothing he could offer that would tempt me to return," she proclaimed. "I like my life."

He pressed his hand flat against her stomach, his touch deliberately possessive. He was willing to spend part of their time in New Orleans if that made her happy, but he intended to make sure that she shared his home in the bayous.

"He's not going to be the only one trying to convince you to return to the Wildlands."

"Whatever you say."

Rage frowned at her flippant words, turning them over in his head. There was some sort of message in them. He knew women well enough to realize that there were always hidden meanings when a woman was acting as if it didn't matter. A smart male learned to decipher them.

It took several minutes, then, like a bolt of lightning, it hit him.

Hell. She'd decided he was a frivolous flirt. A male who drifted from one bed to another. And right now, there was nothing he could say that was going to make her believe that he wanted more than a casual affair. Obviously he was going to have to prove his sincerity with deeds.

A grim smile of determination curved his lips. "You can doubt me, Lucie, but eventually you'll accept you're not getting rid of me."

"That sounds like a threat," she muttered.

His fingers skimmed up until they were just an inch from the delicate curve of her breast. "A promise."

She shivered, reaching up to turn off her Bluetooth. Rage smiled. She could try to shut him out as much as she wanted.

Nothing, not even her stubborn distrust, was going to stop him from claiming her as his own.

* * * *

Lucie pretended an all-consuming concentration on navigating the five-and-a-half-hour drive to Bossier City. Not that she was stupid enough to think for a second that she was fooling Rage. They both knew that she'd have to be dead not to be aware of the six-foot plus male who was snuggled so tightly against her back she could feel every inch of his hard body. That didn't even include the sparks of awareness that were sizzling between them. She wouldn't be surprised if her skin was scorched from the heat.

Thankfully, she managed to arrive at their destination without crashing. Or halting the bike so she could rip off Rage's clothes and have her evil way with him, which had been way more likely than crashing.

Pulling the bike to a halt a block away, she nodded her head toward the large warehouse that overlooked the Red River.

"That's the place."

Rage stepped off the bike and removed his helmet, his gaze locked on the brick structure that looked abandoned from a distance. Lucie, however, didn't miss the new chain link fence that was ten-foot tall and topped with barbed wire. Or the bars that'd recently been added to the windows. Someone didn't want any stray trespassers having a peek inside.

"Stay here while I check it out," he murmured.

Lucie reached out to lay her hand on his arm. Shit. She didn't want him going in there alone.

"I should come with you."

He shoved back his hair with impatient fingers, clearly anxious to be on the hunt.

"You're staying here."

"But—"

"When it comes to geeky stuff, you're in charge," he interrupted, tugging off her helmet so he could stare down at her with a ruthless air of authority.

The casual charmer was replaced with the lethal predator.

"Geeky stuff?"

"When it comes to hunting the enemy, I'm in charge." He reached to cup her chin in his hand, forcing her to meet his steady gaze. "Deal?"

Lucie hesitated. Once she agreed, she would be giving her word that she would be stuck waiting for him, even if her every instinct screamed she should be with him. What if he went in and never came out? What if she truly lost him?

The thought made her heart clench with panic.

Unfortunately, she knew that he wasn't going to leave until he had her promise.

Stubborn cat.

"Deal," she grudgingly conceded.

Easily sensing how difficult it'd been for her to accept his demand, Rage leaned down to brush his lips lightly over her mouth.

"I'll come and get you once I'm sure it's safe."

She reached up to grasp his sweatshirt, a strange sense of premonition inching down her spine.

"Be careful."

"Always."

He paused long enough to steal one last lingering kiss before he was straightening and jogging down the street, staying in the shadows of the nearby buildings. She held her breath as he reached the fence and scaled it with fluid ease. He was fast, but they didn't know anything about the enemy's security.

No alarms sounded as he jogged across the empty parking lot and entered through a back window, but Lucie knew that didn't mean anything.

Crawling off the bike, Lucie stored the helmets before she pulled out her phone. She wanted to call Parish and ask the leader of the Hunters what Rage had said to him earlier. And more importantly, she wanted to make sure he was sending backup in case things went to hell.

She frowned as she scrolled through her contacts, feeling an odd prickle in the center of her back.

It felt as if she was being stalked.

The thought had barely formed when she caught the unmistakable scent of a human male. Glancing up, she watched as a man jumped from a second floor window to land directly in front her. The stranger was dressed in camo pants and a green henley that was stretched tight over his bulging muscles. His face was square with blunt features, and his dirty blond hair was pulled into a short tail at his neck.

Lucie grimaced. Damn. She didn't need the edge of musk that clung to the man's body to realize he'd been drinking Pantera blood. That leap would have broken the legs of an average human.

Shoving her phone back into her pocket, she pinned a faux smile to her lips. The man might have juiced himself on Pantera blood, but that didn't make him any match for the real deal.

"Nice trick, stud," she murmured as she strolled forward. A few more feet and she would be in striking distance. "I was just waiting for my boyfriend, but the jerk is late. Again. Maybe we should—"

"Don't move, bitch," the man snapped, reaching into a holster to pull out...was that a dart gun?

She narrowed her gaze. "You have no idea what kind of bitch I can be," she growled.

He pointed the gun at the center of her chest. "Hands behind your back."

Yeah, right. Like she was going to give him an opportunity to cuff her with those zip-locks she could see dangling from his belt.

"Fuck off," she snarled, surging forward.

She'd managed to get her fingers wrapped around his thick neck when he squeezed the trigger and she was hit by a small dart. Instantly, a crippling pain exploded through her.

It wasn't the tranq gun she'd assumed.

Instead, the dart was filled with malachite, the one thing that could decapitate a Pantera. The mineral not only hurt like hell, but it cut her connection to her cat, leaving her as helpless as an injured human.

Shit, shit, shit.

Nearly paralyzed by the poison pumping through her blood, Lucie didn't even put up a fight when the man grabbed her by the waist and tossed her over his shoulder.

"Bad little kitty," he mocked, smacking his hand on her ass. "I have ways of punishing you."

Her head bounced against his back as he headed down the street and through a narrow gate in the chain link fence. Lucie gave a low groan. They were going to the warehouse where Rage had so recently disappeared. She could only hope that he was well hidden.

Entering the building through a side door, the man carried her up a set of metal stairs to the loft on the fourth floor.

"I got her," her captor called out.

Lucie caught the scent of two more males, both humans who'd used Pantera blood to enhance their power.

"Put her in the cell," one of the males commanded.

There was the sound of the man's heavy boots hitting the wood plank floor as she was carried across the room and roughly dumped into a cage made of iron bars that was shoved against the wall. She hit the ground with a bone-jarring thud, glaring at the man who slammed the door shut and locked it.

He ignored her seething fury, turning on his heel to head toward the two men who were standing beside a long folding table that was loaded with various computer and surveillance equipment.

It was obviously a temporary setup. The numerous cords were hanging from the rafters, the monitors were resting on cheap TV trays, and the only places to sit were plastic patio chairs. Once the auction was done, they intended to pack up shop and get the hell out of Dodge. Or Bossier City.

Despite her pain, her heart skipped a beat.

This was exactly what they'd come here to find.

If she could get out of the cage, she could...

Her thoughts were brought to a sharp end as one of the men strolled toward the cage, eyeing her with a vulgar heat that made her skin crawl.

"She's a pretty little thing," he drawled, his narrow face and thin frame reminding Lucie of a rat. "I think I might have a taste of her."

Lucie tensed, cursing the malachite that continued to cripple her. She wasn't sure if she could fight off the jerk or not.

"You can have fun with her later," the oldest of the men thankfully snapped, pointing toward one of the monitors. "First we need her to capture our unwelcomed visitor."

Lucie made a strangled sound as she crawled to the edge of the cage to catch the image in the monitor.

Rage.

Oh, hell. They knew he was in the building. And they were going to use her to try and capture him.

On cue, the older man, who was clearly the leader of the trio, reached to touch a button on a silver panel arranged in the center of the table.

"Pantera, we know you're here," he said into and old-fashion microphone, the words echoing through the warehouse. "Move to the doorway and go to your knees with your hands behind your head until my guard can arrive."

Lucie watched the monitor as Rage came to a startled halt, his gaze lifting toward the ceiling of the room he was standing in before he was flipping off the camera pointed directly at him.

"Now, now, that's not very nice," the human continued, his tone taunting. "You should be more grateful. After all, we have your pretty companion all safely tucked in her cage waiting for you. It was so rude of you to leave her waiting on the street. Anyone could have come along and hurt her."

Rage's eyes filled with the golden fury of his cat. He couldn't shift away from the Wildlands, but his animal gave him a speed and strength that no human could match. Which was obviously why they'd taken Lucie as their hostage.

Silently praying that the Hunter would be smart enough to escape and wait for backup, Lucie's stomach twisted with dread as he slowly lifted his hands in surrender.

"No, Rage," she screamed. "Get out."

The man standing near the cage reached through the bars to smash his fist into her face, the blow violent enough to snap her nose. She felt the rush of blood as she tumbled to the side, smacking her head on the floor. Weakened by the malachite, she couldn't battle back the darkness that rushed up to claim her.

Her last thought was that she'd never, ever had anyone sacrifice themselves for her...

Chapter Six

Lying in the center of the cage, Rage pressed his body against the unconscious Lucie, silently contemplating the various ways he intended to kill his captors.

Ripping out their throats was always the easiest. But there was a certain satisfaction in the thought of slowly peeling off their skin. Or maybe he'd wait and let Lucie decide how she wanted them to die.

That seemed fair considering they'd broken her nose.

A low growl rumbled in his throat. Even though she'd healed over the past few hours, he was never going to forget his first sight of her crumpled in a heap with blood pouring down her face. If he hadn't been able to pick up the steady beat of her heart, he might very well have torn apart the three humans with his bare hands.

Instead, he'd allowed the men to shove him into the cell. Idiots. It was exactly where he wanted to be.

He'd known from the second he'd heard the human's voice over the intercom that he was going to have to change his plans. It was no longer a matter of finding the mystery man and forcing him to halt the auction. He had to get to Lucie.

End of story.

Thankfully, he'd managed to make a quick call to Parish before the guard arrived. He'd asked for the backup Pantera that were on their way to the warehouse to stay hidden in the neighborhood until he had Lucie away from the humans.

She was, he'd swiftly determined, their only hope to stop the auction.

His little time with the leader of the trio had already convinced him that the bastard wasn't going to give up his shot at a fortune. The human had clearly sacrificed everything to join Benson Enterprises. His reputation as a legitimate researcher, his place in the academic world, and his morals. Now that it was collapsing around him, he was obsessed with getting what he'd been promised.

Money. And a lot of it.

Parish had given him until eleven p.m. to escape with his soon-to-be mate. Then the Hunters were coming in. Which meant that they had less than an hour for Lucie to wake up before the cavalry came charging in and they lost this last opportunity.

Burying his face in her hair, he breathed deep of her primrose scent, his cat pressing against his skin as it tried to comfort his female. Then, without warning, he felt her stir in his arms.

"Rage?" she murmured in a husky voice.

Sitting up, he carefully scooped her in his arms so he could cradle her in his lap. "I've got you, sweetheart."

She blinked in confusion, her face still pale from the malachite that had ravaged her body. Although the poison had worked its way out of her system, she would be weak for hours.

"Where are we…" Her words trailed away as she realized they were sitting in the middle of a cage.

Then, astonishingly, she wiggled until she could free her arm to punch him in the center of his chest.

Rage scowled. Not because it hurt. Even at full strength she couldn't do much damage. She was a Geek, not a Hunter. But in sheer surprise.

Perhaps he was crazy, but he'd expected some gratitude that he'd come to save her.

Just a smidgeon.

"What was that for?" he demanded.

She scowled right back at him. "What the hell is wrong with

you?"

"My mother would tell you nothing," he assured her. "As far as she's concerned, I'm perfect."

She rolled her eyes, not nearly as impressed as she should have been.

"If you were perfect then you wouldn't have been stupid enough to surrender to the enemy."

He shrugged. "You needed me."

"That's not the point." She gave him another punch, but Rage didn't miss the hint of vulnerability that softened her features. She'd never had anyone who truly cared about her. She didn't know how to deal with his concern. "It's your duty to escape so you could stop the research from being sold."

He grabbed her face in his hands, staring down at her with a grim intensity.

"I couldn't risk you," he growled. "Nothing is more important to me than your safety." He tilted his head down until they were nose to nose. "I will sacrifice everything, including my duty, to protect you."

Their gazes locked, the weight of his words vibrating in the air.

It was a pledge not even Lucie could dismiss as his usual flirtations.

She licked her lips, a rapid pulse fluttering at the base of her throat. "You are…"

"What?" he prompted as her words faded away.

The emotions she usually kept so rigidly contained slowly darkened her eyes. Need, hope, and something that Rage desperately wanted to believe was love.

"Impossible," she at last muttered, reaching up to tangle her fingers in his hair as she planted a possessive kiss on his lips.

Pleasure exploded through him.

It was the first time she'd initiated a kiss. It made the caress all the more sweet.

Stroking his fingers down the slender arch of her throat, he savored the feel of her lips as they demanded his response. Deep inside, his cat purred with contentment, even as it twitched with the need to get his female out of this cage and back to the safety of the Wildlands.

Lifting his head, he gazed down at her with a faint smile. "Obviously you're dangerously addicted to males who are impossible," he teased.

She rolled her eyes, but even as her lips parted to punish him for his smartass comment, she was sucking in a sharp breath.

"Shit, what time is it?"

Rage reached down to pull out the cell phone he'd hidden beneath his sweatshirt. The idiots hadn't bothered to frisk him before throwing him in the cage.

"Just after ten."

Scrambling off his lap, Lucie shakily rose to her feet to glance around the empty loft.

"Where are the humans?"

Rage shoved himself upright to stand next to his female. She was too stubborn to lean on him, but he'd make damned sure he was close enough to catch her if she fell.

"The leader just stepped out of the room," he told her, nodding toward the door across the room. "The other two are keeping watch on the lower floor. They seem to think there might be other Pantera on the way."

She arched her brows. "Are there?"

He leaned down to speak directly in her ear. He couldn't be sure they weren't being monitored by a hidden camera.

"They're waiting for my signal."

Following his lead, she kept her voice soft enough that it wouldn't carry. "Then why haven't you signaled?"

"I needed you awake so you can stop the auction."

She blinked, as if caught off guard that he'd managed to fight his natural instincts to ensure she was rescued as swiftly as possible. It spoke of his absolute faith in her. Not only as a computer whiz. But as a loyal Pantera who was willing to take risks to protect her pack.

Reaching out, she placed a hand in the center of his chest, a soul-deep gratitude etched on her pale face.

"Actually, I can do better than that," she promised, glancing toward the door of their cell. "But in case you didn't notice, we're locked in a cage."

"I can take care of the cage." He laid his hand over hers,

pressing it tight against the steady beat of his heart. "Are you feeling up to doing your thing?"

A slow, wicked smile of anticipation curved her lips. "Yeah, I think I can manage my thing. What about the humans?"

"They're my thing," he assured her. Lifting her hand, he pressed his lips to the center of her palm. "Ready?"

She lifted herself on her tiptoes to place a fleeting kiss on his lips before she was stepping back with a determined expression.

"Ready," she said, clearly expecting him to do something "James Bond" like pick the lock or discover some hidden lever that would open the door. Instead, he moved forward to grab the iron bars, and with one massive burst of strength, ripped the door off its hinges. "Shit, Rage," she breathed in shock.

He pointed toward the computer. The humans might have limited hearing, but even they couldn't have missed the screech of metal. They'd have only seconds before their captors were rushing to the loft.

"You concentrate on making sure that intel doesn't get out. I'll make sure you're not interrupted."

He turned to head toward the door, only to halt when she reached out to grasp his arm.

"Rage…" Her words trailed away, as if she couldn't force them past a lump in her throat.

"I know," he murmured softly, leaning down to press a tender kiss against her forehead. "I'll be back for you, Lucie. I swear."

Not giving himself the opportunity to waver from his decision to leave her alone to work her magic with the computers, he jogged across the wooden planks and slipped out the door. Then, holding onto the steel handle, he gave it a violent twist, jamming the lock so no one would be able to open the door if something happened to him.

At least…no human would be able to open it.

A Pantera would be able to get into the loft and rescue Lucie if necessary.

Pausing to take a thorough survey of his surroundings, Rage at last moved to the bottom of the metal steps. The door was the only entry to the upper floor. As long as he could block the stairs, no one was going to get to Lucie.

He had less than a second to glance around the large, open storage room before a shadowed form was entering through an open doorway, quickly followed by one of the guards.

"What the hell..." The leader of the humans came to an abrupt halt as he caught sight of Rage in the faint moonlight that spilled in from a small window. "How did you get out?"

"Did you really think that flimsy cage was going to halt a full-blooded Pantera?" he taunted, folding his arms over his chest with a nonchalance that he hoped would unnerve his prey.

The older man scowled, glancing around the room. "Where's the woman?"

Rage shrugged. "She already escaped."

The goon standing behind the leader turned back toward the doorway. "I'll get her."

"Don't be an idiot," the leader snapped, pointing toward the stairs. "She's still upstairs. We have to stop her before she can disrupt the auction."

The goon frowned. Clearly he'd been hired for his oversized muscles, not his intelligence.

"You said it couldn't be stopped once it started."

"Not unless someone gains access to my computer," the leader snarled. "I have to get up there."

The goon nodded, grimly glancing toward Rage, who flashed a wide grin.

"I don't doubt you have limited brain power, human, but do you really think you can take on a full-blooded Pantera?"

The man narrowed his gaze, stepping forward. "I'm not afraid of you, beast-man."

Rage resisted the urge to roll his eyes. Beast-man?

Whatever.

"It's your funeral," he said, his lips twisting into a humorless smile as the goon fumbled for the gun he'd shoved into the waistband of his jeans.

Sloppy.

The tight material meant that he couldn't draw his weapon cleanly. It was all the opening that Rage needed.

With a low growl, he leaped forward, grabbing the man by the neck. His fingers sank into the thick muscles, lifting the heavy body off the ground. Reaching down, he grabbed the weapon and tossed it into the corner. He didn't want to attract any more guards with the sound of gunfire.

Distantly, he was aware of the older man rushing toward the stairs, but he wasn't foolish enough to allow his attention to stray from the man who was struggling to get free of Rage's iron grip. The goon might be human, but he'd been injected with Pantera blood, which meant he was faster, stronger, and possessed more endurance than a normal person.

Squeezing even tighter, he grimly shoved the man against the wall, trying to avoid the kicks that were aimed at his knees. Was the bastard half mule? At the same time, he was forced to dodge the massive fists that were aimed at his face.

His grip, however, never faltered.

The man grunted, his face turning a strange shade of puce as his eyes slowly glazed over. Still, it was several minutes later before the large body at last went limp and Rage allowed him to drop to the floor. Then, just to make sure that the goon wasn't faking, he stepped forward and kicked him in the face with enough force the make his head slam back against the wall.

Okay, it wasn't just to ensure he was truly unconscious.

He wanted the bastard to pay for hurting Lucie.

For now a busted nose, split lip, and concussion would have to do.

Confident the man wasn't going to be moving for several hours, Rage paused to suck in a deep breath. He could smell the other human guard two floors down, no doubt watching the entrance.

Which meant he only had to worry about the man who had climbed the stairs and was currently pounding on the door of the loft, as if that would magically make it open.

Climbing the steps in two long leaps, he watched in satisfaction as the human turned to stare at him in blatant horror. It was always nice when his prey had the opportunity to regret making an enemy of the Pantera.

Licking his lips, the leader pressed his back against the door and lifted his hands in a pleading gesture.

"Look, there's no reason we can't work together," the man

said, beads of sweat trickling down his thin face. "There's going to be plenty of money to share."

Rage curled his upper lip in disgust. "You think I would betray my people for money?"

"What do you want? Women? Power?"

A growl rumbled in Rage's chest. "Your head mounted on my wall."

The man shook his head. "There has to be something—"

His words broke off as the door was suddenly wrenched open from inside to reveal Lucie. She flashed a smile as she caught sight of Rage and the trembling human.

"It's done," she said with blatant satisfaction.

"Done?" The man paled as he glanced over Lucie's shoulders to his table of computer equipment.

Rage didn't bother asking technical questions. It wasn't like he was going to understand Geek-speak. If Lucie said it was done...it was done.

As simple as that.

Which meant it was time for him to complete his job.

Reaching out, he grabbed the man by the material of his designer shirt, roughly hauling him down the steps and out of the storage room.

"No." The human squirmed, futilely attempting to dig in his heels, and Rage hauled him across the floor to the long bank of windows that overlooked the river. "We can make a deal," he rasped. "Just tell me your price."

"My price?" With a quick motion, Rage had the man lifted off his feet and with one brutal movement, he was shoving him through the nearest window. "This is my price."

There was the sound of glass shattering and a shrill scream as the man flew out the window and down to the parking lot below. He landed with a sickening thud.

Moving forward, Rage studied the limp form that was spread eagle on the pavement, his lips twitching as he watched the second guard dash out of the building to take in the sight of his dead leader. The guard glanced up to catch sight of Rage, his face draining of color before he was ducking his head and running away like a true coward.

Rage shook his head. The Pantera that surrounded the area would catch the idiot before he managed to escape.

Which meant that his job was done. At least for now.

Stepping away from the window, he turned to discover Lucie standing just a few feet away, studying him with a faint smile.

"Happy now?"

"Not yet," he admitted, prowling forward to wrap his arms tightly around her slender curves. Instantly his cat purred in approval, savoring the knowledge his female was safe and exactly where she needed to be. Tucked against his body. Planting a kiss on the top of her head, he sucked in a deep breath of her primrose scent. "But I intend to take you back to the Wildlands and get very, very happy."

Epilogue

Rage watched his female with a growing sense of frustration.

Okay, he was delighted to see her surrounded by a crowd of admiring Geeks as she explained exactly how she'd managed to destroy over a hundred computer systems, expose two terrorist cells to Homeland Security, and nearly topple the dictator of a small country.

She deserved every single pat on the back, not to mention more than one apology for not reaching out to her years ago.

But, enough was enough.

This was *his* female.

He wanted some up close and personal time.

No doubt sensing he was on the edge of shoving his way through the crowd that filled the long meeting room on the top floor of the Diplomats headquarters, Parish moved to stand at his side, placing a restraining hand on his shoulder.

"She's a hero," the leader of the Hunter's softly murmured.

"Yep," Rage readily agreed, his heart swelling with pride. "It was a brilliant idea to booby-trap the payload."

While Rage had been dealing with the humans, his genius mate had been layering the files that were being auctioned with a hidden code. It was the sort of snare only a hacker could have created.

"And even more brilliant to make sure that they were all

chosen as the highest bidder. Every asshole involved in the auction was hit with the nasty virus that created a backdoor that Xavier could use to download the information from the computers involved before wiping their hard drives."

Rage chuckled. "Xavier said that the howls of pain were epic across the Internet."

"And most blame Benson Enterprises," Parish said, soul-deep pleasure shimmering in his golden eyes. They were all celebrating the chance to strike such a decisive blow against their enemies. "It will be a while before Christopher recovers from this latest catastrophe."

Rage grimaced. None of them would be safe until they managed to track down the mysterious leader of Benson Enterprises and put an end to him.

Thankfully, that was someone else's problem. For tonight, Rage intended to devote himself to his beautiful mate.

First, however, there was a question that had been nagging at him.

"Are you going to tell me why you sent me to find Lucie instead of going yourself?" he demanded of his companion.

Parish smiled. "Because I knew that Lucie was always fascinated by you." The older man rolled his eyes. "The goddess knows why. But since she is more deserving of happiness than anyone else I know, I thought I would try my hand at playing cupid."

Rage narrowed his gaze. "So you set me up?"

"Absolutely."

Rage abruptly wrapped his arms around the large man and gave him a hug. "I owe you one, my man."

"Stop that." Parish shoved him away, a gleam of satisfaction in his eyes. "And don't think I won't collect your debt."

"Later." Squaring his shoulders, Rage prepared himself to battle his way to his mate's side. "I have a long overdue date with my female."

The End

Killian

Chapter One

Nostrils flared, green eyes narrowed, Rosalie sprinted across the clearing toward the border. Overhead, the quarter moon was barely visible behind a wash of gray clouds.

A storm was coming.

From above.

And from below.

Rosalie's cat grinned with feral menace as she slowed just enough to weave in and out of a trio of massive cypress. Most of the Pantera either feared the truth of the latter—humans invading the Wildlands—or hoped the threat would just go away and the Pantera would be left in peace once again. Hidden once again. But not Rosalie and her cat. They were looking—hoping—for bloodshed.

Human bloodshed.

Thunder growled around her, fueling her desire. Every night now she'd taken to prowling these lands, the border. From dusk to sunrise. Alone. Granted, she never started off alone. That wasn't the Hunter way. Normally, she was put in a group of three. But inevitably, conveniently, she lost them. Ditched them. Most of the other Hunters liked to patrol in their two-legged form; talking, discussing what they'd done that day as well as the strategy for the night's watch. Rosalie wasn't interested in chitchat, planning, or donning her female form. She preferred a solo hunt these days and the protective layer of her puma. Her cat preferred it too. Its heart was heavy and needy.

Pain.

Loss.

Mercier.

The puma's belly contracted with the thought of the massive gold cat, and the broad, sable-eyed male who'd been her lover and friend and…savior. Were they looking down at her, watching her? Cat and male. Two separate entities in the beyond. Did they miss her as she missed them?

Night consumed the sky above now, its inky blackness interrupted only by a fissure of diamond-colored lightning every now and again. Rosalie's ears pricked up, catching the cries of Bayon and Jazz about a quarter mile off. Near the east border. They were looking for her. Probably worried about her. All the Hunters seemed to be, even though she'd assured them she was fine. That she'd forgiven Hiss, the Hunter male who'd indirectly brought on Mercier's death. That she'd moved on. They didn't believe her lies. Oh, that ever-present expression of concern on their faces. It was irritating as hell. Parish had even gone so far as to insist she take time off. Said that dealing with both her mate's death and the trauma of the abduction that had nearly claimed her life too, was vital to her sanity and productivity.

But Rosalie didn't do time off.

She was in.

Always in.

Even more so as the war between the humans and the Pantera gained ground. And intensity.

The scent of her kind rushed her nostrils as she neared the bayou. She opened her mouth and inhaled deeply. Not Bayon and Jazz. Nor any Hunter she knew. A whisper of unease moved through her as the sound of splashing lured her closer. Who would be swimming at this hour? Two Pantera…lovers, perhaps? Her lip curled. That's all she needed tonight. *Foolish, unthinking cats. Playing in the water while the enemy lurks right outside our borders.*

And sometimes inside them as well.

She'd give them a stern talking-to. Or her claws would.

She stalked through the thick foliage, ready to pounce, to scare the shit out of some Geeks or Suits or Healers. But she only found one female Healer. And something else entirely.

In that moment, Rosalie ceased to exist, and her cat took full control, an event that was happening a lot lately.

"Fuck, woman," a deep male voice barked from the sleepy waters of the bayou. "I don't want to hurt you."

Eyes narrowed, nostrils flared, ears pricked, Rosalie's cat remained behind a moss-coated cypress. She wanted to spring. Attack. Without even knowing what was happening. She didn't care. No. The cat didn't care.

It scented human.

"You can't come here," a female cried out.

No. Not a female, Rosalie puma's confirmed. Not a woman, either. One of the rescued lab rats who had come to stay in the Wildlands. Something halfway between Pantera and human. Rosalie narrowed her eyes on the female figure in the water. She worked with the Healers. Karen...that was her name. She deserved claws and fangs herself for even engaging with this enemy.

A low, feral growl rumbled in Rosalie's throat. Maybe the male wasn't an enemy to *Karen*. Was this a meeting of lovers? Did the rat have a human male lover?

"Stop!" Karen called as the male swam away from her, toward the shore. "You'll be killed the second you step foot onto the Wildlands."

Rosalie's puma grinned. *Or maybe even before that.*

Her cat leapt from the flora and raced to the shore. The second the dark-haired male was out of the water, she attacked. Teeth sank into wet T-shirt, and with a growl of fury she dragged him onto the mossy bank.

But he was no fragile human with dead instincts. In seconds, he rolled away and sprang to his feet. Wasting no time, Rosalie's puma leapt onto his chest and sent him stumbling back. Cursing, he pushed her away, then found his footing again. Wet, his T-shirt clinging to his hard muscles, he crouched into a fighting position. Deep blue eyes raging at her, taunting her, his lip curled. He wasn't remotely afraid. He knew how to fight. Had been trained to fight.

Her Pantera heart sank while her cat's boiled.

He knew how to fight a Pantera.

She snarled and once again leapt at him, claws extended. He ducked, then flipped her over his back. Recovery was less than five seconds, and again she attacked. This time he turned to face her and swipe her legs out from under her.

Fuck you, Human.

The rat, Karen, was on the shore now, and as thunder boomed and lightning flickered in the sky, she tried desperately to calm the situation. But both Rosalie's puma and the man were oblivious. They were circling each other now, eyes narrowed, nostrils flared.

"I don't want to hurt you, kitty cat," he said, his tone dark and dangerous as his blue eyes hardened. "I just want to see—"

Rosalie didn't let him finish. She sprang forward and took him out at the ankles. This time, the man went down. All six foot three inches of muscle and bone. She wrestled him to his back, then stood over him, pinning him to the cold ground. For a few brief seconds, she stared down at him in the quarter moon's cloudy light. Every part of him was hard, from his mouth to his eyes to his body. He was wet, his short black hair plastered to his head. And scented of sweat and the bayou. Some females might call him...*sexy*.

Rosalie would call him dinner.

"Fucking cats," he growled. Then Rosalie's legs were suddenly thrust apart, hands closed around her throat and she was being rolled onto her back.

Panic flooded through her and she unleashed her claws, tried to reach his flesh. Any bit. Draw blood. But...no. Goddess, no. He was so strong. Shockingly strong.

She tried to turn her head, get her teeth on him, in him...

Fuck!

Poised above her, his massive, unyielding body weight pinning her cat down, he stared at her. Intently. Curiously. With those blue shark eyes. "I'll let go, Kitten," he whispered. "If you sheath your claws, close your mouth, and listen to what I have to say."

Hatred threatened to consume her...the puma. A human was not only demanding things from her, but he was imprisoning her. Her nostrils flared. Her puma had never felt such a desire to draw and consume blood. If this bastard thought she would ever allow herself to be imprisoned again, he was an idiot.

"What do you think, Kitten?" he said, his tone low with warning, his hard body digging into the flesh of her cat. "Can you control yourself?"

Rosalie granted him the puma's equivalent of a fuck-you grin, then followed that up with a quick and painful butt to the forehead.

The shock was immediate. The pain, too. He cursed, but his grip on her never wavered. Who the hell was this man? That he could contain her? A deadly beast of a Hunter? That he could suffer the pain she inflicted and not retreat?

And why hadn't she scented him when he was in the bayou with the rat?

Shit. The rat. Rosalie glanced around. Gone. Unbelievable. Or maybe not... It had abandoned a Pantera. What did she expect from a hybrid? From something developed in that goddamned lab. Mercier would've ripped this man apart then laughed as he fed on the bastard's heart.

The puma's insides deflated in instant pain. Unfortunately, the emotion caused not only her instincts to slow, but the man to get the upper hand.

He'd pulled some type of thin rope from his back pocket and was binding her puma's wrists. She roared into the cold night air for her fellow Hunters and fought against the rope. But it was too late.

"You give me no choice, Kitten," he said. "You drew first blood. You won't get another chance to touch me."

Touch you? Oh no, Human. Consume you is what I want. What I'll have the moment you turn your back. Or expose your jugular.

Granted, it was nearly impossible to cool, calm, or regulate the puma in that moment. It wanted only to struggle, get free, fight. *Kill.* But Rosalie had forced herself inside its brain now, and she knew that none of those things would happen if she continued to thrash and snarl. She pushed deep inside herself, to the cat's heart, trying to urge the puma to stop fighting. But it refused her. It was her alpha now. Had been for weeks. It ran the show, and it wasn't backing down or playing dead. Even to get the upper hand.

As her puma snarled and fought and wriggled against the hard, wet earth, the man pressed on. He was shockingly strong and incredibly fast. In under thirty seconds, he had both her back paws tied together, as well as her front.

Panic sliced through Rosalie as she fought for movement. Being bound, contained. It reminded her…

Tears scratched her throat. *Her* throat this time. Not the puma's.

No. Stop and remember where you are. The Wildlands. Not in that—

"Fuck no," the man growled, his eyes searching hers before moving over her puma's face. "I'm not turning into this. Those pieces of shit…"

Pain lanced through her, stealing her breath. Pantera. Puma. What was she? Her eyes clamped shut. *Oh Goddess. Goddess, no, please…* But it was happening anyway. Her fur stood on end and her bones started to ache. Without her consent. A shudder built inside her and she felt her cat's thick skin shrink. Tears pricked her eyes as claws, sharp and protective, drew back into the beginnings of fingers. She gasped for air, a strangled cry into the heavy early winter air.

"Shit," uttered the man.

For several brief seconds, Rosalie lay there, naked, her back to the hard earth, her wrists and ankles still bound. On any other night, she'd be fighting, scrambling to get loose, cursing and snarling at the intruder. Promising him a long, arduous death. But not tonight. Humiliation and pain and grief anchored her body to the ground, stiffened her spine. She was that prisoner of the lab again.

Slowly, she allowed her eyelids to lift. Stunned, confused, almost guilty blue eyes blazed down upon her. They held hers momentarily, then blinked and started to descend. A quick sweep. Down her body, then back up again. Assessing. Almost…professional. And yet Rosalie didn't miss the shards of heat he hadn't been quick enough to hide.

Naked. Female.

She couldn't care less. She had never been a prude. With or without fur, she was Pantera.

As he stared at her, Rosalie took stock of her situation. No longer did those ropes encircle thick puma limbs. On her female wrists and ankles the coils were loose. He hadn't noticed. Her mind revved. *Keep his eyes on yours as you slowly slip from your bindings.*

As she moved a centimeter at a time out of the ropes, she

stared at him. She despised the way he looked. How tall he was—all the hard muscle, the close-cropped black hair, and the arrogant, sharp-angled face. But she especially despised those blue eyes. They changed too swiftly. From blank to predatory to thoughtful. As if he had a soul—or worse, a conscience.

Rosalie knew there were humans living in the Wildlands. Good, decent, kind humans. But they were all female. The men...well, every single human man she had ever known was a terror. Unfeeling. Sadistic. Would do anything to get what he wanted no matter who got in the way or who got hurt.

Like our friend here.

Ankles and wrists free now, Rosalie held her position. The man was staring at her mouth. Like he was hypnotized. *Fool.* With barely a breath, she attacked. Her knee slammed into his hard stomach just as the heel of her hand thrust up into his chin. A grunt of pain met her ears, but she didn't stop. Squeezing him tight, she rolled hard right, and once he was on his back she dropped down on his chest and wrapped her hands around his neck, her thumbs instantly pressing into his windpipe.

Shock and fury registered first in those blue eyes, then, as his eyes flickered down her body to her breasts and belly and sex, desire blazed.

Fuck you, Human, she thought blackly even as her body betrayed her with a wash of sexual awareness. *You don't get this. Me. Ever.*

No longer bound, no longer a prisoner, it was the easiest shift in the world. From Rosalie back to her puma. And the cat ruled. It was alpha. It carried the anger with no grief. It desired blood, not touch or taste or connection. It was the ultimate strength.

With a flourish and a snarl of fury, the cat emerged. Claws dug into thick muscle, and mouth opened to reveal sharp, impressive teeth—ready...so ready.

But just as the puma was about to sink its fangs into the male's neck, it froze. For a voice.

"No, Rosalie."

Master and commander.

Not Parish. That would have her puma slow but not stop. It was Raphael. Leader of the Pantera. And every male and female, no matter what form they took, listened and obeyed.

A growl vibrated in her cat's throat. It didn't want to obey. It wanted vengeance.

"Get off now," Raphael continued in a voice so quietly threatening it buried itself within her.

Rosalie, the female inside the puma, tried to obey. Really. Tried. But it was...

"We have him, Rosalie," Raphael whispered near her ear.

No. I have him. And I want his blood.

Blood for blood.

The last words she heard were, "Take it," before something pricked the back of her cat's neck and she was being pulled off the human, her strength—that reliable, impenetrable strength—now gone.

Chapter Two

Propped up on a hospital-type bed, Killian watched as the doctor—
or whatever they called them here…Healer?— stitched him up.
Three fairly deep puncture wounds on his left shoulder. That damn
wildcat.

That fucking gorgeous wildcat.

Killian erased the thought from his head immediately. It had
no place there. He was in the Wildlands on a mission of survival.
Not to entertain attractions. Especially to a creature who'd nearly
gutted him like a fish on the bank of the bayou not two hours ago.

Something flickered on inside him and he glanced up. The
leader of the Pantera was now in his hospital room, standing next to
one of the guards who had been stationed here since Killian was
brought in.

What the fuck? How had Killian not heard him?

*Shit…*he'd felt him, though…hadn't he?

Killian took a second to assess the man. He looked exactly like
his picture. The one in the dossier kept at the lab, that is. Not the
ones online or in the newspapers. Those all looked Photoshopped.
His features had been softened, making him look less threatening.
More approachable, for a mysterious shape shifter from a hidden
world called the Wildlands. A declawed cat in an Armani suit. But

the truth of it was that this guy was as deadly as the Glock Killian had lost at the bottom of the bayou a couple of hours ago. Maybe even more so.

"So," Raphael started, looking up. His gold eyes were reserved. "Tell me, Killian O'Roarke. Why has a member of the United States military crossed the border into the Wildlands and demanded to see me?"

A muscle flickered in Killian's jaw as he held the man's stare. The only information he'd given the Healer working on him was his first name. "Don't know any O'Roarke, and I never claimed to be military."

Those eyes burned instantly. Clearly, Raphael didn't enjoy lies or games. Or time wasted. He pushed away from the wall and came over to the exam table. He eyed the Healer. "All right, Billie?"

The woman with the dark, short hair and ivy-green eyes nodded. "Almost done."

"They're fine," Killian told her, not liking the position he was in. On his back while the leader of the Pantera stood over him. "I'm an exceptional clotter."

"Oh, yeah," Billie answered with heavy sarcasm, holding him in place. "You're a real super soldier."

Her words caused his lip to curl. She had no fucking clue. "I'm not a solider."

"Maybe not anymore," Raphael said. "But you were."

Killian's gaze lifted and locked with the man.

"Everything about you says armed forces, Mr. O'Roarke. Build, attitude, fighting stance, and technique. And then there's the tattoo on your shoulder."

Killian's mouth thinned. "That has nothing to do with the military."

Pale brows lifted. "Doesn't it?"

What the hell? There was no possible way this man could know… Killian pulled his arm away just as the Healer finished her last stitch. "We're done. I need to speak to your leader alone."

"No we are not, you stubborn asshole," Billie countered, flashing him a green-eyed glare. "You need balm."

"I wouldn't argue with her," Raphael put in. "Or any Pantera female, actually. You'll just end up with—"

"Claw marks?" Killian supplied.

Raphael's lips twitched.

"If you're lucky." Billie snorted as she slapped some goo on his arm then quickly bandaged him. "You're welcome, by the way," she added as she got up and left the room.

"Your women are…interesting," Killian said as the door slammed shut.

"Females," Raphael corrected. "And yes, they are."

"Exceptionally strong. Bold. That…Rosalie." He sniffed, remembering how the wom—*female*—had both bloodied him and sat on top of him naked without even a hint of fear or embarrassment. "Definitely beautiful, but completely out of contr—"

"Don't speak of her." Raphael's eyes and his tone were grave now. "What she's been through, she's allowed to—"

Killian's brows knit together as the male cut himself off. "What has she been through?" *And why do I even give a shit? Maybe because you want some reason, other than that she hates humans, for how feral she was toward you.*

For a second, Raphael looked pissed at himself for saying anything. Then a forced mask of ease came over his expression. "It's really none of your concern, Mr. O'Roarke. Now. Tell me. What is it you want? And why didn't I let my Hunter gut you on the bank?"

"I think that's a question for both of us to answer, but I'll go first. I need your help."

"I don't offer help to humans who wander onto my land. Not anymore."

Killian expelled a heavy breath. He eyed the guards, who he knew weren't going anywhere, then turned back to Raphael. "If I was only human, I wouldn't have wandered onto your land."

Something that didn't seem like surprise flickered in Raphael's eyes. "What are you saying? You are human, Mr. O'Roarke. I smell you."

"But that's not all you smell, is it?"

"You are military," he said in a quiet voice.

"Was," Killian agreed.

Raphael's eyes closed for just a second. Pain registered on his face, in the set of his jaw and the furrow in his brow. When he finally opened them again, it wasn't pain Killian saw there, but Raphael's killer puma. "So they've done it," he ground out.

Killian's jaw tightened. The Pantera knew about the plans the secret black ops group operating within the military had to create an army of super soldiers. Well, of course they knew. Or at least their leader did.

"I was told it was therapy for some lingering PTSD I was going through," Killian explained through gritted teeth. "Injections. Isolation. Therapy. But every day I felt angrier, more combative. And at night, I dreamed..." He cursed under his breath.

"What?" Raphael pushed.

"That I was this massive black puma."

A muscle pulsed below the leader's right eye. "How many injections did they give you?"

"Twelve before I escaped and came here."

"And you came here because..." Raphael began with an edge to his tone. "What? You think you're one of us now? That you belong here?"

Anger pulled at Killian's insides. That same anger he'd felt in the lab. "I'm here, commander, because I *don't* want to be one of you."

Raphael stared at him.

"I'm here," Killian continued. "Because I need you to take whatever they put inside of me—out."

Raphael opened his mouth to speak, but before he did, the exam room door burst open. A man with a ton of tats and piercings, wearing a lab coat, strolled in. And following right behind him—*holy shit*—was none other than Kitten, aka Rosalie.

Aka, the one who'd nearly gutted his ass.

A flash of memory assaulted Killian's brain as he sat up in the bed. The ground near the bayou. Her on her back. Him on his back. Naked, sweaty, tantalizing flesh...

"Sorry, Raph," the tatted guy was saying. "I couldn't stop her."

"It's fine, Jean-Baptiste."

Jean-Baptiste raised his eyebrows, like *Are you sure? She's super pissed.* But after getting the nod from Raphael, he turned and headed back out.

"Rosalie?" Raphael began.

Killian turned to look at her, ran his gaze from the tips of her black combat boots, up her denim-clad legs to the short dark-gray sweater that exposed an inch of her trim belly. She was physical perfection. Drop dead. Dick to stone. Too bad she was hell-bent on killing him.

His gaze landed on her face. Skin like porcelain, hair the color of the morning sun, green eyes that tried to suck out your soul, and pink lips that were ready to swallow it right down.

"Unbelievable," she ground out, her eyes narrowed on the leader of her species.

"What is?" Raphael asked her calmly.

She jabbed a finger in Killian's direction. "You're keeping him, aren't you? *Sir.*"

The man's eyebrows lifted. "Keeping him? He's not a pet, Rosalie."

"Damn right, he's not," she returned. "He's the enemy. He fucking attacked me!"

"Okay, come on," Killian interrupted. "It was you who attacked me. Yanked my ass right out of the water. Got my back to the dirt, claws inside flesh. I'd think you'd be proud of the fact."

Her eyes cut to his, emerald fire bearing down on him. "Pride comes with a job well done, Human." One pale eyebrow jutted upward. "You're still breathing."

"Rosalie," Raphael warned.

"For now," she added.

Killian's mouth twitched with a grin. "Such hostility."

She sneered.

"He's not a pet," Raphael confirmed. "And he's not a prisoner. But...he will remain under guard as we sort some things out."

"*Not* a prisoner?" she repeated, stunned.

"That's what I said."

Killian turned to the male. He wasn't telling Rosalie about the injections. About the reason Killian was here. Why? Were the other Pantera not aware of what was happening? About the super soldier program?

"Fine," she said tightly.

"Fine?" Killian repeated, his gaze finding hers once again. "The fight is over already?"

She ignored him and looked at Raphael. "I'll guard him."

Raphael practically snorted. "I don't think so."

Her lip curled. She had a very sexy mouth. "You need someone on him."

"I have two someones right here," Raphael said, pointing behind him to the male guards.

"They're Suits," she said, as if that explained everything. "You need a Hunter on this. Why not me?"

Raphael exhaled. "Honestly, I don't think you're stable enough."

Her expression went tight and she lifted her chin an inch. "What is that supposed to mean?"

"You'll kill him." The words were simple. Honest. Obvious. And Raphael didn't allow her to counter. "He has information we need. That I need."

She sniffed, disgusted. "Don't they all."

The leader of the Pantera didn't answer. His eyes were strangely kind as he stared at her. Killian wondered if the latitude he was giving her was due to that mysterious something that she'd been through.

Her shoulders drooped. "Don't you get it?" she continued, her tone softer now. "The humans, they don't give a shit about us, Raph. Or about sharing anything with us. They only want to destroy us. You keep letting them in here. Giving them chances. Working with them. When are you going to make them pay?"

"Your anger is understandable, Rosalie, but—"

"Don't give me any of that shit." She didn't say it with any amount of menace. But Raphael wasn't about to let her defiance slide this time.

"Watch yourself, Hunter." His eyes had darkened. "I believed that when you came to me about forgiving Hiss you'd let go of—"

"Hiss is Pantera," Rosalie cut in.

Killian sat up even taller. Who was this...Hiss?

"He showed me that when we broke into the lab." Her eyes swept over Killian. "I have no forgiveness for anything human."

Jaw tight, Raphael nodded. "Then go. And leave this one to me."

"No," Killian broke in.

They both turned to stare at him. "What?" Raphael asked.

"I want her." The words slid from his tongue like honey. Slow and easy. His eyes locked with Rosalie's. "If you insist on someone shadowing me, guarding me while I'm here, then I want her."

The leader cursed, low and black. "I can't allow it. She wants your blood."

Killian laughed. "I'm sure she's not the only one. At least she's honest about it. I know where she stands."

Green eyes flickered with heat, but if it was sexual interest or the possibility of getting him alone and removing his heart with her puma's teeth, he couldn't tell.

"It's settled, then," she said, her lips curving into a smile.

"Nothing is settled until I say it is," Raphael returned tightly. "Rosalie, if this man ends up dead, you will not be able to remain in the Wildlands. Do you understand me?"

She gasped and turned to look at the leader of her kind.

"Do you want to take that risk?" he asked.

Her jaw tightened, but she nodded.

"I need your word, Hunter," he pushed.

"He will not die, Raphael. I give you my word." *But he might feel some pain*, her eyes said.

Killian could handle pain. He might even enjoy it if it was coming from her.

"And," Raphael said just as she was turning Killian's way, "no puma."

She whirled back to face him, eyes wide, nostrils flared.

"When you're around him, the cat is caged."

Her face reddened. "Why?"

"You know why," he stated pointedly, piquing Killian's curiosity. What was this about? So much mystery surrounding the beautiful and terrifying Rosalie. "Now, take him over to the garden house."

"That's very near your home," she said, looking confused. "Why not one of the secure units?"

"Take him, Hunter."

She growled softly. "Fine. Follow me, Human."

With a nod at the leader of the Pantera, Killian grabbed his now-dry shirt and pushed off the bed. As Rosalie walked out the door, her strides confident, her ass swinging from side to side, a thought slammed into his mind before he could stop it. *Follow you? Anywhere, Kitten. Any-fucking-where.*

Chapter Three

She'd been to the garden house only once. It was about an acre away from Raphael and his mate Ashe's two-story antebellum, and overrun with vines and flowers and late tomatoes climbing up the porch railings. The last resident had been an older female who'd kept mostly to herself and had loved everything green and growing, so the exterior of the small two-bedroom cottage appeared to be constructed almost entirely of moss and spotted bee balm. Under the cover of night, the scent of all the living things was intoxicating.

But Rosalie only scented human.

"Are you really going to stand outside the house all night?"

Her back to the front door, Rosalie stared straight ahead, across the long expanse of moonlit yard. The human male had been trying to engage her since they'd arrived an hour ago, this time coming to the open window to speak to her.

"You've gotta be hungry," he added.

She said nothing. Just as she'd said nothing when Raphael, Genevieve, and Lian had brought over food and supplies. While the leader of the Pantera spoke with Killian, the Suit female and the Hunter had tried like hell to not only discuss the human, but get her to relinquish her post as his guard. Lian had even offered to take her place. Said any of the Hunters would. But she'd refused them with a shake of the head.

They thought she'd break. Would give in to her puma's desire for human blood and get sent away from the Wildlands for it. She understood their worry, and she appreciated their care. But no one "handled" Rosalie except Rosalie.

"There's a great spread in here," the human called.

She rolled her eyes. Forget the human part—this man was going to *irritate* her into killing him. "No thanks," she ground out. "Unless you're offering me your blood."

"And if I am…?"

"Then you'll be dead before dessert."

"You know you just smiled when you said that, right?"

Her lips twitched. Again. "I don't doubt it."

He released a breath. "Come on. Eat with me."

"No."

"Rosalie—"

Her head came around fast and she hissed at him. "Don't call me that. You don't get to call me that."

He wasn't at all put out by her ferocity. "What should I call you, then?" His thick, dark eyebrows lifted. "Hunter? Mistress?" He grinned. "Kitten?"

Oh, the puma wanted out so badly… "Listen, Human. I'm not coming in there and eating with you. Period. End of discussion."

"All right." He shrugged, then left the window, disappeared inside the house.

Finally. She heaved a sigh of relief. She didn't like being around him. Not just because he was human, one of *them*. But because, unfortunately, she found him attractive. She shook her head. *Very attractive*. Like when he spoke, she watched the way his lips moved.

Goddess, she didn't deserve to breathe. For the fifth time since leaving Medical, she asked herself why she was doing this. Guarding the human. Why she'd insisted on it. Especially after Raphael had made her swear she wouldn't hurt him. Well, kill him is what she'd actually promised. But one would surely lead swiftly to the other, wouldn't it?

Why hadn't she walked away right when the leader had announced the human was staying? She should be patrolling the border, looking for more of them. Groups of them. Enemies of the Pantera.

The screen door pressed against her back then, and instantly she whirled around, her puma ready to spring. *Down girl. You're not getting me kicked out of my home. Not today.*

"Making a break for it, Human?" she snarled as the door opened and Killian emerged.

"For the porch, absolutely," he returned, moving past her with a snort.

She watched him as he headed for the faded floral loveseat with the small table in front of it and proceeded to set up dinner. A dinner for two. He was wearing the new clothes Lian had brought over: a pair of jeans and a blue Guns N' Roses T-shirt. Granted, this man was no Pantera male, but he surely equaled one in size. From his height, to the bulging biceps, to the way the shirt clung to hard abs and how tight his ass looked in that denim.

Her lip curled with disgust. But at the same time her belly warmed. *No. Just…no.* "You're not allowed to leave the residence, Human."

"I don't know how you divvy property here in your Wildlands, but where I come from this is still the residence."

"Where you come from." She sniffed. "They have porches attached to Locke's laboratories now, do they?"

"Who's Locke?"

She rolled her eyes. "Please."

He didn't say anything for a second. He was pouring lemonade into glasses. But when he took a seat, he said, "Iowa."

"What?"

He turned to look at her, those blue eyes annoyingly friendly. "I'm from Iowa. Originally. Farming family. Mostly soybeans."

She stared at him. She didn't want to know this. Any of this. Personal information. It made one weak and vulnerable to attack. She would never be weak again. Her stomach growled.

"Oh come on," he said. "Your body's in a state of revolt. This fried chicken's delicious. And it'll tide you over until something more human comes along."

She sneered at him. "The only human I'm interested in eating is you."

Rosalie didn't realize how that sounded until the man's mouth curved up into one of the sexiest smiles she'd ever seen. Then she

354/Alexandra Ivy & Laura Wright

wanted to just curl up in a ball and roll right off the porch.

But of course she didn't. She lifted her chin and said arrogantly, "You know what I mean."

His blue eyes flashed. "You're scared to get too close to me." He nodded. "Understandable."

"No. That's not it. At all."

"You sure?" He smiled, then started making soft clucking sounds.

She shook her head and heaved a sigh. "You're super annoying."

Didn't stop him from continuing on.

"Also, that's really inappropriate when you're actually eating the chicken."

His grin only widened as he clucked.

"Oh, fine!" she heaved, walking over and grabbing a chicken leg off the table. "I'll eat if you stop."

He did, then patted the seat beside him. "Come on, Hunter. I won't bite."

"Of course you won't," she said, tearing into the chicken as she remained standing. She was starving. Hadn't realized how starving until right that moment. "You're a weak-blooded human."

He tossed her the side-eye. "Who had you bound and on your back in under a minute."

She glared at him.

He grinned. Again. "Can I ask you something, Kitten?"

" 'Hunter' is fine."

He pouted for one quick second, then said, "I understand the dislike of humans now that your world has been outed, and they're filled with curiosity and fear. I understand the distrust. But your hate runs deep. Blood deep. Why?"

Her insides clenched. "Hand me that lemonade."

He did, but didn't let up on the questions. "Raphael alluded to something...something you're going through."

Rosalie reached for a biscuit, though her stomach was in knots. "You're right. This food is good."

He sniffed. "Okay. Got it. None of my business."

Damn right it wasn't. But not only that, she refused to go personal with this human. It was the first rule of guarding a prisoner, which he pretty much was. You don't ask or answer anything that could make you vulnerable.

But as she finished off her biscuit, she broke that rule. "So, you grew up on a farm?"

"Yup," he said, taking a bite of an apple. "Loved it. Open air, miles and miles of land. It was simple."

"Sounds pretty perfect."

He nodded. "Was."

"So why did you leave?" *And head for Locke's lab? Glory? Money?*

"My parents passed away in an accident my senior year of high school. After I graduated, I just didn't want to stay, you know? They were the only family I had, and it was lonely..."

Her heart squeezed a bit. Loss was really something they shared. "I'm sorry."

He nodded. "I sold the place to a nice family. Then, I joined the army."

Rosalie's head came around so fast she nearly gave herself whiplash. All softness and understanding gone, she stared at him. His jaw was tight, like he knew what he'd just said would be controversial.

Controversial? Try outrageous!

"You're a solider?" she ground out, her appetite now gone. There it was. She'd only been guessing that he might be from one of Locke's labs, but this... "Does Raphael know?"

"Yes."

Shit. That's why the leader had wanted this man to stay. Needed all the information. "Why did you come here? What do you want from Raphael? From us?"

He turned to look at her. His eyes were shuttered now. Back to the shark who was giving nothing away. "That's between Raphael and myself. For now. If he wants someone to know, he'll tell them."

Someone? "I'm not just someone." She stood up. "You're part of them," she snarled. "Those bastards. Fuck you!" Goddess, her cat was pushing to get out. And she wanted to let it. Let the puma handle this. Let the puma handle everything. "We're not helping you people create some hybrid monster for your battlefields."

His eyes flashed with anger and his lips parted to retort. But before a word was uttered, he took stock in her demeanor. Her barely controlled demeanor. He was off the loveseat and at her side in an instant. "Are you all right?"

Fuck, she was shaking. Like a scared cub. Couldn't stop herself. But she refused his touch. "Get away from me."

"You look like you're going to pass out."

"No, *Human*," she snarled at him. "I look like my puma is trying to get out and tear you to shreds."

She expected him to step away. Hell, he should be running into the house and locking the door, if he was smart. But instead he courted death and did the most insane thing ever. He pulled her into his arms.

Rosalie stiffened, growled, "What the hell are you doing?"

"Isn't it obvious?" he asked, pulling her even closer.

"Only if you have that rope again." Something strange was happening. Her puma was suddenly nowhere to be found, and the female part of her was…breathless…

He laughed softly, his hand moving in slow circles on her back. "I'm not trying to contain you, Hunter. Just give you a bit of comfort."

"I don't need comfort," she uttered, her tone strangled.

"I think you do."

She cursed through her uneven breathing. "You are so…human."

"Damn right I am." He made a low sound in his throat, and the rumble went from his chest into hers. It was… Goddess, it was—

No! No, this was wrong. Why wasn't she pulling away? Biting his shoulder? Taking off his ear? Desperate for blood? Why were her nostrils flaring? And why were her lungs pulling in his scent as though they couldn't bear to have anything else inside them?

The human was the first to pull back, release her. But he didn't look happy about it. In fact, he looked confused and troubled. *Join the club.*

His expression tight, he stared down at her. "Is the cat okay?"

Okay? Goddess, nothing was okay. About this. About him. About her. And where was her cat? Her protection? The one thing that was always there to stomp out feelings and emotions and…attraction?

Rosalie gazed up into those deep blue eyes. Okay? The cat was more than okay. It was…quiet.

With a surge of deep fear and guilt, she pulled completely away from him and stalked over to the door. Held it open. "Time for bed, Human."

One dark brow lifted over those ever-changing eyes, but he didn't say anything. Instead, after a few seconds, he went and gathered up all the food, then walked past her into the house.

"'Night, Hunter," he said in a pensive tone that mirrored the feelings running through her.

After the door closed, she pressed back against it and tried to breathe normally again. But it was no use. Her throat felt tight now, scratchy. Her lungs didn't seem to be making enough air. What was wrong with her? Why had she allowed herself to be touched…hugged? And why did she want to call that human back again right this very minute and tell him to call her…Rosalie?

Chapter Four

"Stay away!" Tim Donohue shouted, barely visible in the rubble. "Fuck, O'Roarke!"

Exhausted, eyes burning, Killian dragged an unconscious Mac Fields another three feet out of the wrecked building, then left him with the others. One more. Just one more.

"Stop!" Tim screamed at him. "Another one's coming, man!"

Killian didn't listen. You don't leave a comrade. Never leave a comrade. Not even with the threat of an IED.

Something nicked his arm. Fuck! The sting. He'd been hit. Suddenly, rounds of gunfire broke out less than forty meters away. No cover. Shit!

His men. He had to get to his men.

He had to hunt. Hunt the enemy!

But Tim...

An incoming round zoomed past his head. Eyes right and left. Nowhere to take cover. No-fucking-where!

"You gotta do this for me, man," Tim yelled. "Tell my wife I love—"

The blast of the IED sent Killian flying back. He hit the ground hard, air stolen from his lungs, blood leaking from his arm. When he looked up, Tim's head was down.

And he was silent.

A gasp woke Killian. Not his own. Or was it? Eyes open, he

realized where he was and who he was on top of. Shaking, sweat coating his skin, he rolled off her instantly. "Shit, I'm sorry."

He lay there on his back, breathing hard, staring at the ceiling, remembering where the fuck he was, totally exposed to whatever Rosalie wanted to do to punish him for assaulting—

He blinked, shook the sleep—the nightmares—from his mind for a second, then... He turned his head to look at her. "Why are you in my room?"

He'd taken the smallest one, stripped down to his underwear and fallen asleep around midnight. Alone.

She was sitting up. Wearing sweats and a tight tank top, her blonde hair loose around her shoulders. If he wasn't kind of pissed off at her in that moment—and shit, coming down from another memory mind-fuck—he might consider running his fingers through that hair.

"You were yelling," she said. "In your sleep. You sounded like someone was ripping your heart out. I was trying to wake you up."

Oh, fuck. She'd heard him...

He scrubbed a hand over his face. "I'm surprised you came in." He sort of half laughed, though in that moment it didn't seem all that funny. "Isn't ripping out my heart the very thing you're trying to do?"

"No."

"Only because you made a promise to your senior officer."

"He's not my senior officer."

"Right. Your leader. *El Presidenté.*"

She didn't say anything to that. In fact, she was way quieter than normal. Maybe he'd done more than yell. Maybe he'd said something...about combat or a mission. Or shit, his time in the lab. Well, he wasn't getting into any of that. Not until he knew what Raphael was going to do, or offer him.

"Well, as you can see, I'm fine," he said. "All intact."

Her eyes ran over him. To check. Or maybe for another reason. Whatever it was, it made his gut clench, and shit below his waist fill with enough blood to be obvious.

"You can go," he continued, not liking the idea of pitching a tent in front of her. "Back to your guard station."

But she didn't move. She sat there on the bed, looking all hot and sexy with her tight tank top, no bra, hair all wild and eyes that kept darting his way.

Yep, full hard-on now.

"Rosalie," he began. "Sorry, Hunter—"

"I have nightmares, too."

Killian stilled, not sure he'd heard her correctly. "What's that?"

"Or I did have them..." she continued. She sighed. "They were a lot like that. Like yours. No words, just..." Her eyes lifted to meet his. "Pain."

He stared at her, couldn't believe she was sharing anything with him. Much less something so personal.

"I don't know what you're doing here, Human—" she started.

"Killian."

"Human," she returned. "But I know real pain when I hear it."

Shit. What was this? He really wanted to know. Wanted to ask. But he didn't. He was pretty sure she wouldn't tell him anyway. "So they're gone?" he asked. "The nightmares?"

She nodded. "When I let my cat form take over. Sleep in it twenty-four/seven."

But Raphael hadn't wanted her in the cat form. Said she would kill him if she was. So... Killian sat up on one elbow. "But you can't be in your cat form when you're around me."

Her eyes met his. "Really?"

"Why don't you stop this, Hunter? Let someone else guard me. Go back to what you were doing. Go back to your puma and...sleep." His eyes roamed over her beautiful but very guarded face. "That really made the dreams stop?"

She nodded.

With a sniff of derision, Killian mumbled under his breath, "Maybe I should give it a try."

But she heard him. "Humans can only be human, Human."

"Yeah, you'd think, wouldn't you?" he ground out.

Her eyes narrowed. "Tell me why you're here."

"Help," he said.

"What kind? Immunity? Did you do something on the outside? Are you trying not to go back into combat? Do you know something about the military's plans for the Pantera and our very unique and highly sought-after DNA?"

He remained silent.

Which pissed her off. Not like that was a hard thing. "You're a soldier," she snarled. "But you don't know who Locke is. You're a human, but you're not a criminal or Raphael wouldn't have let you—" She stopped, blinked at him. Killian could see her mind working, and it was fast and sharp. "When I came up on you and the rat in the bayou...I didn't scent human right away. Only Pantera."

"Is that right?" he said softly.

Her lips parted then, and she leaned in. All the way until the tip of her nose brushed his throat. Killian inhaled sharply. He didn't know what she was pulling off him, but her scent was intoxicating. Like a rare flower, whose fragrance existed only for him. He growled at the ridiculous, romanticized, almost insane thought. But when her nose moved up to his jaw and her breath caressed his neck, he lost all brain function whatsoever. His hunger, his desire were on a level he'd never experienced before. An almost animalistic...

Fuck. No.

Slowly, she started to sniff him. His jaw, his ear, the corner of his mouth.

"What do you scent, Hunter?" he uttered in a voice he didn't recognize.

She drew back a few inches, her eyes finding his. They were confused and anxious, and...hot. She bit her lower lip, giving his already hard cock another surge of blood, and whispered, "Pantera."

Before he knew what he was doing, Killian's hand stole around her head, fisting into her hair as he pulled her in for a kiss. The instant their mouths connected, he groaned. It was like having every fucking fantasy he'd ever had since puberty come to life. She was so warm, hungry, and proved the latter with her tongue when he turned his head and deepened their kiss. Christ, he'd never experienced anything so stunning. Like fireworks going off inside him. Constantly. Each one more perfect than the last.

Each one driving him insane with lust.

He fell back onto the pillow, taking her with him. And she responded instantly. Getting on top of him, straddling him, growling at him as he worked her mouth. He left her hair and plunged both hands underneath her tank top. Hot, smooth skin assaulted his unworthy hands. She groaned into his mouth and arched into his touch. The need to flip her onto her back, strip her naked, and drive his cock deep inside her was so intense, he had to fight with himself about it.

And shit, if he was going to admit it, fight with something else too...

He raked his palms up both sides of her waist, up her ribcage, until he felt the soft curve of her breasts. His chest ached to feel her pressed against him. And his cock, fuck, his cock was already leaking at the tip. Anticipation. His own personal hell. He cursed his need into her mouth as she lifted her chest just enough for him to slip his hands underneath and capture her breasts.

Shit, he was going to lose it.

And why did that "thing" inside him keep snarling the word *mine* over and over again? Maybe because it wanted her. All of her. Every inch. First with his hands, then his tongue—then his cock.

He kneaded her breasts, played with them as he played with her tongue and sucked it into his mouth. Rosalie held back nothing, and he loved it. She had his thigh between her legs and was dry-fucking him. No. Not dry at all. Very, very wet, even with the cotton sweats between them.

As one hand teased her nipple, Killian slipped the other under the waistband of her sweats. It wasn't easy. She was grinding against him. So strong. Christ, he was into her strength. It was so goddamned hot.

She was so goddamned hot.

The second his hand met smooth, wet pussy, Killian was gone. On another planet. One he wanted to exist on for eternity. He slid his finger through her warm lips and found her clit swollen and ready. As he consumed her mouth, played her nipple and stroked her clit, he listened to the sounds she made against his lips. Moans of pleasure, snarls of animalistic hunger.

And he understood the language of both.

Leaving his thumb to work the needy bud, Killian slipped two fingers inside her pussy. Instantly her hot, tight walls clamped around him, suckling him. Jesus...he was going to fucking come without her having even touched him.

"I feel it," he uttered against her mouth as he started to thrust inside her. "Come for me, Rosalie."

She froze.

Utterly and completely.

From the top of her head to her feet.

And so did Killian.

"What..." he uttered. "What's wrong?"

She was scrambling off him before the last word was even out of his mouth.

"What the hell?" he said, sitting up. Shit, she was off the bed, her back to him. "Are you okay?"

She didn't have to say the word *no*. He could feel that word radiating off her shaking body. What had he done?

"Never. Never again." She glanced over her shoulder and gave him a look of such hate, he felt it in his marrow. "Human."

She slammed the door when she walked out.

Leaving Killian to stare after her.

His second nightmare of the night.

Chapter Five

As the sun awoke in the sky before her, guilt and self-hatred swam in Rosalie's blood. Not only had she let another male kiss and touch her, but he was a human. She refused to believe what she'd scented last night. He may have been infused with something to try and pass as a Pantera, but he was no true puma shifter. He was human. The very species that had taken her mate from her. Tears threatened, but she pushed them back. She didn't deserve the sweet relief they would bring. She deserved the cold morning air assaulting her still-heated skin. She deserved exhaustion. She deserved the hard wood surface of the porch steps against her ass.

She deserved pain.

"Have you been sitting out here all night?"

She glanced up. Backlit by the early morning's light, Raphael was coming up the walkway. He looked totally put-together in a dark-gray suit, crisp white shirt, and maroon tie. All business. As usual.

"Just doing my job, sir," she said with a mock salute.

"And yet you didn't scent me until I was almost on top of you," he said, stopping at the bottom step.

She laughed. Bitterly. "You and Ashe have a nice romantic morning?" When his eyes widened slightly, she nodded. "Oh, I scented you, sir. From the second you walked out your front door."

His gaze moved over her, assessing as he always did. "Are you all right, Rosalie?"

"Never better," she answered with a false smile. "So, are you here for the prisoner? Am I taking him to the border and kicking his ass out of the Wildlands?"

"No."

"Didn't think so." She shook her head, slowly. "Am I taking him to his lovely new cabin near the bayou, serving him breakfast, and welcoming him to the Wildlands as an honored guest?"

The male pushed out a breath. "What you're going to do is go home."

She grunted.

"Get some sleep," he continued. "Take a shower and report to Parish at midday."

"Fuck that," she tossed out.

"Rosalie," he said, his nostrils flaring as his chin lifted, "you're pushing me. Forcing me into disciplining you."

She snorted. "Boy, the daddy thing is really going to your head. How is little Soyala, by the way?" One brow lifted sardonically. "I imagine an excellent sleeper, by the way you smell."

"Your anger is growing out of control."

"You have no idea." The words rushed from her mouth without thought. Instantly, she wished she could bite them back because Raphael's expression changed from aggravated to worried in an instant.

"You need to see one of the Healers," he said,

Yep. Biting them back would've been awesome. "I'm curious, Raphael," she said calmly. "Would you say that to me if I was a male?" She stood up. "Or would you pat me on the back, invite me out for a drink at The Cougar's Den, then halfway through a game of pool tell me I should get laid?"

Most males would've gotten immediately defensive, but Raphael was totally unaffected by her candor—or her baiting, depending on how one looked at it. "I treat grief as it should be treated, Hunter. With compassion, care, understanding, *and* a kick in the ass if needed. Male or female. Now." He gave her a pointed look. "Go home."

"The human is mine to guard," she fought. "Until he no longer needs it."

"Why?"

"What do you mean *why*? It's my job. I'm doing my job." She sounded as though she barely believed it herself.

"And I'm doing mine," Raphael said softly. "Go home. Lian will take over."

"No," came a male voice behind them. "Rosalie stays with me."

Both Rosalie and Raphael turned to find Killian standing at the doorway. Shit, she hadn't scented him, but she sure *saw* him. Hungrily, her gaze ran over his six-foot-something frame. Jeans, black tank, hard muscle, bare feet, wet hair. A rush of lust shot through her body as her mind conjured images of herself on her knees, pulling down that zipper with her teeth.

Sudden, unwanted tears pricked at her eyes with the thought, and she quickly swiped at them with her hand. She was in trouble. And the kind she'd never had to deal with before. She needed to stop fighting. Follow Raphael's orders and go home. Shower. Sleep. Get her head on straight and never see this human again. He was screwing with her mind. Had since he'd crawled up onto the shore like a gorgeous laboratory-grown mistake.

Goddess, she needed her cat. Her heart jumped inside her chest. If she walked away from this, from him, she could walk away in her puma form. As long as she wasn't around the human—

"You seem to think you have a say in this, Mr. O'Roarke," Raphael returned, his tone cool.

"Maybe I do," he said casually, but Rosalie didn't miss the dogged set of his shoulders and jaw. "I'm about to let you dissect me, mentally and physically, and I only want two things out of it. The first you know. The second." His gaze flickered to Rosalie. "Unless she wants out, of course."

Rosalie felt the weight of both their stares and wanted to disappear. Behind Raphael's intense gaze was a need to understand, and concern. Lots of concern. And behind the human's... Attraction, challenge, curiosity.

What would she do? After last night's idiocy, what *should* she do? And Goddess, what had the human asked Raphael for?

So many questions. Ones she'd have to wait to have answered.

Well, she had time.

"Where do you want him?" she asked the leader of the Pantera in that all-business tone he appreciated. "And when?"

As the seconds ticked by, it seemed as though the Head Suit might continue to argue the point with her. But, for whatever reason, he held off. "Have him at the clinic in thirty minutes. Jean-Baptiste and I will meet you there."

"Yes, sir."

She watched him go, stride across the lawn in his oh-so-fine suit, then she headed back into the house. Killian's scent was everywhere. In the air, the furniture…maybe even her lungs. She growled with irritation at the fact, yet followed it like a hungry cub into the kitchen. The man was seated at the table, tucked into a bowl of cereal. She went and stood over him, fuming.

"Problem, Hunter?" he asked, pouring milk onto his Lucky Charms. *Typical Lian, bringing that over here.* The Hunter was obsessed with that shit.

"I don't need you coming to my rescue," she ground out. "Human."

He glanced up. His jaw was brushed with dark morning beard. "Is that what you thought I was doing?"

Rosalie wondered what the stubble would feel like against her tongue. Around his mouth. Biting his bottom lip. He liked that…responded to—

Fuck. Me. "Just hurry up and finish," she growled.

He shook his head and went back to his cereal. "So I'm gathering we're not going to talk about last night."

She leaned against the wall and crossed her arms over her chest. "You mean the nightmare?"

"Honey, I'd never call you, your kisses, or what you did to me a nightmare." His eyes flashed with humor, and something else…

That something else made her nipples tighten.

"Eat," she hissed.

He took an enormous bite, crunching away, then asked, "Are you starving yourself again?"

"No. I already had breakfast."

"When?"

"Before the sun came up."

"Couldn't sleep, huh?" He nodded. "Yeah. I had a real *hard* time of it myself." He grinned before scooping up another spoonful of cereal.

She wanted to slap that grin right off his face!

No…wait. That's not what she wanted to do at all.

She wanted *to kiss* that grin right off his face. Then make him groan. Then let him make her groan…

Panic spread through her blood and she uttered a terse, "Be outside in five minutes."

She stormed from the room and out the front door, stopping only when she hit the top of the steps. She gripped the railing. Her heart was slamming against her ribs, her mouth was dry, and she wanted to cry. Again. Fucking pussy.

Mercier… She glanced up into the powder blue sky. *I'm sorry. I've betrayed you.*

Chapter Six

"You're going to leave me with a few pints, right?" Killian asked the technician who'd just taken his tenth blood sample of the day.

Ford—the male with black eyes and a scar down the right side of his face—replied dryly, "Try and think of it like we're already removing our DNA from you."

Killian sniffed. "Just feels like you're bleeding me dry. Not exactly what I thought was going to happen."

Jean-Baptiste, who left the three other techs on the opposite side of the room to their computer screens and DNA processing and analysis equipment, walked over to him. "What were you thinking?"

"Well, I was hoping you'd have...an antidote. Something that could go right into my bloodstream and kill whatever they injected me with."

The massive, tatted-up doctor laughed. "Oh, if only it was that simple. We've got urine, saliva tests, MRI...but we're going to need more blood. Blood tells us everything. A basic metabolic panel to reveal any diseases you might have, how the organs are functioning. And then an analysis of proteins, DNA and RNA—see what's happening from those all-powerful injections."

"Sounds like you have some experience with this already," Killian said. "A protocol in place." Back in the lab, toward the latter part of his "stay," he'd heard talk of Pantera prisoners who had been experimented on. It was those days especially when he couldn't help despising his own species. Nothing was sacred. Not even life.

Raphael walked in then, took a quick look around, and headed straight for Killian.

"Do what you gotta do, Doc," Killian told Jean-Baptiste, dropping back against the pillow. "I think I'm going to be hanging out here a while."

"Five hours and counting." Raphael handed him a donut wrapped in a napkin. Chocolate glazed. Then pulled up a chair. "Eat it. It'll help."

"I'm fine, man."

"That's right. I forgot. Super solider." His brows lifted. "But loss of blood is loss of blood. No matter who or what we are."

True that. And his stomach was making all kinds of noise, so...he took a bite. Then another. "Thanks."

Raphael nodded. "Now, Benson Enterprises. What do you know about them?"

The male wasted no time. Not that Killian blamed him. They both wanted answers. "Benson was the name of the clinic. Given to me by my commanding officer when I requested an eval, or something to help with my PTSD."

The leader's pupils dilated. "Commanding officer's name?"

Killian stalled out for a second. The guy had a family, wife, and kids. He didn't want to—

"Just need all the information, Mr. O'Roarke," Raphael said as if reading his mind. "I've got to connect the dots."

Killian eyed the male. "I've known the guy for years, served under him. I'm sure he knew nothing about what was going to happen to me. He'd never send a man under his command into danger unprotected like that. I don't want him or his family hurt."

Raphael nodded.

Killian wasn't at all sure that the Pantera followed the same honor code he did, but they were trusting him, letting him inside their world. Helping him. Maybe he needed to do the same.

Killian released a breath, along with the name of his commander. "Brad Vanco."

The name didn't seem to register with the male, but he typed it into his phone anyway. "Had you heard of Benson Enterprises before Mr. Vanco mentioned it?"

"No."

"And when you went there, initially, who did you speak with?"

"The main doc was a woman. Marcia Copper. A head-shrinker. She was the one who insisted I stay at the facility. I just wanted to talk to someone. Therapy, maybe some meds to keep the nightmares at bay. But she insisted that this was the best way of doing things. Inpatient treatment." Killian's desire for the donut faded and he set it on the side table. "Then there was no choice on my part. It was like being a goddamned prisoner of war."

Raphael glanced up. "The coordinates you gave us for the lab—"

"Did you burn that piece of shit to the ground?" Killian interrupted with undisguised menace.

Raphael shook his head. "It was only an abandoned building."

Shock rolled through Killian and he sat up. "That's impossible. I was just there. Broke out two days ago."

"So you said. Are you sure that's where you were being held?"

"That's where I went when I came in for treatment."

Raphael paused for a second, his brow furrowed. "Was it possible you were moved? Without knowing it?"

His chest tightened as his mind was inundated with questions. "I would've known," he said to himself as well as to the leader of the Pantera. "I would've had to have known. Despite the labs and the room where I was held, The Christopher had this smell—"

"The Christopher," Raphael interrupted sharply. "What's that?"

"Sounds like a swank hotel, right? Like in Vegas or something. Shit, it was anything but." He shook his head. "Wasn't my thing. The guards, the techs, the docs, everybody called it that. Named after the guy who funded the place."

A cold, hard look stole over Raphael's face. "Did you ever meet this man?"

"I saw him around the lab. Granted, he was always with a military escort, so I never got close to him. I noticed him checking in with the doctors though, pushing the technicians for more data—"

"We've got to get that motherfucker," Raphael said on a snarl.

"That's who you're..." Killian trailed off.

A scent he recognized was drifting into his nostrils, and for a moment he was completely captivated by it. His eyes closed and his mouth opened, and inside his chest that...*thing*...rumbled to life. In the back of his mind, he heard Raphael speaking, but it was too far away. He wanted more of that scent. What was it? He grinned. Whatever it was, it belonged to him.

Suddenly, a hand clamped around his arm, causing his eyes to burst open. But instead of looking for the one who'd touched him, his gaze was completely pinned to the open doorway.

Puma.

My puma.

"Shit! Baptiste, what the hell did you do?"

"Nothing."

"He's shifting! How the...fuck!"

The voices were there. In the background. They didn't matter to him. Nothing mattered but the golden female, her green eyes calling to him. A growl escaped his throat.

"It's her," Jean-Baptiste exclaimed. "Rosalie. She's in the hall. In her puma state."

The last thing Killian remembered before his mind dissolved was the deep hunger of the animal inside him.

Wanting out.

Wanting her.

Chapter Seven

Fur as black as the night.

Eyes so pale blue they reminded her of ice.

Rosalie watched as Killian's puma paced inside the cage.

Puma.

How was this possible? He was human. So human. And yet, she'd scented him last night, and at the bayou. Goddess, maybe she'd believed he'd been *played* with, like the rats. But she hadn't believed him capable of this. Shifting into a full-blooded puma. It wasn't possible. Except maybe it was. Raphael would tell her what he knew, explain things to her.

Right before he grounded her ass, or kicked it out of the Wildlands, that is.

She curled her hands around the bars of the large cage and stared at the gorgeous puma, who she was pretty sure didn't understand what was happening. Poor guy. Learning to separate the puma from the Pantera mind took practice. From the time you were a cub, you tried to break that code. And right now, Killian was pushed to the back, and all that occupied the cage was animal.

Her shoulders fell as she scented Raphael. *Shit hitting fan, here we come.* Goddess, she was such a moron.

He came to stand beside her. Didn't look at her. Instead, he stared at the pacing cat. "What were you thinking?" he asked in a dangerously quiet voice.

That I'm a moron? "That I could have a little time in my cat," she said aloud. "The human was with you and Baptiste and the other Healers. Surrounded. And for hours." She broke off, shaking her head—confident in what was coming next.

"Fine. Understandable and acceptable." He turned to face her. "*Outside* the clinic."

Moron!

"Why did you come back here, Rosalie?" he pressed. "To him, in your puma state?"

She looked over at the leader of the Suits, knowing her eyes were a perfect mirror into her confused soul. "I don't know." She shook her head. "I wanted to check on him?"

"Is that a question?"

"No," she said on a sigh.

"You care about him."

She shook her head. "No."

"You're attracted to him."

"Please stop." Her cheeks were burning. Thankfully, Killian couldn't hear this. Or could he? She didn't want to look too closely at him to find out.

"Your job was to keep him safe, Rosalie."

Her heart squeezed painfully, but she nodded. She'd screwed up big time. Granted, Killian wasn't dead, but this was huge nonetheless. She prayed Raphael would only suspend her from hunting duties or shit, toss her in one of the secure units. Because leaving the Wildlands… Goddess, her home—that would be unbelievably painful. And yet, she'd set herself up for punishment. What was wrong with her? Making foolish mistakes. Living inside her puma. Scared, angry—filled with grief and guilt all the time. It was no damn life that she was living. But she'd made her bed, so to speak. If Raphael went hardcore on her, well, she wouldn't walk out of the Wildlands crying for herself or begging for a second chance. She was a proud Pantera, after all.

She turned to go. "I'll prepare to leave."

Raphael grabbed her arm and cursed to himself. "No."

Her heart stuttered as she turned back to face him.

He shook his head. "For now, you're on probation. Until I decide what I'm going to do." He glanced back at the cat that was Killian and released a weighty breath. "You may hate humans for all the right reasons, Rosalie, but this one wasn't a part of what happened to Mercier."

She felt the tears again. Behind her eyes. In her throat. But she refused them. "How can you be sure of that?"

"I had him checked out. Had his story checked out. He's a good man. Fought for his country, saved many of his fellow soldiers, and went into a program he believed would help him deal with his grief over losing a close friend."

She remembered the dream—the nightmare he'd had. He couldn't get back to his...friend. "But the program didn't help him, did it?"

Raphael shook his head. "Was a false front. A way to experiment on soldiers without their knowledge or consent."

A lump formed in her throat, and for the first time in a long time, she didn't wish for her cat. They'd used him. Just like they'd used her and Mercier, and so many others. It was time to face and accept the truth... Humans weren't the enemy. It was Christopher and Benson Enterprises, and all those who turned a blind eye to the lives they were destroying.

She lifted her gaze to meet Raphael's. "I think I need some help. To deal with my grief. While I await my fate." Tears broke and swam in her eyes. But this time she didn't try to hide them or wipe them away.

A soft smile touched the Pantera leader's mouth and he covered her hand with his own. "You deserve to be happy, Rosalie. Mercier would've wanted nothing less."

Just hearing his name...she was about to break. "I'm going to go. Check in with Parish. All the Hunters. I have some...apologies to make."

He nodded. "I'll let you know when I've come to a decision."

She turned around to leave, but before she even got halfway to the door, the snarl of Killian's puma stopped her in her tracks. She didn't have to turn around to know what was happening, what he was feeling. What he wanted.

Her.

In the room.

Close by.

And when he started to rage, go insane inside his cage, she could do nothing but oblige him.

Chapter Eight

When Killian came to, or awoke, or whatever it was that was happening to him, he felt like he'd been hit by a truck. His eyes were heavy and his mouth felt dry. He glanced around. He was in the same room, lying on the same gurney-style bed. Same…people. But there were no IV's or needles or tubes in his arms, and it felt…late. Felt like…night, if you could actually feel that without having visual access to the outside world.

He spotted the technician with the scar, reading a chart and typing something into a computer.

"You took too damn much," Killian said, though his voice was pretty much a whisper. And his throat hurt. What the hell?

"What's that?" Ford asked, glancing up.

"Blood," Killian ground out. "You took too much. Passed out."

The guy's brows lifted, but his eyes descended—back to the file and the computer.

"And with all the donuts I gave you." It was Raphael's voice. He was walking over to Killian's bedside, his mouth curved up in a sardonic smile. "Pussy."

That elicited a soft yet painful chuckle from Killian. "There was one donut. And, if I remember correctly, I only ate half of it." He gave the leader of the Pantera a strange, I'm-fucking-confused look. "My throat's killing me, man. In fact," he winced, "my whole body feels like it's been run over by a Humvee. Did I fall off the bed or get into a fight or something?"

"No." The male's expression tightened.

Okay, something was going on here. Something was wrong. Maybe it had to do with the tests on his blood. Maybe they'd found a way to take the DNA from him. Shit, maybe that's what the pain was from...they'd already done it. But then why—

His mind came to an abrupt halt. Not only was the most delectable scent in the world wafting into his nostrils, but every cell in his body was screaming that it belonged to him. Fucking strange. Then Rosalie walked into the room and strange upgraded to downright bizarre.

He let his gaze move over her. She was wearing jeans and a tight black tank top. Her hair was piled on top of her head, and her eyes—those sexy, green daggers—met his right away. His gut clenched. The same expression he'd seen in Raphael's gaze a second ago was shimmering in the Hunter's. Something like "*Shit's gone down and we're not sure how to tell you.*"

"Okay," he started, sitting up in the bed, shaking off the lightheaded thing that was making him feel like a weak-ass recruit on the first day of boot camp. "What the hell is going on here? Am I cured? Am I dying? Did the gallons of blood you took from me give you any clue—"

"Killian."

He shivered and groaned. It was Rosalie saying his name. *Rosalie.*

And her face was all...what was that? Sympathy?

Shit. Maybe he really was dying.

He glanced over at Raphael, who was stone-faced and silent, then his eyes came back to Rosalie. "Why are you calling me that?" he demanded on a low growl.

She bit her lip. The lower one. Something he'd love to do. But not now. Not here. Maybe when the pain in his body eased up a bit he'd see if she was agreeable. *Screw that. She's worth the pain.*

"It's your name," she said.

"Not to you," he countered. "I'm Human, remember?"

Her gaze flickered to Raphael as she headed over to the chair beside Killian's bed and sat down. What the hell was going on? It was like a damn funeral in progress.

"Somebody better tell me something," he began with a slight snarl. "Or shit's going to get—"

Rosalie jumped in. "When you were...out—"

"Passed out?" he corrected.

"Yes."

"What? I snored? You watched? Or, maybe you took advantage of me?" he said with a dark edge.

"No." Her cheeks flushed as her eyes dipped to take in his naked chest and low-hanging gray sweatpants.

Damn. Those sweatpants were about to get tight if she kept that up. He cocked his head to the side and whispered, "You *wanted* to take advantage of me?"

"No."

"Your mouth says no, Hunter, but your eyes say—"

"You shifted into a puma!" she blurted out.

The room went still and Killian's heart ceased beating. Or it sure as shit felt that way. As he tried to remember how lungs worked, how breathing worked, he replayed the words she'd just tossed at him. Then again. There were only five of them, but that packed a significant punch. He felt strangely empty inside. Hollow. His mind too. Except for the five words. He started to shake his head. This could not be true. She was lying to him. Or he was still knocked out and this was a nightmare.

Another fucking nightmare.

His eyes captured hers and compelled her to speak or explain or... But—nothing. She wouldn't give him a damn thing. Raphael either. The room just remained silent.

For another five seconds, anyway. Then—

"What the fuck did you guys do to me?" Killian exploded, leaping off the bed. "You were supposed to take it out! Not turn it on! Fuck!" Thank Christ he wasn't wearing one of those hospital gowns. He would've ripped the shit off and been standing there buck naked.

Raphael and Ford looked appropriately sympathetic but crouched slightly—ready for whatever was coming their way. And that thing inside Killian? That hybrid monster that Rosalie had talked about? Yeah, that thing in his gut or chest? It moved, woke.

The puma.

A sneer touched his upper lip. Was that really his truth now? His state of being? How could he accept that?

"It wasn't them," Rosalie said, her voice even and strong.

Eyes pinned to the two males, Killian shook his head. "Bullshit."

"It wasn't, Killian," she continued. "It was…me."

Killian's head came around fast. She was standing up now, across the bed from him. Breathing hard, his heart slamming against his ribs, he glared at her.

"I came by your room, in my puma form," she explained. "It…triggered something in you." She shook her head. "I don't understand why it would. I mean, there are plenty of puma females—"

"You don't understand?" Killian exclaimed. "Why you would trigger something in me?" He shook his head, snarled at her. "After last fucking night?"

She immediately blanched. "Don't—"

"I'm attracted to you, Hunter!" he continued. "Goddammit! You walked out on me last night, and today you come back in your puma form? You really do want to kill me, don't you?"

"This is inside you, Mr. O'Roarke," Raphael said before Rosalie could answer, his tone calm, sensible, though his body language warned there'd be a battle if Killian got any more out of control than he already was. "Benson Enterprises put it there, and I'm afraid we can't remove it."

"Now," Killian ground out, feeling out of his mind, out of control. "Right? You can't remove it now that I've shifted into one of you. There's no way to reverse course."

"The shift isn't the reason for the permanent state," Ford put in. "I believe, as does Jean-Baptiste, that this started to take form with the first injection." His eyes were firm, but kind. "I'm sorry, Mr. O'Roarke."

The dark, desperate emotions inside Killian rolled and pitched like a boat on an angry sea. He wanted to attack the technician, even Raphael. He wanted to spill blood and tear apart the room. And then he wanted to turn on the Hunter.

His eyes caught and held hers. Whatever she saw in his blue orbs made her cheeks flame and her nostrils flare. Not fear, not desire—but something definitely and ferociously in between.

He took a step toward her...

"It's late," Raphael intervened quickly. "You should have something to eat, Killian. Get some sleep. We'll talk more in the morning. Discuss your options."

"My options," Killian uttered blackly, his eyes still pinned to the Hunter.

"There are some, I assure you. Come on, Rosalie. Let's leave the male to process."

She swallowed thickly but did as her leader instructed, yanking her gaze from Killian's and walking past him and out the door.

He called me *the male*, Killian thought blackly, as he stared after her. *Like I'm one of them*. No longer a man. No longer a human. No longer recognizable.

His gaze found Ford's and he growled at him. Like the *male* he was. Like the animal he was. What this really happening? What this truly his fate? He'd come to the Wildlands for salvation, only to discover what he should've known all along.

He was doomed.

Chapter Nine

It was close to midnight when Rosalie was finally able to slip into the clinic unseen and catch Killian's guard on a quick trip to the bathroom. No doubt Raphael would kick her ass out of the Wildlands without a second thought if she got caught. But she didn't plan on getting caught. Breaking, entering, retrieving...it was what she lived for.

Inside his large room, the lights were dimmed enough that Rosalie could only make out shapes. The computer tables, covered lab equipment, monitors...bed. Her breathing surprisingly even, she moved swiftly and quietly toward it. No doubt he was fast asleep. Dreaming. Hopefully not the same nightmare she'd caught him in last night. She really didn't want to scare the shit out of him, but they didn't have much time. Her gut clenched momentarily as she wondered what kind of reception the human—no, *the male*—was going to give her after today's news regarding his permanent state of being. And what he believed to be her part in it. But she had to try. She owed him that much—

A sudden gasp ripped from her throat, but she stifled it by clamping a hand over her mouth. What the hell? Where...

She swallowed hard. The bed was empty.

In fact, it didn't looked slept in at all.

Her heart plummeted into her stomach. This was bad. Really bad. He'd escaped? How was that possible? Well, he was military...But where could he have gone? Wherever it was, she had to find him before Parish or one of the Hunters did. They didn't know what was going on. What he was. They'd just assume he was either an out of control human, or an out of control puma.

She turned and headed for the door only to be stopped in her tracks by six-plus feet of hard muscle, sinister expression, and shimmering blue shark eyes.

Her heart stuttered inside her chest. Was it possible that he had become a *male* in one day? Her gaze ran the length of him. He sure looked like one of them.

"K-killian...what are you...where were you..." she uttered like a scared fool. Which she was not. Refused to be. *Hunter, female. You're a fucking hardass Hunter. Act like it!*

"Couldn't sleep," he said. .

His voice was husky, like his cat's growl, and it made her entire body tense. Flare with a heat she refused to acknowledge. It sounded hungry, demanding. Goddess, she remembered that sound. When Raphael had called her back to the cage, to a crazed puma who had instantly calmed and softened the moment she'd wrapped her hands around the bars and given him her attention.

"I'm not surprised," she said. "Sleeping in here can't be easy."

His eyes dropped to her mouth, making everything south of her navel stir. "Not in the mood for any new nightmares."

"Sure. Of course." Why did she sound so breathless?

Those eyes lifted to connect with hers. "Unless I do what you do to block them out."

She licked her dry lips. What the hell was happening to her? Every inch of her skin was tight. Hot. Ready to be touched. "I think you should wait on that. Shifting is an art. Takes practice to master."

"Is that why you're here, Hunter?" he asked with just a touch of sarcasm. One dark brow lifted. "To teach me?"

Her sex actually clenched at his words. Dammit! She shook her head. Not here to teach him, anything. Right? Right? "I want to take you somewhere," she managed to push out.

Those brows drew together. "Why?" A growl rumbled in his

chest. His very broad chest. "To finish the job you started on the bank?" Even in the dim light, she saw his eyes suddenly cloud over. "I just might let you."

Her heart clenched at his words this time. As she'd said to him once, she knew pain when she heard it. And fuck her, she heard it now. "Don't say shit like that."

He sniffed. "It's true."

"I don't care."

"I feel..."

"I know," she said, then added, "It's overwhelming and shocking and scary and you have no clue what you want or what this means."

His eyes were tightly fitted to hers. "Yeah. Something like that."

"I'm sorry, Killian." His nostrils flared at her use of his name. "For everything. How I attacked you on the bank. Treated you last night. Then, coming around in my puma..."

He shook his head. "You heard the tech and Raphael. It was already done. Sealed-fate kind of thing."

"Killian?"

His nostrils flared and a soft groan rumbled in his throat. "It's so weird having you call me that."

"You don't like it?"

"Shit, Hunter, of course I like it."

Her insides melted, both at his words and the soft lust reflected in his eyes. She reached for his hand. "Come with me? I want to show you something."

He nodded, even threaded his fingers with hers. "But how, Kitten? The guard's back."

Rosalie froze, inhaled. Yes, of course. How hadn't she caught that? *Maybe because you're so wrapped up in this male's scent, and his mouth, and his eyes...* "How did *you* know that?" she asked him.

"Clearly I have the scent thing now too." He smiled wickedly, his voice low. "By the way, I smelled you coming. Shit, I smelled you an hour ago when you started watching the guard."

Flames erupted inside her, and she wanted nothing more than to pull up on her toes and attack his mouth. That full, heavy bottom lip that would feel delicious between her teeth. But she forced herself to stay cool. "So, you're a real Pantera now, are you?"

He shrugged. "Not sure what I am," he said, leaning in. "I'm curious. What do you want to show me, Kitten?"

Oh, the things that instantly came to her mind. She nearly started purring. "Might have to wait. At least until the guard needs to go to the bathroom again. Or when they have a shift change."

He gave her an almost arrogant look, then pulled on her hand. "Come on, Hunter."

"You know you can call me Rosalie now," she said, going with him. *I want you to. Want to hear my name on your lips. Maybe when you kiss me...*

"I think I'm used to Hunter now," he said. "Or Kitten. We'll see." He led her past the bank of lab equipment and computers, into the darkness, to a concealed door she'd never seen before.

"What is this?" she asked, suddenly yanked from her sexual haze into all business. Hunter business.

"A small office attached to the room." He opened the door. "Hidden."

She moved inside quickly, stealthily, and started checking out the space. Plain walls, office furniture, computers, bank of windows. Heavy moonlight. "How did you find it?"

He laughed softly, and said, "Combat Search and Rescue, Kitten," like that explained everything. And maybe to a human it would. Or a military-type human.

To Rosalie, it just sounded unbearably sexy.

"Ready?"

Her gaze flew to the window. He was already there; had the thing unlocked and open.

Yes. Very sexy.

"You'd make a damn fine Hunter," she said with a bit of a growl, slipping past him.

"Come on."

"Just sayin'."

They dropped down onto the damp earth, and before Killian could even question her about where they were going, Rosalie took off into the night, motioning for him to follow.

* * * *

"What is this?" Killian asked, his confused gaze trained on the moonlit cottage surrounded by cypress.

Rosalie came to stand beside him. She couldn't believe she'd actually come here, brought someone here. Especially a man. *A male.* She couldn't believe her cat had allowed it. That it hadn't fought her on it. In fact, the puma was so quiet, Rosalie almost didn't feel it breathing inside her. It was incredibly strange.

And yet, she was grateful.

"This is the house of a friend of mine," she said, her eyes running over the dark green paint and white trim.

There was a moment of silence. Just the wind blowing in the trees and night sounds of the animals. Then Killian asked, "A good friend?"

"Yeah."

Another pause. "More than a friend?"

She turned to look at him then. This male standing beside her as she paid her respects and said her good-byes. Killian was tall, strong, handsome, brave. A good male. A Pantera, for all intents and purposes. And she wanted him to know her—as more than just the angry puma chick who was out for human blood. She wanted him to know her as a female. "His name was Mercier," she said as he turned to look at her, too. "He was my mate."

Killian's nostrils flared instantly, and his eyes darkened. "Was?"

Rosalie nodded, tears in her throat. She wasn't a crier. Especially lately. She hadn't allowed herself that pleasure since she'd returned from the lab. Didn't feel like she was worthy. But they were coming now. Whether she'd welcomed them or not. "He and I were taken to one of the labs by some piece-of-shit humans," she explained. "We managed to escape, but..." Her voice broke. "Mercier was killed. Trying to protect me."

"Fuck..." Killian uttered on a breath. "No wonder..."

"I was blaming you because you were human. I was blaming you because I couldn't contain all the anger I felt. I was blaming you because..." Her voice broke. Again. And tears filled her eyes. "I was attracted to you."

His eyes filled with sadness and warmth. And understanding. "I'm sorry, Hunter."

"Please," she begged, her eyes pleading with him. "It's Rosalie. I don't want to be a Hunter to you."

A soft smile touched his mouth. "What do you want to be to me?"

The Wildlands seemed to grow quiet in that moment, as he stared at her, wondering, waiting. And she tried to gather her courage—the kind that came not from physical strength and power, but from being vulnerable.

She bit her lip. "A friend?" she whispered, though it sounded more like a question for him to answer. *Don't do this, Rosalie. Don't be a liar. His friendship is the last thing you want.*

"Walk with me?" She didn't wait for his answer. Just reached for his hand and started walking out of the trees and down to the bank—away from the house. It was time. To be thankful for the past, but to put it behind her too. "I can help you," she said to him as she headed for the bank of the bayou. "I can help you figure out how to shift, how to control your cat."

She scented his reticence before he even uttered the words, "I don't know."

She looked up at him as they walked. "What does that mean?"

His jaw was tight, his gaze predatory. He was looking more like a Pantera male with every second that passed.

Or maybe it was her. How she was seeing him. How her heart was seeing him...in a new light.

"I don't know if I want that," he said. "I don't know what I want. Where I belong. Is it true you can't shift outside the Wildlands?"

A hum started inside her. Loud and painful. *Outside.* Was that what he was thinking of doing? Leaving? Even after knowing what he was? What he'd become? "It's true," she said. "But I don't know about your...situation. You could be different."

He sniffed. "I'm most definitely different. I have to figure out where I belong now. *If* I belong anywhere."

"Don't talk like that," she said passionately.

"After what's happened today, how can I not?"

She cut him off, stood in front of him. Moonlight washed over his handsome face. "If you wanted to stay here, you could. I know Raphael would allow it."

He cursed, looked anywhere but at her. When he spotted a massive cypress down near the bayou, he left her and headed straight for it. Rosalie watched as he went over and sat down, pressed his back to the thick trunk.

She didn't want him to leave. This male she'd tried to push away, hate, hurt... She wanted him to stay in the Wildlands. With her. See what happened. Maybe heal from their respective pasts together.

But she wasn't going to ask him or push him.

Rubbing the chill from her skin, she went over to the tree and sat down beside him. She was quiet. Watched the bayou dance against the bank in the moonlight as she breathed in his scent and felt the warmth of him against her side.

"I don't want to be somewhere because I'm allowed to be there," Killian said after a few minutes had passed.

"I know," Rosalie said.

"I want to feel wanted. I want a home. After losing my family, my military career, I just want a home."

Her heart squeezed painfully, because, Goddess, so did she. A home. And all that it meant. So much more than just four walls and a roof. She'd wanted it for so long, she'd refused to admit it—or even acknowledge its possibility. "I understand," she said softly.

"But it sounds pathetic, right? Weak?"

"No!" She turned to him, scrambling to her knees. "No way." She shook her head, eyes imploring him. "When I said I understood about wanting a home, I do." She closed her eyes for a second and sighed. "I'm really sorry, Killian. For the way I treated you. What you saw...how I acted...that's not who I am." *Or who I want to be.* "Except for maybe—" She cut herself off, bit her lip.

"Except for what?" he asked, his expression intent.

Last night.

Kissing you.

Feeling happy for the first time in a long time.

Not needing the puma to breathe.

His eyes were blazing down into hers, trying to read her mind, her heart, and her soul. She wanted him to see it—all of it. And she nearly did. But something happened...inside of her—and it wasn't the cat. A fear of rejection? Of losing someone she cared for—

again? Whatever it was crept in, took hold, and stole her vulnerability.

She turned away, back to the tree. "Look up, Killian," she said as her heart threatened to break out of her chest. "Look at those stars."

His eyes were on her for the longest time. Or it felt that way. The weight of those blue orbs... How long could she last before she gave in...and just—broke?

Then he turned.

Slipped his arm around her.

And as she exhaled weightily, he pulled her close and gave his attention to the sky.

Chapter Ten

The dreams that came at him now were nothing like they'd been. There was no death. No pain. No one to rescue. In fact, it was him who was being rescued. By green eyes and healing hands. Urgent whispers and a wild mouth.

The Hunter.

Kitten.

Rosalie.

Bright warmth soothed the backs of his eyelids and a breeze blew crisp over his skin. He groaned at the fucking wonder of it all.

And the wonder groaned back.

What the hell...? Eyes rocketing open, Killian looked around sharply. It was habit. Enemy could be anywhere. But there was no enemy here. Only grass and trees, wide bayou, and a very naked female kissing her way down his torso. Along with his cock, every inch of him hardened. It was the very female who'd ripped him from the water, then from his nightmares. The female who'd made him smile and hope, despair, then hope again. The female who made him want to...stay...

He groaned as she lapped at his navel with her tongue.

What was his name again?

"Morning," she whispered, her eyes flipping up to meet his as her fingers eased down his sweats.

Seriously? They were going to do this—

Fuck! His cock popped right out, hard as the trunk of the cypress above him. "Tell me this isn't a dream," he said gruffly, taking in her soft, tanned curves. She was the most incredible sight. Perfection. Seduction. Bathed in soft yellow, the sun coming up behind her...

She smiled at him, then wrapped her hand around his erection and kissed the tip. "Does that feel like a dream?"

He groaned, his ass tightening. "Fuck yeah."

She laughed, then started to stroke him. Up. Down. Soft palm, warm fingers. "I've been thinking about this since dawn."

Shit. It was like the perfect pressure. He sucked air through his teeth and jacked up his hips. "Next time, don't think," he growled. "Or wait."

"Next time?" she purred.

Teeth gritted, body rigid, his eyes captured hers and held. Was that hope he saw there? She wanted a next time? More? Him? This? Or his own hope mirrored back? He needed to know. Had to know...

But the question died as his brain started to spin. After stroking him, up and over, then down to the base, Rosalie guided his cock to her lips. Her eyes still clinging to his, she very slowly drew him in.

Instantly, Killian started to move. Thrust. Shit, he couldn't help himself. Her mouth was so hot, her eyes, too—and her tongue was pressing against the base of his shaft. Christ, what was that? He felt like his dick was drowning in pure pleasure.

She made sounds too. Soft growls, hisses, moans of hunger. And as she took him all the way to the back of her throat, over and over, Killian tried like hell to tamp down his need to either come or get her on her back and fuck her until they both exploded. But it was impossible. As she continued to blow the living hell out of him, drawing him in and out of her sexy mouth, she lifted her ass up in the air and was wiggling it, back and forth. Like it had a fucking tail on it.

Mind gone.

Balls tight and ready.

He. Was. So. Going. To. Have. Her.

And not alone. The thing inside him. The puma—*his puma*— wanted her, too.

She released him for a moment, to yank his sweats down to his knees. It was the opportunity both Killian and his cat had been waiting for. He was up and pressing her back to the ground in seconds. As he loomed over her, a snarl exited his throat. The cat was with him, inside him, wanting, needing, hungry... *Was this normal?* he wondered, grabbing her legs. Did the cat and the male coexist? Feed together? Fuck together?

Well, he was going to find out.

He pressed her knees to her chest, then stared down at what he'd created. A perfect feast. Rosalie gazed up at him, looking feral and excited and ready. Her eyes were wide and bright; her mouth wet and curved up into a challenging smile.

Yes, Kitten, you'll get as good as you give.

It was the last thing Killian thought for a full minute as he dove between her legs and fed off her hot, juicy pussy. She was shaved bare and her scent... Christ, her scent. It was a drug he would never quit. A welcome addiction.

She was his. His and the puma's.

Now he just had to make her see it too.

Her fingers were threading in his hair, fisting, then scraping his scalp as he flicked her swollen clitoris with his tongue. She liked it fast and light. Every time he changed the rhythm, her hold on him slackened, so he kept it up, just right, perfect—until her nails dug into his scalp.

That's right, Hunter, make me bleed.

As she fucked his mouth, thrusting and grinding, he watched her. She was unbearably beautiful. She was watching him too. Her skin pink, her mouth parted, panting, her eyes at half-mast, her brow furrowed as she neared orgasm.

The puma was whispering something to him. It was the only way Killian could describe the sensation. *Suck. Suck her like she sucked you...*

Without question, he wrapped his lips around her clit and drew her in. Rosalie went wild. Crying out, writhing, releasing his head and grabbing her perfect breasts, pinching her nipples as he continued to suckle her. Come leaked from the tip of Killian's dick, but he only sought her climax. And with one deep pull, she broke open. Her body tensed and as her clit swelled against his tongue, he sucked her, taking each beat, each moan of orgasm into his mind and heart and skin, and offering it to the being that had given him this.

This female's pleasure.

Their female's pleasure.

Rosalie barely gave her climax time to ease before she groaned the words, "Inside me. You. Inside me. Now."

As insane and hungry as Killian felt, he couldn't help but grin. He loved this. This female who said what she wanted, was tough and strong, but sensual and female at the same time.

He pulled away and rose over her. She was ready for him, wrapping her legs around his hips the very second he had his cock at her entrance—and pulling him down for a kiss the second he pushed inside of her.

No. Killian was no longer a man. He'd felt the switch. Last night. This morning. It all ran together. He was a male. A shifter.

Hers...

Hot desire flooded him and he could do nothing else but move. Deep, possessive thrusts as he slipped his hands beneath her ass and kissed her. Around them, the sun was streaking through the treetops, illuminating their bond.

Something stunning was happening inside Killian. The pain that had once landed and taken root within him was trying to break free. Fear and guilt couldn't survive where there was this...him and Rosalie. There wasn't room to house it.

Pulling his mouth from hers, he eased back so he could see her. The stunning female that was his. All that yellow hair, spread out around her gorgeous face. Lips wet and pink from his kiss. Cheeks flushed. Neck strained as another orgasm built inside her. Heavy breasts bouncing with each hard thrust.

He shook his head. "The perfect rose. I understand your name now." He sucked air between his teeth as her hot walls tightened around his cock. "Beautiful, soft, proud and a scent so intoxicating, I want to get drunk every fucking night."

That elicited a wide grin and a soft laugh interspersed with gasps as he gave her three punishing thrusts.

He pulled one hand from her backside and reached between them, brushed his thumb over her still-swollen clit. Instantly, she cried out.

"Like that, Kitten?"

She nodded, her breath labored. "Goddess, yes."

As he gazed into her eyes, he brought the pad of his thumb to his mouth and licked her cream. *Perfection.* "This is what I like."

Before she could say another word, or even make a sound, his thumb was back on her clit, and he was pumping inside her brutally fast. Her eyes closed and her nostrils flared. The combination was too much. Once again, she broke, flying over the edge of happiness and pleasure. Bucking wildly, squeezing against his dick.

And Killian wasn't about to be left behind. Sweat on his brow, every muscle straining, he moved, driving into her, over and over, until...

"Oh, fuck!" he snarled, thrusting deep and holding as he released a wash of come inside her.

"Rose," he uttered, then pulled her into his arms, rolling them to one side. Still connected, he held her both possessively and protectively. *I'm never letting you go. You're mine. Mine.*

For long moments, they lay there on the cool ground, under the dappled morning sun and fragrant flora, touching and tasting, stroking and kissing. Rosalie's leg was tossed over Killian's hip and his hand was cupping her ass.

"What is this?" she asked, running her nails over the black barren tree with the words *"There is no secret here"* interwoven in branches tattooed on his shoulder.

"A reminder," he uttered between kisses to her neck.

"Of what?" Her voice carried the delectable strains of jealousy.

He eased back, looked at her, smiled gently. "To never leave things unsaid. If you care about someone, love someone, make sure they know it."

A soft growl rumbled in her chest. "Was it for a female?" she asked, yanking him closer with her leg. "In your past?"

His cock pulsed, started to harden inside her once again. Oh, they were going to have fun together. Painful sometimes, pleasure always. He grinned at her. "A female inspired it."

Her eyes narrowed, and that growl became a snarl.

"Easy, Kitten," he said, then gave her one deep kiss. "She wasn't my female," he whispered against her lips. "She was the wife of a Ranger I wasn't able to save. A guy who hadn't been able to say good-bye or I love you."

Her entire being changed. "Oh." And her eyes softened.

He didn't know which Rosalie he adored more. The possessive she-cat or the soft, supple female. He leaned in and kissed her gently on the mouth. "Come on, baby. You're the only female I—"

Killian froze. Rosalie too, as the sound of movement in the undergrowth caught their ears. It wasn't a random skunk or possum. It was predatory. It was Pantera.

Hunter.

Rosalie was the first to scramble away and leap to her feet. Naked and flushed from sex, she crouched into a fighting stance. His cock hard against his abdomen, Killian moved in front of her. But something was happening. To him. To the world around him. Eyes growing sharper, scent intensifying... No! But before he could stop it, his mind receded and he was no longer the Ranger, the man—or the male.

He was puma.

The puma who would kill anything or anyone who even looked at his female.

Chapter Eleven

"Just say what you have to say." Rosalie stood near the border of the Wildlands. It was midday and warm for winter, and she was about to be kicked out on her ass. Had to be. Killian was still breathing, but shit, she'd broken every rule in the Pantera book, and now she was going to have to live with the consequences.

Raphael and Parish stood before her. The judgment police. Giving her the stink eye and a formal good-bye. After, of course, a thorough dressing down about the many ways she'd screwed up in the past couple of days.

"What if he'd taken off?" Parish demanded, his gold eyes furious. "We don't know what he's capable of. What if he can shift outside of the Wildlands? What if he'd gotten hurt? Or hurt a human?"

"I wouldn't have let that happen." Even as she said the words, she knew they were useless.

"You're reckless," Parish said.

"And arrogant," Raphael finished.

"Better than angry," she tossed back. "Or miserable or guilty or bitter."

Neither male said a word to that. Just stared at her. Clearly, it wasn't the reply they'd expected. For the twenty-four/seven puma female to realize—no, to admit that she'd been anything but *fine* over the past several months.

She took a deep breath, looked to her right at the beautiful Wildlands, her home since she knew what home was. Killian was in there, somewhere, probably back at the clinic, recovering from the tranquilizer dart Parish had shot him with. Bastard. Forget about her cat's insane reaction, she'd nearly lost her mind when the leader of the Hunter's had done that.

She felt their eyes on her. Waiting. Needing an explanation. Her heart squeezed painfully. "When Mercier was killed," she started, almost as if she was speaking to herself, "I truly thought I'd never feel hopeful again. Maybe because I didn't think I deserved to feel it. Not when he couldn't. But now I know that kind of thinking doesn't honor his memory at all. It defiles it." She turned back to face the two males who held her future, at least in the Wildlands, in their hands. "I know what I did was wrong. For you, Raphael, according to the rules and the promises I made, I wouldn't blame you…"

"Rules are there for a reason, Hunter," Parish said tightly, though his eyes weren't nearly as hostile as they were a moment ago. "We can't function as a society without them."

"I get that," she said. "But this time, this rule breaking, it wasn't wrong for me or for Killian. It saved us both, I think. I don't regret it."

"Oh, shit," Parish ground out.

"I'm prepared to go," Rosalie continued, her chin lifted proudly, though inside she was wilting. "Not into the regular world, of course. I couldn't stand that for long."

"Then where?" Raphael asked, his expression thick with concern.

"Hiss and his mate are in the Wetlands. I'm hoping I'll be welcome there."

The scent of him came seconds before the voice.

Killian.

He came through the brush with two Hunters, Ice and Keira,

Parish's twin sister. He was all male, not a prisoner or a tagalong. He was flanked by both Hunters, as if he was one of them. A smile came to Rosalie's lips as pride touched her heart. He looked so right with them.

"You' re not going anywhere," he said, though his blue shark eyes were trained on Raphael.

"This is between us and Rosalie," the leader of the Pantera told him with an edge.

The once human man, who seemed utterly and completely Pantera now, shook his head. "She's not leaving the Wildlands, Raphael."

"That's not for you to say," the male told him.

"You offered me a home here," Killian countered, stepping forward, coming to stand beside Rosalie.

"Yes."

"And if I wanted to take a mate, she would also be welcome here."

"Of course, but—"

"Well, I took one."

Rosalie's growl broke over the border, and she turned on Killian and snarled out her demand, "Who. Did. You. Mate?"

He stared into her eyes and grinned. Wide. Rosalie bristled, and her cat backed down. Unbelievable. Not only wasn't he afraid of her wrath, claws, puma, or fangs—he was turned on.

She could scent it.

Her lip curled.

Males.

"Answer me, Human," she hissed, pressing up against him. Oh yeah, definitely turned on.

He licked his lower lip and a rumble sounded in his chest. "Goddamn, I love it when you call me Human," he said. "Don't think my cat does though."

"Who did you mate, damn you?" she nearly cried.

The smile on his face and his eyes died. He looked at her like she was crazy. "Jesus, Hunter. It's you, for fuck's sake. You're my mate."

She must've gone both pale and blank because Keira and Ice started laughing. She turned on them and snarled. Which only made them laugh harder.

"Fuck the both of you," she spat. "And you." She turned back to address Killian. "I never gave myself to you." She lifted her chin, trying to act all cool and haughty, when secretly, relief and happiness were pouring through her. Such a phony.

Killian cocked one eyebrow and said in a voice for all to hear. "You want me to go over the many ways you gave yourself to me? Now, I don't give a shit if these four hear it, but you might." He grinned wickedly, and those blue eyes flashed. "I'm going to be very detailed, Kitten."

Her body responded instantly, erupting into flame, and she leapt at him—wrapped her arms around his neck. Her heart pounding with the wondrous rhythm of new love, she kissed him. Hungrily. Desperately. Hopefully. When she pulled back, she eyed him and growled against his wet lips, "Ask me, Killian."

He knew exactly what she meant, what she wanted. His hold on her tightened. "Be my mate, Rosalie?"

She smiled back. "All right."

"And my home?"

"Sure."

"And my heart?"

"Okay."

"And my partner in all things Pantera?" His expression downgraded to grim. "If there's one of me, the super solider, then there are more."

She nodded solemnly. "I'm with you. All the way. By your side."

His eyes warmed with the kind of happiness that only came from feeling understood and cared for.

"Us too," Keira called out. "It's about time we went on another field trip."

"Fuck yeah," Ice agreed.

But Killian and Rosalie weren't listening. Killian had pulled her even tighter to him, and was uttering against her mouth, "And you'll help me figure out the shifting thing? How to control—"

Rosalie shut him up with a hard, hungry kiss. She was his and he was hers. And all she wanted in that moment was to revel in the beauty of forgiveness, and letting go of fear and guilt. Her hands drove into his hair, and he growled and sucked on her tongue. At some point, she ripped her mouth away from his to tell the four suddenly silent Pantera to go away—that they could kick her ass out later.

Parish grumbled of course. And Raphael said in his most authoritative tone, "We'll have a strategy session tomorrow at noon. And I *will* see you both there." But they left.

Because really, no one messes with a Pantera female in love.

Except maybe the male, the mate, who loves her in return.

About Alexandra Ivy and Laura Wright

Alexandra Ivy is a *New York Times* and *USA Today* bestselling author of the Guardians of Eternity, as well as the Sentinels, Dragons of Eternity and ARES series. After majoring in theatre she decided she prefers to bring her characters to life on paper rather than stage. She lives in Missouri with her family. Visit her website at alexandraivy.com.

* * * *

New York Times and USA Today Bestselling Author, Laura Wright is passionate about romantic fiction. Though she has spent most of her life immersed in acting, singing and competitive ballroom dancing, when she found the world of writing and books and endless cups of coffee she knew she was home. Laura is the author of the bestselling Mark of the Vampire series and the USA Today bestselling series, Bayou Heat, which she co-authors with Alexandra Ivy.

Laura lives in Los Angeles with her husband, two young children and three loveable dogs.

Also From Alexandra Ivy

Guardians Of Eternity
WHEN DARKNESS ENDS
DARKNESS ETERNAL
HUNT THE DARKNESS
EMBRACE THE DARKNESS
WHEN DARKNESS COMES

Masters Of Seduction
VOLUME ONE
MASTERS OF SEDUCTION TWO
RECKLESS: HOUSE OF FURIA

Ares Series
KILL WITHOUT MERCY

Bayou Heat Series
BAYOU HEAT COLLECTION ONE
BAYOU HEAT COLLECTION TWO
ANGEL/HISS
MICHEL/STRIKER

Branded Pack
STOLEN AND FORGIVEN
ABANDONED AND UNSEEN

Dragons Of Eternity
BURNED BY DARKNESS

Sentinels
ON THE HUNT

Also From Laura Wright

Mark Of The Vampire
ETERNAL HUNGER
ETERNAL KISS
ETERNAL BLOOD (ESPECIAL)
ETERNAL CAPTIVE
ETERNAL BEAST
ETERNAL BEAUTY (ESPECIAL)
ETERNAL DEMON
ETERNAL SIN

Bayou Heat Series
RAPHAEL & PARISH
BAYON & JEAN-BAPTISTE
TALON & XAVIER
SEBASTIAN & ARISTIDE
LIAN & ROCH
HAKAN & SEVERIN
ANGEL & HISS
MICHEL & STRIKER
RAGE & KILLIAN

Wicked Ink Chronicles (New Adult Series- 17+)
FIRST INK
SHATTERED INK
REBEL INK

Cavanaugh Brothers
BRANDED
BROKEN
BRASH
BONDED

Masters Of Seduction
VOLUME ONE
MASTERS OF SEDUCTION TWO

Incubus Tales

Spurs, Stripes And Snow Series
SINFUL IN SPURS

Kill Without Mercy
Ares Security Book 1
By Alexandra Ivy
Now Available

From the hellhole of a Taliban prison to sweet freedom, five brave military heroes have made it home—and they're ready to take on the civilian missions no one else can. Individually they're intimidating. Together they're invincible. They're the men of ARES Security.

Rafe Vargas is only in Newton, Iowa, to clear out his late grandfather's small house. As the covert ops specialist for ARES Security, he's eager to get back to his new life in Texas. But when he crosses paths with Annie White, a haunted beauty with skeletons in her closet, he can't just walk away—not when she's clearly in danger...

There's a mysterious serial killer on the loose with a link to Annie's dark past. And the closer he gets, the deeper Rafe's instinct to protect kicks in. But even with his considerable skill, Annie's courage, and his ARES buddies behind him, the slaying won't stop. Now it's only a matter of time before Annie's next—unless they can unravel a history of deadly lies that won't be buried.

* * * *

Friday nights in Houston meant crowded bars, loud music and ice-cold beer. It was a tradition that Rafe and his friends had quickly adapted to suit their own tastes when they moved to Texas five months ago.

After all, none of them were into the dance scene. They were too old for half-naked coeds and casual hookups. And none of them wanted to have to scream over pounding music to have a decent conversation.

Instead, they'd found The Saloon, a small, cozy bar with lots of polished wood, a jazz band that played softly in the background, and a handful of locals who knew better than to bother the other customers. Oh, and the finest tequila in the city.

They even had their own table that was reserved for them

every Friday night.

Tucked in a back corner, it was shrouded in shadows and well away from the long bar that ran the length of one wall. A perfect spot to observe without being observed.

And best of all, situated so no one could sneak up from behind.

It might have been almost two years since they'd returned from the war, but none of them had forgotten. Lowering your guard, even for a second, could mean death.

Lesson. Fucking. Learned.

Tonight, however, it was only Rafe and Hauk at the table, both of them sipping tequila and eating peanuts from a small bucket.

Lucas was still in Washington D.C., working his contacts to help drum up business for their new security business, ARES. Max had remained at their new offices, putting the final touches on his precious forensics lab, and Teagan was on his way to the bar after installing a computer system that would give Homeland Security a hemorrhage if they knew what he was doing.

Leaning back in his chair, Rafe intended to spend the night relaxing after a long week of hassling with the red tape and bullshit regulations that went into opening a new business, when he made the mistake of checking his messages.

"Shit."

He tossed his cellphone on the polished surface of the wooden table, a tangled ball of emotions lodged in the pit of his stomach.

Across the table Hauk sipped his tequila and studied Rafe with a lift of his brows.

At a glance, the two men couldn't be more different.

Rafe had dark hair that had grown long enough to touch the collar of his white button-down shirt along with dark eyes that were lushly framed by long, black lashes. His skin remained tanned dark bronze despite the fact it was late September, and his body was honed with muscles that came from working on the small ranch he'd just purchased, not the gym.

Hauk, on the other hand, had inherited his Scandinavian father's pale blond hair that he kept cut short, and brilliant blue eyes that held a cunning intelligence. He had a narrow face with sculpted features that were usually set in a stern expression.

And it wasn't just their outward appearance that made them so different.

Rafe was hot tempered, passionate and willing to trust his gut instincts.

Hauk was aloof, calculating, and mind-numbingly anal. Not that Hauk would admit he was OCD. He preferred to call himself detail-oriented.

Which was exactly why he was a successful sniper. Rafe, on the other hand, had been trained in combat rescue. He was capable of making quick decisions, and ready to change strategies on the fly.

"Trouble?" Hauk demanded.

Rafe grimaced. "The real estate agent left a message saying she has a buyer for my grandfather's house."

Hauk looked predictably confused. Rafe had been bitching about the need to get rid of his grandfather's house since the old man's death a year ago.

"Shouldn't that be good news?"

"It would be if I didn't have to travel to Newton to clean it out," Rafe said.

"Aren't there people you can hire to pack up the shit and send it to you?"

"Not in the middle of fucking nowhere."

Hauk's lips twisted into a humorless smile. "I've been in the middle of fucking nowhere, amigo, and it ain't Kansas," he said, the shadows from the past darkening his eyes.

"Newton's in Iowa, but I get your point," Rafe conceded. He did his best to keep the memories in the past where they belonged. Most of the time he was successful. Other times the demons refused to be leashed. "Okay, it's not the hell hole we crawled out of, but the town might as well be living in another century. I'll have to go deal with my grandfather's belongings myself."

Hauk reached to pour himself another shot of tequila from the bottle that had been waiting for them in the center of the table.

Like Rafe, he was dressed in an Oxford shirt, although his was blue instead of white, and he was wearing black dress pants instead of jeans.

"I know you think it's a pain, but it's probably for the best."

Rafe glared at his friend. The last thing he wanted was to drive a thousand miles to pack up the belongings of a cantankerous old man who'd never forgiven Rafe's father for walking away from Iowa. "Already trying to get rid of me?"

"Hell no. Of the five of us, you're the…"

"I'm afraid to ask," Rafe muttered as Hauk hesitated.

"The glue," he at last said.

Rafe gave a bark of laughter. He'd been called a lot of things over the years. Most of them unrepeatable. But glue was a new one. "What the hell does that mean?"

Hauk settled back in his seat. "Lucas is the smooth-talker, Max is the heart, Teagan is the brains and I'm the organizer." The older man shrugged. "You're the one who holds us all together. ARES would never have happened without you."

Rafe couldn't argue. After returning to the States, the five of them had been transferred to separate hospitals to treat their numerous injuries. It would have been easy to drift apart. The natural instinct was to avoid anything that could remind them of the horror they'd endured.

But Rafe had quickly discovered that returning to civilian life wasn't a simple matter of buying a home and getting a 9-to-5 job.

He couldn't bear the thought of being trapped in a small cubicle eight hours a day, or returning to an empty condo that would never be a home.

It felt way too much like the prison he'd barely escaped.

Bonded
The Cavanaugh Brothers Book 4
By Laura Wright
Now Available

The New York Times bestselling author of Brash returns to the Triple C Ranch in River Black, Texas, for more cowboys, romance, and danger...

Ranch hand Blue Perez's once simple life is spinning out of control. He's discovered he has three half-brothers, and they're not ready to accept his claim on the ranch. Also, Blue's girlfriend may have betrayed him in the worst way possible. And after one evening of drowning his sorrows at the bar, there's someone he can't get out of his mind, a woman who says she's carrying his child.

Following a night of breathtaking passion in the arms of the man she's longed for all her life, waitress Emily Shiver is contemplating her next step. With everything that's going on in Blue's life, she doesn't want to force him into fatherhood. Yet as hard hearted as he may seem, Blue can't turn his back on her, particularly when she becomes the target of someone's dark obsession....

* * * *

Last thing she wanted was someone getting hurt because of her. Especially someone with such a beautiful face. That hard, sexy jawline . . .

This time when she rolled her eyes it was internal and at herself.

She reached for a napkin on the table behind her. "Your lip . . . Let me clean it up for you."

"Naw, it's nothing."

"You're bleeding," she said.

He swiped at his lip and the blood with the back of his hand. "All gone."

"Well, that wasn't very sanitary," she said.

His eyes, those incredible blue eyes, warmed with momentary humor. Then he touched the brim of his hat and turned to head back to the bar. "Ma'am."

Emily stared after him, confused. What was that? Saves the day and on his way? "Hey, hold on a sec," she called out. "I didn't thank you."

"There's no need," he called back, sliding onto the same barstool he'd occupied earlier.

Well, that's not very neighborly, she mused. She followed him. "Maybe not," she said, coming up to stand beside him. "But I'm going to do it anyway."

He turned to look at her but didn't say anything. Good night, nurse, he was handsome.

She inclined her head formally. "Thank you."

Those incredible eyes moved over her face then. So probing, so thoughtful. They made her toes curl inside her shoes. "Something tells me you could've taken those men out yourself."

"What tells you that?" she asked.

He ran a hand over his jaw, which was darkening by the minute. "Just a guess."

Her gaze flickered to the bruise, to his mouth, and she frowned. "Are you in pain?"

"Constantly," he said, then turned back to his drink.

The strange, almost morose response made her pause. But before she could ask him anything about it, Dean slid back behind the bar and asked, "You want something, Em? After having to deal with those assholes I'd say you're done for the night. But first, a drink."

"And it's on me," Blue said, then tossed back his tequila.

Dean gave the cowboy a broad grin. "After what you did for our girl here, it's me who's buying."

"Well, thank you kindly." Blue held up his empty glass. "Another, if you please. And what would you like . . . ?" He turned to Emily and arched a brow at her. "Em, is it?"

The soft masculine growl in his voice made her insides warm. "Emily," she told him. "Emily Shiver."

"Right." He cocked his head to one side and studied her. "The girl with the flowers in her hair," he said, his gaze catching on the yellow one behind her ear.

Emily smiled. Couldn't help it. She liked that he'd noticed. "Started when I was little," she told him. "Stole flowers from my grandmother's garden every time I was over there. I'd put them everywhere. My room, the tables here, in my hair." She shrugged. "It became kind of an obsession."

His gaze flickered to the flower in her hair again, then returned to her face. "Pretty."

Heat instantly spread through Emily's insides. Granted, plenty of men came into the Bull's Eye and looked at her with eyes heavy on the hungry—either for food or for her. Hell, sometimes both. But no one had ever looked at her like Blue was now. Curious, frustrated, interested . . .

"Drink, Em?"

Swallowing hard, she turned to see a waiting and mildly curious Dean. "Just a Coke for me, boss. Thanks."

Blue groaned as Dean filled a glass with ice.

"What's wrong?" Emily asked him, wondering if his jaw was paining him.

But the man just chuckled softly. "Come on, now. Have something a little stronger than that.

You're gonna make me feel bad. Or worse." Under his breath he added, "If that's even possible tonight."

Curiosity coiled within her at his words. The way he looked at her, spoke, acted . . . clearly he was working through some heavy feelings tonight. Was it about the fight with the jerkweeds? Or something that came before it? She bit her lip. Did she ask? Or did she wait for him to tell her? But why would he tell her? They barely knew each other.

Maybe she should just ignore it . . .

Dean set the Coke before her and poured another round of tequila for Blue, which the cowboy drained in about five seconds flat; then he tapped the bar top to indicate he wanted another.

Oh yeah. Definitely dealing with something. She'd worked at the Bull's Eye long enough to know that drinking like he was doing had nothing to do with relaxing after a long day. Dark feelings were running through Blue Perez's blood. And maybe some demons to go along with them.

"Everything all right tonight, cowboy?" she asked.

"Yep." He turned to look at her again, his gaze not all that sharp or engaged now. The liquor was starting to do its thing. "I remember you. Flowers, and a ton of strawberry blond curls."

Emily's breath caught inside her lungs. What a strange and very suggestive thing to say. Not that she minded. Just wished he'd have said it before the double shot. And the way he was staring at her . . . like he was trying to memorize her features or something. Then suddenly, he reached out and touched her hair, fingered one of those curls caught up in a ponytail.

A hot, powerful shiver moved up her spine.

"Here you go," Dean interrupted, filling Blue's glass once again.

"Thanks," Blue said, though his eyes were still on Emily. Even when his fingers curled around the glass, his eyes remained locked with hers. "Sure you don't want something stronger, Em?" he asked.

Emily's brows shot up, and her belly clenched with awareness. "I think you're doing fine for the both of us," she said, reaching for her Coke and taking a sip. Her mouth was incredibly dry. "And I'm going to assume that you'll be walking home."

He downed the contents of the glass and chuckled. "Not to worry, darlin'. I got my truck."

Oh jeez. Not to worry? She shook her head. People could be so stupid sometimes. So reckless. Even gorgeous cowboys with eyes the color of a cloudless Texas sky— and a pair of lips that kept calling to her own.

Like the meddlesome gal she was, she reached over and grabbed his keys off the bar top. Blue's gaze turned sharply to hers, and under the heat of that electric stare, Emily tried not to melt. Well, outwardly at any rate.

Yes, you're hot and sexy and annoyed at my ass now. But I'm not going to let you be a shit for brains.

She held up the keys. "No rush, cowboy. I got my Coke here, and nowhere to get to. I'm going to take you home when you've sufficiently drowned yourself."

Blue didn't like that one bit. He released a breath and ground out, "Not necessary."

"I say it is," she returned.

"You don't want to do that, darlin'. I'm not fit to be around tonight."

"Maybe not. But there's no use arguing the matter. I always win arguments. Right, Dean?"

The bartender chuckled. "Don't even try anymore."

"If you're really going to push this, I can call someone—" Blue started, then stopped. His eyes came up and met hers, and it was impossible to miss the heavy, pulsing pain that echoed there.

This wasn't about the jerks or a bad day. This was deep and long lasting. Emily knew some of what had happened to him in the past couple of months. Finding out— along with the whole town— that his daddy was Everett Cavanaugh. That he had part claim to the Triple C. Along with a set of three new brothers. But clearly there was more that was weighing on him. So much more, she'd venture to guess.

She slipped the keys into her jeans pocket and settled back in front of her Coke. This wasn't how she'd wanted the night to go. Watching over a hot, drunk cowboy. She'd had visions of a bathtub, a great book, and some buttered noodles afterward. But tonight this man had offered up his protection, and she couldn't help but do the same.

Dragon King
A Dark Kings Novella
By Donna Grant

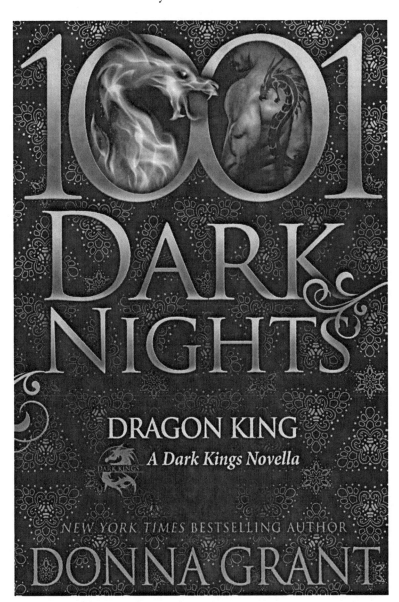

1001 DARK NIGHTS

DRAGON KING
A Dark Kings Novella

NEW YORK TIMES BESTSELLING AUTHOR
DONNA GRANT

Chapter One

Grace was screwed. Royally screwed. As in, her career was over. Finished. *Finite.*

She turned on the windshield wipers and slowed the car as she drove through the rain in the mountains. With a renewed grip on the steering wheel, she sent a quick prayer that the rain would stop.

A little sprinkle she could handle. A storm...well, that was another matter entirely.

She puffed out her cheeks as she exhaled. If only she was in Scotland for a holiday, but that wasn't the case at all. In a last-ditch effort to give her muse a good swift kick in the pants, Grace decided to travel to Scotland.

All her friends thought she had lost her mind. Her editor thought it was just one more excuse in a very long line of them as to why she hadn't turned the book in.

Grace wished she knew the reason the words just stopped coming. One day they were there, and the next...gone, vanished. Poof!

Writing wasn't just her career. It was her life. Because within the words and pages she was able to write about heroines who had relationships she would never have. It was the sad truth, but it was the truth.

Grace accepted her lot...in a way. She might realize the string of miserable dates were complete misses and admit that. However, the stories running through her head allowed her to dream as far as she could, and encounter men and adventures sitting behind a computer never would.

Not being able to find the words anymore was like having someone steal her soul.

She breathed a sigh of relief when the rain stopped and she was able to turn off her windshield wipers. In the two hours since she checked into the B&B, it hadn't stopped raining.

Rain was a part of being in Scotland, and she was pushing herself with her fear of storms to be out in it as well. It proved how far she would go to find her soul again. She needed to write, to sink into another world where she could find happiness and a love that lasted forever.

Now she was armed with her laptop and steely determination. She would find her muse again. Just as soon as she found the right place. The scenery along the highway was stunning, but the noise of the passing vehicles would be too much.

Grace needed somewhere off the beaten path. Somewhere she could pretend she was the only person left in the world.

Already three months past due on the book, she felt the pressure to write. Which wasn't helping her creativity in the least. Her editor had already informed her if she didn't turn the book in three weeks from now, then the contract would be canceled.

A full book in three weeks. Yeah, Grace was nothing if not optimistic. She was aiming for having at least half done by then. Perhaps her editor would take mercy on her and allow her to finish the book.

She laughed at her optimism. Based on the last e-mail from her editor, it was either the entire book or nothing. Her entire future and career was on the line.

Grace exited off the highway. She had no idea where she was going. She would know the perfect place when she found it. Narrow roads had her driving slower, which allowed her to take in the sights.

A couple of times she pulled off the road and rolled down her window, but the sounds of civilization could still be heard. So she kept driving deeper and deeper into the mountains.

She didn't worry about getting lost. The GPS on her phone would get her back to the B&B in one piece. No, her entire focus was on finding a place to write.

When drops of rain began to land on the windshield, Grace glanced over at the passenger seat to her rain jacket. All she could hope for was that it remained sprinkling.

If there was a storm, Grace knew her fear would kick in, and she'd be done for. Astraphobia it was called, and it sucked. One wouldn't think there were many storms any given month, right? Except when it was your fear, and it felt as if they followed you around.

No amount of research she'd done on thunder and lightning storms stopped her fear. Just hearing the rumble of thunder sent chills down to the very marrow of her bones. And lightning? She shuddered just thinking about it.

Some thought such awesome displays of nature were beautiful. All Grace could think about was hiding any time lightning zigzagged through the sky. She was in complete flight mode during those storms.

It's why she constantly checked the weather. She rarely got caught unawares anymore, unless a storm cropped up at night. But she wasn't in Los Angeles or Paris right now. She was in Scotland—a country known for its rainfall.

"I'm in a country with daily rainfall while trying to get past my writer's block because of this need to have my story set in Scotland. Oh, yeah. This was a fabulous idea," she told herself while glancing at the sky to see how dark the rainclouds were.

Grace didn't know how long or how far she drove. Taking back roads and roads that weren't roads at all put her further and further from human contact, just as she wanted.

Until she was driving on grass and came to a dead end at the base of a mountain. Grace was about to turn around when she paused. She stared at the jagged peaks and the grass covering the rocks. After a moment, she turned off her engine and opened her door.

The quiet was broken only by the wind and the sounds of birds. Peace. That's what the place emanated. She looked down at her mobile and saw that the service wasn't working.

There was a brief moment of panic when she couldn't check the weather, but then she looked up at the sky. The sun was peaking out of the clouds.

"Just what I need. No noise from the city or constant interruptions. If I'm going to write, I've got to take this chance."

Grace grabbed her laptop and raincoat and got out of the car. She hiked up the mountain about fifty feet before she found a boulder that made a perfect seat.

For several minutes, she simply sat and looked out over the area. Mountains rose up all around before giving way to breathtaking valleys—or glens, as the Scots called them.

Glens were inspiring places that were as unique as each mountain around them. Many of the glens remained unchanged for thousands of years.

Grace spotted a small waterfall that fell into a stream that wound down the mountain and into a valley. The beauty was unmistakable.

It was the first time in ages that Grace felt released, boundless. Unrestricted.

As she watched the clouds move briskly across the sky, she let her mind drift to her book. Excitement flared when she saw a scene play out in her mind.

For so very long, her characters had refused to talk to her, denied to show her anything of their story. But now they had begun to come alive once more.

Grace opened her laptop with the document waiting. She typed as fast as the words came to her. She didn't stop to correct spelling, didn't halt to see if what was happening would work. She simply wrote. Bad pages were easier to fix than blank ones.

The words continued to pour out of her. She became so focused on them that she didn't know how many pages she had written. She went from one chapter to the next, her smile growing bigger and bigger as everything finally began to come together.

It was the first fat drop of water in the middle of her keyboard that halted her. Her heart seized, panic threatening to take hold. But she was finally writing!

Grace's hands were shaking as she looked up to see a rather dark cloud settling above her. This couldn't be happening. Not when she was writing again.

Anger mixed with her dread. She briefly thought of returning to her car. Another drop of rain landed atop her left hand.

The drops were small and coming irregularly. She could retreat as she always did with the rain, or she could try to get past her fear and keep writing.

She stood and looked around, turning in a full circle as she scanned the area for someplace that would shield her from the rain.

"Yes!" Grace said triumphantly as she spotted an overhang of rock from the mountain off to her right. It was just big enough to keep the rain off her.

Grace saved her work and closed her laptop before she began the climb, her heart pounding so hard she thought it might burst from her chest. With every step farther from her car, she knew she was pushing herself all in the name of her story.

The spot wasn't that much higher, but the climb wasn't nearly as smooth. It didn't help that the spattering of rain became a drizzle. She stopped and put on her raincoat, tucking her computer inside to keep it dry.

Several minutes later and out of breath, Grace settled on the grass and opened her computer. Her hands were still shaking, but the rain hadn't increased. She could do this. She could sit through a rain shower and write. As long as there was no thunder and lightning.

She took a deep breath and opened her mind to her characters once more. Surprisingly, it was just as easy to fall back into the story. Grace could hardly believe her luck. If only she had thought to come to Scotland months ago.

To live so close to the very place she set her book and not visit. It was ridiculous, really.

Grace forgot about the past few months as the words flew from her fingers onto the page. Before she knew it, she had written forty-five pages. In one sitting!

She shivered in the cool air and looked up from the screen to see that the rain was beginning to taper off to almost nothing. The overhang kept the water off her, but the steep decline down to her car looked treacherous.

And it wasn't as if Grace had worn the best shoes. Her tennis shoes were adequate for a short stroll, but not for a walk down a rain-soaked mountain.

Grace went back to writing, intending to reach the fifty-page mark. She was on a roll, and nothing was going to stop her now.

* * * *

Arian paced the cavern in his mountain in agitation and a wee bit of anxiety. He was shaking off the dragon sleep from the past six hundred years. Not only had it been six centuries since he had been in human form, but there was a war the Dragon Kings were involved in.

Con and the others were waiting for him to join in the war. Every King had been woken to take part. After all the wars they had been involved in, Arian wasn't happy to be woken to join another.

Because of Ulrik. The banished and disgraced Dragon King hadn't just made a nuisance of himself, but he somehow managed to get his magic returned.

Which meant the Kings needed to put extra magic into keeping the four silver dragons sleeping undisturbed deep within the mountain. They were Ulrik's dragons, and he would want to wake them soon.

But it wasn't just Ulrik that was causing mischief. The Dark Fae were as well. It infuriated Arian that they were once more fighting the Dark. Hadn't the Fae Wars killed enough Fae and dragons?

Then again, as a Dragon King as old as time itself, they were targets for others who wanted to defeat them.

For Ulrik, he just wanted revenge. Arian hated him for it, but he could understand. Mostly because Arian had briefly joined Ulrik in his quest to rid the realm of humans.

Thoughts of Ulrik were pushed aside as Arian found himself thinking about why he had taken to his mountain. When he came here six hundred years earlier, it was to remain there for many thousands of years.

The Dragon Kings sought their mountains for many reasons. Some were just tired of dealing with mortals, but others had something they wished to forget for a while. Arian was one of the latter.

There were many things he did in his past when the King of Kings, Constantine, asked. Not all of them Arian was proud of. The one that sent him to his mountain still preyed upon him.

He didn't remember her name, but he remembered her tears. Because of the spell to prevent any of the Dragon Kings from falling in love with mortals, Arian had easily walked away from the female.

Six centuries later, he could still hear her begging him to stay with her, still see the tears coursing down her face. Though he hadn't felt anything, it bothered him that he had so easily walked away. Because Con had demanded it.

Loyalty—above all else.

The Dragon Kings were his family, and Dreagan his home. There was never any question if he were needed that Arian would do whatever it took to help his brethren in any capacity asked of him.

Arian wasn't angry at himself for choosing loyalty for Dreagan. It was expected. What he had grown tired of was the monotony of his existence.

He halted, a shiver of awareness overtaking him. With his mountain being one of those closest to the border, Arian was attuned to anything that crossed through their dragon magic barrier.

And something significant just crossed onto Dreagan.

Arian shifted into human form. He flexed his fingers several times before fisting his hand. Then he rotated his shoulders. Next he dropped his chin to his chest and rolled his head from one side to the other, stretching muscles that hadn't been used in centuries.

He had no clothes, but then again there wasn't a need for any. Con visited each King who was sleeping every ten years and passed on everything that was going on in the world.

And a lot had happened.

When Darius , another Dragon King, woke him, he informed Arian of the recent happenings regarding the Dark Fae and Ulrik. It could be a Dark Fae out there, or it could be an MI5 agent.

No way was Arian going to let anyone onto Dreagan—mortal or immortal. They were going to die before they could go a step further.

Arian strode from the cavern through the tunnels in his mountain until he came to the entrance. Before him stood a large pool of water that was as still as glass.

Stalactites hung from the ceiling in various sizes. Only a paltry scrap of light penetrated the thick darkness from the cave entrance.

Arian eyed the opening that was large enough for him to fit through in dragon form. He made his way around the body of water, his feet making nary a sound. Then he paused at the cave entrance.

The world was cast in a gray sheen that made him blink several times for his eyes to adjust. A light smattering of rain fell, wetting everything.

He kept to the shadows of the cave and peered outside where he felt the intruder. Arian spotted a bright orange shoe. What had Con called them when he visited a few years ago? Aye. Tennis shoes.

Arian closed his eyes and used his dragon magic to sense who he would be fighting. Instantly he felt the human. His eyes snapped open. It was going to be an easy fight.

Just as he was about to step outside, the rain began to fall harder. He heard a curse from what sounded like a female. Arian frowned. He didn't like fighting females, but he would do what he had to do.

"Shit. Shit, shit, shit, shittttttttttt," said the distinctly feminine voice with a slight accent to it he couldn't quite place.

There was fear in her tone that stopped him. He stilled as she stood and clumsily began to come closer to the entrance, an entrance she wasn't supposed to be able to see because it was cloaked in dragon magic.

So she had found his cave. It made no difference. She would get no farther than where he was. And…he was going to learn how she was able to see through the magic.

She barreled past him, her back to him as she shook out her blonde locks that stopped at her chin. She raked her hand through her wet hair and sighed loudly, her gaze never leaving the rain.

Visibly shaking, he wasn't sure if it was due to the cold or if she was filled with terror. By the pallor of her skin, he was beginning to think she was frightened.

After several moments, the female relaxed a fraction. It was almost as if she had been waiting for something.

"It's just rain. Only rain." She briefly closed her eyes. "I was making such progress too." She held up a thin rectangle object and spoke to it. "You better not have gotten wet. I need you."

Arian raised a brow. Was she daft? Or was it some trick to keep him off guard.

She turned around before glancing outside again. Her gaze slid right over him, never seeing him in the shadows. Arian was taken aback by her earthy beauty.

Her creamy skin was flawless. She had large, thick-lashed eyes that were a blue so dark Arian had never seen the like. His gaze raked over her heart-shaped face, from her forehead and slightly arched brows to her high cheekbones, and finally her plump lips.

She hugged the thin object against her and shivered in the green jacket that hid her figure from him. But if her slim legs encased in denim were any indication, he was going to like what he saw beneath.

Her blonde hair was a soft yellow that made him think of daisies bending slightly in the wind. With her locks hanging thick and wet against her damp skin, all Arian could think about was touching her hair, running his fingers through it.

She sighed, drawing his eyes back to her mouth. A mouth that was too seductive by far. The fact he was wondering how her lips would feel against his was a prime indication that the last thing Arian should encounter after six centuries of sleeping was a beautiful woman who made him ache to touch her.

Chapter Two

Grace couldn't believe her luck. It seemed too good to be true to find a place that opened up her creativity and allowed her to get the book written.

Of course, she'd only written fifty pages out of four hundred. That wasn't nearly enough. But it was a great start. If only it hadn't begun raining harder. It was like someone had turned on a faucet. Add in the gusting wind and Grace was quickly soaked.

It was by sheer chance alone that she'd seen the cave. Thankfully, it was close enough that she was able to get to it without too much effort. The fact she'd been able to move through her fear was an improvement.

She opened the laptop and sighed when the screen lit up. With the amount of water that hit her, she'd been worried it had been too much for the computer.

Grace felt her muscles ease as the tension began to subside. Every moment that passed without thunder or lightning made her anxiety diminish.

Then a chill raced down her spine. Slowly, she turned and looked behind her. She suddenly realized that she had no idea how big the cave was. Or if she was the only occupant.

She grabbed her mobile and turned on the flashlight. Her eyes widened as she took in the size of the cavern. The ceiling began just a few feet above her, but the deeper the cave went, the higher the ceiling soared.

Small and insignificant. That's how the cavern made her feel.

The light from her mobile then met the water, and she sucked in a breath. Slowly, she moved the light from one side of the water to the other, noting the expanse of it all.

"Wow," she said in a whisper.

If only she could see it better. The meager light from her phone showed a lot, but not as much as she wanted to see. She wanted to walk around the water, but she hesitated when another chill snaked through her.

The weight of her laptop in her hand reminded her that she should work while she could. Grace turned off the flashlight and pocketed her mobile.

Then she sat her laptop down and removed her raincoat. Once she was seated and leaning back against a rock, she placed her raincoat over her damp jeans for warmth then positioned the computer atop her legs.

A quick check of her watch for the time told her she had been on the mountain for almost three hours. She smiled, happy in all she had accomplished so far. Even with the rain.

In moments she was back to typing, immersed in the story once again. Despite her stomach growling, Grace kept going. The rain couldn't last forever. Could it?

She didn't know what caused her head to jerk up and look to her left. Grace stared into the shadows as she fumbled for her mobile and turned on the flashlight.

A loud sigh escaped her when she saw nothing but rocks. It was her imagination playing tricks on her. With the deafening sound of the rain hitting the rock at the entrance and the quiet of the cave, it was a tad unnerving.

Looking around, she realized just how dark it was in the cave. The light from her laptop made her forget until she looked up from the screen.

Grace saved her progress after she saw she had now written another ten pages. Maybe it was a good thing she was stuck on the mountain. It was obviously just what she needed to write.

Please no thunder and lightning.

She closed the laptop to save battery and stretched her arms over her head. Her pants were drying, but still damp. How she hated wearing wet jeans.

The dampness from the cave was beginning to sink into her. Grace put on her raincoat and got to her feet. She walked to the entrance and looked out.

The rain hadn't slacked off at all. If anything, it looked like it was coming down even heavier. She leaned out to see if she could spot her car, but she didn't have any luck.

She was well and truly stuck until the rain stopped. Grace wrapped her arms around herself. Her stomach soured as she imagined a thunderstorm rolling in.

"Please no," she mumbled.

At least she wasn't without resources. She might be hungry and thirsty, but she had a source of water behind her. Not to mention she still had plenty of battery on her laptop to get more writing done.

That is if she could with the rain continuing. She was doing all right in the day, but at night? That was another matter entirely.

The only thing that made her worry was if she had to stay overnight. It wasn't that Grace minded sleeping on the ground. In fact, she loved to camp. Never mind that it had been over twelve years since she had done it.

Sleeping bag or not, she would be fine if she was forced to have an overnight visit in the cave—as long as it stopped raining. And things could definitely be worse. She could be outside in the weather.

Or it could be thundering.

Or someone could be in the cave with her.

Grace chuckled to herself. A heartbeat later the hairs on the back of her neck stood on end. She whirled around. Someone was there. She knew it. She might not be able to see them or hear them, but it was an instinct she couldn't ignore.

Unless...it wasn't a person at all. It could be an animal.

Which didn't make her feel any better about the situation.

Grace turned on the flashlight on her phone again. She walked far enough from the entrance so that she could hear. Halting next to the rock where she had been writing, Grace slowly moved the light from one side of the cave to the other. She pointed it specifically into the areas with the most shadows.

She was just about to turn it off when she felt a presence behind her. Grace stilled, her heart jumping into her throat.

"What are you doing here, lass?" asked a deep, masculine voice with a thick Scot's accent.

Grace whirled around. His face was hidden by the light from the entrance behind him. He was so tall she had to look up at him. And if he was trying to intimidate her, he succeeded without much effort at all. The shadows hid him almost completely. "Who are you?"

"It doesna matter. You're on private property."

She blinked, wondering if she could reach the entrance before he could grab her. That would put her out in the rain, but it was either that or deal with a crazy man. Damn, but she hated her options.

Grace decided to take another approach. Truth and meekness. It might buy her enough time to get away. "I didn't know."

"You expect me to believe that?"

Well, hell. Could his voice be any sexier? It had a rough edge to it. As if he hadn't used it in a very long while. And why did she yearn to see his face? It shouldn't matter if he was as gorgeous as his voice.

Yes, it does.

"I do expect you to believe me," she stated. "I'm not from here."

"Aye. I gather that from your accent."

There was no denying he wasn't happy she was in the cave. As intimidated as his size made her feel, she didn't feel threatened. Odd. Very odd.

Grace pointed outside. "Have you seen the rain? If I go out in that now, I could fall to my death."

"How did you get inside?"

At this she nearly laughed. "Um…well, I saw the entrance and walked in."

"How did you see it?"

Was he for real? Was he messing with her or high on some drugs? "With my eyes."

"You shouldna have come here."

"Here?" she asked as she looked around, her arms out to her sides. "Where is here?"

She could almost feel him raising a brow at her. Oh, if only she could see his face!

"As if you doona know," he replied acerbically.

Grace crossed her arms in front of her chest and gave him the best glare she had. It was more than difficult, especially when she happened to glance at his chest and noticed that he wasn't wearing a shirt.

All Grace could see was his right shoulder all the way to his neck, where his long hair came into view. Even with just a hint of light from the entrance, she could ascertain that his hair was very dark. Black? Or dark brown? Hard to determine.

She could tell it was long, but the shadows kept her from seeing where the ends were. Never had Grace encountered a man with such hair. It should make him appear feminine looking, but even from the partial silhouette and his voice, he was anything but.

It was then she realized she had been staring. Grace lifted her chin. "I don't know where I am. Why can't you believe me?"

He chuckled, but it held no mirth. His head then tilted to the side and she saw more of his hair fall over his very wide, very thick shoulders.

Something stirred within her, as if the longer she looked at him the more aware she became. Every time he breathed she noticed how his chest expanded. With just the slightest movement, his long locks moved.

Was it wrong that she wanted to sink her hands in his length and press against him?

"I doona know you," he replied.

It took her a second to realize he was speaking. Then it dawned on Grace that she shouldn't be getting angry with him. She dropped her arms to her side and pointed to her laptop. "I came to Scotland to write. You see, I'm desperately behind on my deadline, and I must finish. I found this mountain and its beauty. I'm able to write here. Please, allow me to stay during the day and write. I'll be happy to pay for that privilege."

She waited for him to scoff at her words. Instead, there was only silence.

Grace shifted uncomfortably under his gaze. He had full view of her where she could only see one shoulder. Granted, she could make out the detail of corded muscle, but it still wasn't enough. She couldn't see his face or read his expressions.

"Nay. You need to leave."

She opened her mouth in shock. "Leave? Have you looked outside? I can't leave in this!"

She wouldn't. It was raining, and where there was rain, there were thunder and lightning. Not happening. She shook her head to prove her point, even if he didn't know her inner monologue.

"Sure you can. Pick your way slowly down the mountain. You can no' remain here."

Grace snorted in disbelief. "I thought Scottish men were chivalrous. Apparently, I was misinformed. I'm not about to go out there and fall to my death just because you're being stubborn."

Long, strong fingers wrapped around her arms and lifted her to her tiptoes. She could feel the power in those hands, could sense the barely leashed animal inside him.

Yet, his hold was strangely gentle.

"You need to leave," he stated. "Now."

She glanced outside and saw that the rain had stopped. How...odd. If she didn't know better, she'd think he turned it off just by wishing it so. Which was ludicrous. No one could do that.

"Fine. I'll leave. You might've just sealed my fate as far as my career goes, but I'll leave your mountain."

Did she hear him snigger? That only infuriated Grace all the more. She grabbed her laptop and stalked to the entrance. He wasn't even going to let the sun dry some of the water on the mountain. But she'd be damned if she fell and gave him something else to laugh at.

Grace was at the entrance to the cave. She took one step out when she looked down the mountain and spotted four men running toward her.

Good. Maybe they would be more gallant and at least help her to her car. She lifted her hand to wave to them. Her arm didn't rise farther than her face when she was hastily jerked back into the cave and pressed against a stone wall...and a solid wall of muscle.

Her mouth went dry as her free hand landed on his stomach.

She could feel every breath he took, every ripple of his hard muscle.

"Doona move," he whispered urgently.

First, he wanted her to leave. Now he wanted her to stay. What was going on? Not that she could think straight with his body against hers.

She lifted her gaze and felt her breath catch. His face was turned toward the opening as he stared with a severe look in his eyes.

His face seemed to have been cut from the very granite at her back. The hard planes and angles would be too harsh on some men. But not him. He was breathtakingly striking, astonishingly magnificent.

Her hand flattened on his abdomen to feel more of him while she wished she wasn't holding her laptop so her other hand could be touching him as well.

Then his head slowly turned to look down at her. She could scarcely believe the light-goldish hue of his eyes. They reminded her of the champagne she had drunk the night before.

His hair was as black as midnight and hung to the middle of his back. His forehead was high, his nose straight. He had thick black brows that slashed over his intense eyes. His lips, wide and full, turned up slightly at one corner.

His eyes met hers, as if daring her to look at him. Grace let her hand lower to his hip, and she had another shock as she discovered him naked.

Now those lips of his turned up in a full smile. He liked that he had surprised her.

And she kinda liked it to. After all, when was the last time that had happened?

"I..." She cleared her throat and tried again. "I thought you wanted me to leave."

His smile vanished in an instant. "That time is gone."

Something in his words sent up a warning in her brain. "What's that mean?"

"It means you'll get to write your book."

He took a step back from her the same time a bolt of lightning zigzagged across the sky and thunder rumbled. A second later, the skies opened up again.

Chapter Three

Arian wasn't certain whether to believe the mortal. She could very well be with the Dark Fae rapidly approaching his cave.

With a wave of his hand, Arian cloaked the entrance with more dragon magic. No one was supposed to be able to find the cave except another King. Still, the fact the Dark knew which side of the mountain was his cave was enough to cause him alarm.

"I really don't like being ordered about," the female said in a sassy tone as she looked worriedly to the entrance. She tried to move away, but he wouldn't let her.

He had always thought the American drawl was a bit too rough of all the accents Con had shown him through his dragon sleep. But rolling off her tongue, Arian found he quite liked it. He heard another accent as well, though he couldn't pinpoint it.

"You wanted to stay here, did you no'?" he asked as he took another step away from her.

"I'm getting whiplash you change your mind so quickly," she said, her gaze pinning him. Then a crack of thunder filled the silence, causing her to visibly cringe. "Those men could've helped me. I'd be off your mountain and out of your hair."

He glanced out the cave. "As tempting as that offer sounds, you're going to remain."

"Yeah. That sounds good."

"Because I doona trust you." It took him a moment to realize she hadn't asked why as he expected. Arian frowned when he saw she had her arms wrapped around herself while she inched farther away from the opening.

The war the Dragon Kings were in meant that everyone was a potential enemy. The only way they were going to come out of this as secret as before was if every Dragon King assumed one and all was an enemy until they proved otherwise.

And the American had a lot to prove.

"Yep," she said with a nod. "Perfectly understandable. Trust is...trust is... Oh, hell. Nevermind," she mumbled.

Arian glanced at the rain when lightning struck, and she hastily turned away. The way she was breathing shallowly and a fine sheen of sweat covered her were classic symptoms of someone who was terrified.

She looked like at any moment she was going to fall apart, and that's one thing Arian didn't want. A crying female was...well, they were the worst kind of hell for a man—or dragon—to endure. If he could bypass her tears, then he'd consider it a win.

"Perhaps you should leave. It's just a wee bit of rain."

Her navy eyes jerked to him, widening just enough in her outrage. "Not happening."

She pushed away from the wall, her gaze raking down his body as she walked past him, her fear seemingly forgotten in her anger. That scathing look roused him, stirred him.

His balls tightened and his blood heated. Six centuries was a long time to go without relieving his body, and he was feeling the effects of that abstinence profoundly.

The mortal's body was more than adequate. He had the pleasure of seeing—and feeling—more of her. In fact, he found her curves rather enticing. Even the fire in her eyes did something to him.

Arian knew lust well. Aye, he lusted for her greatly. Yet there was something else he couldn't name. Was it because he had watched her fingers punch the keys on her laptop and the words form? Was it because she was scared of him and still had the gumption to stand up to him?

Or was it something else?

Her gaze on him, however, sent all the blood straight to his cock. Arian turned to keep that part of himself in shadow. He didn't want her to know how much a look from her could do to him.

He covertly watched as she returned to her spot near the boulder that stood unmovable about ten feet from the water. She opened the laptop, the light highlighting her face. She blinked quickly before she sat her fingers on the keys. A heartbeat later, she was writing again.

Arian toned down the thunder and lightning. Every Dragon King had a special power, and his was controlling the weather. When he saw her shoulders begin to relax once more, Arian had confirmation that it was storms Grace was frightened of.

While she had been working the first time, he had come up behind the boulder and read over her shoulder. She was really quite good, and he wanted to know how the story progressed. It wasn't just her way with words, but it was how she described things that made Arian feel as if he were in the middle of the story.

In ancient mortal times, she would've been revered for her gifts. And yet, she appeared as if she carried the weight of the world on her shoulders. Then he remembered how she made a comment about needing to finish the book.

"You're not going to stand there and watch me, are you?" she asked with a sigh.

Arian turned his back to her and moved closer to the entrance. The Dark continued to search the mountain for the entrance. How long could he hold them off? The mortal wasn't a Druid, but that didn't mean she wasn't a decoy of some kind.

"It's Grace, by the way."

He frowned and turned his head to the side. "Excuse me?"

"My name. I knew you were about to ask, so I saved you the trouble."

He hid his smile because he liked her sass. Grace. Aye, the name suited her.

"And yours?"

He looked at her over his shoulder. "Arian."

"Arian," she said, letting it roll off her tongue slowly.

His balls tightened again. Damn but she was a distraction he didn't want. Arian needed to get to Dreagan Manor with the other Kings, but with the Dark having arrived, he was glad he remained.

There was a push on his mind. Arian opened the mental link between Dragon Kings and heard Con's voice ask, *"Our barrier was breached near you twice."*

"Aye. It was a mortal woman the first time."

"Did you send her on her way?"

"Was about to when four Dark arrived," Arian explained.

Con let out a string of curses. *"Is the female with them?"*

"I'm no' sure. Yet."

"I'm sending Tristan and Banan to lead the Dark away from you."

Arian looked at the mortal. *"And I'll figure out what the human really wants."*

"Doona take too long. You're needed here," Con stated before he severed the link.

Grace was staring at him again. "Do you always walk around naked?"

"Does it bother you, lass?" Arian asked with a grin.

"Of course not. I'm not a prude."

He turned away so she wouldn't see his smile. Arian had the overwhelming urge to goad her, and he didn't hold back. "Do you no' like what you see?"

"I...yes. You have a nice body."

"Nice," Arian said with a shrug. He glanced at her. "Nice isna that good."

She looked down at the laptop and pressed her lips together. "Fine. I'll admit it's more than nice. It's...very nice. Gorgeous even."

Was she blushing? Arian couldn't look away. She said the words, but she wouldn't meet his gaze. How...enchanting.

Grace shrugged and punched a few keys on her laptop. "You asked."

"So I did."

She peeked up at him before she focused on the screen. Its white light highlighted her face as she began typing. He made himself turn away before he continued their banter—which he was enjoying entirely too much.

Arian's gaze was focused outside. The Dark were still there, and he couldn't help but wonder why Grace hadn't asked about them again. Could it be that she wasn't with them? It was a slim chance. Most likely she didn't mention them again because she was working with them.

And Arian didn't like that thought at all. He enjoyed Grace. Her accent, her feisty nature, her beauty, and her intellect intrigued him. Not to mention her ability to craft a story. In all his years—and they were endless—he hadn't met anyone like her.

Arian surreptitiously looked at her. She seemed absorbed in her work. Her brow was furrowed slightly one moment, and a second before she was smiling at whatever she was typing. How he wanted to know what amused her.

It was the sound of dragon wings that pulled his attention from her. Tristan and Banan arrived quietly, dropping from the sky with wings tucked as they zeroed in on the Dark Fae.

Banan's deep blue claws grabbed a Dark before they were even seen. Tristan opened his amber-colored wings and circled around the group of Dark.

Arian craved to be out there with them. He actually had to stop himself from shifting and joining in the fight, the instinct was so great. But he wasn't about to leave Grace.

Not until he learned if she had wandered into his mountain on accident or not.

If she was innocent, then she didn't need to see the battle taking place on the side of his mountain.

Arian fisted his hands at his sides as he struggled not to join the fight. He needed to be there, wiping the Dark from his mountain instead of standing there watching.

The Dark threw bubbles of magic at Tristan and Banan. Many they were able to dodge, but a few magic balls found their mark.

Arian knew how painful Dark magic could be. He clenched his jaw and struggled to remain in his cave as Tristan and Banan led the Dark away.

Only when the Dark were out of sight did Arian turn back to Grace. A small frown furrowed her brow as she stared at the computer screen. Her fingers rested on the keyboard, but she was no longer typing.

She closed her eyes and took a deep breath before slowly releasing it. When her lids opened, she typed a few words and then halted once more.

"What is it?" he asked, curious.

She slammed the laptop closed and dropped her head back against the rock. "I don't know."

"I hear another accent in your words besides American. What is it?"

Her head rolled to the side to look at him. "French. My mother is from Paris."

"You doona sound like someone who has lived their life in Paris."

"Because I didn't." She set the laptop beside her and pulled her knees up to her chest. "My father raised me after my mom ran off with a musician. She lived in London for a few years until that relationship ended. Then she returned to Paris."

"She left you behind?" Arian could scarcely imagine such a scenario.

Grace gave a half-snort, half-laugh. "She did. She was in love and didn't want a five-year-old getting in the way."

"I doona ken such a thing."

She rested her chin on her knees. "Me either, but she told me that some people just weren't cut out to be parents. She was one of them. It's a poor excuse, I know."

"Aye. It is."

Grace's deep blue eyes focused on him. "I've spent the last three years living in Paris. My father wanted me to see the world."

"Yet, you remained in Paris instead of returning to him."

"He died. It was the last thing he made me promise. To see the world." She smiled, as if recalling the memory. "We'd been planning the trip for some time, so all the destinations were chosen and everything paid for. The only difference was that I traveled it alone."

Arian moved closer to her. "I'm sorry."

She shrugged and blinked rapidly. "It's all right. Our plan was always to end in Paris so I could spend some time with my mother.

I'd already arranged to spend a month in Paris, and after that, I found I liked it."

"So you remained. Did you see your mother?"

Grace chuckled softly. "A bit. She really isn't cut out for parenting. She doesn't have a maternal bone in her body. She had a new man, so I urged her to go with him."

"That was nice."

"Not at all," Grace replied with a laugh. "It was selfish. I didn't want her around either at that point."

Arian found himself smiling. "Who are you, Grace? What are you doing in my mountain?"

She let out a deep breath. "I'm Grace Clark from Los Angeles, California. I'm a writer...er...novelist who lives in Paris."

"What do you write, Grace Clark?"

"Romance novels."

He raised a brow, intrigued. "Interesting."

"It would be if I could get the book written. I turned in the first book of the three-book contract, but I'm beyond late with this second book. If I don't turn it in three weeks from now, they're canceling the rest of my contract."

Arian wasn't sure what all of that meant, but it didn't sound good. "And being here does what?"

"Puts my groove back on."

He might know current events thanks to Con and Darius, but there was obviously still quite a bit Arian needed to catch up on, because he had no idea what she meant.

Grace laughed. "I had writer's block. For some reason, being on this mountain I've written over sixty pages today alone. I've never written that many pages in one sitting. If I can keep this up, I'll meet my deadline."

"It sounds to me, lass, as if there are underlying issues to this writer's block you speak of."

Her eyes fell to the ground. "I'll face that when I get this book turned in. Until then, I must focus." Her gaze returned to him. "So does that mean you'll allow me to stay and write?"

With the Dark gone, there was no reason to keep Grace in the mountain. Arian was relatively certain she wasn't a spy, but then again, she could be a really good mole and actress.

This was going to require him to spend more time with Grace Clark from Los Angeles, California and Paris, France.

"For a wee bit."

Grace's smile was wide as she bestowed it on him. "You're amazing. Thank you so much. This is going to save my ass big time. As soon as it quits raining, I'll leave for the night and return in the morning."

Arian nodded as she spoke, because there was no way he was allowing her to leave. He would make sure the rain continued to keep her trapped.

The only problem was that he was going to have to think about food for her. And light. Because night was approaching quickly.

Arian looked down at himself. And perhaps some clothes as well.

Chapter Four

Grace couldn't write knowing that Arian was watching her. He made her uncomfortable. Not in an "oh my God, he's going to kill me" vibe, but an "I can't look away from that face and body" thing. She would have to be blind not to see how gorgeous he was, even in the dim light of the cave.

A light that was fast fading.

She was thankful that the lightning and thunder had stopped. It hadn't been until she was deep in the story that she realized she had been so caught up in Arian's change of mind for a third time that she had forgotten the storm.

That was a first, to be sure.

Grace checked her battery on the laptop. Fortunately, she had fully charged it the night before. It would last her a few more hours yet, but then what?

"Is something wrong?" Arian asked.

She closed her eyes at the sound of his brogue. How she used to roll her eyes at women who said a man's accent could make them climax. Well, now she knew how true that statement was.

"Grace?"

She bit back a moan. He had to stop saying her name. By all that was holy, didn't he know what it did to her? It was too much. That voice, that accent, *and* her name?

"Are you in pain?"

Her eyes snapped open when she found him squatting in front of her. It was unfortunate that her laptop hid the lower part of him.

She felt her cheeks heat as she pictured him naked in her head. "No. No, I'm fine," she hastily said.

"You didna answer me, lass."

She tried to swallow, but all the moisture in her body seemed to be centered between her legs. "I was thinking."

"Ahh," he said with a nod. "About your book?"

Grace grasped the out he gave her. "That's right. About my book."

She really needed to pull it together. There was no telling how long she would be in the cave with him. Her stomach chose that moment to growl loudly.

His sexy smile did her in. "I was about to ask if you were ready to eat."

"Eat? As in you have food?" she asked hopefully.

He chuckled and stood. That's when she saw he now wore a pair of jeans. Grace saw him walk off, wondering where his shirt and shoes were. Not that she minded him shirtless.

"Of course I have food."

"Of course," she mumbled grumpily to herself as she stood. "Why didn't I think to ask for it earlier."

When she followed him, she found him staring at her. The light from outside was fading, so she was only able to make out his raised brow.

"Sorry," she said with a wince. "I tend to get obnoxious when I'm hungry."

"Then I'll make sure you have plenty of food."

There was a click and light flooded the area from an electric lantern set by the water. Grace looked around in awe before turning back to Arian. She stared into his champagne eyes and forgot to breath. It was wrong for someone to be so handsome that he made all thought vanish.

"Choose whatever you'd like," Arian said.

Grace pulled her gaze from him and looked down where there was a basket of food perched on a boulder that came almost to her waist. And good food like roasted chicken, several kinds of cheese, bread, water, and even a bottle of wine.

She glanced up at him and asked, "This looks like a picnic basket. I hope I didn't interrupt anything with you and your woman."

"I doona have a woman. I bring food with me when I doona know how long I'll be staying."

The words sounded right, but there was just something that didn't sit well with her. Grace studied him, wondering if she could believe him. It wasn't like she had much choice. She was stuck in a cave with him while the next great flood was happening outside.

And he had food.

Grace grabbed a chicken wing, a piece of bread, and water. She stood beside the basket and began to eat, snagging a piece of cheese every few bites.

She wasn't the only one. Arian was also eating as he stood on the other side of the basket. She could feel his gaze on her, but Grace didn't care. She was starving.

"When was the last time you ate, lass?"

Grace took a long drink of water before she said, "This morning when I reached the B&B where I'm staying."

"You should've brought food with you."

"I should've. Then again, I didn't realize the storm of the century was going to happen today and that I'd get stuck in a cave."

He smiled and took a bite of chicken. "Why did you choose this mountain?"

"It was by chance."

"Tell me," he urged.

Grace finished chewing. "Coming to Scotland was my last-ditch effort to get the story written. I've tried everything conceivable that other authors have attempted to break past their writer's block. Nothing worked."

"So you came here."

"I'd been two years earlier and loved it. I thought perhaps if I returned that it might get me writing. I headed out this morning looking for a place that was quiet and beautiful."

Arian's head cocked to the side, allowing several thick strands of black hair to fall over his shoulder. "There are no roads leading here."

"I know." Grace laughed and shook her head at her foolishness. "I decided to find my perfect place I needed to get off the beaten path, so to speak. I took the first road I found. Then I turned off that onto a narrower one. Again and again I did that until I came to a dirt road. I traveled that for a long while, veering different directions at times until I ended up here. To be honest, I'm hoping I can find my way back."

"You will."

He said it with such authority that Grace believed him. She finished off her chicken wing and found a second.

"What brought you to this area of Scotland?" he asked.

Grace was beginning to feel like he was questioning her for something. The queries were worded innocently enough, but they all focused on one thing—this mountain.

"I was here before and liked it," she replied.

He nodded, though his gaze didn't leave her. "A simple enough explanation."

"But you don't believe me? Is that it?"

Arian shrugged and reached for the wine. She watched the play of his muscles as he opened the bottle and held up a glass, silently asking her if she wanted some.

Grace gave a shake of her head. "Look, I don't like games of any sort. Well, that's not true. I love backgammon, but my point is that if you want to ask me something, then just ask it. Stop beating around the bush."

"I want to know why you're on my mountain," he said then took a drink of the red wine.

She popped the last bite of cheese and bread in her mouth and chewed while she observed him. Arian was much too confident. He had been naked earlier, but somehow he managed to find a pair of jeans.

Why hadn't he worn them earlier? And why hadn't it bothered her more that he was naked? She should've been screaming, or at the very least wondering about rape. But she had never thought that about him.

He frightened her, yes. But it was with a feeling that he was protecting something, and as long as it remained protected, he wouldn't unleash his anger.

Grace finished her water and wiped her mouth with the back of her hand. She screwed the cap back on the now empty bottle and placed it inside the basket. "I told you why I'm here. I have no more explanation than that."

"I'm afraid that isna enough."

Wasn't enough? Enough for what? Grace frowned and looked toward the cave entrance. Dusk had fallen. She could just make out the shapes of the trees on the opposite mountain. "Where are the men from earlier?"

"Gone."

She slid her gaze back to him. "Gone where?"

"I'm no' sure. They were no' good men. They would've hurt you."

Grace gave a bark of laughter. "You expect me to take your word about that when you refuse to believe anything I say? Oh, that's rich."

"I knew those men. They were no' good men," he repeated.

"And you are?"

He glanced away. "I didna say that. Though I am better than they are."

"What did those men want?"

"Something in these mountains."

Grace immediately had an idea for her next book. "Really? Like what?" she asked excitedly.

It was the uncertain look on Arian's face that made her realize she had been a bit overzealous.

So Grace tried again. "It gave me an idea for a book is all. Your theories for what those men were looking for could help me decide what I have in my book."

"I doona know what they're looking for," Arian said. "They're trespassers."

"This is your land?"

He lifted one shoulder as an answer.

Grace pinned him with a look. "You expect me to answer your questions. It's only fair that you answer mine."

"That's no' how it works, lass. You're on my land. Uninvited, I might add."

"So what? I'm your prisoner?" she asked in shocked anger.

Arian pointed outside to the rain that still fell. "I'm no' keeping you here. The weather is."

"It'd be just my luck that you control the damn weather."

When he didn't so much as bat an eye, Grace began to wonder if he was. Then she laughed at herself. Being back in the Highlands where the people were superstitious seemed to have rubbed off on her as well.

She laughed. "Thanks for the food. I feel much better."

"Of course."

She was still chuckling at herself when she went back to the boulder where she had been writing. Her characters were nestled in a nice hotel in Inverness while it rained. Real life always fell into her stories, and with the constant rain, of course it was part of her plot.

It also allowed lots of time for her hero and heroine to get to spend time together—in and out of bed.

Grace immediately thought of Arian kissing her. Her stomach flipped wildly.

No, she told herself. She wouldn't think of him that way. He was as gorgeous as sin and had a voice as seductive as silk, but it wouldn't do her any good to pine for a man like him.

They had been together for a few hours. If he found her attractive, he would've said something. And Grace had dealt with enough men to know she wasn't going to put herself out there and be rejected. She had a book to write.

At that thought, she cleared her throat and sat before opening her laptop.

After another hour of writing, the words on the screen began to blur. She was mentally tapped out. A quick save of her document, and she turned off the laptop.

Grace heard the crackle before she saw the fire. She found the fire blazing about five feet from the water near where they had eaten.

She saw no sign of Arian, but that didn't worry her. There was only so far he could go in a cave. As she walked to the fire, she saw several tunnels beyond the water that she hadn't spotted earlier because the light from her phone hadn't penetrated the darkness.

But with the fire and the two electronic lanterns set up, she was able to get a good view of the cave. She sat next to the fire and closed her eyes. It felt wonderful to feel the heat penetrating her clothes.

She hadn't realized how cold she had been until she felt the warmth. Now she wished she had a thick blanket and a mug of coffee. And a comfortable chair.

Grace found herself drifting to sleep. So she curled up on her side with her arm beneath her head. Her eyes hurt from staring at the computer screen for so long, and her brain was complete mush after so many pages.

She drifted in thought as she listened to the sounds around her. The splash of rain onto the rock at the entrance, and the stillness within the cave.

At one point, she thought she heard the lap of water near her, but she was too exhausted to open her eyes. She tried to tell herself to remain awake until Arian returned.

Her trusting nature had gotten her into trouble on many occasions, and yet she still freely gave her trust. With her active imagination, she thought of all the things Arian could do to hurt her.

Then she realized, if he had wanted to harm her, he could've done it hours ago.

Arian. Who was he? Why had he been naked? And what was so important about his mountain?

Grace was going to find out. Right after she woke up.

Chapter Five

Arian emerged from the tunnel to find Grace on her side asleep. He had been watching her. It's all he seemed to do since she walked into his cave.

He found it fascinating how she could stare at the computer screen while her fingers flew over the keys as if they had a life of their own. And somehow, a story came from all of it.

Arian had never been any kind of storyteller. It was amazing to him that people could craft such tales.

It also didn't help that he wanted to believe she just stumbled upon his mountain. Earlier, while she worked, Arian had contacted Ryder, a Dragon King with a craving for jelly-filled donuts and a knack for computers.

Ryder confirmed who Grace was as well as her story. Still, that didn't mean she wasn't working for the Dark or Ulrik. Nor did it mean that she was.

Arian walked past her to the entrance and looked out. With a mere thought, he halted the rain. Grace had no idea the rain was situated atop them. Nor did she know how right she was that he could control the weather.

He didn't like to use his powers that way, but there were

instances where it was needed. And today had been one of them.

Had he left his cave the day before as Darius urged, Arian wouldn't have been there when Grace arrived. He would've arrived soon after, but he doubted it would have been in time to stop the Dark from finding her or his cave.

Tristan and Banan had killed the Dark hours ago, but it still bothered Arian that they had gotten onto Dreagan. Even fortifying the magic on the perimeter of sixty thousand acres wasn't going to be enough.

The Dark were determined enough to push through the invisible barrier despite great pain to themselves. All because of some weapon the Kings had.

A weapon Con hadn't bothered to tell anyone about.

Arian suspected he was one of the few Kings who didn't mind that Con kept such a secret. It would've been nice to know, but the fact Con hadn't breathed a word of it told Arian it was for a reason. And not just because this weapon could be used to destroy the Kings.

There was something else at play here. Something that no one had thought of. Arian knew it was pointless to ask Con. The King of Kings wouldn't divulge anything he didn't want others to know.

As tight-lipped as he was in regards to the weapon, Con wouldn't be telling anyone anything. Speaking of secrets, Kellan knew a great many as Keeper of the History. He had yet to tell a single one.

Arian stepped out of his mountain and lifted his face to the sky. It had been so long since he had seen the moon. As he looked, he spotted dragons flying among the clouds.

He glanced over his shoulder at Grace, and without another thought, hastily removed his jeans. He leapt into the air, shifting as he did.

His giant turquoise wings stretched outward, catching the air and taking him higher. The beat of dragon wings was all around him. He soared higher into the clouds to his brethren, twisting and turning as he remembered what it was to be a dragon again.

The more he flew, the more he missed his dragons. It was a hollow ache in his chest as he recalled the time before humans. Everything changed with the mortals' arrival. That was the one constant throughout time, and yet he never thought he would see the day that dragons weren't in the sky.

Arian usually didn't fly so close to his mountain for fear of mortals seeing him since he was so near to the Dreagan border. But Grace was inside sleeping. He didn't want to be too far away. Not that anything was going to happen, but he wanted to be prepared.

He gave a nod to Nikolai and Dmitri before he dropped his right wing and circled back toward his mountain. The others would remain until dawn, which was only a few hours away. Arian wanted to stay with them. And he would just as soon as Grace Clark was on her way home.

While flying, Arian had decided to let Grace go. Even if she was working for Ulrik or the Dark, she learned nothing from him. Nor would she. And the sooner she was gone the better.

One of the first things he would do was make damn sure she could never find her way back to the mountain again. Her or anyone, for that matter.

The first ray of sunshine crested the peaks. Arian saw his mountain and was getting ready to shift back into human form when he was alerted that Dark had crossed the border once more.

He flew faster when he spotted them on his mountain for a second time. How were they continuing to get in? He'd find that out later. Right now, his concern was getting rid of them.

Arian opened his mental link and told the other Kings there were two Dark that he was taking care of. If any of the other Kings came, it would likely wake Grace. Arian didn't want her seeing anything.

He tucked his wings and dove. Then he stretched out his wings and opened his talons. He managed to grab one of the Dark, but not the other.

Arian crushed the Dark with his talons and tossed him in the air where he let loose a blast of dragon fire. Ash was all that was left of the Fae.

A volley of Dark magic hit Arian. He turned and flew back to his mountain. The Dark was close to the entrance. Too close, actually.

Did they know that there were tunnels deep below the mountains connecting some of them? Was that why they were resolute to get into his mountain?

Arian landed on the side of the mountain with his wings spread as he stared down at the Dark. He took a deep breath, ready to release another round of fire when he spotted something out of the corner of his eye.

It was Grace.

* * * *

Grace knew her knees were going to give out at any moment. She didn't recall why she had woken, only that she had. With the rain no longer falling, she wanted to see how wet it was. Only she saw two men climbing the mountain.

The next thing she knew, a large form dropped from the sky, only to go back up again the next moment. She gaped in horror when she saw the turquoise dragon burn one of the men.

Before that truly registered in her mind, things got stranger. The remaining man threw what looked like a large bubble at the dragon.

"What the hell," she murmured.

Was she really seeing a dragon? A massive beast that was as beautiful to behold as it was terrifying.

"Dragons aren't real. And yet, there's one. Right there. Right in front of me."

More bubbles hit the dragon. It must've hurt because the dragon spun around and flew back to the man.

Only to land on the side of the mountain.

Grace gawked at the immense width and breadth of the dragon's turquoise wings as he spread them out. The scales fairly gleamed in the morning sun, shining brilliantly like metal.

The dragon had two short brow horns and another short horn atop its nose. The head and body were so huge she could barely grasp it, and the tail extended far behind the dragon, twitching as if waiting to be used as a weapon.

Suddenly, the dragon's black eyes turned to her. She froze in fear, unable to move. The last thing she wanted was to bring the dragon's attention to her. She didn't want to get eaten.

What was that old expression? Don't anger a dragon because

you are crunchy.

Well, she didn't want to anger this dragon. She just wanted to go back to the B&B, get some sleep, and then check herself into a mental institution because she was obviously losing her mind if she was seeing dragons.

The dragon's head snapped back to the man, a low rumble coming from its chest. Grace told herself to go back inside the cave and find Arian, but she still couldn't move.

Whether it was from fear or curiosity, she wasn't sure.

But she remained to see what would happen. And as the man began to throw more bubbles at the dragon, she was glad she did.

The dragon was a large target. Even when the dragon knocked the man sideways with its wing, he got back on his feet. As the sun rose higher, Grace got a better look at the man. His short black hair was liberally laced with thick, silver strands.

Everything was odd about the entire scene, from the man to the dragon. It had to be a dream. There was no other explanation for such things.

The man blasted the dragon with several bubbles in a row, and to her shock, Grace watched the dragon disappear in a blink. And in its place was none other than Arian.

He pushed up on his hands and glared at the man. "You're going to die here."

"Not before I find what I'm looking for," replied the man in an Irish accent.

Grace rubbed her eyes. When she opened them and Arian still stood there as naked as she had found him the day before, she wasn't sure what to do.

Then it didn't matter as he and the other man began to attack each other. The fight was vicious in both sight and sound. Arian hit the man hard while more bubbles barreled into Arian.

Then Arian fell to one knee with burns covering his body where the bubbles hit him. Grace covered her mouth with her hand. The shock of seeing him so wounded turned her stomach, but it also made her angry. Who was the man to attack Arian so?

The wounds looked extremely painful. By the way Arian grimaced, they were.

She silently urged him to get up and keep fighting. The fact he was the dragon was something she would face later. She instinctively knew that whoever Arian was fighting wasn't a good person.

The stranger threw another bubble at Arian that caused him to growl in fury. Grace took a step back when she saw the wrath on Arian's face.

He got to his feet and attacked the man again while Grace watched. They were locked together with more bubbles hitting Arian at very close range.

Grace couldn't tell who was winning as the two of them fell together and rolled. For long moments she waited to hear or see something. When nothing happened, Grace walked out of the cave and looked down to find them.

She spotted the black and silver haired man lying face down, unmoving. Arian was on his side with his back to her. And he wasn't moving either.

"Arian," she whispered, worried for him.

Grace briefly thought of getting her laptop and running far away. There was something strange going on at this mountain, and it would be better if she wasn't involved.

But she couldn't leave Arian. He was hurt, and she didn't like how much that upset her. With a sigh, she made her way down to him.

When she reached him, Grace knelt beside him and looked over his body. There were burns everywhere. She bit her lip and gently turned him onto his back. There was no ignoring the fact he was completely naked. His entire torso was littered with wounds. Yet he was still breathing.

She blew out a relieved breath and found herself shaking with a mixture of happiness and concern. Now, she had to get him up and back inside the cave. Since he was so much taller than her, not to mention he outweighed her with all those muscles, she wasn't sure how she was going to accomplish that feat.

Grace glanced at the other guy and picked up a rock to bash him on the head. She got to her feet and cautiously walked to him.

She pushed him with her foot, but he didn't move. Grace gave him a harder push, turning him onto his back. She dropped the rock as she gagged at seeing a gaping wound in his chest where his heart had been.

Whoever the man was, he wasn't going to be bothering Arian anymore.

Grace hurried back to Arian. His eyelids cracked open as she leaned over him. Grace gave him a nod. "We're going to get you back in the cave."

"Scared," he murmured brokenly.

At first Grace thought he was saying he was afraid. Then she realized he was speaking of her. There he was on the side of a mountain injured terribly, and he was worried about her.

Grace could only stare at him, wondering if men like him really existed. Most people would be concerned about themselves, but not Arian. His thought was of her.

Then it hit her. She had seen him as a dragon. Was she afraid? Yes, in many ways. But how could she be scared now as Arian lay wounded?

She licked her lips and met his gaze. "Yes. But my father didn't raise me to leave someone who is hurt. So, I'm going to get you back into that mountain. Then I'm leaving."

The last part had been more for herself than him. She really should leave, but how could she after all she just witnessed? Remaining meant her life was in danger, as was obvious by the battle she had seen.

Then there were Arian's wounds. Someone would need to help him. It was the least she could do since he let her stay and write in his mountain.

Dragons.

Yep, the man she was looking down at was a dragon. Why wasn't she more scared? Most people would've been running for their lives. But there was something about Arian that calmed her. She trusted him.

Arian gave a slight nod in response to her words.

Grace winced as she looked down at him. "This is going to hurt."

At that, Arian rolled back to his side slowly and began to sit up. She was there to lend a hand and keep him steady. He was tall and muscular, and Grace wasn't sure how she was going to get him on his feet, much less up the slope to the cave. But she was going to try.

Once he was on his feet, he only put a small fraction of his weight on her. Grace draped his arm over her shoulder and wrapped an arm around him.

The climb up to the cave was as strenuous as she imagined it would be. Both of them were soon covered in sweat. Grace tried to take more of his weight to help him.

It seemed to take an eternity to reach the entrance. Arian breathed a sigh when they stepped inside the cave.

"Water," he said, motioning with his other hand to the body of water.

Grace walked him to the fire and helped him down. He stretched out on his right side with his eyes closed and didn't utter another word.

She hurried to get a bottle of water from the basket and brought it to him. While she held it to his lips, Arian drank the entire bottle, never opening his eyes.

Grace put the cap on the bottle and sat on her haunches as Arian appeared to slip into unconsciousness. Her mind urged her to leave, but she hesitated. What if there were more of those black and silver haired men about?

She would rather take her chances here with Arian than encounter one of those men. Then she also wanted to see if Arian would speak of what had transpired.

Besides, if she saw something she wasn't supposed to, running would do her no good. Arian and any others like him would find her soon enough. So Grace remained.

She got another bottle of water from the basket and one of the napkins. After she soaked the cloth napkin, she began to clean Arian's wounds.

Her eyes drifted freely over his magnificent body, from his wide shoulders, contoured stomach muscles, and trim waist. Then lower to his narrow hips and his flaccid cock.

She bit her lip at seeing so much of him when he was unconscious, but with a body like his, it should be showed off.

"Oh my," she whispered as she drew in a stuttering breath.

There wasn't a part on Arian that wasn't absolute perfection. And she wanted to touch every inch of him.

Chapter Six

Grace was wondering how to get Arian out of the mountain and to a hospital when she noticed his wounds didn't look quite as bad as before.

As she watched, she saw his injuries begin to heal. The burns disappeared and his skin knitted back together without a trace of any damage.

"Oh, shit," she murmured.

"Doona be afraid," Arian said.

Her gaze jerked to his face where his champagne eyes were open and watching her. "Yeah, a bit late for that."

"I didna mean for you to see any of that. I thought you'd still be asleep."

Grace shrugged and fiddled with the now useless napkin. "But I did witness it."

"Aye. You did." Arian pushed himself up into a sitting position.

She pointed to his now healed wounds. "What was that out there?"

He eyed her for several long, silent moments. Then he said, "Magic."

"Magic," she repeated. Well, she did see a dragon. Would it be too far of a stretch to accept magic as a weapon?

"You didna leave. Why?" Arian asked.

Grace looked at his chest again as she imagined him as a dragon. A huge dragon with the most beautiful turquoise scales that reminded her of the waters off the Bahamas.

The fear she had first felt was melting away. Now, it was desire—hot and insistent—that filled her. "I told you. I couldn't leave you out there wounded. Although, if I'd known you could heal, then I would've."

When she looked up at his face, Arian was grinning. As if her words amused him. He was supposed to be hurt by her words, or at the very least annoyed. Not amused.

She raised a brow. "You find that funny?"

"I like that you speak your mind."

"I probably shouldn't do that," she said as she got to her feet and moved away from him. "You might get angry and turn back into a dragon."

His smile vanished in an instant. He rose to his feet in one fluid motion, with his long black hair falling about his shoulders and his champagne eyes focused on her. "I doona harm the innocent, Grace. That man out there," he said, pointing through the entrance, "wasna a human. He was a Dark Fae, and he was looking for this cave."

Grace held up her hand to stop him. "Wait. Just...wait. I'm sorry, but I don't think I can handle all of this. It's too bizarre. And why are you telling me? Shouldn't you be demanding that I keep my mouth shut at what I've seen?"

"Would anyone believe you?"

She gawked at him, wondering why she hadn't thought of that possibility herself. "I don't believe what I saw."

"Aye, you do."

So she did. He didn't need to rub it in. Couldn't he see she was trying to pull herself together? Grace tossed the napkin in the basket and shrugged. "So what if I do?"

"You want to know more."

Damn. Was she an open book for him to read? This was not going her way at all, especially since she couldn't figure out what he was thinking no matter how hard she tried.

"So you'll tell me all I want to know and let me leave?"

"Aye."

At this, Grace laughed. "That's not how this works."

"And you've been in this situation before?" he asked with a quirked brow.

Grace opened her mouth, then promptly shut it. After a moment, she said, "Of course not. I'm merely going off what I've read normally happens."

"And that would be what, lass?"

"You threaten to kill me if I tell anyone."

Arian smiled, and it was devastating. Like a sucker punch right in her gut. Grace couldn't look away from his mouth and the sexy way his lips tilted.

"If it would make you feel better, then I could threaten you," he said with a half-smile that was by far too seductive.

She knew he was making fun of her, but Grace couldn't get upset. She sounded like a lunatic, which was insane since she wasn't the one who had been in the form of a dragon recently.

"You may no' believe it, lass, but you're safe with me."

Grace scratched her nose. "With a dragon?"

"Aye."

"You were a dragon," she said. "A huge dragon with wings and fire and everything."

He gave a nod. "I ken exactly what I am, lass. Have I hurt you in any way?"

"You know you haven't."

"And I willna. Unless you're here to harm us."

Grace couldn't stop the bubble of laughter that welled up. It escaped her lips. She looked at Arian, wondering about his sanity now. "You're a *dragon*. How could I possibly hurt you?"

"We have enemies. The Dark Fae are just one set. They want to out us to the world so that our existence would no longer be hidden from humans."

She wrapped her arms around her middle. "So there are more of you?"

"Aye."

"Many?"

"Enough."

"Oh." Shit. Grace lowered her gaze. There were dragons in

Scotland.

And she had somehow walked into a cave where one had been. What were the odds that would happen?

He pivoted, causing her eyes to return to him. That's when she caught sight of the dragon tattoo on his left leg. It was done in an amazing black and red ink that she'd never seen before.

The tattoo began at his left hip, where the head of the dragon was looking up at him. The body ran down his thigh with the dragon's wings tucked and its claws looking as if they were sunk into Arian's skin. The dragon's tail dropped to his knee before curling around it.

The design was exquisite, but there was something about the placement that was incredibly sexy.

Grace had trouble breathing. No matter what her brain said, her body was attracted to Arian. It was partly because he was so gorgeous it hurt to look at him, but it was also because of the way he had held her so gently, how he spoke to her in that brogue that made her heart melt, and how he had struggled to help her up the mountain despite his own injuries.

He walked past her, and God help her, Grace turned and watched him, her gaze dropping to his amazing ass. She hastily turned back around when he grabbed his jeans at the entrance and put them on.

Grace drew in a deep breath. How was she expected to think after seeing something so mouthwatering as Arian's body? She had felt that warm skin. She knew how hard his muscles were, how powerful he felt—even injured.

Arian came to stand in front of her with his jeans now fastened. "Sit down with me, Grace. Let me explain since you've already seen who I really am."

When he turned and walked to the fire, she dropped her arms and followed. He was right. She wanted to know. She was insanely curious about him.

If she hadn't seen him with her own eyes, she wouldn't have believed he was a dragon. But she had seen. Up close and personal.

She sat on the opposite side of the fire from him. Grace watched as the flames danced between them, the firelight casting everything in a red-orange glow.

Their eyes met, and she waited for him to begin. Her heart was pounding slow and steady as a thread of exhilaration wound through her.

"We have lived on this realm since the beginning of time," Arian began in his deep, sexy voice. "For millions of years, the only beings on this earth were dragons. It wasn't airplanes that dominated the skies, but dragons."

Grace was immediately sucked into his story. She held her breath, waiting for him to continue.

"There were millions of us. From the smallest dragons, about the size of a cat, to the largest, like me. We were divided into factions based upon color, and there was every color imaginable. Each group was ruled by a king. The one of us with the most power and magic, immortal and lethal. Then there was one above a Dragon King—the King of Kings."

She was trying to imagine all the dragons in various sizes and colors upon the land instead of humans. Grace couldn't fathom it.

"Life was good," Arian continued. "I can still remember what it was like to look up and see dragons flying. Or to be in the sky and look down to see dragons dotting the ground. But those days are long gone."

"What happened?" Grace asked.

Arian looked away for a moment. Then he said, "One day mortals were here. Each Dragon King was suddenly changed into human form to communicate with them. We were then able to shift back and forth at will. We vowed to protect the humans."

Grace worried that the next part wasn't going to be so fun to hear. Especially by the way Arian's face tightened.

"We had peace. For a time. The mortals reproduced at an astonishing rate. Soon we had to move dragons out of areas they had always inhabited to make room for the humans. Even some of the Kings took mortal females to their beds. Some wanted those females as their mates, or wives, if you will."

She raised her brows. The best way to keep peace was an alliance, and what was a marriage but an alliance? It was the perfect solution, especially if there was love involved.

"One of the Kings, Ulrik, was about to take a female as his mate. Somehow Constantine, the King of Kings, discovered that

Ulrik's woman was planning to betray him. She wanted to kill him. Little did she know she would never have been able to do it."

"Why?" Grace asked. "Was she weak?"

Arian smiled, but it was cold and hard. "The only one who can kill a Dragon King is another Dragon King. There isn't a weapon in any of the realms that can kill us."

Well, that certainly explained it. "Oh."

"Con sent Ulrik away, and all the Kings gathered together and hunted down the female. We killed her for her attempted betrayal."

"You killed her?" Grace asked in shock.

Arian nodded. "Ulrik brought her into his home. He clothed her, fed her, protected her, and loved her. Because to be taken as a mate to a Dragon King brings immortality to a human. So aye, Grace, we killed her. But Ulrik was angry at our actions when he found out. He wanted to be the one to end her life. In his grief and rage, Ulrik focused on those he felt responsible."

"Humans," Grace said.

"The mortals retaliated quickly and began to slaughter dragons left and right. There was no end in sight, and nothing any of us could do could stop Ulrik on his quest to rid this realm of humans."

Grace frowned at his words.

"Some of the Kings, myself included, joined Ulrik for a time. Con eventually brought all of us back together. All except for Ulrik. By this time, the mortals were intent on wiping out the dragons."

"But the Kings couldn't die by a human's hand," she said.

Arian nodded. "True. But they were killing dragons. We had no choice but to send all the dragons away. Then, once more the Kings gathered, except this time it wasn't to help Ulrik. It was to bind his magic and prevent him from shifting. We cursed him to walk this world for eternity in human form."

Grace grimaced. "Ouch."

"The war had to end. We hoped with Ulrik taken care of it would cease, but it didna. Even without dragons, the mortals hunted us."

"You could've wiped us out, right?"

Arian gave a single nod.

"Why didn't you?" she asked.

"We made a vow to protect the mortals. We take such

promises seriously."

Grace shook her head, not understanding. "But you lost your dragons in the process. That's not right."

"It's what was decided. We returned to Dreagan and safeguarded it with magic to keep everyone off our land as we slept away centuries waiting for mortals to forget."

"Dreagan?" Why did she know that name? Then she realized it was the famous Scotch whisky.

Arian paused for a moment. "Dreagan is our home. It's the one place we can be our true selves. We hide here. Ulrik, however, has no' given up on his vengeance. He's teamed up with the Dark Fae, another old enemy, to expose us to the world."

She thought back to the questions Arian had asked her. "You thought I was working with Ulrik or the Dark Fae?"

"Aye. They've been known to use mortals to aid them."

"I'm not helping them," she said.

Arian's smile was slow. "Aye. I ken that, lass."

Chapter Seven

Arian tried several times to look away from Grace, but he was drawn back to her dark blue eyes again and again. The fear he had seen earlier wasn't gone completely. But it was tempered, calmed.

She sat casually, listening as he spoke. Her muscles weren't tense, and she was engaged in the story. Even asking him questions. He hadn't been sure how she would react, truth be told.

"How is Ulrik's attempting to show the world there are dragons helping him?" she asked.

Arian saw her gaze lower to his chest and her pulse quicken. His own body reacted viscerally. It was a primal, instinctive desire that flared hungrily through him. His cock hardened instantly, and it was everything he could do to remain on the opposite side of the fire from her.

He vaguely recalled that she had asked a question. Arian searched his mind and tried to get himself under control. "Ulrik wants to defeat Con and take over the Dragon Kings."

"Which means what for all of you?" Her navy eyes rose to his face.

"He could kill us."

Her brow furrowed deeply with concern. "Would he?"

"I doona know. It's a possibility. What I know he'll do is wipe the world of any human, and he'll begin by waking his Silvers and unleashing them."

Grace visibly swallowed. "Oh. Wait. What? There are dragons here? I thought you said they were sent away?"

"Four of his largest Silvers remained with him. We trapped them and keep them sleeping in one of the mountains."

"I see."

"It's no' just ourselves we're trying to save. It's your race as well."

Her gaze moved to the fire as she sat silent for a long moment. She took a deep breath and asked, "Why didn't Con kill him in the beginning, when Ulrik's magic was stripped?"

"Con and Ulrik were as close as brothers. They were opposite sides of the same coin. Con was steadfast and reserved while Ulrik was outgoing and a bit of a jokester. Despite their different personalities, they would've died for the other. Until Con became King of Kings."

Grace shifted, her head tilting to the side as she looked at him. "What happened?"

"That's between Con and Ulrik, but Con doesna talk about it. Or he didna when I was awake."

"Awake?" she repeated.

Arian briefly looked at his hands. "I've been sleeping in my mountain for six centuries."

"Your..." she began, her voice trailing off. Grace looked around the cavern before her gaze returned to him. "This is your mountain?"

"Aye. Each Dragon King has his own."

"I...wow."

He bit back a smile at her surprised reaction. "Many of us take to our mountains for long periods. Some get tired of hiding who we truly are, some have pasts they need to escape from for a while, and others must disappear from the world for a generation or so before reappearing."

"Which one are you?"

"A bit of all of them."

"Six hundred years is a long time though."

Arian lifted one shoulder in a shrug. "I had no intention of waking any time soon. The war with Ulrik and the Dark, however, changed that. Con had all the Kings who slept woken."

"Why were you going to remain asleep?"

"There was no reason for me to be awake. I know mortals have advanced considerably, but that doesna make our lives easier. In fact, it makes keeping our secret hidden even harder. Sleeping through the centuries makes things easier to deal with, like missing my dragons."

"I understand now."

He waited as she took it all in, digesting it bit by bit.

"Back to Con and Ulrik," Grace said. "Did no one think Ulrik wouldn't one day want revenge?"

Arian clasped his hands together as he rested his arms on his knees. "He was never supposed to unbind his magic."

"Um, what?" she asked with wide eyes.

"We bound his magic. Dragon magic is the strongest magic on the realm. No' even the Fae can beat dragon magic."

She nodded slowly, her face frozen in shock. "Yeah, ok. But you just said his magic was never meant to be unbound, which means that he somehow managed to do just that."

"Aye, lass, he did."

"And he says it so calmly," Grace mumbled to herself with a little shake of her head.

Arian found her completely fascinating. He was enthralled with every facet of emotion that crossed her face—and there were dozens. She hid nothing, whether on purpose or not, her emotions were there for all to see.

Grace dropped her head in her hands and blew out a loud breath. "You just said dragon magic was the strongest. What could possibly have beaten that?"

"An anomaly in the form of a Druid."

At this, her head snapped up. "Did you just say a Druid?"

"Aye."

She scratched her eyebrow and looked at the ground. "If there are dragons and Fae, why not Druids?"

Arian was hiding another smile.

When she returned her eyes to him, she shot him a flat look. "You can stop laughing, because yes, I'm wigging out to the Nth degree here."

"You doona appear to be...wigging out," he said, trying the word.

She moved her hands in a vertical circle in front of her chest. "It's all inside."

Arian's smile grew. If she only knew the truth about how he was falling for her. His smile faded as he thought of her leaving, because she would—eventually. He wasn't ready for that yet.

Without a doubt he had been alone in his mountain for a considerable time, and his body yearned to be near Grace again. He longed to touch her skin and feel her lips moving beneath his.

His emotions were so volatile that lightning streaked across the sky, followed immediately by a clap of thunder before the skies opened up once more.

Grace let out a shriek and jumped to her feet, getting as far from the entrance as she could. She faced the rain, backing up as she did.

Arian got to his feet and moved in her path. He used his body to block her from running into a boulder. As soon as he laid his arms on her shoulders, he felt her shaking.

"It's just a storm, lass," he whispered near her ear.

"It's never just a storm."

There was something in her words that caught his attention. Not too much the words themselves, but the depth of emotion in them.

Arian turned her to face him and looked into her deep blue eyes. He needed to take her mind off the storm, because he had no intention of stopping it. As long as it rained she would remain with him.

Once he had his fill of listening to her sweet voice and watching her feelings cross her face, then he would stop the rain.

"Bad things happen in weather like this," she said.

Arian smoothed back her hair from her face. "No' all bad, surely."

"My mother left us in a storm. My father died while a storm howled. I walked into a mountain with a Dragon King who is in the middle of a war with Dark Fae."

He was going to reassure her that all would be fine, but he couldn't find the words. The knowledge that so much pain was associated with storms made him question using his power to keep her with him.

But perhaps there was a way he could help her.

"Rain waters the earth, giving life to plants and flowers that are food for animals. The thunder and lightning are displays of the beauty and fierceness of nature," he said, hoping he could get her to accept his words and erase her fear.

Her body was pressed so enticingly against him. The feel of her breasts made his cock twitch. He looked down at her lips to find them parted slightly. Damn, but he wanted to taste them.

He couldn't breathe. The weight of the need, of the overwhelming desire felt like he was being pulled under. As if he were drowning, and Grace was the only thing that could save him.

The beat of her pulse at her throat was erratic and her chest rose and fell rapidly.

She felt it too.

Arian lifted his gaze to her face to find her eyes heavy-lidded as she watched him. He searched those amazing eyes of hers as he sank, tumbled into the navy depths.

He leaned his head forward until their breaths mingled. Her fingers tightened on his arms. Arian could stand it no more. He put his lips against hers.

She sucked in a quick breath. Arian moved his lips over hers, learning the feel of them before he touched his tongue to them, tracing them.

Grace leaned against him. He wound his arms around her, holding her firmly. A low moan filled him when her tongue touched his.

He was about to explode. Inside was a hunger he could never remember having before, a yearning to claim her right then that shocked and excited him.

The kiss deepened, their tongues intertwining seductively, sensually. Her lips were soft, her taste decadent. He slid a hand into her hair and held her head as their passion grew rapidly.

The soft kiss was turning as untamed as the craving inside him, and the more she responded, the more the flames grew. Her soft moans were driving him wild, but it was the way she breathed that made him burn.

He kissed down the side of her jaw, listening to her short breaths filling the air as she clung to him. His tongue licked her neck, and he felt a shiver race through her.

Then her hands grabbed his face and brought him back up so they could kiss once more. He couldn't get enough of her kisses or the way her hands roamed over his shoulders, arms, and chest.

He had to have her. There was no going back for him now, not after having her kisses.

Not after tasting her desire.

He lifted his head and looked down at her swollen lips. They were still parted, still wet from their kisses.

"Don't you dare stop," she said and rose up on her toes.

Arian felt a nudge in his mind. He could hear Con's voice, but he didn't open the link. Nothing was going to come between him and Grace right now. There would be time enough later to hear what Con had to say.

Grace's finger dipped in the waist of his jeans, and Arian groaned. He jerked when her hand cupped his arousal on the outside of his jeans and gave him a squeeze.

He continued to kiss her as his hand lifted the hem of her sweater and undershirt to feel her skin. He caressed upward until he cupped her breast and massaged the mound.

It was Grace who broke off the kiss this time. She moaned loudly when his finger circled her nipple, causing it to harden. It took but a second to unhook the bra at her back and shove it aside so his palm could feel her breast.

When he held it once more, he tweaked the nipple, causing her to give a cry of pleasure. Their gazes were locked together, their desire palpable.

Arian teased her nipple, enjoying how desire darkened her gaze even more. It was Grace who grabbed her sweater and shirt and pulled them over her head. Her bra followed a moment later.

Now they stood toe-to-toe, hip-to-hip. Arian put his free hand on her neck and nudged her head to the side with his thumb. Then he kissed her neck below her ear, licking and sucking the sensitive area. Her moans spurred him on, urging him to continue.

All the while she unfastened his jeans and spread the opening so she could find his cock.

Arian hissed in a breath when her fingers touched the head of his arousal. Then she began to touch him, tempting and teasing him until he was breathing as heavily as she.

He was rough as he unfastened her jeans and shoved them down her hips. Then he lifted her in his arms and laid her atop her sweater before the fire. With one jerk, he had her boot off. The second followed a heartbeat later. And then her jeans followed. He hesitated when he spotted the red lace panties that he found unbelievably sensual.

After running his fingers along the lace, he removed them so that she was fully bared to him.

Arian was kneeling beside her, looking at Grace's beautiful body, from her pink-tipped breasts to her waist and flared hips, down to her sex. He blinked as he saw she was completely shaven.

"Fuck," he murmured before he leaned down for another kiss.

Chapter Eight

Grace's stomach clutched, her breathing came faster. She didn't know what it was about Arian that made her burn, made her...yearn.

From the moment he'd spoken with that amazing accent, she'd been taken with him. His conversation had by turns irritated and intrigued her, pushing her to believe the impossible after witnessing him in his true form. With his astute thinking and sharp mind, he was more than a match for her intelligently. Seeing that glorious body and to-die-for face only made her crave him more.

Then he had kissed her.

And what a kiss!

It was a kiss like none other. There was fire and a hunger that was both savage as well as tender.

At first.

Then the fire had come. The kiss had charred her, searing her from the inside out. Each touch of his tongue, each time those lips of his moved over hers, had been the most incredible feeling in the world.

Until he lightly bit her bottom lip.

Grace had clutched him as she squeezed her legs together from the intense desire that made her sex throb.

She'd needed to touch him. His skin was warm and the sinew firm beneath her palm. But it hadn't been enough. She wanted to feel *him.*

His thick arousal was pressed against her stomach. It had taken her forever before she got his pants undone, and then she was touching him. She could feel his member pulse in her hand as she stroked him.

Her attention was soon divided when he teased her nipple. All Grace knew was that she wanted him inside her. Now! She burned for him as she had never burned for another.

Then she was on her back, naked. And his voice, husky with emotion and desire murmured, "Fuck."

She had never liked words like that during sex, but from Arian it made her heart race and her stomach flip with excitement. And need.

Grace couldn't find any words, which was a first for her. The feelings of desire, pleasure, and longing swarmed her, but she didn't feel like she was drowning.

No, she felt just the opposite. Like she was just now living.

She swallowed, watching as Arian stood and roughly yanked off his jeans. Grace eyed his tattoo again. She couldn't wait to touch it, but first, she wanted Arian.

He put his hands on either side of her face and leaned over her, kissing her. It wasn't the fiery kisses of earlier. These were more sedate, languid, but still just as sensual and erotic.

She loved the way he could stir her with just a simple kiss. It brought chills to her skin.

He stretched out atop her, his large body covering hers as she opened her legs. Instinctively, her legs wrapped around him, holding him as close as her arms now did.

A moan rumbled in his chest, and Grace held him tighter. What was it about Arian that made her respond so passionately? There was a wildness about her in his arms, and it had never been there before.

She was eager, madly impatient to have him deep inside her. To feel him moving within her.

A sigh escaped when he bent and placed his lips around a nipple. He sucked hard before laving the turgid peak with his tongue until she was writhing beneath him.

But he didn't stop there. He moved to her other breast and

teased that nipple just as mercilessly. Grace's body fairly hummed with desire that coiled tighter and tighter.

Arian scooted down her body, kissing his way as he went. He paused at the scar on her right side where she'd had her appendix removed fifteen years earlier. Then he continued downward until his warm breath fanned her sex.

Grace stared at the stalactites above her without seeing them. She held her breath while he kissed the inside of each thigh softly, slowly.

Then he gently licked her sex. Grace's mouth opened at the wondrous feeling that spread through her. It was quickly replaced by a bright blaze of desire when Arian flicked his tongue over her clit.

The breath rushed from her lungs as her mouth opened on a silent cry of pleasure. He teased, he licked, he laved. Taking her higher and higher each time.

Her back arched from the intense pleasure. He held her hips firmly, refusing to let her escape his tongue. But she had no interest in going anywhere. Not when he was touching her so amazingly.

Grace was floating, allowing the bliss to sink through her. Then Arian's finger touched her sex, stroking just under his tongue.

Before she could even register that, his finger pushed inside her. Grace moaned when he began to move his finger in and out, twisting it as he did.

It was just a moment later before he added the second finger. Grace tried to breathe between the waves of pleasure, but it was too much. She could feel her body hurtling toward the climax and there was nothing she could do about it.

When the orgasm came, it swept her away completely. It was so intense, so powerful that she was helpless to do anything but feel.

It was as if she were falling endlessly through a pleasure-filled void led by Arian. Instead of panicking, Grace didn't fight any of it.

As the climax began to fade, Arian crawled back up to her. Grace pushed at his shoulders and rolled him onto his back as she kneeled beside him. She ran her hands over his chest and leaned over, breathing and kissing on his skin.

She moved closer and closer to his arousal, but each time she got near, she would go another direction.

He was moaning as he watched her, his champagne gaze focused on her face. Grace looked up and met his eyes. The desire she saw there caused her heart to miss a beat.

She stopped with her mouth breaths from his cock. It had been six centuries since he felt a woman or pleasure. Then, still holding his gaze, she took him in hand and let her lips slide over his head.

His fingers dug into her thigh. "Fuck, Grace. That feels so damn good."

Spurred on by his words, she began to move her hand and mouth, taking him deeper. She cupped his ball sac and massaged them with her free hand.

She was enjoying herself, but all too soon he had her on her back once more. Arian held her arms above her head with his. She looked down at their bodies.

Logic intruded through her desire-filled brain. Protection. She needed protection. "Condom," she said, hoping he had one. It wasn't as if she carried one in her laptop.

His brow furrowed. "I'm immortal, lass. I doona carry disease, nor do I pass it on."

"Uh, huh." That was great news. "I don't want to get pregnant."

He leaned down to kiss her nose. "Mortals can no' carry the seed of a dragon."

Oh. Well that was something she didn't expect.

Then all thought fled as he moved his thick cock to the entrance of her sex.

"Do you want me?" he asked.

Grace glanced up at him and nodded.

"Say it, Grace. I have to hear you say it."

"I want you. I want you inside me," she said breathlessly, unable to take her eyes off his arousal.

He shifted his hips forward until the head of him brushed her. Grace sucked in a breath and raised her hips for more.

"Look at me," he demanded.

Grace dropped her head down and looked into his face. He was the most beautiful thing she had ever seen. Even if he was a dragon. Or maybe because of it.

With their gazes locked, she gasped as he entered her. Little by little, he filled her, stretching her as he did.

"So damn wet," he murmured. "And tight."

She wanted to say something, but once more words deserted her.

With one last thrust, he was fully inside her. Since he was still holding her arms, she raised her legs and wrapped them around his waist. She smiled at him when she began to move her hips.

"Minx," he whispered with a grin.

Then he began to move, and all smiles vanished. His thrusts were slow and long, filling her deep. The tempo began to increase steadily.

He released her hands and leaned over her to give himself more leverage. Sweat slicked their bodies as he plunged hard and fast.

His long hair fell over his shoulders, tickling her, but she didn't care. She met his thrusts with her own, silently urging him on with her movement and her cries of pleasure.

To her surprise, she felt a second climax coming. She looked up to see him watching their bodies as they came together.

Grace cried out as the second orgasm seized her. It was even stronger than the first, taking her breath with it.

"I can feel your walls pulsing," Arian said. "Can't. Hold. Back."

She held him as they climaxed together. The strength of it carried them high, as if they were flying.

Grace had no idea how long she lay entwined with Arian. She opened her eyes to see him leaning on his elbow staring down at her.

He touched her cheek gently. She couldn't tell what emotion was on his face, nor did she try. She simply allowed the moment to happen.

Arian pulled out of her and rolled them so that he held her against his chest. She closed her eyes, content where she was. Only then did she hear the rain. The thunder and lightning had stopped, but the storm was far from over.

Chapter Nine

Arian was content to just lay with Grace in his arms. Not only had her body felt good, but it felt *right* to have her next to him now.

He knew she wasn't asleep. She tensed every time the distant sound of thunder reached her. He could end her discomfort with a mere thought, but halting the rain would allow her to leave.

And he wasn't ready for that yet. It was selfish for him to keep making her deal with her fear, but he couldn't let her go. Arian was happy. Actually happy. The last time had been before he sent his dragons away.

How could he even think of losing Grace now?

Arian looked down at the top of her blonde head. He wondered what she was thinking. There was no doubt she enjoyed their lovemaking. Her cries of ecstasy, and the fact she had two orgasms, told him he had pleasured her well.

That should make him feel good about the situation. Instead, he wondered if she wanted to leave. He also worried that she couldn't handle his world.

Arian's thoughts halted immediately.

Why would he care if she couldn't deal with magic and immortality and shape shifting? Grace was beautiful, intelligent, and extremely gifted in her writing, but that didn't make her more to him.

He tried to imagine walking her to her car and seeing her drive away. And it made him want to bellow in fury.

No. He didn't want her to leave.

Ever.

Arian closed his eyes. How the hell had he gotten into this situation? He realized as soon as that thought entered his head that there was no answer. It could be a myriad of things that allowed Grace to sink deep in his soul.

Whatever the cause, she was there. And he was going to hold onto her. It didn't matter what Con or any of the other Kings had to say about it.

"You're quiet," Grace said.

Arian found himself smiling. He noticed that he had been lightly rubbing her back the entire time. "So are you, lass."

"I'm thinking."

"About?" he urged.

She snuggled closer to him. "Don't laugh."

"I would never," he responded solemnly because he had a feeling whatever she was about to say was about them.

Grace flattened her palm on his chest. "I've not been writing it correctly."

"Writing what, exactly?"

"Passion. I forgot what it was," she whispered. "I went off what I saw in movies or read, but I haven't...experienced...it in many years."

He didn't like thinking about other men being with her, but they were in the past. Where they would remain. "Were they no' good lovers?"

"They were all right, but without passion, it all feels...empty."

Arian tightened his arm around her before he rolled her onto her back so he could look into her face. "I'll be happy to show you several times a day."

Her smile was infectious. "You're up for that job?"

He looked between their bodies to his cock that was already hard again. "Oh, aye."

Her smile softened as she put her hand on his cheek. "I just met you, and yet it feels as if I've known you forever."

"Is that wrong?"

"No. It's just...scary."

Arian didn't want her to be scared of the storms or the feelings developing between them. "How, lass?"

"I feel there's a connection between us. I've felt it from the moment I saw you. I don't instantly sleep with people I first meet, and yet I was drawn to you. I couldn't stop it, and I didn't want to."

"What we did is natural. There's nothing to be ashamed of."

"I'm not ashamed," she said as she ran her hand down his neck to his shoulder. "All I can think of is doing it again."

Arian returned her grin. "It's our connection that frightens you, aye?"

"Yes. There isn't the normal anxiety I feel around men I'm attracted to. With others there was nervousness and uncertainty, which can make relationships difficult to form. But with you, I'm comfortable. Except when I saw you in dragon form. Then I was scared out of my mind."

She laughed, but Arian heard the truth in her words. "Are you still afraid?"

"Of you?" she asked, eyebrows raised. "No."

Arian once more felt Con push against his head, shouting Arian's name. He opened the link long enough to tell Con, "*I need a moment.*"

"There are more of us," Arian told her.

Grace swallowed. "Yeah. Those I might be a tad nervous around."

"I willna let them harm you."

Her navy eyes softened. "They're your brethren. You would do that?"

"Without question."

Grace closed her eyes for a second before she said, "Where have you been all my life?"

"Waiting on you to find me, lass."

She laughed and pulled him down as she wrapped her arms around him. They remained like that for several moments. Arian knew he couldn't hold Con off forever, but he also suspected that Con would want to interrogate Grace himself. With the war, they were all on edge.

Though Arian was assured Grace was innocent, Con would

have to be certain as well.

Arian rose up to look at her. How he wanted to stay right here in this moment, but it was fading no matter how desperately he clung to it.

"Tell me about you," she pleaded.

Since he wasn't ready to answer Con, he touched the tip of her nose with his finger. "What do you want to know?"

"Everything. We all have pasts. I want to know yours."

"Aye, I do have one." He leaned on one elbow and traced figures on her stomach. "I was the only child of my parents."

"Dragons."

"Dragons," he said with a nod. "I'm glad they were no' alive to see the war with the mortals."

"Did they know you were a Dragon King?"

Arian smiled, recalling that special day. "That they did. They were so proud."

"Do dragons mate for life?"

"That we do."

Grace stretched her arms over her head, causing her breasts to poke in the air as she smiled. "I like that. I like that a lot."

Arian ran a hand down her side, wanting to be inside her again. His gaze followed his hand down to her hip where she had the leg closest to him out straight and the other bent, leaning against him.

"Did you have a mate?"

Arian nuzzled her neck. "Nay. After what happened with Ulrik's woman, Con cast a spell over us no' to feel anything for humans. We couldna fall in love again."

"Oh," she said softly, hurt in her gaze.

That pleased him immensely. "All that changed when Ulrik's magic was returned. It erased Con's spell, and Kings have been mating with mortals for several years now."

"So you didn't have anyone?"

Arian paused briefly. "I had lovers, aye. I didna get attached to them because of the spell. My duty and honor to Dreagan and the other Kings always came first."

"So you chose honor over love?"

"I was never in love," he reminded her. "But aye, when Con gave me orders, I did them."

Grace regarded him solemnly. "You left those women, didn't you?"

"I did."

"Why did you change sides from Ulrik to Con in the war?"

He groaned as Grace brought his attention from her body back to the conversation. Arian focused on her face, glad she had changed the conversation. "I understood why Ulrik was out to kill mortals, but I didna see a good outcome. We made a vow to protect them."

"But they tried to kill you."

Arian shrugged. "We had been around millions of years, Grace. We were the adults and the humans like children. We shouldna have reacted so harshly."

"You didn't. Ulrik did."

Arian thought about how he might feel if Grace betrayed him. For the first time he began to understand a fraction of what Ulrik went through. "Whether the blame is on the female who was going to betray Ulrik, on us for killing her, or Ulrik for starting the war, the fact is, everything changed for both races."

"What does all this mean for me? I know you asked me many questions when I first arrived. Will there be more?"

"Aye, lass, there will be. Con will want to meet you."

Her eyes widened a fraction. "Oh. Well...that...I didn't expect that."

Arian kissed her, loving the feel of her lips and the way she responded to him. "It'll be fine, lass. Answer him as you answered me."

He heard Con's voice in his head again. Arian could no longer hold him off. He lay back and pulled Grace against him.

"*Aye?*" Arian asked as he opened the mental link.

Con's voice was as frigid as a Scottish winter when he asked, "*Should I even begin to guess what you've been doing?*"

"*I'd rather you no'. As I'm sure Ryder has already informed you, everything Grace told me has checked out.*"

"*That means nothing. You know that. Ulrik likes to get humans to work for him. We doona suspect them, or so he believes. I also want to know how she saw your entrance.*"

Arian knew exactly what Con was getting at. "*You want me to bring her to the manor."*

"I do. Immediately. We need to know for sure if she's working for
Ulrik."

"You might ought to know that she saw me in true form."

There was a long pause. *"Did you intentionally allow her to see you?"*

"Of course no'." It was Arian's turn to get angry. *"She was supposed
to have been sleeping when I went out for a flight. I spotted more Dark on my
mountain, and I took care of them. Sometime during that, she woke and saw
the fight."*

"She'll need her memories wiped by Guy."

Arian didn't bother to argue against it now. He would once
they were at the manor and Grace had proven she wasn't with
Ulrik.

*"I'll have one of the Kings drive her car around to the distillery. Bring her
through the mountains."*

"You would show her that?"

Con chuckled. *"Aye. Watch her reaction, Arian. I want every detail."*

The link was terminated. Arian remained where he was, still
unwilling to leave the serenity they had found in his mountain.
Grace was all smiles and kisses now, but as soon as they left
everything would change.

But Arian couldn't wait. The sooner Con realized Grace was
no spy, the sooner Arian could spend more alone time with her.

"How about some hot food?"

She shifted her head so that she was looking up at him. "We
have to leave, don't we?"

Arian nodded. "Aye, lass. We do."

"I figured we might. This couldn't last forever."

"We'll return."

Grace's smile was sad as she sat up and reached for her clothes.
"Sure we will."

Arian caught her hands and made her look at him. "We will.
It's going to be fine."

"It's not that I don't believe you, but I'm a realist. You're in the
middle of a war. Things like this never go easily."

"I'll be beside you the entire time."

She gave him a smile that didn't quite reach her eyes. "Let's get
this over with."

He watched as she rose and began to dress. After a moment, Arian stood and tugged on his jeans. He gathered her laptop and jacket then waited after he left her keys next to the picnic basket.

As soon as she faced him, Arian bent and took one of the logs from the fire. He used his magic to put out the fire and gave a nod to Grace. "Stay close. There are some tricky spots."

She fell in step behind him as they walked to the back of the cavern. Arian took the tunnel to the far left. He had to duck to enter, but Grace passed through effortlessly.

He glanced over his shoulder at her often, but she stayed close to him. The tunnel was narrow at this part with nothing to see. Up ahead was a different story altogether.

"We're going deeper," Grace whispered.

Arian threw her a smile. "That we are. We'll go down and then back up eventually."

"How far do we need to walk?"

"A ways, lass."

"How far is that, exactly?"

He chuckled at her irritated tone. "We're going in almost a straight line to the manor. It'll take us a third of the time than if you were walking over the mountains."

"That means we're going to be walking for a while," she said with a grin.

It had been a long time since Arian had walked these tunnels, but it was something none of the Kings forgot.

"These aren't here naturally," Grace said.

"We made them after we took to our mountains. We had to stay hidden from the humans completely. So we dug tunnels to connect all the mountains."

"But these are only big enough for a human."

Arian paused and looked at her. "The ones we'll be walking are, but there are a few large enough for dragons."

"This is all real, isn't it?"

"I'm afraid so."

She shook her head in disbelief. "I'm still in shock over it, I think. I was ready to walk on water to run away when I saw the dragon. I knew it was you, because I saw you change, but I still have a difficult time grasping it all."

"Few mortals know of us, Grace. Several Kings have taken females as mates, so you'll most likely see them at the manor."

Her lips parted. "I'm glad the Kings have forgiven us."

"Many have, aye. There are still some who may never forgive humans for the war."

"I can't imagine a world with dragons."

He started walking again, holding the torch up so that it shed enough light so she could see where she was stepping. They walked for a long time in silence.

With every step toward the manor, Arian began to worry. Con had never liked the idea of the Kings taking the humans as mates. Yet nine Dragon Kings had done just that.

"How does Con feel about the mates?" Grace asked.

Arian raised a brow as he glanced back at her. "Do you read minds, lass?"

She laughed, the sound bouncing off the stones. "No. Why?"

"I was just thinking that nine of us have taken mates. Though one of them is a Fae."

"Obviously Con is fine with it then."

Arian flattened his lips as he considered her words. "That's no' entirely true. He's been known to step in and try to dissuade pairings."

"Has he succeeded?"

"Nay."

There was a quick intake of breath as she tripped and reached for him. Arian righted her and gave her a nod to see if she was all right.

Grace shoved her hair out of her face and dropped her hands to her side. "Does he want the Kings to be lonely and miserable for however long you live?"

"Eternity. And aye, he does if it means we're no' betrayed."

Chapter Ten

Eternity. That's what he said.

Grace could hardly fathom such a length of time. "You don't die?"

"The only way for a Dragon King to die is—"

"By another Dragon King," she said over him with a nod, remembering his earlier words.

The light from the torch flickered off his face, singeing the edges of shadows with red and orange. It gave Arian's champagne eyes an amber glow.

In such a few short hours her life had changed. Before her stood not just a man, but an immortal dragon. And a King at that.

He made love to her as if he knew everything she wanted and needed. Though he might believe that she wasn't a spy, the others wouldn't be so easily convinced.

Of that, Grace was certain.

"Come, lass," Arian said and took her hand.

She followed him another dozen steps before the tunnel melted away and she found herself standing in a cavern. It was half the size of Arian's, but even with the little light from the torch she could see the glint of gemstones.

Out of the corner of her eye, she saw Arian watching her before he whispered a few words. Suddenly a ball of light flared above them, rising higher and higher while its light grew brighter and brighter.

Grace gasped when she saw not just the gemstones embedded in the rock, but dozens of drawings and etched stone of dragons. Every inch of stone was marked in some way.

"We took turns sleeping those years we waited until the humans forgot us. Those that remained awake dug tunnels. And passed the time with these."

"Wow," she whispered.

There were no words to describe the magnificence of what she was seeing. It wasn't just beautiful and amazing, it was wonderful and inconceivable.

And it was a little sad as well.

To know that Arian and the others were trapped below ground for centuries was just wrong. This planet had been theirs until her kind arrived. Humans were like a plague. They destroyed everything and everyone. Just like what they had done to the dragons.

"What is it?" he asked when she lowered her gaze.

Grace turned her head to him. "I saw you in your true form. You were scary, yes, but also incredible. Seeing all of this makes me depressed knowing my race was responsible for keeping you from the skies where you belong."

His arm wound around her waist as he pulled her against him. He kissed her softly, gently before he rubbed his nose against hers.

She laid her head on his chest and looked at the cavern again. It was pretty, but to not see the sun? No wonder so many Kings hated her kind.

"Doona fash yourself about it, lass," Arian whispered.

She straightened from him. Without a word, he dropped his arm and continued walking. Grace followed as they skirted one part of the cavern. She could see several different tunnels that could be taken.

Arian walked past four before he took the fifth one. They encountered no one, but Grace had the feeling that others were there. Other Dragon Kings, that is.

She didn't see them. It was just a feeling. Or perhaps it was the weight of what the humans had done to the dragons that pressed upon her as she saw more and more drawings and carvings.

Grace touched one dragon drawing she glimpsed from the torchlight. It was no bigger than her hand, and for some reason it struck her right in the heart. Such a tiny dragon after seeing so many huge ones on the walls.

Arian glanced back at her often, but there were no more words between them. The closer they came to the manor, the more worried she became. And the tenser he became.

She was tired. Some parts of the tunnels were relatively smooth and easy to walk. Other parts were like hiking in a minefield with all the boulders and dips and valleys in the rocks.

Thankfully, those treacherous places were few and far between and were only short distances. But her exhaustion and anxiety were taking a toll on her.

Tunnel after tunnel they walked. She lost count of the caverns they either passed through or she saw a glimpse of through an opening. Arian never hesitated in the direction he was taking her.

Grace realized that she was putting a lot of trust in him to be taking her so deep in the earth. He could be a serial killer.

The thought made her giggle. He was a dragon, not a serial killer. And though she knew his secret, she didn't really know him.

Why then was it so easy to be around him and so comfortable to talk to him? She usually only felt that way with people she had known for years. Certainly it had never happened with someone she barely knew a handful of hours.

Her father had often warned her that her greatest gift—and biggest weakness—was that she trusted so certainly.

How many times had that trust been burned? And yet each time she found herself trusting again. It was a weakness, a flaw, and yet it was who she was.

It put her in positions to be deceived, mislead, and lied to on various occasions.

However, it had never put her in a position to lose her life, and that's exactly what she felt was at stake here. Arian hadn't said anything, but he didn't need to. It was in the way he held his jaw.

Just when she was about to collapse and ask for a break, she saw a light ahead of them. Arian said another word, and the torch extinguished instantly.

"We're here," he said.

Grace looked ahead in the tunnel. "I need to know the truth. If I don't answer Con the way he wants, will he kill me?"

Arian's face softened as he smiled and cupped her cheek for a quick, hard kiss. "Nay, lass."

"He won't just let me go though."

"We have our secret to maintain."

"Well, he can't keep me here," she said, thinking of the next viable option.

Arian sighed and dropped his arms to his side. "There's another way."

"What way?" she pressed.

He paused before he said, "One of the other Kings has the ability to wipe memories."

She blinked, unsure if she had heard him correctly. "I'm sorry. Did you just say wipe my memories? So you'd leave me wandering the streets without knowing who I am?"

"Nay, no' at all. Guy will only wipe away anything you've seen or learned while here."

"Meaning you."

Arian gave a single nod.

Grace wasn't about to give up her time with Arian. It was special, and she had the right to hold on to those memories.

Just as the Kings had a right to protect themselves.

"I understand," Grace said. "I don't like it, because I don't want to forget you, but it's better than being killed. Still, I don't want my memories wiped. I'm going to do my best convincing that I'm telling the truth."

"I know you will, lass."

How she wished she could see his face better as he stared at her, but the shadows had taken over once more. Grace was relieved when he slid his fingers in hers and took her hand.

Together, they walked toward the light as the tunnel opened wider. When she saw the door that seemed to go into the house, she knew the time had arrived for her to face the King of Kings, Con.

Grace took a deep breath and slowly released it. Arian opened the door and she walked into the manor from what appeared to be nothing more than a wall. A hidden doorway. As if she would expect anything less after all she had learned.

"It's going to be all right," Arian whispered as he closed the door behind them.

She followed him through the house where there were once more dragons everywhere. Some were obvious, like the iron dragons that seemed to come from right out of the wall while holding a light in a claw, to others, not so discernable in paintings.

They passed near the kitchen where she could hear female voices and laughter, followed by a deep baritone. Arian didn't so much as look in the direction as he led her onward.

When they came to the stairs, Grace looked outside to see that the rain had finally stopped as morning dawned. At least that was one thing she wouldn't have to deal with.

She placed her hand on the banister, only noticing then that the wood was a dragon as well. A glance back at the newel post showed the head of the dragon, with every detail from its scales to its teeth painstakingly carved.

Grace ran her hands through her hair, trying to straighten what she could. She probably smelled, and she knew she looked awful. She'd much rather meet Con showered and dressed properly, but that wasn't going to happen.

Arian reached the landing and proceeded down the corridor. Grace wondered where the next set of stairs led to, and she had the insane urge to find out right then.

Anything to delay seeing Con. She felt like a kid being sent to the principles office in elementary.

As if sensing her nervousness, Arian smiled at her. Grace attempted to return it, but her nerves were too wound up to manage more than a slight tilt of her mouth.

All too soon Arian stopped next to a closed door. He gave her an encouraging nod, then opened the door. There was no time at all for Grace to collect herself before she was standing before a tall man with penetrating black eyes that were as cold and desolate as a desert.

They were in stark contrast to his bright blond hair that was cut short on the sides and longer on top. Con wore a pair of black dress slacks and a burgundy dress shirt that was unbuttoned at the neck and his sleeves rolled up to his elbows.

Arian and Con clasped forearms like something out of the middle ages. Whatever was passed between them was done silently, because no words were spoken aloud, but Grace was sure something had been said.

Then Con's midnight gaze was on her again. He looked her up and down without any emotion on his face. Grace was beginning to think he was a robot to not show any kind of reaction—good or bad.

"Grace Clark," Con said in a deep, clear voice. "Thank you for coming to see me."

"I didn't have much of a choice."

Arian spoke up then, "But she came freely, Con."

Con looked from her to Arian and back to her. "Freely?"

"Arian told me you needed convincing." Grace shrugged. "That's what I'm here to do. I also know that if what I say isn't satisfactory that my memories will be wiped."

"It seems Arian told you a great deal," Con said, showing his first signs of annoyance with the tone of his voice.

Grace lifted her chin. "Shall we proceed? I have a book that has to be written."

Con turned to the side and motioned to the chairs before his desk with his arm. Grace walked past him and took the one on the right. Only once she was seated did Con move to stand behind his desk.

He stared out the window for a time. Grace tried not to fidget in her chair, but the silence was cruel and unusual punishment when she knew Con wanted answers.

She drummed her fingers on the arm of the leather chair and looked around the room, seeing a medium-sized chest with a rounded lid off to one side. It looked ancient. There was a sideboard where a decanter filled with a gold liquid and several crystal glasses sat.

It was the pinging on the window that drew her attention. Grace looked outside to see the sky had darkened, as if night had changed its mind about allowing the day to break.

Lightning flashed in the distance, forking over the mountain. Grace barely noticed the dots of white on the mountain until the sheep began to run in a group to shelter.

Another storm. This was the last thing she needed. She gripped the arm of the chair and tried desperately not to show how she was affected.

Then Con turned and pinned her with a look.

And she knew it was too late.

Chapter Eleven

Arian didn't look around the manor at all the changes that had taken place while he had been sleeping. With Con visiting each of the sleeping Kings and updating them on the goings on in the world and how humans had advanced, Arian was up to date on technology.

No, Arian's attention was on Grace. She gripped the arms of the chairs tightly, making her knuckles white in the process. She was nervous, and she had every right to be.

Constantine hadn't changed in six centuries, not that Arian expected him to. If anything, Con had gotten colder, more aloof. He was completely detached from the world.

"Keep the storm going," Con said in his head.

After everything he and Grace had shared with each other, Arian felt ashamed for what he was doing. Yet, he told himself that the sooner Con got his answers, the sooner Grace wouldn't need to endure her fear anymore.

Arian turned away from the window and grabbed the shirt folded on the edge of Con's desk. It was plain and white, but Arian didn't really see it. His focus was on Grace.

She convinced him of her innocence. All she needed to do was persuade Con as well. The problem was that to Con, everyone was an enemy.

Nothing Arian had tried to argue on his and Grace's journey to the manor swayed Con. Con's argument was that Arian hadn't been involved in the shite that had been happening.

In other words, Arian was soft.

Which infuriated him. Arian might not have been fighting these past months, but he fought plenty enough before. He was one of the last to find sleep after the Fae Wars. Not to mention that it took a lot to convince him to change his mind once he made a decision.

Con, however, had used a low blow. He suggested that Arian had been influenced because of Grace's body.

"Tell me what brought you to Dreagan, Grace," Con asked.

Arian could hear the weather getting out of control. That was his doing because he couldn't get a handle on his anger. He drew in a deep breath and slowly released it, the storm abating some.

Grace swallowed and looked Con in the eye. "As I told Arian, I checked into the B&B where I'm staying. From there I went driving, looking for a place that was quiet and where I could be alone. I drove deeper into the mountains. I had no idea where I was going. I drove until I reached the mountain and could go no further."

"There was no road there."

She gave a slight nod. "It's true the road was more of tracks in the grass. I was curious and wanted to see where it would take me."

"How long did you drive before you came to Dreagan?"

"I didn't know it was Dreagan," she said in an unsteady voice, her gaze going to the window as the rain pinged against the glass. "As for how long I drove, I've no idea. I wasn't timing myself."

Con walked around the desk and came to the front of it, leaning his hands and hips back against it. "You don't know what time you left the B&B?"

"It was around ten or so," Grace said with a shrug.

Arian wanted to go to her and stand beside her. To give her strength and to show Con that Arian was going to protect her. It might come to that, but Arian sincerely hoped it didn't. Surely Con would come around to see what Arian already had—that it was merely fate that brought Grace to him.

"When did you arrive at Arian's mountain?" Con asked.

"I don't know. An hour or an hour and a half later. I didn't really look at my watch. I had no one waiting for me or anyone to answer to. Why would I keep track of time?"

Con looked down at her boots. "You dressed for hiking."

Grace laughed wryly as she straightened her leg so that it was horizontal as she regarded her shoes. "These aren't hiking boots. They're old tennis shoes that wouldn't do me a bit of good," she said, her voice growing louder in her anger. "Would you like to comment on my raincoat? Do you think I can make it rain at will?"

"Oh, I'm no' worried about you having that ability," Con said and glanced at Arian.

Arian fisted his hands. He might have told Grace much about his race, but he hadn't told her about his ability to control the weather. He rarely used the ability, preferring to let the realm take care of itself.

But there were instances, like earlier when he needed to keep her in his mountain, that it came in handy.

Grace's gaze swung to him. Arian gave her a small nod. If she saw it, she gave no response as she returned her eyes to Con.

"That's right," Grace said, jerking when more thunder boomed. "I'm just a human. I'm mortal. I've no magic or the ability to shift into a dragon. I am who I say I am—a novelist. I'm sure with the money Dreagan brings in that you have the ability to do a search on me. Do it. Find out all that you need. Hell, go to a bookstore and find my book."

Con raised a blond brow. "Perhaps you made up everything that we'll find. We've friends in MI5, Ms. Clark. We know what lengths someone will go to in order to hide who they are."

"Not me," she insisted. Her voice pitched higher in frustration. "I'm a freaking nobody! I came here to try and find my muse again. My writing groove left me. It said *adios* and vanished months ago. If I don't turn that book in three weeks from now, I lose my contract. My book is set in Scotland. That's why I'm here."

Arian knew Ryder had already given Con all there was to know about Grace. Ryder, in his infinite skill, had dug up every single thing there was to know about Grace from the day she was born until now.

Even Ryder had cleared her. So what was Con up to?

"And how did you find the cave entrance?"

Grace gaped at him. "This again? I saw it. With my eyes. Why is that so odd?"

"Because it was cloaked with dragon magic," Arian answered.

Grace's eyes went wide. "I don't have an answer then. I saw it."

Could Grace have been meant to find his mountain and him? Arian was beginning to think so. Because there was no other explanation. The barrier around Dreagan hadn't kept her out, and she'd seen his cave entrance—both of which had dragon magic.

"I doona believe in accidents, Ms. Clark," Con said in a soft voice. "I doona believe you just happened to find Arian's mountain."

Arian inwardly cringed. That voice had lulled plenty of others before Grace. It belied the anger and awareness within Con, as well as his purpose.

Grace blew out a breath, her face going white as lightning speared from the sky to the ground. "Well, we'll have to agree to disagree then, because I believe life is nothing more than a multitude of accidents and coincidences."

"You make light of your situation?"

"Absolutely not," Grace stated. "I know how serious this is. I also know that Arian believes me. Why isn't that enough for you?"

"Because I believe Arian is being ruled by his cock."

Grace gasped the same instant Arian narrowed his gaze on Con.

"*Trust me*," Con said in Arian's mind.

Arian had always trusted Con, but to have him talk in such a way to Grace was nearly impossible to bear. Slowly, he released the tension in his body.

Grace was shaking her head. "You think so little of Arian then? That's...well, that's just sad."

"Sad?"

"Yes," she said firmly. "I ran into that mountain to escape the storm. A few hours later, I saw Arian in dragon form fighting the Fae. If I'm to believe everything Arian has told me, all of you are in the middle of a war. You should trust your people."

There was a push against Arian's mind and then Con said,

"Ramp up the storm. I need lightning."

Arian hesitated. Never before had he wavered in doing as Con ordered, but now he was having serious doubts. Grace was shaking, her face was white, and she was sweating from her fear. To put her through more was too much. Arian couldn't take it.

"Arian," Con urged. *"Trust me."*

Trust. That's what Grace had put in him. Arian had vowed he would protect her from everyone and everything. He wasn't doing that now. She was innocent. Con would see that. He had to.

With a deep breath, Arian did as Con requested. The first flash of lightning made Grace jump in her chair and squeeze her eyes closed.

It killed Arian to purposefully scare her in such a manner, but if it could end the interrogation earlier, then he would make it up to her later and explain his power.

If she let him.

"Trust is something I doona give lightly," Con said as his head leaned to the side while he studied Grace. "What about you?"

Grace pulled her eyes away from the window to look at Con. Her head nodded jerkingly. "Yeah. I trust easily. Don't bother to tell me it's wrong. Plenty of others have."

"So you trust Arian?" Con pressed.

Grace jumped when more lightning flashed, followed by thunder that sounded all around them. She yelped, then said, "Yep. I do."

Arian exchanged a look with Con. Would this be all Con needed?

"More lightning and thunder," Con demanded.

"She's afraid of it. Can you no' see that?"

"Of course I can."

Arian should've known he wouldn't get an explanation, but then again, it went unsaid. Everything Con did was to ensure their secrecy.

It hurt Arian physically to put Grace in such fear, but he had no choice. If Con didna get what he needed then Grace would have her memories wiped. She would wake up at the B&B never knowing how deeply she touched his soul when they kissed or how he ached to be buried inside her once more.

She would never know how much he wanted to be with her.

Con was in favor of wiping her memories regardless of if she was working with Ulrik or not, but Arian wasn't going to let that happen.

He needed Grace. It was because he needed her that he did as Con asked once more.

After this was all over, Grace might leave and want nothing to do with him. Arian wasn't about to give up on her that easily though. If something was worth having, it was worth fighting for.

That meant against his own kind as well as Grace.

There was something special between him and Grace. It was something profound, something that never came near Arian before.

Until Grace.

He watched her complexion pale with each bolt of lightning. Her body tensed as the thunder rumbled loudly around them. Each moment that passed made her curl into herself.

And it was slowly killing him.

"Get on with it, Con!"

Con cut him a look before he focused on Grace. "Who do you work for, Ms. Clark?"

"Myself," she answered without taking her eyes off the window.

"That's no' true. Who do you work for?"

She shrugged, slinking farther into the back of the chair. "My pub...publisher. I work for my publisher."

"You work for Ulrik, do you no'?" Con pressed.

"No." She let out a shriek when several rounds of lightning struck in quick succession.

The more anxious Grace became, the angrier Arian got. And the more extreme the weather became until he couldn't get it under control.

Arian desperately tried to rein the weather in, but it was nearly impossible as he listened to Con push Grace again and again to see if she would change her answer.

Every trembling "no" that fell from her lips only infuriated Arian more. She gripped the chair so tightly that he heard the wood crack.

"What are you doing at Dreagan?" Con demanded.

"I already told you!" Grace screamed as thunder made the manor shake.

Arian looked to Con to find Con watching him. Even with that icy stare, Arian knew Con's thoughts. Con recognized that somehow in the few hours Arian was with Grace, that something transpired between them. Something more than just sex.

And Con wasn't happy.

"*Finish it*," Arian insisted.

Con's gaze slid to Grace. "Do you work for Ulrik?"

"No! For the twentieth time, no!" Grace screamed.

But there was something in her voice that sent warning bells off in Arian's head. He looked to her then. Grace's gaze moved from Con to the window to Arian and back to Con several times.

Her face crumpled as she rose and hurried around the chair to put distance between them. She shook her head as she stared at Arian with navy eyes that were filled with sadness—and a hint of anger.

"Grace," Arian said and took a step toward her.

She held up a hand to halt him. "Stop," she ordered and blinked past the tears that began to fall. She then pointed to the window. "That's you. You've been doing this. All this time here and in the mountain. You used my fear against me. How could you?" she yelled.

"I ordered him to do it," Con said.

Grace ignored Con as she stared at Arian, wincing as another bolt of lightning struck. "I thought you believed me."

"I do," Arian said.

Grace sniffed and turned to Con then. "Do whatever you're going to do to me, but I'm done here."

"Grace," Arian began.

But Con stopped him. "Give her some time, Arian."

Arian waited for Grace to look his way. After several tense moments, he realized that wasn't going to happen. It took numerous tries to halt the storm. When he had, he left the room with a sick feeling in the pit of his stomach growing with every step he took away from her.

Chapter Twelve

The tears dried quickly as the numbness took hold. It was worse than the day her mother left. Even worse than when her father died.

She had trusted, as she always did, and it had once more come back to bite her. She should've known Arian was too good to be true.

A man like him who was too gorgeous to even look at, immortal, and a Dragon King didn't choose someone like her. It had always been about their secrecy.

If only he had been honest with her from the beginning. But why would he? They were in the middle of a war. Not even that thinking could stop the hurt from spreading.

"Can I get you anything?" Con asked.

She closed her eyes. How could she have forgotten she wasn't alone? Grace blew out a breath and shook her head as she looked out the window. She wrapped her arms around herself while the clouds dissipated and the sun came out. "No, thank you."

"I did what had to be done. I'll no' apologize for that."

"Then don't." She'd had enough of Con. He and everyone else needed to go step on a Lego and fall in a hole.

Out of the corner of her eye, she saw Con push away from the desk and stand. "Remain here, Ms. Clark. I'll return in a moment."

As soon as the door closed behind him, Grace turned and stuck her tongue out. It was immature, but it was either that or cry some more.

Grace couldn't believe Arian had manipulated her fear in such a way. Then again, she could. If her very way of life was threatened, there was no telling what she would do. She recalled vividly the extremes she went to in order to save her father from his heart failure.

On one hand, she didn't blame Arian, but on the other, she did. They'd shared something personal and beautiful together, and she felt manipulated.

Grace glanced at the door. She was supposed to wait for Con. If she were braver, she would take her chances and make a run for it.

She looked at the door again, her heart kicking up a notch at the thought of making a run for it. But that's exactly what she was going to do.

A look around Con's office didn't show her keys or her laptop. But that wasn't going to stop her. She didn't care if she had to steal a car, she was getting out of there.

Grace didn't hesitate. She hurried to the door and quietly turned the knob. When the door cracked open, she looked into the corridor. No one was in sight. She opened the door wider and poked her head out, looking both directions.

There was a small voice in the back of her mind that reminded her something terrible could happen if she got caught. But she wasn't going to get caught. She had been used enough. It was time to leave Dreagan.

Grace slid into the hallway and quickly closed the door behind her. She remained against the wall and half-ran, half-walked to the stairs.

She paused when she reached the steps because once she was on them, anyone could see her. Grace took in a steadying breath and then held her head high as she descended the stairs.

At the bottom she had a moment's fear since she didn't know where to go. Then she decided it didn't matter. She turned left and found herself walking down a wide corridor with windows on one side letting in tons of light. On the opposite wall were paintings and tapestries of dragons of numerous sizes and colors. She came to a door and peeked inside to find it was a library.

Grace pivoted and retraced her steps since it didn't look as if she was going to find a way out in the direction she had been going.

She found the stairs again easily enough. This time she went to the right. After a bit of maneuvering around open doorways with others inside what appeared to be a parlor, Grace found the front door.

As soon as she was outside, she breathed a sigh of relief. She faced forward and saw her rental car parked right in front. Grace ran to the vehicle and got inside. There she found her keys in the ignition, her purse and laptop on the seat beside her. Her hands were shaking as she started the engine and threw the car in reverse.

It wasn't until she was driving away that she felt something heavy in her chest, as if her heart were breaking in two. All that she had shared with Arian was gone. She thought he was different than other men, but she had been wrong. He was a man who cared more about Dreagan and the Dragon Kings than he did about her.

Grace pressed the accelerator. The car gained speed as she turned onto the main road. She didn't have a clue where she was going. All that mattered was that she left the Dragon Kings behind.

Something fell on her cheek. Grace swiped at her face, infuriated to find that it was a tear.

"I'm not going to cry for Arian," she told herself. "He's not worth it."

The sad part was that he was *definitely* worth it. He was the type of guy she had been writing in her novels for years. The type of guy that she only thought existed in her mind. Not once did she ever believe she would find him.

But she had found him. That's what hurt so much. He had been in her arms, real and so wonderful she hadn't been able to stop touching him.

Kissing him had been mind-blowing. So much so she hadn't ever wanted to stop.

He had been kind and gentle, tender and sweet. All while having an air of danger and mystery that made her so hot for him.

His immortality made her a bit wary, but how could she be afraid of a Dragon King who made love to her like he was worshipping her?

She hadn't expected anything of Arian. Well, that wasn't true. She knew what she wanted from him, and she had hoped he wanted more from her as well. Knowing what he was and the war he was part of would've made things difficult, but it didn't deter her.

Arian hadn't just touched her physically. He had changed her. She always thought she had an open mind, but discovering his secret had forced her to challenge herself and her thinking. She had accepted who he was, as well as his story. Grace yearned to help him any way she could.

The few hours with him had altered her mind, her body, and her heart. Now she looked at the world entirely different because she knew there was magic and dragons, Fae, and Druids walking around.

How wonderful she had felt being with him.

Then Arian had to go and ruin it by using her fear against her.

Grace shifted gears and found the signs leading back to Inverness.

* * * *

Warrick stood with Con at the front of the manor, watching Grace Clark drive away. "Are you sure this was the right thing?"

"She wasna lying. She's no' working with Ulrik," Con said.

Warrick raised a brow as he cut his eyes to Con. "That's no' what I'm talking about, and you know it."

"Is it no' enough that one more King has chosen a mate? Arian just woke. He needs to be focused on the war."

Warrick crossed his arms over his chest and faced Con. "You saw how Arian reacted. I believe Grace could be his mate."

"Perhaps."

"Perhaps?" Warrick repeated. "Just what lengths will you go to in order to keep a King from his mate?"

Con turned his black eyes to him. "If I think there could be another repeat of what happed with Ulrik—anything and everything."

"Grace isna that type of woman."

"You doona know her."

"Neither do you," Warrick pointed out. "The only one who knows her at all is Arian. And I tell you, he's no' going to be happy when he learns what's happened."

"And what has happened?" came a voice behind Warrick.

Warrick turned and spotted Arian standing in the middle of the doorway. Warrick hooked his thumb toward Con and said, "Ask him."

Arian met Con's gaze. "Where is Grace? I went to your office, but no one was there."

"She's gone," Con said.

Warrick watched Arian closely. A muscle ticced in his temple and his nostrils flared as he attempted to keep calm. It was just a few days earlier Warrick had felt those same emotions. Just as he imagined, Arian was thinking of throttling Con.

"Gone?" Arian asked tightly.

Con nodded. "You were right. She was telling the truth about who she is."

"And you allowed her to leave knowing our secret?" Arian asked in disbelief.

Con glanced at Warrick and said, "Does that sound like something I would do?"

Warrick watched Con walk from the room. He gave a shake of his head and sat down in one of the chairs. Con had said he would go to any lengths. He had just proven it.

"I didna see Guy," Arian said. "I wanted to tell Grace farewell."

Warrick wasn't going to sit there and allow Arian to think Grace had her memories wiped. And surely Con knew that. Which made Warrick wonder just what the hell Con was up to.

"Her memories were no' wiped," Warrick said.

Arian's head jerked around, his long black hair falling over the white shirt. "What?"

"Con didna have Guy see Grace. He left her alone in his office, and just as he expected, she made a run for it. We stood here and watched her leave."

Arian ran a hand down his face. "I'm going to kill him."

"Ulrik may very well beat you to the punch, my friend."

"Why?" Arian asked helplessly. "Why would Con make me believe Grace was out of reach?"

Warrick shrugged and got to his feet. "Because he's an arse. Because he doesna want us to be happy. Because he doesna want to be the only one without a mate. Because he can. Take your pick."

"Why did he no' wipe her memories?"

Warrick shrugged. "That I can no' answer."

"Fuck, this is messed up."

"I could tell you all the ways that he's made it difficult for some Kings to have their mates, but that would take too much time. You need to go after Grace."

Arian looked out the window. "Con knew you would tell me the truth. I wish he would've done it."

"No' in the bastard's DNA."

"I hurt her, War."

Warrick nodded as he recalled doing the same to Darcy. "Aye, I know that feeling well. If you think there's something there, then go to her and do or say whatever needs to be done or said to get her back."

"Fight for her."

"Aye. Fight."

"That I can do."

Warrick smiled as he watched Arian stalk from the room. He looked upward to the room where Darcy was still asleep in their bed after hours of lovemaking.

He was supposed to be getting them something to eat. He made his way to the kitchen and began to gather items as he thought of all the ways he still wanted to make love to his woman.

Warrick was walking up the stairs when Arian came running down in a pair of boots, his same jeans, and a leather jacket over his tee shirt.

"I doona have a vehicle," Arian said.

Warrick laughed and jerked his head toward the garage. "You've no' actually driven yet, either, but you'll get the hang of it. At least you willna kill a sheep as Kiril did. Take the top set of keys. It's to a white G-class Mercedes. You'll figure it out soon enough."

Arian went down a few steps then stopped again. "Where is

she staying?"

"Ryder," they said in unison.

Arian was all smiles as he ran from the manor to the garage. Warrick hoped Con hadn't interfered too much to stop Arian from finding happiness.

Warrick was beginning to think that Con wanted everyone there to be miserable, which was shite, because they all suspected he had a lover.

The fact they had yet to find a woman he was with told Warrick it wasn't a mortal woman. Which left the Fae.

And no good would come of that.

Chapter Thirteen

Arian adjusted his grip on the steering wheel. He hadn't been awake in hundreds of years. The world had changed drastically from the last time he saw it, but he wasn't looking at the landscape. He was thinking of Grace and how badly things had gone wrong.

He flexed his toes, not yet used to the boots confining his feet. The clothes weren't much better, but then again, he had been in dragon form for a very long time. Nothing was going to feel right.

Except Grace's hands. They felt perfect against his skin.

Arian followed the directions from the female voice coming from the SAT NAV system. Driving wasn't that difficult. After he ran into a couple of things. The damage shouldn't be that bad.

He glanced up through the sunroof to the sky. A sky he wondered if dragons would ever be seen in again. He had a sick feeling they never would.

Pushing aside such morbid thoughts, Arian focused on what he would say to Grace. Everything that ran through his mind sounded awful.

Arian cringed when he heard the scrape of metal as he moved too far to the right and the SUV skidded against a wall of rocks as he drove across a bridge.

Seeing the damage done to the vehicle was the least of his worries. It was just a piece of metal. There was much more at stake—his heart.

His soul.

His future.

Arian didn't stop to wonder how he had come to feel so strongly about Grace in so short a time. All he knew was that he did.

That fear clutching at his heart was the same sensation he felt when he watched his dragons fly across the dragon bridge to another realm.

He had been helpless to do anything then. This time was different. This time he could set things right. And he was going to make sure he did.

No matter what he had to do or say, he wouldn't give up on Grace until she realized she was his. Because she had been. From the first moment she walked into his mountain, she had been his. Their fates had been sealed when they made love.

The B&B came into view. Arian slowed the SUV, his heart kicking up a notch when he spotted the car Grace had been driving.

She was still there. He hadn't realized how worried he was that she might have left until that moment.

Arian pulled over and stopped the vehicle. He shut off the engine. Then he rested his forehead against the steering wheel. He wasn't sure he knew what to do next.

It went without saying that he wanted Grace, but he had never gone after a woman before. If they wanted to be with him, great. If not, then he moved on.

With Grace, it was different. He had chased after her. He was even willing to get down on his knees and beg her forgiveness.

But where to start? A simple apology wasn't going to cut it.

Arian lifted his head and looked at the cottage across the street. Grace was inside, probably still upset. He recalled the fear in her pretty eyes and how they had welled with tears when she realized what he had done.

He'd hated himself at that moment. Though his actions had been to help safeguard his brethren, it had hurt Grace deeply. He'd promised to protect her, and instead he had done the opposite.

No, she hadn't been hurt physically. That didn't mean he hadn't harmed her emotionally and mentally.

Arian palmed the keys and got out of the vehicle. He closed the door behind him as he strode across the street. His hand shook when he knocked upon the bright blue wooden door.

The seconds that ticked by felt like eons as he waited for someone to come to the door. Finally, there was a creak in the floor when someone approached.

A moment later and the door opened to reveal a man in his early sixties with a solid white head of hair and gray eyes. He was beginning to hunch forward, but he stared at Arian with a clear gaze.

"Can I help you?" the man asked.

Arian gave a nod. "I'd like to speak to Grace Clark, please."

One thick, bushy white eyebrow rose. "Grace, aye? Stay here, lad, and let me see if she's in."

That was his way of telling Arian he was going to see if Grace would talk to him. Arian remained on the front step, trying not to fidget. He looked around the area, noting all the houses had taken the place of forests of trees.

Arian fiddled with the keys. He ran his hand through his hair. He kicked at the dirt on the path. He watched cars pass.

And all the while he thought of Grace.

He imagined running his hand along her face, of threading his fingers in her hair.

He thought of her smile, of the way her navy eyes lit from within when she gazed at him.

He remembered the touch of her hands on him, of the way she breathed when he was making love to her.

Then he recalled her fear, a fear he'd exploited. Her terror for storms went bone deep—so deep she might never get over it. He would try to show her the beauty of storms, but it would be asking a lot of her.

Arian knew then that even though it was his power, he was willing to never use it again if it meant he could be with Grace.

The door opened behind him.

Arian turned around, words already tumbling from his lips. But they fell silent as he looked not into the navy eyes of Grace but the old man.

"I'm sorry, lad, but she's no' available," the man said.

Arian looked above him to the windows of the second floor. Grace was up there. He could force his way in and make her talk to him, but what good would that do?

"I see." Arian hated the bitter taste of disappointment.

The old man's gray eyes were steady as he watched Arian. "Perhaps latter, lad," he offered.

"Perhaps. Thank you for your time," Arian said with a bow of his head. He then turned on his heel and walked back to the Mercedes.

Arian got back inside the vehicle and simply sat there. It wasn't a good sign that Grace wouldn't see him, but Arian wasn't about to give up. He would wait however long it took for her to talk to him.

He looked around the village. If the Dark could gain access to Dreagan, they could be there as well. Arian started the SUV and pulled onto the road. No Dark were going to get close to Grace.

* * * *

Grace's hands were shaking as she pulled her laptop on her legs and reclined against the iron headboard. Arian was there. To talk to her.

But she couldn't see him. Not now. Not after what he had done.

Everything bad in her life happened during a storm. For the first time, she had felt safe during the thunder and lightning as long as she was with Arian.

Then she learned he was controlling it, making the storm rage while Con interrogated her.

Grace didn't take an easy breath until she heard the SUV start up and drive away. She had seen Arian pull up, and much to her dismay, she had been ecstatic that he had come for her.

But she somehow found the courage to turn him away.

She opened a new document, the cursor blinking on the blank screen. She tabbed down and typed "Chapter One." Her fingers hovered over the keys for a moment, and then the words came out like a deluge.

She stopped seeing the words as she relived the scenes in her head. The smells, the sounds, the stillness of the water. The cool air, the heat from Arian's body.

His touch, his kisses.

The way he made her laugh and feel comforted.

The way he welcomed her into his world.

Hours later, she looked up to see that it was time for dinner. She surveyed the hundreds of pages she had written, stunned that it had all come so easily.

Words had never flown so effortlessly from her mind to her fingers, and she doubted she would ever again be able to write a story in so quick a time.

Then again, it was her story. She'd lived it, breathed it.

Survived it.

Grace set aside her laptop when there was a knock at her door. She rose and opened it to find Mr. McKean.

"Lass, you missed lunch and tea," he said, concern lining his eyes. "We didna want you going hungry."

At that he stepped aside, and one of the young girls helping at the B&B walked into her room with a tray in hand. The young girl came inside Grace's room and set the tray on the table.

"Eat," Mr. McKean urged Grace.

She blinked her tired eyes. "I will. Thank you for being so kind."

"That young man was brokenhearted that you didna see him, lass."

Grace lowered her gaze as she thought of Arian. She believed he might feel something for her, but more than likely he was concerned she might tell others his secret.

"He'll be fine," Grace said and smiled at Mr. McKean. "Thank you again for the food."

He returned her smile, and he and the girl walked away. Grace closed the door as her stomach rumbled. She sat at the small table and took a large bit of the shepherd's pie.

As she ate, she looked at her laptop. She was at the part of the story where Arian had driven away from the B&B. Grace knew what the future held for her, but this was where she could make it into whatever she wanted.

And since it was a romance story, the couple had to end up together. She might not get her own happily ever after, but her characters could.

Grace finished eating and returned to the bed. With the computer back in her lap, supported with a pillow underneath, she began typing once more.

It was easy for her to lose herself in the story. It was *her* story, after all. Her very own touch with having an HEA of her own. After the books she wrote and characters she lived through before she finally sold, she had never thought she would find anything close to what was in her books in real life.

And yet she had.

The part that hurt the worst was that it was over—before it had barely begun. It wasn't like she could delete parts and rewrite her story.

What happened, happened. There was no changing anything in her life like she could with the words on a page.

As she wrote the epilogue to the story where the characters— really it was her and Arian—remained together with a love that would last for eternity, she found herself crying.

Not just because the characters were in love and together, but because her heroine had been able to get over her fear of storms for the hero—something Grace wasn't sure she could ever do herself.

When the last period was typed, she saved the document, staring at the manuscript. She wasn't worried about her telling of the Dragon Kings, mostly because her books were fiction and no one would believe it anyway, but also because she changed all the names and locations just in case.

With a sigh, Grace closed the laptop.

For long moments she sat without moving, her gaze out the window. It had felt good to get her story out, but she was feeling a plethora of emotions.

Happiness at recalling her time with Arian.

Fear at reliving the storms.

Sorrow at having to say farewell to Arian.

And finally, gratification at being able to once more get her HEA—this time with her very own story, even if it wasn't in real life.

Grace blinked. Night had fallen without her even noticing. Was Arian up in the sky, flying? What did the moon look like reflected upon his turquoise scales?

Grace curled onto her side and closed her eyes as she imaged looking up and finding dragons soaring overhead. The fear she felt when she first saw Arian was gone, as if it had never been.

Now all she felt were possibilities for who the Dragon Kings were and what they could offer the world.

But she also felt desolation because she knew the Kings wouldn't be welcomed by all.

It was no wonder the Dragon Kings stayed hidden. And why they took their privacy so seriously. The world wasn't ready to know about them, magic, immortality, or the Dark Fae.

No amount of movies or TV shows or books could prepare a person for the real thing. The sheer size of Arian in dragon form alone was enough to make her feel as if her heart were going to burst from her chest.

With her eyes stinging from staring so long at the computer, Grace closed them. Her mind drifted once more to Arian and how he had so gently and possessively taken her into his arms and kissed her.

Another tear leaked from the corner of her eye. He was "The One." The one man who could've given her the great love she had always dreamed of. The one who was the other half to her soul.

To have held him so close only to lose him seemed too cruel for it to be real.

Chapter Fourteen

Arian paced Con's office. He had searched the village and didn't find a single Dark Fae or anyone who looked suspicious. Yet they had killed three more Dark who dared to try and enter Dreagan.

"You're making my head ache," Con said from his chair behind his desk.

Arian cut him a dark look. "You've never had a headache. You wouldna even know what one felt like."

"Oh, you'd be surprised."

Con's cryptic words halted Arian. He faced the King of Kings. "What are you no' telling me?"

"A lot, but that is the nature of my position." Con tossed his favorite moon pearl Montblanc fountain pen on the desk.

"You've always hidden things well, Con. Your anger, worry, anxiety. Even your fear."

"Fear?" Con asked with one blond brow raised.

Arian nodded and crossed his arms over his chest. "I want Grace as mine."

"You doona even know her."

"Are you my parent that I must convince?"

Con grew even more still. For long minutes he simply stared at Arian. "What I am is your king. What I do is for our continuation and survival."

"We'll always survive here," Arian argued. "Tell me, why did you no' wipe Grace's memories?"

"She left before I could."

Arian grunted. "You allowed her to leave. Admit it."

Con simply returned his stare.

"What are you up to?"

"I've told you."

"Do you have a lover, Con?"

"As if that's any of your concern."

"It is. As long as you interfere in my love life, I'll interfere in yours. Who is she, Con? Who is the woman you've been spending time with?"

"None of your goddamn business."

Arian blinked, taken aback by Con's words. It hadn't been an outburst as some who might have shouted those words. Instead, they were spoken in a cool tone. Entirely too controlled, which confirmed that whoever Con was seeing was important to him.

"One way or another I'm going to convince Grace to be mine." Arian dropped his arms to his sides. "I'll take the time to get to know her and for her to know me. But she'll be mine."

Con put his hands on the desk and slowly stood. He leaned on the desk and held Arian's gaze. "You're claiming her? Even though she may no' want you?"

"I am." Arian knew how she responded to his touch. She may not want him now, but he wouldn't give up until she remembered her initial reaction to him.

"All right," Con said and straightened. "I'll welcome her as I have the others. But I'll also warn you as I have the other Kings. I killed a human who betrayed one of you. I'll no' hesitate to do it again if need be."

"We were all right there with you, Con. You didna kill Ulrik's woman on your own."

"I was prepared to."

"Grace isna like that. She wouldna betray me."

"Ulrik thought the same of his woman. We may look like the mortals in this form, Arian, but we're no' them. And they are no' us. They doona think as we do."

Arian thought of Grace and her acceptance of him. "Perhaps

no', but there are many other ways our two species are the same."

"We mate for life. Verra few of the humans even grasp that concept. They take marriage vows no' thinking forever. It's for the here and now. That's why so many commit adultery or leave the marriage when things get rough instead of working through it."

Arian put his hands on the back of the chair in front of Con. "You make it sound like we've no' made any mistakes. We've made plenty. We're no more perfect than the mortals."

"I could argue differently."

"Do you hate them?"

Con's black eyes became distant. "I doona know what you mean."

"I get the feeling you do, but then why do you defend them so fiercely? If you hated them, why no' allow Ulrik to rid the realm of them once and for all."

"We took an oath."

Arian shrugged one shoulder. "So you do despise them."

"I didna say that."

"You didna deny it, either."

Con adjusted the gold dragon-head cuff link at his wrist. "My feelings toward the mortals doona matter one way or the other. My first duty is to all of you and our way of life. Only after that do I consider the vow I took regarding the humans."

Arian looked past Con to the window. Night was still upon them. It was time to stretch his wings and look in on Grace.

After all, debating anything with Con was an exercise in futility.

* * * *

Grace's eyes snapped open. She sat up in the darkened room and glanced at her mobile. It had only been two hours since she finished the book.

She tried to lie back down and sleep once more, but her eyes wouldn't remain shut. She couldn't stop thinking about Arian. Or seeing the cavern in her mind's eye.

After another thirty minutes of tossing, Grace rose and took a shower, thinking that might help her relax and get back to sleep. But once out of the shower, she was more awake than before.

She dried off and put on clean clothes before she tugged on her hiking boots. Grace walked from her room with nothing but her mobile phone and a jacket.

As she strode from the back door of the B&B, Grace saw the rolling landscape before her. The moon didn't shed much light as it filtered through the clouds, but she had the flashlight on her mobile if she needed it.

The fresh air and a nice walk were just what she needed to empty her mind so she could find some peace. She strolled across the terrain. Occasionally she glanced upward, not that she expected to see anything. There were too many clouds for one, and for another, she didn't think any of the Kings would be this far from Dreagan.

Why then did she keep looking up? She tried to deny it, but the simple fact was she wanted to see a dragon. Correction. She wanted to see Arian.

She knew what he looked like with his wings spread as he soared through the sky. She knew how his turquoise scales glinted metallic in the sunlight. She knew the feel of the heat from the fire he breathed from his mouth.

Powerful. Dignified. Commanding. Mighty. Imposing. Noble.

They were all words she would readily use to describe Arian in both his dragon and human forms.

Grace was breathing heavily when she crested a hill that was a lot steeper than she had originally thought. She stood looking over the land even as a cold breeze blew past her.

She wrapped her arms around herself. Though she had traveled extensively all over Europe, she continued to set her stories in Scotland.

Her father used to laugh about it, telling her that there must be something in Scotland drawing her to the land. She used to roll her eyes at his teasing. Now she wondered if he hadn't been right.

Her father had believed in fate and destiny. Whereas Grace thought each person decided their own path with the choices they made.

Now she was beginning to believe that perhaps her father might have had it right all along. It felt as if she were supposed to have met Arian and experienced all that she had with him.

Destiny? Or choice?

There was a whoosh overhead. Grace looked up but saw nothing more than the clouds from before. She started walking forward down the hill.

Grace reached the bottom when she heard something above her. This time when she lifted her gaze she saw a dark shape begin to emerge from a cloud.

She gasped, mesmerized as Arian flew over her, circling back around by dipping one wing. The beat of his wings was so loud she wondered how no one else heard it.

Her gaze was riveted as he descended in one fluid motion with his wings outspread while he hovered over the ground before landing.

He tucked his wings against him and watched her with his black eyes. Arian didn't move, and it took Grace a moment to realize he was waiting on her.

She licked her lips. What should she do? She was torn, wanting to go to him and wanting to run away. He had already come to see her once as a human. He had returned again. This time in his true form.

Grace walked to him one slow step at a time. Her heart was racing, but not because she was scared of him. Because she was frightened of how he made her feel.

She halted before him, looking up into his black eyes as he towered over her. Arian lowered his giant head, and Grace hesitantly stroked him.

A laugh escaped when she felt the warmth of his scales. They were hard beneath her hand, but not cold. It was so unexpected that she couldn't stop touching him.

He closed his eyes, a low rumble coming from deep within him. Grace rested her cheek against the side of his head. In all her wild imaginings, she never pictured herself caressing a dragon.

As odd as it seemed, it also felt as if she had been destined for it.

If only he hadn't used her fear against her.

Grace squeezed her eyes closed. Why did she have to be afraid of storms? Why couldn't she let go of the fear? If she could, she might have a future with Arian—because she had already forgiven him for what he did.

Because she loved him.

Arian blew out a breath and lifted his head. Grace stepped back as she watched him. For long seconds, he held her gaze, and then in a blink the dragon was gone. In its place was Arian, standing naked and proud before her.

Grace let her gaze run over him from his face to his feet and back up again, stopping to admire the dragon tat on his left leg.

It must be the trick of the light because she could've sworn it moved.

"Grace."

Her eyes lifted to his face, where she found him staring at her. His expression melted her heart instantly. He allowed her to see his sorrow, his anxiety, and his...love.

She took a step back when she realized what he was offering. Grace hadn't thought anyone could tell another of their love without words, but the proof stood before her now.

"I promised to protect you, and I didna," Arian said. "I let you down."

Grace didn't move, didn't so much as blink.

"I'm sorry. So verra sorry, lass." Arian looked at the ground for a moment and ran a hand through his hair. "Those words are so inadequate. I could say I did it for my brethren and Dreagan, but even that doesna sound right."

She looked at his wide shoulders. Those same shoulders where she had rested her head after they made love. She looked at his arms. The same arms that had held her so passionately and protectively.

"Say something, Grace. Please," he implored.

But she didn't know if she could. The words were stuck in her throat. Yes, she had felt wonderful with Arian, but she had also experienced her greatest fear while with him.

She loved him and already forgave him, but he chose loyalty over love. Would he do it again?

Arian let out a deep breath and gave a single nod. "You'll no' see anyone from Dreagan again. Of that, I vow. No one will take away your memories. Unless you want them gone."

Did she? It would be easier not having to remember Arian and his kisses, but was that really want she wanted? No!

"Anything worth having is worth fighting for," her father used to say.

His second favorite quote was, *"Sometimes the most complicated things in life are the ones that end up bringing us the most satisfaction."*

Arian and the Dragon Kings were definitely complications. And she wanted to be a part of that world. As alarming and thrilling and terrifying as it all was.

"I forgive you," she said as Arian turned to leave.

He jerked back to her. "Say it again. Please."

This time she had a difficult time not smiling. "I forgive you."

He was before her in a blink. Hesitantly, he hooked a finger with hers. "I'll never hurt you again, Grace. I put my loyalty to Con and Dreagan above my feelings for you. I did it because I wanted Con to believe you, so I thought that if he could get his information you'd never have to endure his question again. I'm sorry, lass."

Her eyes closed when he pulled her against his chest and wrapped his arms around her. Despite everything, in his arms was where she knew she belonged.

Chapter Fifteen

Arian held Grace tight. He let her go once. He wasn't going to do it again. Kissing the top of her head, he said, "I doona want to scare you, lass, but I've fallen for you."

There was a beat of silence. He felt her tense in his arms then. Arian knew he shouldn't have told her that yet. He was going to frighten her away just as he got her back.

"Arian," she whispered.

It was the thread of panic in her voice that alerted him. He jerked his head to where she was looking and saw the three Dark Fae approaching.

"*Dark Fae!*" Arian shouted through his mental link to the Kings.

He pushed Grace behind him as he looked around for more Dark.

Behind them another two came their way. It was their smirks that set Arian off. The Fae thought they had them cornered, but Arian wasn't about to let that happen.

"Do you trust me?" he asked Grace.

She clutched his arm and nodded her head quickly. "Yes, I trust you."

"Climb on my back. And hang on tight."

There was a strangled screech as he shifted as soon as she had her legs wrapped around him. Arian unfurled his wings, knocking two of the Dark back.

Another sent a blast of magic at him, hitting him squarely on the neck. Pain radiated through him as the magic sizzled along his scales.

If only he had thunder to mask a roar, but he wouldn't put Grace through that fear again. He would find another way to beat the Dark.

He opened his mouth and blasted the Dark with dragon fire. Grace had a death grip on him, but even so Arian was afraid to jump into the air and knock her off. It was her first ride, and he needed to be gentle.

But there was no such thing as gentle in battle.

A growl left him as he was hit with several more rounds of Dark magic. If he didn't get out of there soon, the Dark magic would make him shift back into a human.

Arian swiped his tail behind him. He severed a Dark in half, leaving only three more to fight.

"Make it rain!" Grace yelled.

Surely Arian heard her wrong. Grace would never tell him to make it rain.

Arian turned, using his tail to keep the Dark at a distance. His wings he used to deflect magic aimed at Grace. He took a couple of steps forward to take off when he was hit in the side with a volley of Dark magic.

"Arian! Do it!" Grace demanded. "Make it thunder."

His heart swelled at the trust she bestowed upon him. Despite her fear, she believed in him.

He let loose his magic. The clouds gathered quickly overhead, and a second later, lightning split the sky viciously again and again. Thunder rumbled so loudly that it masked Arian's roar as he was bombarded with Dark magic.

There was no mistaking the feel of Grace shaking as she clung to his neck. He had to get her away from the Dark and the storm. But the tempest was the only cover to get them out.

He took a huge chance dropping from the meager clouds to see Grace to begin with. Getting away without the storm would be impossible as the Dark tried to keep him there. Not to mention, the

Dark didn't care who heard or saw them.

Arian prayed Grace held on. He jumped into the air, spreading his wings, and caught a current. With a quick turn, he dodged another round of magic. As he swung back around to deliver a blast of dragon fire, two dragons came up on either side of him.

He met the royal purple gaze of the gold dragon. Con. With a nod, Con tucked his wings and dove toward the ground. Arian looked on the other side of him to find Warrick. Lightning flashed around them, giving Arian a glimpse of War's jade scales before he joined Con in taking out the remaining Dark.

Arian contained the storm to where they were and quickly flew Grace out of it. He kept as low to the ground as he dared without being seen as he glided through the sky toward Dreagan.

Finally, Grace lifted her head from his neck and looked around. He heard her whispered, "Wow," which caused him to smile.

Though he reached Dreagan swiftly, he didn't land. Instead, he wanted to show Grace the other side of being a Dragon King.

He dipped lower, taking them in the valley between mountains. Arian felt his heart swell when he heard her laughter.

"Arian, this is amazing!" she yelled.

Her grip eased, but it didn't loosen altogether. Finally, after another thirty minutes, Arian turned and headed to his mountain.

He slowed, using his wings to hover him over the entrance. After he landed, he walked through his entrance to the cavern. Only then did he lower his neck so she could slide off him.

Arian used his magic to start a fire for light. Then he shifted and yanked her into his arms. He buried his head in her neck. "I'm so sorry I had to use the weather."

"It's all right."

"Nay. It's no'."

She leaned back to look at his face. "No, it really is. I knew I was safe with you. I knew you would control the weather so it couldn't hurt me. I should've realized that sooner. It was us in danger that made me face what I already knew."

"I'll never let anything hurt you, Grace. Ever," he vowed.

She glanced down at his chest. "Before the Dark arrived, you were saying something."

"It doesna matter. It can wait."

"Say it again," she urged.

He looked into her navy eyes and felt the steel band of anxiety ease from his chest. "I'm falling for you."

"Falling? Or fallen?"

"Fallen," he admitted. "I fell for you the minute you walked into this mountain. Does that frighten you?"

She gave a small nod. "It does."

Arian knew he shouldn't have told her his true feelings. Not yet anyway. She needed time to adjust.

"It does because this isn't suppose to happen," Grace said.

"What?"

"Love at first sight." She put her hands on his chest and smiled. "Everyone says it can't possibly happen, but I know that it does."

Arian's heart beat faster. "And? What do you think it means?"

"I'm not sure. All I know is that I like how I feel when I'm with you. I love how protective you are and that you aren't afraid to say you're sorry. I like how you touch me and kiss me. I like how you hold me, but more than anything, I like the possibilities that are before us."

"We're in the middle of a war," he warned.

She shrugged and ran her hands up his chest and over his shoulders to clasp around his neck. "Every couple has their own issues to get through."

He threw back his head and laughed. "I do love how you can make me laugh in such a way."

"I do, too. I also really like how you can make me hot for you with just a look."

Damn. Did she really just say that? Arian moaned, feeling his cock harden at the thought.

"That," she said breathlessly. "That's the look."

Arian kissed her hard, his arm holding her so tight he knew he was hurting her. But he couldn't loosen his hold. She was too precious to him.

He ended the kiss and simply held her, amazed that she had come into his life. "You found your muse again at Dreagan. Will you stay?"

"What of Con?"

Arian leaned back so he could look at her. "Con let you leave Dreagan. He watched you."

"What?" she asked, her brow furrowed.

"He believes you. I think he wanted to see how far I was willing to go and how much you could take."

She rolled her eyes. "I don't think I like him very much, but I know why he did what he did."

Arian smiled and tugged a lock of blonde hair. "Stay here with me, Grace. I want you as mine. Always."

"You don't know me."

"We'll take the time to get to know each other. But please stay. I need you."

She rose up on her tiptoes and placed her lips on his. "As if I could refuse such a request. I'm all yours, Arian."

"Damn, baby. That's just what I wanted to hear," he said as he claimed her lips for another fierce kiss and began to undress her.

Epilogue

Grace couldn't stop fiddling with her purse strap. The book was turned in to her publisher. Arian even liked the fact she used their story. But that's not why she was nervous.

Arian's hand came to rest atop hers gently. She looked at him and returned his smile as she gazed into his champagne eyes. "It's going to be fine," he assured her once again.

He had been saying that all morning. She believed it when they went to gather her things at the B&B with Mr. McKean smiling knowingly. She even believed as they drove away.

But the closer they came to Dreagan, the more worried she began.

"You trust me, right?" Arian asked.

"Of course."

"Then trust me when I say it's going to be all right."

She nodded. "My things are really being packed up in Paris?"

"The joys of being involved with such a large corporation. Things get done."

"That's money, Arian."

"Same difference," he replied with a grin.

She released a deep breath and sat back in the Mercedes. It was dented on both sides badly, though it made her smile to know that Arian had driven for the first time the day before to look for her.

His fingers threaded with hers when they turned onto the drive that wound through thick woods leading toward the manor. She caught a glimpse of red roofs and knew that was the distillery based on the descriptions Arian had told her.

He was going to take her on a tour later and show her everything. She was also going to meet everyone.

The manor came in sight then, the gray stones standing strong against the backdrop of the Highlands. The sky was bright blue without a cloud, and the sun was blinding. A perfect day.

Arian parked the SUV and turned off the ignition. He lifted her hand to his lips and kissed her fingers. "Ready?"

"Yes."

They got out of the car. Grace looked around at the mountains as she closed her door. Arian came up beside her and wrapped an arm around her. They stood together for several minutes.

"You're part of Dreagan now," Arian said as he looked at her. "Just as you're a part of me. That means our enemies could focus on you, but it also means everyone here will protect you."

"I don't know what to say."

"Say you'll be mine."

She smiled then. "I was yours from the moment I saw you."

"Then lets get your new life started."

They walked arm-in-arm to the front door. When they drew close, it opened and Con stood in the doorway. He gave a nod to Arian, and then bestowed a smile to Grace.

"It looks like another King has found his mate," Con said.

With that, they walked into the manor to a crowd of people waiting to meet her.

Through it all, Arian never left her side. His arm remained around her, offering comfort and support when she needed it.

Grace found herself looking at him often. And each time he was watching her. She couldn't believe she had gotten so lucky to find the man of her dreams.

It was only made better knowing he was a Dragon King.

About Donna Grant

New York Times and *USA Today* bestselling author Donna Grant has been praised for her "totally addictive" and "unique and sensual" stories. She's the author of more than thirty novels spanning multiple genres of romance. Her latest acclaimed series, Dark Kings, features dragons, the Fae, and immortal Highlanders who are dark, dangerous, and irresistible.

She lives with her two children, three dogs, and four cats in Texas.

For more information about Donna, visit her website at www.DonnaGrant.com.

Also From Donna Grant

Don't miss these other spellbinding novels!

Dark King Series
DARK HEAT (3 NOVELLA COMPILATION)
DARKEST FLAME
FIRE RISING
BURNING DESIRE
HOT BLOODED
NIGHT'S BLAZE
SOUL SCORCHED
DRAGON KING (NOVELLA)

Dark Warrior Series
MIDNIGHT'S MASTER
MIDNIGHT'S LOVER
MIDNIGHT'S SEDUCTION
MIDNIGHT'S WARRIOR
MIDNIGHT'S KISS
MIDNIGHT'S CAPTIVE
MIDNIGHT'S TEMPTATION
MIDNIGHT'S PROMISE
MIDNIGHT'S SURRENDER (NOVELLA)

Chiasson Series
WILD FEVER
WILD DREAM
WILD NEED
WILD FLAME

Larue Series
MOON KISSED
MOON THRALL

And look for more anticipated novels from
Donna Grant

MOON STRUCK (LARUE)
PASSION IGNITES (DARK KINGS)
DARK ALPHA'S CLAIM (REAPER – DARK KING SPIN OFF)

coming soon!

Passion Ignites
Dark Kings #7
By Donna Grant
Now Available

He consumed her with that kiss, leaving no question that whatever was happening between them was meant to be-that it had always been meant to be...

HE LOVES FOR ETERNITY

Thorn is the bad boy of the Dragon Kings, a gorgeous, reckless warrior whose passions run wild and fury knows no bounds. When he sees the brave, beautiful Lexi being lured into the Dark Fae's trap, he has no choice but to rescue her from a fate worse than death. But by saving this tempting mortal, he exposes himself to his fiercest enemy-and darkest desires. As the war between Dragons and Fae heats up, so does the passion between Lexi and Thorn. And when love is a battlefield, the heart takes no prisoners...

SHE LIVES FOR VENGEANCE

Lexi is on a mission of justice. Every day, she searches for the monster who murdered her friend. Every night, she hides in the shadows and plots her revenge. But the man she seeks is more dangerous than she ever imagined. He is one of the Dark Fae who preys on human life, who uses his unearthly power to seduce the innocent, and who is setting a trap just for her. Nothing can save Lexi from a creature like this-except the one man who's been watching her every move...

* * * *

For two weeks, Thorn had been in Edinburgh with Darius hunting the Dark Fae. He wasn't exactly thrilled that the Dragon Kings were spread so thin throughout Scotland to kill the bastards.

Then again, he was killing Dark Fae, which made him extremely happy.

He liked Darius, even if he had his own demons to battle.

Darius wasn't the issue. It was Con.

Thorn halted his thoughts as he jumped from the roof he had been on and landed silently behind two Dark. He came up to them and smashed their heads together. Then, with his knife, he slashed their throats.

Both Fae fell without a sound. Damn, did he ever like his job. Thorn threw both Dark Fae over his shoulder and hurried to the warehouse where he and Darius were stashing the bodies.

He did most of his killing at night when the Dark came out to prey on the mortals, but Thorn never passed up an opportunity to kill the buggers.

There were half a dozen Dark laying dead in the warehouse. With merely a thought, he shifted, letting his body return to its rightful form—a dragon.

His long talons clicked on the concrete floor as he looked down at the Dark. Thorn inhaled deeply, fire rumbling in his throat. Then he released it, aiming at the bodies.

Dragon fire was the hottest thing on the realm. It disintegrated the Dark Fae bodies instantly. When there was nothing left but ash, Thorn shifted back into his human form.

He clothed himself and returned to the streets that were overrun with Dark. The humans had no idea who they were walking beside or having drinks with. Many mortals he and Darius had saved from being killed by the Dark, but there were so many more that they couldn't reach in time.

With just two Dragon Kings in the city against hundreds of Dark Fae, the odds were stacked against the humans.

Thorn didn't understand why the mortals couldn't sense how dangerous the Dark were. Or perhaps that's exactly what drew them to the Dark—that and their sexual vibes the humans couldn't ignore.

The Dark weren't as confident as they were a few weeks ago. Their ranks were dwindling, and though they suspected Dragon Kings were involved, they had yet to find him or Darius.

If two Dragon Kings could do so much damage, imagine what twelve could do? That brought a smile to Thorn's face. The Dark thought they were being smart, but they had begun the war a second time. And Thorn knew it would be impossible for the humans not to learn just what inhabited their realm with them.

His smile faded when his gaze snagged on a woman he had seen daily for the past week. She kept hidden, but it was obvious she was following the Dark.

She had a determined look on her face, one that had anger and revenge mixed together. Thorn knew that expression. It was the one that got mortals killed.

Her pale brown locks hung thick and straight to her shoulders. She tucked her hair behind her ear and peered around the corner of a store.

Thorn slid his gaze to the three Dark she was trailing. They were toying with her. They knew she was there.

"Damn," Thorn mumbled.

He and the other Dragon Kings vowed to protect the humans millions of years ago. They fought wars and sent their own dragons away to do just that. He couldn't stand there and let the Dark kill her.

Nor could he let them know he was there.

He flattened his lips when she stepped from her hiding spot and followed the Dark down the street. They were leading her to a secluded section.

Thorn didn't waste any time climbing to the roof of the building. He kept to the shadows and jumped from roof to roof as he tracked them.

He let out a thankful sigh when she ducked into an alley. Thorn jumped over the street to the opposite building before landing behind her.

"Not this time," he heard her say.

An American. Southern by her accent. He reached to tap her on the shoulder when his enhanced hearing picked up the Darks' conversation. They were coming for her.

Thorn wrapped a hand around her mouth and dragged her behind a Dumpster. "Be quiet and still if you doona want them to find you," he whispered in her ear.

She was struggling against him, but his words caused her to pause. A second later, she renewed her efforts.

Thorn held her tightly, her thin form easy to detain. The more she struggled, the more he could feel every curve of her body.

It wasn't until the Dark reached the alley that she stilled. He couldn't even feel her breathing.

"There's no one here," one of the Dark said in his Irish brogue.

"She was here."

The third snorted. "Not anymore. Come on."

A full minute passed before the three walked on. The woman's shoulders sagged as she blew out a breath. Thorn released her and held up his hands as she whirled around to face him.

Slate gray eyes glared at him with fury as her full lips pulled back in a scowl. Her cheekbones were high in her oval face.

She wasn't a great beauty, but there was something about her that wouldn't let Thorn look away.

"You're in way over your head," he told her.

Ignite
A Legacy Novella
By Rebecca Yarros

IT ONLY TAKES A SINGLE SPARK...

ignite

FROM THE AUTHOR OF *HALLOWED GROUND*

REBECCA YARROS

Chapter One

River

Fuck my life, I was exhausted. Squinting into the sun, I walked out of the Midnight Sun's Hotshot Crew house at 10:45 p.m. I'd never known a more fitting name for a hotshot team in my life. We'd lived here the last seven years—as soon as I'd been accepted to the University of Alaska—but the sunlight situation in late July still caught me off guard from time to time.

Guess my brain always diverted back to Colorado.

"Damn, that was a long one, Riv," Bishop said, swinging his arm over my shoulder and squeezing. He'd done the same thing after every fire we'd ever been on together. I knew he hated that I'd followed him into this life. What the fuck did he think I was going to do? Let my big brother follow in our dad's footsteps and not tag along? Hell no. As soon as I was old enough, I'd applied, worked my ass off through college getting my degree in forestry, and now here we were.

"I'm just glad it's over. It was getting dicey there for a while." I unlocked the doors on my F250 as he ruffled my hair like we were kids again. Strands of the dark, heavy stuff caught in the scruff of my beard as it settled back around my face. Chin-length was as far as I could handle my hair, I had no clue how Bishop managed to keep his down his back.

Our mother is Cheyenne, he always said in explanation.

"It did go to shit," he admitted. "You could always take a cushy job with the forest service. No fires, safe hours, nice scenery…" he said before unlocking the doors to his truck, too.

"Like that's ever going to happen," I said as I tossed my dirt-covered bag into the bed of the truck.

"Yeah, well, I wish it would," he mumbled.

"Gym tomorrow?" I asked, ignoring his jibe. For only being three years older than me, he took his brothering seriously.

"Same as usual," he answered, climbing up into his truck.

I did the same, sliding behind the wheel and shutting the door. A crank of the engine later and I was on the road out of Fairbanks, heading toward my house in Ester. Bishop was a mad man when it came to gym time. *You'd better be able to outrun the fire,* he'd always told me.

So he pushed me like the flames were constantly licking at my heels. Not that I minded the body it gave me—hell, it attracted more than my fair share of female attention. Though I'd definitely sampled the buffet of women up here, my exploits were nothing compared to Bishop's.

We were both the same in one regard, though: we'd never been with one woman longer than six months or so. Bishop tended to leave around that time, and as for me…well, the girls always figured out that they weren't my first priority, which rightfully pissed them off.

As I turned off route three into Ester the sun finally started to set. For God's sake, it was 11 p.m. I missed warm summer nights under the stars in Colorado. Not that Northern Lights weren't amazing…they just weren't the same.

Don't complain about the sunlight. It will be dark nearly all day soon enough.

The lot in front of the Golden Eagle Saloon had an empty parking spot, and I took it, jumping down from the truck once I killed the ignition. I smelled like smoke and ten days of hard firefighting, but I knew she'd lose her shit if I didn't stop by.

Besides, I was itching to see her.

The music was up when I walked into the old-fashioned log

cabin saloon. Good crowd for a Saturday night.

"River!" Jessie Ruggles called out from the bar, her skirt a hell of a lot shorter than those long-ass legs of hers called for. Not that I was complaining. "Everybody make it home okay?"

"Yeah, we're intact," I answered. "Have you seen—"

"River!"

I turned toward her voice and was immediately met with a hundred pounds of perfection. She swore it was more. I never believed her.

Avery jumped, and I easily caught her. Her arms wrapped around my neck, one of them cradling the back of my head in that way of hers that always fucking melted me.

"You're okay," she whispered in my neck.

Even in the bar, she smelled fantastic, all apples and warm cinnamon.

"I'm okay, Avery," I promised, my hands splaying on her back. "Everyone is."

She nodded but didn't say anything, just held me a little tighter. I'd come home from countless fires in the years that she'd been my best friend, and this was always how she welcomed me home.

There was nothing better on the planet.

I stood there in the middle of the bar, letting her hold me as long as she needed. Mostly because I could never get enough of her in my arms.

Avery Claire had been my best friend since I was eighteen.

I'd also been silently in love with her for just as long.

Maybe one day she'd be ready to hear it, but I knew that today was not that day. Hell, the next year didn't look promising, either.

Taking in one more deep breath, Avery slid from my grasp, backing up a couple feet once her toes hit the wooden floor of the bar. Then she looked me over, inspecting for anything that might slightly resemble an injury. She tucked her long blonde hair behind her ears and nodded, appeased. Avery was fair everywhere I was dark, her skin pale where mine was deeply tanned by the sun and my mother's Cheyenne heritage. She was tiny where I was broad, curved where I was straight, and those shorts she wore didn't disguise much of her toned legs.

"See, I'm fine," I said with a little grin.

"Promise?" she asked, narrowing those gorgeous blue eyes.

"I smell like smoke and I'm fucking exhausted, but other than that, I'm in one piece. I'm actually headed home, but I figured you were working tonight—"

"And that I'd kick your ass if you didn't tell me you were home."

"I could always text."

"Not the same." Her smile grew until she could have lit the world with how bright it was. "I'm glad you're home."

"Me, too. Did Zeus miss me?"

"Your husky is the neediest, wimpiest dog I've ever met, but yes, he's content and full of treats at your house."

"He's a big baby," I admitted.

"Just like his owner," she teased.

"Avery, were you thinking about getting back to work?" Megan asked from behind the bar in her pack-a-day rasp. She was ageless, frozen somewhere in her fifties. The woman hadn't changed since I got here seven years ago.

"Yeah," Avery called out. "Sorry, I have to go."

"I know. Don't worry. I'll see you tomorrow—"

"Riv!" Adeline came running at me, a tangle of hair and knobby knees.

I caught her easily and squeezed her tight. "Hey, Addy! What are you doing here?"

She pulled back and glanced at Avery. "I was supposed to stay with Stella, but she had to go out of town with her parents."

I nodded and looked over to Avery, who was biting her lip. I knew she hated when she had to bring Addy in—she was only thirteen—but not nearly as much as she hated leaving her home alone with their father.

"Why don't you come spend the night in my guest room?" I asked.

Her eyes flew wide with excitement. "Can I watch *Game of Thrones*?"

"Nope," I answered. "But I think I have every episode of *Arrow*."

"Okay, I can rock that. Stephen Amell is hot."

"If you say so," I said, grinning at her. Addy never failed to bring a smile to my face.

"Are you sure you don't mind?" Avery asked, her hands wringing.

I wanted to cup her face, brush my thumbs across her cheekbones, and lay a soft kiss to her lips. Instead, I squeezed her hand. "It's no problem. Why don't you come over when you're done? Bunk with Adeline, and we'll go for breakfast in the morning?"

She nodded with a grin. "Yes. I close out at two, and then I'll head over."

I would have said anything to see Avery smile like that—carefree and happy. She was always beautiful, but that smile shot her straight to gorgeous, and I never saw enough of it. "You have a key, so just come on in. Addy, you ready?"

"Yes!"

I laughed at her excitement. "Okay, but don't get too excited. Zeus might want to share your bed, and he's a hog."

"True, but he's nice and warm."

"That he is," I admitted before turning back to her big sister. "See you in the morning?"

She nodded and leaned up on tiptoes to hug me. It was the only way to cross the difference between my six-foot-five frame and her five-foot-six. "Thank you for taking her," she said, holding me tight. "I just couldn't leave her there on her own. He gets so mean at night."

When he's been drinking.

"No problem." I hugged her back and let her slide from my arms.

Then I took Adeline home.

"I love your house," she said as we climbed the steps to the porch.

"It's not as big as yours," I answered, slipping the key into the lock. I'd built the house myself—with Bishop and contracted workers, of course, and I was fond of its traditional log-cabin design, but I knew it wasn't much.

"It feels more like home," she said as I opened the door.

"Umpf!" My breath was knocked out of me as Zeus barreled out the door, tackling me to the ground. All hundred and twenty pounds of him lay on my chest, licking my face as he whined. "Yeah, I missed you, too, buddy," I said, petting his thick fur.

He looked at me with disapproving blue eyes, like I'd had any control over how long the fire had taken, and let me up. I massaged his head a few more times, and he started to forgive me. "Come back when you're done," I told him, and he raced off into the woods. There was something to be said for having ten acres to myself.

I brought two of my fingers to my mouth and then pressed them to the framed picture of my dad that hung just inside the entry. Some rituals had to be kept—and this was definitely one of them. "Made it home, Pop," I said.

"Why did you do that?" Addy asked.

"Because I always tell him I made it when I get home from a fire," I told her, hauling my bag in with me.

"Because he didn't?" she asked.

The innocent question caught me off guard. "That's right. He died with his whole Hotshot team when a fire took our hometown."

She looked up at the photo of my dad in his gear and then back to me. "How long ago was that?"

"Ten years." *Ten years in a couple weeks.*

"That's sad. I'm sorry."

"Thank you. It's hard to lose your parent, huh?"

She nodded. "I don't really remember my mom, though, so…" She shrugged.

"I don't think that makes it any easier. Loss is loss."

She nodded, examining the photo of my father. "He was handsome."

"My mom sure thought so." They had loved each other in a way that told me I'd never settle for less in my own life. "Your stuff is still in the dresser in there," I told Addy as she walked into the living room. This wasn't the first time she'd slept over while Avery worked, and I knew it wouldn't be the last.

"Thanks!" she said, skipping off to the guest room and its seventy-inch television that I bought mostly for her.

As much as I loved Avery, I was a sucker for Adeline.

Zeus cried at the door, and I let him in, then took my bag to the washer. As usual, all of my clothes smelled like smoke. It never really bugged me until I got home. Once I walked into my house, I couldn't wait to get the reek of smoke out of my clothes, my hair, my skin. I tossed them in, dumped detergent, and started the load. Hopefully the smell would come out on the first wash.

It took a long shower to do the same for my body.

After I was clean, I grabbed a beer, turned on the news to catch up on the world, and pulled my laptop onto my lap, checking my social media. Zeus curled up next to me, and I absently pet him while I scrolled.

Drama.

Drama.

Cute baby.

Drama.

Shit, when did he get married?

I'd been gone from Colorado so long that I'd completely lost touch.

After a few minutes I closed the computer, leaving my friends—both from college and home in Colorado—behind as I changed the channel and tuned the world out for a little while.

I'd made it home from another fire. I glanced up at my dad's picture and tipped the beer toward him in salute. Then I took a long pull and leaned my head back on the couch.

"Riv?"

I blinked at the soft voice and raised my head as my beer was pulled from my hand. "Avery?" I asked, my voice husky from sleep.

"Yeah," she said, running her fingers through my hair. "You must have fallen asleep."

"Mmmm." I leaned into her touch. "What time is it?"

"Two fifteen."

I sat up and shook the sleep from my eyes. "No shit?"

"You must be exhausted," she said, snuggling into my side.

I wrapped my arm around her and with the other arm pulled a blanket over her. "I am," I admitted. "I bet you are, too."

"Mmmhmmm," she said, her head finding that perfect spot on my chest as she let out a jaw-cracking yawn.

Do it now. Every time I was in a fire, I swore that I'd come home and tell her how I felt. I knew she didn't want to be in a relationship with anyone—that taking care of her nearly bed-ridden father was all she thought she had time for. That her two jobs and basically raising Adeline on her own were her only priorities...

But I wanted her to know that she was *my* only priority.

So what if it got complicated? Messy? I wasn't going anywhere, and neither was she. We'd find a way to work out whatever got in the way, and even if it took years, I knew she'd be the only one I'd ever want.

Every other failed relationship had already taught me that there was no substitute for Avery Claire.

I took a deep breath and tried to find my proverbial balls. "Hey, Avery?"

She didn't answer.

I moved just enough to see her closed eyes and parted lips, her breath even and deep. She was asleep.

I should have moved her. Instead I leaned my head back on the couch and savored the feeling of falling asleep with her in my arms.

It had only been five minutes when there was a pounding at my door. I sat up with a start, barely catching Avery before she tumbled to the floor. "Who the hell?" I mumbled, glancing at the window. The sun was up already, but that didn't mean much.

"Whoa, it's eight," Avery said, stretching next to me.

I did not look at the way her breasts pressed against the thin material of her tank top.

I did not appreciate her sleepy yawn, where her tongue curled like a little kitten.

I did not immediately picture putting her sleep-warmed body under mine and waking her up fully with an orgasm that would leave that raspy voice screaming my name.

Not at all.

Fuck.

The pounding continued, and I got up and headed for the door, where Zeus was already wagging his tail. I opened the door and he flew out, past where Bishop stood with his lips pressed together. That face was never a good sign.

"Some guard dog you have there," he remarked as he walked in.

"Zeus knew it was you," I said. "Besides, I'm twenty-five years old. Get off my ass. You're only older by three years."

"Yeah," he said, looking up at Dad's picture before striding into the living room. If he didn't rise to that bait, there really was something drastically wrong.

"Hey, Avery," he said into my kitchen where she was putting on coffee.

"Bishop," she said with a smile. "Coffee?"

"That'd be great," he said before turning back to me. "You awake?"

"I answered the door, didn't I?" I crossed my arms over my chest. "We're not supposed to meet up for another two hours, so why are you here?"

His jaw flexed. "I had an early morning phone call."

"From?" Unless it was our father calling from the grave, I couldn't think of a reason good enough to jolt me out of Avery's arms.

"Sebastian Vargas."

"Bash? No fucking way." I shook my head, certain I'd heard him wrong. "Is something wrong at home?" Why the fuck would Bash call? He was on a Hotshot team in California. Hell, he'd left Legacy the same time I did.

Bishop swallowed and flexed his hands. "They're resurrecting the team."

My jaw hit the fucking floor. "I'm sorry. You're going to have to say it again."

He nodded. "Yeah, I made him say it like six times. I honestly didn't believe him until Emerson Kendrick got on the phone."

"Emmy is in on this, too?" Emmy and Bash had both lost their fathers with ours, buried them next to each other on Legacy Mountain.

"I never thought it was possible, but they got the town council to agree on one condition."

"Which is?" Every emotion possible assaulted me, scraping me raw with disbelief, hope, pride, and a touch of wariness. Was resurrecting a team that had been annihilated the best move? Would it do them justice? Was it cursed to suffer the same fate? We'd buried eighteen out of the nineteen of them.

It was everything we'd fought for during the first years after the fire, but as time passed, and we'd been denied over and over…well, it became the impossible.

"It has to be made up primarily of Legacies. Blood of the original team."

I stood there, staring at my brother while it sank in. He nodded slowly, like he understood the time it was taking me to process the news of the impossible.

My eyes drifted back to where Avery pulled a steaming mug of coffee from under the Keurig. "Say it," I nearly growled, knowing his next words were about to rip my plans to shreds.

"They can't do it without us. If we want the Legacy Hotshot Crew to be reborn…"

Fuck. My. Life.

"We have to go home."

Chapter Two

Avery

He has to what?

The idea of River going anywhere was enough to nauseate me. Maybe I misheard. Maybe Bishop didn't mean it. Maybe that awestruck look on River's face meant something completely different.

The heat from the coffee radiated through the mug, finally burning my hand before I realized I still held it. I rounded the half-wall that separated the kitchen from the living room and handed the cup to River, who looked at me with shocked, deep brown eyes and mumbled his thanks.

"What does he mean?" I asked River.

His strong jaw tensed as he looked back to Bishop. With the stern set of their faces, they'd never looked more like brothers. Their Native American heritage proved dominant, giving them chiseled features, strong noses, high cheek bones, and raven black hair. But although Bishop was an inch or so taller than his little brother, River had at least thirty pounds more muscle on him. Thirty pounds of insanely cut, incredibly hot muscle.

Whoa. No thinking about River like that.

"What exactly *do* you mean?" River asked Bishop.

Every muscle in my body clenched.

"We'd have to move back to Colorado." Bishop's eyes flickered toward me, but mine were on River.

He nodded slowly, like he was working details through his head. That was one thing about River—he never made a decision without thinking it through. "And they have to have us?" he asked.

"They do. They're going to be tight to hit sixty percent as is. Bash said he can't be sure of final numbers yet."

"How long does he have to come up with names?"

A year. Say a year. Nausea hit my stomach hard. I couldn't fathom a life without River around. It was already hell when he was on fires for a few weeks at a time.

"Two weeks."

Okay, now I was going to puke. I must have made some kind of sound, because River's arm came around my shoulders, pulling me into his side where I always thought I'd be. We weren't together or anything, but he was an integral part of what made my world turn.

"Two weeks," he repeated, rubbing the bare skin of my arm with his hand.

"Council only gave him until the ceremony."

"Well, that's just fucking fitting," River growled.

"I don't understand," I said quietly.

River hit me with those impossibly deep eyes, two little lines furrowing between his eyebrows. "Remember I'm headed back to Colorado for the weekend in a couple weeks?"

I nodded.

"That's the deadline they gave Bash," Bishop answered. "They're making this as impossible as they can, even though he's footing the bill for everything. The firehouse is up and everything, it's just missing a crew."

"Damn. I knew he was rich, but not *that* rich." River took a deep breath, and let it out slowly. "Okay, so if we move back, we get to reform the Legacy Crew?"

"That's the plan."

"And if we don't?"

"They fail. There's no mathematical way to do it without the both of us."

River smirked with a sarcastic laugh. "And to think you never wanted me to fight fires."

"Still don't. This isn't an order, River, it's a choice."

"Are you in?" River asked.

"I'm going," Bishop said.

My breath left in a rush. If Bishop was going—

"Then I have to go. There's no way you're doing this on your own. We keep each other alive. Isn't that what you always tell me?"

Pain ripped through me, so intense that I felt the emotion singeing my nerves as though someone had taken a branding iron to my soul.

"Yeah," Bishop said quietly. "Are you sure this is what you want to do?" His eyes passed over me again, like I would make any impact on River's decision. I'd never crossed the line that would give me a say—never given in to the intense chemistry we shared, or the longing I'd always had. It wouldn't have been fair of me, not with the responsibilities I'd taken on.

He deserved better.

River's grip on my shoulder tightened. "It's Dad, Bishop. There's not really a choice. It's his team and our home. If there's a chance to bring Legacy back to life, then I'm not sitting it out."

This was it. He was leaving Alaska. Leaving me.

* * * *

"Where the hell have you been?" Dad yelled out as Adeline and I walked into our home.

She winced. I gave her a reassuring smile. "I'll take care of him."

"Are you okay?" she asked.

"Yeah," I lied. "Why?"

"You've been on the verge of tears since we left River's house. Did something happen between you two?"

I tucked a strand of blonde hair behind her ear. "No. River and I are fine. It's never been like that between us."

"Well, it should," she said as she walked off.

He was my best friend. It wasn't that I hadn't ever thought of what it would be like—actually being his. I was a woman after all. I already knew nearly every plane and hollow of his body, the way the corners of his eyes crinkled just a little when he full-out grinned. Hell, he'd even starred in some of my most blush-worthy fantasies. But I lived in reality.

"Avery!" Dad yelled from the living room.

A reality with my dad. I steeled my nerves with a deep breath and headed in. "Yes, Dad?"

"Where the hell have you been?" he repeated his earlier question. "You didn't bother to come home after work." He was laid out on the living room couch, wearing yesterday's clothes and reeking of alcohol. Or maybe that was the nearly empty bottle of Jack on the floor next to him. Dishes littered the coffee table, just within his reach.

"We stayed with River last night," I said, stacking the dishes.

"Well, you should have been here, not whoring around with the Maldonado boy."

He didn't even bother to look at me, just went back to watching *Family Feud*. Not that he had any clue what family was. In his mind, that word had only extended to my mother, and with her gone...well, we weren't worth much.

"We're just friends, Dad," I said, taking the dishes back into the kitchen.

"Like hell. Bring me my meds, would you?" he asked, his tone suddenly sweet at the end.

I set the dishes in the sink and turned the warm water on to help loosen the dry, stuck-on food. Then I gripped the edge of the counter and lowered my head, taking in deep breaths.

River was leaving. This was my life. There would be no bright spots of laughter with him, of star-gazing, or stealing the comfort of his arms under the guise of friendship. This was it.

My heart felt like it was being mashed, squeezed until I bled out. The life I led wasn't glamorous, or even really fulfilling. It was duty. Duty to raise Adeline. Duty to take care of Dad.

Duty.

I slammed the pill bottle onto the counter with more force than I'd intended.

Duty.

I twisted off the cap, Dad yelling again from the living room because I was taking too long.

Duty.

And that had seemed fine last night because I had one small

thing that I kept for myself: River.

But now I felt like I was staring across the path my life would take…and suddenly the emptiness was overwhelming.

"Avery!" Dad yelled.

"Yeah, Dad. In a second," I answered, knowing that if I didn't, the shouts would only get louder until they turned to yells. Until he started throwing things. And if I put my foot down and made him get up for it…well, shit got broken. Not us—he'd never laid a finger on Adeline or me—just everything we loved, to make his point.

Mom had died in the car crash that had resulted in Dad's fused spine, and we would forever pay for losing her and his never-ending pain and the loss of his job on the force. After all, they'd been on their way to pick us up from a weekend with our grandmother. In Dad's mind, if we'd never been born, she'd still be alive and he'd be whole—still a police officer.

I knew better, whether or not he would ever admit it.

It was the secret between us. He kept it because he'd never willingly expose himself to the consequences of his actions. I kept it because he was Addy's guardian, and the minute I opened my mouth, he'd kick me out of her life, and then what would happen to her? Even if I reported him for neglect, there was no guarantee she'd end up with me.

I rinsed the dishes and put them into the dishwasher, then grabbed Dad's pain meds from the top of the cabinet, where I'd chosen to hide them for the week. Moving them around ensured that he never took more than he was allotted.

I grabbed a bottle of water from the refrigerator and carried the pills to him.

"It's about time," he grumbled and cried out as he sat up on the couch. He swallowed the pills and some of the water, then scratched his hand across his unshaven beard. I'd given up trying to get him to shave years ago. "You think about cleaning this place up?" He motioned around the general dishevel of the living room.

"Maybe later," I answered. "I need to run into the office for a few minutes."

"At the *paper*?" he sneered.

"Yes, at the paper. Where I have a job." *So I can keep the lights on.*

He laughed. "That's not a job. Jobs make real money. Why don't you quit that one and take up more shifts at the bar? Pretty girl like you can make good tips."

I did make good tips. Enough to save up almost a full semester's tuition for Adeline. Five more years and maybe I could get her through college without the loans I'd taken out for my journalism degree. But that degree had also led me to River, which was worth every cent of the debt I'd accrued.

"Okay, well, if that's it, then I have stuff I need to get done."

He turned the channel. "Get me clean clothes and make me breakfast."

I bit the insides of my cheeks and something in me snapped. "Say please."

"I'm sorry?" he asked, finally looking at me, his eyes drug-hazed but wide.

"Say please," I repeated.

"Why should I?" he snapped like a petulant toddler.

The pain of River's inevitable loss morphed into red-hot anger. "Because I haven't changed from work yet. Because I'm holding down two jobs to keep the taxes paid, utilities on, and everything Adeline needs. Because River is moving back to Colorado and this is my life, so I need you to be a little understanding today, Dad, okay?"

"Losing your boyfriend, huh?" he asked, turning his attention back to the television. I had the overwhelming urge to throw that goddamned remote through the screen.

"He's not my boyfriend."

"Then why do you care so much? Let him move on, find a woman who can take care of him. Be happy that he's getting the hell out of here, because we never will."

I never will.

"Nice. Really supportive."

"You're right," he said with a little shrug.

My chest lightened just a little, like the man I'd loved more than life was peeking through the clouds that had covered him the last eleven years. "Oh?"

"This is your life. You earned it. Now get my clothes, these smell."

"Shower once in a while," I threw over my shoulder as I walked away from him and the smell of funk that had become the norm of that room since he'd decided he was done walking to bed.

"Watch your mouth!" he yelled.

I made my way up the stairs and into my bedroom where I flung myself onto the bed and stared up at the ceiling.

Put him in a home.

Move out and leave.

You're an adult now; you don't have to stay.

The words of advice all of my friends had given raced through my head as I lay there. But those friends had all moved on. They'd gone to warmer climates, bigger cities. They weren't responsible for the care of their parents.

Family has a way of pushing us to our limit...but we just keep moving the limits for them. River's voice overpowered every other thought. He'd always understood why I stayed when everyone else left.

I looked over at the picture of us from last summer on the water. His arms were around me, his chin resting on my head as we both grinned at the camera. His chest was bare, the tribal tattoos stretching across his chest and bringing more attention to the definition of his muscles, the tight, honed lines he worked so hard to keep perfect.

As he reminded me constantly—it wasn't vanity but the way he stayed alive and one step ahead of the fires he fought.

Then again, I'd never seen him argue when he turned the head of every woman within fifty miles. He'd just smile back, wink, and I knew their panties would happily drop to his bedroom floor.

Not that I was allowed to be jealous. For starters, we weren't together. He could sleep with every woman in Fairbanks and I wouldn't get to say a damn thing. Not that any of them were good enough for him. But I also had a part of him that none of them ever would. Our friendship had outlasted every failed relationship on both our parts. If there was a constant for us, it was each other.

How the hell was that going to work with him in Colorado?

Would he move, find a hometown girl?

Would I get a wedding invite? A birth announcement? Would his world widen into something beautiful while mine stayed stagnant here—without him?

It should, I told myself. River deserved everything. A beautiful, kind wife who would give him little boys with his eyes and little girls with his hair and courage.

How was I going to put on a brave face while he prepared to move? I couldn't make him choose—and it wasn't like I had much to offer.

Here, River. You have the world at your fingertips and every woman in the country to choose from, but pick me. I come complete with a little sister to raise and an invalid, drunk father. Aren't I a bargain?

I pulled my pillow into my chest, like it could fill the emptiness threatening to make me implode, simply crumple into myself until there was nothing left.

My phone rang with his ringtone and I swiped to answer.

"Hey, Riv."

"Hey, Ava. You ran out of here pretty fast this morning."

Silence stretched along the line while I composed my answer. It wasn't fair to unload on him, to take all of my insecurities, all the responsibilities in my life, and thrust them on him. "Yeah, I just had a lot to do, and it sounded like you did, too."

"My head is kind of swimming, honestly."

My teeth sank into my lower lip. "I bet."

"I never thought they'd restart the team," he said quietly. I knew what it meant to him, his father's literal legacy.

I wanted to talk to him. I did. I just didn't know how to bury my misery deep enough to not lay it on him. He didn't need my selfish shit on top of everything else.

"I totally get that. But hey, can we talk later? I have to run by the office." I congratulated myself on not letting my voice crack.

"Yeah, of course. Avery, are you okay?" he asked.

My eyes slid shut as a sweet pressure settled in my chest at his concern. He always made me feel precious, protected. In a world where I spent almost every waking moment taking care of everyone else, he was the only one who cared for me.

And now it was my turn to take care of him.

"Absolutely. I'm fine."

The lie was sour on my tongue and nauseated me the moment it left my mouth. This was anything but fine. The thought of losing him hurt so deeply that I was almost numb with shock, afraid to look at the damage or see the hemorrhage.

But he could never know that.

Chapter Three

River

Could this day get any fucking worse?

The realtor told me the state of the housing market up here meant I was going to lose money when I sold my house, I'd just had to tell Midnight Sun that I needed to give notice, and Avery was fucking *avoiding* me.

Even when I'd been in my most serious relationship, she'd never pulled that shit. It had been two days since she'd told me she was "absolutely fine" and ran off to work.

In those two days I'd signed a listing agreement with a date to be determined, arranged to stay an extra day in Legacy for house-hunting, and contacted a moving company about getting my crap down there.

I'd been so busy that I'd pushed every emotion onto the back burner. That plan had actually been pretty successful until this moment. But now I was standing in front of Avery's house and every single doubt came crawling back to the surface. How could I leave her? How could I move to Colorado and never see her again? Never put my arms around her? Never help her out when she protested but so obviously needed it?

I swallowed and knocked on the front door.

A few moments later, Adeline answered. "Hey, Riv."

"Hey, Addy. Is Avery around?"

"She's just getting off work from the paper, but she called to say that she was on her way. Want to come in and wait?"

Normally I'd say no, that I'd call her, and then I'd intercept her drive home in order to steal a couple quiet moments with her. But since she hadn't answered any of my calls and had replied to my texts with one-word answers, this was probably the only way I'd get any face time with her.

"Yeah, that sounds great," I said, walking into the house. It was nice, spacious enough for a family, and had been built with care, but the last eleven years had been tough on it, and it wasn't like her dad was going to jump up and volunteer to grab a hammer. *Speaking of which, I should fix that bannister while I'm here.*

"Avery? Is that you?" her dad yelled from the living room.

"Nope, Mr. Claire, it's me—River."

"Get in here, boy."

I rolled my eyes at not just his word choice but his tone. I sure as hell was not his boy. My father would have kicked this guy's ass ten times over for the man he'd let himself become. But for Avery, well, I could handle him.

"Sir," I said as I entered the living room. Jesus, there was shit everywhere. Dishes on the coffee table, trash on the floor, and he smelled like he hadn't seen water in at least a week…if not two.

As much as I longed to pick everything up before Avery got home, I knew she'd die of embarrassment. So I did what I learned to do the first year we'd been friends—ignored it.

"You're leaving for Colorado, eh?" he asked, shifting his weight enough to reach for the beer on the floor.

"That appears to be the plan."

"Find greener pastures?" He took a swig, and I briefly wondered if he was mixing the alcohol with his meds, or if Avery had successfully hidden the bottles before she left for work.

"No, sir. My father's old Hotshot crew is restarting, and they can't get the job done without me."

"Well, aren't you just important."

I wanted to sigh, to curse him, to steal Avery away from this life he thought she owed him. Instead, I offered him a tight smile and said, "It's just a numbers game, really."

He grunted. "Well, I imagine Avery will be a little put off."

"I imagine so."

An awkward silence settled over us, which was—thank God— soon interrupted by the sound of the door opening.

"Riv?" Avery's voice carried through the downstairs.

"In here," I answered.

She came through the arch of the living room, all frayed ponytail and well-worn Beastie Boys T-shirt. "I saw your truck out front. Is everything okay?"

"He just came to see you," her dad answered.

"Oh," she said, looking between the two of us. Then she nodded toward the door.

"It's always a pleasure to see you, Mr. Claire," I said.

"You, too, River. Good luck in Colorado." He hadn't even looked away from the television.

I followed Avery through the hallway and up the stairs, my eyes front and center on the way her shorts hugged the sumptuous curve of her ass. Trying hard to do the right thing, I looked away, but that only took me to the tight, toned thighs that I was already picturing locked around my hips.

She led me into her room and shut the door behind us. I took in the space that still boasted high school and college pictures. "Nothing here changes much," I said.

"It's my own personal time capsule," she replied, sitting on her bed.

I took the chair from her desk, swinging my leg over and sitting on it backwards to keep some kind of barrier between us. Ever since I knew I was leaving, it was like the control I showed around her— the constant checks I kept on myself and my need for her—was fraying, like my sex drive knew our time was limited. "I like it. It's you."

She laughed in a self-deprecating way that I hated. "Never changing, stuck, and gathering dust."

"Steady and loyal."

We locked eyes, and the zing of electricity between us was palpable. Did she feel it, too? If so, why would she deny it?

Because you've never given her a reason not to, asshole.

"I've been avoiding you," she said, her eyes open and honest.

"I know."

"I don't know how to handle this, and it seemed easier to bury my head in the sand and just not deal." She hugged her pillow to her chest.

"You talk to me. I talk to you. That's how this friendship has always worked."

"But how is it going to work with you in Colorado? I know I'm supposed to be happy for you. This is your dad's crew, and I know what that means to you. But selfishly..." She shook her head.

"What? Don't clam up on me."

She shrugged. "It's just... The day you bought the land to build your house was one of the happiest days of my life."

I blinked. "Wait. What?"

"Stupid, I know."

"I didn't say that. I just don't understand." *Talk to me, Avery.*

"That was what? Three years ago?" she asked.

"About. You were dating that dickhead math major."

Her eyebrows rose. "Good memory."

"I remember everything when it comes to you," I said, then cursed myself when her eyes widened even more. *Smooth. Real smooth.* "The land?" I prompted.

"Right. You buying that land felt like you were putting down roots. That you'd stayed when you graduated—when everyone else left—it felt solid. Dependable."

"Are you talking about me or the house?" Those weren't love words, or even attraction words. Hell, she'd just described my truck.

"You, and it's a good thing. That moment felt like you would always be here, that you were the person I could lean on. I've never looked into my future and not seen you in it. This scares the shit out of me."

I gave up the chair and sat down on the bed next to her. "Me, too. But I can't not go."

She leaned her head on my shoulder, and I rested mine on hers. "I'd never ask you to stay," she whispered. "I know you can't."

"But I can't imagine leaving you, either."

"Then it seems, we are at an impasse."

* * * *

The clock on my dash changed to 1:36 a.m. I'd been sitting in my truck for the last hour in front of the Golden Eagle Saloon, trying to figure out how to explain the crazy plan I'd concocted between the hours of leaving Avery's house and sitting here now.

The bar closed in twenty-four minutes, so I had exactly that long to pull my shit together before I went in.

The door opened, and I stopped breathing until I saw that it was just two local girls. Kris waved and I unrolled my window.

She climbed up on my running boards and leaned her pretty face into the cab, reeking of alcohol. "Hey, River," she slurred.

"Hey, Kris. What brings you out tonight?"

"It's my birfday."

"Happy birthday. So you're legal now, huh?"

She slow-winked a brown eye at me and then blew her hair out of her eyes. "Yep! What are you doing?"

"Waiting on Avery."

Her head lolled back in exasperation. "You two. Ugh. Why she'd keep a fine piece of man flesh like you in the friend zone is beyond me. I'd climb you like a ladder." She snorted. "Like a ladder. Get it? Because you're a fireman?"

"Absolutely," I answered. The girl was three sheets to the wind, but I'd known her since she could barely drive.

"River, I'm sorry," her friend Lauren called out. "She's trashed."

"I am not!" She licked her lips. "Want me to wait with you? I can keep you plenty busy."

Usually I'd think about it. Kris was a gorgeous girl, and it wasn't like I was celibate. But first, she was drunk, and that I never took advantage of, and second, well…she wasn't Avery. I wanted Avery. "Not tonight, but happy birthday. Lauren, can you get her home?"

She nodded and guided her friend off my truck. "Stone-cold sober, no problem. Good to see you, River!"

By the time the girls piled into Lauren's car and left, it was 1:45 a.m. My heart pounded, my stomach dropping slightly just like it did before I walked into a fire, before I took a step that had the potential to change my life.

I was already out of my truck, climbing the steps to the saloon, before I'd decided that I couldn't wait until two. I couldn't wait another second.

I swung the door open and Avery looked up, startled, from where she was washing down a table. "River?"

I didn't answer her, just looked at Mike, who sat at the end of the bar as usual for a Tuesday night. "Mike, go home."

"It isn't two," he said.

"Close enough."

The forty-something guy got off his stool, tossing cash on the bar. "Thanks for the company, Avery."

"No problem," she answered with a smile.

"River," he said as he walked by me.

"Thanks, Mike."

He nodded and left, the door closing behind him. I knew he wasn't drunk—he came here every night to escape his wife, had one beer around eight thirty, and then sipped soda the rest of the night.

Small towns, man. Everyone knew everyone's business.

"What are you doing here?" Avery asked, licking her lips nervously.

"Are you alone?"

"She will be," Maud said as she popped up from behind the bar where she'd obviously been stocking. "You two have fun." She wiggled her eyebrows at Avery. "I'll go out the back and lock it up."

"Maud," Avery pled.

"Nope, not listening!" she sang with her fingers in her ears like she was five. I knew I liked her for a reason. She sang her way through the back door, and then I heard the exterior door close, too.

Avery leaned back against the table, white-knuckling the edges. "So what's so important that it couldn't wait until morning?"

I leaned against the table opposite hers so that there was only a few feet separating us. "I know how to fix our problem."

"Oh, do you? Because short of you not moving to Colorado, and then subsequently hating me because I took away everyone's chance to have that team back, I'm really not seeing where there's an option."

"Option one: I could go seasonal. Live there during the summers and be back here for the winters."

She shook her head before I even finished what I was saying.

"Nope. You can't afford that. There are no jobs up here that would take you on that stipulation, even your crew here couldn't. Next brilliant idea?"

"Okay. Then you move to Colorado with me."

Now I was the one gripping the table as her face drained of color. "What? Are you kidding?"

Fuck, was that my heart in my throat, or had I just swallowed something huge? "I've never been more serious."

Silence stretched between us as she blinked at me, her mouth slightly agape, her unreadable eyes never wavering from mine.

"I'm serious, Avery," I repeated quietly.

"I can tell," she answered.

"I've thought it through—"

"Obviously, because I just talked to you twelve hours ago. Seems perfectly thought out."

"You have always wanted to leave here." I started laying out the reasons like I had planned.

"And you know why I can't!" she shouted. "What are you thinking, River? I can't just pick up and leave. I'm not you. I have responsibilities here. I have Adeline and my father to think of."

"I know. I've watched you struggle every day that I've known you, and I've seen you grow into an amazing, strong woman."

"Stop!" She put her hands over her ears and squeezed her eyes shut, little lines appearing between her eyebrows.

I crossed the distance between us, lightly pulling her hands away from her face. "Open your eyes," I begged.

Her eyelids fluttered open to reveal blue eyes swimming with so much emotion that I nearly lost my breath. "Tell me one thing. If it wasn't for Adeline, for your father, and every piece of obligation that anchors you to this place, would you want to come with me?"

Her eyes flickered back and forth, her tell for when she was hashing something out in her head.

Avery had always been immovable in her loyalty to family, her insistence that she was responsible for them both. It was something I'd always loved about her, but now I needed that to give just an inch.

"Would you want to come with me? Get out of here? The Rockies are just as gorgeous, and the sun is a little more dependable.

And best of all, you'd have me."

Her eyes flew to mine. "But I'm not free, no matter how pretty you make it sound."

My thumbs lightly stroked the insides of her wrists. "I know our lives aren't prefect, but I'm asking you, in a perfect world—I'm asking you to pretend—if you didn't have the obligations you do, if it was just you and me making this decision, would you want to come with me? Would you take that leap?"

"To Colorado?" she asked.

"To Colorado," I affirmed just in case she thought I meant back to my house for tea.

Her eyes slid shut. "Yes," she whispered.

My breath abandoned me in a rush, my entire body letting go of the tension that had plagued me since Bishop told me we'd have to go. "Oh, thank God."

"But it doesn't matter," she cried, her face distorting as she fought tears. "What I want doesn't matter. That I would give anything to move somewhere new with a fresh start where I'm not 'that drunk's' daughter, or to have the chance to keep you as my best friend...none of it matters. My life is what it is."

"It doesn't have to be." I took her face in my hands, cradling the back of her head.

"It does. What about Adeline? What would she do?"

My chest tightened at the way she always put everyone else first. "She'd come with."

Avery's jaw went slack in my hands. "What?"

"Legacy has a great high school. Brand-new facilities. It's a small town, but there's a kindness there I haven't seen anywhere else. Addy would be welcome there, with us, and so would you. Stop looking at me like I'm dreaming. This is possible."

"You'd bring her with you? With us?"

"Of course. She's a part of you, and she needs to get out just as much as you do."

"And my father?"

My jaw flexed. This had been the one point that had been hard to swallow, but I knew I had to if I wanted to keep Avery in my life. And she was worth any hurdle I had to jump, or any length of broken glass I had to walk across barefoot. I had no doubt the girl standing in front of me was the key to the rest of my life.

"He can come, too," I said softly.

"Now I know you're joking." She tried to pull her face from my hands, but I wouldn't let her. "You hate him."

"I hate how he treats you," I corrected her. "I've never understood why you take it."

"He's Addy's guardian," I explained. "I could never abandon her." No matter what I'd promised my mom—to keep quiet, to keep family business private—Addy came first, and if that meant I had to live at home and commute to college so I could provide some kind of future for her, then fine. It was a small price to pay.

"Then if he's what I have to put up with to keep you in my life, to keep you near, then fine, I'll do it. There are treatment facilities in Colorado, and maybe if we can just get him clean—"

She sobbed—one long whimper, which was the one reaction I wasn't expecting.

"Avery," I whispered. "Don't cry."

"Why? Why would you do that? Drag the worst part of my life into yours?"

A smile tugged up the corners of my lips as I wiped away her single tear that escaped. "Because I get you. I can't leave you. It's never been Bishop keeping me here. It's always been you."

"But why?" she squeaked.

"God, don't you know by now?"

"No," she whispered as something that looked like hope passed through those blue eyes.

"Yes, you do. You've always known, just the same as me." I sent up a quick prayer that she wouldn't smack the hell out of me, and then I kissed her.

She gasped in surprise, and I kept the caress light, taking my time with her lips as I waited for her response. She was so soft. I ran my tongue along her lower lip, savoring the delicate curve. I sipped at her lips with soft kisses for so long that I was about out of hope. While she was letting me kiss her, she wasn't responding.

I pulled back slowly, scared to see what lingered in her eyes, and prayed it wasn't disgust. What the hell had I been thinking to kiss her like that? We'd never shown any signs of crossing the line, and I'd just jumped across it. Her eyes were closed, giving me no hint of what she was feeling. "Avery?" I asked softly.

Her pulse raced under my hand.

Her eyes fluttered open and there was no anger, just surprise. "You want me?"

"I have *always* wanted you."

With a soft cry, she met my mouth, opening hers in a hungry kiss. My tongue swept inside the mouth I'd dreamed of for years, and *holy shit*, she tasted even better than I'd ever fantasized. She tasted faintly of the peppermint tea she loved and pure, sweet Avery.

I explored her mouth with sweeping strokes of my tongue, and she rubbed back against me with every one, creating a friction that sent heat streaking through me, pooling in my dick.

My hands shifted, tilting her head so I could kiss her deeper. If this was the only time I'd get to kiss her, then I was sure-as-fuck going to leave her with a memory that haunted her at night the same way she already did for me. She melted against me, our bodies molding effortlessly into each other.

At some point I was hit with the stunning realization—*Holy shit. I'm kissing Avery.* And she was kissing me back like her life depended on it. One of my hands left the curves of her face and drifted down her back, giving her every chance to protest—she didn't—before I grasped her ass and lifted her up to set her on the table. I stepped between her outstretched thighs, and she ground against me, moaning into my mouth when she discovered my erection.

I'd never been so hard so fast for any woman in my life. But Avery wasn't just any other woman. She was everything I'd ever wanted. The woman I'd compared every girl to since I met her. The only one who had my heart without ever knowing it.

She threw her head back, and I pressed kisses down her neck, careful not to mark the tender flesh. We weren't eighteen anymore, and I wasn't going to paw at her like an inexperienced teenager no matter how loudly my body screamed at me that she was finally in my hands.

Her fingers threaded through my hair, and she rocked against my hips and whimpered my name. It was the most beautiful sound I'd ever heard.

I brought my mouth back to hers for one last, long, luscious kiss, pouring everything I had into it. I almost forgot my own name as I gave myself over to everything Avery was.

Then, with the patience of a saint, I pulled back from her. She looked up at me with hazy, passion-filled eyes and kiss-stung lips. *Yup, sainthood.*

"River?" she asked, her voice husky and so damn sexy that I had the immediate urge to see what color her panties were and how they'd look on the floor of the bar.

Instead I kissed her forehead and took my hands off her— before I fucked my best friend in the bar that she worked at. Avery deserved so much better than that, and for how long I'd waited, I did, too.

"I want you," I said, my voice so low I barely recognized it.

Her mouth opened to speak, and I pressed my thumb against her tempting lips.

"Don't say anything. I just wanted you to know that you have options. That *I* am an option. And whether it's in friendship or something more, I want you in Colorado with me. I leave next week for a weekend there, and I've already bought you a ticket. It's just a weekend—not a lifetime commitment, but I want you to come and see if you could make a life there. A life with me or without me— that's your choice."

I stroked her lip with my thumb and leaned forward, stealing one more kiss. "God, I've waited so many years to do that."

"River…"

"Don't," I ordered softly. "Don't talk. Just think. I'll wait outside for you to lock up, and then maybe we can talk tomorrow?"

She nodded, and I backed away slowly, refusing to notice the rapid rise and fall of her breasts, or that her lips were still parted like she was waiting for me to come back and kiss the hell out of her again.

Maybe I'd just fucked everything up. Maybe I'd thrown away the best relationship of my life by pushing for something that she didn't want, but when I looked back and saw her touching her lips as I walked out the door, I couldn't help but smile.

Maybe I'd just made the best decision of my life.

Chapter Four

Avery

I flipped through the magazine at Dr. Stone's office, not really seeing the print on the pages. My mind was too focused on River.

He'd kissed me. My eyes slid shut as I remembered his lips against mine, the feel of his tongue, his hands, his sweet taste. My fingertips slid over my lips like I could still feel him there.

How could one moment change everything?

Just like that.

It had been the best kiss of my life—hot enough that had he not stopped us, I wasn't sure where we would have ended up.

On the table. The bar. His bed.

I felt heat rush to my face and opened my eyes, smiling. God, he just made me happy, which was something I hadn't been in such a long time. Kissing him hadn't been the awkward first kiss of friends trying out something more. It had been like two magnets finally flipped so they were unable to do anything but collide.

"What has you all happy?" Dad grumbled, sitting on the exam table.

"River," I answered honestly. He'd texted me all day yesterday from work, but our schedules hadn't meshed and we hadn't gotten a chance to see each other.

His eyes narrowed. "Don't get too attached to that boy, Avery. He'll just break your heart when he leaves, and you'll be downright bitchy. Hell, it's bad enough already." He pointed at me. "Watch yourself."

I soothed my hackles, which begged to go up in my own defense. "Actually, I think I'm going with him next weekend to Colorado."

Dad's mouth hung open, his eyes ready to shoot fire. "You. Are. Not."

"I am," I said with a certainty I hadn't felt this morning when I woke up. *Guess you made that decision.* "It's just for a weekend, Dad. Aunt Dawn already said she'd come up and stay." She'd actually been all too happy to do so when I'd called her this morning.

"You can not put her out like that!"

"Dad, she lives thirty minutes away and she's retired. It's hardly putting her out to ask her to spend a weekend with her brother."

He grumbled, tapping his foot against the side of the exam table. "And what about Adeline?"

"What about her?" I closed the magazine, giving up any pretense of reading.

"Are you thinking of moving there? With him? Why else would you go?"

I should have waited until we were home to say anything, or told him before this appointment. "Let's just talk about this later."

"No, the doc is late as usual. Let's talk about it now." He crossed his arms around his chest. His fingernails were too long, but at least I'd gotten him to shower this morning.

For the smallest second, the potential of a different future washed over me—a future where every day wasn't fighting with him, where I could live for me, step fully into the independent adulthood I'd always been so scared to want. A future where River kissed me, where I finally allowed myself to really examine my feelings for my best friend.

"What if I wanted to move?" I asked softly. "What if I wanted to have an actual life, Dad?"

"One where you're not tied down by an invalid father? Is that what you mean?"

"You're not an invalid. And River already said you could come with us—"

"Enough!" he snapped. "I'm not moving to Colorado and neither are you. Your life is here, with me. I know it's not the life you wanted, but this isn't what I wanted, either. We're in this together. It's always been you and me, Avery. What would I do without you? What would Adeline do? You know we can't make it without you. So you can go for the weekend and live out your little fantasy, but you know you'll come right back here, because you're not the kind of girl to walk out on her family."

He lifted his eyebrows, challenging me to say that I was.

Was he right? Did it matter what I wanted?

The doctor knocked, saving me from going down that tunnel.

"Mr. Claire," Dr. Stone said as he sat in front of the computer on the desk and flipped through the screens. "Okay, so how have you been feeling this month? Your weight is up."

"I like to eat," Dad joked, bringing out his charming side, the way he always did with Dr. Stone. After all, he had something Dad wanted.

He's playing you, too.

I kept my thoughts to myself as Dr. Stone examined him, prodding and asking the same questions he did every month.

"And how is your pain level?" he asked.

They had my full attention, now.

"It's bad, doc," Dad said, grimacing as he pushed against his lower back. "It's getting worse."

Dr. Stone nodded thoughtfully, rubbing his goatee. It was hard to believe he was the same age as my dad, or maybe it was just that there were healthy men that age, in general. "I'm not going to lie to you, Jim. The pain is always going to be there. There's no guarantee with a spine fused where yours is. I know it hurts."

"Can we up my meds? Give me a little relief?"

Dr. Stone sighed and sat back at the computer, going through the screens again. "I really think you're at your max on the opioids. I can't safely prescribe any more without putting you at risk for overdose."

"It hurts," Dad snapped, startling me. He never showed his angry face outside the house. No, that side of him was reserved for Adeline and me, of course.

"I know," Dr. Stone said, leaning back in his chair. "Maybe it's time to discuss other options."

"Something stronger?" Dad suggested.

For the love. If they got Dad any higher, he'd be an astronaut.

"No, but there are new methods out there. Ways of going directly after the nerves." He tilted his head. "And we should look at your weight. Other patients with this same fusion live relatively active, normal lives. Yes, they're still in pain—that is absolutely real, but we've been able to decrease pain meds by natural means."

"Well, I'm not interested in that. I want it to stop hurting. Now. So can you help me?"

Dr. Stone looked at me, and I dropped my eyes. The repercussions from outing Dad would be disastrous at home. "Avery, can I talk with you outside?"

"Why do you want to talk to her alone?" Dad questioned.

"Just some caregiver stuff. She still has your medical power of attorney, right?"

"Yes," Dad grumbled.

"Then there shouldn't be an issue, right? Unless there's something you don't want me to know?"

"It's fine," Dad answered.

Shit.

I didn't need to look at Dad to know that his eyes bore into me. Hell, I could feel the heat from here.

Dr. Stone shut the door behind us as we stepped into the hallway. "How is he, really?" he asked.

Angry. Drunk. Verbally abusive. Legally Adeline's guardian.

"Fine."

"Avery?" He gave me the Dad tone he'd probably used on his daughter Michelle…Michelle who'd gone to college in Texas after we'd both graduated. Michelle who, no doubt, had a life.

I could lie, send Dad further down the rabbit hole. Or I could take the smallest step to force some change into his life. If not for my own good, then Addy's.

"He's angry," I said, my eyes dropping to the floor as I betrayed the only parent I had left. "He drinks too much, he won't get off the couch, and the farthest he'll go is for the remote unless we're coming here on our monthly trip to refill his meds."

"Jesus," he muttered.

"You asked," I said, raising my eyes. "He's destroying himself."

"And taking you down with him," he noted.

I shook my head. "It's not about me. But it is about Adeline."

He nodded slowly.

"I need you to keep this between us," I whispered.

He sighed, rubbing the bridge of his nose. "Okay. Thank you for being honest with me."

I took a deep breath and hardened my defenses as we walked back in. Between this and the bombshell of going to Colorado that I'd just dropped on him, I might need some of those pain meds for the headache all his yelling would give me.

"Well, Avery says nothing much has changed," Dr. Stone forced a smile. "We'll keep you on the same dose you're at. I don't want you in pain, but let's explore some of those other treatments, shall we? I really want you to go back to physical therapy. Really make a go of it this time."

"No," Dad said simply, like the doc had asked him if he wanted mashed potatoes with dinner.

Dr. Stone scribbled on his pad and then ripped off the sheet as he gave Dad a smile. "Well, I'm not asking. If you want me to refill this prescription next month, you'll call this number," he said, adding a business card to the sheet as he handed it to Dad. "Dr. Maxwell is great, and I'll check in with her to make sure you're attending whatever sessions she recommends before we meet again next month."

Dad's eyes snapped toward mine. "What did you say?"

"Dad," I pled. It was shitty enough having the hermit, drunk dad who everyone talked about, but public embarrassment? That was a new level of hell I hadn't had since I'd had to pull him off a barstool at the Golden Saloon when I was sixteen.

Now I worked there.

"She said you're doing well on these meds, but your pain has you uncomfortable, Jim," Dr. Stone answered. "This isn't a punishment. We're looking for a long-term solution for you to return to feeling fully functional. Physical therapy is going to help strengthen your back muscles and maybe lose a little of that weight. It will be good for you. Good for the girls who are taking such good care of you, too."

Dad grunted.

Because the truth was he hadn't cared about us in such a long time that I wasn't sure he knew how to anymore.

* * * *

"Oh em gee!" Adeline squealed and danced around me, acting every single day of her thirteen years.

"Shhh!" I said as we made our way out to my car.

"You can't shush me!" she said, taking the passenger seat as I climbed into the driver's side.

"I can, too."

"No way! You and River! Finally!"

I could practically see the hearts dancing above her head. "Stop!" I laughed. "Look, I only told you because I need to make sure that you're okay with Aunt Dawn coming up next weekend to stay with you."

"Absolutely. Dad will be on his best behavior with her in the house."

She chatted on, stating easily a dozen times that she couldn't believe it took us this long to get together. I reminded her every single time that it was just a kiss and we weren't together.

"Yes, you are. You're going away together!"

"I'm going with him to check out his home town and see where he'll be living. He doesn't know how soon he'll have to move." *Too soon.*

"You should go with him," she said, playing with her phone.

"What?" I said, my hands tightening on the wheel.

"You. Should. Go. Get the hell out of here."

"Don't swear," I said automatically. "And that's a huge thing to even think about."

"Why? Because life is *so* great here?" She snorted. "Seriously. If you have a chance to get out, do it. I'm leaving the first chance I get."

"You're not happy?"

She shrugged, her eyes still on that damn phone. "Sure. But it's not like I have a ton of friends. Everything is"—she shrugged again—"stagnant. Nothing changes. It feels like one of those ponds that just grows crap and mosquitos."

"But there are good things, too, right?"

"Yeah, of course. You're here, and it's nice to see Aunt Dawn when she comes around. But I'm not going to stay here. I'm leaving for college, and then once I've seen what's out there, maybe I'll come back. But I don't want to feel like I stayed because it was the only option. You're not mad, are you?" She looked over at me.

"Not at all," I said as we turned onto her friend's street. "I had those exact thoughts at your age."

"But then Mom died."

I nodded slowly. "Then Mom died." *And my entire future went with her.*

I pulled into the driveway and put the car in park, quickly touching Adeline's wrist before she could open her door. "Addy, if it was your choice, would you go? If you were me?"

"In a heartbeat," she said without blinking. "Dad puts you through hell. Once River leaves...I just think you deserve a chance to be happy. Both of you do."

My heart stuttered, knowing I needed to ask her. I couldn't make these kinds of choices without her. "Okay, and if there was a way for you to come with me? Would you? I know it's more complicated than that, and that you have friends and a life, and Dad, but just for the purpose of this conversation, would you?"

She tilted her head in a way that reminded me so much of our mother. "I'd pack a box tomorrow. In theory."

"In theory," I repeated.

She lunged across the console of my SUV and kissed me on the cheek. "Don't hurt your brain, sis. Catch you later?"

"Yeah."

A couple I-love-yous later, I left her at Mandy's for the sleepover. My thoughts raced as I drove. What would it even take to bring her with me? *If you go.* I couldn't leave Adeline. I could barely process the thought of leaving Dad. It didn't matter how far he'd sunk, he was still my dad.

I would have given anything for five minutes with Mom. What would happen if I left here, lost him, and had that same regret?

I'd parked in front of River's house before I even realized I was headed there. I meant to go home, but I guessed my subconscious knew what I really needed.

Zeus didn't bark as I approached the door, so I knew he wasn't inside. That meant he was out for a run with River. My hand paused on the door handle. Was I allowed to just walk in anymore? I still had a key, of course, but we'd done some really weird transitioning, and I didn't know where we stood.

Keys for best friends? No big deal.

A key for your girlfriend? Huge. Like iceberg and *Titanic* huge.

Like moving to Colorado huge.

I opted for the three o'clock sun, which hung directly above me, and stretched my legs out on the steps that led to the porch. Peace seeped into me in the quiet, filling more of my chest with each breath, spreading through me in the way only being near River—or even just his house—could.

Gravel crunched nearby, and my breath caught as I opened my eyes. *Holy. Shit.* River ran with Zeus unleashed at his side, his strides eating up the ground as he came closer.

He was shirtless, all of that gorgeous, bronzed skin basking in the sunlight. I'd always known he was hot. I wasn't blind to the girls who flocked to him, or my own attraction. But my need to check my own drool level was new. The tribal tattoo that stretched across his chest rippled with his movements, and as he came toward me, I made out the tiny rivulets of sweat that slipped down the cut lines of his torso to his carved abs.

The man was a walking advertisement for sex.

I shifted my legs under me as he slowed, a smile spreading across his face. "Hey, you," he said, breathing heavily but not over-exerted.

"Hi," I said, suddenly shy. The last time we'd spoken had been right after he'd pulled his tongue out of my mouth.

The way he looked at me—blatant hunger in those brown eyes—made me feel like he was thinking the same exact thing.

"What are you doing out here?" he asked as Zeus licked my face.

"Waiting for you."

His forehead puckered, but he pulled me to my feet easily. "Good answer, want to come in?"

I nodded, and he led us inside, heading straight for the kitchen. He pulled two bottles of water out of the fridge and offered one to me. "No thank you," I said, scared that if I drank the water it would come right back up in a second.

"Okay," he said, then chugged the water.

Damn, even the muscles of his throat were sexy.

"So why were you sitting on my porch like some kind of stranger? You have a key," he said as he put the empty bottle into the recycling bin.

"I feel like that key just became complicated," I said, dragging my eyes up the muscles of his back as he turned away to grab the other bottle. I knew Bishop pushed him at the gym, but damn. Just...*damn*. In the past, he'd always thrown a shirt on around me unless we were at the lake, and to be honest, I hadn't looked.

No point wanting what you knew you couldn't have.

But now I could have him. It was like seven years of pent-up sexual frustration were hitting me all at once, hitting the walls of my defenses with a battering ram made out of pure steel...kind of like his body.

"Uncomplicate it. You have a key, so use it."

He hit me with those eyes, and I nearly melted. Was this the charm the other girls at the bar raved about? Had he simply never used it on me before?

"You gave it to me...you know...before."

"Before what?" he asked.

I blew my breath out through a rumble of my lips. "Come on, you know."

His smirk caught my panties on fire. *Good thing he knows how to put those out.* "Say it."

"Before you kissed me and I stopped being best-friend Avery and turned into...I don't even know. Kissable Avery?"

He stalked forward until he stood just a breath away, close enough to touch, but not. "You have always been kissable Avery, I've just never been allowed to kiss you like I wanted. You're also fuckable Avery—"

"River!" My cheeks ran hot.

His grin was wide and so very beautiful. "Oh no, I have nothing to lose. I'm done pulling my punches. Done being careful around you. Done trying my best not to let it show how badly I want you."

Oh God, he was *good*. His words alone had me ready to strip him in the kitchen. *Or maybe that's a year plus without sex.*

"Okay," I whispered. *Lame.*

He stroked my cheek with his thumb. "But you're still best-friend Avery. That's never going to change no matter how many times I get to kiss you or how often you'll let me touch you. If you decide that was the only kiss we'll ever share, you'll still be my best friend."

The thought soured my stomach. "You'd be okay if I cut you off?"

"No. I'd just work my ass off to convince you otherwise."

"Oh."

"Oh," he repeated, and kissed my forehead lightly before backing away.

A stab of disappointment hit me right between my thighs.

"So what made you stop by?" He looked at his phone and put it right down. "I know you have to be to work in twenty mintues."

"I just kind of ended up here."

"That's okay. I like seeing you." He lifted the second bottle of water to his lips and took a sip, never once looking away.

There was something so ordinary about the motion, the ease there was between us that made me long for a different future—made me wonder if it was possible to change my course in life.

"I'll go," I said suddenly. "For the weekend," I corrected.

"Really?" His face lit up like the time I'd given him Mumford & Sons concert tickets for his birthday.

"Yes," I answered.

I was in his arms before I finished the word as he swung me around the kitchen against his very hot, very sweaty chest. "You're going to love it!" he promised as we spun.

Laughter bubbled from my chest, and I felt lighter than I had in years, like he'd picked up more than my weight—he'd lifted my soul.

"Can I kiss you?" he asked, his eyes dropping to my lips.

"Yes," I said. "But you'd better make it fast. I have to leave in five minutes."

I sighed when his lips brushed over mine, relearning the feel of them. Then our mouths opened, and the sweet kiss turned hot so fast my head spun.

Good God, the man could kiss.

He consumed my every thought, until my only concerns were how close I could get and how much deeper I could kiss him.

Finally he pulled my hands from around his neck. "You'd better go before I keep you here with me."

"I'm not sure I would mind."

He groaned and set me down, backing away slowly. "Go. Now. Just be ready for the perfect trip to Colorado, because then you're mine."

"I like the way that sounds...*mine*."

"Me, too," he said softly.

This was good. No, this was better than anything I'd ever felt. And when he looked at me like that—like he'd been waiting a lifetime to sample me and now he was planning his attack—I melted.

How had we done this? Flipped from friends to horny teens in the span of two days?

"Go, Avery." He ran his tongue along his lower lip, and I knew if I stayed a moment longer I'd never make it to work. Ever.

I ran.

Chapter Five

River

Damn, that thing was long. I looked back at the trench we'd dug in to the south side of the fire and examined it for weak spots. We'd chosen the only feasible place to dig in and tried to clear as much of the fuel as possible.

"You good?" Bishop asked, sliding his chainsaw into its case.

"Yeah, finished." Sweat ran in rivulets along my face. I couldn't wait to get down from this ridgeline and get my helmet off.

The fire was a small one compared to our last blaze, but when the call had gone out shortly after Avery left my house, I'd answered. I would always answer. I thought of it as my last hoorah with the Midnight Sun crew.

I'd also cursed like a fucking sailor. This fire, as small as it was, had cost me four days with Avery. Maybe in the larger scheme of things, four days didn't mean much. But when I was only guaranteed a couple of weeks with her, four days was forever.

"Let's get out of here," Bishop said, hoisting his chainsaw to his shoulder.

I gave the ridgeline one last look. Would this be the last time I was called to the Alaskan wilderness? It was a bittersweet thought. Next year this time I'd be on the Legacy crew, as long as we could pull back the numbers the council wanted.

"River?" Bishop called as the team started down the mountain.

"Yeah, I'm coming," I said, turning to join the line of guys. If we got down in the next couple hours, there was a chance we'd make it back in time for me to see Avery tonight.

"You ready to head home?" Bishop asked as I fell in next to him.

"Which one?" I asked.

"Both, I guess."

"I'm ready to see Avery."

A grin spread across his face. "So that's how it is now, eh?"

"To be honest, I don't really know how it is. She agreed to come to Colorado for the weekend, so I'll take it."

"And anything else she has to offer?" He shot me a little side-eye.

"I'll take anything she's willing to give," I answered softly.

Never one to talk about his feelings, Bishop's jaw tightened. His mouth opened and closed a few times, until it was downright painful to watch.

"For fuck's sake, just say it. Whatever it is."

"Do you want to reconsider the Legacy crew? You have a life here, a house, a great team, and a great girl. I wouldn't think any less of you if you didn't want to go."

I thought about it—the simple act of staying. I loved Midnight Sun, my house, the landscape…hell, even the crazy hours the sun kept were growing on me. Staying gave me a shot at keeping Avery, really seeing what we could turn into. If being in a relationship was as easy as being her best friend, then I knew we could be extraordinary. But as certain as I was of how perfect we'd be, I also knew that the actual chances of her moving with me were insanely small.

She'd never leave her father, and he'd never agree to move.

But if I didn't go, Legacy wouldn't get her Hotshot crew back, and I'd lose the last piece of my father. So would Bishop and every other Legacy kid.

So I was pretty much fucked either way.

"River?" Bishop asked again as we continued our descent.

"Sorry, just a lot on my mind. I haven't changed my mind about the crew. I'm just hoping that visiting Colorado is enough to make

Avery want to come with."

Bishop whistled low. "That's a lot to ask of a girl you've been dating for a week."

Were we dating? We hadn't really had the whole "what are we" talk. "It's a Hail Mary. The whole thing with her is, but I couldn't just leave and not try."

"You're in love with her."

My grip tightened on the axe handle. "How long have you known?"

He shrugged, moving the chainsaw. "Since the first year we were here. I figured you'd get your shit straight sooner or later."

"It's pretty much the latest moment possible."

"Yeah, well, we don't remember the easily won games, right? The victories we remember are the ones where the outcome came down to the last minute, the overtime."

"The Hail Mary," I said.

He slapped my back. "The Hail Mary."

* * * *

The bar was busy for a Tuesday, but it was Ladies Night, which brought the women out for the drinks, and the men out for the ladies.

I made my way through the crowd and took a tall table at the back, sitting so I could see Avery at the bar.

Fuck, she was beautiful. Her hair was up in a ponytail, swishing with her every movement as she poured drinks.

"So you and Avery, huh?" Jessie said, grabbing the empty chair to my right.

"How did you know?" I asked, my eyes still locked on Avery. She went up on her tiptoes to grab a bottle off the shelf, giving me a perfect view of her ass, and I sucked in a breath reflexively. We were in a room with at least thirty of our neighbors. Common sense told me that this wasn't the place for me to ogle, let alone fantasize about propping her up on the bar and sliding her jeans down her thighs so I could taste her. I'd never had an issue controlling myself around Avery. Sure, my body had always reacted to the sight of her, but now that I'd had a taste and knew that she wanted the same thing...well, my body was trying to overrule my common sense.

And the bar really was perfect height.

"Please. Like you can keep a secret in this town? Just about everyone has seen the way you guys have been looking at each other these last few years. We were just waiting for Avery to find the courage to say something and you to stop fucking around in Fairbanks with co-eds.

"The way we look at each other?" I parroted, focusing in on Avery. I could see how I'd been obvious. Hell, I couldn't take my eyes off her if we were in the same room—hence my cycle of breakups—but Avery had never once hinted that she wanted more than what we had. If she'd so much as breathed in my direction, I would have jumped before she said how high.

But she'd never thrown me signals. Maybe that was one of the reasons this whole situation was terrifying. Was she only kissing me back because she didn't want to lose her best friend? Was I pushing her for something she didn't really want?

Feeling unsure of myself was a foreign concept and damned inconvenient seeing as I had less than a week in Colorado to convince her to uproot her whole life for me.

"Please." Jessie snorted, playing with her beer bottle. "You look at her like you're ready to eat her alive."

"Fair assessment," I admitted, done hiding how I felt about her. I swallowed, my throat suddenly tight. "And her?"

"Seriously?" She arched an eyebrow at me.

"Seriously."

"She looks at you like you're everything she's ever wanted, dipped in chocolate and ready for a tasty bite. Always has."

I ripped my eyes from Avery to look at Jessie. She nodded slowly as she laughed. "You should see your face right now. If your jaw was any lower you'd be hitting the floor."

My gaze went back and forth between the two women. Avery looked at me? Why the hell hadn't I noticed? Was I blind? Or was she really that good at hiding her feelings?

"Never thought I'd see the day where River Maldonado was speechless."

"First time for everything," I said softly. Maybe this would work. Maybe she really did want me enough to leave. My mind raced with different scenarios as I swiped open my phone. She could stay through the school year if Addy needed that much time, or just to give her dad a few more months to come around, and be in Colorado by summer. I'd have the house set up by then, and they could stay with me until they figured out what they wanted to do.

Or maybe Avery would never move out. Maybe my house would become *our* house.

My chest tightened to the point of pain as she smiled at Maud. I couldn't push her too fast—just because I'd been in love with her for the last seven years didn't mean that she felt the same. But I didn't exactly have another option with the deadline for the Legacy crew.

As much as I loved watching her, I also couldn't wait another minute to get my arms around her.

River: what are you up to?

I hit send and watched as she pulled out her cell phone, grinning as her thumbs worked on the small device.

Avery: working. you? how is the fire?

River: fire's one hundred percent contained. i'm thinking about taking this really hot blonde out.

Her eyebrows puckered together and her face fell.

River: it's definitely the green ribbon in her hair that has me turned on.

Her eyes shot up, wide and excited as she scanned the bar, her ribbon moving with the swish of her ponytail.

She jumped when she saw me, racing around the end of the bar. I had barely pushed away from the table and stood when she was in my arms, all sweet-smelling and soft.

"Hey, baby," I said into her hair as I held her to me, lifting her against my chest.

She wrapped those incredible legs around my waist and burrowed her face into my neck. "River." She sighed my name like a prayer. "Why didn't you tell me you were back?"

"I wanted to surprise you," I said, easily supporting her weight and loving the feel of her pressed against me.

Her arms tightened around me, and her fingers moved through my hair, lightly scratching my scalp. "I was so worried."

Damn, I loved her. "I was fine. Promise. I'm sorry we were out of service up there, but it really was an easy one."

"Good. I didn't know if you'd make it home before we had to leave."

I urged her back and she met my eyes. "Nothing's going to stop me from taking you to Colorado this weekend."

Nothing. Not her dad, or even Addy—as much as I adored her. This weekend was for us.

Her eyes dropped to my lips and want slammed into me, more intense than any time I'd ever come home from a fire. "Keep looking at me like that and you'll get kissed in front of all these people. I've never minded gossip, but you might."

Her tongue snuck out to wet her lower lip. "I don't care."

Fuck it. My fingers threading through the base of her ponytail, I crushed her mouth to mine. I tried to remember where we were, that I couldn't strip her down in the middle of a crowded bar. I tried to keep the kiss short, just enough to satisfy the craving I'd had for her mouth since I'd been called away.

I failed.

Her tongue moved against mine and I was gone. I sank into her, tilting her head so I could find a deeper, sweeter angle, and I forgot where we were. Hell, I forgot there was anyone else on the planet besides us.

Her ass pushed into my hand as she arched, her breasts stealing my breath as they pressed against me. She made that sexy little noise in the back of her throat, and I was ready to carry her the hell out of there and take her in my damned truck if it meant the throbbing in my dick would ease up just a little.

Someone cleared her throat near us, and I remembered that we were, in fact, the very opposite of being alone. I pulled away, but Avery held my lip with gentle suction, her teeth grazing the skin lightly as she finally released me.

Holy. Fucking. Shit.

My breathing was too fast, too uncontrolled, and I was way too turned on to be this public at the moment.

"Welcome home," she whispered, those blue eyes hazy with passion and happiness.

"I love the sound of that," I admitted as I let her down. Her curves rubbed against me every. Inch. Of. The. Way. "You're killing me."

"Feeling's mutual."

"It's about damn time!" someone in the bar called out.

He was followed by a round of applause that had Avery burying her beautiful, flushed face in my shirt. "Yeah, yeah," I said as the clapping died down.

"Oh my God," she mumbled.

I tilted her chin and kissed her scrunched nose. "I'd better get out of here and get packed for tomorrow."

"You are cutting it pretty close."

"Yeah, well, you know me. I have to do everything at the last possible second." *Like tell you that I want you.*

She grinned and kissed me lightly. "Pick me up in the morning?"

"Wouldn't miss it."

I kissed her goodbye just because I could, then made my way to the door before I ended up kissing her again. She waved when I looked back, and suddenly the eight-or-so hours I had to wait to kiss her again seemed like an eternity.

She was all I thought about as I packed a small suitcase, and all I thought about as I tried to get a few hours of sleep. After the last seven years, it was hard to believe that everything would come down to the next few days.

I had to find a way to convince her that she'd be happy in Colorado—that I was worth the risk. It wasn't a small thing I was asking. Hell no. I wanted her to uproot her whole life and transplant it thousands of miles away, all because I knew that the only way we'd thrive was together.

But what if her dad wouldn't come?

What if she wouldn't leave him?

The clock ticked steadily on the nightstand, reminding me that I had to be up in a matter of hours, but that didn't stop my brain, or the nauseating turn of my stomach that reminded me that no matter how much I loved her, she'd never abandon her family.

I couldn't let my dad's crew die before it even had the chance to be resurrected, but I also knew I'd be a shell of who I was if Avery stayed in Alaska.

I had to make these next few days as perfect as possible.

Chapter Six

Avery

"What do you mean you've lost our bags?" River asked the airline attendant as we leaned against the counter the next day. After a delayed flight from Fairbanks, to running through the Seattle airport and barely making our connection to Denver, and then taking the smallest plane I'd ever been willing to get on to Gunnison...well, this trip was definitely off to a rocky start.

We'd been traveling for ten hours, and as happy as I was to be here and to see River's hometown, I was also about to go full-on zombie apocalypse raid on that vending machine in the lobby if we didn't find some food soon.

"I've tracked them as currently in route from Seattle to Denver, sir," the small girl said as she pushed her glasses up her nose with a look that pretty much said, please don't eat me.

Not that River was intimidating. Liar. River was huge and rather cranky at the moment. "It's okay." I put my hand on his bicep.

"It's not okay," he told me. "All your stuff—"

"I can buy what I need until it gets here." I looked over to the girl who was furiously typing. "Can you have it delivered to Legacy when it gets here?"

She nodded. "Absolutely. The next flight comes in from

Denver…" She typed, her eyes never going higher than River's chest. "Tomorrow morning at seven thirty."

"You have got to be kidding—"

I squeezed his arm lightly, then looped mine through it and hugged myself to his side. "That will be just fine."

Her fingers flew over the keyboard as she took down our contact information. With each moment, River grew more tense, until I thought his muscles might snap under my fingers.

The attendant's eyes widened to impossible dimensions when she looked behind us, and I turned my head. Bishop walked toward us, a scowl deepening with every step he took. Maybe I wasn't the only one getting hangry over here.

"What's wrong?" River asked.

"All the rental cars are gone. They overbooked or something."

"How is that even possible?" River snapped.

"It's pretty much just par for the course today," I responded, laughter bubbling up.

They both looked at me like I was nuts.

"I called Knox, and he's on his way here. We've probably got about another forty-five minutes before he shows up."

"Perfect, just in time to grab food!" I said.

"Actually, the airport café closed about a half hour ago. I'm so sorry," the attendant said, cringing as all of our gazes swung to her. "They close after the last flight of the day…which was yours."

River's jaw locked. "It's only eight."

"Small airport."

"Let's go wait outside," I said. "I've never seen the sunset in Colorado." Or anywhere outside of Alaska. I plastered a smile on my face and prayed it was enough to convince River to leave the poor girl alone. It wasn't her fault that we'd had rotten luck today.

A slight tug on River's arm and he followed me out, Bishop on his heels.

A Snickers bar later I felt somewhat human. River slipped my forefinger into his mouth, licking away the last of the chocolate on my skin, and my thighs clenched. He ran his teeth over the digit and released it, smirking at the way my mouth hung open.

"I'm so sorry today has been a disaster," he said, running his fingers through the strands of my travel-abused ponytail. The evening breeze wrapped a few strands around my neck, and he chased them as we sat on a bench outside.

"This isn't a disaster," I told him. "It's just a kaleidoscope of inconveniences."

"Kaleidoscopes are beautiful."

"And so is this. Think of it this way. We just finished a delicious bit of chocolate as we're watching the sun set behind the Rocky Mountains. The weather is gorgeous, and this just might be the best first date I've ever had."

A corner of his mouth tilted upward. "First date, huh?"

"What would you call it?"

"A sneak peek."

"At what?"

"Everything we could have," he whispered and then brushed his lips over mine, his tongue tracing my bottom lip. Was I ever going to get tired of kissing him? I only craved more and more. For that matter, what was the appropriate amount of time I had to wait before I could kiss other places on his body? Where was the rule book that governed hey, I know we just got into a relationship, but I've wanted to lick your abs for years?

I sucked in a breath as he pulled away, my chest burning. "Wow, even just kissing you makes me breathless."

He laughed. "That, my dear Avery, is the altitude. But I'll absolutely take credit. We're almost at eight thousand feet here, and almost nine where we're headed."

"Easier to get you drunk at," Bishop said as he came around the corner.

My cheeks flamed, wondering how much he'd seen.

"No worries," he said as if he'd read my mind. "I've been waiting on you two to get your shit together for years. And there's Knox," he said as a black SUV pulled up to the curb.

"How can you tell?" River asked.

"We're the only ones here, and they locked the airport doors twenty minutes ago."

"Good point," River answered as we stood. When an incredibly hot guy got out and headed toward us, River pulled me under his arm.

Subtle.

"Knox," Bishop said as the two shook hands and then hugged in that tight guy way with lots of back-slapping.

"Good to see you, Bishop." Knox turned his eyes on River and grinned before pulling him into a hug. "River. Damn, you're huge. What the hell are they feeding you up in Alaska?" he asked.

"Moose, mostly," he joked.

Knox held his hand out to me, and I shook it as he made an obvious appraisal. "And who might you be?"

"Avery," I said with a smile. The guy was gorgeous in a Scott Eastwood kind of way, with eyes that held laughter and the promise of a really good time.

"She's with me," River said, pulling me to his side.

"Obviously." Knox grinned and nodded toward the car. "We're about forty-five minutes from home. Let's get you guys settled in and then figure everything out."

We loaded into the back of the SUV, and as we pulled onto the highway out of town, the gentle hum of the car on the pavement sent my exhaustion into sleepville. When my head bobbed for the third time, River unbuckled my seat belt and slid me over to his side, buckling me in the middle.

"Get some rest," he ordered softly.

My head hit the perfect place just under his shoulder. With his warmth and steady heartbeat, I was asleep before a second song could play on the radio.

I vaguely felt River's strong arms lifting me and the crisp mountain air brushing over my skin as he carried me somewhere. "It's okay, you can sleep. I've got you," he said, kissing my forehead.

A few blinks later we were in a hotel room. I brought the room into focus as he lowered me onto the bed. "Food or sleep?" he asked, setting my backpack down on the floor.

I weighed my options, but the three hours of sleep I'd had coupled with the long travel and altitude won out. "Sleep. What about you?"

"It's already ten. I'm game for sleep if you are." He leaned over me, brushing a kiss against my hairline. "I'll be next door with Bishop, just let me know if you need anything, okay?"

A sharp flash of panic hit me when he pulled away. We were in Colorado, where he would be moving, and while I had him now, nothing was guaranteed past this weekend. "Stay with me?" I asked.

"Avery," he whispered, his dark brown eyes soft in the lamplight. He stroked my cheek with his thumb.

"It wouldn't be the first time we've slept together."

A smirk played across his face. "Yeah, well..."

"That's not what I meant." But now that the words were out there...well, would it be a bad idea?

River was undeniably sexy. Hell, my heart rate picked up just thinking about what his hands would feel like on my body. His lips were sinful, and the look in his eyes told me he wanted me just as much as I wanted him. I knew, without so much as removing a single item of clothing, that we would be incredible together.

Explosive.

"River?" I whispered.

His eyes narrowed slightly as he decided. "You know how badly I want you?"

"I think so."

"I can control myself, Avery. I'm not going to pounce on you, but there's every chance that we could cross a line you're not ready for."

I ran my hands through his hair, the black strands stopping just above his chin. "I know. But if I only have this little bit of time with you, I don't want to give any of it up. Even if we're both sleeping."

He nodded slowly. "Agreed."

I cracked the unsexiest yawn in the history of yawns, and he chuckled.

There was a knock at the door and he answered it, taking a plastic bag from Bishop. "That's all they had downstairs, sorry, man. The bags should be here in the morning."

"I just wanted it to be..."

"Perfect?" Bishop asked, his voice low.

"Yeah, and it's anything but. Could one more thing get fucked up?"

"Let's not chance fate," Bishop said before saying a quiet good night and shutting the door.

River disappeared into the bathroom momentarily. "Avery, there's toothpaste and stuff in the bathroom if you want it, okay?" He said as he came back out.

Shirtless.

Holy shit. I'd always appreciated his body. How could I not? But seeing those yards of muscle and soft, inked skin, and knowing that I could touch them were two different things.

"Teeth. Right." I nodded, forcing myself from the bed. My feet felt like they weight a bajillion pounds, but I brushed my teeth with the new toothbrush and got ready for bed.

What the hell was I going to sleep in? Capris and a blouse weren't really conducive to the whole REM thing. River's T-shirt lay folded on the counter, and my fingers caressed the soft cotton. Perfect.

A few minutes later I walked out of the bathroom to see River sitting up in bed reading the book he'd brought along. He did a double take as I came into his line of sight, and warmth rushed through me.

He really wasn't faking it, trying to keep me as his best friend by feigning some kind of interest. He honestly wanted me.

I pulled back the covers, and his eyes followed every motion, heating more with every second. "I hope it's okay that I borrowed your shirt."

"Yeah. More than okay."

He turned off the light as I slid into bed, pulling the covers up as my head hit the pillow.

"I'm so sorry today was a disaster."

"It wasn't." I remembered what he'd said to Bishop and scooted my back toward him until I was against his chest. His arm found its way around my waist, and I sighed in contentment as he pulled me closer.

His nose ran along the line of my neck, and I arched to give him better access. "It was."

"Maybe," I said, intertwining our fingers. "But this is worth it. This is pretty perfect."

"Yeah, you are."

His arms flexed around me and I melted. River relaxed me in a way no other man had. In so many ways this could still be just my best friend holding me, but it wasn't. Sure, it was still River, still the guy who had changed my flat tire freshman year, the guy who'd punched Troy Williams when he'd kissed me during sophomore year after I'd said no. He was the guy who had helped me with Addy, Dad, and my life in general.

He was my best friend.

But this desire to roll him over, climb on top of him, and explore every line of his body until I'd wiped away the thought of every one of those bar-bunnies he'd taken home over the years...well, that wasn't so friendly.

Was our friendship—and this blatant craving I had for him—enough to uproot my entire life?

"Avery?"

"Yeah?"

"Stop thinking about it."

"How did you—?"

"Because I know you. Stop thinking there's any expectation for this weekend and just be with me, okay? Try to forget anything else. Can you try?"

If this was really my only chance to be with him, then I had to try. I had to throw myself into this headfirst and see what was really there, because if his leaving didn't kill me, then the never knowing would.

"Yeah."

Chapter Seven

River

There was something to be said for waking up with Avery in my arms. She was soft, warm, and fit my body like she'd been made to do exactly that.

I'd already been up this morning, untangled her hair from the stubble of my beard and snuck off for a shower. Once I'd finished brushing my teeth, it was already eight thirty and she still wasn't awake.

I should have gone downstairs and found us food—I was fucking starving, but instead I crawled back into bed with her. As soon as I slid between the sheets, she rolled at me like a heat-seeking missile, using my chest as a pillow and tossing one of her thighs right across my dick.

Her best friend—I was.

A saint—I was not.

I wrapped my arm around her back, tangling it in the thick blonde strands of her hair. She felt perfect wrapped around me, and it was far too easy to envision this as our life.

My free hand rested on her knee, then lightly stroked the soft skin up her thigh. I kept myself to a six-inch limit, savoring the silk of her skin under my fingers but going no higher because I knew my shirt was bunched around her waist and there was nothing between my hand and her softness besides her panties.

When she'd walked out in my shirt last night I'd had a moment of primal possession, and it had taken everything in me not to send my hands beneath the fabric.

Even thinking about it had my dick hardening, or maybe it was the way her thigh moved against me. Either way, my body had zero issue reminding me that she was nearly naked, and so was I.

"Mmmmm," she moaned, moving even closer.

Her head shifted until her lips were pressed against my neck, and my pulse pounded beneath her innocent caress. If she honestly knew how badly I wanted her—the effort it took to keep my damn hands to myself—she never would have wanted me in bed with her.

Avery usually liked time to think things through. To examine every consequence of a possible action and then take the course she thought safest. I was damn lucky to have even stolen her away for five whole days, let alone be thinking of how easy it would be to slip my fingers inside her and bring her to orgasm before breakfast.

Not helping the hard-on situation.

She shifted again, lightly kissing my throat, and my hand tensed on her thigh, gripping the toned limb.

"Good morning." Her voice was husky from sleep and sexy as hell.

"Hey there," I said, waiting for her to understand the situation we were in.

Instead of moving away, she slid over until she rested on top of me, still pressing kisses to my neck.

"Avery." I groaned, my hands filling with the barely covered globes of her ass. Fuck me, her panties were lace.

"Hmmm?" she hummed, the vibration streaking through my nervous system and lodging in my dick. She rocked gently until I was settled directly against the heat between her thighs.

She was trying to kill me. That was the only logical explanation I could come up with. "Are you awake?"

"Yep," she said, her lips trailing down to my collarbone.

"Do you—?" I hissed when her teeth lightly grazed my skin. Damn, that felt good. "Do you know what you're doing?"

She slid farther down my body, the friction so good that my hips moved against her. Her fingers traced the lines of my abs. "Do you mean am I aware that I'm on top of you? Kissing you?"

"Yes, that." One of my hands cupped the back of her head while the other fisted the sheet next to me.

"Do I realize that you're hard for me?" she whispered, looking up at me under her lashes with eyes so blue they rivaled the Colorado sky.

"That, too." My dick twitched in agreement.

"Yes," she said, before kissing her way down my stomach.

Holy shit. Her lips on my skin were the most exquisite torture.

"I've always wanted to do this," she said, just before tracing the lines of my abs with her tongue.

I sucked in my breath as every muscle in my body tensed. She was every fantasy I'd ever had come to life.

"Your body is incredible. I'm sure you've been told that a million times—"

Oh hell no.

I flipped her so fast that she landed with an *oomph* underneath me. Then I stretched both her arms above her head and settled in between her thighs. "Nothing mattered before you. *No one* mattered before you. Do you understand?"

She nodded, tugging her lip between her teeth.

I leaned down and sucked it free. "Speaking of incredible bodies..." My hands followed her curves, her gently tucked waist and the flare of her hips. "God, what you do to me, Avery."

Her hips rolled in my hands, and I set my mouth to her neck, loving her gasp, the way she softly said my name. Every tiny motion or sound she made drove me higher, wound me tighter.

My shirt was bunched a little higher than her waist, leaving her stomach bare to my lips. I kissed my way down her belly, letting my tongue and teeth linger where she whimpered. The skin just along her hipbone was the most sensitive, and I had her squirming under me in a matter of minutes.

"River." She moaned, her fingers in my hair, urging me on.

"I want to touch you so badly," I admitted, breathing against the band of her blue lace panties.

"So touch me."

Her words sent me into a level of need I'd never known before. I wanted to roar, to mark her as mine, to let the world know that this woman deemed me good enough to put my hands on her.

I ran my hand up the inside of her thigh, my eyes locked on hers to watch for the first sign that she didn't want this. My fingers grazed the line of her underwear and then slipped under until—

Knock. Knock. Knock.

"No fucking way," I muttered. "What?" I called out as Avery giggled beneath me.

"Mr. Maldonado? I'm from the airline."

I left the warm haven of Avery's body and strode across the room, flinging the door open. "Bags?"

"Here," he said, his eyes wide. I took the bags from his hands and put them inside the door, well aware that my boxers weren't doing a damn thing to disguise my erection.

"Can you sign?" he asked.

I scrawled my signature across the paper. "Thanks for bringing them out," I said, and promptly shut the door.

Avery had sat up in bed, her hair a tousled, glorious mess, and my T-shirt pulled down to meet her thighs. I couldn't wait to strip it off her. She grinned at me and crooked her finger.

Hell yes.

Another knock at the door sounded and I cursed. "What now?" I asked as I opened the door.

Bishop was already fully dressed as he stood there with his arms crossed. He glanced down and then back up, sighing. "Play around later, little brother. We have shit to do today. We're meeting with Knox in half an hour."

"Half an hour?" Avery squealed and ran for the bathroom, dragging her small suitcase in with her.

"You seriously couldn't give me another hour?" I asked him as she shut the door.

"Consider this payback for cock-blocking me with Sarah Ganston."

"I was fourteen!" I yelled as he walked away.

"Nothing personal," he said, repeating my exact words when I'd been sent to find him for breaking curfew.

I dressed in clean clothes and then waited for Avery. We might have a full day planned, but the only thing on my agenda tonight was her.

* * * *

"This is amazing," Avery whispered as we looked around the Legacy crew's clubhouse as they affectionately called it.

"Bash pulled out all the stops," Knox said as he gestured to the main room of the complex that boasted floor-to-ceiling windows and a kick-ass view of the mountains. "He wanted to make sure the Legacy crew had everything it needed."

"What about people?" Bishop asked, his eyes taking in the row of glassed-in offices on one side and the huge dining tables along the other.

The complex was massive. Double kitchens, eating areas, offices, a great room, gym, and enough rooms in the downstairs walkout level to sleep every member of the proposed twenty-two member team.

"Not going to lie, we're short," Knox admitted. "But both Emerson and Bash are working on it, and we've called every firefighting Legacy kid. So far they've all said that they're coming home, but we'll find out tomorrow."

"What's tomorrow?" Avery asked, lacing her fingers with mine.

"The council meeting," Knox answered. "We have to present them with the crew. If we have the numbers, we'll take the Legacy name."

"If we don't?" I asked.

"Ever known Bash to fail?" Knox replied.

"Ever known any of us to?" I countered.

"Exactly."

I could almost feel Avery rolling her eyes. "Okay, well let's say hell freezes over and your unfailing masculinity isn't quite enough. What then?"

Knox grinned at her. "I like you."

"Don't," I said.

Avery looked between him and me. "Are all your friends this good looking here? Because if so, then maybe Colorado really is a good idea..."

My mouth hung agape for a second while she smiled up at me.

"Maybe commuting from Alaska is a good idea."

Knox laughed. "If we don't have the numbers then we'll still establish the team, it just won't be under the same banner."

"Your dad's," Avery said.

"Right."

"Either way, we're in," Bishop answered. "Even if we don't have the Legacy name, this is still their crew. Their mountain."

"Good to know," Knox said. "Now let's get to the fun part. Follow me."

He walked ahead, leading us to one of the offices with a map of Legacy on the wall. "You okay?" Avery asked quietly as we followed.

"Yeah."

"You're all tense."

I tried to relax—and failed. "The only reason I'm willing to leave Alaska and risk losing you is that it's Dad's team. It's the one they wouldn't let us restart years ago, and if we have that chance now…"

"You have to take it," she finished, looking up at me with understanding and a soft smile. "I get it. I respect you even more for it."

"But if it's not the real Legacy team, then what am I doing?"

She squeezed my hand. "Wait and see how it goes tomorrow, and then answer that question. For now…" She trailed off, looking where Bishop stood next to Knox at the map.

"What?" I asked.

"Can we just pretend for a couple of days?"

"Pretend what?" My free hand cupped her face, tilting it so she wouldn't look away.

"Pretend that this is a given? That I'll come here with you for sure?" A slight hint of panic crept into her eyes.

"Is it just pretend?" I asked softly.

"I don't want it to be, but you and I know it's so much more complicated than we're willing to admit."

I kissed her, letting my lips promise what terrified my heart. "Yeah. We can pretend. Maybe it will give you a better idea of what it would really be like if you opened yourself up to the possibility that life exists beyond the limits you've accepted."

She swallowed, then nodded. "Okay. Shall we?" She nodded toward the office.

I squeezed her hand in answer and then walked in with her at my side.

"You two good?" Bishop asked, his eyes narrowing in my direction.

"We're fantastic," I said, leading Avery over to the map.

"Right. So here's the fun part. Bash is beyond loaded now. He knew what it would take to relocate an entire Hotshot crew here, and once he realized it would be Legacy kids last week, well…he made a few calls to realtors."

Bishop and I locked eyes. He shrugged.

"That means you can either take the signing bonus that will cover the house you'd like to buy, or he'll sign you over one of the eleven he's already bought."

"No shit?" I asked, stunned.

"No shit," Knox answered. "He wasn't letting anything get in the way. Of course there are barracks here, but if you're bringing your family"—he looked at Avery—"then he wants to make sure it's a smooth transition. Trust me, this money is nothing for him."

"Tech," I answered Avery's unspoken question. "He's sold a few apps and invested really well."

"Obscenely well," Knox added.

"Apparently," Avery said, her eyes huge.

"What do you say? Want to house hunt with me?" *Come on, Avery. Pretend.*

"I do," she said with a smile that rivaled the sun.

* * * *

Five hours later, I'd fed her twice, showed her some of my favorite spots around town, and even walked her into the newspaper office.

Old Mr. Buchanan was still in charge, but he told her he was looking for a new reporter/editor/graphic designer.

"Small-town life," I said to her as we walked back to the Jeep Knox had lent us from the crew's new garage. The thing was brand new, and the weather was perfect for keeping the top off.

"I love it," she said, dropping her sunglasses down as she buckled in to the passenger side. "And thank you for driving by the high school. Addy wanted pictures."

"My pleasure," I told her as we pulled out onto the main street. "How is she doing?"

"She says Aunt Dawn has everything under control. Then again, I'm pretty sure if the house was burning down she wouldn't tell me right now."

"She knows you need the break," I said. "Where's the next house?"

She gripped the paper tightly as the wind rustled it. "Six-fifteen Pine Ave."

I entered it into the GPS and we turned left, heading for the edge of town. "I'm not sure where that is."

"Has a lot changed since you left?"

"There's more here. They'd finished a lot of the rebuild before I left for Alaska, but there's been some growth, too. I bet we're up to four thousand people by now."

"It's beautiful," she said, her eyes on the mountains around us as we left the town limits.

"What did you think about the first six houses we saw?"

"They're nice. Not exactly what I picture you in—us in," she corrected. "A little trendy, a little too close to each other."

"Agreed. I want an easy commute to the clubhouse, but I think Alaska spoiled me. I like being away from people."

"You've gone savage," she joked.

"Just a little wild," I countered.

We followed the road deeper into the mountains until we were a good three miles outside of town. "Pine," I said, turning onto a dirt road.

"Much more your speed," she joked, reaching over to rub the back of my neck.

The road took us another mile before a house appeared on the left side of the road. "Wow," Avery sighed.

Wow, indeed. We made our way up the lengthy driveway and parked. It was log-cabin style, similar to my house back in Alaska but bigger.

"He said it was new construction," I told her as we got out of the Jeep. "Landscaping isn't finished."

She looked around the front yard. "You'd have to put in some beds there. I could plant some gorgeous flowers. The tall kind that would bring color up to the porch level."

I intertwined our fingers as we took the steps up to the porch. "Rocking chairs?" I asked.

She shook her head. "A swing."

"A swing," I agreed as I punched the code into the lock box. It popped open and I turned the handle. Then, before I could stop to think, I swung Avery up into my arms, her weight slight against my chest.

"River!" She laughed. "We're not married."

"Pretend, remember?"

She looped her arms around my neck as I carried her inside. "Wow," she said.

"You already said that," I told her as we both took it in.

"I might say it about twelve more times."

The entry and great room were open to the second floor, where there was a walkway that connected one suite of rooms to the others above us. There were more windows than walls, all looking out over the mountain range and forest.

"It's like we're the only ones on the planet," she said as I set her down. We walked over the hardwood floors of what was staged as the living room, to take in the views from the windows and sliding door to the deck.

"Want to explore?"

She nodded in excitement and took off. As was par for the course in my life, all I could do was follow her.

There was a gourmet kitchen with full appliances, a dining room, a full, finished walk-out basement, and that was before we headed upstairs. The entire house had been staged to sell, and even though the furniture wasn't exactly my style, the space was.

"Wow," Avery said again as we walked into the master bedroom. It was separated from the other three by the bridge we'd passed under downstairs. There was a bed against the far wall, two walk-in closets, a giant master bath, and an entire wall of windows that looked over the mountains, mirroring the downstairs. A door led out to a private balcony, and we stepped onto it, both leaning against the railing that held us three stories up.

"I've never seen something so beautiful," she said, tucking the stray strands of her topknot behind her ears.

"Me either," I said, never looking away from her. She was still my Avery, but here, she felt freer, less burdened. I couldn't help but wonder how she would bloom if she were allowed the freedom to define who she was without others telling her.

"I can see it," she said softly, turning to face me.

"See what?" I was desperate to know how she envisioned life, what this house, this place looked like through her eyes, because all I saw was her.

"I can see living here. I could work at the newspaper office, and Addy could go to the high school. I see the fresh start as clearly as I can smell the new paint, and it's…"

"Scary?" I offered.

"Beautiful. It's such a beautiful picture. I can see you here, cooking in that kitchen, waking me up in the mornings with soft kisses."

"That's exactly what I want," I said.

"This house is you. You should take it." Her profile was framed by the sun-kissed strands of blonde in the afternoon light as she looked out over the sizeable backyard that ended in forest—trees and the mountains I loved almost as much as I loved her.

"This house could be us," I said, taking her hand. "I want you here, sleeping in that bedroom. Kissing me in the kitchen, racked out on the couch while we binge-watch something awful on Netflix. I want to explore these mountains with you, talk to you, laugh with you, make love to you." I brought her fingers to my mouth, kissing each one as her lips parted. "I want to make a life with you here. It's not just about leaving my best friend behind, it's about what we have between us—what we can be if we just give this a chance."

My chest tightened as I waited for her to respond, her eyes moving between mine and the landscape. I'd been so careful with her these last seven years, cautious with my feelings and how much I let her know. But laying it all out on the line was both freeing and terrifying.

I'd rather be at a fire. At least those were the flames I knew how to battle—Avery I'd just let burn me if she wanted.

"It's a beautiful dream," she said softly.

"It can be reality." *Don't give up, Avery.*

She sighed. "And Addy?"

"You are under no obligation to live with me. You know that. But there's plenty of room here. I want nothing more than to wake up next to you every day, and the bedroom down the hall on the left has a great view that I think she'd like."

Her eyes swam with tears. "You'd do that? Live with Adeline?"

"Adeline is pretty much my little sister, too. I have no problem helping you raise her. You've done a damn good job already, and I'd love to ease some of that. Besides, the room at the end is a three-story drop, so it's the hardest for a boy to sneak in."

She laughed, two tears racing down her face. "I don't know what to say."

I brushed the tears away with my thumbs. "Say yes. Say you'll make the crazy choice to come with me. Say you'll jump with me. For once, let's do something reckless."

"How can you be so sure we'd work out?"

The fear in her eyes might have given me pause if not for that tiny glimmer of hope I saw there, and that was what I latched onto. "Because you're already my longest relationship. You've always been the woman I've put before everyone else. I would never hurt you, never betray you, never stray from your body if I knew you felt the same."

"How do you feel?" she whispered, opening the door I'd done my damndest to keep shut all these years.

"Avery, don't you realize that I'm completely, madly, whole-heartedly in love with you?" I didn't wait for her answer, simply sealed my mouth over hers and showed her that I meant every single word.

Chapter Eight

Avery

His tongue consumed my mouth the way his words invaded my soul—completely and without apology.

His confession had done what I thought was impossible and brought down every last one of my defenses against him. This wasn't some fling—this was River. My River.

God, could the man kiss. It was a blatant, carnal exploration that had me arching against him, reaching for his head to hold him closer. He grasped me under my ass, lifting me easily, and my legs wrapped around his waist.

He brought us into the bedroom and headed for the massive four-poster bed that took up the center of the room, never once breaking the kiss or pausing. He lowered us to the mattress, and my senses ignited. The feel of the fur coverlet beneath me combined with River's taste, his scent, the weight of him as he rested between my thighs all merged together to awaken every nerve ending. The need that had pulsed in me that morning came back tenfold, demanding appeasement.

He kissed me deeper, with care and carefully checked passion. I felt his restraint in the tension of his arms, the flex of his fingers. He wanted me, but he wasn't going to do anything I wasn't fully ready for. The knowledge was heady, relaxing and inflaming all in the same moment because I knew he would give me whatever I wanted.

And he loved me.

Sweetness filled my chest and expanded outward, lingering in my limbs until his hands stroked up my rib cage, and then desire overpowered it.

I stretched my arms above my head, silently urging him to take off my shirt.

"Are you sure?" he asked.

"I want your hands on me," I whispered against his mouth, gently tugging on his lower lip with my teeth. "Here. Now."

This would be his home. I had zero doubt. For this moment, it was mine, too, because he was here. No matter what happened with us in the coming months, I wanted this with him. I wanted him to have a piece of me here even if it was only in memory.

My blue shirt came off with little fuss, and then River sucked in his breath. "Incredible," he whispered as he framed my lace-cupped breasts with his hands. His mouth collided with mine, a new edge taking over.

His thumbs grazed my hardened nipples through the lace, and I pushed into his hands, needing more.

His hand slipped beneath my back as I arched, and with a simple flick of his fingers, my bra was undone. With a motion of my arms, it found its way to the floor, and then his mouth was on me, drawing my nipple into his mouth.

"River!" I cried out as he worked the sensitive flesh. My thighs restlessly rubbed against him. I'd never been so turned on from a few touches, never been so desperate to get a man naked before...but I'd never been with River.

"Off," I demanded, yanking the fabric of his shirt.

He sat back on his heels with a wicked grin. "Your wish is my command," he said, gathering the shirt by the neck and pulling it off in one smooth motion.

My brain didn't have words for him—for the cut of his muscles, the deep tan of his warm skin, the desire darkening his eyes. He was the definition of sex, and for right now he was mine.

I kicked off my flip-flops as he stretched out over me again, leaning his weight to the side so he didn't crush me. "You are exquisite," he said, running his mouth along the underside of my jaw.

Chills raced down my body, my hips rocking involuntarily.

"So fucking sexy and finally mine." His words echoed my thoughts as he kissed me again, robbing me of every thought beyond his body and the magic he spun around mine. If I was this lost after a few kisses, how would I feel when he—

"River!" I gasped as his fingers slid past the waistband of my shorts.

"Tell me no," he whispered as those fingers reached my panties.

"But then you'd stop," I said, my hips moving to meet him.

"That is the rule, yes."

His hand paused just above where I needed him the most, where a dull throb had begun.

"Don't stop," I told him as my hands threaded through his hair. I loved the silky texture, the way it slid through my fingers.

"Avery." My name was a prayer on his lips as his fingers parted me and brushed my clit.

I cried out, my hips moving, my back arching, my fingers tightening their hold.

His breath stuttered in his chest. "God, if you only knew how many times I fantasized about this." He circled my clit again, then lightly rolled it.

I whimpered and kissed him as one of my hands dug into the muscles of his shoulder. "How does it live up to the fantasy?" I asked, barely able to hold on to a thought as he pressed down on me. Pleasure shot through me like electricity, tension coiling in my belly. The space was almost too tight, but he slid one finger inside me and my back came off the bed.

"There's no comparison. You're hotter, wetter..." He slipped his hand free of my shorts, then—holy shit—licked the finger he'd had inside me. "Sweeter than I ever imagined."

"More." It was the only word I could say because it was the only thing I wanted. I'd had sex before—I wasn't a nun—but I'd never felt this driving need, this utter desperation for someone.

He kissed his way down my stomach, then flicked open the button of my shorts and slid them over my ass and down my legs. "These have to go, too," he said, and my panties followed.

There was no shyness, no awkwardness as he looked me over

like he needed to memorize this moment. The need in his eyes was enough to make me feel like a wanton goddess. His hands started at my breasts, squeezing with just the right amount of pressure, then slid down my curves, over the seam of my thighs until they reached under my ass.

He didn't look away as he brought his mouth to my core. I screamed as he licked me, sucked at me, made love to me with his fingers and then his tongue. My mind lost all control of my body as he worshipped me. I rocked against his face, loving the scrape of his stubble against my inner thighs. My hands fisted in the sheets, then his hair, anything I could grip onto as I shamelessly reveled in every sensation skyrocketing through me.

He laved at me until my body grew so tense that I could barely stand it, my need for release pounding at me. It was so damn good, the pleasure nearly unbearable until I fractured into a thousand pieces of light, his name the only word on my tongue.

His lips made their way up my body, over my navel, between my breasts, until they found mine with a surprisingly tender kiss. "God, I love that," he moaned.

"Which part?" My smile was weak as I struggled to find my breath.

"All of it. Your reactions, your taste, the way you say my name. God, especially that."

"River," I whispered and kissed his neck.

He groaned. "Yeah, that."

"River," I said again, my hands exploring the glorious muscles of his back. His skin felt like warm satin draped over knotted steel. He gasped as my fingers traced the fuck-me lines that led to his shorts. "Take these off."

A few quick motions and he was naked, his erection hot and heavy where it rested along my thigh.

"Are you sure?" he asked, looking deeply into my eyes, his thumb stroking over my lower lip.

"Yes. I want you to be mine," I answered, then kissed his thumb.

"I'm already yours in every possible way." He kissed me, reigniting the flame I was sure my orgasm had doused.

A tear of foil, and we were protected.

He picked me up easily, flipping us so that I straddled his thighs as he sat. He gave me the precious gift of control, and I reveled in the ability I had to drive him wild. I ran my hand along his length, wishing I'd taken the time earlier to taste him.

He cradled my face in his hands as I raised up on my knees and guided him to my entrance. Eyes locked, breaths ragged, hearts hammering, I lowered myself slowly, taking him inside me inch by exquisite inch. He swallowed my cry with a deep kiss, and we were joined in every possible way. My flesh stretched to accommodate him, and he was utterly still as I adjusted to him.

But then still wasn't enough. Not when he was this full, this hard inside me.

His hands kneaded my hips as I began to move, his grip digging into my flesh as I rode him. "You feel. So. Perfect," I said between glides.

"We," he corrected, kissing my neck. "We feel perfect."

And we were. It didn't feel like sex—more like fulfilling the union our bodies demanded because our souls had always had it. The lines of his face grew taut as he concentrated on our movements, sweat making our skin slippery as we rocked against each other, pleasure streaking through me with each motion.

His hand shifted from my thigh to strum his thumb over my clit, the nerves hypersensitive. "You don't..." I gasped as he pressed, then circled again. I tried to gather my thoughts to speak again. "You don't have to...I don't think I can..."

"Yes you can," he said, his breath warm in my ear. His free hand reached for my ponytail, wrapping it around as he gently tugged my head back. His mouth attacked my neck, licking and sucking every sensitive place. "I have seven years of fantasies, Avery. Seven years of imagining the way you'd scream my name, how tight you'd grip me as I slid into you. Seven years of waiting to feel you come around me. I have more than enough to get you there again."

I groaned, already feeling that tension starting to ravel. He shifted our angle so he could stroke deeper, our bodies undulating in perfect rhythm. It was as if we'd been making love for years, already so in tune, in sync.

"I love you." He groaned. "I'm never going to get enough of this—never going to get enough of you."

Yes, more. I moved faster, until my world was a blur of sensation and River—his breath, his body, his scent, his heart. My orgasm built until I was ready to splinter. "River," I begged.

"Yes," he hissed, then brought his mouth to mine. A few deft movements of his fingers and I came apart, my cry swallowed by his kiss.

The moment I started to sag over him, he turned, putting me on my back. Our kiss deep, he drove into me, pounding out a rhythm that had me keening, my orgasm kicking back aftershocks.

He yelled my name as he came, his muscles straining above me, and through the haze of my pleasure I could think of nothing more than how beautiful he was.

A salty kiss later, he collapsed, rolling us to the side.

Our breathing was ragged as we stared at each other. "I think we might be pretty good at that," I said.

He grinned, and my heart clenched, screaming out an emotion I couldn't—wouldn't—name.

"Yeah, but I think there might be room for improvement with practice."

"Lots of practice," I nodded.

"As much as you can handle," he promised, kissing my nose. Then all traces of laughter faded. "That was... I don't have words for it. Perfect isn't enough."

Earth shattering. Mind blowing. "Perfect is just about right."

He kissed me, holding me like I was infinitely precious to him.

"Hello? River?" A female voice came from downstairs.

We scrambled for clothes, throwing them on while he called out, "Just a minute!"

I tripped trying to put on my flip-flop, River barely catching me before I tumbled to the ground.

"All I wanted was—"

"Perfection," I said, kissing him lightly once we were right. "We've got it. Now let's see who that is."

We walked hand-in-hand down the stairs to find a petite, curvy blonde in the kitchen examining the refrigerator. She turned when she heard us, her green eyes wide with joy. "Oh my God!"

"Harper?" River asked.

By the way she jumped into his hug, I guessed she was.

He set her down and she turned to me, enveloping me in the same warm hug. "You must be Avery!" She pulled back and smiled. "Bishop said you two are pretty much fated for the diner wall. I'm Harper. Ryker's sister."

"Diner wall?" I asked as River slid me under his arm. "Ryker?"

River kissed the top of my head. "You haven't met Ryker yet. He's on a fire with Bash right now. They're Bishop's age, but I graduated with Harper. And the town has a little tradition where we carve our names into the diner wall when we're ready to declare undying love."

My heart melted. "That might be the sweetest thing I've ever heard."

Harper sighed. "It really is. Until there's a divorce or an affair and you see some crazed wife hacking at the wall with a pocket knife."

River nodded. "It happens. I love seeing you, Harper, but what are you doing all the way out here?"

"Oh, well, Knox told me that the breakers weren't on out here, and when you didn't come back, they figured you might not want to stumble around in the dark if you stayed any later."

"How did you know we were at this one?" he asked.

"I didn't. I've checked four other houses," she admitted. "Anyway, the breakers are on now, if you two want to get back to"— she gestured at us—"the amazing sex you were having."

I sputtered, my eyes flying wide. "We weren't…"

She waved us off. "Your shirt is on inside out. Anyway. Ceremony is tomorrow afternoon, and then the council meeting is tomorrow night, so you two can frolic all you like."

I wanted to die. It was like that nightmare where you're caught at school with no clothes…except mine were on inside out and this was real.

"Thanks for coming out to check on us. Does anyone deliver out here?"

She tilted her head. "Magnolia's might. Should I tell Knox you'll take this one?"

"Knox, huh?" River grinned.

She turned redder than the tank top she had on. "Shut up."

River laughed, his entire chest rumbling. "Good to see not much changes around here. Has Emerson taken Bash back yet?"

"How did you know?"

"Oh, come on. Emmy and Bash are a given. Almost as much as you dancing around Knox and praying he and your brother don't notice."

She narrowed her eyes at him. "Ugh. You've been in town for all of a day." Then she looked over at me, a small smile playing over her lips. "You and I are going to be great friends. I need someone on my team against this one."

I nodded. "I think we can manage that." I liked her openness, the way she didn't beat around the bush, and I loved the way she didn't flirt with River. Then again, I'd seen how hot Knox was, and if River was right, and that's the way her world tilted, then I couldn't blame her.

"Tell Knox we'll take this one," River said. "Do you think we have the numbers for this meeting tomorrow?"

Her smile faded. "We'll have them, one way or another."

The determination on her face was the same I'd seen on River's over the years, the same Knox had shown when he'd led us on the tour of the clubhouse. There was a steel in this generation, a tenacity that I felt simply by looking at them.

I pitied anyone who stood in the way of them getting their crew back.

Chapter Nine

River

I traced the letters on her headstone, grief wrapping around my heart, uncaring that it had been eight years since we lost her.

"Man, I miss you," I told her before looking up to where Avery stood, flowers in her arms. "She would have loved you."

"I'm a hot mess."

"You're my hot mess," I corrected her. After the handful of times I'd taken her in the last twelve hours I was pretty sure she'd have a hard time arguing that she wasn't mine.

She placed the flowers on Mom's grave as I stood, then stepped into my arms as I held them out to her. The cemetery was quiet, peaceful.

"I'm sorry you lost them both."

"I'm glad they went close to each other. Losing Dad in the fire, that was brutal, but when cancer took her a couple years later..." He shook his head. "For a long time I wondered if I was cursed. If I wasn't supposed to have anything good."

"You deserve the best," she said, her voice soft.

"It all changed when I saw you. Frustrated, ponytail a mess, fighting with the tire iron and rusted lug nuts."

"Ugh. I'd been on the side of the road for a half hour."

I brushed her hair back from her face, loving that it was down and free. "You were beautiful, and I fell in love with you in that moment."

Her lips parted. "Because I couldn't change a tire?" she whispered.

"Because you hadn't given up. There was zero chance you could have gotten those bolts off, but you weren't giving up. When I realized that you were raising Addy, caring for your dad...there wasn't a force in this world that could have stopped me from loving you."

"Why didn't you say anything?"

"You weren't ready and I was terrified. I'd lost everyone I loved except for Bishop. When the wildfire came, when Dad died, there was a part of me that shriveled, that started to expect heartache. I couldn't show it, of course. The whole town was in mourning, and there were sixteen of us left behind without fathers. Indigo was left without a mom. In our collective grief, we weren't allowed to break down, not when there were so many eyes on us."

"River..." she whispered, holding me tighter in her support.

"Then the rebuilding began, and Mom got sick. She died the summer of my junior year, and we had the new high school open by my senior year."

"Then you and Bishop came up to Alaska."

I rested my chin on the top of her head, loving how well she fit me. "And you know the rest."

"I wish I knew how it ended."

My heart sank, knowing as much as she loved pretending, she hadn't really decided. Because as fierce as my love of this crew and my family was, hers was just as intense for hers, and she wouldn't leave her father.

In a place that had always brought me so much loss, I couldn't help but wonder if the biggest heartache was yet to come.

"Me, too, baby."

* * * *

The ceremony was somber. Bishop and I took the wreath up for our father, and then placed it at the new memorial where it stood with seventeen others.

Ten years later, and I still missed him like hell.

He'd been larger than life, a force of nature. In so many ways Bishop was just like him, but the years of raising me had hardened him in ways Dad hadn't been. Where Dad was optimistic, Bishop saw the pitfalls of everything. Where Dad loved Mom with the same kind of intensity I felt for Avery, Bishop held himself away from everyone who could leave.

As I looked around at the other Legacy kids, the ones who had grown up without their dads or mom, I realized that the casualties of that day were far more reaching than the firefighters laid to rest in Aspen Cemetery.

The entire town had lost. Homes, businesses, and memories were ash by the time the fire had finished with us, but it always felt like we had lost a little more. We took our seats, and the bells rang— one for each loss, each sacrifice, each choice that had been made the day they headed up Legacy Mountain with the odds and the weather against them.

Avery took my hand, steadying me like always. I concentrated on the feeling of her fingers with mine and tried to keep the memories at bay. But the harshest ones fought through—the order for evacuation, the way he'd held us, kissed our mother. The way he'd told Bishop to keep me out of trouble while he was gone.

My resolve sharpened with each bell. The council could be afraid of the liability of having another Hotshot crew. They could deny us the Legacy name, and they could claim it was to salvage the tender hearts of this town.

But the Legacy crew had been family, and damn it, we were getting it back.

As the ceremony cleared out, the sixteen of us stood in a line facing the monument, from the youngest kid, Violet, who had never met her father, to the oldest, Shane Winston, who'd been away at college when it happened.

Those who wouldn't be joining us on the crew—the ones who were too young or who had no interest in firefighting—left, until it was just those of us who were.

"Are you sure about this?" Bash asked, Emerson by his side. Time had turned the dark-haired, reckless guy into a hell of a stubborn man.

I looked around as we all nodded.

"They're going to fight us tooth and nail," he warned. "They don't want this. They're terrified of what could happen." He looked pointedly at our youngest members who couldn't be older than twenty.

"We're with you, Bash," Bishop answered from next to me. "They're not taking this from us."

"We're with you," we all agreed.

Avery's soft smile was forced as I looked down at her, and I sent up a fervent prayer that she would stay, because I knew in that moment there was no way I could leave.

Chapter Ten

Avery

"So which one is that?" I asked Harper as we looked over the packed clubhouse.

The Legacy crew had gotten their needed numbers, and the council had begrudgingly approved the team after Spencer—the only surviving member of the original team—showed up and agreed to lead them.

"That's Ryker," Harper answered. "He's my brother."

"Right," I said, trying to remember names with faces. "And the one standing next to River is Bash."

"Yup. Sebastian Vargas, but everyone's called him Bash since he was little. And Emerson is the brunette standing next to him. She's my best friend."

"Too many names," I muttered.

She laughed and took a sip of her beer. "You'll figure it out. Don't worry. The crew is a giant family. We're together a lot, so you'll learn."

If I'm here.

The longer we were here, the more I wanted to—hell, needed to. I loved everything about the little town, the people, the crew…and River. All I had to do was convince Dad to come, that maybe the change would be good for him, too. River was pretty much a saint to offer for Dad to live with us, but maybe he'd get to where he could live on his own...and I could have my own life.

The texts Addy had sent me said everything was under control, so maybe it was possible.

Yes. I could do it. Maybe.

"What's up, Avery?" Bishop asked as he walked over.

"Can we take a walk?" I asked him, needing a sounding board that wasn't River.

His forehead puckered. "Of course."

He helped me up and we walked out the side door of the clubhouse. I sucked in a deep lungful of air, grateful for the quiet we had outside. My lungs burned, but I was adjusting to the altitude. Kind of.

"What are you going to do?" he asked, never one to beat around the bush.

"I don't know," I answered.

"What do you want?" he asked. "Not what River wants, what your dad wants...what do you want?"

I thought about the last two days. The peace, the freedom, the pure happiness I felt at the possibility of a fresh start with River. "I want to be here."

"Then that's your answer."

I scoffed. "What I want and what's possible are almost never the same thing."

"Avery, if you're willing to tear up everything, move from Alaska, and build something fresh, then you've already jumped the biggest barrier. Well, that and chancing your life on River's cooking."

My lips turned up at the corners. "Okay, there's that. Do you really think I can convince my dad to come? Adeline is all for it, but it's not just me in this decision. I can't leave them any more than you'd leave River."

His face scrunched. "Eh, you know, River is a grown-ass man. If he didn't want to come here, I would have left him in Alaska. He makes his own choices. Of course, I'm glad he's here with me. If he's going to be firefighting, then I want him on my crew, but don't think for a second that I wouldn't have come without him. He deserves his own life, and you do, too."

"And what if I come here, and it doesn't work out with River?" I asked, giving voice to my biggest fear. "What if I leave everything I know behind, and come here, and we have a horrid breakup and then I lose him anyway?"

He grasped both of my shoulders and ducked to look in my eyes. "That's a risk you're going to have to take. Nothing is guaranteed, not in life and sure as hell not in love. But I can tell you that he has loved you for as long as he's known you. There is nothing he won't give you—nothing he won't do to make this work. That kind of love, the one that's rooted in a friendship as deep as you two have...that's not easy to come by. It's worth the fight. I'll tell you the same thing I told him. You guys are worth the gamble."

"Thank you," I said softly.

"Don't thank me. You have a hell of a road ahead of you. I just wish that I could be there to help you with it."

"You're not coming back with us?" My stomach dropped.

"Nah. I boxed up my shit before I left. River is going to sell my truck and pack send up my stuff with his. Bash needs my help here. We have a ton of relocating to do, and there's not much up there for me anyway."

"I guess I thought when they told us you could have until spring..." My voice drifted off because we both knew where it was going. When Bash had gotten approval for the team to be together by spring, I figured we'd been given a reprieve. Another few months to work everything out. Time to convince my dad. Time to coordinate.

"River might take it," Bishop said. "Like I said, we make our own decisions. If he chooses to stay the winter in Alaska, then I'll support that. He doesn't have to be back until April."

"I just need time."

"I know that, and he does, too. It's just that time might not be something we have a lot of to spare right now."

The door opened behind us and River stepped out. "Hey, are you stealing my girl, or what?"

Bishop gave my shoulders one last squeeze. "Nope, she's all yours." He went for the door but turned before going in. "Remember what I said, Avery. His cooking really will kill you." He tossed a grin at River and went inside, leaving us alone.

"Asshole," River muttered.

"Are you going to take the time?" I asked. "Are you going to stay in Alaska until spring, or are you moving right now?"

His eyebrows shot high. "Well, I guess that's what you two were talking about."

"Answer, please? Because I'm kind of freaking out."

He took two steps and enveloped me in his arms, pulling me close. I rested my head on his chest, letting his familiar scent and heartbeat surround me.

"I'll do whatever you need," he said, his chin resting on the top of my head. "If you want to move now, we'll get Addy, your dad, and move. If you want to wait until spring, I'll have to come back a few times, but we can make that happen, too."

"You'd wait for me to get everything together?"

His arms tightened around me. "If I know that you're coming here, making your life with me, I'll wait forever."

I took a stuttering breath, knowing that what I was going to say would change everything. Then I looked up at him, meeting his dark eyes in the bright moonlight. "I want to come. I want to live here with you. Well, not here, here, but at our house here. I want to make this work. I'll do it."

Saying the words set my heart free in a way I'd never known. Every possibility for my future was so clear, so vibrant that I could taste it, and then River was all I could taste as he kissed me.

This was what I wanted for my life. River's kisses, his arms around me, his love. I wanted it all.

His kiss was passionate, claiming, and I found my back against the building as he pinned me between him and the wall. It didn't matter that I'd already kissed him dozens of times in the last week. Each kiss felt new, and at the same time like coming home.

"This is yours," he said, his lips brushing my ear as something cold and metal pressed into my palm.

"A key?" I asked, examining it in the pale light.

His smile could have lit the world. "I just signed for the house. This one is yours. No pressure. It's just a key."

It wasn't just a key. "I love it," I said, my hand closing so tight the ridges bit into my skin.

"I love you," he said.

My heart soared, erupted, as if by saying what I wanted, I'd finally cut loose the chains I'd tightly bound myself with. "River," I whispered, pulling him back so I could look into his eyes when I said it. "I—"

My phone sounded with Addy's ringtone. Calling wasn't in her nature, she was more of a text girl, so it had to be urgent.

"Ugh." I sighed, pulling my phone from my pocket. "One second." I swiped the phone and answered. "What's up?"

"Avery?" she sobbed.

My stomach soured and my world narrowed to the small voice on the other end. "What's wrong?" I asked her.

"It's Dad. He…" Another sob came through, and I forced oxygen through my lungs. "Aunt Dawn didn't move the meds, and he found them."

"Oh, God." I would have fallen if River's arms hadn't caught me, holding me upright. "Addy, is he…?"

"He overdosed. They have him on a ventilator and they don't know…" Her voice faded into hiccupping sobs. "Can you come home?"

I looked up into River's eyes and realized he'd heard her through the phone when he nodded. The earth shifted beneath my feet; the reality I'd been so certain of a few minutes ago disappearing as a new one took its place.

"I'm on my way."

Chapter Eleven

River

I took another sip of hospital coffee and tried to stay awake. We'd been traveling sixteen hours, having driven to Denver the night before to get the first flight out. Avery couldn't wait to fly out of Gunnison in the morning.

We'd come straight to the hospital where her dad was in the ICU, and I'd been sitting out here for at least another two hours, just hoping that she was okay in there with him.

"They say if he makes it through the night, he should be okay," Adeline said, curled into my side.

"He's a tough guy, your dad," I told her. It didn't matter what an ass he'd been; no kid deserved to lose her father this way.

"I hate him," she whispered. "Why can't he just be like other dads?"

I put my coffee down and wrapped my other arm around her. "I know, and you know what? It's not fair. But I do know that you and your sister are some of the strongest, smartest women I know, and I think that has a lot to do with what you've been through. Don't hate him, Addy. He struggles with something we can't understand."

Problem was, I hated him. I hated that the moment Avery found out he'd overdosed, she'd clammed up. She went distant. Gone were the soft looks, the warm touches. Gone were the kisses, the talks about our future. She stared out the fucking window on every airplane and responded to questions in one-word answers.

My Avery was gone in the span of a heartbeat as we'd packed, driven, flown, and arrived. It wasn't even that she'd pulled away romantically that pissed me off. It was that she'd blocked me as her best friend. She'd closed herself down and built a wall so high I'd need a damn ladder.

"Do you want me to take you home?" I asked Addy.

"No. I'm scared that if I leave..."

He won't be alive when I come back. I heard it loud and clear without her uttering a word.

"I understand."

Another hour passed before Avery walked out.

I moved to sit up straight, but she shook her head. "He's still... He's alive," she whispered as she motioned to Addy. "How long has she been asleep?"

"About a half hour," I said softly.

She nodded, taking the seat on the other side of me. Her skin was pale in gross contrast to the dark circles under her eyes. The worst part was that they were flat, giving away no hint of whatever emotion she was feeling.

"How is he?" I asked.

"Stable." She shrugged. "Aunt Dawn is a mess. I never told her how bad it really was. Figured if I could handle it on my own, why air the laundry, you know?"

I threaded our fingers and squeezed lightly. "You've done a damn fine job. Better than anyone else could have. What happened here is not your fault. It's his."

She nodded slowly, repetitively, which moved to slight rocking motions. "I should have been here."

Boom. I heard my heart hit the floor with every word. "This isn't your fault," I repeated. "You have to know that or it will eat you up."

She kept rocking, but the head nod changed to her shaking it. "I should have been here. I know to move the meds. I know what he's capable of."

"Avery," I begged.

She stood up, dropped my hand, and walked back into the ICU.

* * * *

Two days later he was still alive.

I wasn't so sure about Avery. She was gaunt, quiet, and barely left his room unless the nurses told her she had to. She slept on the waiting room couches and only went home to shower.

I'd given up on trying to get her to talk to me yesterday. Avery would open up when she wanted to, and until then it was like chipping away at Fort Knox with a fucking toothpick.

So instead of sitting there for hours, waiting for her to realize I was right next to her, I started on the list Bishop had texted me.

"Friday is great," I told the moving company. "I'm just impressed you can get it done by then. Thank you."

I hung up and crossed coordinate movers off my to-do list as I chugged down a glass of water.

I'd already put his truck on Craigslist and had an appointment to show it to a potential buyer. Not bad for a Tuesday morning.

On the flipside, he was having the satellite installed at our new place in Colorado.

Is it ours? Is she even coming?

A knock at the door startled Zeus, but he was wagging like a puppy when I opened the door to find Avery standing there. Her hair was up in a messy knot, but it was clean, and her jeans and baseball tee were different than the outfit I'd seen her in this morning.

"Hey. You didn't have to knock."

She shrugged, preoccupied with petting Zeus. "I didn't want to barge in. Do you have a couple of minutes?" Finally, she looked up at me, but the cool, detached look in her eyes had my stomach somersaulting.

"Of course. Come on in."

She passed me in the doorway, careful not to brush against me, and my senses went on high alert, warning bells screaming in my ears. "Dad's awake," she said, crossing her arms in front of her chest. The move didn't look defensive, more like what she would do to hold herself together.

"That's great!" He was going to be okay. My relief was short-lived because when I reached for her, she stepped away. "Avery?"

She shook her head, her teeth sinking into her bottom lip momentarily. "Just stay over there. I can't think when you touch me."

"Okay," I said slowly, tucking my thumbs into the pockets of my shorts to keep my hands off her. She looked so small, defenseless, and it was ripping me apart that she didn't want me to touch her.

"He's awake and talking since this morning, right after you left, actually."

"That's good. What's wrong? This is good—no, great news. He's going to be okay. Maybe this will be a turning point for him."

She laughed, the sound bitter and empty. "He won't change. He's never going to change. And he won't go to Colorado. He refuses. Says that this whole thing was my fault for being gone, and that the minute I leave he'll do it again."

"Avery…" God, I wanted to strangle him with my bare hands. None of this was her fault, but he'd gotten it into her so young—the guilt, the obligation—until it became part of her very being.

"It wasn't even intentional, that's the kicker. He didn't take the whole bottle or anything, just upped his pain meds. But the dosage he was already on gave him an accidental overdose."

"This wasn't your fault. I will say it every minute of every day until you realize that. He's an adult. He made a choice."

"But it is my fault," she cried. "I left. I believed that someone else could care for him, and this is what happened. None of this would have happened if I'd been here—where I'm supposed to be, taking care of my family." She rubbed her hands over her bloodshot eyes, the blue even brighter than usual. "What was I thinking?"

I walked over to her, damning her instructions, and gently lifted her wrists so I could see her face. "You were thinking that you deserve happiness, too. You deserve a life, love, kids, a future that isn't all about when he decides to go off the rails."

"But I don't." Her voice was quiet, her eyes pleading for something I didn't know how to give. "Sometimes we draw the short straw. You lost your dad, then your mom. Are you telling me you wouldn't feel the same if it was them? If you had a chance to be there for them, would you leave? Or would you suck up the bitterness because it's the straw you were dealt, and just be thankful you have them around?"

The small piece of hope I'd kept cradled close screamed out its defeat and died. "You're not coming back to Colorado with me right now."

She shook her head. "I can't. Look what happened when I left him."

I took a deep, steadying breath and pulled out plan B. "Okay, then we'll spend the winter here, get him healthy, and talk about it again in the spring. By then maybe his head will be clear enough to make a better choice."

"No," she whispered. "He said he'll die in that house before he moves. It's where we all lived when Mom was alive, and that's all there is left."

"I typically draw the line at relocating an entire house, but I can make some calls," I tried to joke. I was grasping at straws as they slid through my hands.

"He's lonely. He said that I'm never there, and he's right. Between working both jobs and seeing..."

"Me," I offered, my tone tensing.

"You," she agreed softly. "With all that, I'm not around for him, and there's no one else he'll let in."

"What are you saying?" I asked, the pit in my stomach growing to black-hole proportions.

She looked up at me, the sadness of the world pouring out of her eyes, and I knew. I fucking knew. "You're not coming at all."

"I can't. I would never forgive myself if something happened to him."

My mind swam, trying to come up with plan C. "Okay, so I'll go seasonal. I'll work with the Legacy crew in the summer, and come back for winters. It will suck, but we can manage it."

She shook her head. "No. It wouldn't work. We'd both be miserable, and eventually you'd resent me. We'd just be prolonging the inevitable."

"Don't do this."

She tugged her wrists free and cupped my face with her hands, scratching her palms over my day's worth of stubble. "You are the most beautiful dream. What we could have had...that was another life, with another girl who could walk away from her responsibility.

That girl is never going to be me. Maybe if Adeline was grown, but there's just too much here."

"I can call Bash. I'll back out of the team. There's one other guy they could call, and I'll make sure he takes the slot."

She brushed her thumb over my lower lip. "You staying won't fix anything. I'd cost you the chance to be on the Legacy crew."

"I don't care. Nothing matters without you."

Her hands fell from my face, and I realized that I was wrong. I wasn't grasping at straws—I was desperately clutching at her, and she fell through my fingers like running water, impossible to hold and yet even harder to whisk away in its entirety. She'd already soaked into my soul.

"I can't be with you, River. Not now. Not ever. I can't go, and you can't stay. Our dream was beautiful—the happiest few days of my life—but it's time to wake up. I'm not a child. I can't do selfish things, and not everyone gets the fairy tale."

"You are my fairy tale," I argued. "You are the only woman I have ever loved. The only woman I will ever love, and I'm not giving up that easily."

"I'm not giving you a choice!" she yelled, backing away from me. The lack of physical contact felt like having a limb severed. My nerves screamed to have her back. "God, can't you see? I'm still the girl with the goddamned rusted lug nuts on the flat tire. I'm not going to back down. I'm not going to leave him. That's not what good people do!"

I raked my hands down my face. "So what am I supposed to do? Leave you because you're honorable? Because you stepped up to do what no one else would? Do you expect me to be less than the man you know by walking away?"

She shook her head, two crystal tears streaking down her cheeks. "No. I expect you to do what you need to for your family. Go to Colorado. Become what you were destined to be. Live in that house and be happy, River. Just be happy!"

"I can't be happy without you! Is that seriously what you think of me? That I can move, start over? Forget that you exist? You're in every single breath I take, every thought I have. I'm not leaving you here to carry this by yourself. To raise Addy, to take care of your dad, to work yourself to death. That's not in my nature."

"It's not your choice to make," she said, furiously wiping her tears away. "Whether or not you're still here, we're over. I won't sit by and watch you resent me, watch you kiss that picture every time you come home from a fire. That will kill me far more than knowing you're happy somewhere else...with someone else."

Pure, white-hot rage choked me, and I had to swallow a couple times before I was under control. "If you think you're that easily replaceable, then you never really knew me."

"We only had a few days," she said quietly.

"We had seven fucking years."

"And they're over. We're over."

"Avery..."

"What's your solution, River? What happens if you stay here and Bishop is killed on a fire? You wouldn't ever recover from that. The guilt alone would destroy you. What if I go there and my dad dies because I wasn't here to take care of him? I'm his daughter. His flesh and bone. I owe this to my mother. I promised her, and as much as I—" My heart stopped as she sucked in a breath, closing her eyes for a moment. "As much as I care for you, it would turn to hate for putting me in that position where I have to choose to abandon my family to be with you."

Hate. The word drove a knife through my chest, and as sure as if it was a physical wound, my heart bled out on my hardwood floor. "You're really ending this."

"I don't have a choice."

I shook my head. "No, you have all the choices, you're just refusing to make them. I'm not saying they're easy choices, but at least you have them. Me, on the other hand, I get to stand here while you shred me because you're not willing to take a fucking chance!"

"There's no chance to take! This is a certainty."

"You have no idea what could happen over the winter. None. You're letting him manipulate you, as usual. As your best friend, I stood by and watched you put yourself last over and over. But as the man who loves you, openly and out loud, I can't stand to watch you do this to yourself."

"I'm telling you not to watch. I'm telling you to go."

"It's bullshit that you think you get to make that choice for me!"

"You're like this kid in a car, speeding toward the cliff, knowing that it's coming but refusing to turn, or just stop."

"And you're too scared of the cliff to find another way," I threw back.

"Do you realize what happens when you jump off a damn cliff? You fall. You die. The ground crushes you."

"Or maybe you fly. Damn it, Avery, why do you make it so hard to love you? Why can't you just let me love you?"

She looked like I'd slapped her, those eyes huge and pooling with tears as we stood facing each other, the only sound in the room the pounding of my heart, the rush of blood through my ears.

"I never wanted it to end this way," she whispered.

"Yeah, well, I never wanted it to end."

"I'm so sorry," she whispered.

"That makes two of us."

She nodded and walked to the door, pausing at the frame to look back. "Goodbye, River."

I fought against every one of my instincts that demanded I go after her and kiss some sense into her, force her into seeing that we could make it. No matter how imperfect our circumstances, we were perfect for each other. But I was done forcing her to see the possibilities. This was her choice.

Every muscle in my body locked as I spoke the words she wanted.

"Bye, Avery."

The sound of the door closing reverberated though every cell of my body. Only then did I say the word I needed.

"I love you."

The future I'd planned, dreamed of, yearned for disintegrated in front of me. My heart shattered with the glass I threw against the wall, water dripping down the wall and soaking into the paint.

Chapter Twelve

Avery

"I'm the one in the hospital, but you're the one who looks like shit," Dad said as I walked into his room.

"Get off her case, Jim," Aunt Dawn said from the chair next to his bed. "Honey, are you okay?"

"I'm fine," I replied, giving the same answer I had for the last three days since I'd left River.

I said it to everyone at work when they asked about how red my eyes were. I said it to Addy when she caught me staring off into space, thinking about him. I said it to myself every time I felt my walls crumble and the not-fine emotions surface.

"Fine or not, you look like crap," Dad repeated, sitting up in bed with a wince. "I wish they hadn't lowered my meds."

"You have to be able to function," I said. "Besides, with the new physical therapy, maybe we can wean you off them."

"I'm not seeing a physical therapist," he grumbled.

"Yeah, why bother with something that might help you?" I snapped. "Why not just up the pain meds until we're here again?"

"Watch your tone!" He seethed. "Your mother would be ashamed!"

My mouth snapped shut, heat flushing my face. She had handled him with more grace than I ever would manage...and she had died for it.

"Jim," Aunt Dawn warned. "Avery didn't put you in this hospital. You did that yourself."

Before he could snap back at her, the doctor came in to discharge Dad. I stared out the window in the direction of River's house, wondering what he was doing, how mad at me he still was.

Did I make a mistake? I shut that line of thinking down before it could destroy me. There hadn't been a choice to make. I had to set him free before we destroyed each other.

Too late.

I listened as the doctor gave the discharge instructions to my aunt. The pain meds he was allowed, the therapist he needed to see. It should have been me the doctor gave the instructions to. After all, I was the one who was responsible for Dad. But this doc wouldn't know that. In appearances, it made sense that the fifty-ish woman was caring for the fifty-ish man.

Not the twenty-five year old.

A little over an hour later, we had Dad settled back on the living room couch. "Give me the remote," he demanded when Aunt Dawn went to grab his bag from the car.

I handed it over without a word, too tired to fight with him over manners.

"Give me one of those white pills."

"No, it's not time yet," I told him, removing the medication.

"You're not the adult here!" he screamed.

"Of course I am!" I fired back. "That's what you made me! You want to be the grown-up then you have to act like it."

I put the meds in the small breadbox on top of the refrigerator, gripped the counter, and leaned over, trying to get a breath. Everything suddenly felt stifling, as if the walls of my life were suddenly moving closer—like I was stuck in that trash compactor on Star Wars.

But I'd let my Han Solo walk away.

Gasping for air, I stumbled to the front door, grabbing my car keys on the way out. I needed to see him. Even if it was only for a second. Even if he told me to go the hell away, I needed him.

"Avery?" Aunt Dawn bumped into me on the bottom steps.

"Are you okay?"

"I'm fine," I replied automatically, sucking in the clean, sweet air. "I just need to run an errand. Do you think you could stay with him?"

"Of course."

"Thank you," I said, nearly running to my car.

"Honey," she called out. "You don't have to do this—take care of him on your own. I didn't know how bad it was, you were that good at caring for him. But I'm here now. I'm not leaving you to do this on your own, do you understand?"

"He's my father," I said with a shrug.

"He's my little brother. He was my responsibility long before he was yours. Don't you let your father's actions stop you from living your life. Do you understand me? I won't stand for it, and neither would your mother."

I nodded, unable to think of anything to say, then slid behind the wheel. She waved before disappearing into the house, and I backed out of our driveway, more than desperate to get to River.

Maybe River was right. Maybe if I had Aunt Dawn to push Dad, he'd get better—at least well enough to move to Colorado. Maybe all he needed was the winter.

Maybe there was something at the cliff's edge.

I sped across the back roads toward River's house. I'd never gone this long without talking to him unless he was on a fire, and we'd never been in a fight this severe, but I knew it could be fixed.

He was River. I was Avery. It was as simple as that.

I pulled into his driveway and killed the ignition, running for the house before I heard the car door fully shut behind me. Zeus wasn't barking, so maybe they were out for a run.

I fumbled with my keys, pulling out the small bronze one he'd given me years ago, and opened the door.

"River? I used my—" The air rushed from my lungs as I looked into his perfectly clean, perfectly empty house. "Key."

Everything was gone. The furniture. The dishes. Zeus's bowls. The house I loved had been transformed into an empty shell. Somehow I got my feet to move, to carry me to the kitchen counter where there was a stack of papers. There was a listing agreement and a note to Mindy Ruiz, a local realtor.

Hey, Mindy,

Here's the listing agreement. Sorry I had to leave so fast. It just made sense to send all my stuff with Bishop's. You'll find his listing agreement under mine. If you need anything else, I'll forward my new number from Colorado. All the keys are here except one. Avery Claire has it. Let her keep it. I'll pay to have the locks redone when you find new buyers.

Thanks,

River Maldonado

He was gone. Really and truly gone. Because I told him to go.

My back hit the cabinet and I fell to the ground. Hugging my knees to my chest, I finally succumbed to my emotions, letting them out of the cage I'd locked them in.

I loved him. I'd always thought if I didn't acknowledge that fact, it wouldn't have the power to hurt me, but I was pulverized all the same. Whether or not I'd told him, or even myself, didn't matter. The love was still there, and the ache was pure agony.

I'd had him. Touched him. Loved him. I'd held his heart in my hands and then thrown it back at him.

My sobs echoed through the empty house until my body ran out of tears. By the time I left, it was dark—and I was broken.

* * * *

"I want to move to Colorado," Adeline said as she helped me load the dishwasher.

"They have some really great colleges there. Why don't we do some research? It's only five years away." I slipped another glass into the top rack.

"Because I want to go now."

My stomach tightened. "Yeah, well, we can't. Look what happened when I left last time." It had been three weeks since he'd overdosed. Two since River moved to Colorado.

One since he posted a photo of his new house on Instagram with the caption that he was home in Legacy for good.

"Where's that beer?" Dad called out from the living room.

"That was his choice," Addy whispered.

I grabbed a clean glass from the cabinet, filled it with ice and water, and walked out of the kitchen without replying. How could she understand? She was only thirteen. I'd been two years older when Mom died, and even then I hadn't fully understood.

"Here we go," I said to Dad as I put the glass within his reach on the coffee table.

"What is that bullshit?" he spat.

"That is water. Doc said no booze, remember?" I counted to ten in my head, reminding myself that he was an addict.

"I don't give a fuck what that doctor said. Get me a beer before your aunt Dawn gets back from the store."

"No," I said with a shake of my head.

"Girl!" he yelled, and I heard Adeline go silent in the kitchen. The water was running, but no dishes clanked.

"I didn't give up everything good in my life just so you could sit there and drink yourself to death," I said calmly.

"Get me the goddamned beer! Gave up everything good? What would you know? Because you broke up with a boy who you dated for all of five seconds? I lost your mother!"

"I did, too!" I yelled. "You aren't the only one who lost her!"

Something went sailing past my head and smashed against the wall. I spun to see water running down the wall into a puddle of ice and smashed glass.

"Clean that up!" he yelled.

"Clean it up yourself," I snapped and walked away.

My chest heaved as I ran outside, gasping for the clean air as I sat on the front steps, my head in my hands. He'd fucking thrown a glass at me. What was next? Would he hit me? Would he hit Addy?

The doc had warned us that he would get worse before he got better. That weaning him down from the pain meds wasn't going to be pleasant, but this was horrid. Maybe I needed to send Addy to a friend's house for the next month or so.

The door opened and shut behind me and Adeline joined me on the step. "I want to move now."

"I know," I said, putting my arm around her. "But we can't just leave him."

"We wouldn't be. Aunt Dawn is here. She's already offered to take care of him, and let's face it—she's the only one he's remotely scared of."

"That's true, but he's our dad."

"He's never going to forgive us for Mom dying," she whispered.

I wanted to tell her that wasn't true, but I'd made a promise to never lie to her, so I stayed silent.

"Avery?"

"Yeah?"

"I did something."

My stomach clenched. "Okay. What did you do?"

"You know my savings?"

"I do." She hated that I made her save half of every birthday gift from our extended family.

"I spent it yesterday."

Before I could flip out on her that she'd need that when she went to college, she unfolded a paper from her back pocket and handed it to me.

Doing my best to keep my hands from trembling, I opened it up. Then my jaw dropped. "You want me to be your legal guardian?"

She nodded. "There's nothing left for us here, Avery. You're already more of a parent than he is. This would just make it possible…"

"For us to move to Colorado without him," I whispered.

"For us to be free."

I hugged her to me, and for the first time in my life, I considered leaving him behind.

* * * *

"You're sure you're okay to get him to his appointment?" I asked Aunt Dawn.

"Yes, Avery. You go to work. Maybe stay out late? Go see a movie?"

It had been a month since River left, and I still hadn't ventured out for more than work, groceries, or getting Adeline to school. Just like River's house had become nothing more than a shell when he left, I was hollowing out on the inside without him.

I stalked his Instagram like a mad woman, savoring the pictures he took of Legacy, of the views from his run, or the deck. Where he told me that he loved me.

As much as those pictures hurt, it was nothing compared to the pain that ripped me in two when his house here sold.

As I reached for a pre-work snack, I saw a pamphlet on the counter. "LaVerna Lodge. What's this?"

"That's an extended rehab center," Aunt Dawn said slowly. "I wanted to talk to you about it later. He's not getting any better with how we're doing things, and I thought maybe he needed a little more structure. A firmer hand."

He hadn't had another violent outburst, but he hadn't cleaned up the glass he'd broken, either. He'd been careful with his words, especially when Aunt Dawn was around. Maybe Addy was right and I wasn't what he needed to get healthy. "You think this is what he needs?"

She covered my hand with hers. "I do. I have the money, you don't have to worry about that. But I think you both need to go. Him to the recovery center and you to that man you love so desperately."

A lump formed in my throat. "That ship sailed."

"Chase it down," she said softly. "You have your whole life ahead of you. Let your dad get healthy. Right now he doesn't deserve you, and there comes a point where you need to recognize that he's not your responsibility, no matter how much you claim otherwise."

Never tell, Avery. You can never tell. Mom's words came back to me as I glanced at the pamphlet. "He'll never agree. His addiction...it was something he would never let on in the public."

"Now that, my dear, is a ship that's sailed. The ambulance and hospital stay outed him pretty damn loudly. I honestly don't know why you didn't come to me earlier."

"I...he..." I stuttered. "I did it for Mom, because I was scared that if I left, or I brought attention to it, the system would take Addy. She was so little, and I was still in high school."

"You're not anymore. You'd be more than fit as a guardian...if you wanted to be. I'm here. I'm not going anywhere, and if you want to go, I can take care of Adeline. Either way, we really need to get him into treatment."

I nodded. She was right about everything. The same fear that had me covering his ass all these years didn't come into play anymore. "Maybe I can talk to him about it." A quick glance at my phone told me I had thirty minutes before I needed to leave. "Let me get dressed for work, first."

Ten minutes later, I walked toward the living room but paused just outside the door when I heard Aunt Dawn talking with Adeline, and I shamelessly eavesdropped.

"They have a great pre-law program, and the campus is gorgeous," Addy said.

"I'm sure it is, baby. I'm so proud of you for thinking ahead. Have you looked anywhere local?" Aunt Dawn asked.

Dad struggled to sit up, and Aunt Dawn helped him, propping a pillow behind his back.

Addy licked her lips nervously, her eyes darting toward Dad before answering. "Not really. I think I belong there. Colorado just kind of calls to me."

I smiled at the wistfulness in her voice, the way her world seemed so open, everything possible. She had the determination to do it, too. Once Adeline put her mind to something, it was pretty much a done deal.

"What about Avery?" Dad asked, turning his eyes soft in a way I had only seen when he wanted something.

Chills raced down my spine.

"What about her?" Adeline asked carefully. "She loves Colorado."

"She does, but she won't leave here. This is her home—your home, too, but I understand you wanting to stretch your wings. Our little town isn't for everyone, is it?"

"No," she said quietly, looking at her hands.

"I guess..." He shook his head, and I leaned closer.

"What?" she asked in a small voice.

"I just guess I never saw you as being the kind of girl who would abandon her family."

Oh, hell no.

"Oh, that's not what she'd be doing—" Aunt Dawn argued, but the damage was done.

Addy's shoulders slumped. "I guess I'd never thought of it that way."

"I bet Avery has," he said, reaching for her hand. "I don't know how she'd get by without you."

Every time he'd used those exact words on me flooded my head, the memories bringing with them the kind of cold rage I hadn't felt since the night Mom died.

It wasn't about family for him. If it was, he'd be content that I was here to take care of him and he would have eventually let Adeline go. No, it was about control.

And I was taking it back.

I walked to the hall table and calmly took out Adeline's folded paper, then grabbed a pen and went back to the living room, Aunt Dawn following me with her head tilted.

"Avery?"

I ignored her and made a beeline straight for my father. "Addy, move," I instructed her.

She jumped, moving out of the way. I didn't look at her, instead I focused completely on the man who'd blamed me for his misery since I was fifteen.

"Sign it," I said, handing him the paper and pen.

"What?" he scoffed, opening the paper. "Like hell am I signing this."

"You'll sign it," I told him. "I'm taking Adeline to Colorado. She's going to have a life. She's going to finish out a real childhood and then be whatever the hell she wants when she grows up. She's not staying here under your thumb so you can guilt her into spending her life in this house. I refuse. Sign the goddamned paper."

"Have you lost your mind, girl?" he spat at me. "She's my child. You want to leave? Go. No one's stopping you. Good riddance. But she stays." He pointed the pen at Adeline.

I sat in the chair, leaning close to him so only he could hear me. "You sign that paper, or I will tell her why our mother is really dead." He tensed. "You were high while you were driving. You see, you can play off your addiction as the result of that crash and get all the sympathy, but I'm old enough to remember. We were at Grandma's because Mom needed to dry you out before your work buddies realized what you'd become. I know because I wasn't a kid when it happened, Dad. I heard her on the phone. I knew what drug paraphernalia looked like."

"You wouldn't," he whispered, his eyes wide with panic.

"I would. For Adeline, I would. You can blame us for being born all you want, but you were an addict way before that accident. And I know that the only reason you weren't put in jail was because you were on the force and your buddy figured losing Mom would change you. He didn't want to take you away from us."

"Avery…"

"I hated you, but I was also so grateful just to have you alive."

"Please don't…"

"But I don't feel that way anymore. I have no problem writing a huge article about it for the paper. Sure, maybe no one will believe me, but chances are they all will—including Adeline. Sign the paper, Dad. Free her. Get healthy. Then come find us, and we'll see if we can ever repair what you've systematically destroyed. Until then… Sign. The. Fucking. Paper."

A simple movement of his wrist, and Adeline was free.

And so was I.

Chapter Thirteen

River

My heart pounded as I finished my run. When the hell was I finally going to adjust to this altitude? I'd been running every day for the last five weeks and I still felt like I needed a lung transplant after four miles.

"It's embarrassing, Zeus," I said as we stretched out near the steps.

He looked up at me with an exasperated expression and laid down while I worked out my quads. I glanced over at the flower beds I'd put in last weekend and wondered what Avery would have planted.

Would she have wanted one around the mail box I'd just put in? Did it even fucking matter? I closed my eyes against the onslaught of pain I knew was coming. Every time I thought about her was followed by an exquisite ache somewhere in the vicinity of where my heart used to be.

I clicked my tongue and Zeus jumped up, following me into the house. All the furniture I didn't like had been taken away, but I was too damn lazy to pick out anything new. I'd donated damn near every piece that had come from Alaska. It just hadn't fit here. It was too much…Avery. I'd kept the bed, though. I couldn't bring myself to get rid of the one place I'd slept next to her, made love to her.

Maybe I should have told Bash that I wanted a different house, one she hadn't been in. He'd already been pissed at me for insisting on paying him for this one. Not that I cared. I wasn't going to live in a house that another man paid for—I didn't care if he called it a signing bonus or not. Maybe another house would have been better. One where I didn't see her smiling, crying out in pleasure, or picture her arching underneath me.

One where I didn't see her standing in my kitchen.

My heart stopped beating, my breath faltered, and the only muscle I moved were my eyelids, trying to blink away the vision of Avery standing at my stove, making breakfast.

Hell, I would have thought she was a mirage, if not for the smell of bacon and Zeus's excited yipping. Damn, that dog turned into a pitiful puppy when she was around…just like his owner.

"Hi," she said softly, the island between us.

"Hi."

She licked her lips nervously, her hair a wild tumble around her shoulders that I was desperate to slide my hands through. "So, I used my key."

"Finally. It only took me moving three thousand miles away to get you to do that." My feet were frozen. No matter how much I wanted to move, to get just the slightest bit closer to her, they wouldn't comply.

She forced a smile, and it was the most beautiful damn thing I'd seen since she'd smiled here six weeks ago. "I'm a little slow to act sometimes."

"Snails are faster," I agreed.

"I'm here," she said softly, her nervousness showing in the way she twisted the spatula in her hand.

"I've noticed," I said. Why? For the first time, I was scared to ask a damn question, scared that this was just a visit. Scared that all she wanted was my friendship when I loved her so much that I ached with it.

She swallowed, taking the rest of the bacon out of the pan and then moving it off the heat. "I thought maybe I was too late," she said, looking up at me as she came around the island in a pale blue sundress that matched her eyes to a T. "I wondered if you'd moved on. It's not like you're hard to look at," she muttered.

My forehead puckered, trying to figure out what the hell to say to her that wouldn't send her running back to Alaska.

"I had Harper drop me off. She has Adeline at the school right now, picking up enrollment papers."

My heart slammed to a beat again, life rushing through my veins. She was moving here. She'd brought Adeline.

She was staying.

"And when we pulled up, I was terrified that I'd find some other woman here, you know? Because I was so fucking stupid to let you go."

I stepped forward, and she put her hand out, taking a step back and shaking her head. "No. I told you once, I can't think when you touch me."

My feet stayed planted only with the utmost effort.

"But then I got out of the car and saw the flower beds," she whispered. Then she smiled so brightly that her entire face lit up. "And I saw the swing you put on the front porch, and I knew."

"Knew what?" I asked her, needing to hear the words.

"I knew that you hadn't moved on. That this was still our house, even if I'd pushed you away. I knew that you still loved me."

I almost laughed. Almost. "I've loved you for seven years. It would take a hell of a lot longer than a month to stop. It would take about seven eternities."

Her breasts rose and fell quickly as she struggled for control. "Thank God," she said as her voice broke. "Because I'm so in love with you that I don't know what I'd do if you ever stopped loving me."

Three steps and she was in my arms, my mouth fused to hers. The kiss was desperate, hungry, with an edge to it that I hadn't intended, but it was there all the same. I picked her up, and she wrapped those legs around me, her bare feet digging into my back as I carried her to the counter and set her ass on it.

"I missed you so fucking much," I told her in between kisses down her neck, the tops of breasts that peeked just above the fabric.

"River," she moaned, her hands tight in my hair, threading through where I had it pulled back. I'd never heard a more beautiful sound. "I can't think."

"Good," I told her, stroking my hand up her dress, caressing her thigh. "I let you think too much and look where that got us. From now on no head, just heart."

Her hand covered my heart. "What does yours tell you?"

I smiled, happiness bursting through me in ways I never thought would happen again. "That I'm going to love you until the day I die."

"Good," she said. "Now you'd better be quick. You've got maybe an hour before Addy is back."

"Welcome to life with a kid." I laughed, kissing her as my fingers slipped under her panties. "I haven't showered," I told her.

"I could not care less," she said, ripping my shirt over my head, then gasping as I parted her and ran my fingers from her slick entrance to her clit. "Just don't stop."

"There's no chance of that," I promised. "You're all I've thought about since I left Alaska." I stripped her panties off her and dropped my shorts to the ground, pulling her to the edge of the counter, my mind focused on getting inside her, fucking her until she couldn't ever think about walking away from me again, and then making love to her until she agreed to marry me. "Shit. Condoms are upstairs."

"I'm on birth control," she said, her voice breathless as she brought her mouth back to mine. "Now, River."

Raising her dress to her waist, I nudged her entrance with my dick and then thrust home.

Holy. Shit.

"I didn't imagine it," I said into her mouth between kisses. "We really are this good together."

She rocked her hips against me, her feet digging into my ass for leverage. I groaned and gave up trying to talk. I used my body to tell her everything I needed to say. Every thrust was my vow of love, every kiss my plea that she never leave me again.

Every gasp from her lips told me how much she'd missed me. Every rake of her nails told me she was as desperate for this as I was.

I grasped her hips and pulled her closer, changing our angle to hit her where I knew it would make her writhe.

"Yes, River. Yes." She chanted my name as I thumbed her clit, kissing her deeply, stroking her mouth with my tongue the same way I moved within her.

She was molten, pouring over me, setting me on fire as I thrust again and again, never giving her a chance to catch her breath.

She tightened around me, her cries growing louder, her breath catching and then holding as she came apart in my arms, arching against me. I was helpless against her, my orgasm ripping through me, shredding everything I was and rebuilding me as nothing more than Avery's man.

It was perfection.

She was perfection.

Our breathing was ragged as she stroked my hair, my lips pressed to her neck. "Wow," she said, reminding me of the first time she'd seen our house.

"Is that all you can say?" I asked her with a laugh.

"Do you have something better?" she asked with a grin as I pulled back to look in her eyes. She was so beautiful, her lips swollen from my kisses, her hair wild from my hands.

"I do."

She arched a delicate eyebrow at me.

"Welcome home, Avery."

Epilogue

Avery
Two years later

"Midnight. Do you understand me?" River's voice was low and menacing.

"Y-y-yes, sir," the boy said as he stood in our entry hall.

"I don't care if it's homecoming. I don't care if you think you're getting lucky tonight. You touch her in any way she doesn't expressly ask for and they will never find your body."

The kid paled, and I did my best not to sputter in laughter as I watched my husband from the stairs. "Yes, sir," he said a little stronger now.

"Do you have condoms?"

"W-what?" the kid asked.

"Do you?" River barked.

"No, sir?" The kid panicked, looking back and forth like there was someone who might save him.

"Is that because you don't believe in safe sex, or because you are well aware that you won't be getting anywhere near her tonight?" River snapped.

"I…uh…I do believe in safe sex, I just haven't had any yet," the kid squeaked.

"Yet?" River barked.

"I'm not planning on starting tonight, sir!"

"Good answer. Midnight, or I come looking for you. I grew up here. I know all the spots, and I know exactly where your parents live. Do you understand me?"

"I do, sir." The kid managed to stand upright, which I knew got him a little more respect in River's eyes.

"Okay. As long as we understand each other, Devin."

"We do," the kid said.

"Is he done scaring him yet?" Addy asked, coming down the stairs in a silver, knee-length homecoming dress that made my little sister look like an angel.

"I think so. Maybe you should save him," I suggested.

"Did you get enough pictures?"

I thought of the three dozen or so on my camera. "I think so. I sent a couple to Dad already, and he said you look gorgeous. Did you find your purse?"

"I did." She hugged me. "Thank you."

"I love you. Be safe. Call me if you need anything, do you understand?"

"I do," she said.

Then she walked over to her date, kissing River's cheek first. "I'll be home by midnight, I promise."

"Uh huh," he muttered. "You're more likely to break the curfew than he is."

"Yeah, yeah. Love you," she told him before they headed out to the dance.

I came up behind River as he watched from the front bay window. "He opened her door," he said with approval.

Once they were out of the driveway, he pulled me into his arms. "She's going to be the death of me. I swear."

"You're good at this dad thing," I told River, reveling in the feel of him. A year of marriage and I still hadn't tired of this. Longest honeymoon period ever.

"You think?"

"I do. And I'm glad."

"Oh, are you?" he asked.

"Yeah, considering you'll get to do it from the beginning in about seven months." My teeth dug into my lower lip as I watched his every reaction.

He blinked down at me. "For real?" he whispered.

"Confirmed with the doc this morning," I told him, tears prickling my eyes.

Sheer wonder filled his eyes. "A baby."

"Our baby," I confirmed.

He kissed me deep, his hand protectively covering my belly. "Amazing. Just…perfect."

I sighed, leaning into his kiss. This was the kind of happiness I'd never dreamed of having, and yet here it was in overflowing abundance, filling every nook and cranny of my heart until I thought I'd burst.

His eyes flickered to the window and back to me. "Oh, God. What if it's a girl?"

I laughed. "Would that be so bad?"

"I know you Claire girls. I'm going to need another gun."

"Yeah, well, I can't wait to see how much trouble a Maldonado girl will be."

He paled. "Maybe two guns."

He kissed me again, and I sank into him, losing myself in his love and the promise that forever gave us.

Moving here, choosing a life with River, it hadn't just set me free.

It had brought me home.

The End.

About Rebecca Yarros

Rebecca Yarros a hopeless romantic and a lover of all things coffee, chocolate, and Paleo. She is the author of the Flight & Glory series, which includes *Full Measures*, the award-winning *Eyes Turned Skyward*, *Beyond What is Given*, and *Hallowed Ground*. She loves military heroes, and has been blissfully married to hers for fourteen years.

When she's not writing, she's tying hockey skates for her four sons, sneaking in some guitar time, or watching brat-pack movies with her two daughters. She lives in Colorado with the hottest Apache pilot ever, their rambunctious gaggle of kids, an English bulldog who is more stubborn than sweet, and a tortoise named Phillip who is faster than you'd think. They recently adopted their youngest daughter from the foster system, and Rebecca is passionate about helping others do the same.

Want to know about Rebecca's next release? Join her mailing list: https://app.mailerlite.com/webforms/landing/g3b7h1

Or check her out online at www.rebeccayarros.com.

Also by Rebecca Yarros

The Flight & Glory Series
FULL MEASURES
EYES TURNED SKYWARD
BEYOND WHAT IS GIVEN
HALLOWED GROUND

The Legacy Series
POINT OF ORIGIN
IGNITE

Coming September 2016
The Renegade Series
WILDER

WILDER

The Renegade Series
By Rebecca Yarros
Coming 9/19/16

He's Paxton Wilder.

Twenty-two- year-old, tattooed, smoking-hot leader of the Renegades.

Five time X Game medalist.

The world is his playground—especially this year—and for the next nine months I'm stuck as his tutor on the Study at Sea program.

He's too busy staging worldwide stunts for his documentary to get to class.

But if I can't get him to take academics seriously, I'll lose my scholarship…if I don't lose my heart first.

Six unlikely friends on a nine-month cruise with the Study at Sea program will learn that chemistry is more than a subject and the best lessons aren't taught in the classroom…but in the heart.

Fated Identity
Red Starr, Book Six
By Kennedy Layne

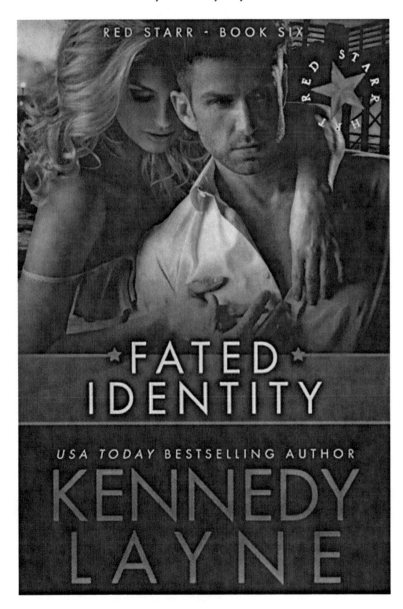

Dedication

Liz Berry and M.J. Rose—Thank you so very much for including me in such a talented group of women who make up the 1,001 Dark Nights Discovery Authors. I'm honored and appreciative of such a prestigious opportunity.

Jeffrey—Fate can be very fickle. I love that you are a part of mine and that I am a part of yours.

Chapter One

Grady Kenton stormed through the glass security doors of the CIA's Near Eastern and South Asian Analysis Desk in the Intelligence Division located in the maze of halls at Langley. He was looking for the one woman who could give him the answers he sought. He didn't care about the curious stares he was receiving as he made his way through the sea of cubicles facing the multitude of executive offices lining the outer wall. The analysts who worked here didn't get an office with a view—at least, not until they had been promoted to the level of their incompetence.

When Grady had a choice between the two separated hallways, he veered down the left corridor with a purpose. The office he was targeting was the last one on the left, offering a view out of the specially designed windows of multiple rows of pine trees. The vista was definitely a one-way experience, deliberately constructed to keep prying eyes from determining what was going on inside one of the world's most secretive buildings. It would also prevent anyone from seeing or hearing the upcoming argument that was about to ensue.

"Sir, you can't—"

Grady held up his agency identification badge dangling from his company lanyard without breaking stride, most of these employees knowing exactly who he was and the influence he had at the highest levels within the National Clandestine Services (NCS) Division at the

Agency. He'd worked hard in garnering the rank of Lieutenant Colonel from his career in the Marine Corps within the Intelligence field and he'd been recruited as a senior planning and operations advisor to the CIA after his retirement from the military.

He was good at his job and worked closely with those within his particular department. This young administrative assistant was notably not among them, but at least he had the wisdom to step aside while lifting his coffee mug out of the way of Grady's headlong path.

It didn't surprise Grady to find the dark wooden door to Brienne Chaylse's office currently closed. Their paths had crossed numerous times throughout his years in the military, especially during his lead role in dismantling the fledgling IRG leadership cabal formed shortly after the invasion during Operation Iraqi Freedom. He was always conscientious of their personal boundaries and it was rare he ever entered into the Intelligence Division's territory without at least a courtesy heads-up, but he was too irate to mind his manners or professional protocol at the moment. He glanced back at her assistant as the man buzzed him in and opened the door a little harder than necessary, but he might as well get his point across early on.

"When were you going to tell me, for Christ's sake?" Grady demanded, seeking Brienne out and finding her seated behind her cluttered desk as expected.

She'd been conducting a meeting with Bob Jensen, one of the other office POG analysts Grady didn't particularly like, when she broke off the conversation. The fact that she didn't seem too surprised to see Grady when he should be on a plane to Florida on a counterintelligence case told him all he needed to know about her motives. She'd gone behind his back with information related to an old friend's death and she hadn't had the decency to inform him.

Jensen immediately stood after clearing his throat, the slender man not needing an invitation to leave what he had to know would be a volatile discussion. He didn't lack common sense and ducked out of the office quickly, closing the door behind him as he muttered something about picking up the discussion at a later date. It would be a long wait if Grady had anything to say about it.

"I did everything exactly by the book, Grady," Brienne informed him in a rather confident tone, which only made him more intent on .

forcing her hand on this one. She was too self-assured in what she'd done to see the irreparable damage she had most likely caused to a very dear friend of his. "It's my case. I dotted every I and crossed every T before I made that phone call. It was the right thing to do, given the situation."

"For who?" Grady wanted to know, shaking his head at her naïve knowledge of the situation. It was times like these that highlighted their age difference and level of experience. His proficiency at the tradecraft required to operate in the field had taught him better than to react with emotion. "You? So you could claim you did your job well, according to procedure?"

Brienne leaned back in her chair with conviction brimming in her blue eyes over what Grady believed to be a terrible decision, looking every bit as poised as he knew her to be. Her long blonde hair had been pulled back into a bun, but in such a manner that a person could see the soft natural curls while she maintained her professionalism. Her features reminded him of the actress Gene Teirney, whose classic beauty reigned back in the mid-1940s. He had a penchant for the black and white films, and at the moment he would have given anything to go back to an era where things hadn't been so complicated. Brienne had made a terrible mistake and it wasn't something he could easily fix.

"Catori Starr is a good friend of mine…and that of the director's as well," Grady explained slowly, not telling Brienne anything she didn't already know. He purposefully closed the distance to the front of her desk, leaning down to rest his knuckles on the hard surface. He needed to get across to her the damage she'd done. "Starr's been through hell and back after losing her husband, and you calling to tell her about some outdated intelligence from an unknown source to give her an unrealistic hope he might still be alive wasn't your best work, Brienne. And I will have to justify your position while discussing this whole incident with the director, because what you did affects operations. Starr is the owner and operator of Red Starr HRT, and she has every right to know that the bodies of her original team were never recovered because there *is* no official record of their deaths according to the Pakistani government. You have no idea what you have set into motion. You should know better than most."

"Don't you dare go there, Colonel." Brienne abruptly stood, causing her black leather chair to roll into the windowsill behind her with a thud. Her white jacket was unbuttoned and revealed a red camisole he'd never seen her wear before. Another thing she never did was call him by his nickname used by those around the Agency, preferring to use his given name, but it proved he finally had her attention. Good, because her saying she'd just been doing her job didn't cut it when it came to the shakers and movers within their community. Her hands started waving in her usual manner as she tried to explain a decision he would never agree with, but he didn't think it was charming at the moment. "I'm not saying they are alive, but they were *not* killed the day they made their way into that Christian enclave to rescue those mission workers as we originally suspected. She deserves to know and more importantly, she has clearance from people farther up the ladder than I could ever hope to be. My hands were tied and I did what I had been directed to do. You don't get to pass judgment on me for doing my duty. Besides, the intelligence I received was good or else I would never have forwarded it on."

"Based on what? Who?" Grady shot back, demanding to know the identity of Brienne's source. He had a personal stake in this and had every right to know where she was getting her information. "Starr and her team are a primary operational independent contractor for the NCS. You may have just fucked that up. We're talking years old information and most likely from someone who's requesting a lighter sentence in exchange for a pack of fucking lies. Hell, you weren't even the chief liaison back then. And now you're allowing this bastard to give false hope to a woman who's already gone through the grieving process and picked up the pieces of her life and moved on. You never should have made that call without first talking to me."

"Why?" Brienne countered fiercely, leaning down and setting her manicured hands in front of his. Her red lips, perfectly outlined with her favorite lipstick, were inches from his and her warm breath caressed his clean-shaven chin. Grady should have been more prepared for where she was going to take this, but her brutally honest words were still like bullets striking his hardened flesh. "Because you never got over the death of your wife?"

Grady couldn't have heard her right, but damn if Brienne didn't appear a little shocked at her own words. He pushed off of her desk as slowly as he could, doing his best not to pick up the clear paperweight she'd had in the same place for the last four years and throw it through the exceptionally expensive electronic window behind her. He inhaled deeply to give himself balance and turned away from Brienne, not wanting her to see how her accusation stung. She knew based on personal facts better than most that he'd moved on with his life.

"If I recall correctly, it was *your* bed I left this morning." Grady was willing to fight fire with fire as he turned back around to witness Brienne's reaction. This was a battle she'd never win. "I'd say my grieving process has been quite comprehensive, wouldn't you?"

Grady hadn't meant for this conversation to come around to them, but Brienne had been the first one to throw down the gauntlet. Yes, his wife had died and left him a widower over five years ago now. Had he loved her? More than his own life, and he would have traded places with her in a split second if he'd known a suicide bomber was going to make his way into the makeshift hospital tent during one of Madison's mission trips with Doctors Without Borders. He'd grieved and he'd moved on...most recently with Brienne. They made excellent bed partners and both were happy with the way things developed, so he was confused as to why she would throw Madison's death into the conversation like she had. It was unfair and it was downright uncalled for.

"Touché," Brienne murmured with one brow arched higher than the other before she straightened from her desk and pulled her chair back in place. Grady would have sworn he saw a flicker of hurt flash in her baby blues, but her professional mask was back in place by the time she was seated. She gestured toward one of her guest chairs, but he walked to the corner window and stared out over the numerous rows of enveloping pine trees basking in the morning sun. He was still on edge and he needed time to collect himself. "Grady, this isn't about us. I had a job to do and I felt it in Starr's best interest she be furnished with all the available information on hand to do with as she wishes. It's pointless to even discuss this. Technically, the case has been reviewed by the after action board and closed. The original members of Red Starr HRT were officially declared dead for legal purposes a while back and we aren't pursuing this unless we are given a mandate or something more concrete is developed. It's over and done with."

"Which is precisely the reason you never should have communicated any further information to Starr. Did you know she and her team were the ones who rescued those Nigerian girls a couple of months ago? She received your message during that mission and it was a distraction we didn't need on our side of the house." Grady shook his head at this endless circle they were traveling in, deciding to appeal to Brienne's softer side. He knew it well and she wasn't the hardass her office personnel thought she was. "You know of my friendship with Red, as well as the fact that I keep in contact with Starr personally and not just professionally. I'm directly requesting you to keep me in the loop from here on out—before making any further calls. I'd rather she hear anything of importance from me than a—"

"Complete fucking stranger?" Brienne asked, not so subtly pointing out the barriers each had put into place back in the day. Grady shot her a cross glance, noticing she'd closed her eyes in irritation as if she were the one with the right to feel betrayed. The words she used in place of what he was going to say didn't sit well with him. "This is the way you wanted it, Grady. We lead separate lives, inside and outside of this office. My professional dealings don't always require your review."

Grady waited for Brienne to say more, but she fell quiet. It made him think she knew more than she was letting on. He could easily go over her head to obtain the means in which she'd acquired her intelligence, but he didn't want to have to do that. She'd been pulling away from him little by little this last year and he wasn't quite sure of the reason why. He'd actually put it on the back burner to deal with after his trip to Florida, which apparently wasn't going to happen now. He made a mental note to get in touch with the FBI Special Agent-In-Charge, because it was clear he was staying in Virginia to deal with personal matters.

"You want to know what I revealed to Starr? I was able to gather intel on the day Red and his team were supposed to meet with their contact at the rendezvous point near a village outside Islamabad. My source gave names, dates, and times corresponding with the hostage rescue mission Red Starr had been assigned to. Red and his team never arrived, Grady."

"We had solid intelligence Red and his team ran into a large group of well-armed insurgents," Grady countered, wanting the name of Brienne's source, but knowing she wouldn't give it. Pakistan was technically considered an ally, but those within the Agency knew better. Any intelligence given on behalf of America always made it back to the factions who were closely related to those same terrorists the United States was fighting against. It made it very hard to get things done. "I was at Starr's side when she received confirmation. Your guy doesn't have the slightest idea what he is talking about."

"My source is a woman and she's not wrong." Brienne picked up a pen from her desk and rolled it in between her fingers as she appeared to think over what she was going to say next. Grady leaned a shoulder against the windowpane, feeling the slight electronic vibration while studying her features and trying to get a fix on what was different today than any other for the past four years of their relationship. She was right, to an extent. They always tried to maintain their professional roles during work hours, but there was a chill in the air he didn't like. "Should anything else arise as a result of this source's information, I'll judge then if it's something you should know professionally."

Grady stiffened at Brienne's dismissal, not liking this side of her and not willing to let her put any more distance between them at the moment than he'd already allowed. He leisurely crossed her office floor and walked around her desk, leaning down until his hands rested on the arms of her chair. He always gave her his full attention and now was no different. He was at eye level and it took her a moment to meet his stare. It was then he realized she'd made another decision without consulting him…this time on a subject a little more personal, and he hadn't thought that was possible.

Brienne was leaving him.

Chapter Two

"This isn't the time nor place for this, Grady," Brienne said, her heart rate spiking at the way his dark eyes looked into her, past her carefully erected barriers. She'd thought she had the coming week to personally come to terms with her decision since he was supposed to be in Florida, but it looked as if she wasn't going to get her anticipated reprieve. "We'll talk about this later."

"We'll talk about this now. You want to tell me what is really going on?" Grady knelt in front of her so she couldn't avoid the question. He was searching for answers, but she was very good at camouflaging her thoughts and eliminating her tells. She refused to get into their personal lives while at the office. She'd certainly had years of practice and she could prove quite the adversary when the need arose. The thing of it was, he wasn't used to being in this position and it was clear he didn't appreciate the sliver of unease she'd dangled in front of him. She hadn't meant for the conversation to go this way. "You seemed fine when I left your apartment this morning."

"Things haven't been fine in quite a while," Brienne said softly, doing her best to cushion the blow while avoiding the bait. She realized she'd surprised him by kicking her black heel against the clear mat underneath them, but she wouldn't allow him to take control of this discussion like he had the tendency to do. She might like to give up some measure of control in the bedroom, but not when it came her professional life. She rolled her chair far enough away to regain the advantage of her personal space. She stood to her full height and tossed the pen onto her desk. The ball of anxiety she'd been living with started to unravel and she wasn't able to suppress the words that spilled over her lips. "You still love her with your whole heart. You still love Madison. I could accept that if there was some room in your life for me, but there isn't even an inch. I refuse to compete with a ghost from your past, so I've made some decisions for my own personal growth."

It was a rare occurrence where Grady was ever speechless, but Brienne had apparently managed to render him so now. She hadn't meant to hit him with something so far out of left field, but she was tired of fighting a losing battle. He unfolded his lean muscled frame and straightened his suit jacket, his sophisticated style being one tiny part of his overall charisma. She was younger than him by a good ten years, but never once had that made a difference in their relationship.

"My love for Madison has never been a problem before," Grady reminded Brienne somewhat cuttingly as he walked back around to the other side of her desk as he seemed to reinforce his offense. His previous anger came back twofold, but she stood her ground. She had too much to lose should she give an inch at this juncture. It was time she changed the rules of engagement, in and out of the bedroom. "She was my wife. For you to ask me to forget her—"

"I never said you should forget her or that you shouldn't have loved her," Brienne sharply clarified, not wanting to revisit this recycled conversation and find that he'd put words in her mouth. She stepped around the desk and held her head high for a battle she'd long been prepared to have. "I accepted long ago that I was nothing more than a filler for Madison's presence, and at the time I was more than okay with that, given both our needs. I'd just returned from a field assignment where I'd experienced things that still remain in my nightmares. You nevertheless manage to ease those terrors when they revisit me in the dark."

"Then why are we even having this conversation, Brienne?" Grady ran a hand through his dark hair that was peppered with silver, clearly not understanding where she was heading with this. Part of her felt guilty for having kept the truth from him, but her time was running out and she needed to make a decision. "We're both content with the way things are or were."

"That's just it. *You* are content." Brienne closed the distance between them until she was able to lightly rest her hands on the lapels of his jacket and stare up into the dark brown eyes she'd woken up to every morning for the past four years. They had both kept their separate residences, taking turns staying the night in each other's beds. It wasn't hard considering their travel schedule, but she was being offered something a little more permanent, which would essentially end whatever *this* was between them. "I need more, Grady. I've been trying to tell you that for a while now, albeit subtly. You've just turned a deaf ear to what I've been saying."

Grady gently placed his warm hands on either side of Brienne's neck and didn't stop the upward caress until he was cradling her face. The tender gesture was in total contradiction to the gathering storm settling over his features and her heart could almost feel the blow he was about to land.

"I've listened to every word you've ever said to me, sweetheart," Grady murmured, pulling her closer if that were even possible. She wished it were for something more intimate, but this was his way of making a point. "Never once have you said you wanted more than what we have had and I've reiterated multiple times that I could never bring myself to remarry after being widowed. You accepted that. So you tell me where my misunderstanding comes into play?"

"I guess it doesn't," Brienne whispered in regret, praying her heart didn't shatter into a million pieces while he looked on. She slowly inhaled, wishing now she hadn't as the sensual fragrance of his cologne enveloped her as if to remind her of what she would be missing so very soon. She gave herself a few more seconds before slowly pushing against him until his hands fell at his sides. She immediately missed his touch. She cleared her throat to say what she should have voiced long before now. "I've been offered a permanent position with the State Department Bureau of Diplomatic Security at our embassy in Cairo. You can understand how my current assignment uniquely qualifies me for the work that needs to be done there. I'll let them know my decision in the morning."

"Is there a reason you didn't share this with me when you were first given this new job proposal? It would seem that you've been keeping a lot of secrets from me lately." Grady's brown eyes became even darker if that were possible, with what emotion she couldn't say. It hadn't been Brienne's intention to hurt him, but neither one could continue with the way things were. "What exactly is it you want me to say to you? Of course I want you to stay here with me, but I wouldn't stand in your way if this could further your professional career."

Brienne would have laughed at the most appropriate of answers he'd just given her if she thought she wouldn't cry instead. Grady wanted her to stay, but yet he didn't want to hold back her career advancement of all things. He couldn't love her the way she needed to be loved, and therein lay the crux of the problem.

"I don't want you to say anything," Brienne said sadly, wishing she hadn't said anything and given them one more day. "My decision is made. I'm taking the position in Cairo. I'll be leaving at the end of the month."

"You don't need to throw away what we have." Grady wasn't a man to plead for anything, but Brienne could have sworn there was a hint of despair in his voice. "I want—"

"Brienne." Gus Wilson knocked impatiently on the office door after he'd opened it abruptly, not apologetic in the least for interrupting. The alarm written on his features conveyed the emergency. "We have a serious problem. There is chatter coming in over the wires and it's bad. I mean, really bad."

"What happened?" Brienne asked, reaching for her favorite coffee mug with the remnants of the cold liquid from the first pot still inside. She would take whatever reprieve Gus was offering her to get out of this office before she lost her thin veil of composure in front of Grady. She needed a better, solid emotional footing before she collected her things from his apartment. Her mind understood this was how things needed to be done, but her heart was obviously still protesting. "Are we talking about the mission in Kandahar or the one in Damascus?"

Brienne brushed past Grady, ignoring his penetrating gaze promising her this conversation was far from over. She was well aware of that, but this allowed her a brief reprieve, a moment to breathe and focus on something she had the ability to change. Critical missions, such as the ones in the Middle East or southern Asia, were vital in the success on this fight against terrorism. She had her professional priorities and right now...this took precedence. The ringing of Grady's cell phone aided her ability to follow Gus out of the office without having to say anything else.

"It's neither," Gus said rather distractedly, so unlike his usual demeanor. Her colleague was normally focused on the task at hand, and pulling his attention elsewhere was like pulling teeth out with nothing but her fingers. Right now, he appeared at a loss as he led the way down the hallway toward the Sensitive Compartmented Information Facility (SCIF). Every department within the Intelligence Division had their own satellite version of this secure area where sources and methods were stored, used, processed, or discussed. Had one of the embassies been attacked? "This is more of a personnel issue."

Gus walked at a faster pace, his erratic movements telling her more than his words. He was leading her to Supervisory Special Agent James Telfer's office located just outside the SCIF. The door was open and she could see the small gathering of other agents. Brienne crushed the anxiety that tried to surge through her body, but it didn't prevent a fine sheen of perspiration to coat her skin. She was now wishing she'd left her coffee cup back on her desk.

"Agent Chaylse, we have a problem," SSA Telfer explained without even glancing her way. He was in the middle of looking at his phone, but it was a blow to her chest when he finally did look her way. Jim Telfer was worried; therefore, she should be scared as hell. She tightened her fingers around her cold mug and braced herself. "Your personal identity as an agent for the Central Intelligence Agency has been compromised."

No one else in the office said a word. As a matter of fact, only the muffled sounds from the bullpen could be heard through the door Gus had closed behind them. The other three agents—Samuel Frye, Connor Vaupel, and Chloe Hammond—all appeared stunned as they were apparently hearing this for the first time as well. It didn't make Brienne feel any better to realize she wasn't the last to know.

She took a moment to step forward and set her cup gently down on SSA Telfer's desk, careful not to spill what little was left of the contents. She took notice of how organized the surface was maintained. Her life had been very much like that until this very moment.

The pencil holder must have been made by one of Telfer's children, but it only held sharpened pencils and pens with black ink. The inbox had a few folders meticulously centered in the middle of the wooden container, while the outbox contained more files just as well-ordered. The mouse for his computer was centered on its pad parallel to his keyboard and his desk phone was within perfect distance of his reach at a forty-five degree angle.

What would it look like if she were to take an arm and swipe it across this immaculate surface?

Chaos.

Wreckage.

Her life—as it stood at this very moment.

"In what manner?" Brienne asked, grateful she was able to get the words out without hesitation. Depending on the leak, everything she'd worked for could be gone...depleted. "Is it something that can be mitigated?"

"There was an article published in the *Daily Express Urdu* newspaper today stating your name as the lead CIA liaison to the Pakistani government for the Near Eastern and South Asian Analysis Desk here at Langley," SSA Telfer stated bluntly, cutting to the chase and giving Brienne what she needed to know. Her career as a covert agent for the CIA was officially over. "We're doing what we can to locate the source of the leak, but you'll be placed on administrative leave as the board reviews the damage this has caused to your current caseload, as well as to the other agents involved on your desk. You know the process and we'll..."

Administrative leave. Brienne suppressed the manic laugh that built within her as SSA Telfer continued to outline her immediate future. Her employment—the very thing she'd invested her life in— within any branch of the United States government was now tainted. She was going to be terminated because of a simple article written in a Pakistan newspaper and there wasn't a thing she could do to change that. She would deal with the emotional fallout in private. Right now, there were things that needed to be addressed and she would handle it like the definitive professional she was.

"I will turn over all of my files for..."

Three hours. That was how long it took Brienne to delegate her current caseload and her life's work over to her desk's executive replacement within her section's hierarchy. She hadn't allowed herself to comprehend the raw emotion burning inside of her or to acknowledge the compassion her associates were trying to convey. She would have completely come undone had she permitted anything other than maintaining a distant demeanor.

It was only when she was by herself that she leaned against her office door for support and laid a hand over her chest to prevent the physical pain from becoming overbearing. All she needed now was the courage to walk out of the Company with her head held high.

"Are you ready to leave?" Grady asked from his position by the window, only turning toward her after he'd spoken. It surprised her to find determination within his dark eyes instead of sympathy. His appearance was as immaculate now as it had been this morning and his composure was something to envy. It wasn't until he continued his train of thought that she understood the reason why. "We need to get in touch with Catori Starr. She has the contacts we need to take care of your problem."

Chapter Three

The long, flat ride through downtown Washington D.C. was made in silence. Traffic was at the usual near stall rate, held up by the ever-present red stoplights and eternal flow of jaywalkers. The annoying sounds of car horns and shrilling brakes being applied too quickly were muffled by the premium ride package of his Mercedes-Maybach S600. The smell of vehicle exhaust was minimized by the cabin fragrance system injected through the vents as other vehicles crowded around, trying to cut in front of one another, jousting for position. These city people were like well-oiled machines as they gathered at the intersections waiting for the crosswalk lights to turn, allowing them to move in a somewhat staggered line.

City life. It wasn't for everyone.

It could raise anyone's blood pressure.

Grady gripped the Napa leather-wrapped steering wheel harder than necessary. It was better than the alternative. He wanted nothing more than to reach over the center console and hold Brienne's hand to let her know everything was going to be all right.

It wasn't.

At least, her professional life wouldn't be anything like it had been before. As for her personal life…well, she'd stated she wanted that to change as well. It wasn't fair to bring up their relationship given the extraordinary events that had transpired since her personal revelation. His brooding platitudes regarding her current situation weren't going to be welcome.

"What exactly do you think Starr can do to rectify my situation, Grady?" Brienne asked, her steady voice cutting through the relative silence of the car.

Grady admired Brienne's ability to keep her composure under the mounting stress, but then again, she'd been trained by the Farm. Grady applied the brakes and came to a standstill behind the navy blue Honda Accord he'd allowed into the flow of traffic a block back. He took advantage of the stop to look Brienne's way. She was holding herself together, considering the initial shock of her public outing as an agent was wearing off.

"It's over," Brienne said somewhat dejectedly. "My name is out there and now all of my cases are compromised, as well as possibly other assets who I work with. The only thing that matters at this point is finding out who leaked the information to the newspaper, how they uncovered my personal data to begin with, who else is next based on my association with them, and then try to prevent any further damage from happening. SSA Telfer has the Director's assurance that the Technical Collections boys from the Science and Technology Division is all over this. There's nothing Starr can do that our resources can't accomplish on their own."

"You would be surprised at what Starr can achieve," Grady informed her, catching sight of a grey Ford Focus pulling alongside of them a little too close for comfort. The man driving was singing along to his radio and clueless as to what was going on around him. "She has the seemingly magical ability to get things done in a timely manner without causing even a ripple in the water. You and I both know the CIA and the FBI have a tendency to overshoot these things and make the situation worse."

Grady admired Brienne's sense of right and wrong. She saw things black and white in a grey world, which was how she conducted her business. She fit right into the Agency's mold and was able to make calculated decisions based on the collection of solid, supporting facts.

It did run through Grady's mind that Brienne was handling their relationship in the same lock-step manner, but again, this wasn't the time or place to get into that. She was a true professional and this violation of her covert status was ultimately a tragedy for the Agency and a setback in the region her desk managed. Would he be able to convince her to make a mutually beneficial deal with Starr in an attempt to salvage her career?

"Grady, do you happen to have a backup piece on you?"

Brienne's question was said with the calm of a seasoned field agent. No one else would have caught the concern lacing her soft-spoken words. It helped that Grady had already caught sight of the male figure beside them drawing his weapon a little higher than he'd realized, giving away the reason he'd furtively pulled so close to Grady's vehicle. He'd essentially blocked Brienne inside the car. She wouldn't have known that from the direction she was looking, though, meaning an additional threat was present and within her line of sight.

"Glove box. It's condition one."

Grady hadn't finished saying his last word before Brienne had efficiently opened the compartment in front of her in one fluid movement. The weapon was smaller than his preferred Kimber 1911 TLE, as was par for the course when it came to a spare weapon. She would have known he'd kept a round in the chamber without his statement to that effect, which was why she didn't hesitate to bring the Berretta PX4 Storm in .40 S&W up with a purpose. He'd already done the same and the discharge of both firearms inside such an insulated luxury sedan instantly compromised their hearing. Only time would tell just how much damage had been done on a permanent basis.

That didn't stop Grady from reaching for his door handle, ignoring the shards of glass that had shattered everywhere upon the bullet's impact with the vehicle's safety glass. He rammed his shoulder into the door, confident Brienne had neutralized her target or she would have followed up with continued fire. She was an accurate shot, on and off the range.

The ringing in his ears overtook the city noise, as well as the construction zone up ahead. It was apparent from the way people were ducking down in their cars and running in a staggered fashion away from the scene that they were terrified about what had unfolded, especially with two men dead. He took hold of Brienne's hand as she maneuvered herself across the driver's seat over fragmented glass. He didn't let go until they started to jog down the street against traffic.

There wasn't a chance in hell they were going to wait around to see if more men showed up to try and finish the job. Brienne wouldn't be able to hear what Grady said, so he motioned for them to head for Union Station. It would provide an opportunity to get lost in the general public, as well as give them the time needed to analyze the situation.

Grady could see from people's expressions and the way they were craning their necks that the police were arriving on the scene. It wouldn't be long before someone pointed in the direction they had taken, but they'd already made a right at the next block and were putting lateral distance between them and the carnage left behind. He needed to speak with either SSA Telfer or someone higher up the chain immediately. Brienne was being targeted, which meant that article in a Pakistani newspaper had a far wider reach than any of them had initially anticipated.

Brienne slowed down and took the time to hide the weapon she'd taken from his glove compartment underneath her jacket. She placed her fingertips against her ears with a wince and rubbed the areas as she examined their surroundings. He moved his jaw from side to side as well, trying to subdue the ringing. He took her cue to holster his weapon, albeit reluctantly. The less attention they brought to themselves, the better at this point. They were about a block away from Union Station, but it was enough of a distance to allow them to reevaluate.

"I think we need to catch a cab," Brienne shouted, her words getting caught up in the incessant buzzing. It was apparent she was talking too loud and he signaled she needed to lower her voice. A few curious stares were shot their way. "Staying visible out on the streets will only put us and other innocent pedestrians in the line of fire."

"We need to get you underground." Grady noticed that Brienne's attention was on his lips since her hearing had yet to fully return. He repeated his statement and waited for her to nod her understanding. "Stay close."

Brienne's quick nod of acquiesce had Grady changing direction. The adrenaline produced by what had just happened was starting to wear off. Damn, that was a close call. Had Brienne been by herself during that ambush, she never would have had time to stop both converging tangos coming at her from opposite directions. He couldn't even fathom that scenario. *Why* was she being specifically targeted and not any other agents within the section?

The temperature was above normal for this time of year and the sun was beating down on the asphalt, producing an uncomfortable heat. The normally delicious aroma drifting from the hot dog stand did nothing but generate nausea. Once they were able to blend in with the crowd, people weren't watching where they were headed and Grady didn't have a spare minute for pleasantries. He was determined to get Brienne to safety and he didn't stop until they were at the Georgetown Law School off of New Jersey Avenue.

Grady didn't waste time heading directly for McDonough Hall, where the office of the Dean of Students was located. There were advantages to still being in the field, one of them being established contacts who were dependable.

David Pierce was the current Dean of Students, as well as a source for the FBI and CIA to tap into regarding foreign students coming into the university with less than stellar goals of education. The student visa ruse was usually quickly spotted and many a terrorist plot had been diverted using this method of detection. Dave was currently with another staff member, but quickly dismissed the younger man once Grady and Brienne appeared outside his door.

Dave's office was small, but the furniture was an immaculate red oak with ornate handles and matching bookcases off to the side. Literature and history books adorned the shelves, but it was the miniature metal models of World War II planes and tanks that gave the room a unique look. His office furnished the impression that the professor was a historian managing his own tiny museum.

"You're bleeding." Dave was already standing when he took some tissues from a box he kept on his desk, handing them over with a look of concern. Grady had dismissed the small cuts as insignificant seeing as it wasn't Brienne who'd been hurt. He could take care of himself at a later time, but he would clean up the best he could seeing as it was distracting Dave. "Grady, what happened? Do I need to alert security?"

"No," Grady replied, pressing the thin white material against the small cuts on his hand. The blood quickly soaked in, but the majority of the wounds were superficial. Only one was still bleeding. "I need your vehicle. I can't explain right now, but we're in a bit of a bind."

"Of course," Dave replied, his gaze drifting to where Brienne was looking at her cell phone. Grady had thought she'd left it in her purse back in the car, but she'd apparently had it on her person. She was holding it up before he could give her a dressing-down on security protocol. She'd already turned the device off, as he had done with his own back when they'd stopped running. "I'm parked..."

Dave continued to give instructions on how to reach his vehicle, leaving Grady to scrutinize Brienne. She was standing to the left of the door with her right arm straight at her side, giving her the opportunity to draw the weapon from underneath her white jacket with little effort should the need arise.

Brienne appeared calm and collected, her breathing even. There wasn't even a tremor in her hands, though there were a few smears of blood on her sleeve from when Grady had pulled her from the car. The pallor of her face had whitened and caused the red lipstick on her lips to become even brighter. He would have given anything to be able to pull her into his arms and tell her everything would be okay, but he made an effort to never lie unless it was a life and death situation.

"I appreciate this, Dave." Grady tossed the used tissues into the trashcan, taking time to pull the desk phone toward him. It was the standard black and silver model installed in most offices. He'd be able to place a call without turning on his own cellular device. "Would you give us a moment alone? We won't be long."

One of Dave's best qualities was that he never asked questions, though he was always willing to provide answers and toe the line. He vacated the office without a second glance. Grady had already dialed the number of SSA Telfer and pressed the speaker button before the door had completely shut.

Brienne hesitated and shot a sideways look at the doorknob. She most likely wanted to lock it, but Grady wasn't concerned with anyone walking in unannounced. Dave wouldn't have gone far and would be monitoring the traffic in and out of the department.

"Telfer."

"We ran into a problem en route to our meeting," Grady informed Brienne's SSA, keeping an eye on Brienne to see if she wanted to add anything to the conversation. She stepped forward, about to speak when Telfer cut in with a directive no agent wanted to hear.

"Agent Chaylse is in the crosshairs of ISI. Bring her in now."

The line disconnected, leaving Grady and Brienne to deal with the aftermath of such a decree. He didn't hesitate to reach for her, bringing her into his embrace and wishing it were that easy to shield her from what was to come. The ISI was Pakistan's premier military-operated intelligence service. These weren't amateurs who were after Brienne and they had to have had help from inside the Agency to pull off what had almost transpired today.

"We're going out on our own," Grady murmured, pressing his lips softly against her temple. Brienne nodded slightly in agreement, because even she knew there was only one logical choice to make given their circumstances. "There isn't a chance in hell you're going back to Langley to ride this out."

Chapter Four

Brienne removed her soiled white blazer and tossed it on the couch before sitting on the edge of the middle cushion. The décor of the beach house located on the Jersey shore was modern, but she was too exhausted to care if she scuffed the cream twill fabric with her dirt-stained pants. This morning's events had certainly put things into perspective. She rested her forehead onto the palms of her hands, wondering how her day had spiraled so out of control.

It had taken Grady and Brienne around six hours to reach their destination, but two of those had been used to switch vehicles at no less than three different locations. She'd only ever worked with Grady on overseas missions, so seeing his impressive reach with little to no notice here in their homeland was quite a sight.

It was no wonder the Agency, along with the FBI and other notorious government organizations, hadn't wanted him to retire. She would have taken the time to state how impressed she was had she not been so damned busy trying to figure out who was responsible for leaking her identity and doing their best to eliminate her.

"Why don't you go and take a shower?" Grady said, finally stepping away from the front door where he'd been resetting the security alarm code. The beach home they were currently using did not have a garage, so they'd left the last car Grady had borrowed near the boardwalk with hordes of other tourist vehicles. They eventually made their way to the beach and walked the winding sand trail as if they were nothing more than the typical vacationers. Her high heels had been dropped on the tile he was now vacating as he made his way to the kitchen. "I have a few calls to make."

"Don't you mean *we* have a few calls to make?" Brienne restated his declaration, finally having enough of the brushoff. She stood, in spite of the fact that her body protested, and made her way into the pristine cream shoreline kitchen with light gray granite countertops. Everything else in here was cream as well, if she discounted the bowl of green apples sitting on the stone-topped island. The owners could have done a lot more if the adornment was to add color. The somewhat sterile design matched her mood though. "I'm more than capable of conducting this investigation as if it were any other assignment. You need to trust me, Grady."

Brienne couldn't stand the clip in her hair any longer, especially considering the taut prongs were only adding to her pounding headache. Someone wanted her dead and it was all related to Brendan "Red" O'Neill. She had no other connection to Pakistan or to the ISI. She finally released the clip, running a hand through her hair and closing her eyes in relief as some of the built-up tension faded away as her hair fell.

"I never said you weren't capable, Brie. And you know for a fact that I trust you with my life."

Grady's affectionate nickname for her was unexpected. Brienne stilled her movements as their gazes connected across the small island and the little appalling bowl of green apples. His dark eyes were narrowed, as if daring her to dispute his statement. His normally immaculate suit jacket was wrinkled from the long ride and his tie was slightly askew. He'd been by her side this entire time, doing everything needed to ensure her safety. She had no doubt that he cared for her, but his love for Madison was holding him back from living his life with someone else.

"I know," Brienne admitted softly, conceding a bit and accepting the fact that she was relatively safe here. She'd always been independent, but she'd have to continue to stand on her own two feet now that she'd made the decision to be reassigned away from D.C. and the memories she and Grady had made together. Only she didn't have that escape route anymore. "I'm not a victim, Grady. I refuse to be a victim for anyone."

"But you *are* a target," Grady reminded her, taking the time to remove his suit jacket, fold the sleeves just so, and lay it across the counter. She couldn't help but look at the wounds on his left hand, wondering if there were any shards of glass still embedded into his skin. She was surprised when he came around the island and tenderly slipped his fingers in her hair until his thumbs were underneath her chin. "Your safety is my primary concern. You. This is my specialty, Brie. I don't mean to take over and exclude you from any decisions, but—"

"It comes naturally," Brienne finished in a whisper, giving in to what she needed. The warm comfort of his touch was everything she required to breathe easy and release the built-up tension running through her. "I'm so scared, Grady. The ISI? What the hell did I get caught up in that would cause this kind of reaction?"

"Your source apparently had some very accurate and meaningful information, making the ISI a little too uncomfortable with what she revealed. The first thing we need to do is confirm she is still alive. There are too many balls in the air right now and some are going to crack when they hit the ground." Grady smiled tenderly, the way he usually did when he told her he was leaving town on assignment. He didn't say that this time, but instead leaned forward and softly brushed his lips against hers. "Go and use the SAT phone I gave you to make contact. I'll follow up with Telfer, since he's going to be rather displeased at the fact we didn't follow direct—and might I add lawful—orders. We'll then clean up and decide afterward what our next move will be."

Brienne breathed deeply to capture the subtle masculine fragrance of Grady's cologne. He'd worn the same brand since she'd known him...he was a creature of habit. She didn't appreciate the emotional wavering she was experiencing at having made the decision to end their relationship. It was the right thing to do and yet the regret for what could have been was beyond anything she'd ever experienced. Her throat constricted when his fingers gradually drifted away from her. It was as if their ship had sailed into the mist and the gathering darkness was what was left of their relationship.

Grady moved silently across the tiled floor and into what Brienne assumed was the bedroom. The width of his back told her more than the size of his lean upper body, but of the baggage he carried from his past. Could he not see that she was more than willing to carry some of the weight?

Brienne hadn't expected Grady to stop before crossing the threshold into the next room, but he paused and turned only enough so that he could see her expression at what he had to convey. She now wished more than anything that he hadn't.

"You deserve more than what I've been giving you. On that we can both agree."

Grady lifted one corner of his mouth as if to convey his understanding, but did he? Brienne couldn't draw air until he finally turned on the heel of his dress shoe and quietly closed the door behind him. She continued to stare at the barrier, knowing there was much more than a wooden portal between them. Madison's essence lingered like another woman's perfume, but it wasn't Grady's wife who was the issue…it was his inability to let her go from his everyday existence.

Brienne wiped away a tear that had escaped and then did her best to compose herself. She'd always had the ability to mentally compartmentalize her life and she did so now out of necessity. She'd like to be alive come tomorrow morning to be able to face the same obstacles she was now. She wasn't sure that didn't make her an emotional masochist, but that was the only way she could view things at the moment.

"Get yourself together," Brienne whispered to ground herself, sometimes wishing Grady wasn't ten years her senior. Their age difference had never really played a part in their relationship, but his life experience far surpassed hers and she'd come to realize maybe that was part of the problem. He'd already experienced his proverbial love while she'd found hers too late. "Focus, Brienne. Stay alive to deal with this tomorrow."

Survival had become day-to-day at this point. Brienne understood how this situation worked, seeing as she'd been a liaison to several missions with the same types of dangers they faced now. She identified what needed to be done and walked across the cold floor to where she'd set the SAT phone on top of her jacket. Grady had taken possession of them from the last person they'd had contact with, along with a go-bag filled with a change of clothing for each of them, weapons, plenty of ammunition, and a few additional items that might come in handy.

Brienne took a minute to rehearse what she would say over the line, hoping her contact comprehended the severity of what had taken place. She dialed the number that would connect her to another time zone in another country, another source, and the woman who might very well have information that could keep them both alive. It took over a minute for the connection to finally establish a link.

"Raheela," Brienne started out, ensuring the tone in her voice conveyed conviction as she continued to nurture the personal connection she'd established with the Pakistani woman long ago, "there's been a slight problem. Have you spoken with anyone else besides me in the last few months?"

Brienne listened carefully to Raheela, her broken English not too hard to understand if the time was taken to string the words together. It had taken a couple of years to form this give-and-take relationship. Raheela had become a very reliable source for the CIA, handing over information in exchange for cash payments in rupees. Whatever the woman was doing with the currency was of unimportance. That didn't mean the CIA wasn't aware of Raheela using the payments as a means to conceal the movements of women wanting to escape the tyranny of their families or their husbands.

"…you are in danger. The man was asking…"

Raheela's broken words finally strung together at the end, giving off a dire warning that came a little too late. Brienne had learned a lot from this brief exchange, but not the name of the insider who'd leaked her identity. The more she thought about it, the more she realized there hadn't been a cyber attack on the Agency's network to uncover her identity. Someone had personally given up her name and it was only a matter of time before her source was eliminated as part of a mass campaign to eradicate her influence in the AOR.

"Raheela, I want you to cease contact with everyone," Brienne stressed her order, ignoring the sound of Grady reentering the room. "You won't hear from us again until it's safe."

"What the hell do you think you're doing?" Grady asked in a somewhat harsh tone, conveying his displeasure at the way she was managing the conversation.

Brienne turned her back to Grady to finish what she'd started. Another group of agents was already well-positioned within Pakistan and was currently using Raheela, along with several others, as their information source. Brienne didn't have the authority to terminate such a viable informant, but she would deal with the fallout at a later time. Raheela's life was in jeopardy and it was still Brienne's duty to ensure this woman's safety.

"I'm not sure who to trust on my side, Raheela, so you'll have to do this on your own," Brienne revealed, knowing that warning alone would be enough to make Raheela cautious. "I'd suggest implementing precisely what you've been setting up for other women. Good luck."

The line disconnected and Brienne didn't have to wait long for the censure.

"You don't have the authority to—"

"I have every right to warn my source that she has a chance of being compromised in the same manner I was," Brienne stated, spinning on her bare feet to face Grady and wanting answers. "What was Telfer's explanation to our assertion that ISI was involved with this morning's events?"

"Telfer wants you in protective custody, as well as a rundown on all your most recent dealings in Pakistan." Grady wasn't one to show his frustration, but he ran his fingers through his military cut and then rested his palm on the back of his head. The peppered grey on his sideburns only made him appear more distinguished, but that didn't mean she wasn't of some influence as well. "He's under the assumption—"

"That I somehow foolishly let my source know my real identity," Brienne finished, already seeing how this was going to play out. Only no one was aware that she was holding an ace. "I'm good at my job, Grady. Telfer knows better than that. Just as he knows there wasn't a cyber attack on a secure network. As a matter of fact, my source had nothing to do with the leak, of that I'm certain. We were right all along with thinking there was a turncoat within the Agency, especially since those operatives had my exact location…which was with you."

"I've already reached out to some people who can help with that, but it still doesn't explain why ISI—"

"My source *is* the wife of an ISI Major. It's the perfect framework to ensure my termination. I basically handed them both me and my contact over on a silver platter with all of the trimmings." Brienne tossed her SAT phone back on the couch, wishing she could collapse into the cushion and hide away from the world in the same manner. She couldn't and now Grady's life was on the line as well. "You see, I'm the only one who is still actively engaged in trying to locate the remains of the former Red Starr HRT unit, which means someone within my own department is actively trying to prevent me from discovering exactly what happened to Brendan O'Neill on that ill-fated mission. Red must have discovered our turncoat and was eliminated to secure their identity."

Chapter Five

Grady had already walked the property's perimeter, surveying the area for likely avenues of approach for threats along with making liaison with the special security firm he'd called in for extra protection. There was no immediate danger and he hadn't spotted any overtly obvious team members who should have moved into the area a few hours ago, but then again he hadn't expected to see any amateur bullshit.

Gavin Crest ran a tight unit over at Crest Security Agency, hiring only the best of the best from former military operators to men and women who had sharpened their skills in other paramilitary black ops teams serving the intelligence agencies. His old friend would see to it that Grady and Brienne could actually sleep tonight without fear of waking up with a gun in their face.

"I don't like delaying the inevitable," Brienne said tersely, taking the spatula and turning over the omelets in the large frying pan. She had already showered and changed into the pair of jeans and white T-shirt that had been in the bag Connor Ortega had given Grady. He'd been the first of CSA's agents to land on the ground, supplying Grady with what he would need over the course of the next few days. "We know it's someone on the inside. We should head back to D.C. and—"

"We're not going anywhere while your name is on the ISI's hit list. Apparently, they have moved a group of their own operators into Washington to finish the job." Grady understood the need to feel like he was contributing, but he'd learned a long time ago that some things were better handled when delegated to those who were more practiced at that particular skillset. Brienne needed to step back while those with that demonstrated capability got the job done. "We're staying put until we have enough information to confirm the identity of the leak, as well as possibly fix your long-term predicament."

Grady didn't blink when Brienne shot him a disbelieving look at the last part of his declaration. She reached across the stove and turned the dial with a little more force than necessary. She was sure there was some way to find a resolution to her career-ending problem. Her future ability to work at the Company after a fuckup of this magnitude was going to be difficult to overcome, but she didn't like going outside of her comfort zone by allowing someone else to do her own work.

Grady reached into the cupboard for what he was searching for, noticing Brienne's hair was still slightly damp from her shower. Her blonde hair had always curled into loose waves if she didn't immediately blow the strands dry. He personally liked it this way, loving the natural beauty as well as the silky texture when he ran his fingers through the tresses. She wouldn't appreciate the gesture now, so he refrained from reaching out to her.

"What if we—"

"Arguing won't change the fact that we have a few days to ourselves. Besides, we have things to discuss that affect our future." Grady finally set two glasses of ice on the small table overlooking the ocean. They'd closed the colorless blinds, but they could still hear the distant thunder of the waves crashing against the sandbar to only then dissolve as the tide pulled the water back into its endless void. His soul could relate to the infinite abyss, but maybe it was time to replenish it. "Unless, of course, it's too late."

Grady continued setting the table, not willing to let this slide when they didn't know what tomorrow would bring. The light noises Brienne had been making in the kitchen had gone relatively silent, but she'd yet to confirm his last statement. At least she'd acted as if she was willing to work with him.

"Let's eat before—"

"We lose our appetite?" Brienne said wryly, slipping one of the omelets onto the plate Grady had set down on his side before she did the same to hers. This place wasn't the most well-stocked safe house, but the kitchen had enough ingredients to keep them from starving. "That's already been accomplished."

"Eat anyway," Grady instructed firmly, taking the frying pan and spatula from her hands. He motioned for her to take a seat while he placed the items in the sink and retrieved the pitcher of sweet tea from the refrigerator. He then joined her at the table, filling both of their glasses. "The first rule in a situation like this is to eat when you can and sleep if time allows. Walk me through the scenario of what you think happened."

Brienne's shoulders gave way a bit, telling him that she thought he'd want to talk about them over their meal. He did, but it wasn't the type of conversation one could have while eating. They had too much at stake to discuss it as if they were talking about the weather and he would wait until they were more comfortable, thus giving her more time to acclimate to the fact that they needed to discuss Madison. He wasn't sure he was ready. She was a part of him that was no longer here. That part of him was gone forever. That was a very hard concept to put into words.

"The Pakistani source I acquired was when I was a subordinate. The chief liaison officer was training me in the art of pulling together informants in specific demographics the Agency had been targeting. I managed to excel in that area and we were able to gather rather detailed information regarding the ISI from an insider." Brienne picked up her fork, but had yet to take a bite of the omelet she'd made. Grady looked pointedly at her food, not wanting her to get so caught up in her theories that she didn't eat. They paused long enough to make a dent in their meal before she continued, finally making the connections he'd only speculated on. "I had given this woman's contact information to the chief of mission. I haven't been inside Pakistan in a couple of years, my current assignments being elsewhere in the latest Iraq and Afghanistan wars. It was only recently that my informant reached out to me through one of the cultural attaché connections at the embassy. We were reconnected and then told about the possibility of locating the remains of the former Red Starr HRT's unit."

"Who was privy to your most recent conversation?" Grady asked, taking a sip of the sweet tea. He studied Brienne over the rim of his glass, her blue eyes darkening in determination to discover who had betrayed her so recklessly. Who was willing to throw his or her life down the drain by committing treason by betraying a fellow American Intelligence Agent? "Telfer, obviously. Anyone else?"

Grady didn't want to believe that an SSA of Telfer's standing would ever divulge the identities of his subordinate agents beneath him, but there had been far more devastating treason than that within the Agency over the years. There would have to be a money trail, which was why Grady had brought in CSA. Gavin Crest had just as many avenues to pursue those leads, but without the hindrance of being hunted.

"Samuel Frye, Connor Vaupel, and Chloe Hammond are the agents I worked most closely with, along with Gus Wilson and Bob Jensen. Pretty much the entire desk, along with the supporting analysis staff," Brienne disclosed with a frown, lowering her fork after eating only half of what had been on her plate. She pushed it away, sitting back after she'd picked up her glass of iced tea. "I need access to the SCIF. There has to be a data trail to follow. We should head back to D.C. and—"

"I already told you that was out of the question." Grady finished his meal, unable to give Brienne what she wanted. "The ISI will be watching every single location you might decide to show your face, and that includes all the roads leading into Langley. You're not going anywhere near D.C. until we can confirm the leak's identity and how to go about minimizing the damage. Your name is out there on the wind. Nothing can change that, but we can target the ISI in ways to shut down their team and prevent another physical attack."

"Which coincides with Red Starr and Starr's inquiry," Brienne surmised, looking off into space as she continued to process the reasoning behind such an assault. "Why is it that the ISI doesn't want us to have knowledge of the location of Brendan O'Neill and his team's remains?"

"Numerous motives come to mind, such as the fact that maybe it wasn't rebel insurgents who attacked the Red Starr team." Grady started to clear the table, motioning that Brienne should stay where she was. This wasn't uncommon, seeing as they used to confer with each other on numerous assignments. Having another viewpoint was an advantage. He didn't want to lose this, but that meant making changes he wasn't so comfortable with. "It appeared to be cut and dry, but it might be that something more is in play with what your informant has stirred up."

"You think the ISI were the ones to attack Red Starr's infiltration route?" Brienne asked, setting her empty glass on the table. She was biting her lip in thought as she slouched in her chair the way she was prone to do after a meal in the privacy of one of their apartments, crossing her arms in what looked like a petulant manner. It wasn't. He couldn't prevent a half smile at the habit that had been formed long ago. "What would they have to gain by eliminating a government contracted paramilitary hostage rescue team inside Pakistan who had ISI-supported intelligence about the terrain and local factions? I recall the hostages being with a mission group from the United States, so there shouldn't have been any opposition from the Pakistani government or the ISI."

"Have you considered the possibility that the missionaries weren't taken by a group of insurgents, but instead the ISI had a part in it or were supporting the faction that did?" Grady set their plates into the sink. He didn't return to the table, but instead walked the open layout of the small beach house to the living room. It was a better location to have the upcoming conversation he'd been waiting for. "It's the only logical explanation for why the ISI would want to silence your inquiry."

Brienne didn't reply right away, which had Grady looking over the couch to see that she was still seated at the table. She was regarding him with wariness, her blue eyes tapered in the corners and deep in thought. Her blonde hair was wild with untamed waves falling around her shoulders and the beautiful sight before him was something he wanted to see for many years to come.

"Cairo is off the table now that your identity has been compromised and your Agency association has been revealed," Grady said, starting down the path that was sure to be a maze of flickering, dangerous flames. He could handle the heat, so he forged ahead. "Does that change things for us in the near term?"

"You tell me, Grady." Brienne uncrossed her arms and stood, taking her time as she slowly made her way around the couch to join him. Her chin was tilted up in a way that told him she wasn't going to take any prisoners. That was good, because neither was he. "Is there any room in your life for someone other than Madison's ghost and a house full of reminders of your life together?"

Chapter Six

Brienne had been on pins and needles ever since she and Grady had set foot into this damned beach house that was more sterile than any hospital room she'd ever had the misfortune to be in. She wasn't one to shy away from confrontation and she stood her ground when she needed to do what was best for her. Why, then, did being completely honest with Grady make her experience vulnerability in a manner she'd never encountered? Maybe it had to do with the fact that no one possessed the ability to hurt her as much as he did at this very moment.

"Madison was my wife, Brie." Grady's tone of voice was as calm as ever, similar to when he was discussing politics. It grated Brienne's nerves at how composed and self-assured he was in himself. Maturity, maybe, but she would say it had mostly to do with how comfortable he was in his life. She disrupted that and he must have assumed he could domesticate her like some errant puppy. "She will always be a part of me."

"She *is* you," Brienne countered in understanding and acceptance. Could Grady truly not see it? "The two of you had known each other since high school. You walked by each other's sides hand in hand through the good times and bad. You molded each other into adulthood, and it was never my intention to change you to be anyone else. She had a great deal to do with making who you are today and I'm grateful for that, but you clearly do not understand where I'm coming from."

Brienne purposefully kept the couch between them. She couldn't be touched and it was more than apparent Grady didn't want to be either. She leaned up against the cream-colored fabric, resting her hands on the soft cushions when all she wanted to do was ball them into tight fists and continually pound the couch until all of her frustration faded away. It was so hard to breathe while describing what the coiled anger inside of her was doing to her.

"I was okay with a small amount of distance between us, Grady," Brienne admitted through the constriction of her throat. It hurt to speak, because she understood she was pushing him further away with each word. Maybe that was why she'd put off having this conversation and why she'd treated this perilous situation with more poise than what it called for. Anything was more bearable than witnessing the disintegration of their relationship "We both had our reasons to start out that way, but as with anything in this life…situations change. Your presence in my life wasn't just for physical pleasure anymore and the two of our lives integrated somehow, someway, in a manner where *this* became more to me than just a casual relationship."

Grady remained silent, his stoic expression not changing in the slightest as he slipped his hands into his front pockets. The muscle in his jawline strained underneath his five o'clock shadow, the black whiskers peppered with a few bristles of grey. Even annoyed, his virility was unmistakable. He thought he had no control here, but she was more than aware that wasn't the case. Everything that made up who they were as a couple rested in the palms of his hands and had for quite some time.

"You have no idea…" Grady's voice faded away as he shook his head in what Brienne would have said was despondency. He shot her a sideways glance before turning away from her and walking to where the alarm system panel was in the small foyer. He stared at it for a moment and she was unsure of what the significance was until he ever so slowly opened a part of himself that she'd never witnessed before. "Word of the suicide bomber walking into that makeshift hospital tent made out of cheap canvas hit the airwaves while I was in the communications bunker in Kandahar. I didn't even pick up the phone when it rang. Why should I have someone tell me what I already knew? Just to hear the words I already understood to be the end of her? I'd never known pain like that…shattered, slicing agony to the point a person can't physically move."

Brienne wondered just how far her selfishness went as she held back her tears. She hadn't meant for Grady to share with her that devastating moment upon discovering his wife had died. All she'd wanted was for him to say there was room in his life for her. A happy ending. Wasn't that what she'd been brought up to hear?

Nothing was ever simple though. Grady was describing exactly what she would go through if he were taken from this life. Walking away was something Brienne could physically carry out, but to go through life knowing his presence wasn't somewhere in this world making a difference? That was beyond her ability to understand.

Grady removed his right hand from his pocket and pointed toward the security panel. He shook his finger as if he were admonishing the device and all it stood for. Brienne wanted to move closer, but couldn't bring herself to make the effort.

"Madison didn't know it, but I'd sent additional security for the mission she'd been assigned." Grady barked out a humorless laugh. The loud sound caught Brienne off guard and she realized that he wasn't even here with her. He was back there…in the darkness where she couldn't reach him. "The contracted agents all lost their lives as well, leaving behind wives and children. A mass loss of life on a scale that was beyond imagining, and yet I didn't think of them once that night."

The disparaging rebuke Grady had undertaken wasn't fair to himself, but Brienne doubted he would ever see the situation any differently. Those agents had understood the risk they were taking in the place that they found themselves. The only ones to carry the blame of lost lives were the insurgents, but they had been too busy celebrating to know that they had destroyed more than just a tent full of aid workers.

"I went through our lives together…memory by memory," Grady whispered hoarsely as he started to walk the perimeter of the room. Brienne wanted to tell him to stop, that he didn't have to talk about this anymore, but he cleared his throat and spoke over her. "I stared at Madison's photograph for hours, wanting to memorize each feature to ensure her image never faded from my memory. It didn't work. I lost the small imperfections first. There are times when I try to recall her face and it's blurred. I did that. You also had a part in that."

Brienne jerked back from her place behind the couch as if Grady had physically hit her. He might as well have. The accusation was like a direct blow to her stomach and she realized she could no longer do this. She desperately needed to leave and take a moment to regain her equilibrium, but he stopped her.

"Don't you dare walk away from this, Brie," Grady demanded in a voice filled with so much pain, Brienne could no longer hold back the tears. They slid down her face as she turned back to him, shaking her head in response. "You wanted this. I was foolish to think you wouldn't, but here we are."

"I wanted the chance to love you," Brienne confessed, choking out the words as she took a step closer to him. Grady's eyes were filled with so much pain that she stopped her advancement. "I wanted the chance to hold your hand through whatever the future holds instead of watching you from the distance that you insisted on. You were pushing me away, Grady. What would you have done if the roles had been reversed? I never meant—"

"To replace Madison?" Grady asked, getting to the heart of the problem. His lips formed the saddest of smiles and Brienne braced herself for the final blow. She'd known it would end like this, but imagining it and experiencing it were two very different concepts. "You didn't replace Madison and you certainly didn't erase her memory. We both had a hand in that, but it's the progression of life that is responsible for time passing and memories fading. *That* is what I'm having trouble accepting."

"You—"

"You're asking me to risk going through that again, Brie."

The brutal honesty of Grady's words stole her breath. He finally closed the distance between them and cradled her face in the palms of his hands in the tender manner she'd come to cherish. Brienne closed her eyes against the accusation in his, accepting the blame.

"Yes," Brienne answered genuinely as she opened her eyes to see Grady's acceptance and knowing from this moment forward that everything would be as it should be. He was willing walk through hell all over again...for her. "Yes, that is what I am asking of you. But it's nothing that I'm not demanding of myself, Grady. Horrific scenarios run through my head every time you leave my office, my apartment, the city, for another country where we walk around with targets on our backs. I can't possibly imagine what it is like to lose the person you love, but I do know what it is like to have found him. The love I feel for you can physically bring me to my knees and I don't want to live without that, Grady. I don't want to walk through the rest of my life without you by my side."

Grady pressed his forehead against hers, as this time it was he who closed his eyes against the emotional turmoil they'd brought to a boil. Brienne had thrown down the gauntlet at a time in which he feared the most—her life was in imminent danger. There wasn't a thing either one of them could do about that at the moment. Her fate was out of their hands and yet she was still asking that he walk by her side through it all. Yes, maybe she was being selfish.

"Madison would have loved you, too," Grady murmured, taking Brienne by surprise at his admission. He pulled her close to him, wrapping both arms around her so that she was tucked in nice and close against him. She rested her ear over his heart, listening to the reassuring rhythmic beat as the warmth of his body invaded hers. She hadn't realized just how cold she'd been until this very moment. "She would have appreciated your sense of duty to others, your strength in commitment, and your unwillingness to settle for less than you deserve."

Grady pulled slightly away until he could see her, shaking his head in what she assumed was wonder. He brushed away another tear from her face with his thumb and then did the same to her other cheek. The stuttered breath he pulled through his lips told her just how fragile his emotions were. They matched her own.

"I do love you, Brie. No more, no less, no different than the love I have for Madison." Grady paused and it was apparent he was trying to form his words in a manner that wouldn't offend her. Brienne could only nod her understanding. "My love for you is enduring, encompassing, and one that has the capability to destroy me if I lost you. I hope you understand the lengths I will go to in order to keep you safe and that you have the ability to forgive me for the damage I might have to leave in my wake."

Chapter Seven

Grady's mental struggle with allowing himself to truly and freely love Brienne was finally at an end. He experienced a freedom he'd never expected after anguishing over his decision, but there was also a fierce need to protect her in a manner he hadn't been cognizant of with Madison. He would try his best to not overcompensate, but he'd given Brienne fair warning and he wouldn't apologize for the lengths he'd go to in order to achieve his goal. He was a protector by his very nature...of his country and now of her.

"Make love to me, Grady," Brienne whispered with need, her hand on the back of his neck, drawing his lips down to hers. "Show me what it is like to love knowing it is both our futures from now until the end."

Grady bent and lifted Brienne into his arms, cradling her securely as he walked to the bedroom. He didn't stop until he was able to set her on her feet at the end of the bed. Without a word, he kissed her—passionately and possessively. He drank from her like he was stranded in a desert and she was his sole oasis. He would never satiate his thirst for her, but he would damn well test her reserves.

Brienne's long and delicate fingers slipped beneath the shoulder holster he'd secured to his chest earlier. Once he'd removed it and positioned it on the bed for easy reach, he allowed her to tug at the cotton shirt he'd put on after his shower. The soft fabric stretched and he pulled away long enough to draw the shirt over his head. He dropped it to the ground and then proceeded to do the same with her clothes. One by one, the articles of her apparel joined his. It wasn't until they were both nude that he slowly guided her down onto the bed.

Grady used one arm to hold himself up, taking in the breathtaking sight of Brienne's body. She might be blonde, but her flawless skin was exquisitely sun-kissed by those trips overseas. Her muscles were well toned from the training the Agency required of their field agents. She was able to physically keep up with him in a manner that didn't make him feel as if he would break her with his rough touch. Her breasts were ample enough and firm, filling the palm of his hand, and her mound was bare of any hair, as was her habit. The slight scar on the left side of her ribcage she'd gotten while protecting a child from a hand grenade in Damascus only added to her beauty.

"Wait," Brienne said somewhat breathlessly, her palm against his chest. Her blue eyes were clear of tears and only love remained. "Protection. I don't—"

"I do," Grady promised, rolling onto his back and taking her with him. Brienne's blonde hair fell all around them until he gathered the thick strands over one of her shoulders. He pressed his lips to her other one. "I have one in my wallet."

Neither one was sure how long they would be here, but one condom definitely wasn't enough. Grady would worry about that at a later time, needing this moment to love her like she deserved. What had she said? Show her what it was like to love knowing it will never end. He could do that for her, but she apparently had other plans first.

"Brie—"

Grady was cut off when Brienne trailed the tips of her fingers down his chest and wrapped them around his already hardened cock. Her lips slowly followed behind, leaving a trail of moisture from her tongue. She veered to his right, gently biting his pelvic bone. There wasn't a chance in hell she was going to suck him without him bearing witness.

He gathered up her blonde hair once more, keeping a hold of the thick mane in his hand. There was something about the intimacy in watching a woman love her man with her mouth that shouldn't be missed. Adding on his ability to control her movements in doing so was even more arousing.

Brienne's lashes lifted, those crystal blues connecting with his just as her soft lips sealed warmly over the head of his cock. Grady had to remind himself to breathe as she glided her tongue over the slit, gathering the pre-cum that had gathered from anticipation.

"What you do to me," Grady murmured, barely getting the words out after she slowly took the remainder of him into her mouth. The gradual insertion caused his heart to speed up its usual steady rhythm. "Brie…"

Brienne ran the tips of her fingers up his inner thigh until she was able to take his large sac into her hand, massaging him a manner that would end this act faster than he'd like. She sucked him until she was back at his tip, settling herself between his legs. He held onto her hair, not allowing her to take him back inside her mouth until he had himself under control. He ignored the knowing look she gave him.

Grady prevented himself from hauling her above him, flipping her over, and plunging himself deep inside of her. He didn't want this rushed and he wanted to deliver to her what he'd promised, but damn if she wasn't making that a hard undertaking to achieve.

Brienne pulled against his hold until he reluctantly allowed her to pleasure him the way she wanted. He closed his eyes against the wicked, delicious sight. Her tongue stroked against the underside of his shaft as she continued to take him to the back of her throat. It was one of his preferred sensations and when she swallowed, the soft pressure around his cock was euphoric.

Grady needed to control things from here, so he used the hold he had on her hair to set the pace of her pleasuring exploit. He started watching Brienne once more, taking in how her lips fit perfectly around his member as her cheeks hollowed in a sensual motion. She never stopped massaging his sac and it wasn't long before he could feel the gathering presence of his release.

"Stop." Grady had just enough energy to stop Brienne, wanting them to reach that blissful precipice together. He pulled her back up his body until he could roll her over onto her back. They were both breathing rather heavily, but that didn't stop him from talking. "It's my turn, Brie."

* * * *

Brienne grabbed the pillow above her head, giving herself something to hold onto. She arched into Grady as he took her breast into his hand, closing his lips around her nipple. The heat of his mouth was a drastic shock against her cool skin, hardening the peak even more. He stroked his tongue over the sensitive nub until she could literally feel the arousal travel from her breast to her clit like a bolt of lightning.

"Grady…"

Of course, he didn't answer her. Instead, Grady started to roll her nipple with his tongue in small circles. Every once in a while he would draw the delicate tissue in between his teeth. The pleasurable pain caused her body to spiral into an awakening, aided by the coarse brush of his five o'clock shadow against her skin.

Brienne wasn't sure how much more decadent indulgence she could take, so she released her hold on the pillow and wrapped her fingers around Grady's neck. He wouldn't budge and she swore she was going to come just from nipple stimulation itself. She cried out when he bit a little harder than usual, the sharp, arousing stinging sending her even closer to that edge.

"Damn it, Grady," Brienne cursed, wishing his hair was long enough so that she could use it like he did hers. That didn't stop her from trying to pull him away to give her a brief reprieve. She finally breathed a sigh of relief when he released her nipple, but she should have known it wasn't his intention to stop. "Hmmmm."

That low moan was all Brienne was able to get out when Grady transferred his attention to her other nipple. It had been throbbing in the absence of his touch, but now the intense stimulation was almost unbearable. He had rolled to her side, giving him full access to her body.

"Open your legs for me, Brie. Put your arms back and allow me to pleasure you."

Brie recalled those words being said before. It wasn't easy for her to lay back and allow someone to pleasure her while she did nothing. Grady wasn't like the other men she'd been with. She wasn't sure if it was age, experience, or just knowing how to please a woman…but he excelled at it. He'd explained that he attained his pleasure through her and after experiencing firsthand his lovemaking…she had finally understood.

Grady continued to draw on her nipple, every so often using his tongue to stroke the tip. He waited until her arms were above her head before caressing her abdomen with his fingers. He didn't stop until his hand cupped her mound. She widened her legs and waited for…that. Brienne parted her lips in rapture. It was that moment where his middle finger dipped in between her folds and gathered her cream.

"Spread your legs wider, Brie. Give me what I want."

Unprecedented access. Brienne widened her legs, only to find one knee captured by his. She tightened her grip on the pillow as he drew the moisture up and over her throbbing clitoris. Grady started to move one finger in tiny, tiny circles over the swollen nub. A whimper escaped her as he awakened more nerves, if that were even possible.

"Look at me."

The directive shot a jolt of arousal through her, but it was nowhere near as stimulating as when Grady pressed even more firmly than before, initiating a small orgasm that took her by surprise. His watchful eyes took in every ounce of pleasure she experienced in this vulnerable position.

"I want more."

With those three words, Grady lowered his mouth to her nipple before moving lower and positioning himself between her legs. He pushed her thighs even farther apart and licked away any trace of her original orgasm, from which she was still coming down. She tried to tell him that she was too sensitive, but the words never left her mouth as he ever so slowly slid two fingers inside of her.

Brienne wasn't sure how her nails hadn't punctured the pillow by now, because her grip couldn't get any tighter than what it was. Grady had bent his fingers slightly forward, stroking over that sweet spot at the exact same moment his lips closed over her clit. He drew the overly sensitive tissue into his mouth, sucking gently and yet firmly enough that it was as if her orgasm had never ended.

Grady took her higher and higher, to a point where Brienne was floating in something far beyond a mere awakening. Her mind had soared to another plane, although she couldn't quite reach that ultimate high. He maintained a slow, even pace that was, quite frankly, torturous. She couldn't even have described what he'd just done with his tongue, but it was enough to light the fuse of her impending explosion.

Brienne called out his name as she came apart into a million pieces. The shattering was an exquisite eruption of pleasure that lasted longer than anything she'd ever experienced at the touch of his hand. She was subjected to an indulgence that took on another meaning altogether—this was the reaction to unrestricted love.

Chapter Eight

Grady heard the ringing of his SAT phone right when he'd pushed off the bed to retrieve the condom he'd planned to put to good use. His gaze connected with Brienne's before he reached down to where his clothes lay. The black device had ended up near her shirt, so he immediately snatched it up and addressed the person on the other end after first glancing at the screen.

"Crest, what have you got for us?"

Grady motioned for Brienne to crawl underneath the covers, but she was too intent on hearing what was being said from the other end of the line. He couldn't blame her and sighed in resignation, coming to stand near the side of the bed where she'd come to rest on her knees. The sensual pose would have had him disconnecting the call had this not been such a dire situation.

"The entire family of Brienne's informant has been terminated."

Brienne slowly closed her eyes and then rested her forehead in sorrow against his chest. Grady wrapped one arm around her while keeping the phone upright in order for her to still hear the conversation. Loss in the field was never easy for an agent to accept because the people putting their lives at risk were doing so for the very families who suffered.

"And Raheela?" Grady asked, not even bothering to inquire how the murders were committed. It didn't matter. Death was death. "Was she among the casualties?"

"No," Crest replied confidently, delving into the next topic of importance. Grady could literally feel the relief wash over Brienne. "She's gone underground somewhere, but we have our contractors on the ground looking for her. I've also touched base with Starr, although the only thing I told her was that you were otherwise occupied and would be calling her soon. I want confirmation of the location of the lost Red Starr unit's bodies before going to her with this. We have the potential of recovering both Brienne's asset and the remains of the founder's unit if we have to do an amphibious operation in theater using those assets."

Starr wouldn't appreciate the gesture of protection Crest was offering her, but Grady agreed it was the right thing to do. There were too many irons in the fire and someone was bound to get burned. The Agency had all of its divisions searching for who could possibly be the one responsible for betraying Brienne, Telfer was taking a closer look in-house at his own team, and Grady had hired Crest to figure out a way to minimize the threat posed by ISI's mission to terminate Brienne. Several time-critical issues needed to be resolved before tugging on the string she'd started to unravel.

"Any progress with the ISI team?" Grady asked, backing up a step so that Brienne could move off of the bed. She made her way to the bathroom, retrieving both white robes he'd seen hanging behind the door. "Brienne informed me that Raheela is married to Shujaat Qalat, an ISI Major. The connection is there. Brienne and I went over some things this evening and we've come to the conclusion that members from ISI might have been the ones to halt Red Starr's insertion in the region and Qalat is doing his best to cover his tracks. It's the only reasonable explanation."

"It would also explain why Raheela was able to gather intel on such an old mission. Qalat has gone off the radar, but we'll find him wherever he ends up."

Crest didn't need to say it wouldn't be a legal interrogation. There was no physical evidence Shujaat Qalat had anything to do with Red Starr's fated mission or the threat on Brienne's life. It was all assumption through the bits of intel coming through. There were things that American citizens didn't need to know regarding the safety of the very Agents who worked to keep the United States free of terrorism.

"Raheela most likely already knows about her family, but she'll do what needs to be done to escape," Brienne offered up, knowing more about the underground conduit. "She uses the port of Karachi to slip the women and children out of the city. She's either close by Karachi or she's already at her destination."

Grady could tell by Brienne's voice that she wasn't sure where that final destination was located, thus not fully illuminating the path they had to follow. She had belted her robe and then handed him the other. She took a hold of the SAT phone, but he laid the garment on the bed. He wasn't one to wear robes. She still had enough spark in her that she lifted a corner of her mouth in humor as she watched him don nothing more than the pair of jeans that had been in the go-bag.

"We'll check that out immediately," Crest answered, covering his end of the phone to give the order to one of his agents. It was his next statement that caused Brienne to freeze in her steps. "I think we're all in agreement Brienne's name was leaked by someone inside the Intelligence Division. Raheela had too much to lose. As a matter of fact, it was most likely done by someone assigned to Brienne's own section."

"Telfer is taking care of that issue," Grady said, not bothering to hide his skepticism. It was damned hard to be objective with the piles of shit that were being dumped on Brienne's supervisor's desk. "He's solid, Crest. I can vouch for him."

"You and I both know he's not got the time to brush his own teeth, let alone find out who within his department is the guilty party."

"Brienne can't get within a mile of Langley without becoming a target in someone's scope, and you damn well know it," Grady asserted irritably, not backing down on this. It was apparent Brienne was actually giving it thought from the way she was touching the bracelet on her wrist, so he grabbed the phone from her and took it off speaker. "Find another way."

"I have," Crest replied without hesitation. This man was the embodiment of a warrior. If he said he had a solution, he did. It just wasn't what Grady had expected. "You, Kenton. You have to go back to Langley and finish this so Brienne can get her life back."

* * * *

Brienne recalled Grady's sentiment regarding the lengths he would go to in order to keep her safe. She understood at the time, but now it was different. She was a seasoned agent, this case was regarding her career, and her life was literally on the line...she had a right to hear the other side of the conversation.

"You have no right to cut me out of this, Grady."

Brienne had never had the pleasure of meeting Gavin Crest, or even Catori Starr for that matter. She was sure that would change, but right now it didn't matter. These people were making choices for her and that had to stop.

"Telfer is getting flak from the higher-ups within the Agency, especially those with important connections to the Pakistani government." Grady snatched his weapon, which was still in its holster, and walked out of the bedroom. Brienne's stomach rolled a bit as she realized Crest had told him something of importance. She followed close behind, not willing to allow Grady to make decisions without her. It was as if the last hour they'd spent together hadn't even taken place. "Crest is under the assumption he doesn't have time to flush out the guilty party."

"We're assuming the person responsible is within the section based on some reasonable suppositions," Brienne pointed out distractedly, already feeling their time together slipping through her fingers. She didn't want to be proven wrong and have her death occur before they ever stood a chance. She swallowed down the desperation and tried to compose her emotions. She needed to treat this like any other assignment. "It could very well have come from one of my own sources. I could have slipped and—"

"You didn't do anything of the sort, Brie," Grady replied, resignation in the tone of his voice. He set his weapon on the counter and then retrieved a bottle of water from the refrigerator before leaning back against the hard granite. He unscrewed the cap and took a long drink of water, a droplet of condensation immediately falling onto his chest. It trailed lower to where she'd been earlier, to when they'd pushed aside all that was wrong and loved one another. "Crest is suggesting I go into Langley."

"And do what?" Brienne couldn't believe Grady was even considering such a reckless motion. "The ISI already knows about our association. Either they will take you out on sight or they will have every available source they have here in the United States glued to you, waiting for an opportunity to bring you in and do God knows what in order to get you to talk. You and I both know something of this magnitude takes time. Didn't you sit here during dinner and reiterate those same words?"

"We *don't* have time, Brie."

Grady was considering putting himself in the crosshairs of ISI to gain their attention…on purpose. Brienne needed to find a way to change his mind before he ended up being chained up to a ceiling, beaten, and tortured. That wasn't going to happen.

"You aren't going." Brienne was firm in her stance, ignoring the dark gaze Grady was shooting her way. He never did like being told what to do, but he wasn't calling the shots around here. Neither was Crest, for that matter. She crossed her arms and stood in the middle of the small kitchen, daring for Grady to argue with her. "I won't be responsible for the most likely outcome should you and Crest try to do this. Telfer might be dealing with his superiors and putting out the firestorm this has all caused, but he's good at his job. He will have people in place, such as those within the Technical Collections Section in the Science and Technology Division, to ferret out whoever disclosed my identity."

"This isn't a normal operation and you know it," Grady countered, slamming his half-empty bottle onto the counter. Water droplets sprayed and she wasn't surprised when the plastic practically collapsed beneath his grip. "Damn it, Brie, this is your life we're talking about. People are out there doing their best to see it snuffed out. Crest has multiple angles covered, but Telfer has a leak inside his section. How far do you think he'll get without knowing who he can trust?"

"ISI had to have bought the intel from someone and left—"

"A paper trail?" Grady was already shaking his head in response to what she was implying. "Those agents within your department are seasoned. There is no way in hell they left evidence of their ties to

ISI. This is going to come down to traditional methods of investigation. I need to be onsite."

The evening had been an emotional rollercoaster and it was as if the ride had never been brought to a stop. Their coaster car was still on the tracks and about to go another round. Brienne wanted off, but Grady was in the first seat with his hands high in the air. She wouldn't allow him to ride alone.

"Brie, you and I know how this works." Grady was now standing in front of her, his strong arms pulling her to him. Brienne closed her eyes, wishing she had half the strength to physically prevent him from leaving this sanctuary. "Should ISI be monitoring the approaches to Langley, they'll eventually spot me. It's better we have the upper hand. Maybe they'll make a mistake and call whomever it is they have in their grip. Telfer has those tech boys monitoring every individual cell phone of every person you've ever had contact with."

They could stay up all night discussing this, but it wouldn't change a thing—at least the facts. Brienne needed time to mentally go through everything regarding Raheela, from every word spoken to those that weren't. Had she known? Had she already been in a safe place, knowing her husband was about to eliminate any remaining threat to a mission that had never truly been completed? Crest needed to reach the port before Raheela was able to fade into the masses as if she'd never existed. In the meantime, Brienne wouldn't allow the time she and Grady had left to be wasted by discussing what-ifs.

"Take me back to bed, Grady. Make this all go away for a few hours, at the very least."

Chapter Nine

Grady couldn't sleep at all. The sun was due to rise within the hour and he would soon need to leave for his trip back to D.C. He wasn't comfortable leaving Brienne here, even if it was with a high-powered covert action team assigned to one of Crest's best team members. What if this was what ISI was waiting for? What if they had gone even further in their attempt to eliminate Brienne and her informant? What if they'd manage to infiltrate the NSA and knew exactly where to look all along?

"I think we need to wait until Raheela is found and brought to safety before sending you into Langley," Brienne whispered, still using her finger to trace circles on his chest. She hadn't gotten much sleep either. Another phone call from Crest last night had their minds spinning with questions, so they'd ended up retracing Brienne's steps…only to end up in the same place they started. "Going into this thing blind, hoping for the best, isn't the answer."

Grady couldn't take hearing the strain of worry in Brienne's voice, so he brought her hand up and pressed a tender kiss in the center of her palm. He continued to trail his lips down her arm until he needed to flip her over to continue his progression. Her arms came up in acceptance and pulled him closer.

Neither of them had to say a word. They used to make love quietly on the nights one of them had to leave the following morning.

It was a silent goodbye, just in case. He hadn't realized it then, but he did now.

There wasn't a spot on her body that Grady didn't stroke, touch, or caress with his lips and hands. He started with her front and then continued his exploration on her back. Her lower back had a sensual arch, but he spent more time at curve of her buttocks. Brienne was ticklish on the back of her thighs, but by the time he'd finished...she was more than ready to accept him into her.

"Not yet," Grady whispered, not wanting this to end as she turned to face him. If only he had the power to stop the sun from rising. "I need to taste more of you."

Grady trailed tiny kisses down her abdomen, cherishing the warmth of her skin. Brienne didn't hesitate to spread her legs and give him access to her most vulnerable region. He spread her folds, running his tongue over her swollen clitoris. He savored her sweet taste while taking his time enjoying this intimate act they were engaging in. They could live another two hundred years and it still wouldn't be enough time to love her the way he wanted.

Brienne's breath was becoming hitched as she continued to climb, but Grady didn't want her soaring without him. He slowed down, pulling away from her sensitive nub and gradually made his way back up to kiss her. He allowed her to roll both of them over, giving her access to the condom he'd placed on the nightstand. The sun was starting to shine through the slates of the blinds, kissing the areas of her body he'd already had the pleasure of touching.

Brienne tore the square foil package with her teeth, pulling the small disc out with the pads of her fingers. She placed the condom on the tip of his cock, ever so slowly unraveling the latex over his shaft. Grady couldn't help but stare at the beautiful woman above him. She was a sight that he would never tire of looking at, but it wasn't just her physical attributes that pulled him toward her.

The woman she had become through all her trials and tribulations, the unforgettable painful sights she'd encountered, and the harsh decisions she'd had to make along the way had only given her strength to succeed in her position...not just professionally, but in life. And she was here with him. She chose him to share her life with and it had taken him way too long to accept her love. It was remarkable.

"Take what you need from me, Brie," Grady encouraged lovingly, assisting her in straddling him. "I'm yours and you are mine."

"Don't forget that when you are out there in the field," Brienne whispered, placing the tip of his cock against her entrance. She closed her eyes as she ever so slowly slid down his shaft. Her sheath parted and her warmth surrounded him as she took every inch. "And remember what you have to live for."

Brienne didn't move right away, but instead started to slowly rotate her hips. The pressure she was exerting on him made it exquisitely difficult to refrain from having an orgasm. Grady evened out his breathing, reaching for the strength to control his physical urge to attain release. She wanted this and he would see that she got what she needed.

Grady lifted both arms and cupped her breasts, using his thumbs to caress her nipples. Brienne arched her back in pleasure, even leaning slightly back to rest her hands on his thighs. She never once stopped gyrating against him. A ray of sun moved slightly lower, shining on where they were now connected. Her clit was swollen and the base of his shaft glistened every time she lifted.

"Touch your breasts, Brie," Grady urged, lowering his arms and licking his thumb. He waited for her to do as he instructed, in awe of the pleasure she was experiencing, before pressing on her clitoris. She was uninhibited in her quest for release, the guttural moan sending an ache directly through his cock. "That's right, sweetheart. Roll your nipples for me."

Brienne was mesmerizing as she pleasured herself under his command. Grady watched her through hooded eyes, not wanting to miss a second of this sensual demonstration. Her lips were parted in a silent cry while she manipulated her hardened nipples. He could literally see the goose bumps forming on her silken flesh as they made their way straight to where he was touching her.

Grady pressed slightly harder, never letting up on the circular motions he was administering to her clit. Brienne lifted herself off of him by the strength of her legs, only to then take him back inside of her. She quickened her pace and her sheath started to press against his shaft in response.

"Don't stop, Brie. Keep riding me until you come."

Grady had no doubt the orgasm hit Brienne when she slammed down on him and his name fell from her lips. Her pussy contracted around him over and over, pulling at his seed until he spilled into the condom. She didn't stop until they were both out of breath and she'd collapsed on top of him. He held her while they both recovered, not willing to give this up quite yet.

"I can't let you go," Brienne whispered, her warm lips moving against his neck. Grady was technically still inside of her and neither one of them made a move to leave the bed. That didn't mean he wouldn't when the time came. Seeing her through this threat was his main priority and he would do what had to be done, regardless of her protests. "We'll figure out another way."

* * * *

Brienne never let Grady out of her sight. They'd taken a shower together and he'd made them some pancakes while she literally went over every conversation she'd ever had with Raheela for the second time. She was the key and it was only a matter of time before the door was unlocked. It was going on zero nine hundred and he'd yet to leave, most likely waiting for another one of Crest's team members to arrive. He could wait until hell froze over, but there wasn't a chance he was leaving here without her. The things ISI would do to him if they captured him was unthinkable.

"Whoever it is didn't necessarily need to know about Raheela," Grady offered up, taking his coffee and peering out the blinds of the patio door that overlooked the ocean. They'd not been opened and they wouldn't be, but she would certainly love to be able to breathe in the salt air. "Raheela's husband could have been monitoring her calls and then made the attempt to uncover your identity. ISI is smart enough to know which department within the CIA was keeping tabs on Pakistani relations. From there, it wouldn't take much to find a weakness among the personnel and then exploit them."

"Threats?" Brienne poured herself more coffee out of the glass carafe. Even the cups were cream in color, matching the rest of the décor. The tedious design couldn't prevent the delicious aroma from filling the air. "You know that all of us do our best to prevent that."

"What about those employees who aren't field agents? How about the analyst on your desk?" Grady stepped away from the closed blinds, turning back to face Brienne. He'd changed into the only other set of clothes given to them, which happened to be one of his preferred suits. The grey jacket was currently on the back of one of the chairs, but his blue and charcoal grey tie was perfectly aligned with the buttons on his white dress shirt. "Think about it. How many times have the IRS databases been breached by other countries or even the lowliest hacker who wanted to discover who held those kinds of credentials? With the right amount of time and the correct person at the helm, it wouldn't be too hard to figure out who worked for the government in a certain department. From there, it's a matter of pushing the right buttons, greasing the correct wheels, and using the appropriate people to get what they need."

Brienne thought about the first time she'd been in contact with Raheela. It was years ago, offering up the timetable needed for such a coup against the CIA. Had her husband known all along and it had taken this length of time to actually locate Brienne? The question remained—why was the ISI concerned with Red Starr?

Brienne and Grady were making assumptions based on the last few transmissions she had with Raheela. The whole group of agency field assets stationed in Pakistan had used the woman more often on other related terrorist issues than what Brienne had done in the past. What if she was just a casualty because she'd been the one responsible for bringing Raheela into the fold to begin with? There were so many unanswered questions.

"Do you see why I have to go in?" Grady asked, coming up behind Brienne and kissing the back of her neck. She'd used her clip to pull her hair back, keeping it out of the way. He was using his affection to ease the difficulty of this situation. It wasn't working and she turned around to face him. "Don't give me that look, Brienne. This is our chosen profession and we knew the risks going in."

"Technically, you're retired," Brienne countered, resting her hands on either side of his tie. She raised an eyebrow in challenge as she grasped for straws. "You don't have to do anything. Telfer is my Supervisory Special Agent in Charge. He's the one who—"

"Has his ass in a ring of fire right now," Grady finished for her, not even coming close to using the words she would have. Brienne sighed in frustration, but refused to think that this was their only choice. "You and I both know the shitstorm that brews up within the Agency when an agent's identity is leaked. At this point, we use whatever means necessary."

The SAT phone rang, although not unexpectedly. Crest had radioed in that Connor would be arriving to relieve the night crew, allowing Grady to take his trip to Langley. Connor was to call right before he approached the beach house. It wasn't Connor's voice that came over the speaker, though.

"We have a bit of a problem. Starr is currently heading to Langley," Crest informed them, his tone tight with worry. "I've held her off as long as I could. We're about to have a third party enter the arena. The firepower she has at her disposal could take out a third world nation."

Chapter Ten

Grady and Brienne had both agreed to allow Crest another twenty-four hours to speak with Starr, locate Raheela, and devise a plan that would lead them to who gave up Brienne's identity. Two of those three things had been accomplished and now it was time to make a difficult decision. Grady was ready to walk out the door and act as bait, but Brienne couldn't allow that to happen.

"We go into the city together." Brienne refused to budge on her position. It was apparent Grady was suppressing his annoyance at her deliberate resistance to what needed to be done. These four walls were closing in and she wasn't sure how much longer either one of them would last, but he didn't get to go off alone. "Or at least allow me to speak with Raheela first before you make the drive."

"Raheela is currently en route to a safe house outside of Karachi. That could take hours, which we can't afford to waste. Besides, we both know that there's nothing she can offer that she hasn't already supplied. The—" Grady would have continued had the SAT phone not begun to buzz again. This was becoming repetitive and something had to be decided one way or another. He answered the call on speaker so that both of them could hear the update. "Tell me something useful."

"Bob Jensen."

Brienne stood up from the middle cushion on the couch as the third item on Crest's list had finally been accomplished, wanting to throw her cup of coffee across the room. She needed to hear it shatter, see it being destroyed with as much desire as she wanted Crest to retract his declaration. Her team—make that her former team—was falling apart. She'd yet to fully realize the ramifications that her career was over and her life would never be the same. The safety of those men and women had always come first and she refused to believe Bob had anything to do with betraying her. He was a dear friend of hers.

"That's not a possibility."

"Brienne, they kidnapped his five-year-old son."

"Excuse me?" Brienne lost the ability to breathe as the pressure on her chest became real. Brutal images of what could happen to such a young child entered her mind before she could put those barriers up that she'd gotten accustomed to using during overseas assignments. She could only imagine what Bob was going through. Grady was by her side immediately, indicating she needed to keep grounded. "You're telling me that ISI took Michael Jensen? Is SSA Telfer aware of this? Do they have the FBI's Hostage Rescue Team assembled—"

"Yes, it's being handled," Crest advised over a loud purring sound that could be heard in the background. "Starr is using her operations group to assist in the rescue mission and we're hoping the element of surprise is enough to keep Michael alive. Jensen gave himself over when he was forced to kill one of Shujaat Qalat's lieutenants who wasn't happy with the answers he was being given. He made one too many threats and Jensen snapped. ISI isn't aware their source has turned and their handler terminated."

Crest didn't have to convey that those answers ISI sought had everything and anything to do with Brienne's current location. They were bound and determined to eliminate her for God knows what motive, which most likely added on to their desperation in being unable to locate Raheela. Qalat has lost control of whatever plan he had in motion and now a little boy's life was at stake.

"And what of Qalat?" Grady asked, motioning for Brienne to sit down. There was no telling how long they would be here now, but she couldn't bring herself to stay stationary. She handed the SAT phone over to Grady as she started to pace in order to ease some of her anxiety. She wasn't used to being on the sidelines during the homecoming game. "Do we know of his location?"

"Qalat is still in Pakistan, making it hard for us to reach his location. However, it also makes quick changes in directions difficult for our adversaries. His communications system is coordinated through several take-outs for security reasons. Chief among those was to escape detection by the NSA," Crest explained, the whirring noise fading slightly. Brienne recognized the sounds of a turboprop driven aircraft. "Telfer is on his way there, working a deal out with the Foreign Minister, who the ISI doesn't have control of. In fact, we believe the ISI has been acting outside the government's control on this whole operation. Their government officials are trying to maintain peace within the region, and with the U.S. They weren't too happy to discover Qalat has been using resources for his own selfish means. They aren't willing to go as far as handing him over, but they are prepared to allow a witness when they take him into custody for treason. It's the best we can do given our tenuous relationship at the moment."

Brienne understood the significance of what Crest was saying. The Agency would be allowed to observe whatever interrogation methods the Pakistani officials authorized, designed to garner the desired intelligence. It was more than evident Qalat had a hand in aiding the rebellions and insurgents against the current Pakistani government. That was punishable by death, but the ISI had a unique level of influence when it came to dealing with its own government. They needed to maintain the military's support to govern the people and the ISI had direct ties to the military. The question remained if Telfer would be able to acquire any information regarding what truly happened to the Red Starr unit during that fateful mission. The dots were connecting and it was only a matter of time before the picture was complete.

"Where are you going now?" Brienne asked, turning back so that her words could thoroughly be heard over the satellite phone.

"I'm not going anywhere," Crest advised, his confidence coming across the line loud and clear. "Reinforcements just arrived with their equipment and I'm here to greet them personally."

"The cell that Qalat had managed to organize in the D.C. area has to be strained with trying to find my location while keeping Michael Jensen secure," Brienne said, thinking out loud. Grady was already motioning for her to stop with her train of thought, but she couldn't stand the concept of Bob's son being harmed in any way. "Tell Starr and the FBI HRT to hold off if they find Michael's location. Let me be the distraction the Agency needs to make a safe rescue. The bad guys should leap at the chance. It will put them off balance and weaken their defense of the safe house location where they're keeping Bob's son."

"No," Grady barked into the phone. It was already too late. Brienne had made up her mind and she had no doubt that Gavin Crest and Catori Starr would agree with the strategy. The location where Michael Jensen was being held needed to be thinned out to lessen the risk to his life. The only person capable of doing that was Brienne. "Crest, allow things to proceed as planned. Brienne stays here."

"You explained in great detail what it was like to lose Madison," Brienne exclaimed, not hesitating to cross that delicate line. There wasn't time for pleasantries, selfishness, or ignorance. Grady understood that, but his judgment was being slightly hindered from past experiences. "What exactly do you think Bob and Sharon will experience if their son dies today? Their innocent five-year-old child?"

Silence hung thick in the air and not even Crest ventured into the dampening cloud. Brienne had never seen such anguish in a person as she did with Grady at this very moment. Tears stung her eyes at what she was asking of him, but it was the right thing to do.

"Grady," Brienne whispered, stepping close to the man she'd come to love more than anything in this world. She raised an arm so that her palm rested against his freshly shaven skin, grateful for the warmth that penetrated her cold hands. "If this were any other agent, you would have suggested it out of the gate. Qalat's men are desperate because they've lost contact with the person pulling the strings and their source's handler. They are disorganized without senior leadership, and will most likely end up killing an innocent little boy unless we provide the necessary distraction and the only possible way for them to accomplish their mission."

Grady's jawline was as tight as a piano wire. It was a wonder his teeth didn't crack underneath the pressure. His dark eyes became almost black in his attempt at reconciling what Brienne was suggesting. He'd wrapped his other hand around her arm and his grip became even more constricting, as he had no choice but to accept her proposal. The struggle within him was strikingly obvious and she physically hurt for him. She would have given anything for them not to be here at this moment…but they were.

"This is what we signed up for, Grady. Isn't that what you said? We need to honor that fated identity."

"Alert Starr and the FBI HRT lead that we'll be headed into D.C. within four hours," Grady said harshly into the SAT phone before disconnecting the call. He glanced down at the device as if it was a lifeline, but he wouldn't find the reprieve he was looking for. Brienne's heart tore upon his next words. "That identity you're talking about wasn't written in blood, Brie. Mine was. Not yours."

Grady turned and walked out of the room, leaving Brienne standing there alone as she pondered his words. Yes, he was the one who'd endorsed his life over to the United States Marines. He was the one who'd gone on countless deployments and combat tours, placing himself at the will of the Corps in many battles to defend his country. What he understood but didn't want to accept was that she was bound by the same contract, regardless that ninety percent of the time she was safe behind a desk.

Brienne was dressed in the jeans she'd had on from yesterday, along with the camisole she'd been wearing upon arrival at this safe house. She reached for the matching white blazer, the blood spots still apparent on one of the sleeves. She'd done her best to wash it out, but to no avail. She stared intently at the small dots and even ran her thumb over the stains, recalling the terror she'd experienced when she shattered the window and killed a man. She wasn't just scared about walking back into a similar situation…she was downright terrified of what was to come.

Brienne's fingers trembled when she reached for her cup of coffee still sitting on the small table in front of the couch. How could she convince Grady that he shouldn't be by her side on the drive into the city? It was pure hypocrisy, but she wouldn't have to worry about him and he'd have a better vantage point of anyone coming her way if he were in a chase vehicle. She'd already accepted that it wouldn't happen that way, but it was nice to imagine.

"You have absolutely no idea what you are asking me to do." Grady had come out of the bedroom right when she'd reached the kitchen sink, his words barely above a harsh murmur. The raw emotion was evident and Brienne set her coffee cup next to the drain before pressing her fingers to her lips to prevent herself from breaking down. It had never been her intent to hurt him like this. "I will do this for the parents of Michael Jensen, but we do it my way. No more heroics."

Brienne didn't need to turn around to know Grady had come up behind her. He wrapped his arms around her waist and pulled her back to his chest, resting his warm cheek against hers. She inhaled as deeply as she could, capturing his essence in hopes it would give her the strength to carry out the rest of this assignment. She leaned back and then tilted her face closer to his.

"I will agree to that on one condition," Brienne whispered, closing her eyes to savor this moment. She refused to believe that they'd made it this far only to have history repeat itself. She needed something to hold on to. "From what you told me about Madison, she'll be watching over you today. I want you to take me to her grave when this is all said and done. I want the chance to thank her for having a hand in the man you've become."

"We can do that, if you like."

Grady had granted Brienne's wish, his relief evident at the fact that she wasn't going to try something foolish.

She wouldn't, because he would be there to prevent her from acting out.

Brienne had already accepted that Grady would be by her side today. She could only pray they made it through this alive.

Chapter Eleven

The SUV's temperature was set at a comfortable seventy degrees. The vents were softly blowing the regulated air through the interior, doing nothing to alleviate the concern Grady and Brienne were currently consumed with. This was it. Today was the day this all ended.

Grady and Brienne had spent the first hour of the drive coordinating their arrival with Gavin Crest. His men were in position and they had already scouted the exact access road on which he and Brienne would enter, as well as the assembly site. This, of course, was all being organized in conjunction with the CIA and FBI.

The FBI had been briefed. It had two teams on the ground in two locations in the greater D.C. area, and were now the lead organization overseeing this part of the assignment, although Grady didn't have to wonder who was really calling the shots. The Agency had no doubt withheld specific intelligence, suiting their purposes and taking advantage of the additional reinforcements brought to bear by both private contractors present.

Everyone was waiting for Brienne to make an appearance, drawing the attention away from the location of Michael Jensen. Granted, this undertaking was already underway, but there were multiple goals that needed to be obtained—the main being to eliminate the cell Qalat and the ISI had managed to infiltrate so close to the heart of the nation.

Grady and Brienne had traveled at least a hundred and sixty miles before the critical update they'd been waiting on came through. The tension in the vehicle could have been cut with a knife, but the ringing of the SAT phone had done just as good a job.

"Starr has given confirmation," Crest relayed, being their person of contact. Grady wouldn't have it any other way. "Bob Jensen placed the call in to his contact thirty minutes ago, under the supervision of SSA Telfer. The connection was long enough that the technicians were able to trace the location of the group of men we're targeting within three meters of their cell phone. Not only were they able to trace the initial call, they were able to track others located in the same general area and listen in to the conversations in the vicinity of those phones."

Grady was pleased to hear the accomplishment of this morning's endeavor, but he understood all too well the events that had to take place afterward for this to be a true success.

"Taps were placed on all suspected phones," Crest stated, continuing with the updates. "Telemetry and velocity data were correlated by mainframe computers that tracked movements and placed the targets in surrounding buildings on a three-dimensional mapping system."

This was good. Even if the original caller removed the battery from his or her phone, it would be too late to avoid the collateral collection of all the other surrounding devices' information and location data. Grady appreciated the fact that something was going right today.

"The CIA, FBI, and Red Starr are now en route with precision location and targeting data being constantly updated to each participant's heads-up display on the intelligence network established for this specific operation. By the time they engage the targets, we should know numbers and likely avenues of approach on most of the tangos. Just prior to their assault, however, each of the attacking forces will go dark and their movements toward the two of you will be unseen."

Satellites and drones were deployed and tasked now that contact had been made, courtesy of the FBI and the CIA's Technology and

Science Division. The buildings and outlying area where the call had been triangulated was examined in real time, as well as sensors employed for analyzing heat signatures.

Those signatures were cross-checked with the phone and electronic device collections. A real-time situation display of the area would then be developed. The location of Michael Jensen had finally been revealed and it was only a matter of time before a rescue mission commenced after the additional tangos departed to attack the bait vehicle. Things were going as planned, but Grady was well aware it could go to hell at any moment.

"I take it Jensen gave the time and waypoint for Brienne's return?"

Grady never stopped surveying the area ahead of them, regardless that one of the CSA team members was driving fifty yards in front of their vehicle. Connor Ortega was following fifty yards behind. Everyone was aware that the enemy wouldn't show their faces until they had eyes on their target. The split seconds needed to identify all the attacking cell members would be crucial.

"Jensen played his part well, but he will still be held accountable."

That was all Crest would say on the subject. Bob Jensen no longer had a career within the Agency. He hadn't followed protocol upon his son's abduction while at the same time putting another agent's life in danger, though a felony was still a felony. No one, not even Brienne, blamed Jensen for his error. A parent would do whatever it took to safeguard their child.

"Did he sell it?" Grady asked, knowing that was the key to the success of this cleanup.

"Yes. Jensen was able to continue the charade and give them and us the time needed to put several plans in motion. He read the script where Brienne was turning herself into protective custody, but only into the hands of Gus Wilson. The FBI will cordon off the traffic to and from the Key Bridge just prior to the coordinated assault commencement. They are waiting for your arrival in the immediate area."

Grady continued to drive while Crest gave updates throughout the remainder of the journey. Specific scenarios were proposed and thrown out as they all did their best to strategize the downside of the thousand ways this could possibly go sideways.

"Qalat's men have now been dispatched and are heading toward the target location," Crest advised, his announcement also reaching his team. His unit would be positioned throughout the target area to take out those they could positively verify as being a part of Qalat's cell, but there would clearly be those that slipped under the radar. All of this was being communicated to the FBI's On-Scene Tactical Coordination Center (OSTCC) and into CIA Headquarters where a maze of operations personnel would dissect every angle of every movement for future recrimination. "Eight tangos were spotted leaving, but we can't discount there being more en route from another location. They have gone communications black on all cell assets. The locale where Michael is being kept has four tangos left inside—presumed to be heavily armed males."

The Company usually stayed far away from domestic matters and rarely contributed to missions on U.S. soil, which was why the FBI had to be the lead agency. That didn't change the fact that this wasn't a typical hostage rescue mission. There would be no negotiating. The FBI and CIA contracted groups sent in to retrieve their objectives would complete their mission, eliminating every tango in their way. They took care of business in the most ruthless manner…in a way the majority of the population found contemptible.

"Please keep us updated on Michael Jensen's safety," Brienne instructed, sitting up a little straighter as Grady drove her closer to their destination. They were now passing by Georgetown University. No one spoke of what would happen should Qalat manage to get a call out to his people here on U.S. soil, either abandoning the plan to eliminate evidence or putting into place something bigger than any of them could imagine. "We're switching to tactical communications. Earpieces in. Watch the hot mics."

Brienne handed Grady one of the small earpieces that would connect them to the FBI OSTCC after they disconnected their hands free call with Crest over the vehicle's Bluetooth sound system. She laid the small device in his palm and held on longer than necessary. He needed the intimate contact and lifted the back of her hand to his lips.

Grady wanted more than anything to turn this SUV around and take her far from here. He had a cabin outside of Ashville, North Carolina. It was hardly ever used since Madison's death, but they could easily go there and live out their lives without any thought to anyone else.

Who was he kidding? Neither one of them were cut out for retirement and Brienne was certainly way too young to call it quits for the simple life in the western Carolina mountains. As for him? Well, Grady would no doubt consult for the various agencies until they no longer wanted him and he hoped to have a colleague in that aspect of his life. He already had a partner where it mattered most.

"TAC one, this is Echo Five Charlie. We're sixty seconds out."

"Copy, Echo Five Charlie. Four heavy tangos in sight north side of the bridge."

Grady's grip tightened on the steering wheel in reaction to the summary. That meant at least four more threats remained that had yet to be observed inside the target area. That lowered their odds of getting through this unscathed, but the FBI and CIA teams were crawling all over the place.

"We're making the right decision," Brienne murmured, reaching for the weapon in her side holster. Crest had seen to it that she had her usual Sig Sauer P250 Compact chambered in .40 S&W. She confirmed a round was in the chamber and then slowly inhaled to seemingly give herself a moment of calm. "This will all be over in less than five minutes. Then we get to decide what to do with the rest of our lives."

"I didn't tell you?" Grady asked somewhat nonchalantly, having waited for just this moment to give Brienne something even more to fight for. She quickly shot a glance his way with a raised eyebrow. "Telfer needs another consultant. Obviously, it's not as exciting as a CIA field agent and consultants are behind the scenes more often than in front of them, usually going over endless rows of files, but it passes the time. Oh, and the pay might be shit, but you do get to travel on the Company dime."

Brienne lifted the side of her mouth in a half-smile. The voices coming through the earpieces were updating them on the whereabouts of the four heavily armed individuals within the sights of the snipers' scopes. Grady continued to drive the vehicle onto the bridge where Gus would be waiting for them in the emergency pull-up lane mid-span. No doubt he was outfitted with a bulletproof vest, similar to what Brienne and Grady had on underneath their suit jackets.

"Is a companion written in that job description?" Brienne asked with not even a hitch to her voice when he stopped a good thirty feet behind where Gus was waiting for them. The CSA lead vehicle continued in the slow lane of traffic and the chase vehicle braked twenty yards back, effectively blocking any following traffic in their lane…of which there was none. The transfer would appear to go as planned until the FBI gave them notice of their assault. They were currently waiting for Qalat's other men to make themselves known. "That's my one stipulation."

"Sweetheart, you can have whatever you want written in that contract," Grady answered, leaving the vehicle running as he shifted the gear into park. Gus' face appeared to be set in stone as he stared at them through the side view mirror. "Foxtrot Six, what is their position?"

"TAC One, Foxtrot Six. Tangos on approach twenty yards north. On my count, open the doors on the target vehicles. Five, four…"

The sun was shining bright, the vivid rays making it almost impossible to see in the direction the federal agent had indicated. Grady didn't like the impediment currently blocking their view of the enemy. Their opponents had certainly done well choosing their advantage point. It would have gone their way had this been a genuine meeting point between Brienne and a colleague from her division.

As it stood, these men were about to be terminated with high-powered rifles with fast expanding mushrooming .308 caliber hollow point rounds. It wasn't up to them to choose whether they would surrender of their own will or die today. Their fate had already been decided.

"Are you ready?" Grady murmured, bringing up Brienne's free hand and pressing another kiss to the back of her fingers. He didn't like how cool her skin had become and he swore when this was over he would take her to a place where the sunshine would make it impossible for her to be cold. Her blue eyes met his with a promise…an assurance she would do everything in her power to give them the life they'd talked about. "I love you, Brie."

"I love you, too," Brienne whispered, squeezing his hand before holstering her weapon. It wouldn't do to give up their plan too early and she had to appear relaxed upon exiting the vehicle or Qalat's men might react earlier than anticipated. She looked at him one more time before pulling on the door handle. "I'll accept that consulting position when we're back at Langley."

Grady's chest tightened upon Brienne opening her car door after the FBI agent's countdown. He did the same, knowing he was on the side of where Qalat's men had stationed themselves—well, at least four of them.

The meeting was taking place in the center of Key Bridge, giving the FBI the advantage by restricting the ambush to two entry points. It positioned Brienne, to some degree, and other civilian traffic out of the line of fire while also providing the FBI and CIA the ability to spot the enemy on both sides of their likely line of approach.

"Weapons hot. Tangos are bringing their weapons up. Fire! Fire! Fire!"

Chapter Twelve

Brienne had been in many dangerous situations throughout her career. There was that time in Damascus where she'd witnessed a young boy pull the pin on a hand grenade he'd found on the ground in the bazaar near where the local arms merchants' stalls were located. The split second reaction when she'd grabbed it from his small fingers and tossed it into an exposed sewage pipe had been one of the worst. Or when she'd been in Kandahar and the Humvee in front of her trailing civilian SUV had exploded into nothing but shrapnel, flesh, and bones from those Marines who had been inside.

This time? Brienne was the target and she had no doubt that the enemy had her mop of blonde hair within their crosshairs, their fingers on their triggers. All it took was a miscalculation of mere seconds on the part of the FBI and she wouldn't even know she'd been hit. The 7.62 x 39mm bullet would hit her head at just over twenty-three hundred feet per second and cause her brain to explosively depart her cranium through both the entrance and exit wounds.

Brienne didn't want to die today. She didn't want to be taken away from Grady, leaving him alone to bear more pain upon losing a woman he loved. He deserved better.

Then there was the flip side...the one she really couldn't fathom. What if Grady was the one killed today, leaving her to know without a doubt that she was to blame? He could have easily stayed behind with one of the FBI or CIA agents, overseeing things from a safe distance. She hadn't asked him to do that, because she wouldn't have done so either had the roles been reversed.

Brienne loved him...that meant they faced their enemy together.

"TAC One, four tangos down twenty yards out from the middle span. I repeat, four down."

That meant there were at least four more men at large. Brienne and Grady had stopped just outside of their respective doors on the SUV, still a good forty feet from where Gus was standing. She braced herself for the bullet, not knowing which direction it might be coming from. Where were the others?

The drone above them was scouting for possible sightings, whether it be by land or water. Both entry points were being canvassed and now it was only a waiting game. Hell, Grady and Brienne might actually make it all the way to where Gus was waiting for her without any other attempt on her life. Qalat might very well have reached out to his men here on U.S. soil before being taken into custody. There were too many variables to count, but that didn't mean this current mission could be halted.

Brienne took another step out, this one putting her directly opposite Grady's side of the vehicle and a bit forward toward the bridge railing. She hadn't realized she'd been holding her breath until his voice spoke inside her ears.

"Keep walking to the front of the vehicle," Grady advised, his soothing tone giving Brienne the encouragement to continue forward. She couldn't help but wonder where the next attack would come from. "Slow steps. We're almost halfway there."

The sun reflected off of something to Brienne's right, but she didn't take her eyes off of the agent in front of them. Gus must have noticed it from his location at the back of his vehicle as well, but he maintained position. It wasn't until another agent's voice shouted into their earpiece that all hell broke loose.

"RPG! Get down! RPG! Take cover!"

Fight or flight. Those instincts always managed to take over. As an agent, those reflexes were honed to initiate at the right time. It didn't always happen that way, but their training molded them in a manner where the percentage of success was in their favor.

This wasn't the time to fight. One couldn't fight a rocket propelled grenade. One also couldn't escape the damage that was about to be done. This was it. They would die together in the open between the two armored vehicles.

"Fuck," Grady muttered over the whir of the drone as it repositioned overhead. The weapons that the teams would use to combat individual targets wouldn't stop the oncoming boat below them. The likelihood they could eliminate the threat before the RPG struck was impossible. "Move!"

Grady grabbed Brienne by the hand and together they ran back toward the relative safety of the armored SUV without a snowball's chance in hell of making it to cover before the hiss of the RPG ended in a detonation against the concrete and steel railing directly behind them and showering them with millions of white hot fragments of molten steel. There was absolutely no way they could outrun the shrapnel that was about to rain across the bridge directly into them.

So she thought.

Brienne hadn't expected Grady to drag her over the knee-high cement barrier opposite their vehicle in the center of the bridge. Neither had she predicted he would use the momentum to take both of them over the tall greyish-blue steel railing on the other side, tumbling both of them off of the structure and toward the depths of the filthy water below.

The explosion that rocked the Key Bridge had most likely been heard for miles. It was the only sound that could be heard resounding through the air as Brienne and Grady continued to free-fall toward the churning brown water. She did her best to brace herself against hitting the cold water below, but nothing could prepare her for the impact of an eighty-five foot drop. She'd done her best to stay upright so that her feet hit first. She wasn't so lucky and her thighs took the brunt of the bruising.

Even so, Brienne had little time to suck in oxygen as she was submerged in the cold, dark water. The shock had her fighting against the gravity and she immediately kicked her legs and arms, struggling to get to the surface. She tried her best to wrestle against the panic taking hold, as well as the need to breathe again.

Where was Grady?

Brienne couldn't see anything in the darkness as she thrashed against the water. She was aware that she was rising to the surface, but she wasn't sure it was fast enough. Her chest literally burned and the fiery flames began to travel up her throat, insisting she open her mouth for relief...not understanding it would be welcoming death instead.

Brienne finally broke the surface, her lips parting automatically and sucking in oxygen faster than her body could process. That didn't stop her from frantically looking for Grady. She used her feet to spin in the water, her hands clearing away the debris floating around her while avoiding the rubble still falling from above. The churning of the water from their abrupt entrance, along with the boats, shrapnel, and whatever firepower the FBI had used to destroy those who'd had possession of the RPG made it difficult for her to focus on any one thing.

"Grady!" Brienne continued to yell for him over the engines and the whirling of the blades overhead. The pain and horror Brienne had faced in the water below was nothing compared to what she was experiencing now. "Grady!"

"Here!"

Brienne twisted her body, using what strength she had left in her arms and legs to face in the direction of Grady's voice. There! His handsome, distinguished face was dripping with water, filled with worry, and the most beautiful vision she'd ever seen. He swam to her, pulling her against him as he reassured them both that they were still alive.

"We did it," Grady professed with absolute certainty. "We did it."

There was no time for crying, but Brienne couldn't stop the sob that had gathered in her chest from escaping. She turned it into a laugh of victory, knowing full well she sounded as if she were losing her mind. She wrapped her arms around Grady's neck and held on as tight as she could.

Life as Brienne knew it was over. She was no longer a field agent. She was no longer a liaison to the Pakistani desk at the CIA. She would no longer be an asset to her country the way she'd once been.

The chaos continued around them as Brienne clung to her future and came to terms with her past. There were no regrets. Her identity might have been compromised, but she knew exactly who she was and where she was meant to be.

Brienne released Grady enough to where their lips were inches apart and she could see for herself that he was all right. He was smiling brighter than she'd ever bore witness. His brown eyes were lit with triumph, happiness, and love.

They'd made it.

Grady kissed her without hesitation, with no regard to who was watching them. Brienne kicked her feet harder to stay afloat, not missing this adrenaline rush for anything.

By now, either the FBI or the CIA had a boat coming in their direction. The drone above was pulling away and sirens could now be heard in the distance. The fallout of this operation would be on the six o'clock news and it would fall on the FBI to do damage control. Nothing would be said in regards to Brienne, her identity leak, the CIA or Shujaat Qalat's role in all of this, or the fact that a breach had been made to recover a five-year-old boy from a group of ISI kidnappers. There was still one more mission to carry out—bringing home the remains of the former Red Starr unit.

The engine to a watercraft was upon them way too soon. Grady pulled away from Brienne to make sure they weren't in danger of getting bumped by the large boat. She took the time to glance up at the bridge, unable to see the extent of the damage on the other side. She was able to see Special Agent Gus Wilson looking over the railing, giving them a thumbs up that no casualties had taken place. Agents with FBI vests on their chest were reaching out for Brienne, who Grady had already turned and aided them by putting his hands securely underneath her arms.

Brienne grabbed the agent's hands and allowed him to pull her aboard, taking the blanket they offered with appreciation. She moved out of their way as they assisted Grady into the boat, but she didn't sit down until he was at her side. Together, they sat inside the small cabin and waited to be escorted to land.

"Michael Jensen. Was he rescued unharmed?" Brienne asked, directing her question to the agent facing them.

Grady wrapped an arm around her and pulled her closer, the warmth of his body invading hers. Her teeth immediately started to chatter, but she forced them tightly shut to hear the answer.

"Yes, ma'am," the younger agent responded, making a motion with his hand that the driver of the boat should proceed toward land. "The rescue mission was successful. SA Wilson will meet us on shore and you'll then be taken to Langley."

Brienne shared a victorious look with Grady, both of them grateful the various agencies had been able to come together to save the life of an innocent boy. Michael Jensen's life would never be the same, though. He'd had to face the harsh reality of what hatred could do to a group of people.

Bob Jensen would have to serve out a sentence for committing a felony for disclosing an active agent's identity to a foreign power, though Brienne would do her best to give testimony that there had been extenuating circumstances. She didn't blame him for what he'd done, although she did wish he'd trusted his own people to be by his side instead of choosing a path that could have taken many more lives, including her own.

"Are you ready to start a new life?" Grady asked as he spoke against her ear. "One with a man who's pretty well set in his ways?"

Brienne held up her right hand and waited for him to lace his fingers with hers. She tightened her grip on his and then gave her answer.

"I've always been ready, Grady. It was you who I've been waiting on."

Chapter Thirteen

Grady removed the change of clothes given to him by Gus Wilson back when they'd been at Langley. The pants hadn't been long enough and the dress shirt had been too tight, but the garments had been enough to see them through the debriefings he and Brienne had gone through. The day had been long and grueling, but it had finally come to an end.

Michael Jensen was back home, safe and sound with his mother, while Bob Jensen was being currently being arraigned. Grady and Brienne had yet to speak with Starr in person. She was busy taking care of paperwork since she'd been on hand to provide Red Starr's services. Every I needed to be dotted and every T needed to be crossed in order to show that no position of power had been abused to resolve the magnitude of the situations that had occurred in the past several days. As a matter of fact, Red Starr had not fired a shot during any of the recent exchanges.

As for SA Gus Wilson, he was awaiting word from SSA Telfer who had contracted CSA to secure Raheela at a safe house outside of Karachi. Everyone was waiting to hear what was occurring on their end. Qalat had been taken into custody and it was only a matter of time before the Pakistani government dealt out their punishment for aiding and abetting groups aligned against their government's official policy. Gavin Crest was in the process of reaching out to his contacts, who had found Raheela and were now moving her to another location. There was nothing for Grady or Brienne to do now but wait and see what would happen from here.

Grady opened the door to the master bathroom of his apartment. Brienne had not flipped the switch for the fan, so the steam billowed out once he opened the door. She'd been inside the shower for over twenty minutes and he didn't like her being in there for so long alone. Their adrenaline had worn off and exhaustion was settling in along with the reality of their insane adventure.

"Hey. Planning on using all the hot water?" Grady asked softly, opening the glass door and stepping inside the enclosure. Brienne had been standing underneath the hot spray with her eyes closed in a somewhat relaxing manner, telling him he didn't have to worry about her wellbeing. A smile lit up her face as she opened those baby blues and he realized he'd walked into her trap. "Oh, you were waiting for me to come in here, weren't you?"

"Absolutely, Colonel. And here I thought you were a bit sharper than that," Brienne murmured, sliding her warm hands up his now wet chest. She didn't stop until she wrapped her arms around his neck, bringing him closer. "You see, we'll probably both be in need of a really good masseuse come tomorrow. The impact my body took hitting that water is going to hurt like a—"

Grady kissed her before she could continue, not needing to hear how sore their muscles were truly going to be. He'd already set a bottle of ibuprofen on the nightstand with a glass of water. He made a mental note to call the masseuse Brienne preferred when he got a moment.

"So you decided we should make love in the shower?" Grady asked, finally pulling away and turning them so that his back took the brunt force of the spray. Brienne rested a cheek against his chest, lowering her arms so that they were wrapped around his waist. "I would have thought you've had your fill of fun in the water today."

"The heat feels too good to get out, so I had to wait long enough for you to catch on," Brienne explained, licking away a stream of water as it ran off of his shoulder. He hardened at the soft feel of her tongue against his skin. "Hmmm, it was apparently worth it. Our muscles are reacting just the way I'd hoped."

"I don't even have—"

Brienne held up a small package containing exactly what Grady had been about to name. She must have brought the condom in earlier, meaning this had been her plan all along. She wouldn't get an argument from him, as she knelt before him before he could take the foil from her hands.

"Brie, your knees—"

"Are just fine. Do you want to catch up here?" Brienne asked with a smile after she'd leisurely wrapped her fingers around his cock. She took her time stroking him, although she needn't waste the time. He was already hardening up just fine—ready and willing. Grady looked down to see her blonde lashes flutter against her cheeks as she parted her lips and licked his slit with her tongue. It was then he saw the towel she'd placed on the shower floor, but his thoughts were now in a different place. "Hmmm, you taste good."

"You can play around another time, Brie," Grady responded in a rather hoarse voice. He chalked it up to their bout in the water earlier. "I need you. Now."

Instead of seeing disappointment in her features, all Grady saw was longing. Brienne stroked him a couple of more times before ripping the foiled package open and tossing it toward the soap dish. She lovingly unrolled the latex as she slid the rubber over the head of his cock and down his shaft. The moment it was securely on, Grady pulled her up and turned her to face the wall at the rear of the river rock lined shower stall. He adjusted the selector to multiple sprays and several additional showerheads came to life.

"We're alive, Brie," Grady reassured her, knowing they would need to repeat those words several times over the next few days. Loving each other like this only solidified the fact that they still had a future ahead of them. He trailed his lips down her shoulder blade as he took ahold of her hips. Brienne had already spread her legs and arched her back, waiting to receive him. She didn't have to wait and he thrust forward, seating himself deeply within her. "All we have to do is enjoy the ride."

"Yes," Brienne moaned, spreading her fingers out on the tile before them as she leveraged herself for his long, hard strokes. The wet strands of her hair flowed down her back and barely budged as he continued to drive in and out of her. This wasn't a slow and sensual act. The spray angled in front of her hit her nipples as he stroked away. This was a fast, hard, and well-deserved satiation. "Harder, Grady. Drive me home."

The heat of her sheath was hotter than the water. Grady never once let up the momentum and it wasn't long before their cries mingled together, joining the steam as it rose into the air. Brienne rested her forehead against her arm as she recovered from such a quick, loving incursion. He placed his arms on either side of her hips, doing the same.

"Ten years your senior," Grady said after a while, pulling her back against him when they'd recovered. Their breathing was still quite uneven and he had to laugh. "I'll have to work in a strict workout regimen to keep up with you."

"We could always work daily sex into the regimen," Brienne suggested as she rested against his chest. "That counts for losing calories and stretching muscles, you know."

Grady closed his eyes as Brienne started to talk about all the ways they could stay fit, giving him time to remove the used condom. He washed himself off, pondering if they should have another round. He decided against it, seeing as the water was cooling off and they really would be quite sore tomorrow given what they'd put their bodies through today. Still, he wouldn't change anything that had occurred these last few days.

Grady had been given the opportunity to truly love two women in this lifetime. Most men didn't get to say they found their soul mate even once and he counted himself twice as lucky. For all the sins he'd committed in the name of his country and his freedom, he wasn't certain he deserved such a gift. Either way, he wasn't planning on returning it.

Grady took his time drying her off with one of the extra soft towels he'd purchased just for her. Brienne loved the feel of the smooth Turkish 802 gram bath towel against her skin and he wanted nothing but the best for her. He'd just finished and was wrapping her body in the towel when a noise caught his attention.

"Grady, is someone at the door?"

He was still kneeling on the plush carpet and rested his head against Brienne's abdomen. What she needed was rest. There was still a lot left to do regarding her position within the Agency, but none of that would happen until SSA Telfer wrapped up his own internal investigation. Grady was set to meet up with Starr and Crest tomorrow, so who could be here?

"I'm tempted to ignore whoever it is." Grady sighed in resignation, knowing he could do nothing of the sort. He slowly rose off the floor and pulled Brienne close to him, pressing a tender kiss to her forehead. He would see to her first. "I laid your robe out on the bed. Go ahead and crawl underneath the covers. I'll deal with whoever is here and then I'll use those oils we bought a few weeks ago when we were in Annapolis to see if we can't loosen up the muscles on the back of your legs."

"How did you know—"

Grady just gave Brienne a tender smile. He knew her better than he knew himself. He took in every movement, every gesture, and every word that she emitted. She had a tell for every single thing that affected her and it was his duty to ensure her happiness. He had willingly taken that position and only death could take that responsibility away.

"I will always know, Brie."

* * * *

Brienne tied the sash of her robe as she finally made her way through Grady's apartment to his home office. He hadn't returned immediately and she couldn't help but wonder who'd been at the door. Her painted toes sunk into the luxurious carpet Grady had installed a while back, having done extensive upgrades to his place when she started to spend nights here in his apartment.

The office door was open, so Brienne didn't hesitate to cross the threshold. She really wasn't surprised to see a woman currently staring out the window overlooking St. Stephan's Catholic Church across Pennsylvania Avenue NW in Foggy Bottom.

"Ms. Starr," Brienne said, announcing herself. She wished more than anything she was wearing something other than a blue silk robe.

"It's a pleasure to meet you. I'd like to thank you for your support in Michael Jensen's rescue."

Catori Starr turned, her penetrating brown gaze immediately seeking out Brienne. Stunning was the only word to describe the woman in front of her. Long jet-black hair was currently flowing over her shoulders and the fresh white tailored blouse she was wearing. Her bronze skin practically glowed against the fabric, but it was her high cheekbones and her full lips that drew any admirer's attention. The striking combination of Native American and English heritage had resulted in a classically beautiful, yet dominatingly attractive, woman.

"Ms. Chaylse," Starr countered with just as much respect, reaching out her arm. Brienne shook hands with the retired Master Sergeant, wishing there was more information she could provide about Starr's husband's final resting spot and that of his team. "Contrary to what Grady believes, I truly appreciate you keeping me up-to-date on a mission that ended so long ago."

It hadn't ended though, had it?

Brienne looked over to see Grady pouring two drinks of what appeared to be Crown Royal XR Canadian blended whiskey. The light auburn liquid splashed into the tumblers. She shook her head when he offered her some. She would only stay long enough to tell Starr what was taking place in Karachi, although she suspected that either Grady or Gavin Crest had no doubt already passed along her information.

"Gavin Crest currently has contractors taking care of Raheela. Once she is safe, I will see if she is willing to give up whatever intel she might have overhead from her husband."

"Who is currently dead," Starr shared as if she'd just announced it was raining, taking a step forward to accept the proffered drink from Grady. Brienne gave him a reassuring smile when he joined her, wrapping one arm around her waist while taking a drink of his bourbon. "Shujaat Qalat will be of no help to us now that he is dead."

"I'm sorry," Brienne offered, knowing full well the Pakistani government had terminated the threat to their security before any information was compromised. It was the way these things were done.

"I must applaud you for obtaining Raheela as an informant," Starr said, raising her glass in salute. Her smile didn't reach her eyes and Brienne could only imagine the anguish Starr lived in every day knowing her husband wasn't at rest. "You must have been very good at your job. The CIA has lost a valuable asset, although I do hear they are gaining a well-placed consultant."

Brienne nodded her acceptance of such praise, only wishing she'd been able to do more. Raheela had aided the CIA in numerous missions, but it wasn't until recently that she'd wanted more rupees to benefit the women currently trapped in horrible situations. Raheela had thrown out abundant facts regarding her husband, which had eventually revealed his role in eliminating the former Red Starr team upon their approach while rescuing mission workers.

"Grady wasn't pleased with my role in this assignment," Brienne revealed honestly, "and though I understand where he was coming from…it was still my duty to let you know Raheela wasn't sure what happened to the bodies of your former team. With no bodies—"

"There's no confirmation of death," Starr finished before taking another sip of her drink. "Either way, when the time comes that you're able to speak to Raheela, I would like to be kept apprised of any details she might have been privy to."

"Of course," Brienne responded, wishing she could do more to help Starr reach the peace that was currently out of her hands. There was no guarantee that Crest's contractors would be able to relocate Raheela outside of Pakistan without considerable help. "I will—"

Grady's office phone rang, cutting off Brienne's promise to follow through on a case that she no longer had any influence over. She no longer held the position of a field agent and she certainly wasn't a liaison anymore. She'd lost that privilege once her name was announced to the world. The ramifications of that hadn't even hit the U.S. airwaves, but it would happen soon enough. Maybe by then she and Grady would be off to another country conferring with those who used to be her colleagues.

"Yes, she's right here." Grady had set his drink down on a coaster beside his monitor. He was watching Starr, but holding the phone out to Brienne. Her heart lurched slightly upon realizing this could very well be the final nail in the coffin. "It's Crest."

Had the contractors relocated Raheela to a safe house? Was Crest calling to tell her that the woman had been lost, never to be found again? There was only way to find out. Brienne reached for the receiver, grateful when Grady didn't leave her side. Unfortunately, it might not be her who needed the support.

"This is Brienne." She'd stumbled a bit over her name, usually referring to herself as Agent Chaylse.

"We have her safe and sound."

Gavin Crest's words literally stole Brienne's breath away. She reached for Grady's hand and held on tight as Raheela was finally put on the line, having been connected through a three-way call. She was naturally scared and only wanted to speak with Brienne, who'd been her main contact and had always kept her word. After taking the time to talk to Raheela and soothe her worries away regarding her husband and his tyranny, Brienne finally broached the topic for which she needed answers.

"Raheela, I understand why you only gave pieces of information at the time," Brienne assured, opening up a dialogue that would give Starr the closure she needed. "Those women who came to you for help needed a way out. And you did that for them. But your life there is now over. You'll be brought to the United States under an assumed identity once we have secured passage and documents for your new life. What I need to know is everything you can remember from when that rescue mission occurred. The one your husband prevented from occurring. What happened to those men in that Red Starr unit?"

Brienne listened intently, not truly believing what she was hearing. It couldn't be. She swallowed over the lump in her throat, trying to confirm what Raheela had just revealed.

"Are you absolutely sure, Raheela?" Brienne asked after clearing her throat.

She sought out Grady's gaze. His eyes were filled with questions, whereas Catori Starr had gone completely still. There was no telling what the woman was thinking, but the lethal glimmer in her dark eyes was enough for Brienne to know she was glad she wasn't on the receiving end.

Gavin Crest had taken over the conversation, telling Brienne that he would be at Grady's apartment within the hour. They had work to do. She disconnected the line and finally revealed the truth of Brendan O'Neill's fate.

"Red's alive, Starr," Brienne divulged, a tentative smile forming on her face as her heart tightened with happiness. Raheela's new identity wasn't the only one to be established today. The gift of life renewed was in the air and now all that was left was for Starr to go and retrieve Brendan O'Neill from his bondage. "Your husband is alive."

~THE END~

About the Author

First and foremost, I love life. I love that I'm a wife, mother, daughter, sister… and a writer.

I am one of the lucky women in this world who gets to do what makes them happy. As long as I have a cup of coffee (maybe two or three) and my laptop, the stories evolve themselves and I try to do them justice. I draw my inspiration from a retired Marine Master Sergeant that swept me off of my feet and has drawn me into a world that fulfills all of my deepest and darkest desires. Erotic romance, military men, intrigue, with a little bit of kinky chili pepper (his recipe), fill my head and there is nothing more satisfying than making the hero and heroine fulfill their destinies.

Thank you for having joined me on their journeys…

Email:

kennedylayneauthor@gmail.com

Facebook:

facebook.com/kennedy.layne.94

Twitter:

twitter.com/KennedyL_Author

Website:

www.kennedylayne.com

Newsletter:

www.kennedylayne.com/newsletter.html

Books by Kennedy Layne

Brutal Obsession
The Safeguard Series, Book One
By Kennedy Layne

Join me in a thrilling new romantic suspense series that will leave you on the edge of your seat!

Keane Sanderson never thought he'd survive to see a day past his latest deployment with the United States Marines in Iraq. That was six years ago and he's finally ready to ease off the accelerator. A unique opportunity to work for a top-shelf security and investigations firm in Florida is right up his alley.

Ashlyn Ellis had everything she'd ever wanted—a high-profile career as a federal prosecutor, an upscale apartment in the city, and a beach house for when she needed to decompress from all the stress that accompanied the job. All three are threatened when she realizes someone has been following her every move for a very long time.

When Ashlyn comprehends the lengths her pursuer is willing to take things, she calls in a favor. She never expected her plea for assistance to materialize in the form of Keane Sanderson—the one man who had every reason to revel in her misfortune. She's finally given the chance to rekindle the flames of desire she never should have extinguished, just in time for it all to be taken away when the stalker takes his obsession a step too far.

Series Description: Safeguard Security & Investigations (SSI) is owned and operated by Townes Calvert, a retired Marine Gunnery Sergeant who returned home to the States a bit more damaged than he'd care to admit. Not that anyone could tell outside of a very select group of former active duty buddies. It had taken Townes quite a while to acclimate to civilian life and he'd kept himself busy in the interim working in treacherous situations with even more dangerous friends. The final result is a close-knit unit of highly trained former military men who have the experience to protect the innocent, investigate crimes on the gritty edge, and aid local law enforcement when justice has taken a back seat to political correctness. Follow along as Kennedy Layne conveys each of their gripping stories as they work together on investigations that lead them down perilous paths of passion, intrigue, and suspense...

Sign up for the 1001 Dark Nights Newsletter
and be entered to win a Tiffany Key necklace.

There's a contest every month!

Go to www.1001DarkNights.com to subscribe.

As a bonus, all subscribers will receive a free
1001 Dark Nights story
The First Night
by Lexi Blake & M.J. Rose

Turn the page for a full list of the
1001 Dark Nights fabulous novellas...

Discover 1001 Dark Nights Collection One

FOREVER WICKED by Shayla Black
CRIMSON TWILIGHT by Heather Graham
CAPTURED IN SURRENDER by Liliana Hart
SILENT BITE: A SCANGUARDS WEDDING by Tina Folsom
DUNGEON GAMES by Lexi Blake
AZAGOTH by Larissa Ione
NEED YOU NOW by Lisa Renee Jones
SHOW ME, BABY by Cherise Sinclair
ROPED IN by Lorelei James
TEMPTED BY MIDNIGHT by Lara Adrian
THE FLAME by Christopher Rice
CARESS OF DARKNESS by Julie Kenner

Also from 1001 Dark Nights

TAME ME by J. Kenner

For more information, visit www.1001DarkNights.com.

Discover 1001 Dark Nights Collection Two

Also from 1001 Dark Nights

For more information, visit www.1001DarkNights.com.

Discover 1001 Dark Nights Collection Three

HIDDEN INK by Carrie Ann Ryan
A Montgomery Ink Novella

BLOOD ON THE BAYOU by Heather Graham
A Cafferty & Quinn Novella

SEARCHING FOR MINE by Jennifer Probst
A Searching For Novella

DANCE OF DESIRE by Christopher Rice

ROUGH RHYTHM by Tessa Bailey
A Made In Jersey Novella

DEVOTED by Lexi Blake
A Masters and Mercenaries Novella

Z by Larissa Ione
A Demonica Underworld Novella

FALLING UNDER YOU by Laurelin Paige
A Fixed Trilogy Novella

EASY FOR KEEPS by Kristen Proby
A Boudreaux Novella

UNCHAINED by Elisabeth Naughton
An Eternal Guardians Novella

HARD TO SERVE by Laura Kaye
A Hard Ink Novella

DRAGON FEVER by Donna Grant
A Dark Kings Novella

KAYDEN/SIMON by Alexandra Ivy/Laura Wright
A Bayou Heat Novella

STRUNG UP by Lorelei James
A Blacktop Cowboys® Novella

MIDNIGHT UNTAMED by Lara Adrian
A Midnight Breed Novella

TRICKED by Rebecca Zanetti
A Dark Protectors Novella

DIRTY WICKED by Shayla Black
A Wicked Lovers Novella

A SEDUCTIVE INVITATION by Lauren Blakely
A Seductive Nights New York Novella

SWEET SURRENDER by Liliana Hart
A MacKenzie Family Novella

For more information, visit www.1001DarkNights.com.

On behalf of 1001 Dark Nights,

Liz Berry and M.J. Rose would like to thank ~

Steve Berry
Doug Scofield
Kim Guidroz
Jillian Stein
InkSlinger PR
Dan Slater
Asha Hossain
Chris Graham
Pamela Jamison
Jessica Johns
Dylan Stockton
Richard Blake
BookTrib After Dark
The Dinner Party Show
and Simon Lipskar